BBLE
VN

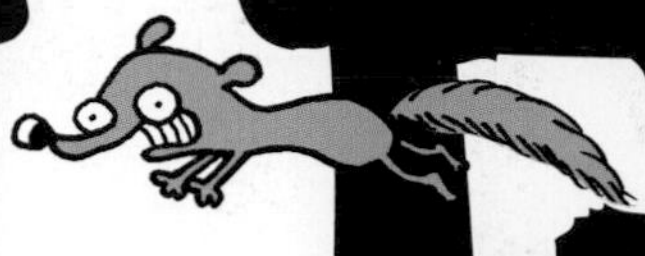

SQUIRREL DO BAD

STEPHAN PASTIS

ALADDIN | New York | London | Toronto | Sydney | New Delhi

This book is a work of fiction. Any references to historical events, real people, or real places are used fictitiously. Other names, characters, places, and events are products of the author's imagination, and any resemblance to actual events or places or persons, living or dead, is entirely coincidental.

ALADDIN / An imprint of Simon & Schuster Children's Publishing Division / 1230 Avenue of the Americas, New York, New York 10020 / First Aladdin edition August 2021 / Copyright © 2021 by Stephan Pastis / All rights reserved, including the right of reproduction in whole or in part in any form. / ALADDIN and related logo are registered trademarks of Simon & Schuster, Inc. / For information about special discounts for bulk purchases, please contact Simon & Schuster Special Sales at 1-866-506-1949 or business@simonandschuster.com. / The Simon & Schuster Speakers Bureau can bring authors to your live event. For more information or to book an event contact the Simon & Schuster Speakers Bureau at 1-866-248-3049 or visit our website at www.simonspeakers.com. / Designed by Karin Paprocki and Stephan Pastis / The illustrations for this book were rendered digitally. / The text of this book was hand-lettered and set in Bodoni. / Manufactured in China 0621 SCP / 2 4 6 8 10 9 7 5 3 1 / Library of Congress Cataloging-in-Publication Data / Names: Pastis, Stephan, author, illustrator. / Title: Squirrel do bad / Stephan Pastis. / Description: First Aladdin edition. / New York : Aladdin, 2021. / Series: Trubble town / Audience: Ages 8 to 12. / Summary: Wendy the Wanderer's overprotective father never lets her go anywhere alone, so when he hires a babysitter, Wendy decides to venture out into Trubble Town alone, where she meets Squirrely McSquirrel and other townsfolk. / Identifiers: LCCN 2021001471 (print) / LCCN 2021001472 (ebook) / ISBN 9781534496118 (hardcover) / ISBN 9781534496101 (paperback) / ISBN 9781534496125 (ebook) / Subjects: LCSH: Humorous stories. / Graphic novels. / CYAC: Graphic novels. / Squirrels—Fiction. / City and town life—Fiction. / Classification: LCC PZ7.7.P273 Sq 2021 (print) / LCC PZ7.7.P273 (ebook) / DDC 741.5/973—dc22 / LC record available at https://lccn.loc.gov/2021001471 / LC ebook record available at https://lccn.loc.gov/2021001472 /

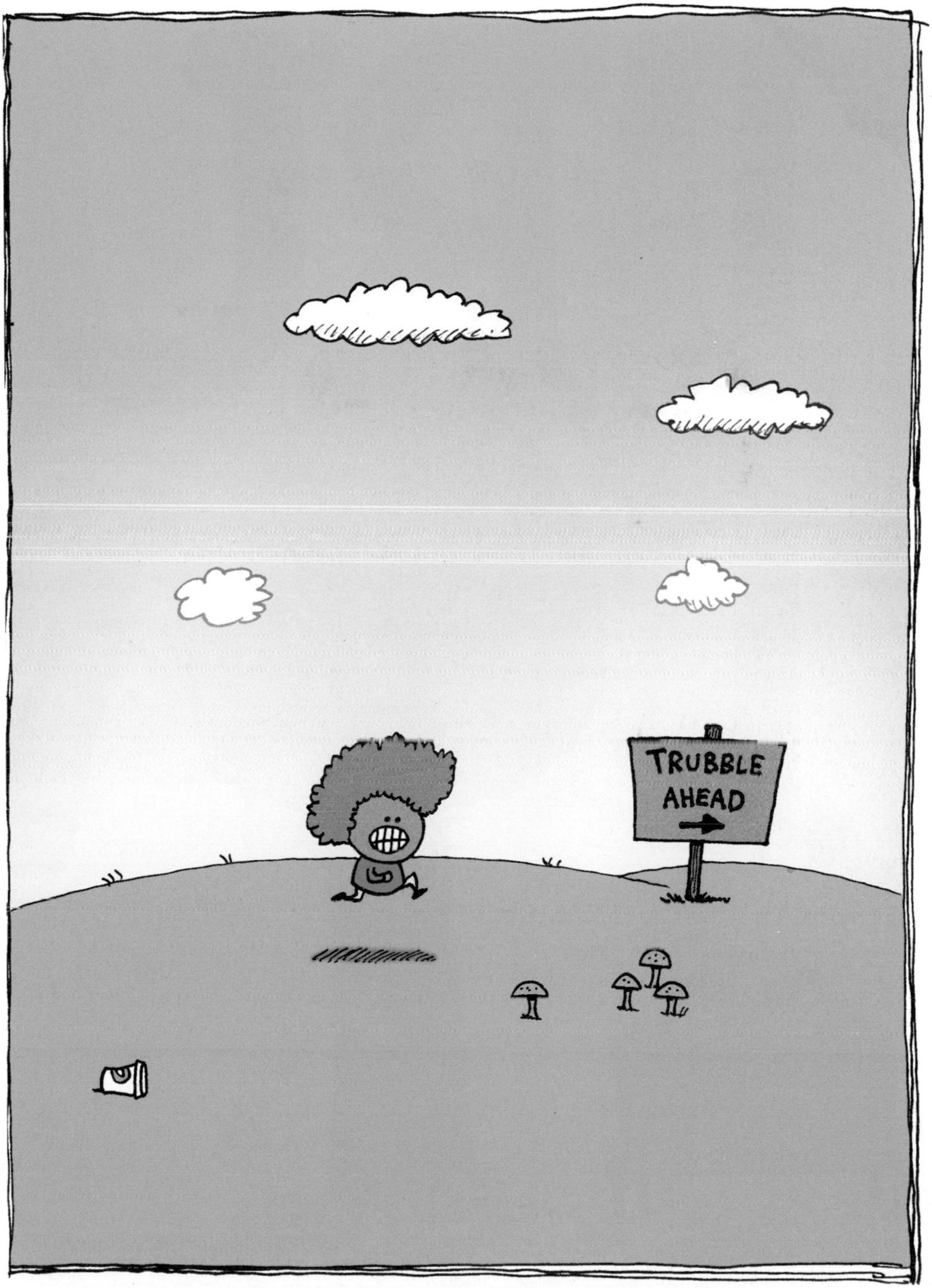
TRUBBLE
AHEAD

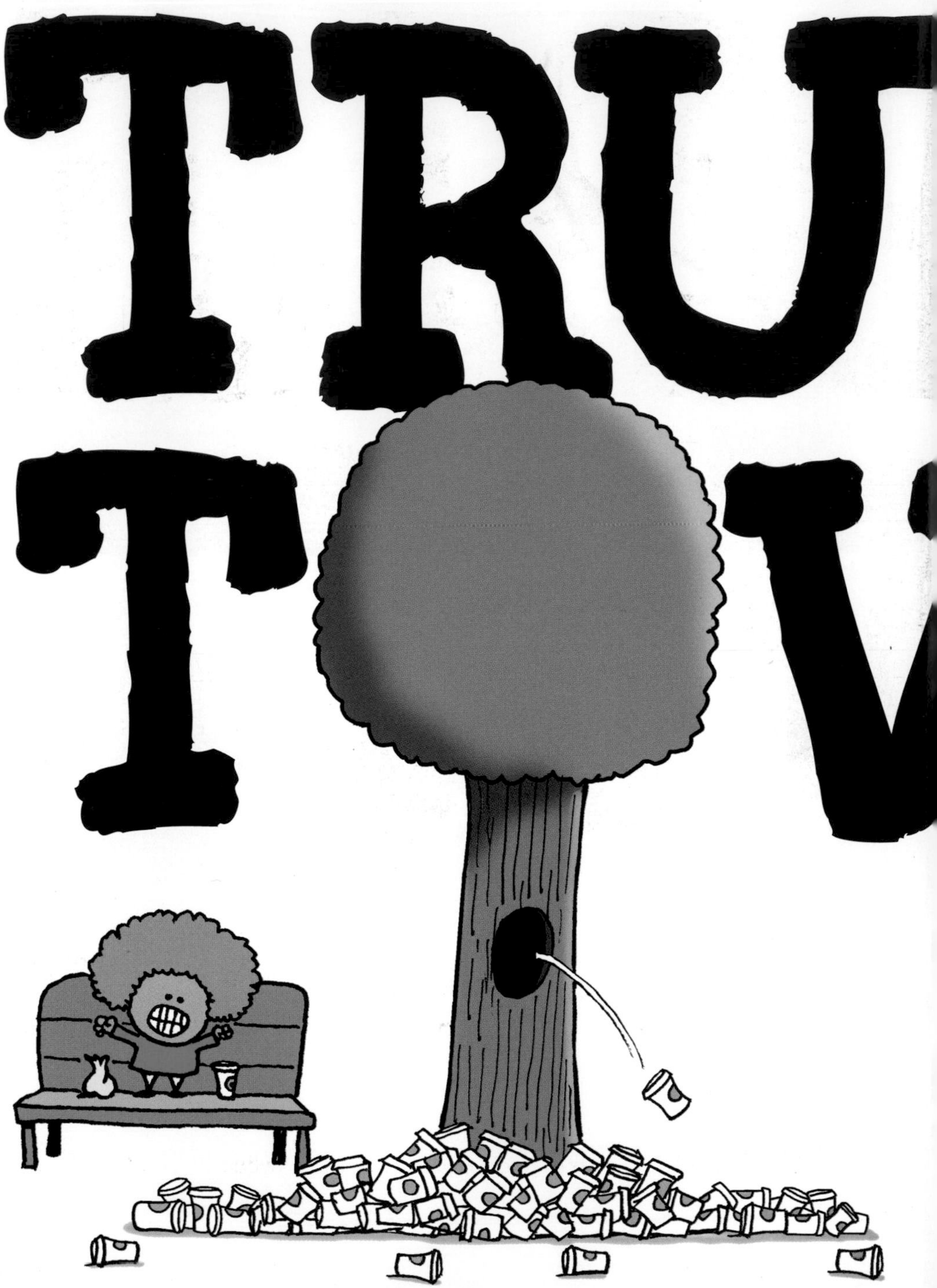
TRU
T

TO STACI...

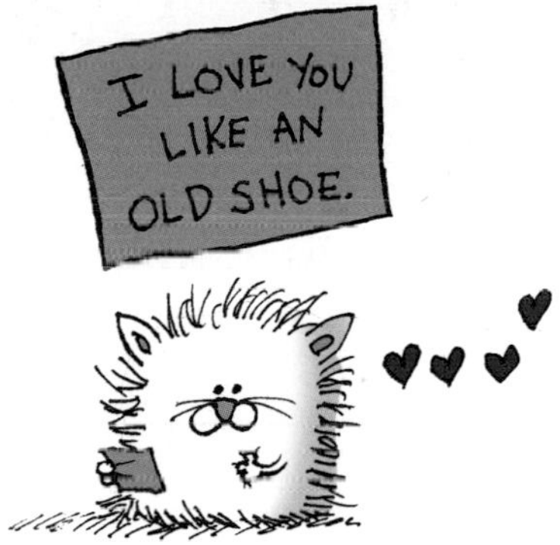
I LOVE YOU
LIKE AN
OLD SHOE.

CHAPTER ZERO

IN WHICH...

WE USE A CHAPTER NUMBER WE DON'T THINK ANYONE HAS USED BEFORE

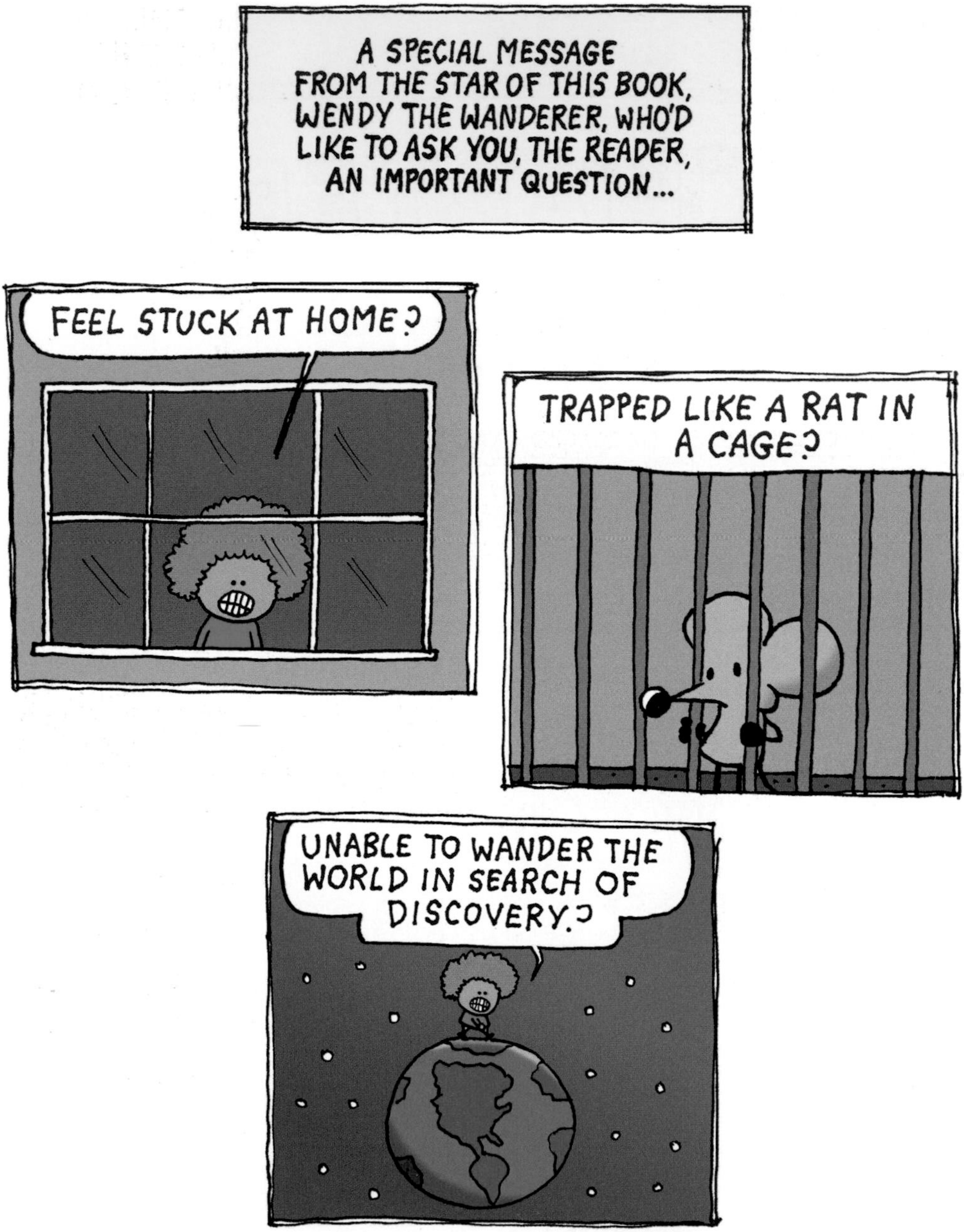
A SPECIAL MESSAGE FROM THE STAR OF THIS BOOK, WENDY THE WANDERER, WHO'D LIKE TO ASK YOU, THE READER, AN IMPORTANT QUESTION...
FEEL STUCK AT HOME?
TRAPPED LIKE A RAT IN A CAGE?
UNABLE TO WANDER THE WORLD IN SEARCH OF DISCOVERY?

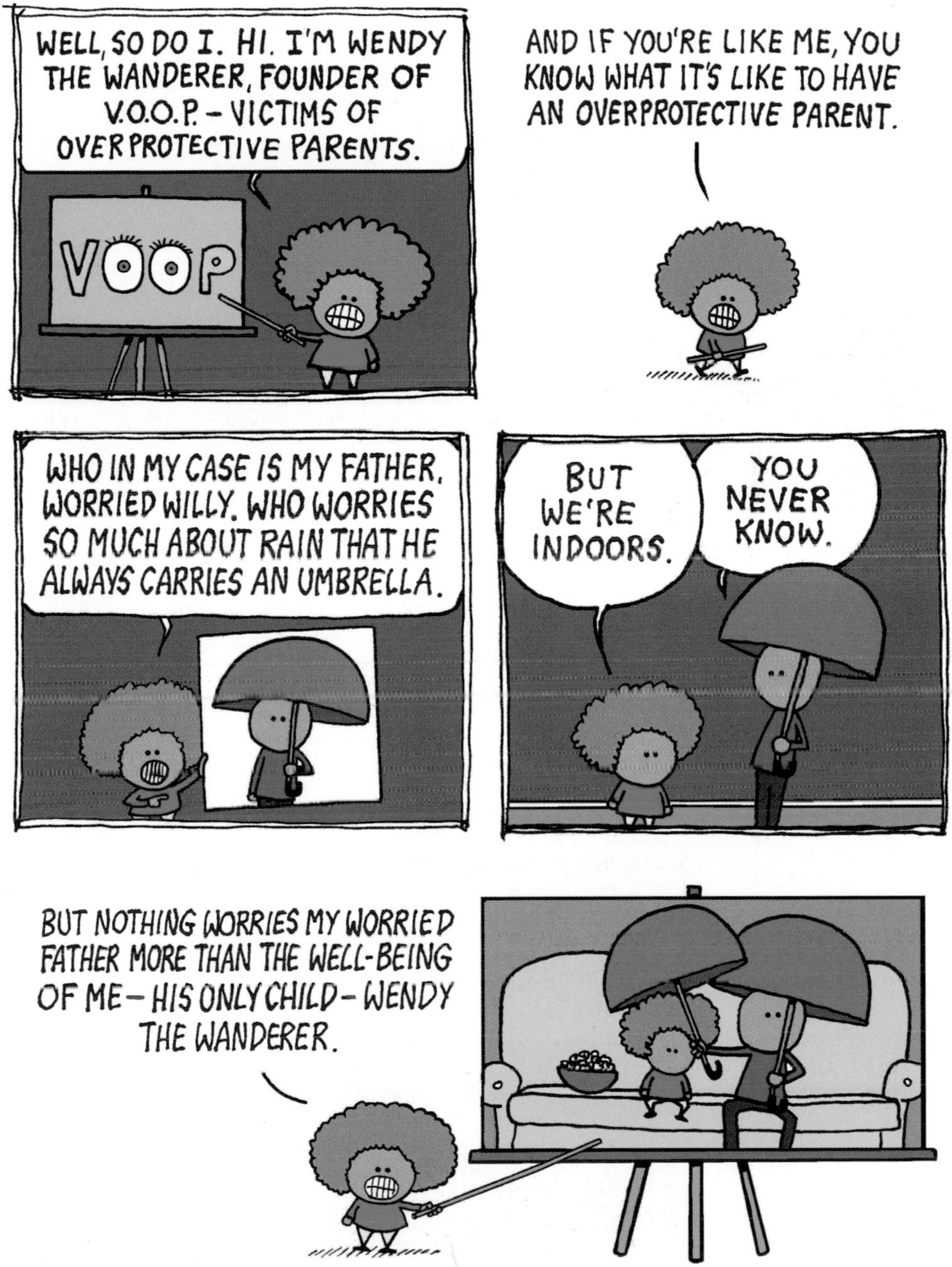
WELL, SO DO I. HI. I'M WENDY THE WANDERER, FOUNDER OF V.O.O.P. – VICTIMS OF OVERPROTECTIVE PARENTS.
VOOP
AND IF YOU'RE LIKE ME, YOU KNOW WHAT IT'S LIKE TO HAVE AN OVERPROTECTIVE PARENT.
WHO IN MY CASE IS MY FATHER, WORRIED WILLY. WHO WORRIES SO MUCH ABOUT RAIN THAT HE ALWAYS CARRIES AN UMBRELLA.
BUT WE'RE INDOORS.
YOU NEVER KNOW.
BUT NOTHING WORRIES MY WORRIED FATHER MORE THAN THE WELL-BEING OF ME – HIS ONLY CHILD – WENDY THE WANDERER.

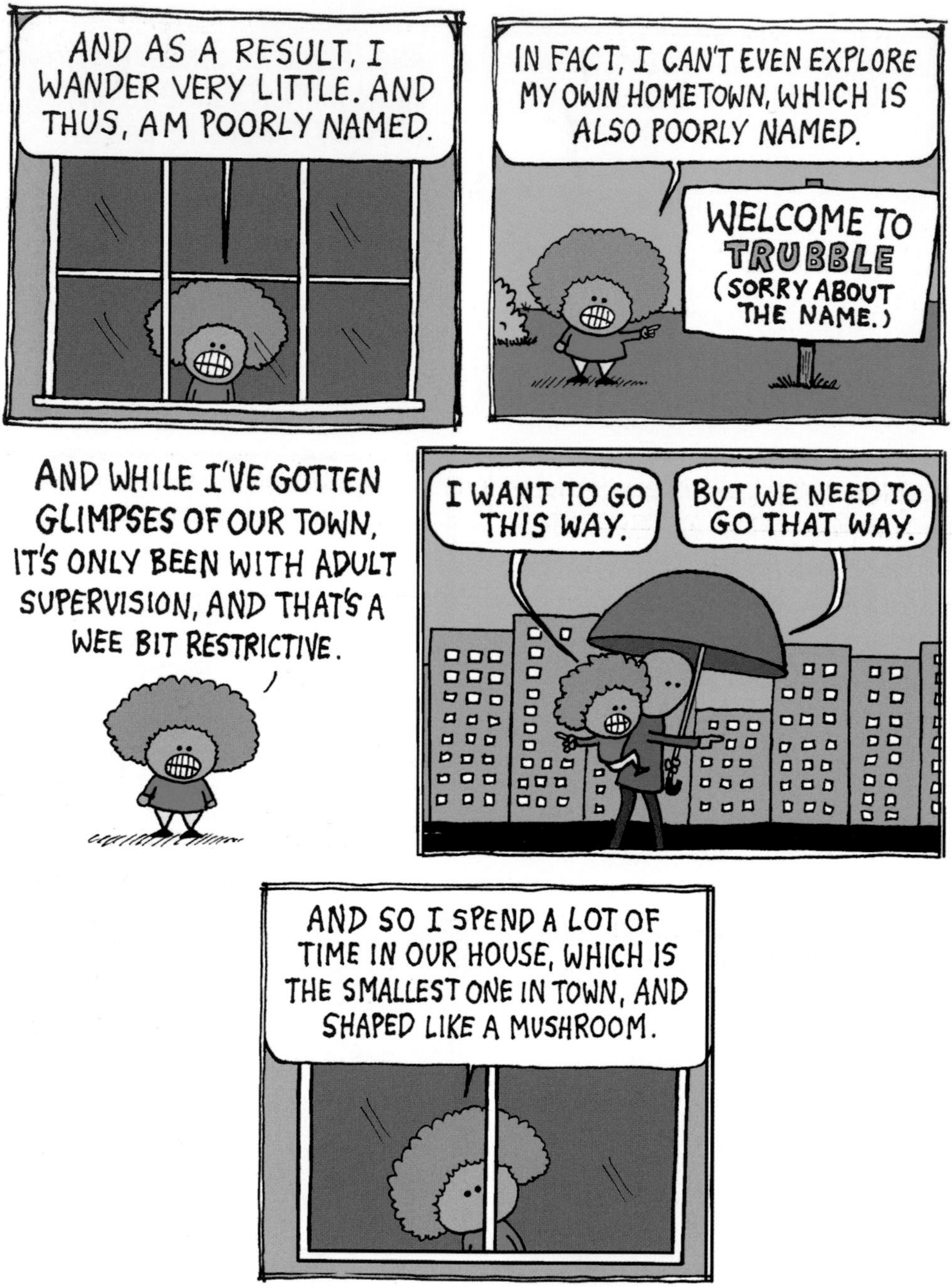
AND AS A RESULT, I WANDER VERY LITTLE. AND THUS, AM POORLY NAMED.
IN FACT, I CAN'T EVEN EXPLORE MY OWN HOMETOWN, WHICH IS ALSO POORLY NAMED.
WELCOME TO TRUBBLE (SORRY ABOUT THE NAME.)
AND WHILE I'VE GOTTEN GLIMPSES OF OUR TOWN, IT'S ONLY BEEN WITH ADULT SUPERVISION, AND THAT'S A WEE BIT RESTRICTIVE.
I WANT TO GO THIS WAY.
BUT WE NEED TO GO THAT WAY.
AND SO I SPEND A LOT OF TIME IN OUR HOUSE, WHICH IS THE SMALLEST ONE IN TOWN, AND SHAPED LIKE A MUSHROOM.

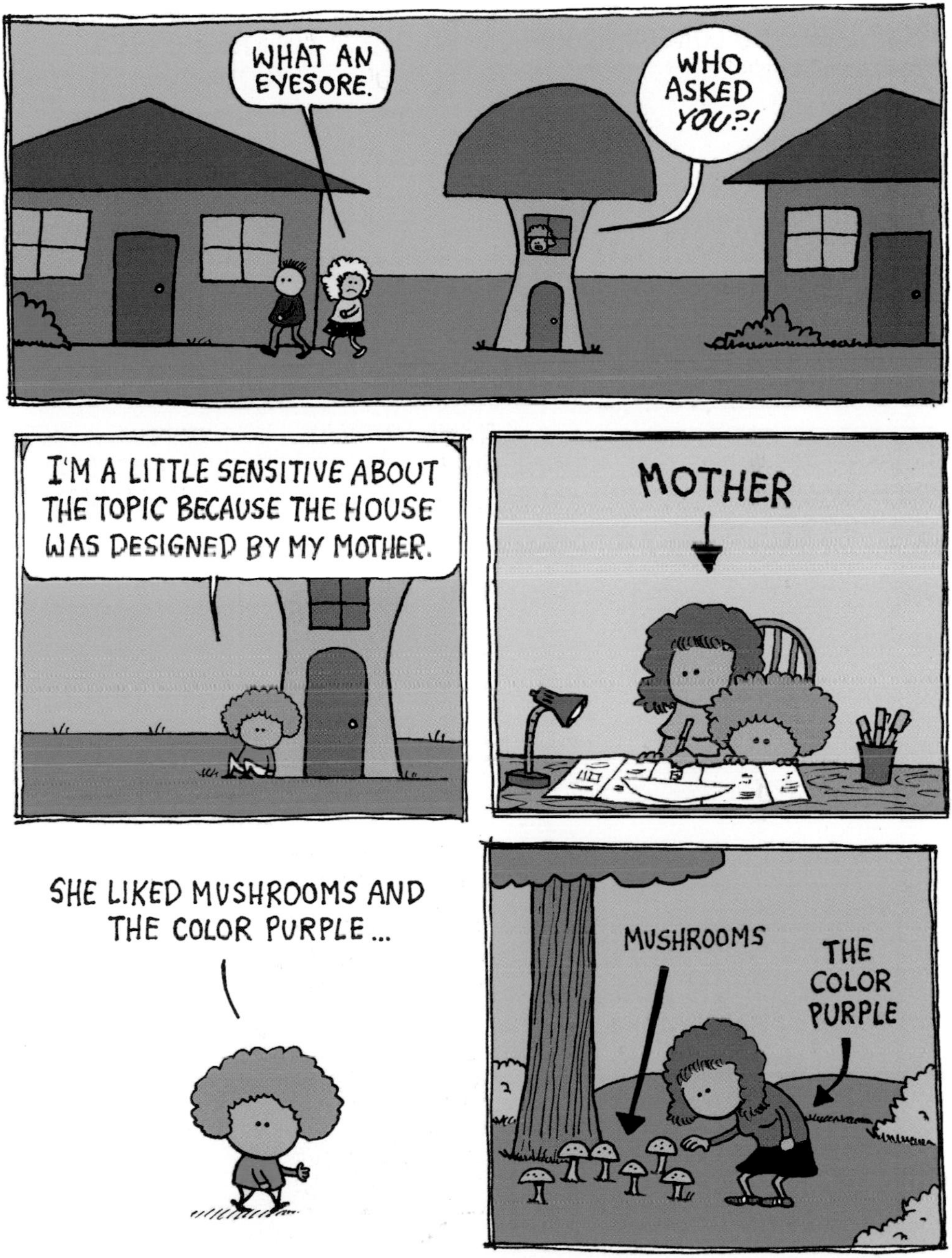
WHAT AN EYESORE.
WHO ASKED YOU?!
I'M A LITTLE SENSITIVE ABOUT THE TOPIC BECAUSE THE HOUSE WAS DESIGNED BY MY MOTHER.
MOTHER
SHE LIKED MUSHROOMS AND THE COLOR PURPLE ...
MUSHROOMS
THE COLOR PURPLE

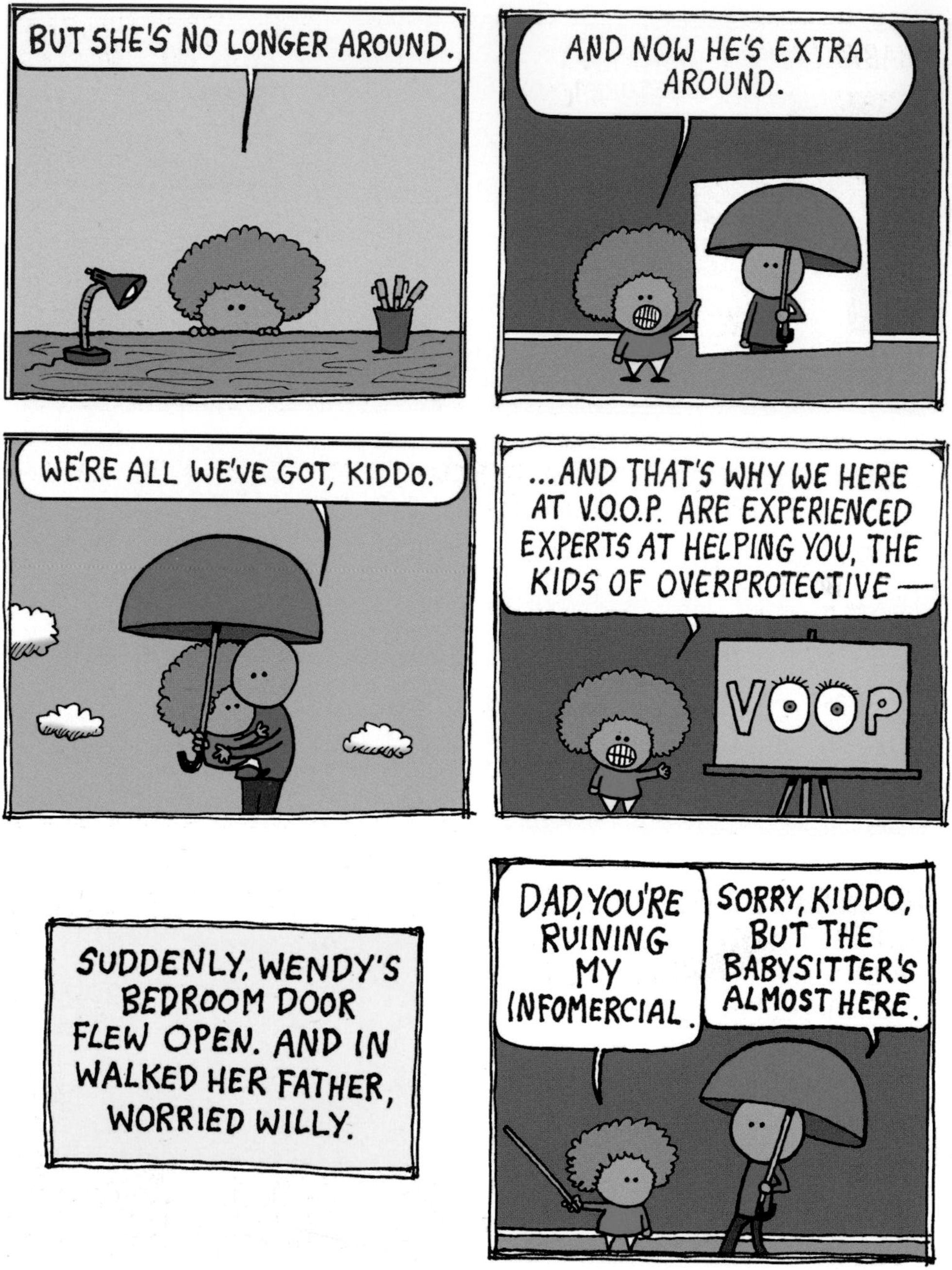
BUT SHE'S NO LONGER AROUND.
AND NOW HE'S EXTRA AROUND.
WE'RE ALL WE'VE GOT, KIDDO.
...AND THAT'S WHY WE HERE AT V.O.O.P. ARE EXPERIENCED EXPERTS AT HELPING YOU, THE KIDS OF OVERPROTECTIVE —
VOOP
SUDDENLY, WENDY'S BEDROOM DOOR FLEW OPEN. AND IN WALKED HER FATHER, WORRIED WILLY.
DAD, YOU'RE RUINING MY INFOMERCIAL.
SORRY, KIDDO, BUT THE BABYSITTER'S ALMOST HERE.

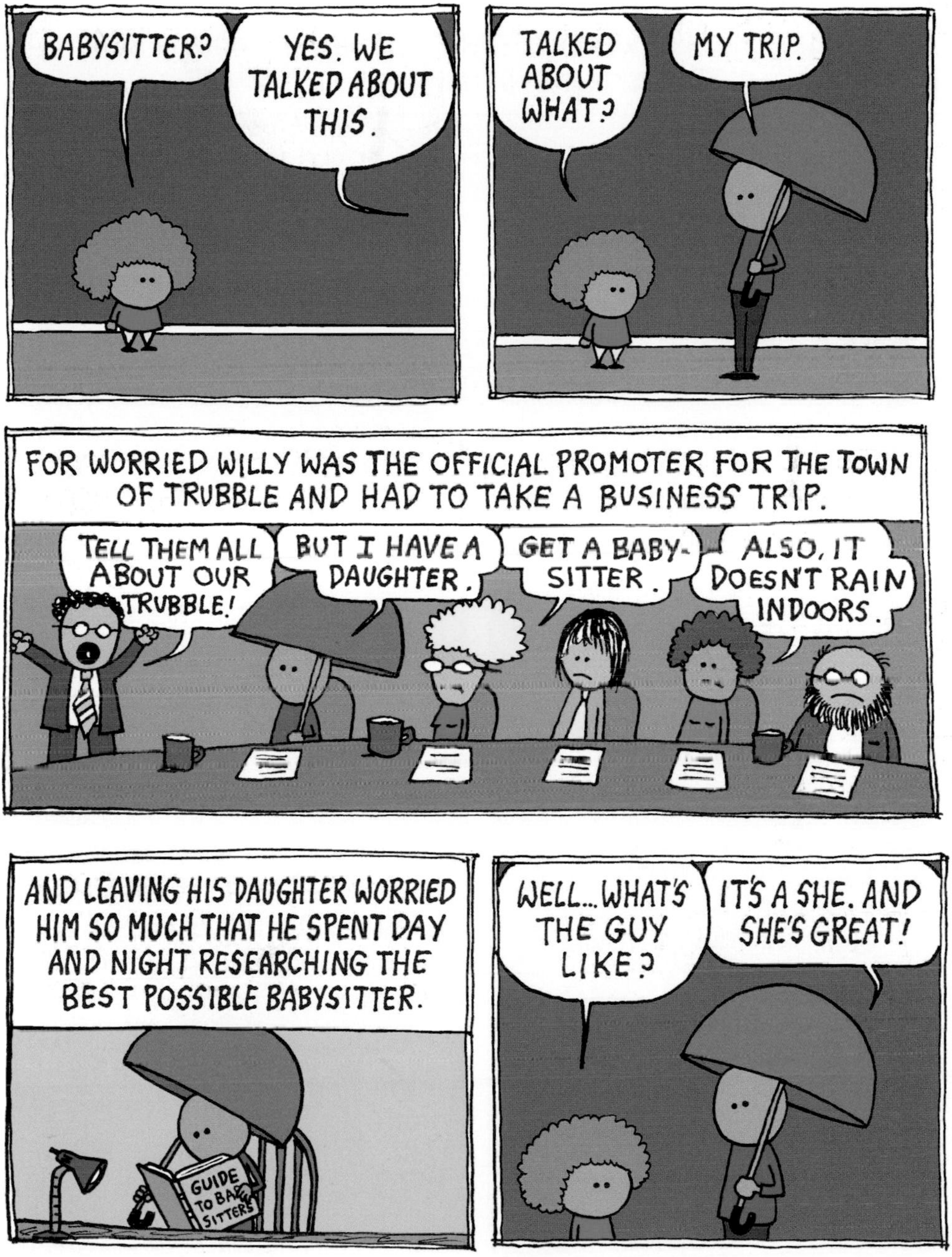
BABYSITTER?
YES. WE TALKED ABOUT THIS.
TALKED ABOUT WHAT?
MY TRIP.
FOR WORRIED WILLY WAS THE OFFICIAL PROMOTER FOR THE TOWN OF TRUBBLE AND HAD TO TAKE A BUSINESS TRIP.
TELL THEM ALL ABOUT OUR TRUBBLE!
BUT I HAVE A DAUGHTER.
GET A BABY-SITTER.
ALSO, IT DOESN'T RAIN INDOORS.
AND LEAVING HIS DAUGHTER WORRIED HIM SO MUCH THAT HE SPENT DAY AND NIGHT RESEARCHING THE BEST POSSIBLE BABYSITTER.
GUIDE TO BA SITTERS
WELL... WHAT'S THE GUY LIKE?
IT'S A SHE. AND SHE'S GREAT!

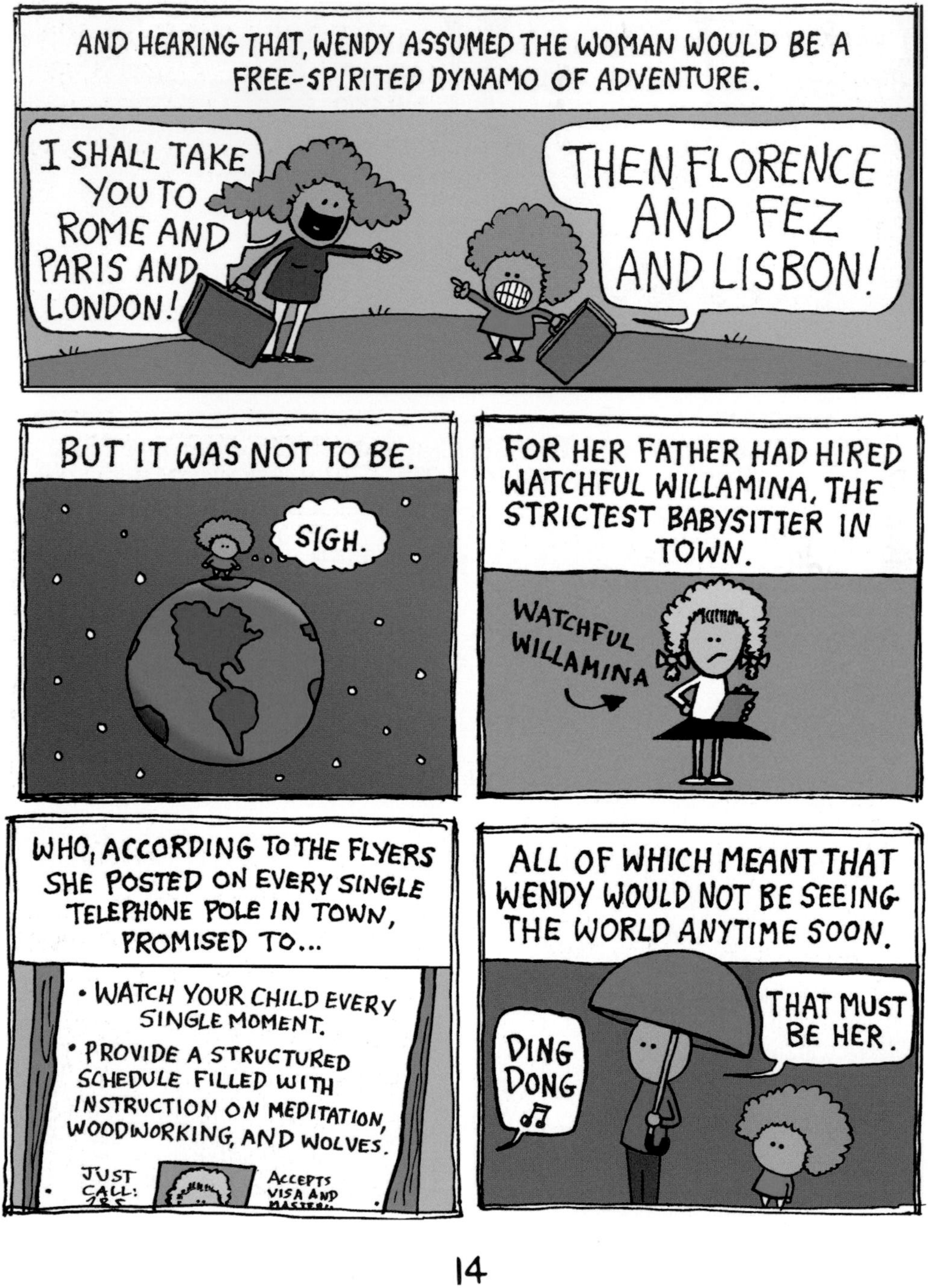
AND HEARING THAT, WENDY ASSUMED THE WOMAN WOULD BE A FREE-SPIRITED DYNAMO OF ADVENTURE.
I SHALL TAKE YOU TO ROME AND PARIS AND LONDON!
THEN FLORENCE AND FEZ AND LISBON!
BUT IT WAS NOT TO BE.
SIGH.
FOR HER FATHER HAD HIRED WATCHFUL WILLAMINA, THE STRICTEST BABYSITTER IN TOWN.
WATCHFUL WILLAMINA
WHO, ACCORDING TO THE FLYERS SHE POSTED ON EVERY SINGLE TELEPHONE POLE IN TOWN, PROMISED TO...
• WATCH YOUR CHILD EVERY SINGLE MOMENT.
• PROVIDE A STRUCTURED SCHEDULE FILLED WITH INSTRUCTION ON MEDITATION, WOODWORKING, AND WOLVES.
JUST CALL:
ACCEPTS VISA AND
ALL OF WHICH MEANT THAT WENDY WOULD NOT BE SEEING THE WORLD ANYTIME SOON.
DING DONG ♫
THAT MUST BE HER.

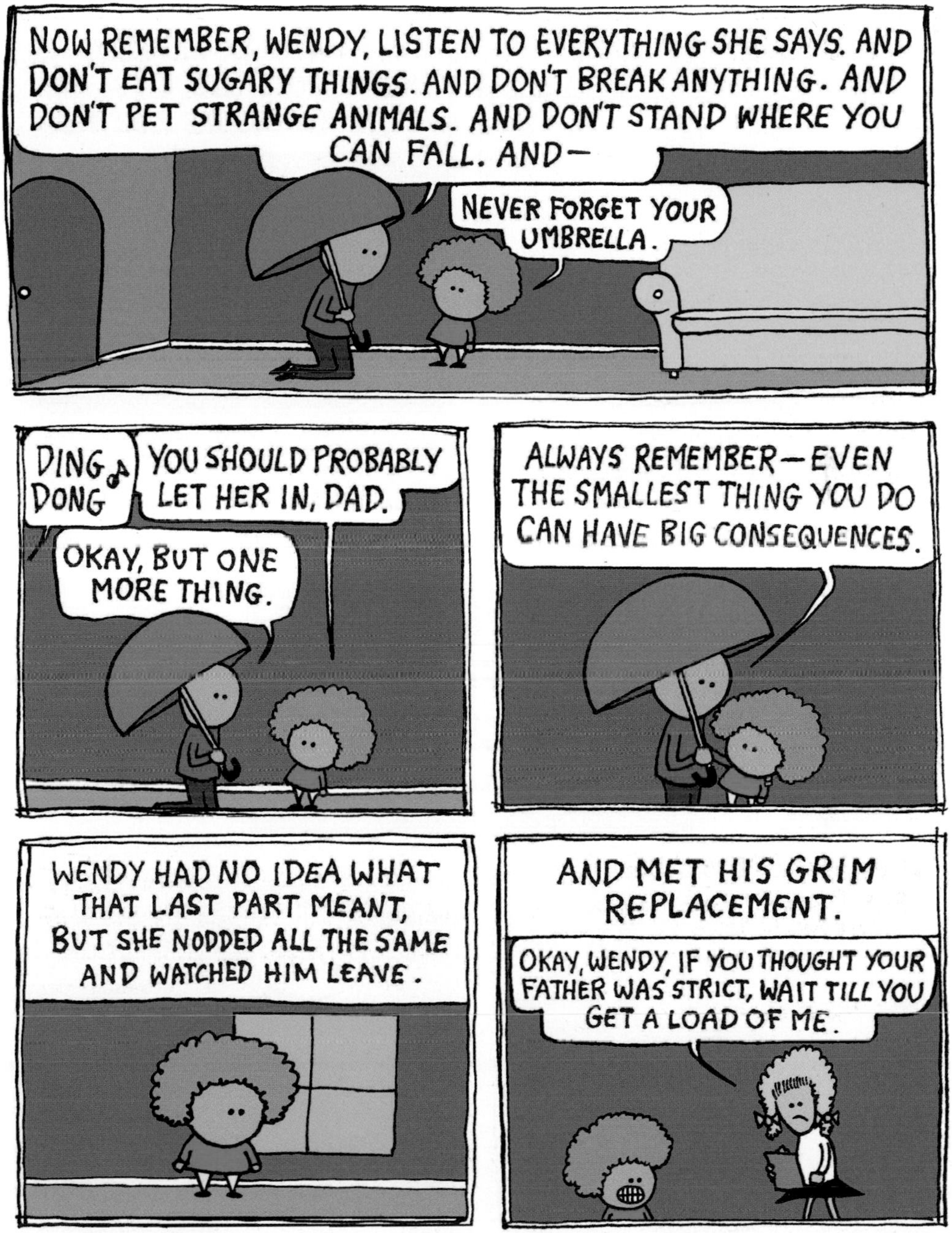
NOW REMEMBER, WENDY, LISTEN TO EVERYTHING SHE SAYS. AND DON'T EAT SUGARY THINGS. AND DON'T BREAK ANYTHING. AND DON'T PET STRANGE ANIMALS. AND DON'T STAND WHERE YOU CAN FALL. AND—
NEVER FORGET YOUR UMBRELLA.
DING DONG
YOU SHOULD PROBABLY LET HER IN, DAD.
OKAY, BUT ONE MORE THING.
ALWAYS REMEMBER—EVEN THE SMALLEST THING YOU DO CAN HAVE BIG CONSEQUENCES.
WENDY HAD NO IDEA WHAT THAT LAST PART MEANT, BUT SHE NODDED ALL THE SAME AND WATCHED HIM LEAVE.
AND MET HIS GRIM REPLACEMENT.
OKAY, WENDY, IF YOU THOUGHT YOUR FATHER WAS STRICT, WAIT TILL YOU GET A LOAD OF ME.

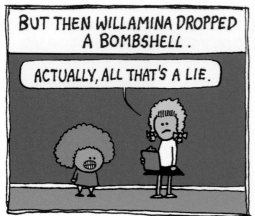

BUT THEN WILLAMINA DROPPED A BOMBSHELL.

ACTUALLY, ALL THAT'S A LIE.

THE STRICTNESS. THE SCHEDULE. THE WATCHFULNESS. I JUST SAY IT TO IMPRESS THE PARENTS.

THE TRUTH IS... I'M GONNA BE ON MY PHONE EVERY MINUTE OF EVERY DAY.

SO IF YOU STAY OUTTA MY WAY, I'LL STAY OUTTA YOURS. JUST DON'T GET INTO TROUBLE. DEAL?

Deal.

AND LEAVING HER UMBRELLA BEHIND, WENDY THE WANDERER RAN OFF TO FIND TRUBBLE.

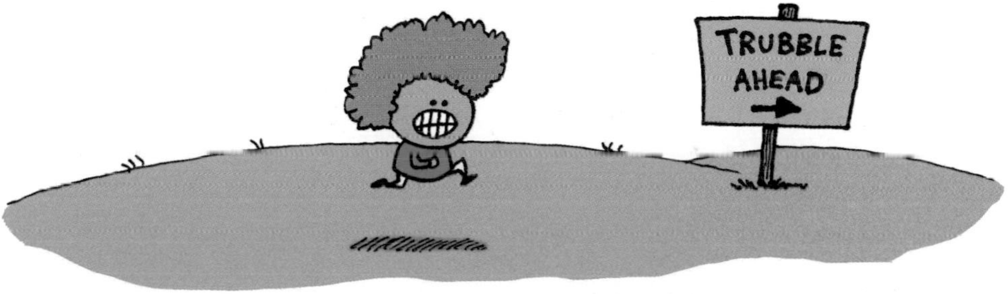
TRUBBLE
AHEAD

CHAPTER ONE

IN WHICH...

YOU WILL BE SHOCKED AND AMAZED

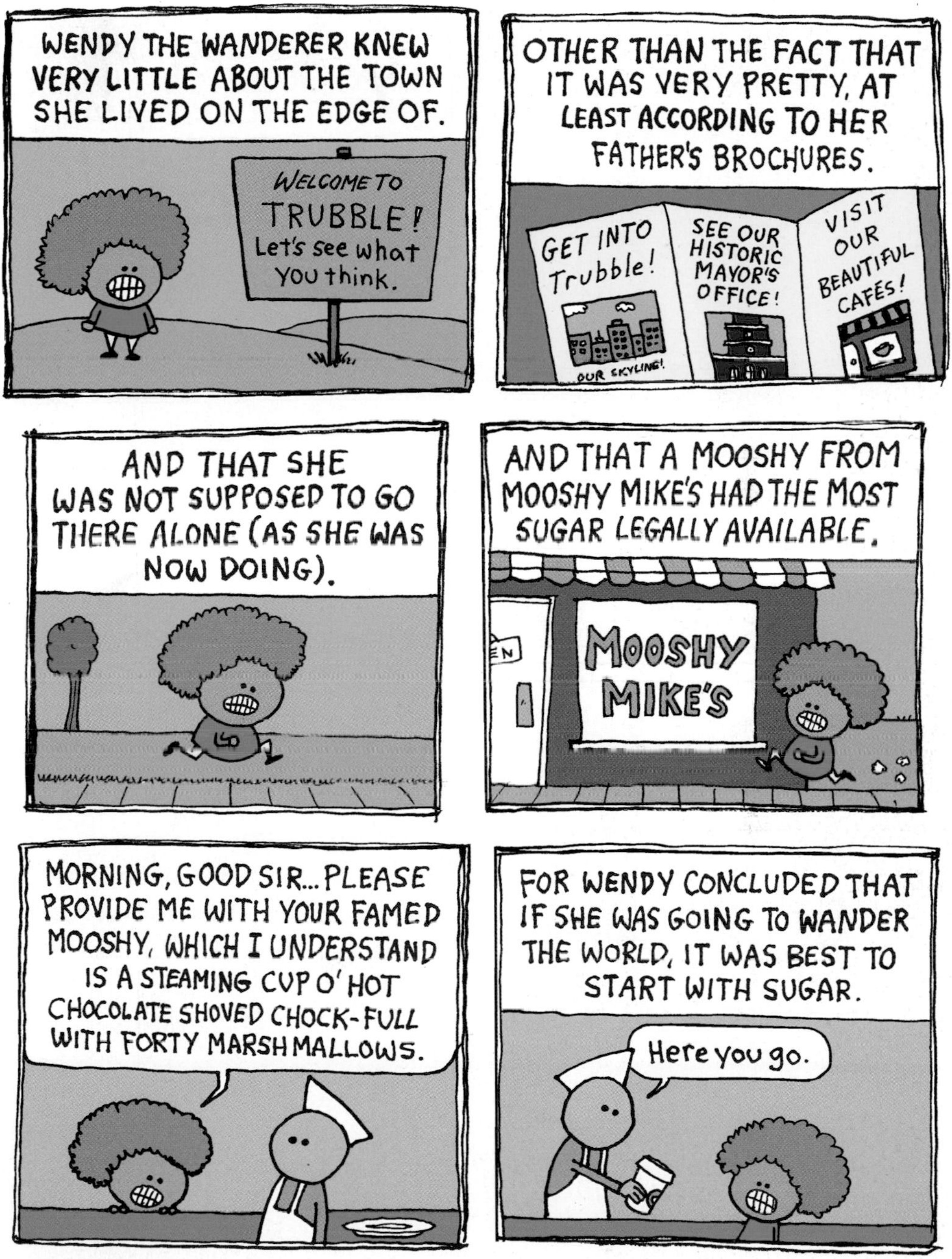
WENDY THE WANDERER KNEW VERY LITTLE ABOUT THE TOWN SHE LIVED ON THE EDGE OF.
WELCOME TO TRUBBLE! Let's see what you think.
OTHER THAN THE FACT THAT IT WAS VERY PRETTY, AT LEAST ACCORDING TO HER FATHER'S BROCHURES.
GET INTO Trubble!
OUR SKYLINE!
SEE OUR HISTORIC MAYOR'S OFFICE!
VISIT OUR BEAUTIFUL CAFÉS!
AND THAT SHE WAS NOT SUPPOSED TO GO THERE ALONE (AS SHE WAS NOW DOING).
AND THAT A MOOSHY FROM MOOSHY MIKE'S HAD THE MOST SUGAR LEGALLY AVAILABLE.
MOOSHY MIKE'S
MORNING, GOOD SIR... PLEASE PROVIDE ME WITH YOUR FAMED MOOSHY, WHICH I UNDERSTAND IS A STEAMING CUP O' HOT CHOCOLATE SHOVED CHOCK-FULL WITH FORTY MARSHMALLOWS.
FOR WENDY CONCLUDED THAT IF SHE WAS GOING TO WANDER THE WORLD, IT WAS BEST TO START WITH SUGAR.
Here you go.

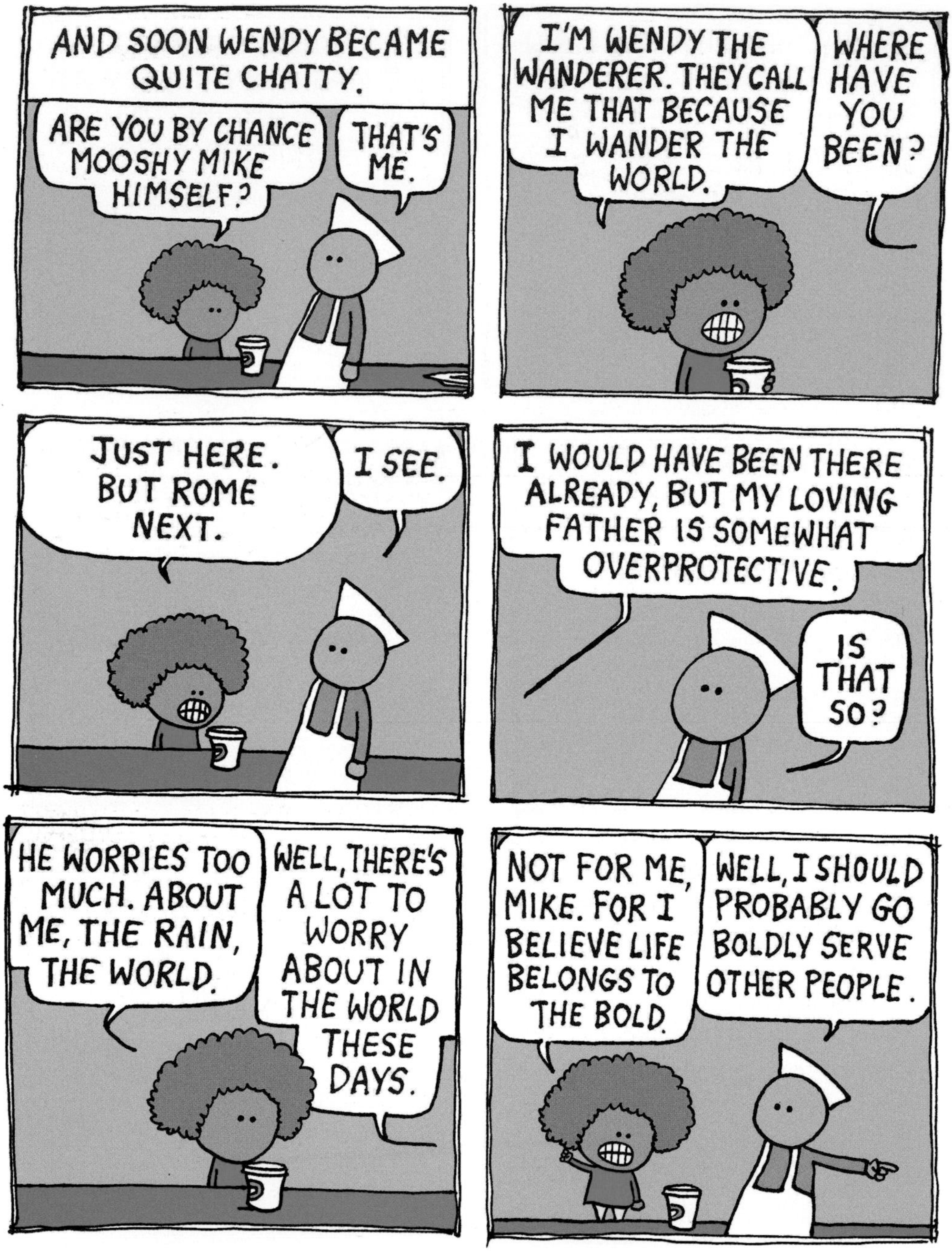
AND SOON WENDY BECAME QUITE CHATTY.
ARE YOU BY CHANCE MOOSHY MIKE HIMSELF?
THAT'S ME.
I'M WENDY THE WANDERER. THEY CALL ME THAT BECAUSE I WANDER THE WORLD.
WHERE HAVE YOU BEEN?
JUST HERE. BUT ROME NEXT.
I SEE.
I WOULD HAVE BEEN THERE ALREADY, BUT MY LOVING FATHER IS SOMEWHAT OVERPROTECTIVE.
IS THAT SO?
HE WORRIES TOO MUCH. ABOUT ME, THE RAIN, THE WORLD.
WELL, THERE'S A LOT TO WORRY ABOUT IN THE WORLD THESE DAYS.
NOT FOR ME, MIKE. FOR I BELIEVE LIFE BELONGS TO THE BOLD.
WELL, I SHOULD PROBABLY GO BOLDLY SERVE OTHER PEOPLE.

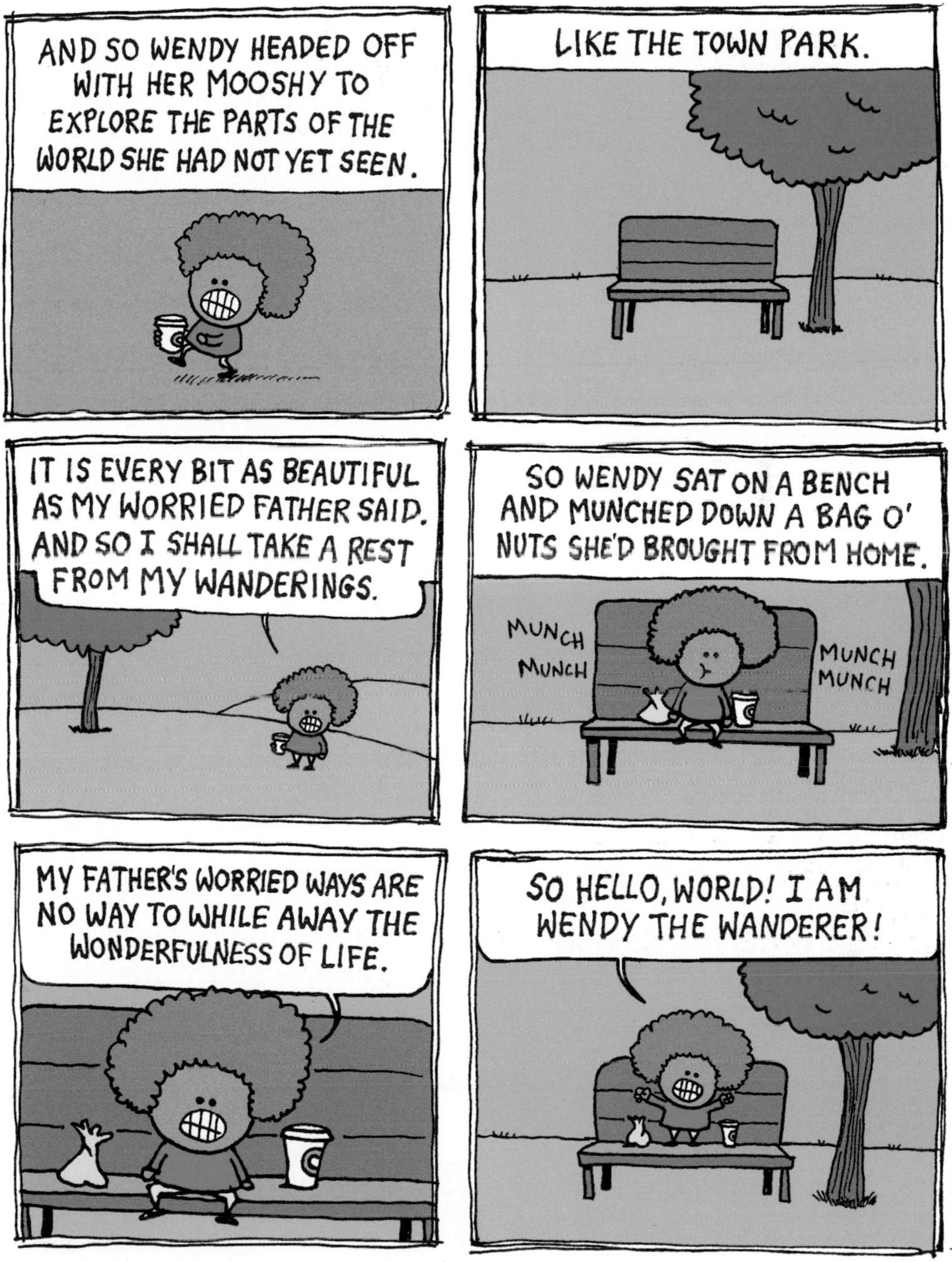
AND SO WENDY HEADED OFF WITH HER MOOSHY TO EXPLORE THE PARTS OF THE WORLD SHE HAD NOT YET SEEN.
LIKE THE TOWN PARK.
IT IS EVERY BIT AS BEAUTIFUL AS MY WORRIED FATHER SAID. AND SO I SHALL TAKE A REST FROM MY WANDERINGS.
SO WENDY SAT ON A BENCH AND MUNCHED DOWN A BAG O' NUTS SHE'D BROUGHT FROM HOME.
MUNCH MUNCH
MUNCH MUNCH
MY FATHER'S WORRIED WAYS ARE NO WAY TO WHILE AWAY THE WONDERFULNESS OF LIFE.
SO HELLO, WORLD! I AM WENDY THE WANDERER!

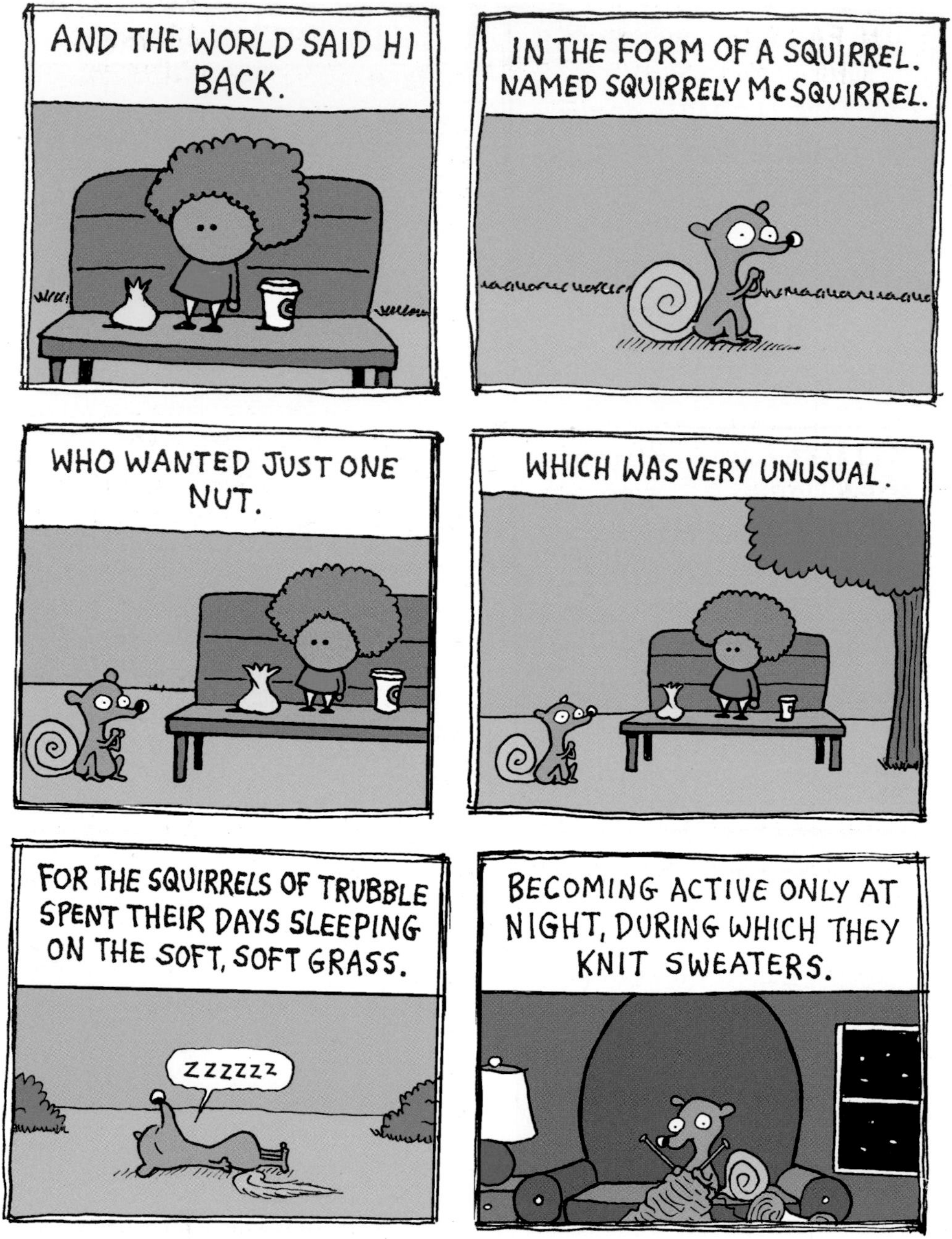
AND THE WORLD SAID HI BACK.
IN THE FORM OF A SQUIRREL. NAMED SQUIRRELY McSQUIRREL.
WHO WANTED JUST ONE NUT.
WHICH WAS VERY UNUSUAL.
FOR THE SQUIRRELS OF TRUBBLE SPENT THEIR DAYS SLEEPING ON THE SOFT, SOFT GRASS.
ZZZZZZ
BECOMING ACTIVE ONLY AT NIGHT, DURING WHICH THEY KNIT SWEATERS.

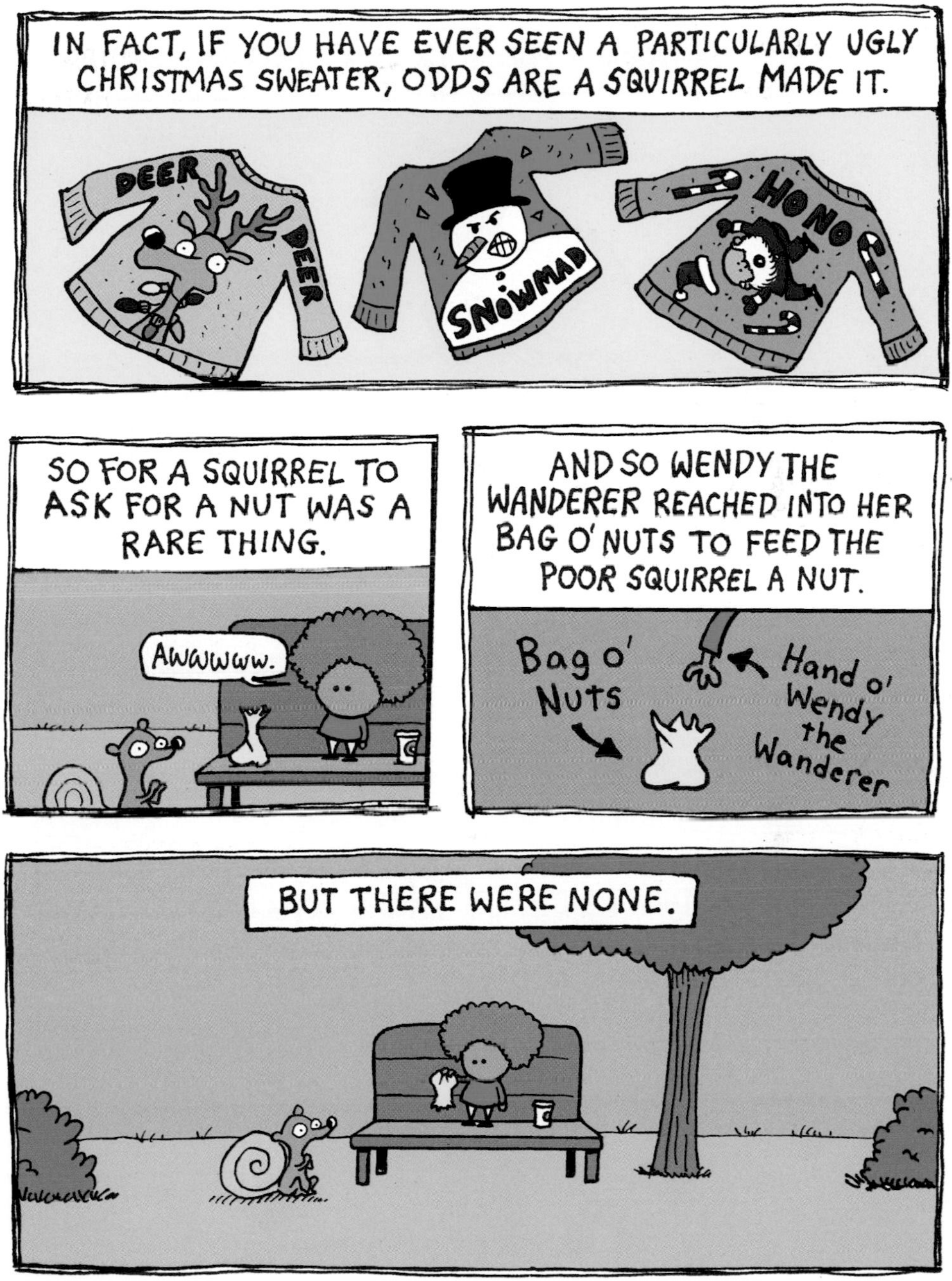
IN FACT, IF YOU HAVE EVER SEEN A PARTICULARLY UGLY CHRISTMAS SWEATER, ODDS ARE A SQUIRREL MADE IT.
DEER
DEER
SNOWMAD
HO NO
SO FOR A SQUIRREL TO ASK FOR A NUT WAS A RARE THING.
AWWWWW.
AND SO WENDY THE WANDERER REACHED INTO HER BAG O' NUTS TO FEED THE POOR SQUIRREL A NUT.
Bag o' Nuts
Hand o' Wendy the Wanderer
BUT THERE WERE NONE.

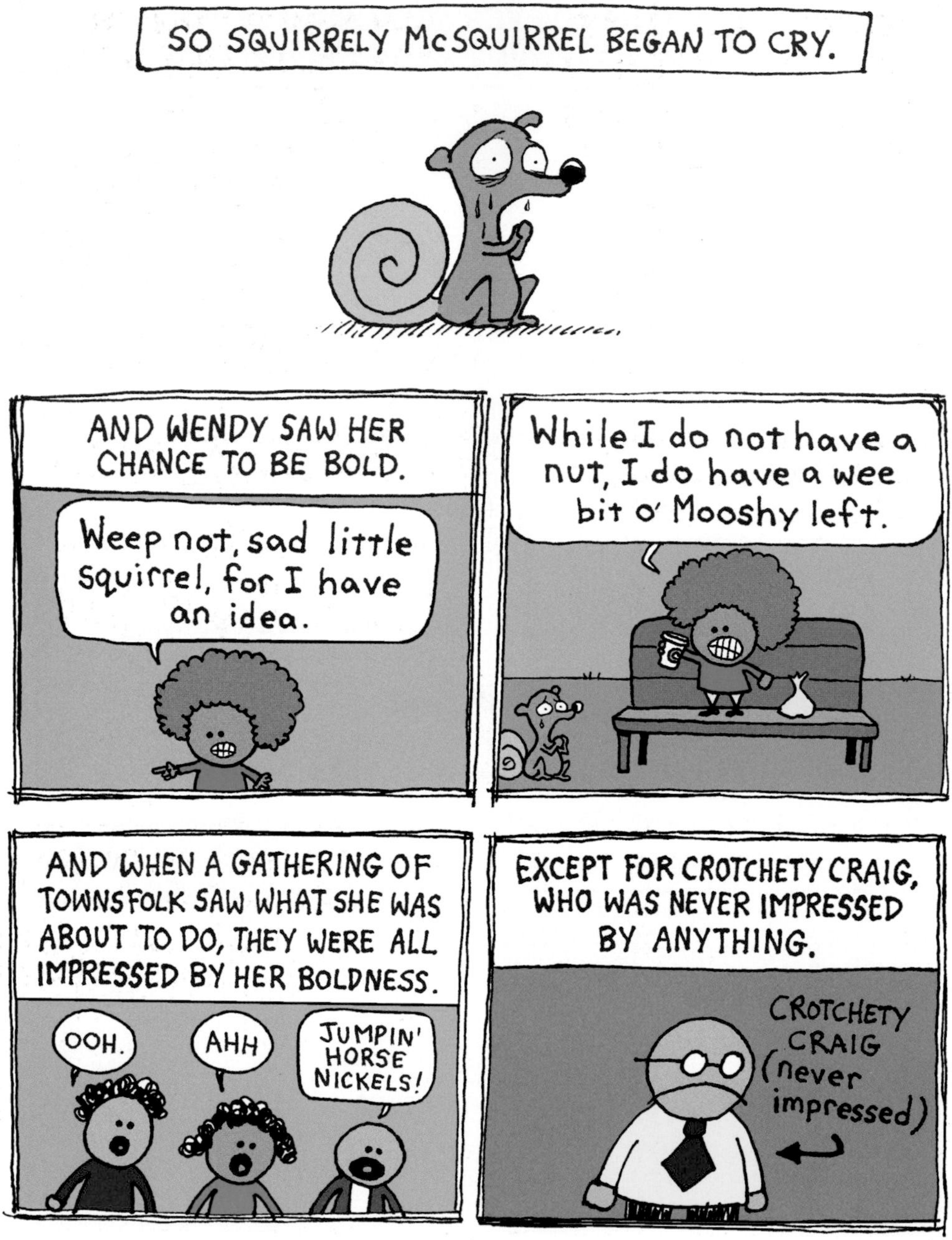
SO SQUIRRELY McSQUIRREL BEGAN TO CRY.
AND WENDY SAW HER CHANCE TO BE BOLD.
Weep not, sad little squirrel, for I have an idea.
While I do not have a nut, I do have a wee bit o' Mooshy left.
AND WHEN A GATHERING OF TOWNSFOLK SAW WHAT SHE WAS ABOUT TO DO, THEY WERE ALL IMPRESSED BY HER BOLDNESS.
OOH.
AHH
JUMPIN' HORSE NICKELS!
EXCEPT FOR CROTCHETY CRAIG, WHO WAS NEVER IMPRESSED BY ANYTHING.
CROTCHETY CRAIG (never impressed)

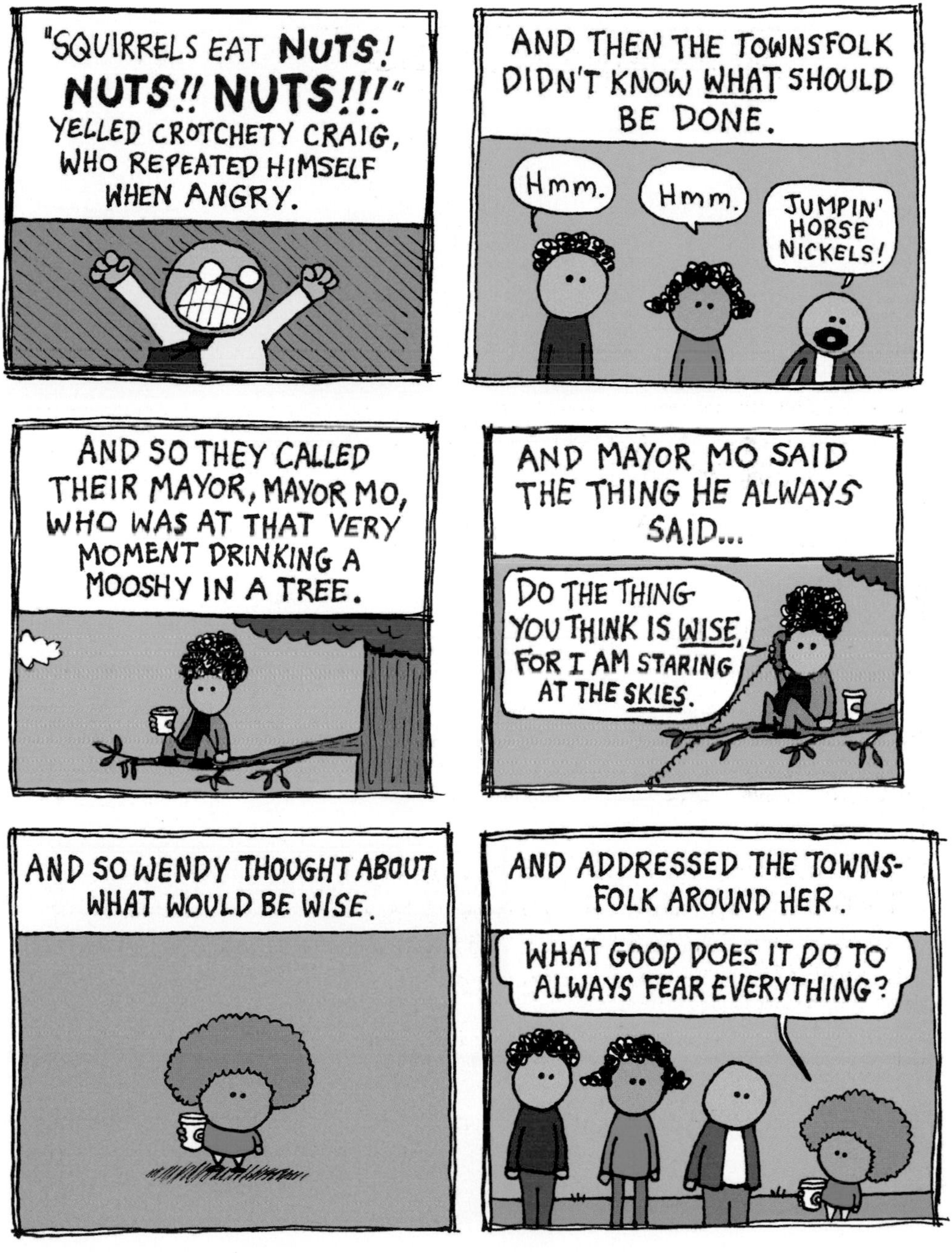
"SQUIRRELS EAT NUTS! NUTS!! NUTS!!!" YELLED CROTCHETY CRAIG, WHO REPEATED HIMSELF WHEN ANGRY.
AND THEN THE TOWNSFOLK DIDN'T KNOW WHAT SHOULD BE DONE.
Hmm.
Hmm.
JUMPIN' HORSE NICKELS!
AND SO THEY CALLED THEIR MAYOR, MAYOR MO, WHO WAS AT THAT VERY MOMENT DRINKING A MOOSHY IN A TREE.
AND MAYOR MO SAID THE THING HE ALWAYS SAID...
DO THE THING YOU THINK IS WISE, FOR I AM STARING AT THE SKIES.
AND SO WENDY THOUGHT ABOUT WHAT WOULD BE WISE.
AND ADDRESSED THE TOWNSFOLK AROUND HER.
WHAT GOOD DOES IT DO TO ALWAYS FEAR EVERYTHING?

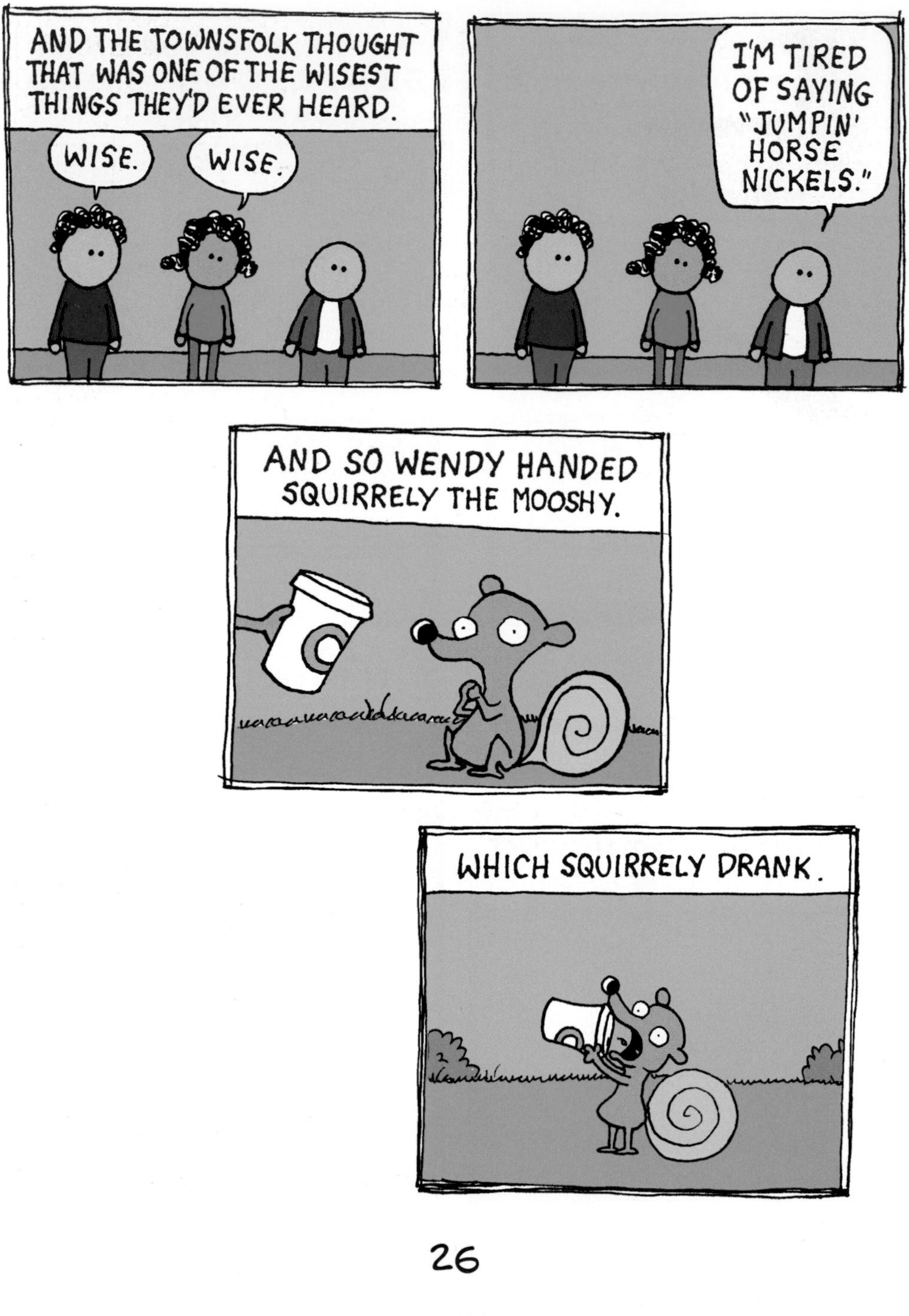
AND THE TOWNSFOLK THOUGHT THAT WAS ONE OF THE WISEST THINGS THEY'D EVER HEARD.
WISE.
WISE.
I'M TIRED OF SAYING "JUMPIN' HORSE NICKELS."
AND SO WENDY HANDED SQUIRRELY THE MOOSHY.
WHICH SQUIRRELY DRANK.

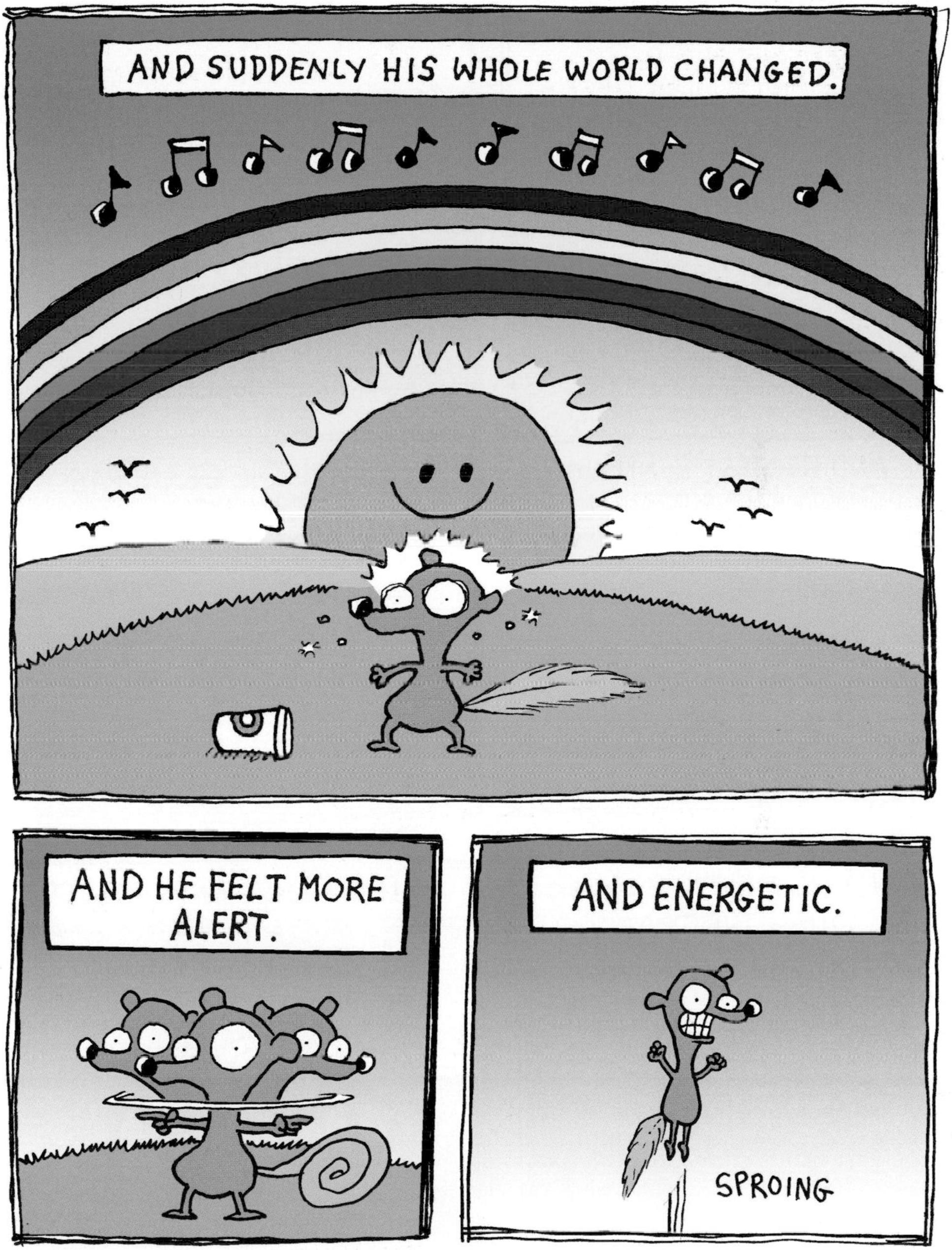
AND SUDDENLY HIS WHOLE WORLD CHANGED.
AND HE FELT MORE ALERT.
AND ENERGETIC.
SPROING

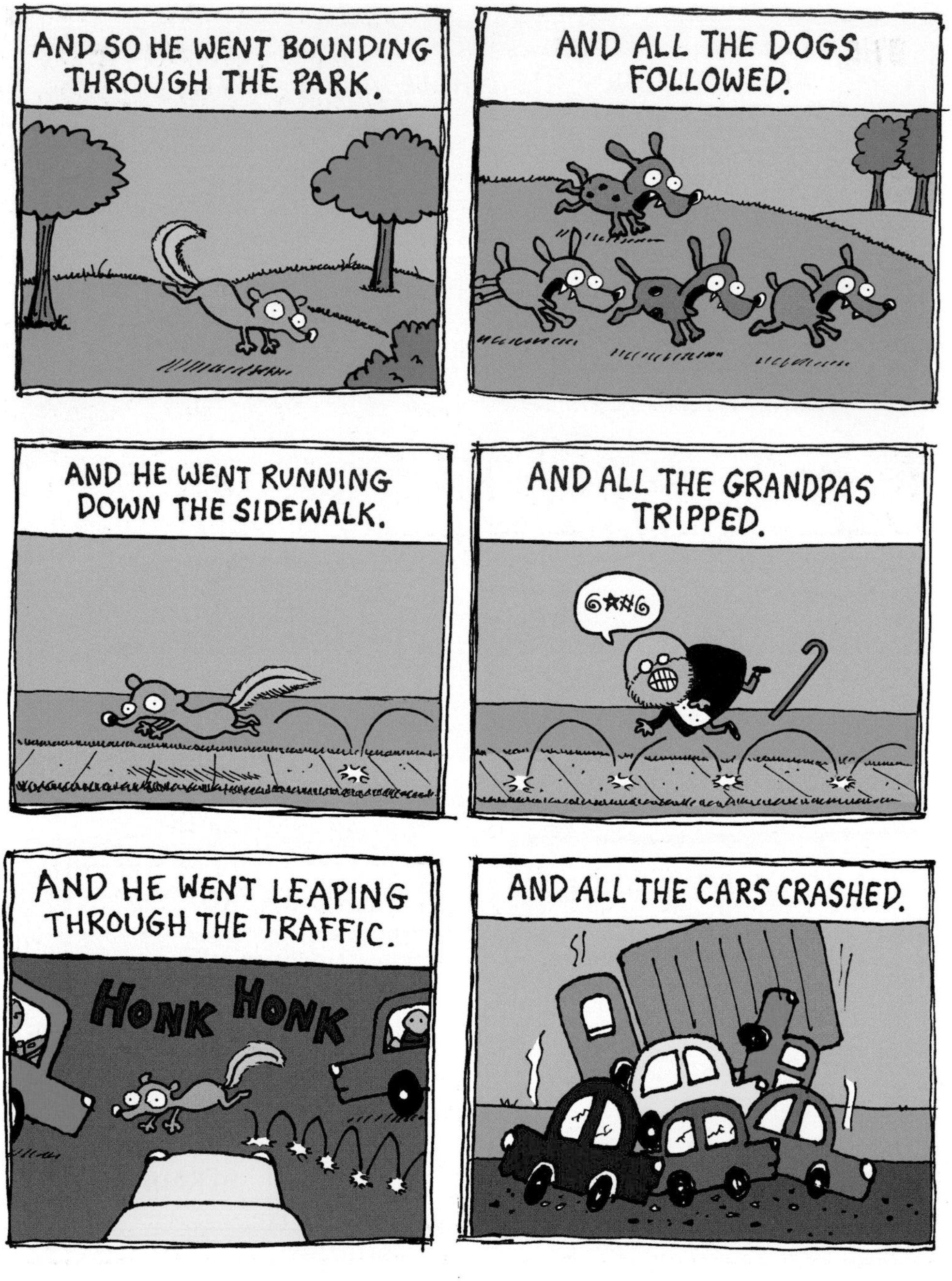
AND SO HE WENT BOUNDING THROUGH THE PARK.
AND ALL THE DOGS FOLLOWED.
AND HE WENT RUNNING DOWN THE SIDEWALK.
AND ALL THE GRANDPAS TRIPPED.
AND HE WENT LEAPING THROUGH THE TRAFFIC.
HONK HONK
AND ALL THE CARS CRASHED.

THE TOWNSFOLK WATCHED IN HORROR.

THE DOGS!

THE CARS!

IT'S FUNNY WHEN GRANDPAS FALL.

"I TOLD YOU SO," SAID CROTCHETY CRAIG EIGHTY TIMES IN A ROW.

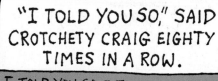

I TOLD YOU SO I TOLD YOU SO I TOLD YOU SO LD YOU SO I TOLD YOU I TOLD YOU SO I TOLL SO I TOLD YOU SO I TOLD TO OLD YOU SO I I TOLD I TOLD YOU SO YOU SO I TOLP YOU SO I TOLD YOU SO I

BUT I DON'T UNDERSTAND. HOW COULD A WEE BIT O' MOOSHY AFFECT A SQUIRREL LIKE THAT?

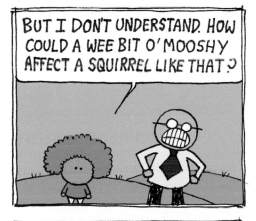

BECAUSE SQUIRRELS EAT NUTS!

AND SEEING THE CHAOS SPREADING THROUGHOUT HIS CITY, MAYOR MO KNEW HE HAD TO ACT.

AND NOT JUST SAY...

Do the thing You think is <u>WISE</u>, For I am staring at the <u>SKIES</u>.

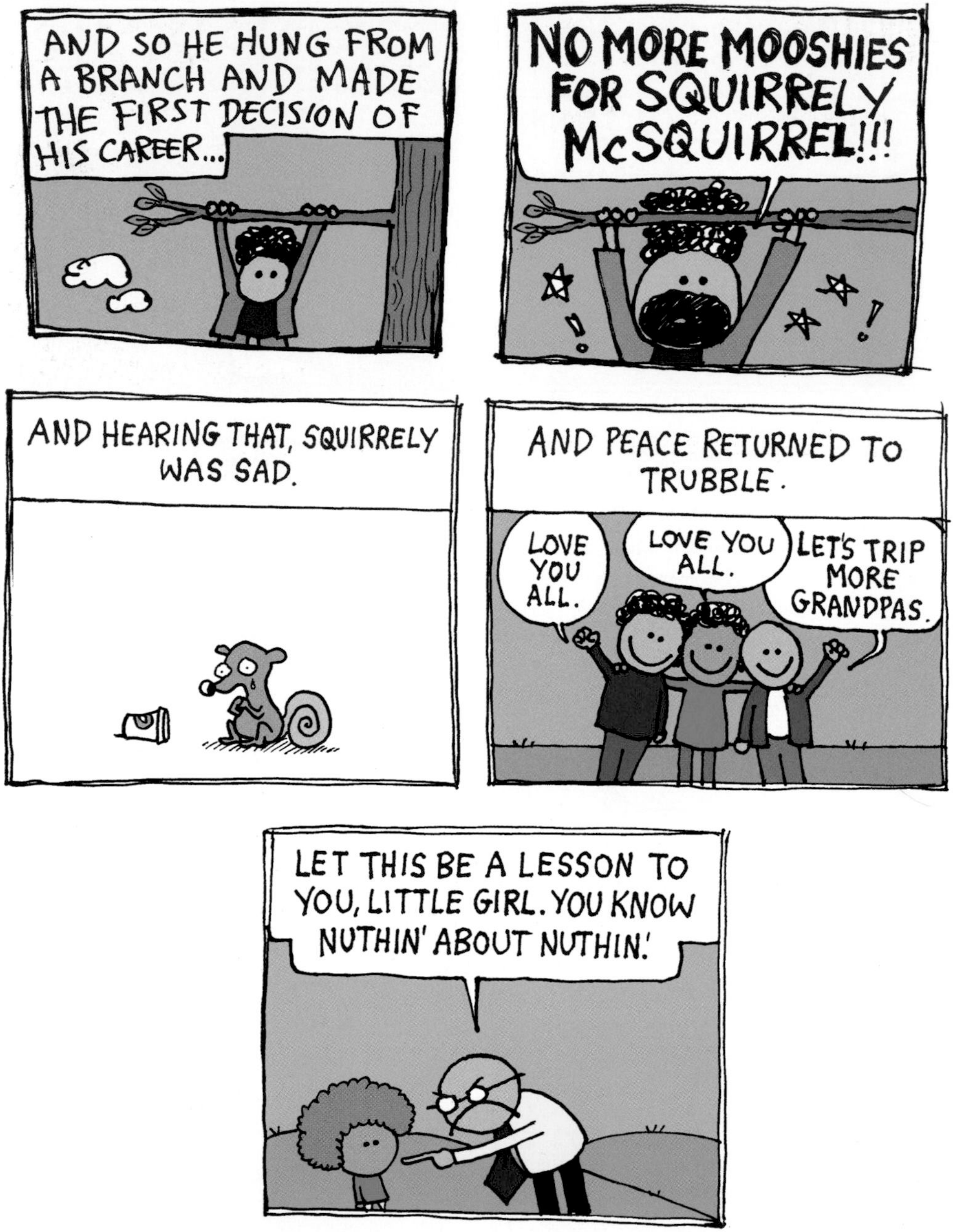
AND SO HE HUNG FROM A BRANCH AND MADE THE FIRST DECISION OF HIS CAREER...
NO MORE MOOSHIES FOR SQUIRRELY McSQUIRREL!!!
AND HEARING THAT, SQUIRRELY WAS SAD.
AND PEACE RETURNED TO TRUBBLE.
LOVE YOU ALL.
LOVE YOU ALL.
LET'S TRIP MORE GRANDPAS.
LET THIS BE A LESSON TO YOU, LITTLE GIRL. YOU KNOW NUTHIN' ABOUT NUTHIN.'

AND LOOKING AT THE CHAIN OF EVENTS SHE HAD TRIGGERED, WENDY THOUGHT BACK TO WHAT HER FATHER HAD SAID.

ALWAYS REMEMBER—EVEN THE SMALLEST THING YOU DO CAN HAVE BIG CONSEQUENCES.

AND HOW SHE HAD NOT HEEDED HIS ADVICE.

AND SO SQUIRRELY McSQUIRREL WENT HOME.

HOME OF SQUIRRELY McSQUIRREL

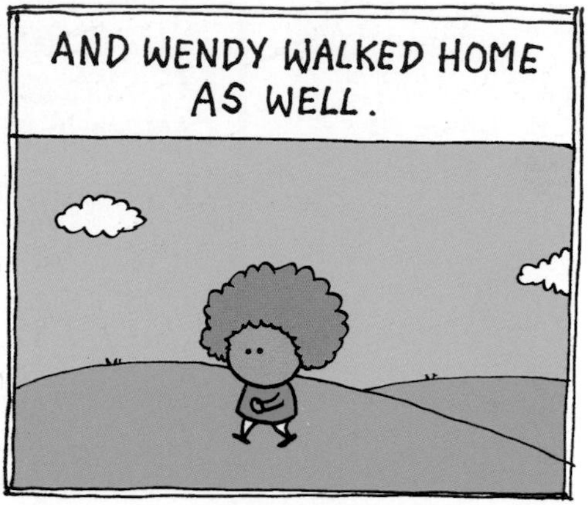
AND WENDY WALKED HOME AS WELL.

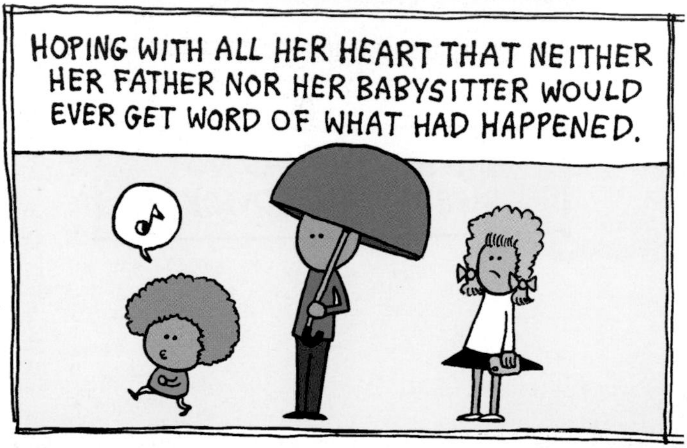
HOPING WITH ALL HER HEART THAT NEITHER HER FATHER NOR HER BABYSITTER WOULD EVER GET WORD OF WHAT HAD HAPPENED.

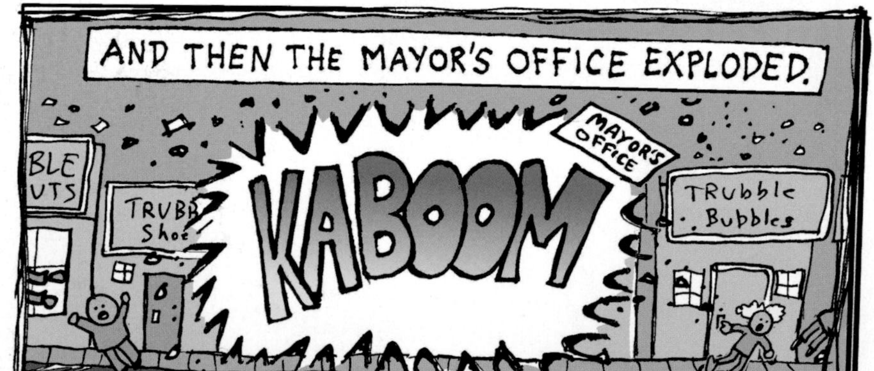
AND THEN THE MAYOR'S OFFICE EXPLODED.
MAYOR'S OFFICE
KABOOM
TRubble Bubbles

CHAPTER TWO

IN WHICH...

THINGS HAPPEN

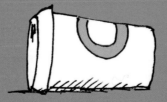

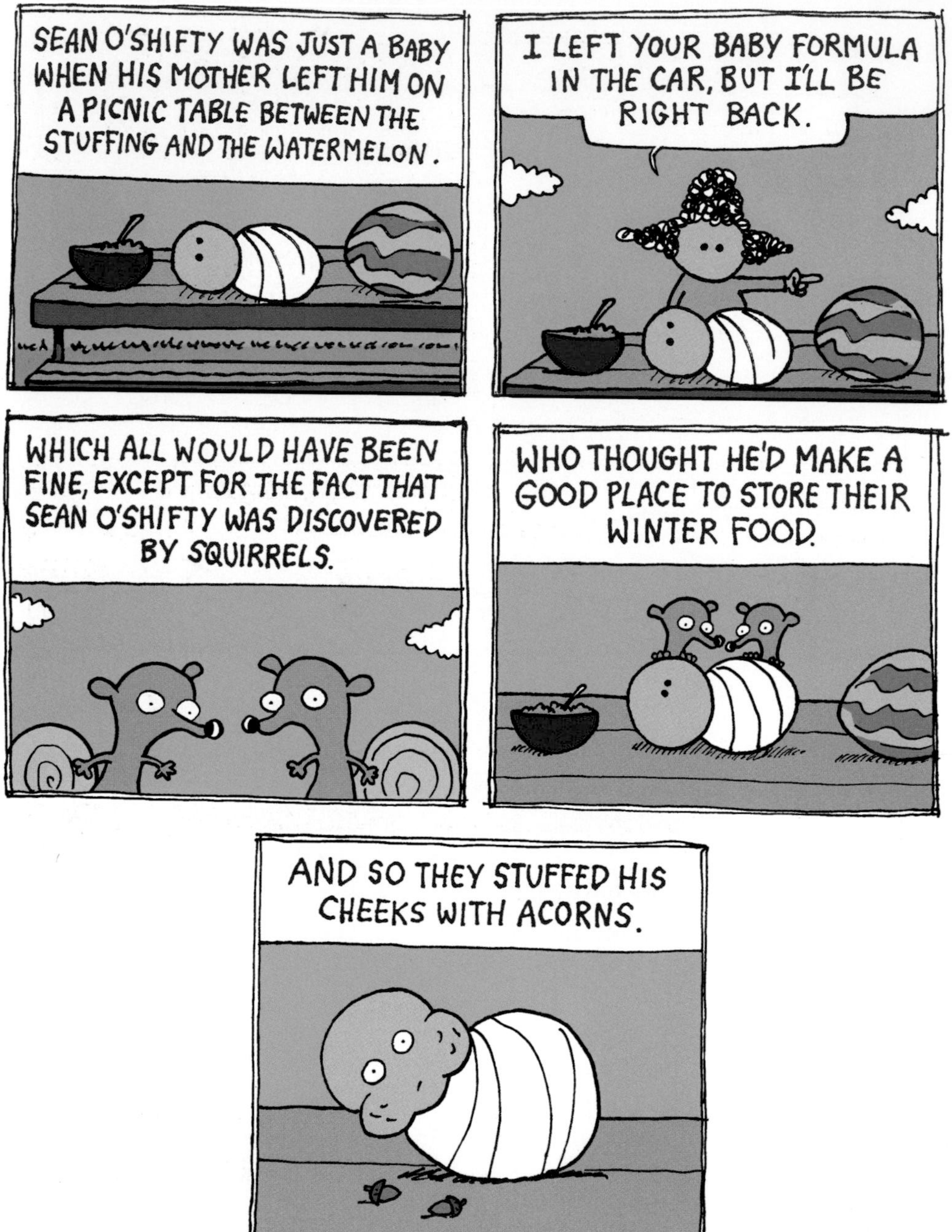
SEAN O'SHIFTY WAS JUST A BABY WHEN HIS MOTHER LEFT HIM ON A PICNIC TABLE BETWEEN THE STUFFING AND THE WATERMELON.
I LEFT YOUR BABY FORMULA IN THE CAR, BUT I'LL BE RIGHT BACK.
WHICH ALL WOULD HAVE BEEN FINE, EXCEPT FOR THE FACT THAT SEAN O'SHIFTY WAS DISCOVERED BY SQUIRRELS.
WHO THOUGHT HE'D MAKE A GOOD PLACE TO STORE THEIR WINTER FOOD.
AND SO THEY STUFFED HIS CHEEKS WITH ACORNS.

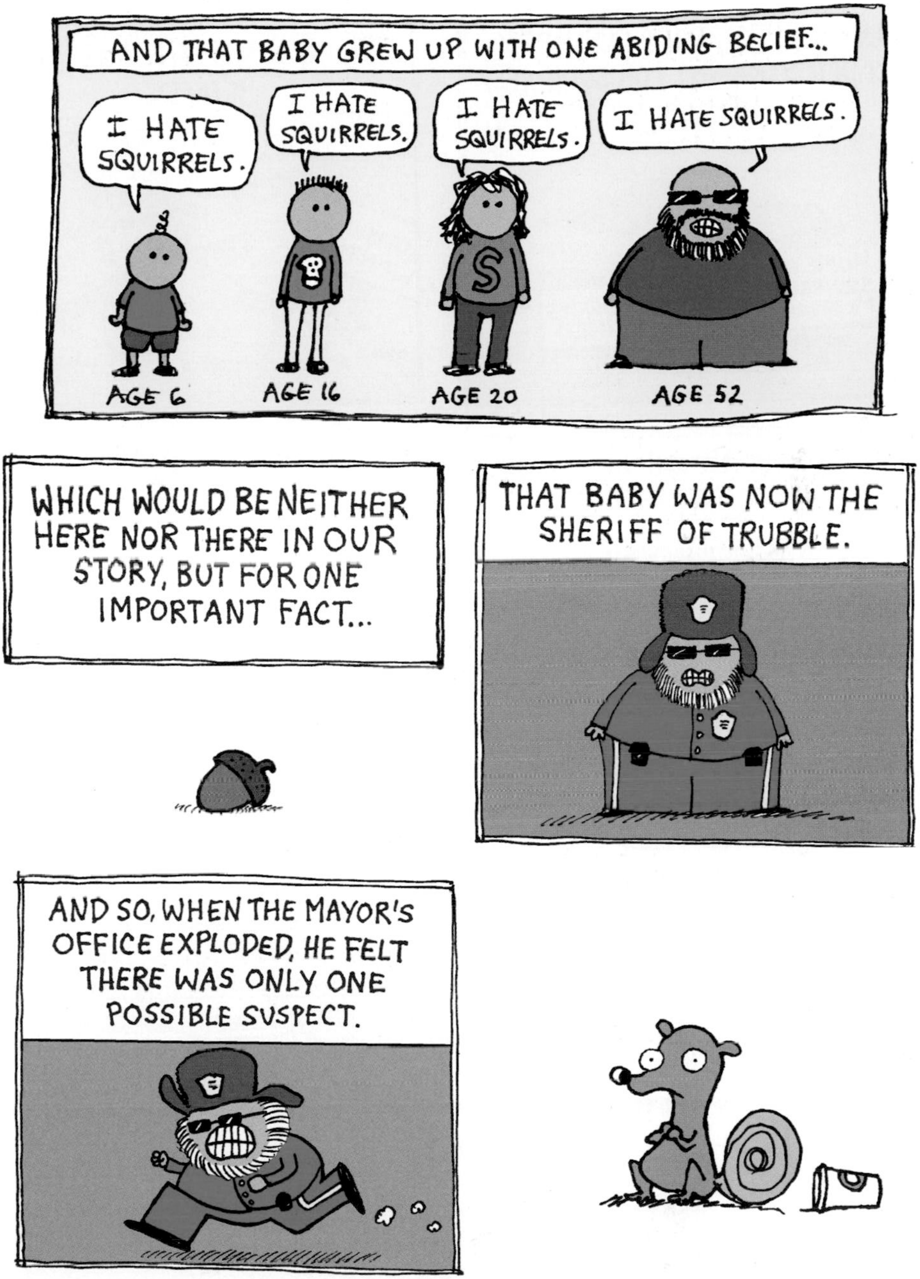
AND THAT BABY GREW UP WITH ONE ABIDING BELIEF...
I HATE SQUIRRELS.
I HATE SQUIRRELS.
I HATE SQUIRRELS.
I HATE SQUIRRELS.
AGE 6
AGE 16
AGE 20
AGE 52
WHICH WOULD BE NEITHER HERE NOR THERE IN OUR STORY, BUT FOR ONE IMPORTANT FACT...
THAT BABY WAS NOW THE SHERIFF OF TRUBBLE.
AND SO, WHEN THE MAYOR'S OFFICE EXPLODED, HE FELT THERE WAS ONLY ONE POSSIBLE SUSPECT.

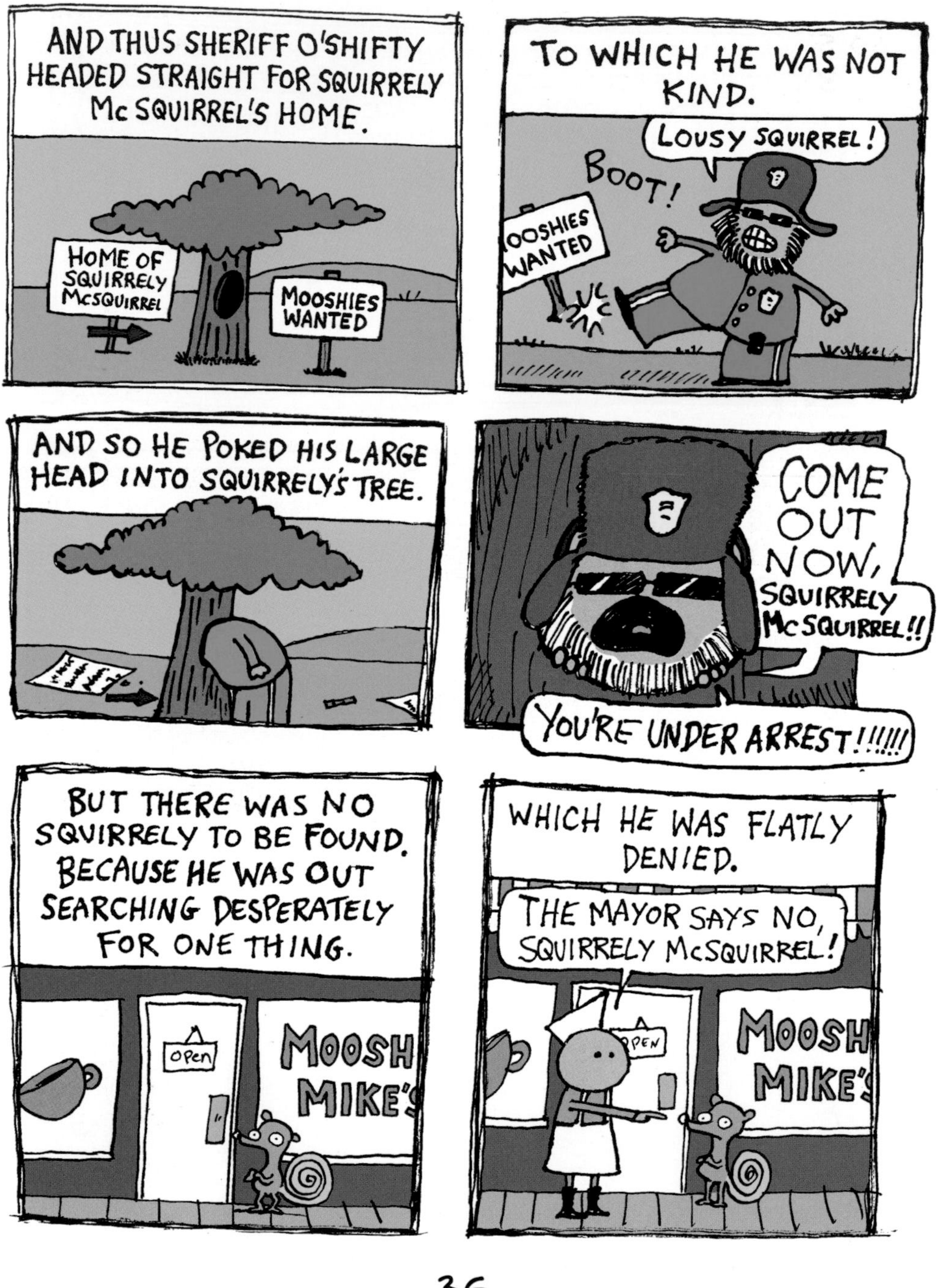
AND THUS SHERIFF O'SHIFTY HEADED STRAIGHT FOR SQUIRRELY McSQUIRREL'S HOME.
HOME OF SQUIRRELY McSQUIRREL
MOOSHIES WANTED
TO WHICH HE WAS NOT KIND.
LOUSY SQUIRREL!
BOOT!
OOSHIES WANTED
AND SO HE POKED HIS LARGE HEAD INTO SQUIRRELY'S TREE.
COME OUT NOW, SQUIRRELY McSQUIRREL!!
YOU'RE UNDER ARREST!!!!!!
BUT THERE WAS NO SQUIRRELY TO BE FOUND. BECAUSE HE WAS OUT SEARCHING DESPERATELY FOR ONE THING.
OPEN
MOOSH MIKE'S
WHICH HE WAS FLATLY DENIED.
THE MAYOR SAYS NO, SQUIRRELY McSQUIRREL!
OPEN
MOOSH MIKE'S

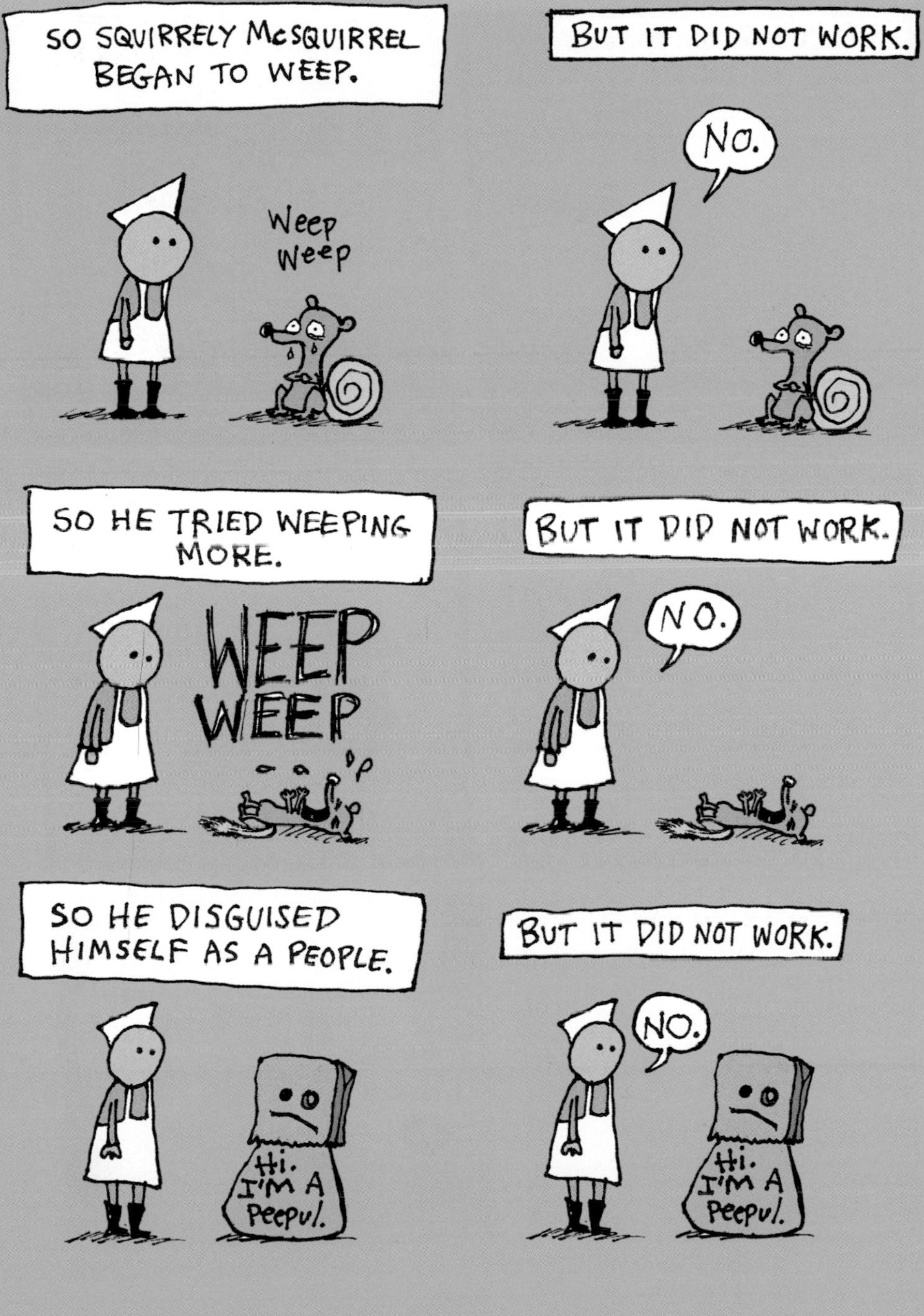
SO SQUIRRELY McSQUIRREL BEGAN TO WEEP.
Weep Weep
BUT IT DID NOT WORK.
NO.
SO HE TRIED WEEPING MORE.
WEEP WEEP
BUT IT DID NOT WORK.
NO.
SO HE DISGUISED HIMSELF AS A PEOPLE.
Hi. I'M A Peepul.
BUT IT DID NOT WORK.
NO.
Hi. I'M A Peepul.

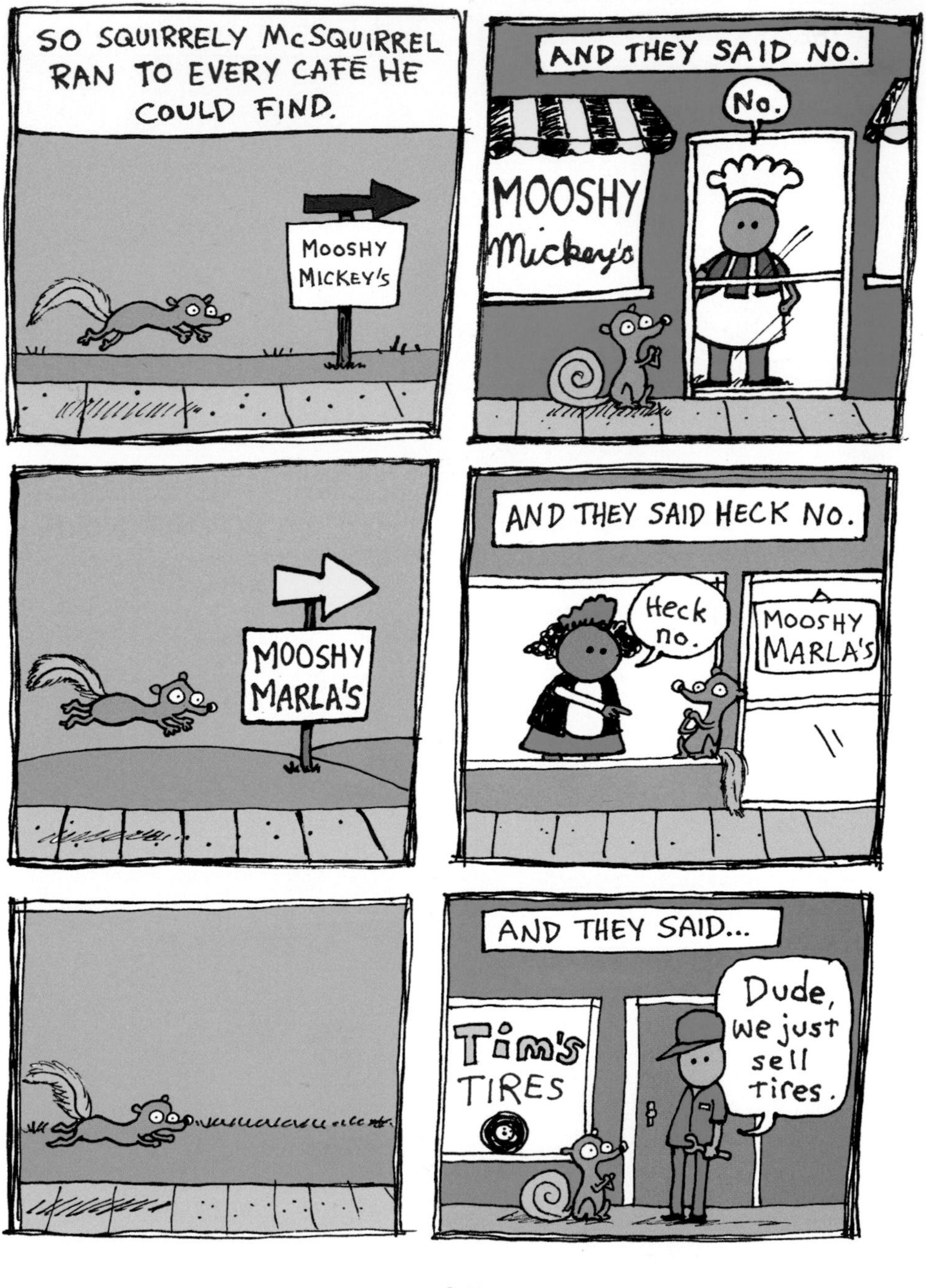
SO SQUIRRELY McSQUIRREL RAN TO EVERY CAFÉ HE COULD FIND.
MOOSHY MICKEY'S
AND THEY SAID NO.
No.
MOOSHY Mickey's
MOOSHY MARLA'S
AND THEY SAID HECK NO.
Heck no.
MOOSHY MARLA'S
AND THEY SAID...
Dude, we just sell tires.
Tim's TIRES

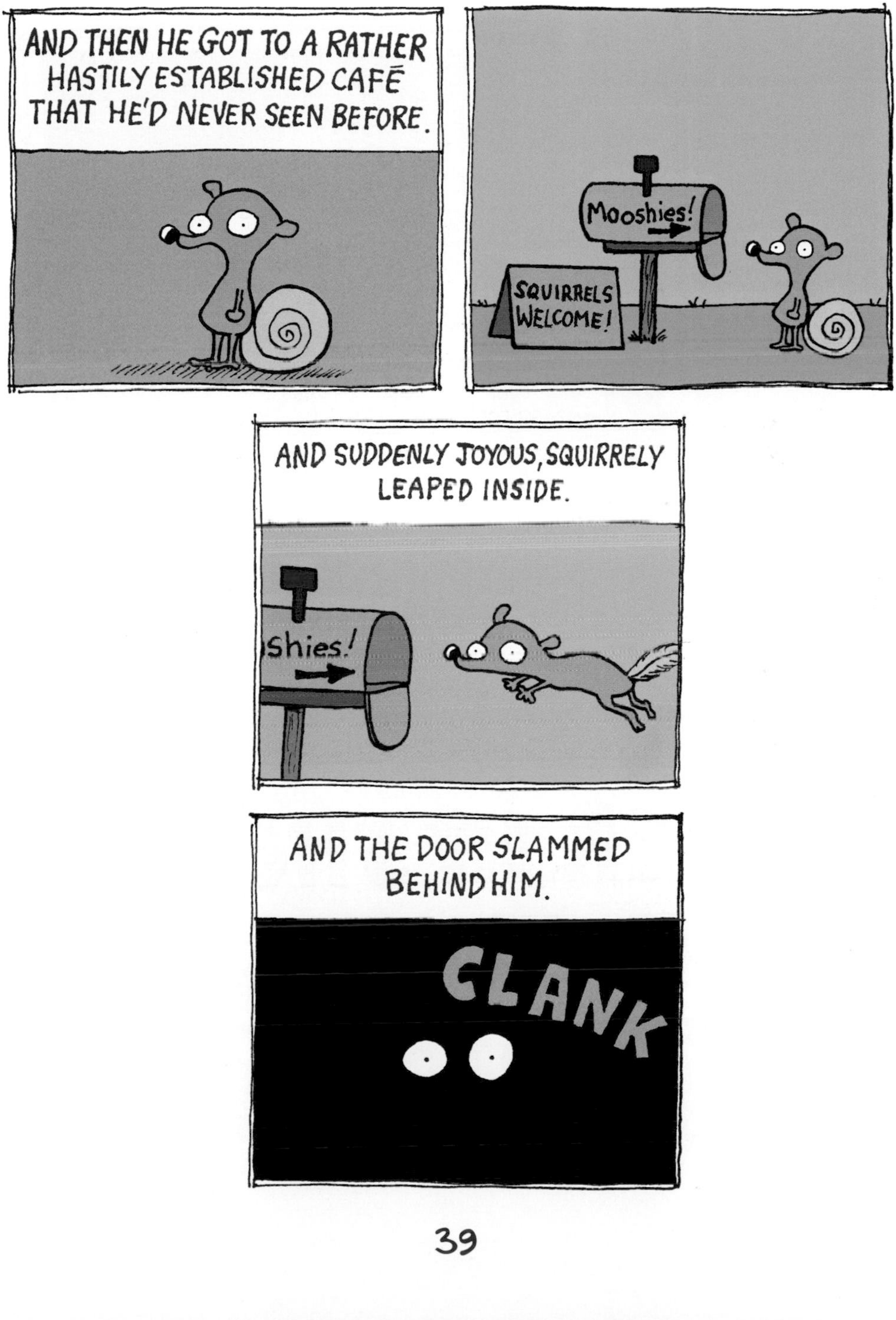
AND THEN HE GOT TO A RATHER HASTILY ESTABLISHED CAFÉ THAT HE'D NEVER SEEN BEFORE.
Mooshies!
SQUIRRELS WELCOME!
AND SUDDENLY JOYOUS, SQUIRRELY LEAPED INSIDE.
shies!
AND THE DOOR SLAMMED BEHIND HIM.
CLANK

CHAPTER THREE

IN WHICH...

YOU WILL FALL OVER IN SHOCK AND CRY, "NO, SQUIRRELY, NO!"

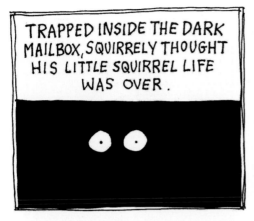

TRAPPED INSIDE THE DARK MAILBOX, SQUIRRELY THOUGHT HIS LITTLE SQUIRREL LIFE WAS OVER.

SO HE THOUGHT ABOUT WRITING A WILL GIVING ALL HIS EARTHLY POSSESSIONS TO HIS FRIENDS.

BUT THEN HE REALIZED HE HAD NO PAPER, NO PENCILS, NO LIGHT, AND NO FRIENDS.

AND THEN HE HEARD A LITTLE GIRL'S VOICE.

NOW YOU LISTEN TO ME, SQUIRRELY McSQUIRREL.

I'M SURE YOU HAD NOTHING TO DO WITH WHAT HAPPENED AT THE MAYOR'S OFFICE.

Mooshies!

SQUIRRELS WELCOME!

BUT YOU NEED TO GO TELL THEM ANYTHING YOU KNOW.

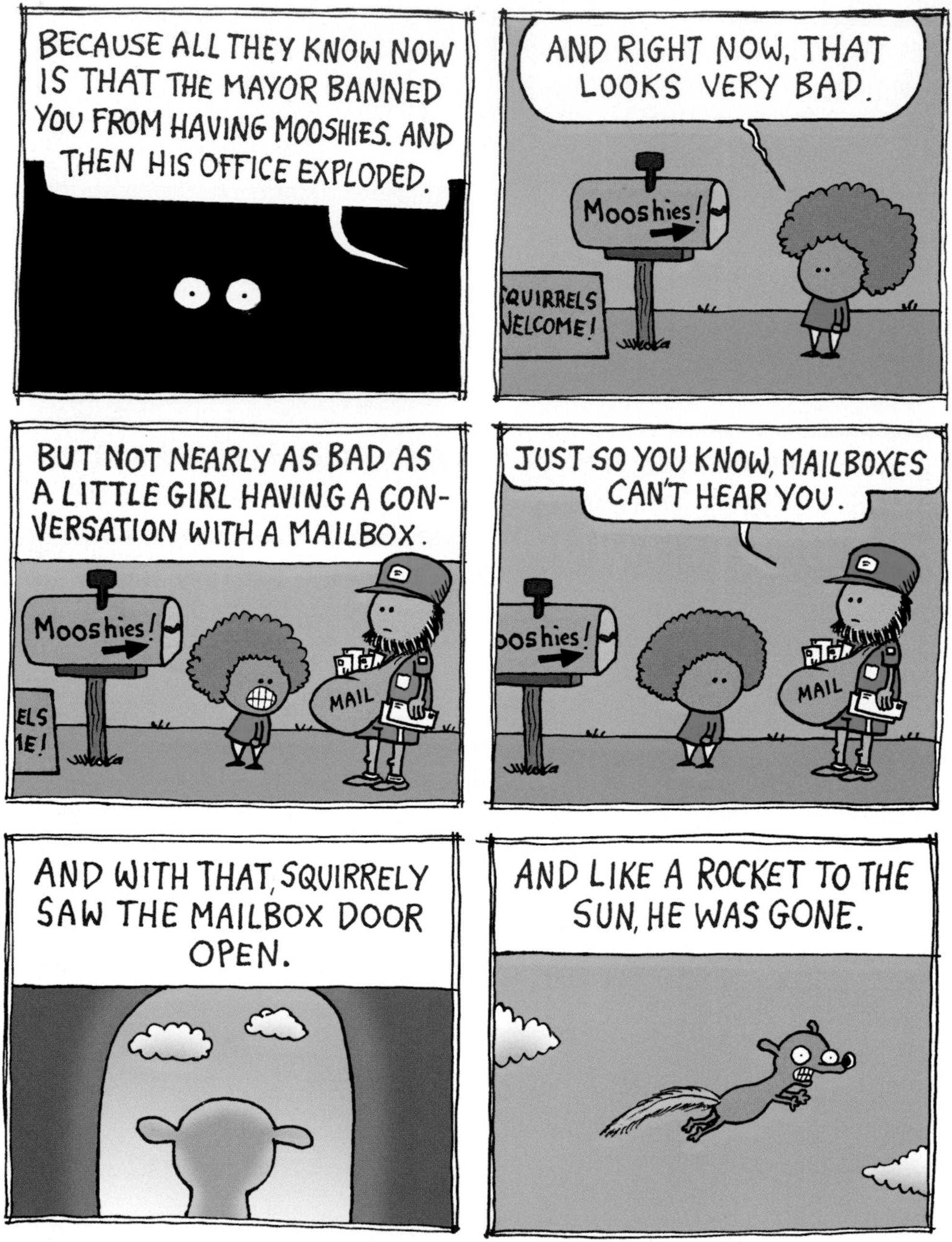
BECAUSE ALL THEY KNOW NOW IS THAT THE MAYOR BANNED YOU FROM HAVING MOOSHIES. AND THEN HIS OFFICE EXPLODED.
AND RIGHT NOW, THAT LOOKS VERY BAD.
Mooshies!
SQUIRRELS WELCOME!
BUT NOT NEARLY AS BAD AS A LITTLE GIRL HAVING A CONVERSATION WITH A MAILBOX.
Mooshies!
MAIL
JUST SO YOU KNOW, MAILBOXES CAN'T HEAR YOU.
MAIL
AND WITH THAT, SQUIRRELY SAW THE MAILBOX DOOR OPEN.
AND LIKE A ROCKET TO THE SUN, HE WAS GONE.

CHAPTER FOUR

IN WHICH...

YOUR ♥ WILL BREAK *

* Provided ye haveth one...

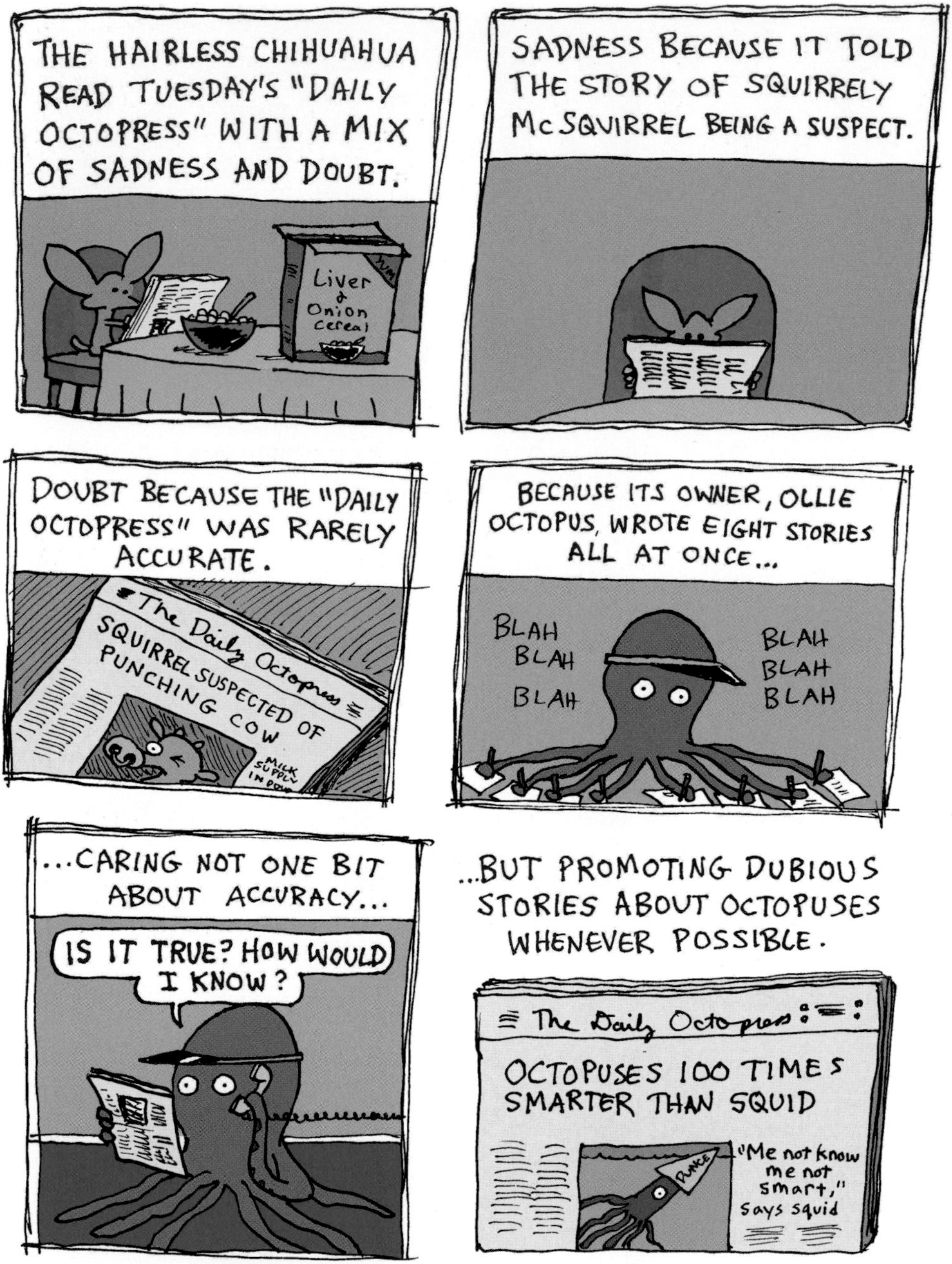
THE HAIRLESS CHIHUAHUA READ TUESDAY'S "DAILY OCTOPRESS" WITH A MIX OF SADNESS AND DOUBT.
Liver & Onion cereal
SADNESS BECAUSE IT TOLD THE STORY OF SQUIRRELY McSQUIRREL BEING A SUSPECT.
DOUBT BECAUSE THE "DAILY OCTOPRESS" WAS RARELY ACCURATE.
The Daily Octopress
SQUIRREL SUSPECTED OF PUNCHING COW
BECAUSE ITS OWNER, OLLIE OCTOPUS, WROTE EIGHT STORIES ALL AT ONCE...
BLAH BLAH BLAH
BLAH BLAH BLAH
...CARING NOT ONE BIT ABOUT ACCURACY...
IS IT TRUE? HOW WOULD I KNOW?
...BUT PROMOTING DUBIOUS STORIES ABOUT OCTOPUSES WHENEVER POSSIBLE.
The Daily Octopress
OCTOPUSES 100 TIMES SMARTER THAN SQUID
DUNCE
"Me not know me not smart," says squid

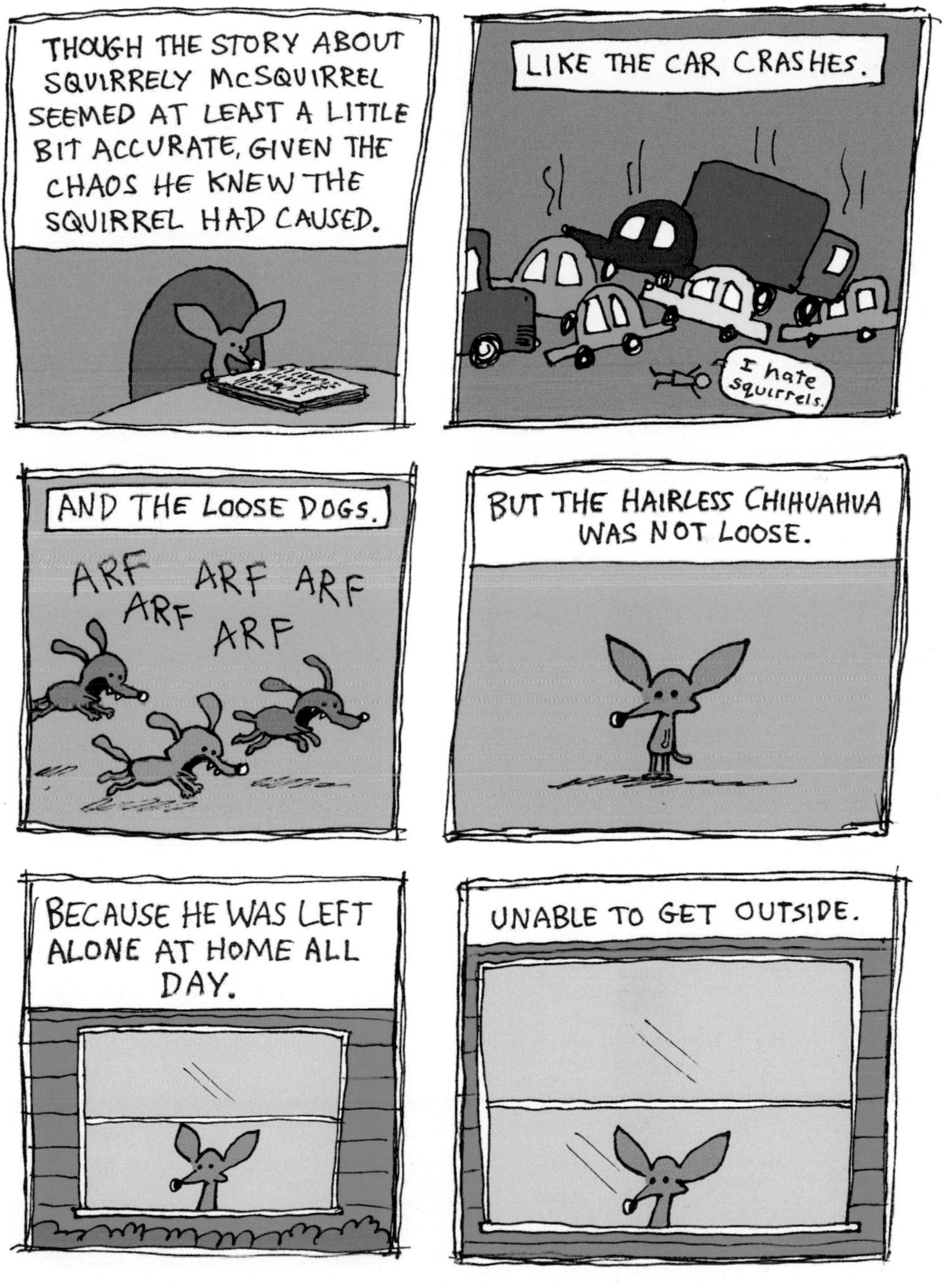
THOUGH THE STORY ABOUT SQUIRRELY McSQUIRREL SEEMED AT LEAST A LITTLE BIT ACCURATE, GIVEN THE CHAOS HE KNEW THE SQUIRREL HAD CAUSED.
LIKE THE CAR CRASHES.
I hate squirrels.
AND THE LOOSE DOGS.
ARF ARF ARF ARF ARF
BUT THE HAIRLESS CHIHUAHUA WAS NOT LOOSE.
BECAUSE HE WAS LEFT ALONE AT HOME ALL DAY.
UNABLE TO GET OUTSIDE.

SO LIKE MOST DOGS LEFT ALONE ALL DAY, HE GOT INTO TROUBLE.

BY STEALING AN ONLINE GIFT CARD FROM HIS OWNER.

OOOH.

AND ENTERING ITS REDEMPTION CODE INTO THE COMPUTER.

TAP
TAP
TAP
TAP

AND BUYING ALL THE POSTER BOARD HE COULD AFFORD.

AND WOOING THE CAT NEXT DOOR.

YOU'RE AS LOVELY AS A BOWL OF

LIVER AND ONIONS.

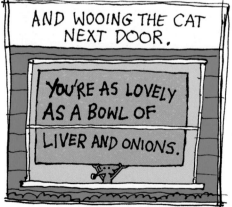

TO WHICH THE UNKEMPT CAT, ALSO TRAPPED ALONE ALL DAY, WAS UNIQUELY SUSCEPTIBLE.

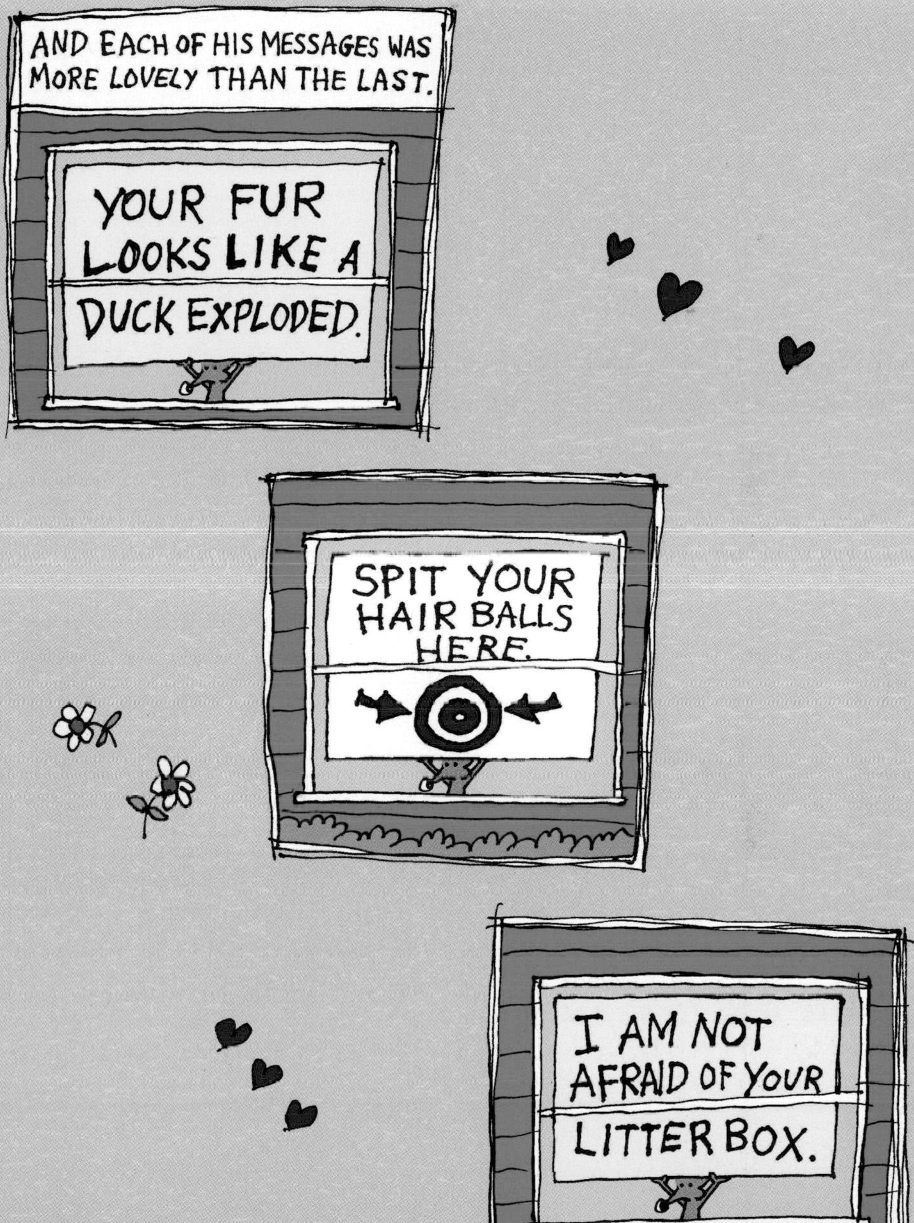
AND EACH OF HIS MESSAGES WAS MORE LOVELY THAN THE LAST.
YOUR FUR LOOKS LIKE A DUCK EXPLODED.
SPIT YOUR HAIR BALLS HERE.
I AM NOT AFRAID OF YOUR LITTER BOX.

UNTIL ONE DAY HE RAN OUT OF POSTER BOARD.

AND HIS WHOLE WORLD FELT LIKE IT WAS CRUMBLING APART.

ESPECIALLY WHEN HE STARED OUT THE WINDOW AND SAW HIS LOVE...

WONDERING WHY HE WAS NO LONGER SPEAKING TO HER.

AND SO, DESPERATE, THE HAIRLESS CHIHUAHUA WROTE A MESSAGE ON A STICKY NOTE...

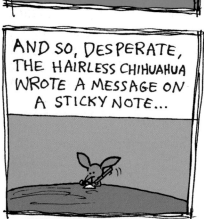

AND RAN TO POST IT ON THE WINDOW.

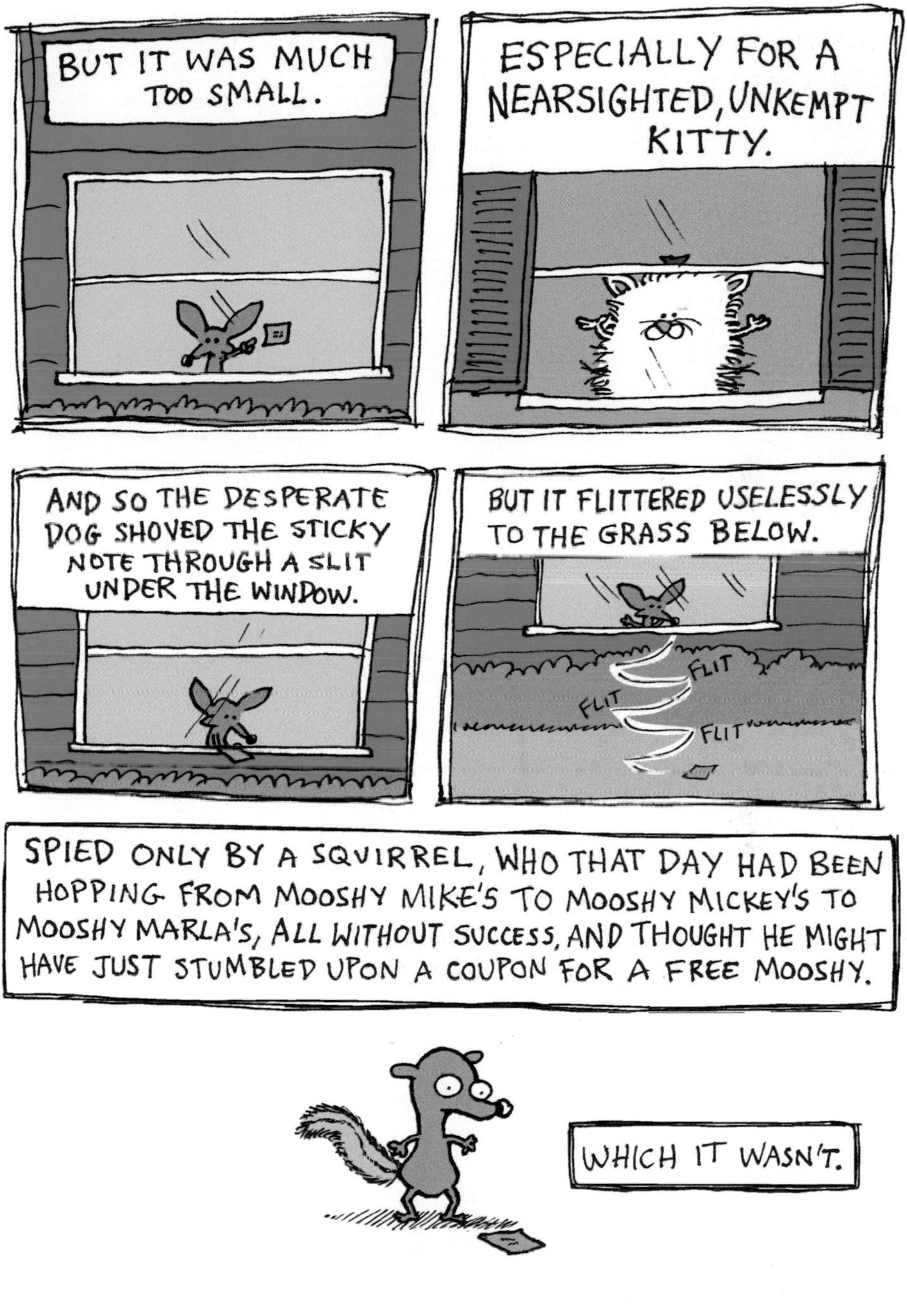
BUT IT WAS MUCH TOO SMALL.
ESPECIALLY FOR A NEARSIGHTED, UNKEMPT KITTY.
AND SO THE DESPERATE DOG SHOVED THE STICKY NOTE THROUGH A SLIT UNDER THE WINDOW.
BUT IT FLITTERED USELESSLY TO THE GRASS BELOW.
FLIT
FLIT
FLIT
SPIED ONLY BY A SQUIRREL, WHO THAT DAY HAD BEEN HOPPING FROM MOOSHY MIKE'S TO MOOSHY MICKEY'S TO MOOSHY MARLA'S, ALL WITHOUT SUCCESS, AND THOUGHT HE MIGHT HAVE JUST STUMBLED UPON A COUPON FOR A FREE MOOSHY.
WHICH IT WASN'T.

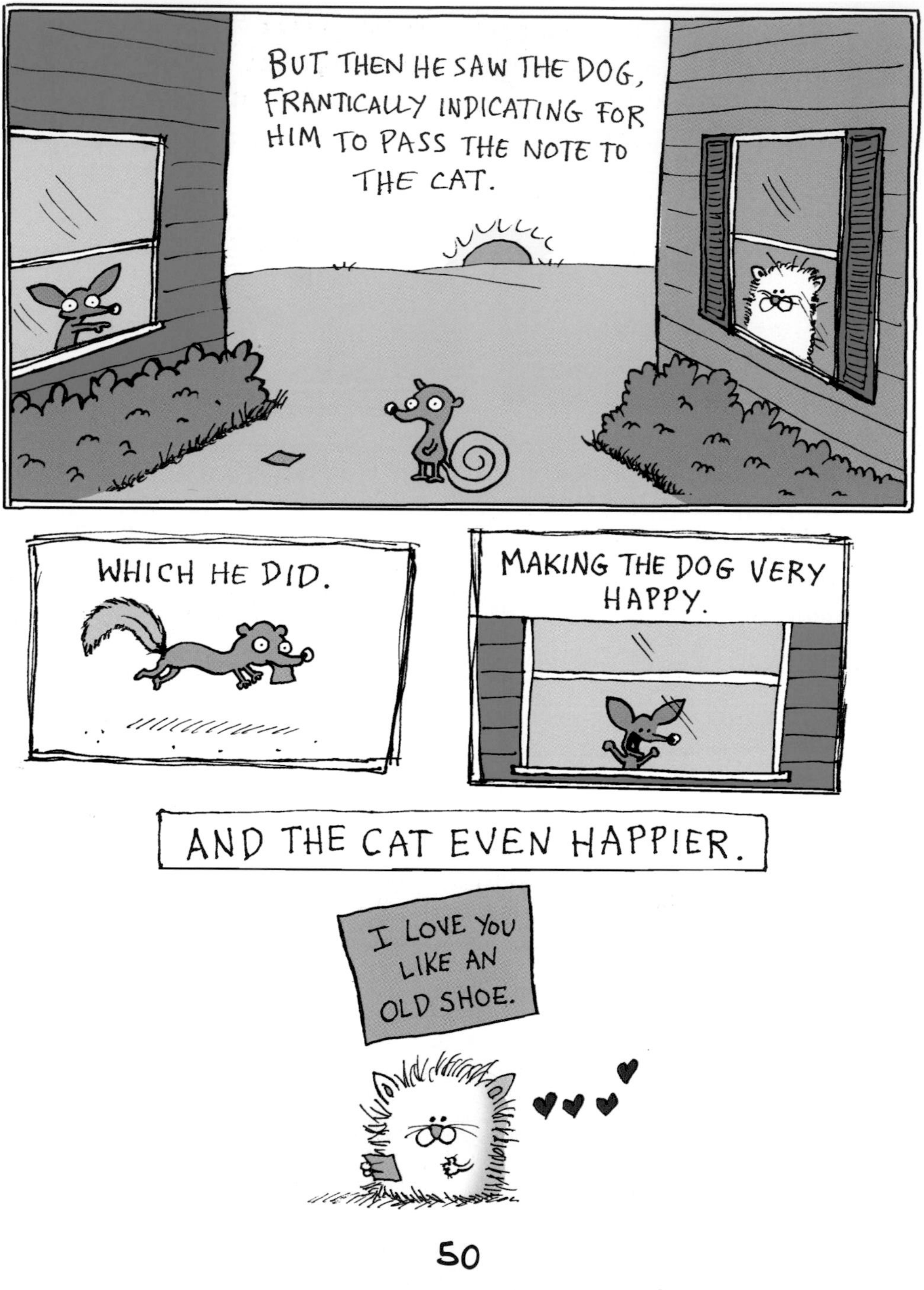

BUT THEN HE SAW THE DOG, FRANTICALLY INDICATING FOR HIM TO PASS THE NOTE TO THE CAT.
WHICH HE DID.
MAKING THE DOG VERY HAPPY.
AND THE CAT EVEN HAPPIER.
I LOVE YOU LIKE AN OLD SHOE.

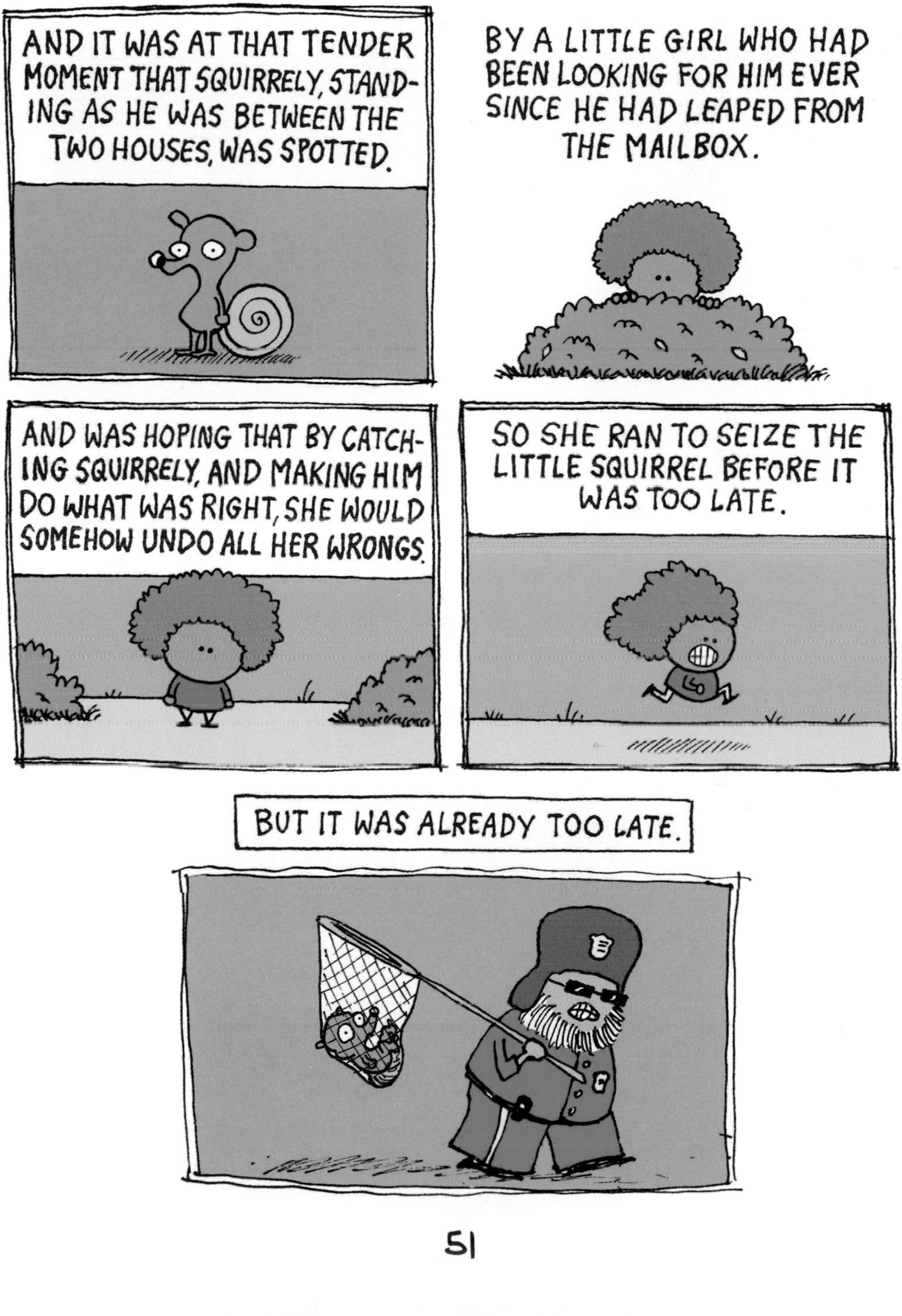
AND IT WAS AT THAT TENDER MOMENT THAT SQUIRRELY, STANDING AS HE WAS BETWEEN THE TWO HOUSES, WAS SPOTTED.
BY A LITTLE GIRL WHO HAD BEEN LOOKING FOR HIM EVER SINCE HE HAD LEAPED FROM THE MAILBOX.
AND WAS HOPING THAT BY CATCHING SQUIRRELY, AND MAKING HIM DO WHAT WAS RIGHT, SHE WOULD SOMEHOW UNDO ALL HER WRONGS.
SO SHE RAN TO SEIZE THE LITTLE SQUIRREL BEFORE IT WAS TOO LATE.
BUT IT WAS ALREADY TOO LATE.

CHAPTER FIVE

IN WHICH...

SO MANY SHOCKING THINGS HAPPEN THAT YOU MAY FAINT

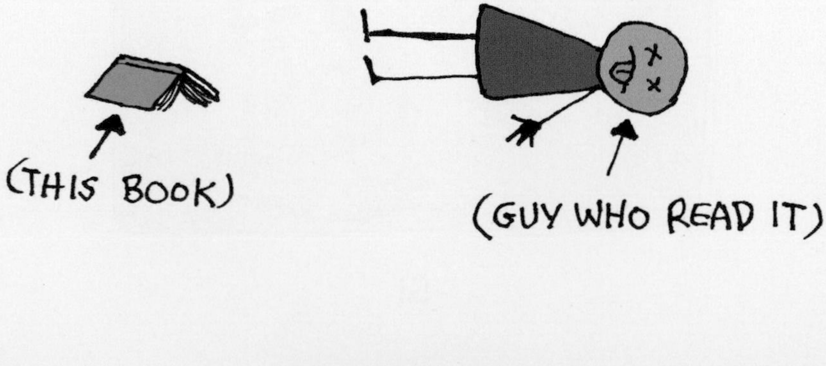

(THIS BOOK)

(GUY WHO READ IT)

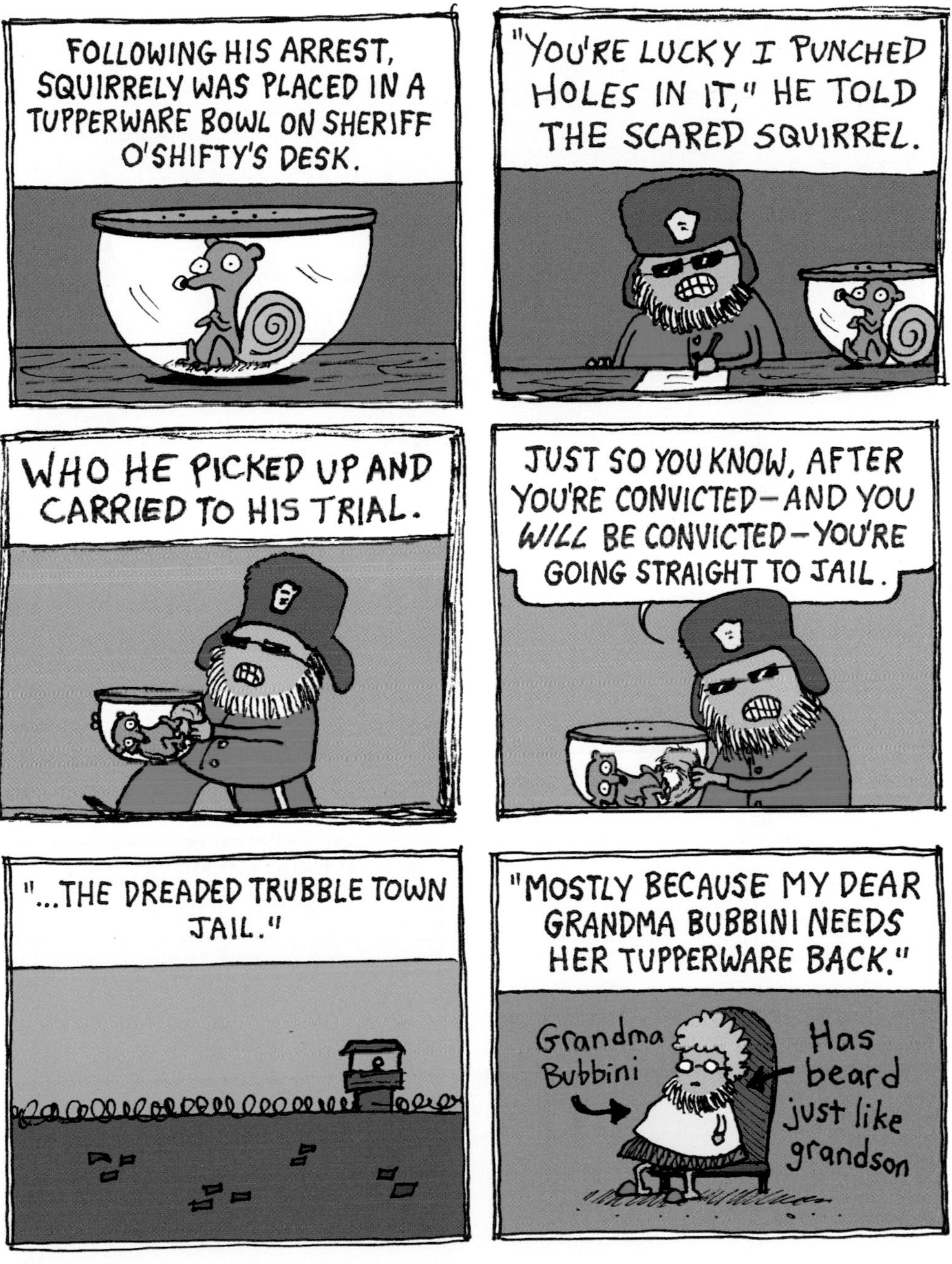
FOLLOWING HIS ARREST, SQUIRRELY WAS PLACED IN A TUPPERWARE BOWL ON SHERIFF O'SHIFTY'S DESK.
"YOU'RE LUCKY I PUNCHED HOLES IN IT," HE TOLD THE SCARED SQUIRREL.
WHO HE PICKED UP AND CARRIED TO HIS TRIAL.
JUST SO YOU KNOW, AFTER YOU'RE CONVICTED—AND YOU WILL BE CONVICTED—YOU'RE GOING STRAIGHT TO JAIL.
"...THE DREADED TRUBBLE TOWN JAIL."
"MOSTLY BECAUSE MY DEAR GRANDMA BUBBINI NEEDS HER TUPPERWARE BACK."
Grandma Bubbini
Has beard just like grandson

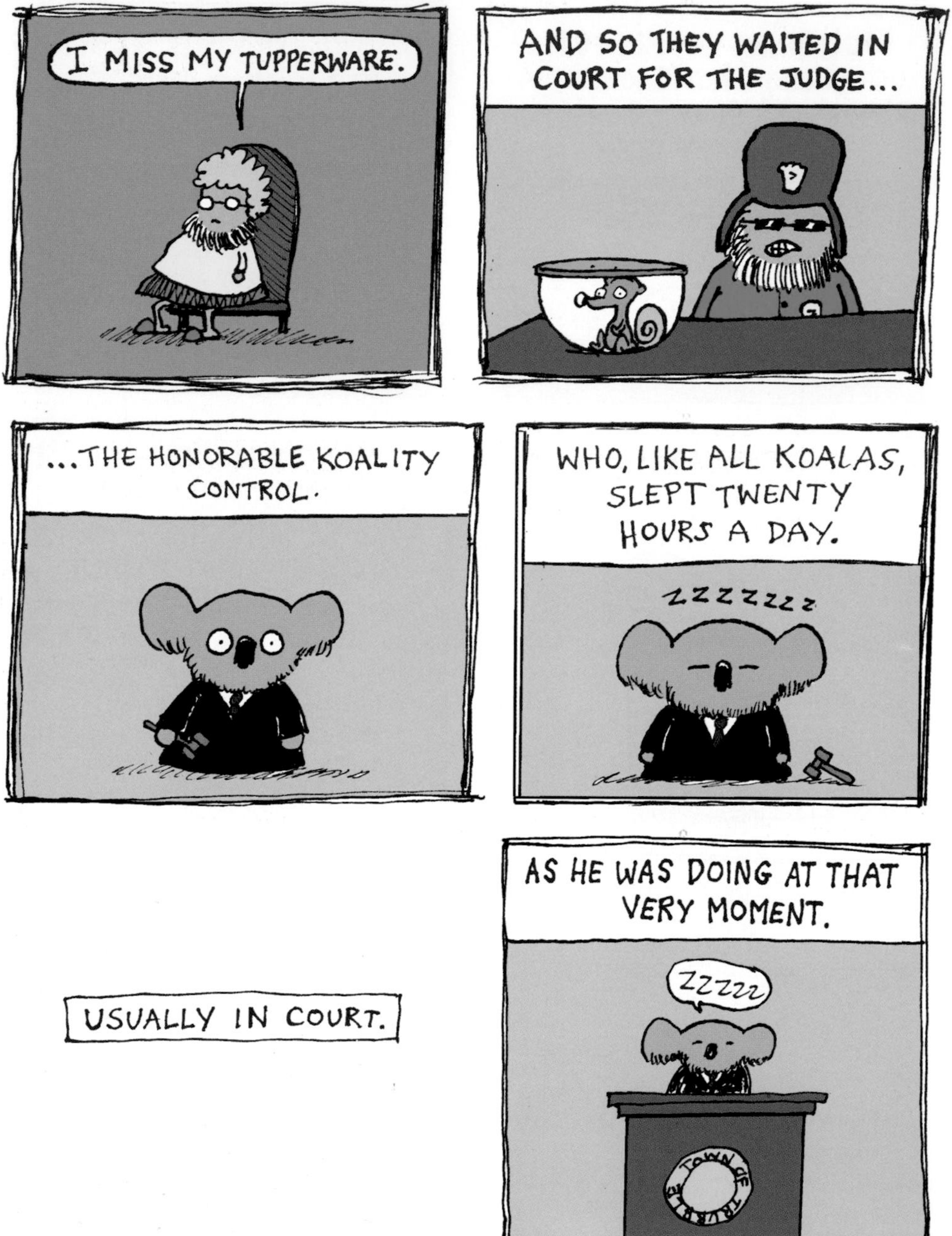
I MISS MY TUPPERWARE.
AND SO THEY WAITED IN COURT FOR THE JUDGE...
...THE HONORABLE KOALITY CONTROL.
WHO, LIKE ALL KOALAS, SLEPT TWENTY HOURS A DAY.
ZZZZZZZ
USUALLY IN COURT.
AS HE WAS DOING AT THAT VERY MOMENT.
ZZZZZ

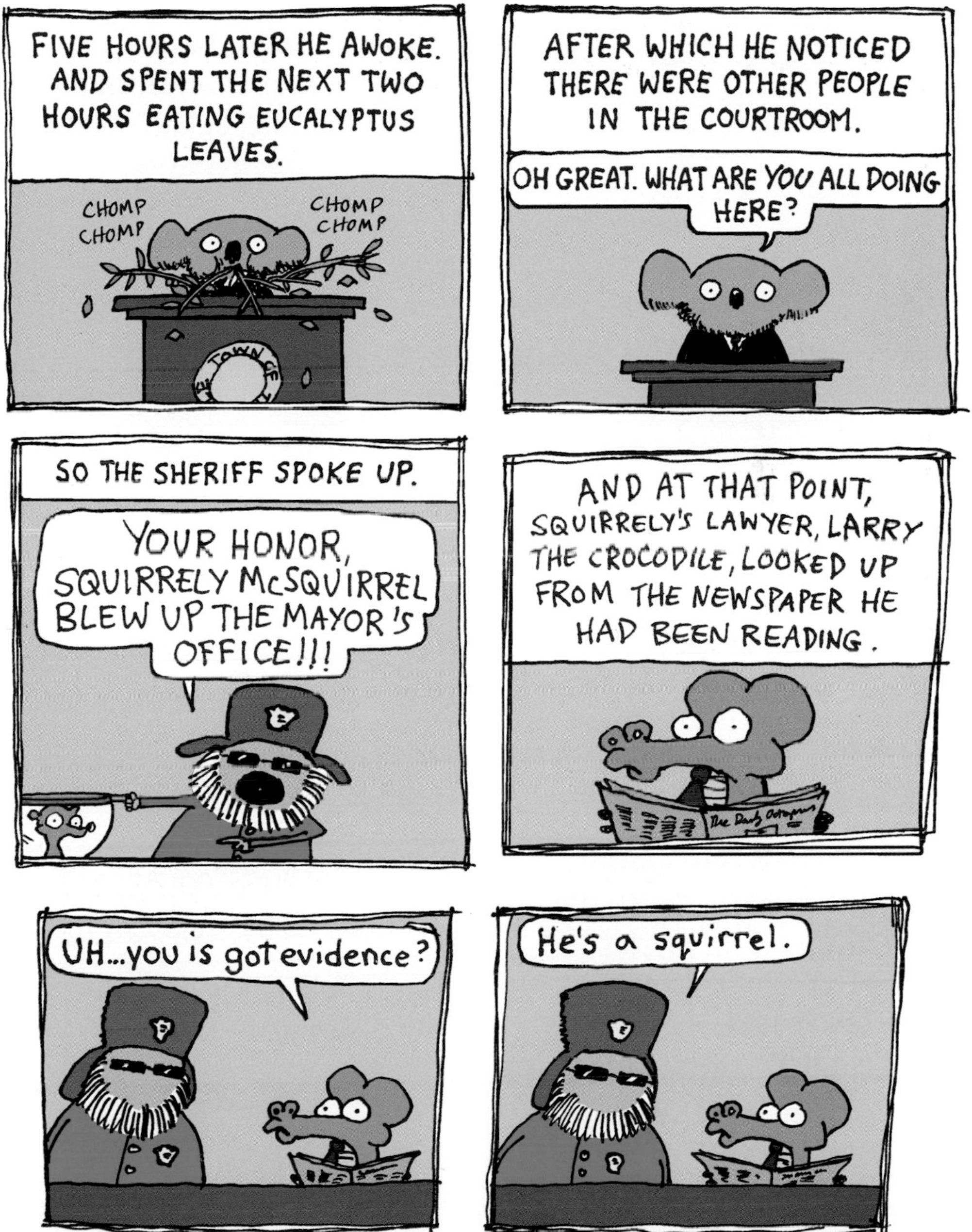
FIVE HOURS LATER HE AWOKE. AND SPENT THE NEXT TWO HOURS EATING EUCALYPTUS LEAVES.
CHOMP CHOMP
CHOMP CHOMP
TOWN
AFTER WHICH HE NOTICED THERE WERE OTHER PEOPLE IN THE COURTROOM.
OH GREAT. WHAT ARE YOU ALL DOING HERE?
SO THE SHERIFF SPOKE UP.
YOUR HONOR, SQUIRRELY McSQUIRREL BLEW UP THE MAYOR'S OFFICE!!!
AND AT THAT POINT, SQUIRRELY'S LAWYER, LARRY THE CROCODILE, LOOKED UP FROM THE NEWSPAPER HE HAD BEEN READING.
The Daily Octopus
UH...you is got evidence?
He's a squirrel.

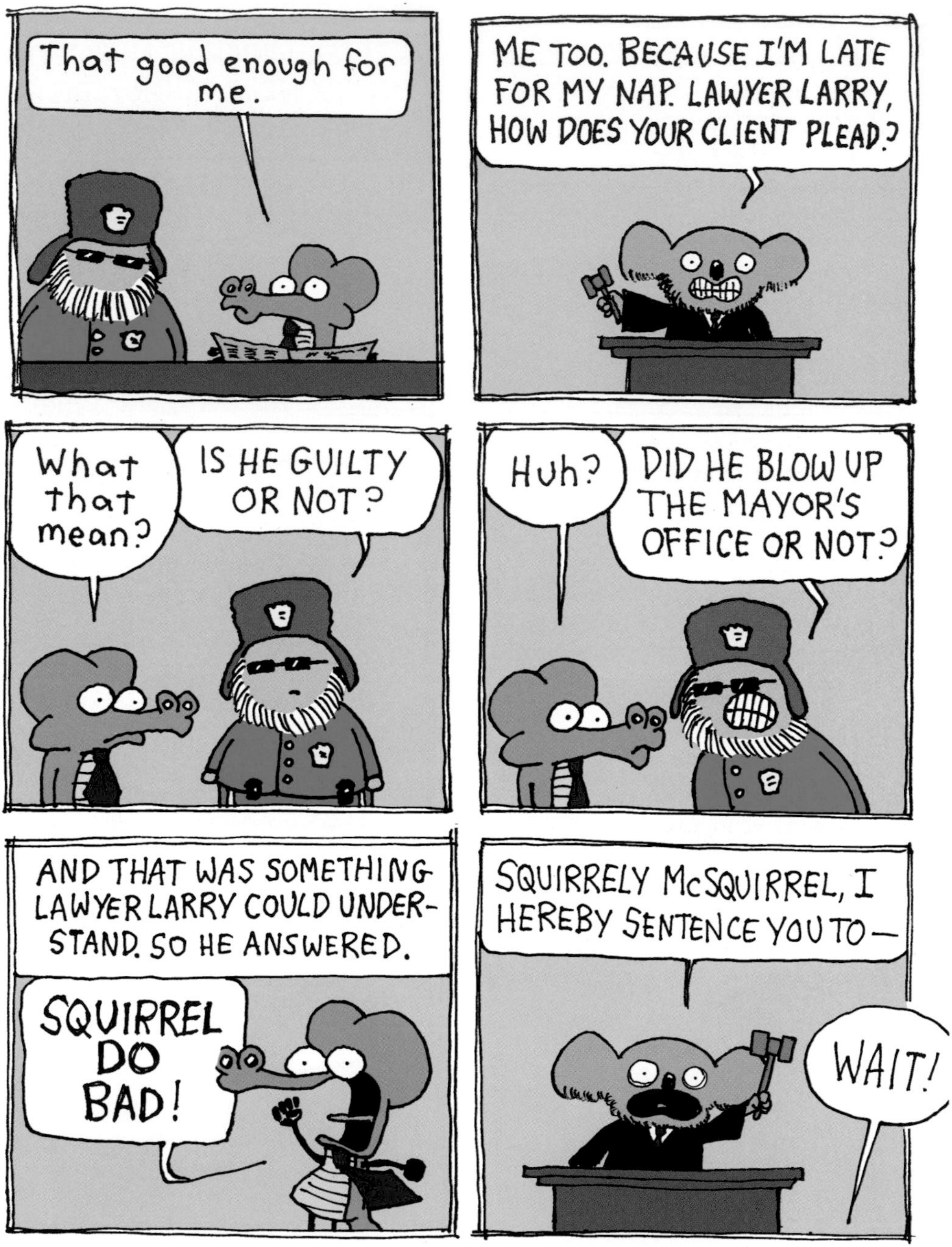
That good enough for me.
ME TOO. BECAUSE I'M LATE FOR MY NAP. LAWYER LARRY, HOW DOES YOUR CLIENT PLEAD?
What that mean?
IS HE GUILTY OR NOT?
Huh?
DID HE BLOW UP THE MAYOR'S OFFICE OR NOT?
AND THAT WAS SOMETHING LAWYER LARRY COULD UNDERSTAND. SO HE ANSWERED.
SQUIRREL DO BAD!
SQUIRRELY McSQUIRREL, I HEREBY SENTENCE YOU TO—
WAIT!

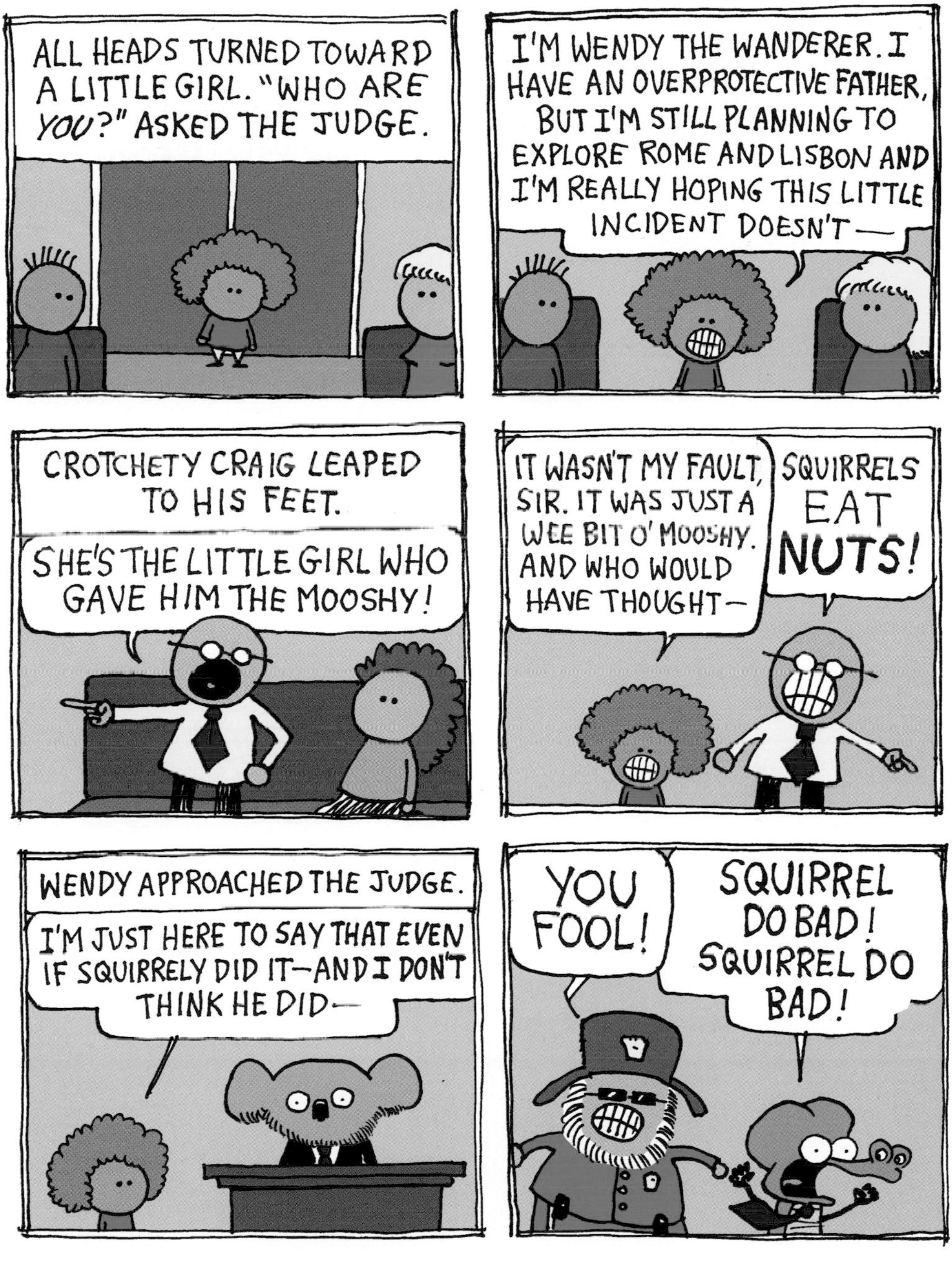
ALL HEADS TURNED TOWARD A LITTLE GIRL. "WHO ARE *YOU*?" ASKED THE JUDGE.
I'M WENDY THE WANDERER. I HAVE AN OVERPROTECTIVE FATHER, BUT I'M STILL PLANNING TO EXPLORE ROME AND LISBON AND I'M REALLY HOPING THIS LITTLE INCIDENT DOESN'T—
CROTCHETY CRAIG LEAPED TO HIS FEET.
SHE'S THE LITTLE GIRL WHO GAVE HIM THE MOOSHY!
IT WASN'T MY FAULT, SIR. IT WAS JUST A WEE BIT O' MOOSHY. AND WHO WOULD HAVE THOUGHT—
SQUIRRELS EAT **NUTS!**
WENDY APPROACHED THE JUDGE.
I'M JUST HERE TO SAY THAT EVEN IF SQUIRRELY DID IT—AND I DON'T THINK HE DID—
YOU FOOL!
SQUIRREL DO BAD! SQUIRREL DO BAD!

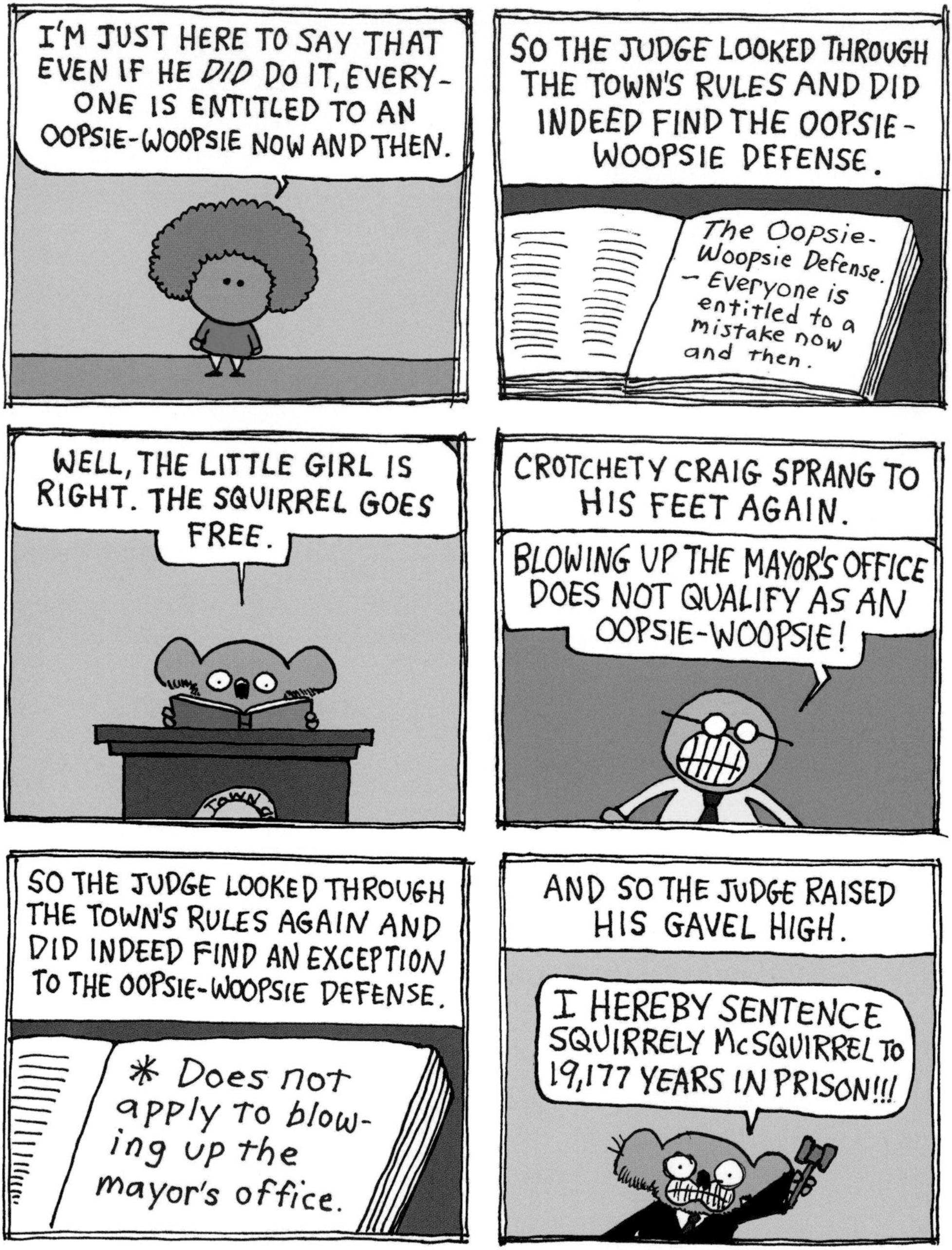
I'M JUST HERE TO SAY THAT EVEN IF HE *DID* DO IT, EVERYONE IS ENTITLED TO AN OOPSIE-WOOPSIE NOW AND THEN.
SO THE JUDGE LOOKED THROUGH THE TOWN'S RULES AND DID INDEED FIND THE OOPSIE-WOOPSIE DEFENSE.
The Oopsie-Woopsie Defense. – Everyone is entitled to a mistake now and then.
WELL, THE LITTLE GIRL IS RIGHT. THE SQUIRREL GOES FREE.
CROTCHETY CRAIG SPRANG TO HIS FEET AGAIN.
BLOWING UP THE MAYOR'S OFFICE DOES NOT QUALIFY AS AN OOPSIE-WOOPSIE!
SO THE JUDGE LOOKED THROUGH THE TOWN'S RULES AGAIN AND DID INDEED FIND AN EXCEPTION TO THE OOPSIE-WOOPSIE DEFENSE.
* Does not apply to blowing up the mayor's office.
AND SO THE JUDGE RAISED HIS GAVEL HIGH.
I HEREBY SENTENCE SQUIRRELY McSQUIRREL TO 19,177 YEARS IN PRISON!!!

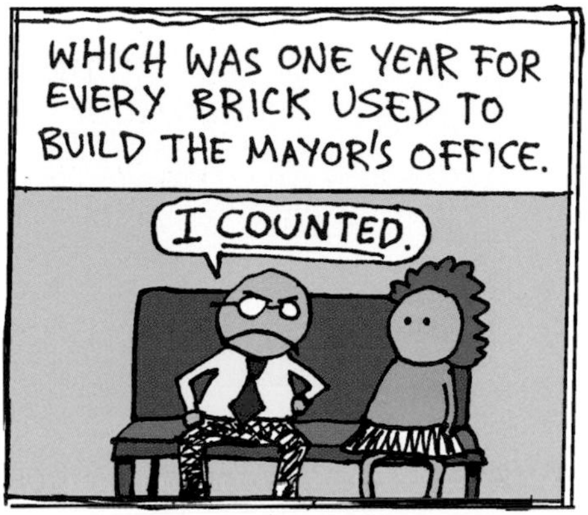
WHICH WAS ONE YEAR FOR EVERY BRICK USED TO BUILD THE MAYOR'S OFFICE.
I COUNTED.

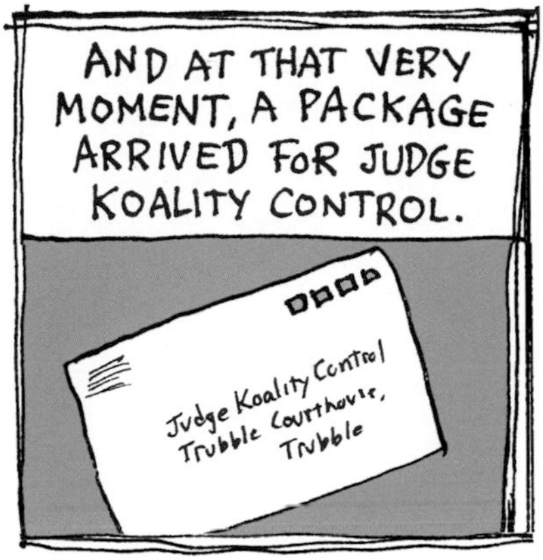
AND AT THAT VERY MOMENT, A PACKAGE ARRIVED FOR JUDGE KOALITY CONTROL.
Judge Koality Control
Trubble Courthouse,
Trubble

"IT'S ANOTHER BOMB!" SCREAMED THE GOOD PEOPLE OF TRUBBLE.

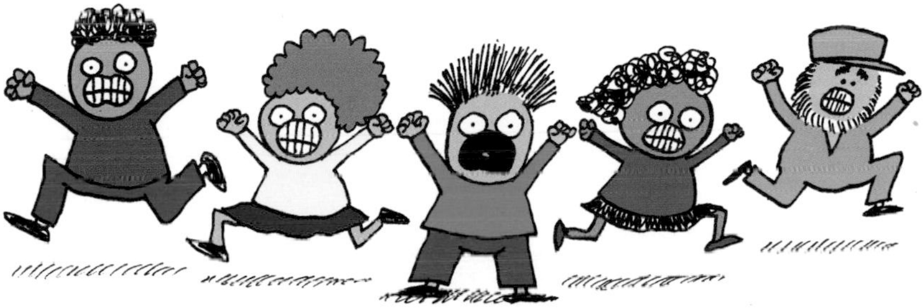

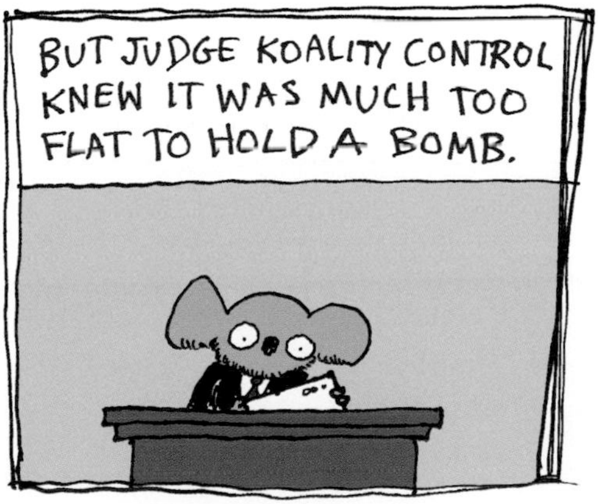
BUT JUDGE KOALITY CONTROL KNEW IT WAS MUCH TOO FLAT TO HOLD A BOMB.

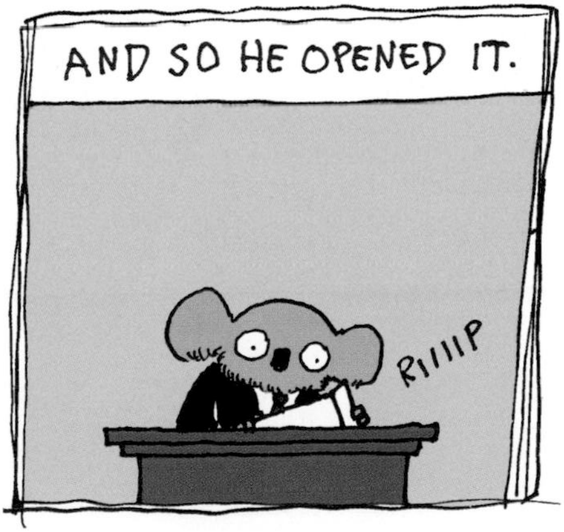
AND SO HE OPENED IT.
RIIIIP

AND OUT POURED HUNDREDS OF EUCALYPTUS LEAVES.

(THE JUDGE'S FAVORITE FOOD)

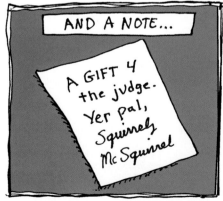

AND A NOTE...

A GIFT 4 the judge. Yer pal, Squirrely McSquirrel

"THAT'S A BRIBE!" YELLED CROTCHETY CRAIG.

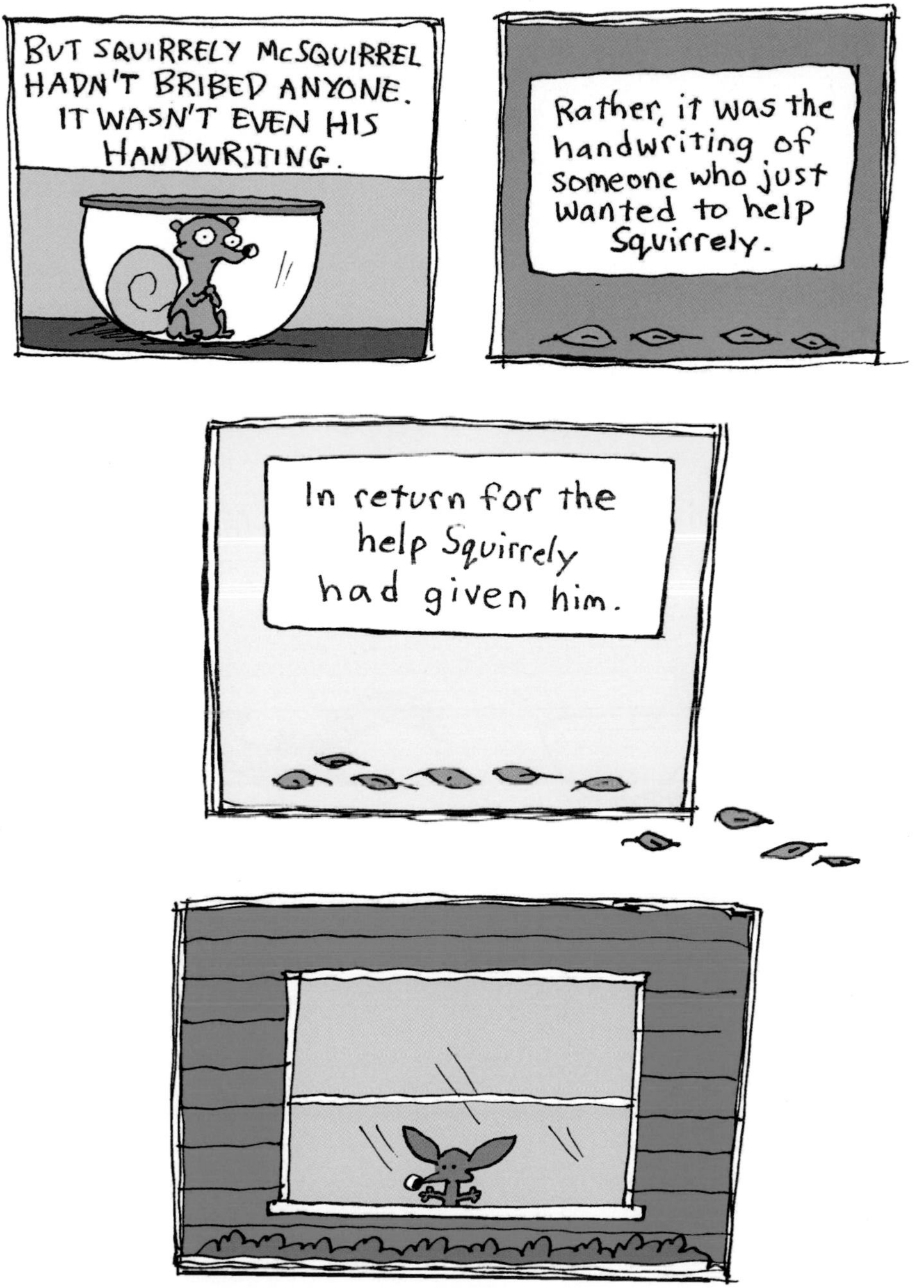
BUT SQUIRRELY McSQUIRREL HADN'T BRIBED ANYONE. IT WASN'T EVEN HIS HANDWRITING.
Rather, it was the handwriting of someone who just wanted to help Squirrely.
In return for the help Squirrely had given him.

AND SQUIRRELY McSQUIRREL WAS A FREE SQUIRREL.

CHAPTER FIVE AND A HALF

WHICH IS...

SUCH A SHORT CHAPTER, IT DOES NOT DESERVE A WHOLE NUMBER

WHEN WENDY GOT HOME, SHE REALIZED THE BABYSITTER APPEARED TO KNOW NOTHING ABOUT WHAT HAD HAPPENED IN TRUBBLE.

OR IF SHE DID KNOW, SHE HAD NOT CONNECTED THE EVENTS TO WENDY.

BUT WENDY DID NEED TO FIND OUT ONE THING.

PARDON ME, BUT DID MY DEAR FATHER CALL?

WHY DO YOU WANT TO KNOW?

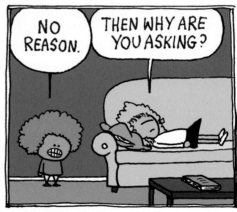

NO REASON.

THEN WHY ARE YOU ASKING?

I JUST ADORE THE MAN.

WHERE HAVE YOU BEEN?

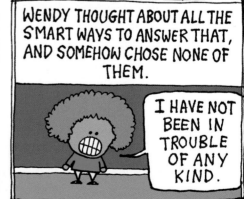

WENDY THOUGHT ABOUT ALL THE SMART WAYS TO ANSWER THAT, AND SOMEHOW CHOSE NONE OF THEM.

I HAVE NOT BEEN IN TROUBLE OF ANY KIND.

THAT'S A REALLY ODD THING TO SAY.

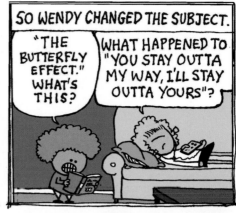

SO WENDY CHANGED THE SUBJECT.

"THE BUTTERFLY EFFECT." WHAT'S THIS?

WHAT HAPPENED TO "YOU STAY OUTTA MY WAY, I'LL STAY OUTTA YOURS"?

JUST ASKING.

IT'S FOR A CLASS. SOME THEORY ABOUT HOW SOME- THING SMALL, LIKE THE FLAP- PING OF A BUTTERFLY'S WINGS, CAN LEAD TO SOMETHING BIG...

...LIKE A TORNADO.

IS THAT TRUE?

YOU BETTER NOT BE IN TROUBLE, BECAUSE I HAVE A PERFECT BABYSITTING RECORD AND MY PERFORMANCE REVIEWS ARE AWESOME.

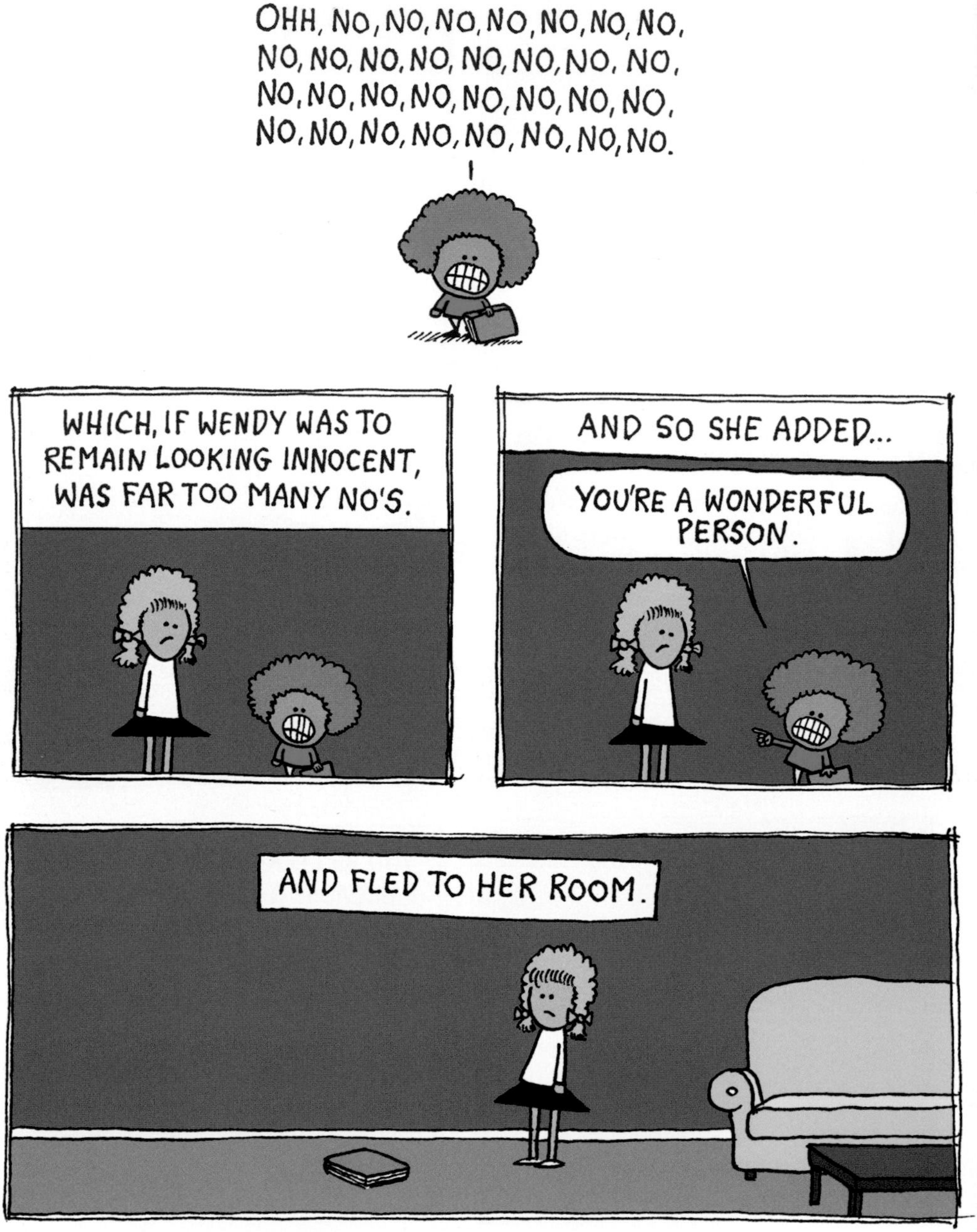

OHH, NO, NO, NO, NO, NO, NO, NO, NO, NO, NO, NO, NO, NO, NO, NO, NO, NO, NO, NO, NO, NO, NO, NO, NO, NO, NO, NO, NO, NO, NO, NO.
WHICH, IF WENDY WAS TO REMAIN LOOKING INNOCENT, WAS FAR TOO MANY NO'S.
AND SO SHE ADDED...
YOU'RE A WONDERFUL PERSON.
AND FLED TO HER ROOM.

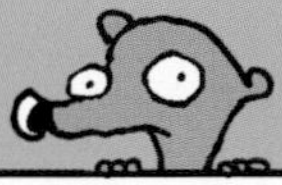

CHAPTER SIX

IN WHICH...

YOU WILL READ THINGS

AND...

TURN PAGES

AS MAD AS SHERIFF O'SHIFTY WAS TO SEE SQUIRRELY GO FREE...

GRRRR

AND AS ANGRY AS CROTCHETY CRAIG WAS TO SEE A BRIBE ACCEPTED...

GRRRR

NO ONE WAS MORE DISAPPOINTED THAN M.O.T.H.E.R.

M.O.T.H.E.R.

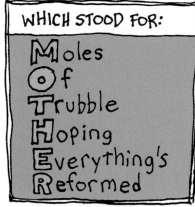

WHICH STOOD FOR:

Moles
Of
Trubble
Hoping
Everything's
Reformed

M.O.T.H.E.R. CONSISTED OF THREE MOLES, MYRTLE, GIRDLE, AND MENACE TO SOCIETY...

(WE DON'T KNOW WHICH IS WHICH.)

AND THEY WERE SAD ABOUT WHAT WAS HAPPENING TO THEIR CITY.

WELCOME TO TRUBBLE
(ONCE WE WERE NOT HORRIBLE)

SAD ABOUT THEIR MAYOR IN A TREE.

SAD ABOUT THEIR SAD NEWSPAPER.

The Daily Octopress
SQUID CAN'T TIE THEIR OWN SHOES
OCTOPUS WINS NOBEL PRIZE

SAD ABOUT THEIR SLEEPING JUDGE.

ZZZZ ZZZZZZz

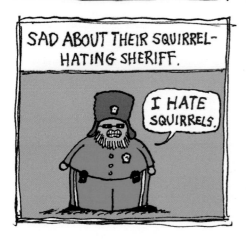

SAD ABOUT THEIR SQUIRREL-HATING SHERIFF.

I HATE SQUIRRELS.

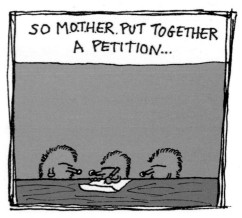

SO M.O.T.H.E.R. PUT TOGETHER A PETITION...

...THAT SIMPLY SAID:

Let's
Do
Better.

BUT NO ONE WOULD SIGN.

NOT CROTCHETY CRAIG.

BAH! WHAT DOES A SILLY MOLE KNOW?

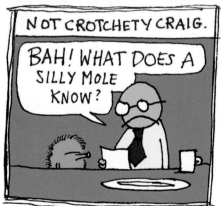

NOT LAWYER LARRY.

Me no care.

AND NOT MAYOR MO, WHO WAS LEAST RESPONSIVE OF ALL.

DO THE THING YOU THINK IS WISE, FOR IF I FALL, I SURELY DIES.

AND HEARING THAT, THE MOLES OF M.O.T.H.E.R. WANTED TO DO WHAT THEY OFTEN DID WHEN THEY GOT FRUSTRATED...

... HIT EACH OTHER WITH A FRUITCAKE.

WHAM

But no one had a fruitcake.

Darn.

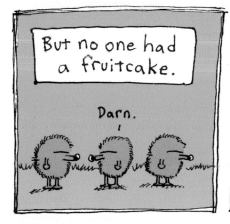

"Well," said Myrtle, "I guess we can do what all other moles do and just give up and live underground."

Because living underground is what moles do when they're disappointed with what's happening aboveground.

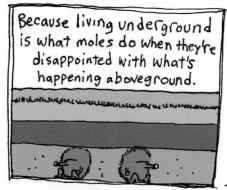

BUT MYRTLE, GIRDLE, AND MENACE TO SOCIETY WERE DIFFERENT.

We cannot give up.

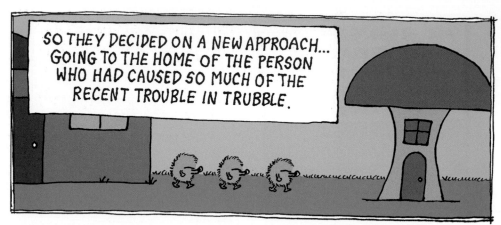

So they decided on a new approach... going to the home of the person who had caused so much of the recent trouble in Trubble.

Oh ye of mooshy-giving fame, undo the damage ye have done!

Wendy rushed to the door.

Hush, whoever you are. You're gonna get me in trouble.

We are the moles of M.O.T.H.E.R. and we want to talk about what you've done to our town.

I didn't do anything.

Oh, but you did.

72

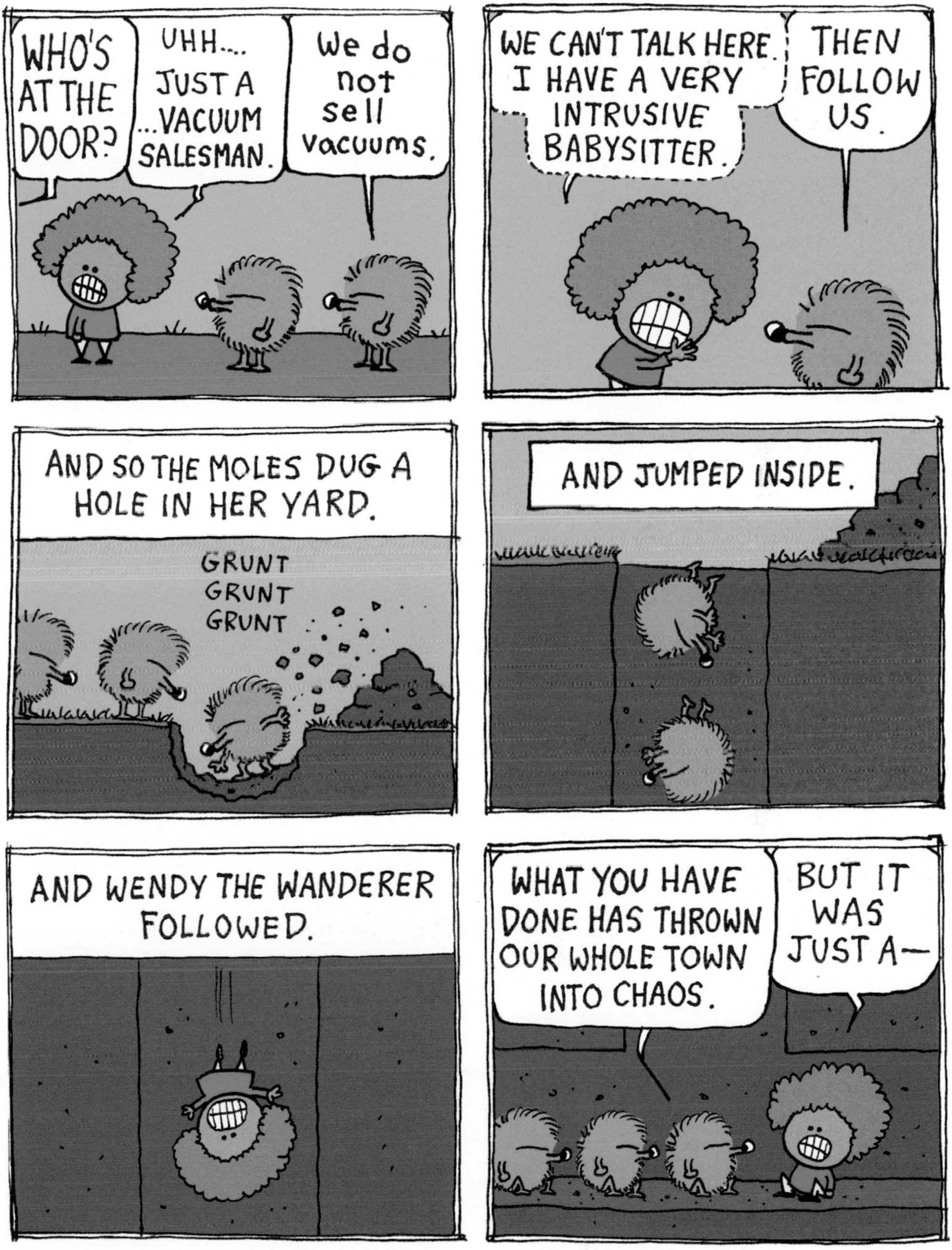

WHO'S AT THE DOOR?
UHH.... JUST A ...VACUUM SALESMAN.
We do not sell vacuums.
WE CAN'T TALK HERE. I HAVE A VERY INTRUSIVE BABYSITTER.
THEN FOLLOW US.
AND SO THE MOLES DUG A HOLE IN HER YARD.
GRUNT
GRUNT
GRUNT
AND JUMPED INSIDE.
AND WENDY THE WANDERER FOLLOWED.
WHAT YOU HAVE DONE HAS THROWN OUR WHOLE TOWN INTO CHAOS.
BUT IT WAS JUST A—

—WEE BIT O' MOOSHY. NEVERTHELESS, IT HAS EXPOSED OUR TOWN FOR HOW POORLY RUN IT IS.

PLEASE DON'T TELL MY FATHER.

WE WON'T. BUT WE NEED YOU TO TELL SQUIRRELY TO NEVER TRY A MOOSHY AGAIN.

OH, BUT I'M SURE HE WON'T. THE TRIAL HAS SURELY SCARED HIM STRAIGHT.

PLEASE. HE SEEMS TO TRUST YOU.

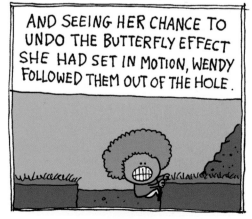

AND SEEING HER CHANCE TO UNDO THE BUTTERFLY EFFECT SHE HAD SET IN MOTION, WENDY FOLLOWED THEM OUT OF THE HOLE.

AND TOWARD SQUIRRELY'S TREE.

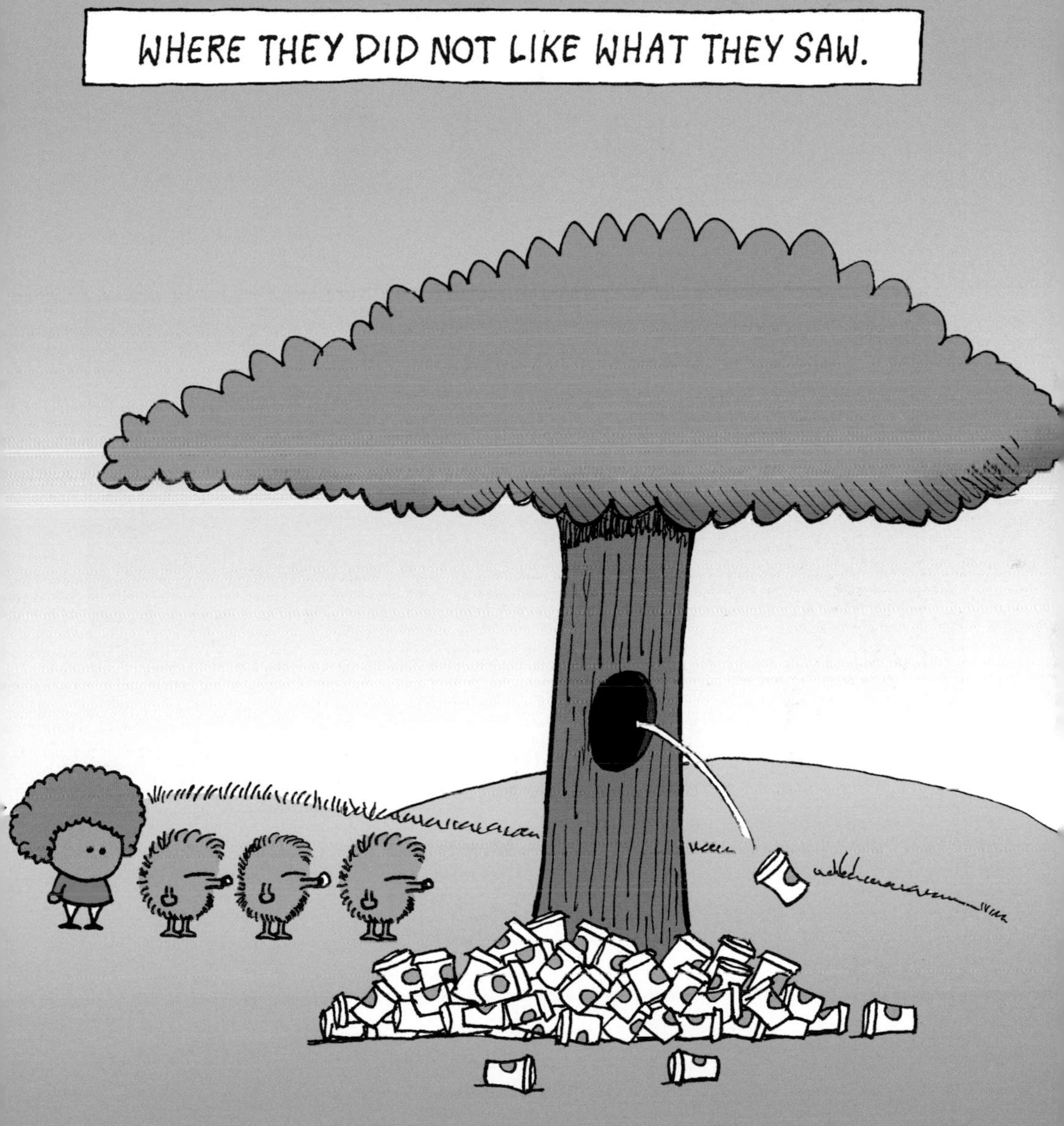
WHERE THEY DID NOT LIKE WHAT THEY SAW.

AND SO M.O.T.H.E.R. LEFT.

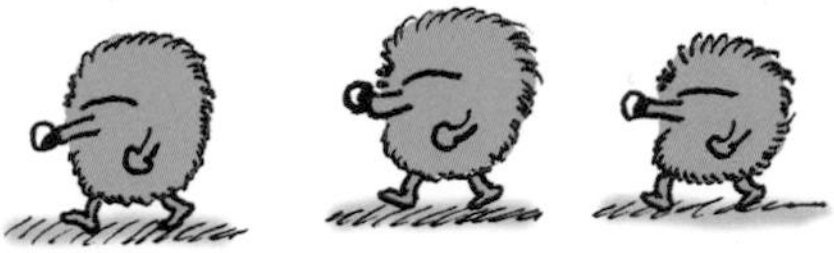

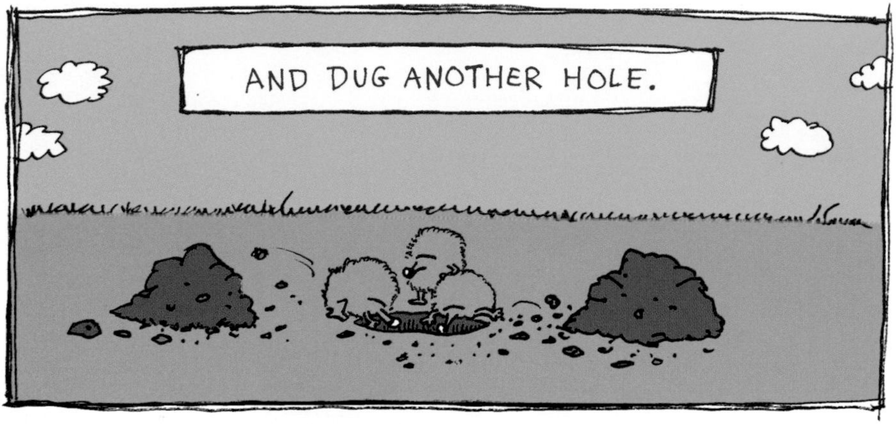
AND DUG ANOTHER HOLE.

AND WERE GONE.

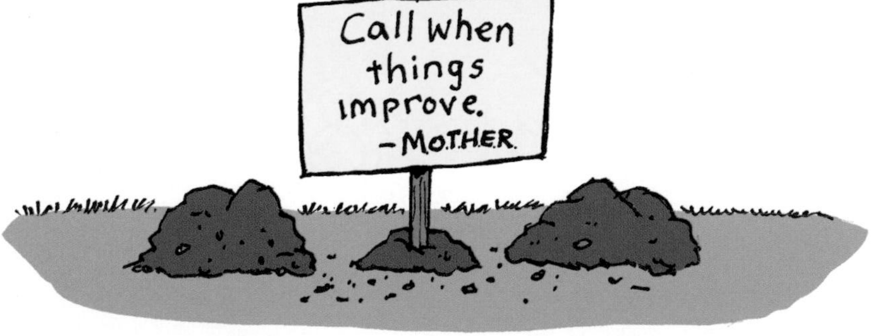
Call when things improve.
-MO.T.H.E.R.

CHAPTER 7

IN WHICH...

YOU WILL GET THAT MUCH CLOSER TO CHAPTER EIGHT

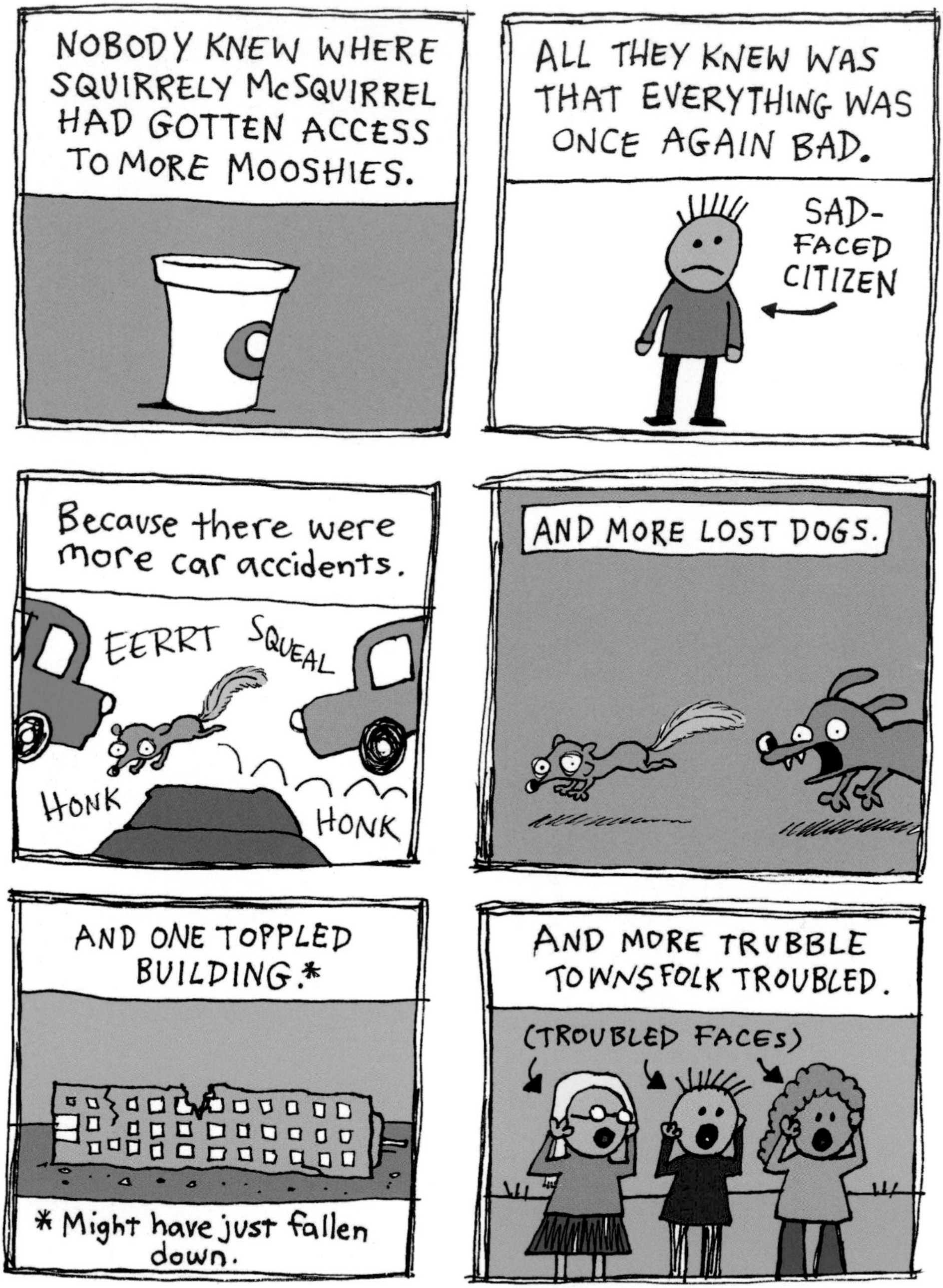
NOBODY KNEW WHERE SQUIRRELY McSQUIRREL HAD GOTTEN ACCESS TO MORE MOOSHIES.
ALL THEY KNEW WAS THAT EVERYTHING WAS ONCE AGAIN BAD.
SAD-FACED CITIZEN
Because there were more car accidents.
EERRT
SQUEAL
HONK
HONK
AND MORE LOST DOGS.
AND ONE TOPPLED BUILDING.*
* Might have just fallen down.
AND MORE TRUBBLE TOWNSFOLK TROUBLED.
(TROUBLED FACES)

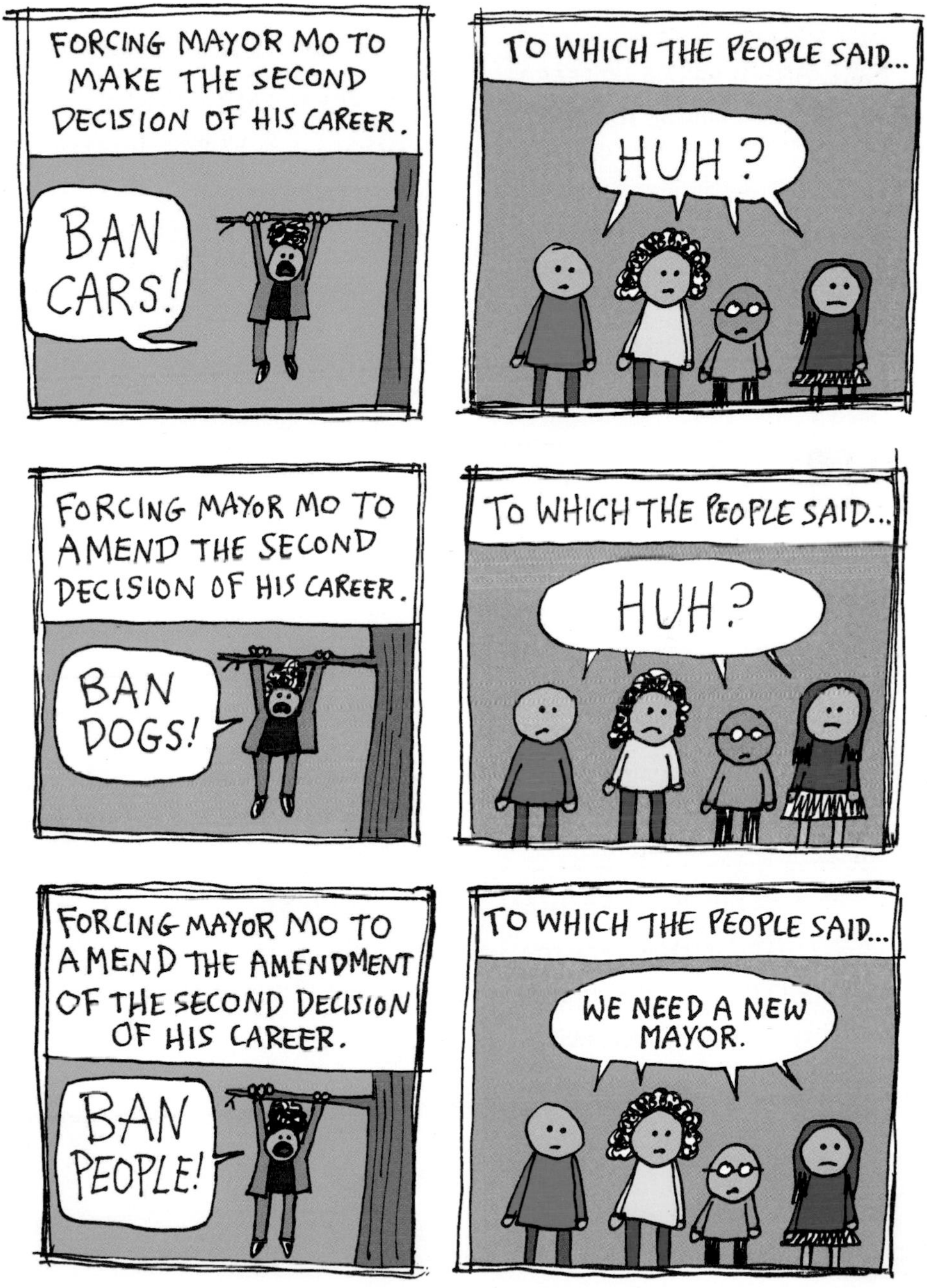
FORCING MAYOR MO TO MAKE THE SECOND DECISION OF HIS CAREER.
BAN CARS!
TO WHICH THE PEOPLE SAID...
HUH?
FORCING MAYOR MO TO AMEND THE SECOND DECISION OF HIS CAREER.
BAN DOGS!
TO WHICH THE PEOPLE SAID...
HUH?
FORCING MAYOR MO TO AMEND THE AMENDMENT OF THE SECOND DECISION OF HIS CAREER.
BAN PEOPLE!
TO WHICH THE PEOPLE SAID...
WE NEED A NEW MAYOR.

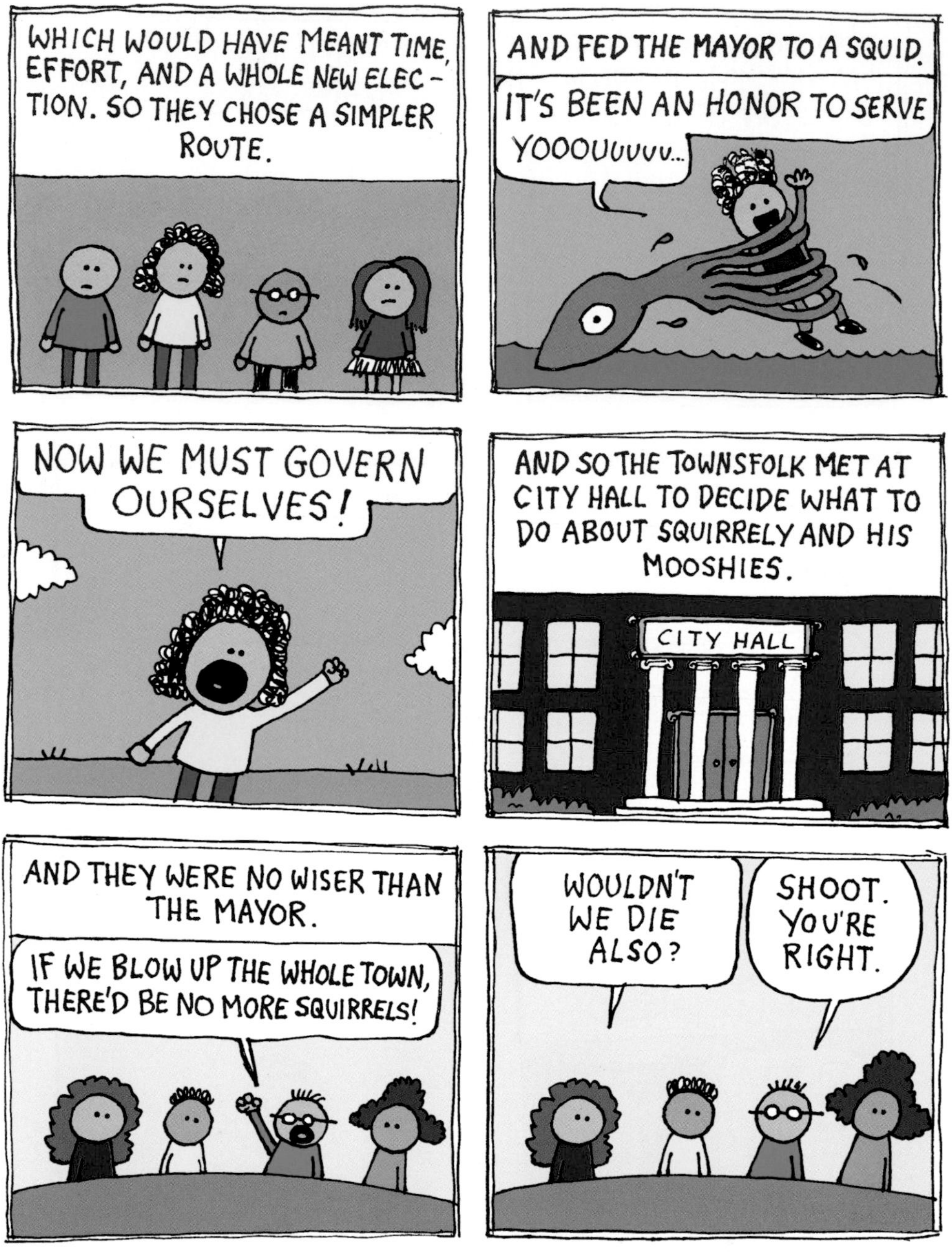
WHICH WOULD HAVE MEANT TIME, EFFORT, AND A WHOLE NEW ELEC-TION. SO THEY CHOSE A SIMPLER ROUTE.
AND FED THE MAYOR TO A SQUID.
IT'S BEEN AN HONOR TO SERVE YOOOUUUUU...
NOW WE MUST GOVERN OURSELVES!
AND SO THE TOWNSFOLK MET AT CITY HALL TO DECIDE WHAT TO DO ABOUT SQUIRRELY AND HIS MOOSHIES.
CITY HALL
AND THEY WERE NO WISER THAN THE MAYOR.
IF WE BLOW UP THE WHOLE TOWN, THERE'D BE NO MORE SQUIRRELS!
WOULDN'T WE DIE ALSO?
SHOOT. YOU'RE RIGHT.

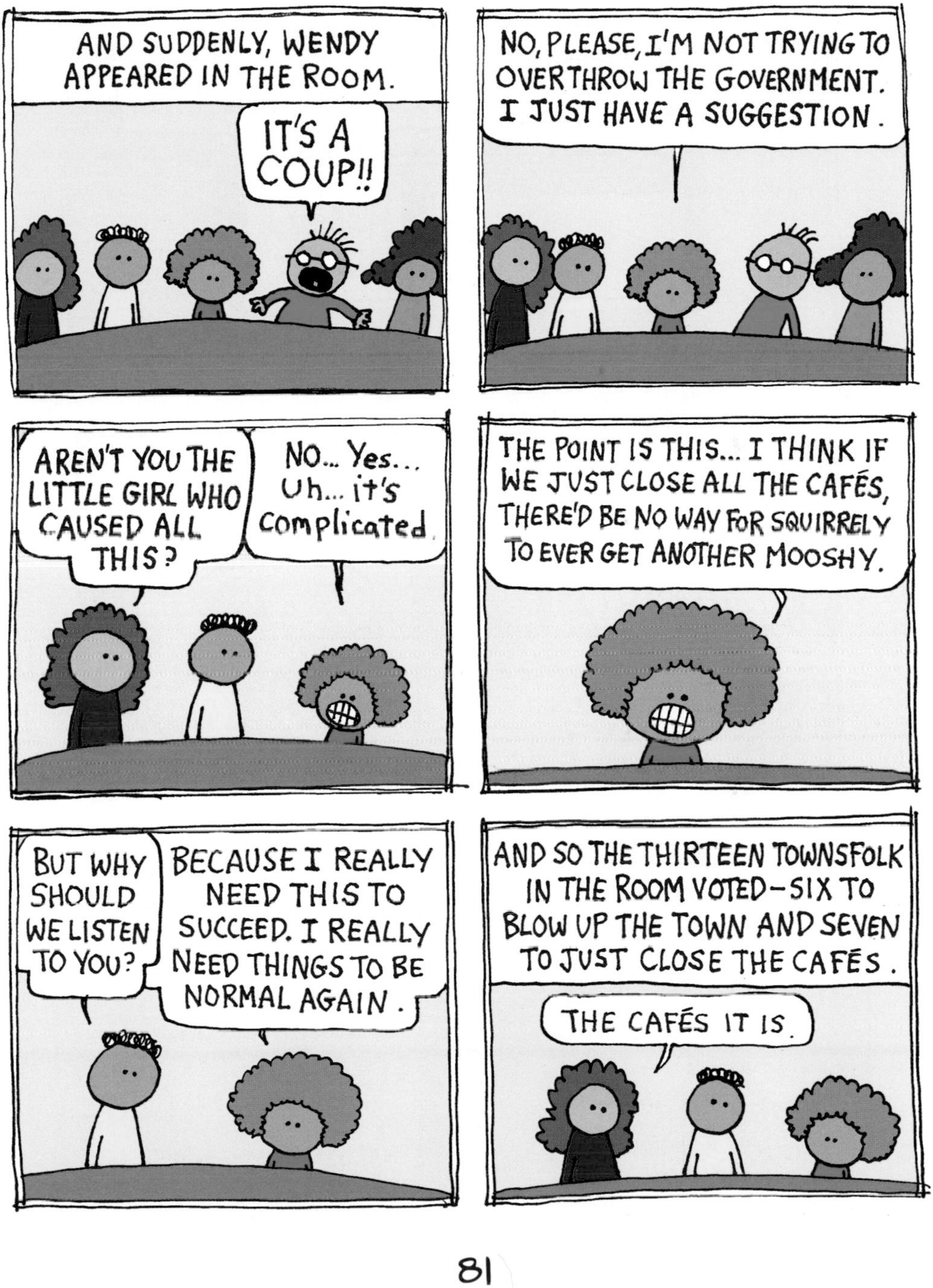
AND SUDDENLY, WENDY APPEARED IN THE ROOM.
IT'S A COUP!!
NO, PLEASE, I'M NOT TRYING TO OVERTHROW THE GOVERNMENT. I JUST HAVE A SUGGESTION.
AREN'T YOU THE LITTLE GIRL WHO CAUSED ALL THIS?
NO... Yes... Uh... it's complicated.
THE POINT IS THIS... I THINK IF WE JUST CLOSE ALL THE CAFÉS, THERE'D BE NO WAY FOR SQUIRRELY TO EVER GET ANOTHER MOOSHY.
BUT WHY SHOULD WE LISTEN TO YOU?
BECAUSE I REALLY NEED THIS TO SUCCEED. I REALLY NEED THINGS TO BE NORMAL AGAIN.
AND SO THE THIRTEEN TOWNSFOLK IN THE ROOM VOTED—SIX TO BLOW UP THE TOWN AND SEVEN TO JUST CLOSE THE CAFÉS.
THE CAFÉS IT IS.

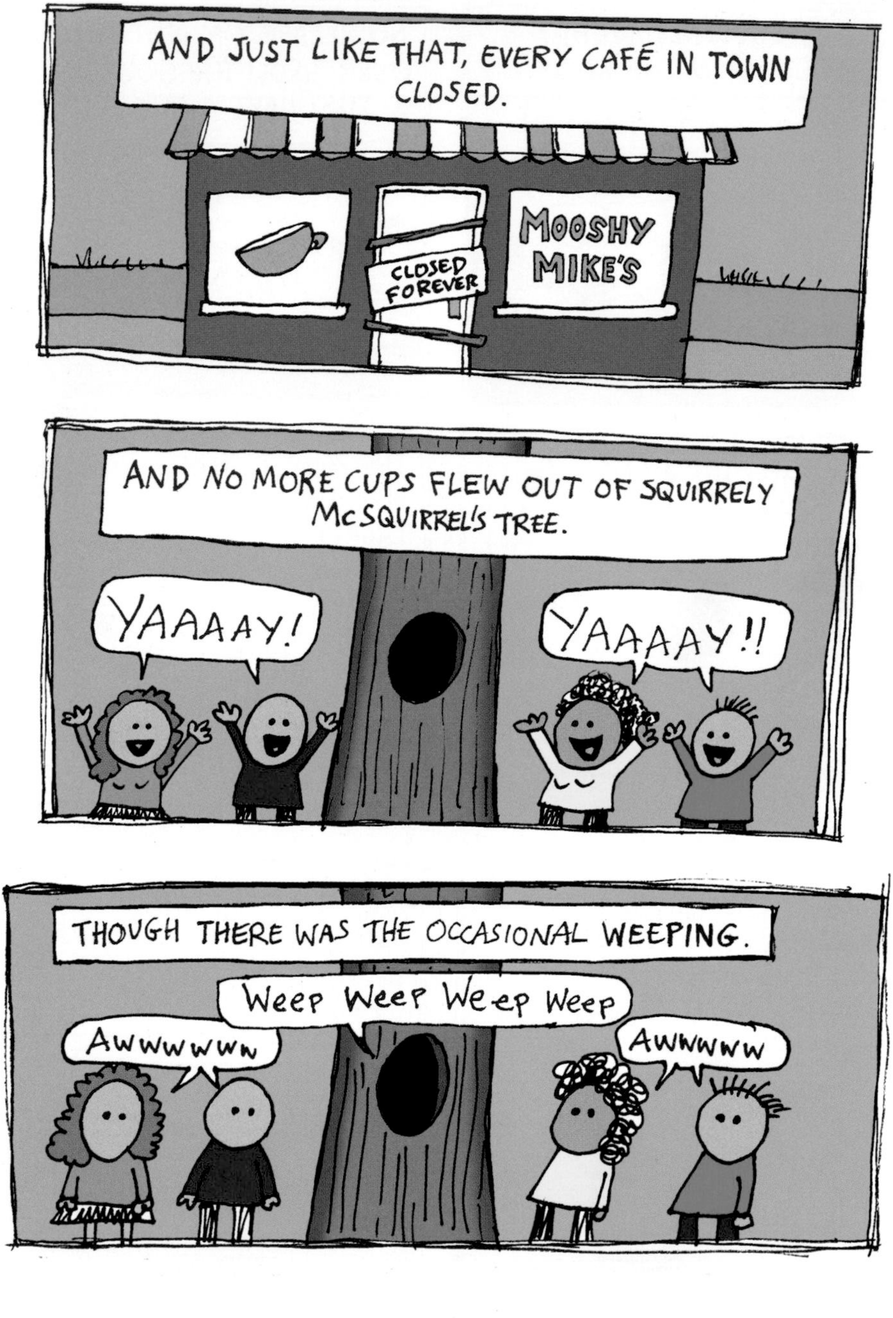
AND JUST LIKE THAT, EVERY CAFÉ IN TOWN CLOSED.
CLOSED FOREVER
MOOSHY MIKE'S
AND NO MORE CUPS FLEW OUT OF SQUIRRELY McSQUIRREL'S TREE.
YAAAAY!
YAAAAY!!
THOUGH THERE WAS THE OCCASIONAL WEEPING.
Weep Weep Weep Weep
AWWWWWN
AWWWWW

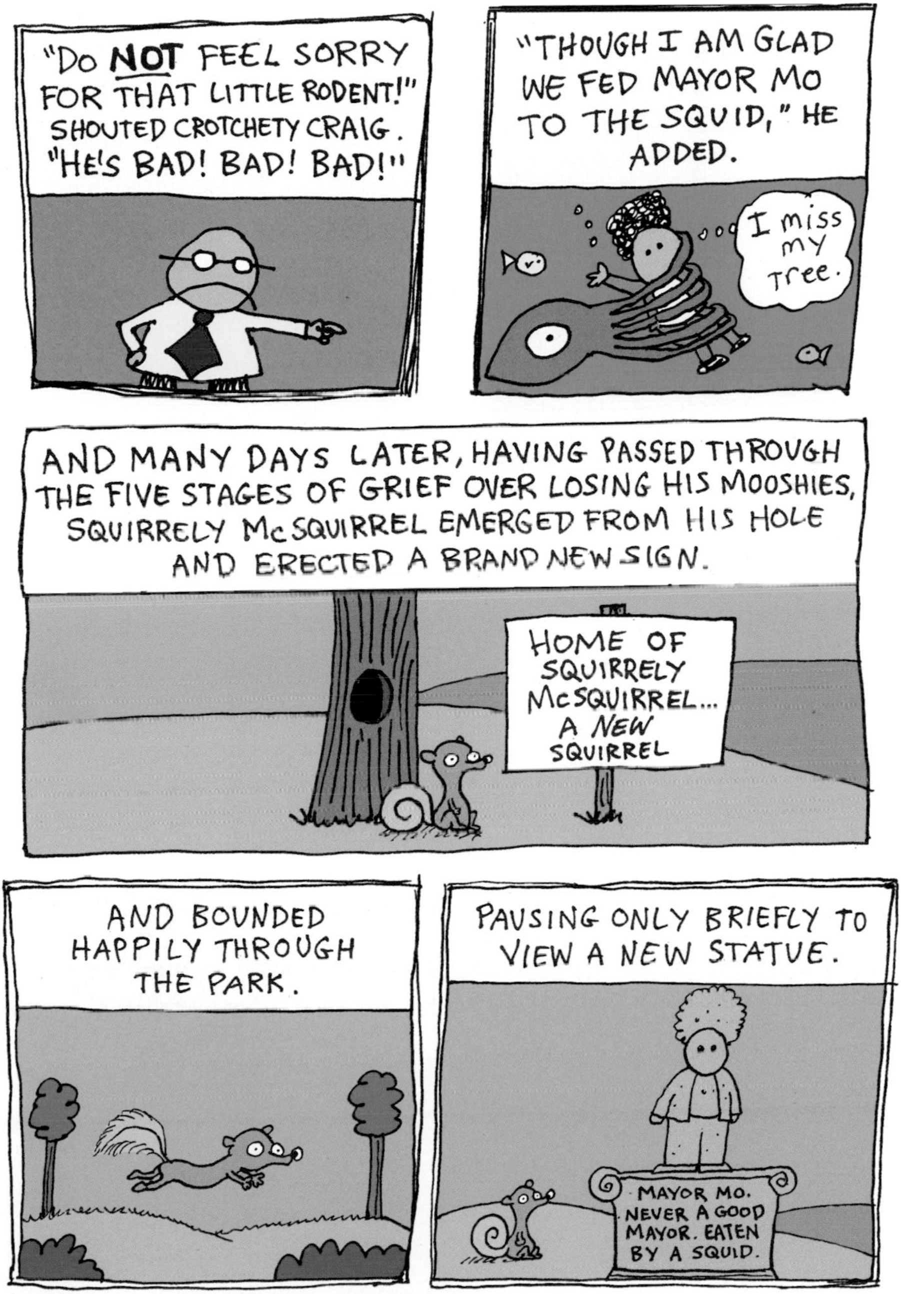
"Do NOT FEEL SORRY FOR THAT LITTLE RODENT!" SHOUTED CROTCHETY CRAIG. "HE'S BAD! BAD! BAD!"
"THOUGH I AM GLAD WE FED MAYOR MO TO THE SQUID," HE ADDED.
I miss my Tree.
AND MANY DAYS LATER, HAVING PASSED THROUGH THE FIVE STAGES OF GRIEF OVER LOSING HIS MOOSHIES, SQUIRRELY McSQUIRREL EMERGED FROM HIS HOLE AND ERECTED A BRAND NEW SIGN.
HOME OF SQUIRRELY McSQUIRREL... A NEW SQUIRREL
AND BOUNDED HAPPILY THROUGH THE PARK.
PAUSING ONLY BRIEFLY TO VIEW A NEW STATUE.
MAYOR MO. NEVER A GOOD MAYOR. EATEN BY A SQUID.

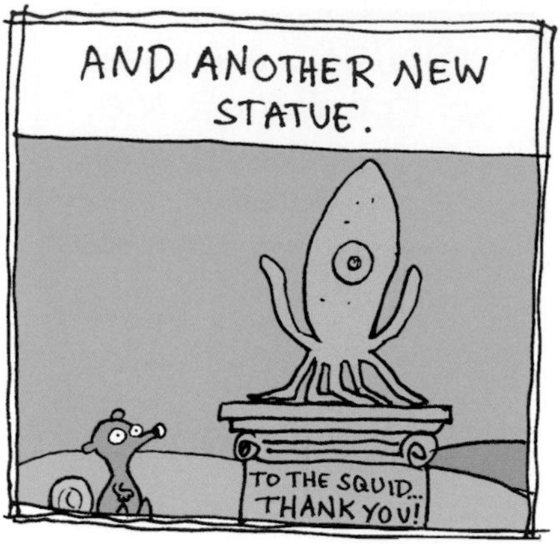
AND ANOTHER NEW STATUE.
TO THE SQUID... THANK YOU!

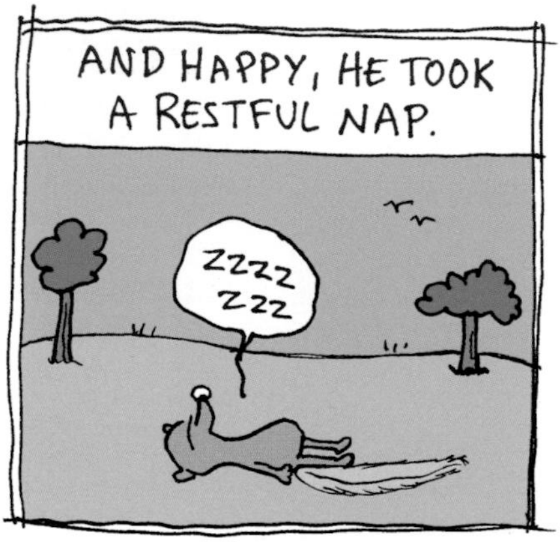
AND HAPPY, HE TOOK A RESTFUL NAP.
ZZZZ ZZZ

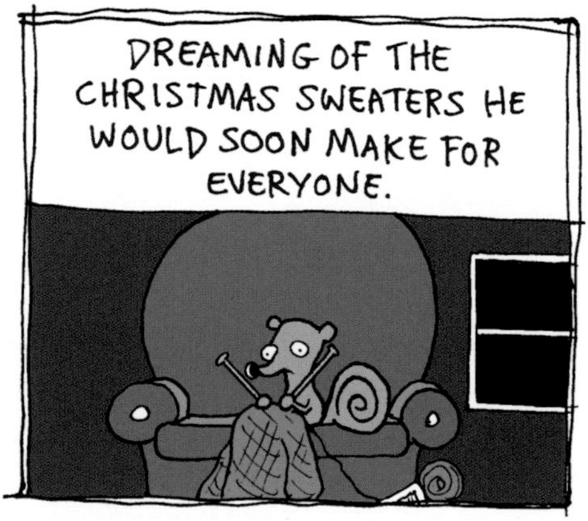
DREAMING OF THE CHRISTMAS SWEATERS HE WOULD SOON MAKE FOR EVERYONE.

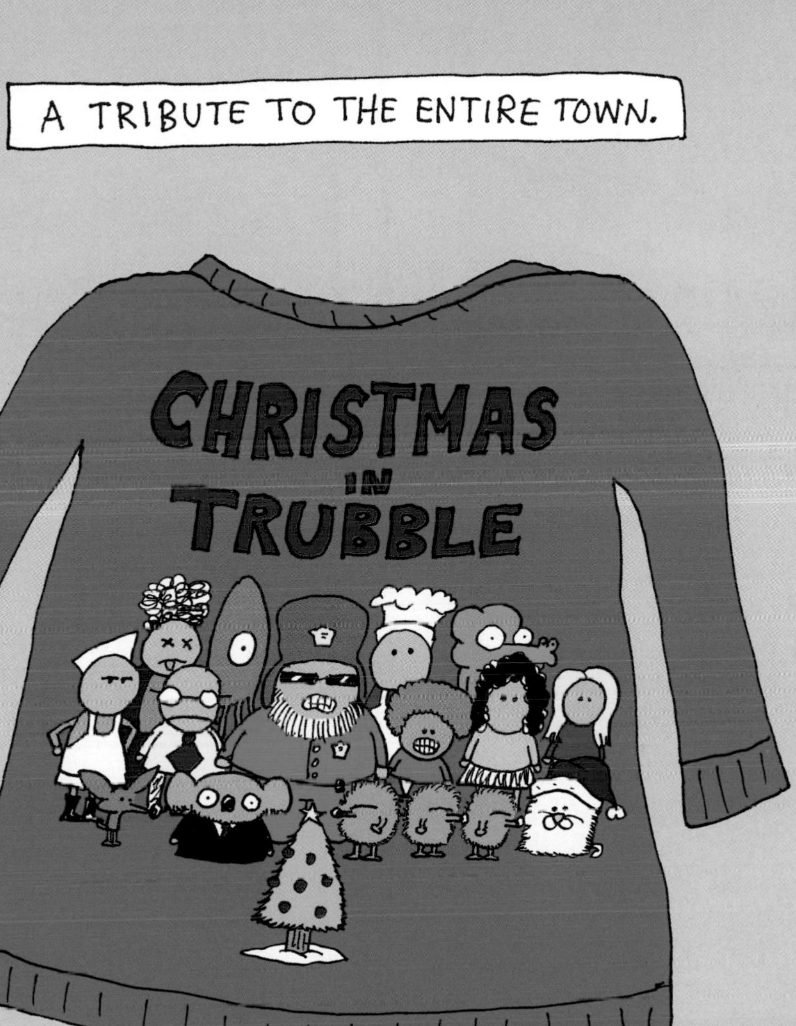
A TRIBUTE TO THE ENTIRE TOWN.
CHRISTMAS IN TRUBBLE

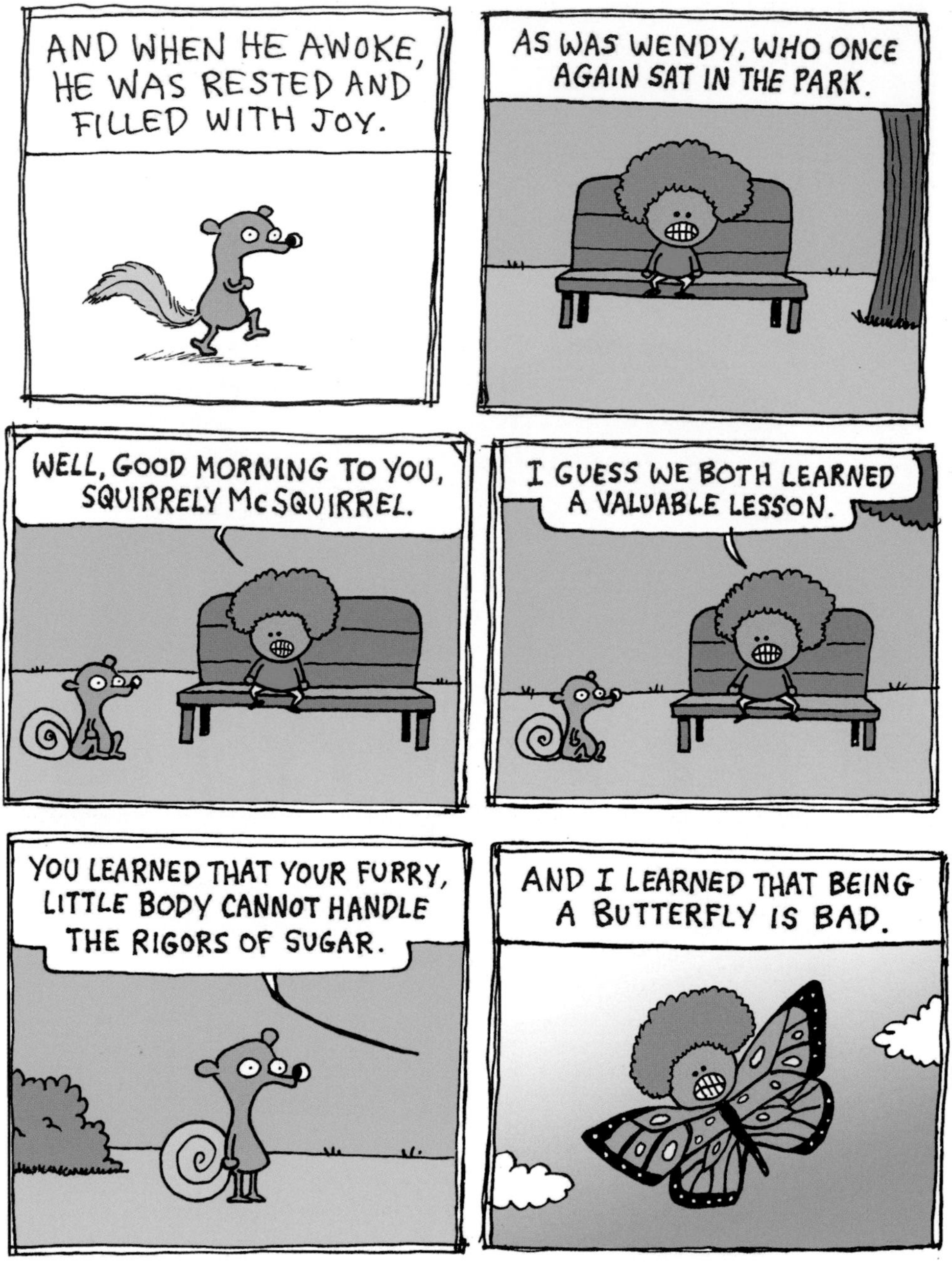
AND WHEN HE AWOKE, HE WAS RESTED AND FILLED WITH JOY.
AS WAS WENDY, WHO ONCE AGAIN SAT IN THE PARK.
WELL, GOOD MORNING TO YOU, SQUIRRELY McSQUIRREL.
I GUESS WE BOTH LEARNED A VALUABLE LESSON.
YOU LEARNED THAT YOUR FURRY, LITTLE BODY CANNOT HANDLE THE RIGORS OF SUGAR.
AND I LEARNED THAT BEING A BUTTERFLY IS BAD.

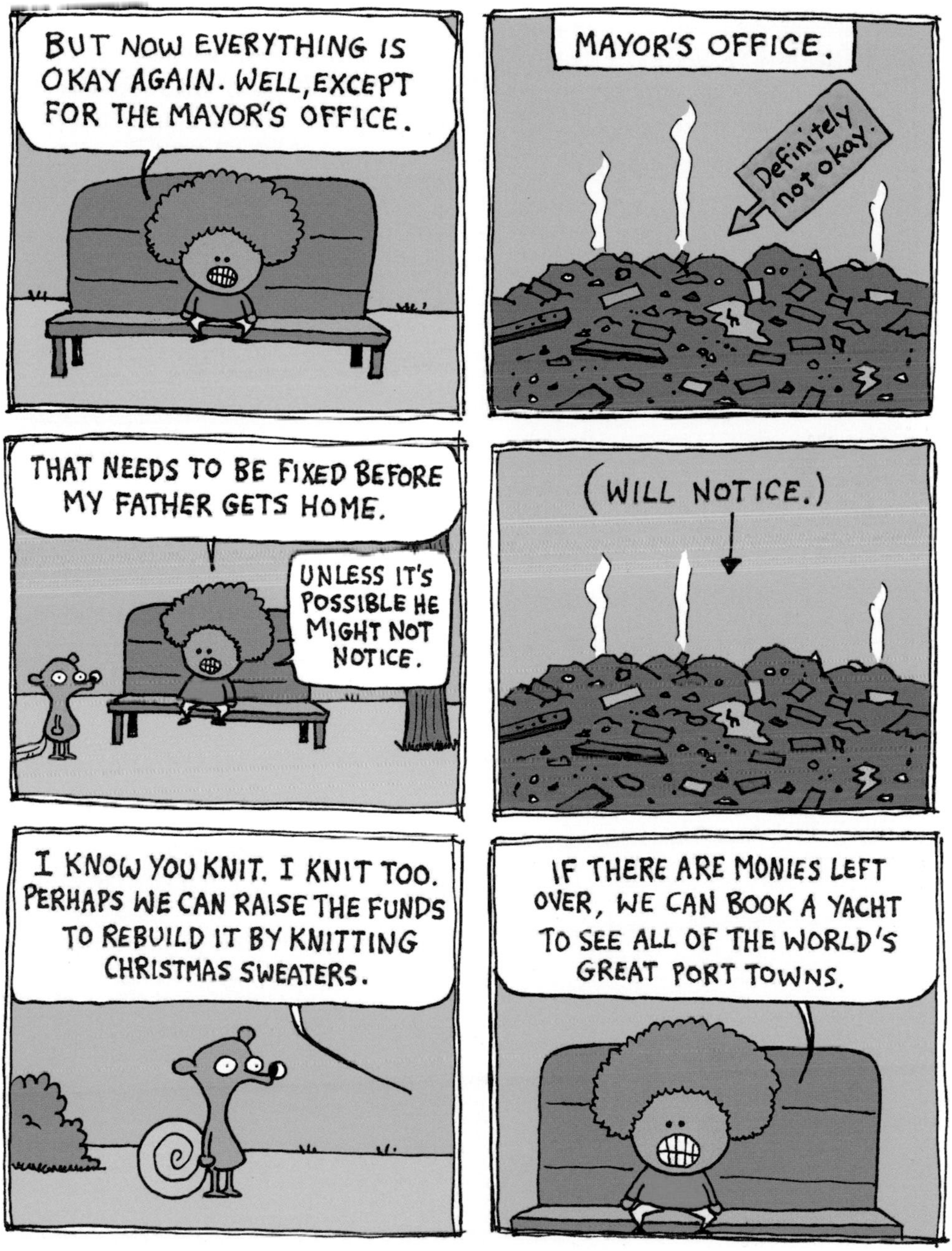
BUT NOW EVERYTHING IS OKAY AGAIN. WELL, EXCEPT FOR THE MAYOR'S OFFICE.
MAYOR'S OFFICE.
Definitely not okay.
THAT NEEDS TO BE FIXED BEFORE MY FATHER GETS HOME.
UNLESS IT'S POSSIBLE HE MIGHT NOT NOTICE.
(WILL NOTICE.)
I KNOW YOU KNIT. I KNIT TOO. PERHAPS WE CAN RAISE THE FUNDS TO REBUILD IT BY KNITTING CHRISTMAS SWEATERS.
IF THERE ARE MONIES LEFT OVER, WE CAN BOOK A YACHT TO SEE ALL OF THE WORLD'S GREAT PORT TOWNS.

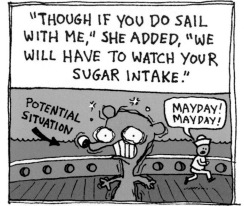

"THOUGH IF YOU DO SAIL WITH ME," SHE ADDED, "WE WILL HAVE TO WATCH YOUR SUGAR INTAKE."

POTENTIAL SITUATION

MAYDAY! MAYDAY!

"BUT ENOUGH ABOUT ME," SAID WENDY, PATTING THE SQUIRREL ON THE HEAD, "WHAT ABOUT YOU?"

PAT PAT PAT

NOW THAT ALL THE CAFÉS ARE CLOSED, WHAT ARE YOU GONNA DO?

SO SQUIRRELY THOUGHT...

...REALLY HARD.

AND EVERY CAFÉ IN TOWN
EXPLODED.

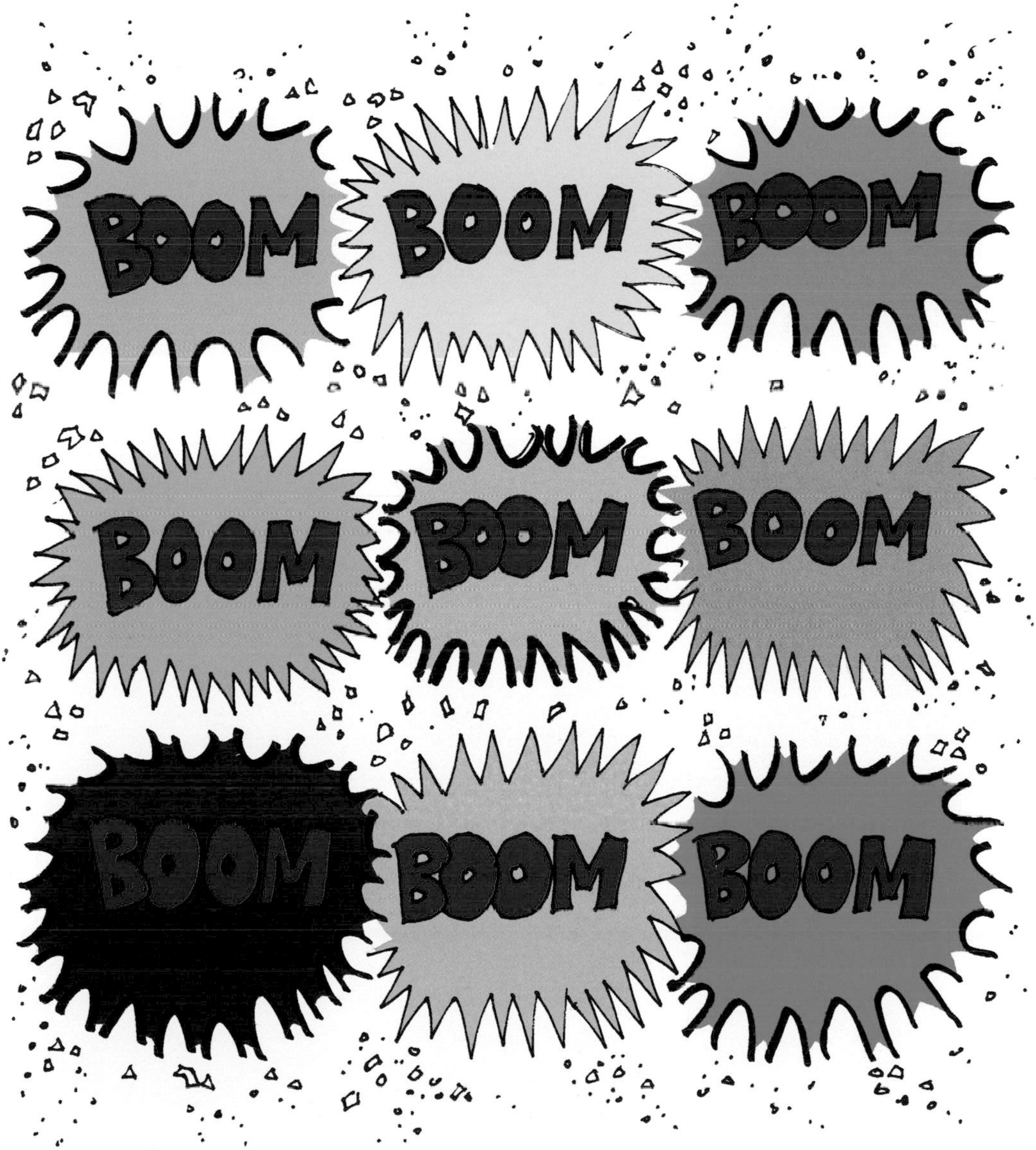
BOOM
BOOM
BOOM
BOOM
BOOM
BOOM
BOOM
BOOM
BOOM

CHAPTER

8

IN WHICH...

THE TENSION INCREASETH

SQUIRRELY RAN AS FAST AS HIS LITTLE SQUIRREL LEGS WOULD TAKE HIM.

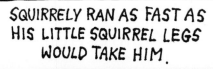

OVER THE RIVER.

AND THROUGH THE WOODS.

TO GRANDMOTHERS' HEADS HE WENT.

FOLLOWED CLOSELY BY WENDY THE WANDERER.

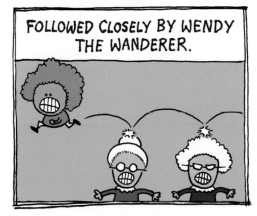

YOU APPEAR TO BE MAKING VERY POOR LIFE CHOICES!

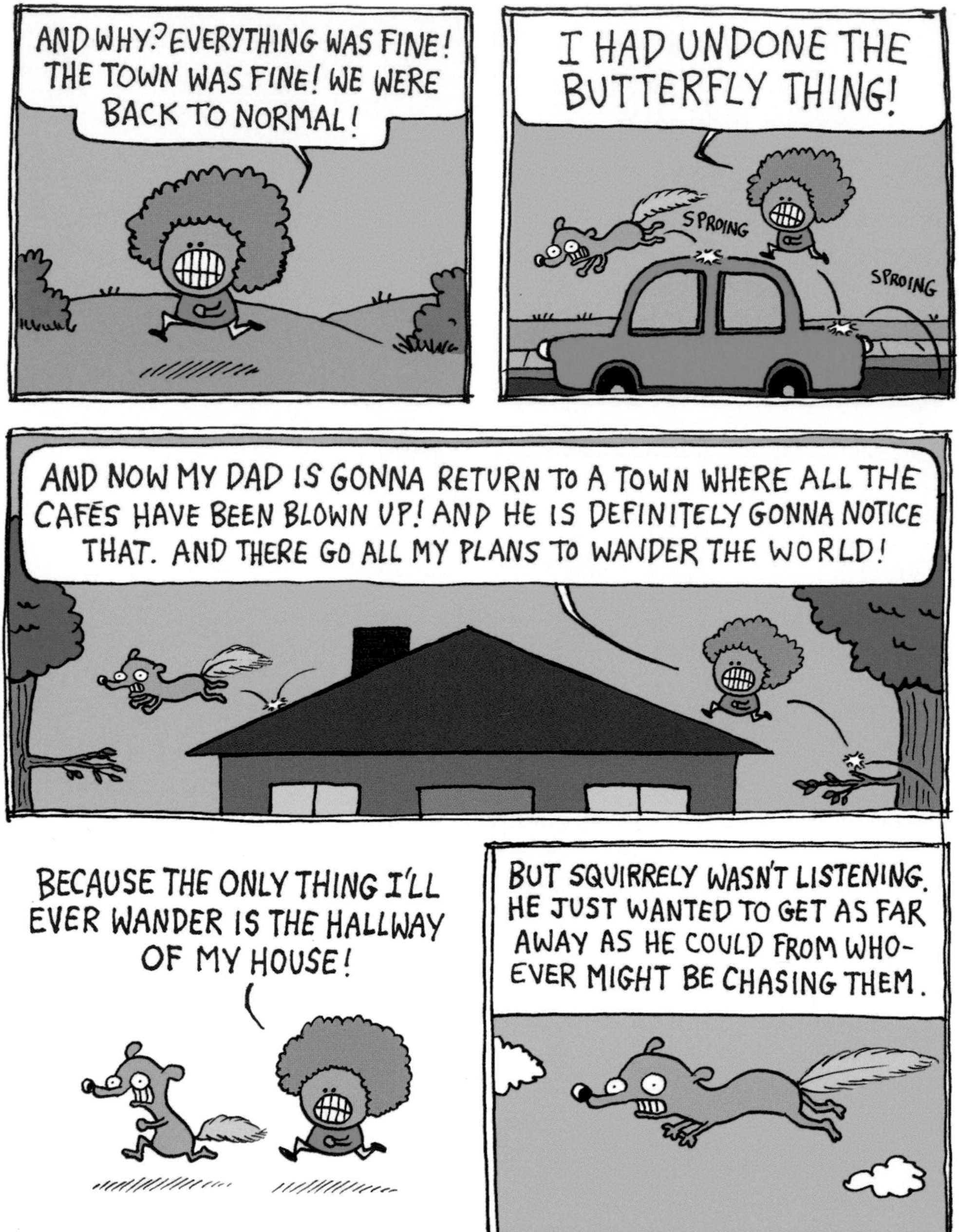
AND WHY? EVERYTHING WAS FINE! THE TOWN WAS FINE! WE WERE BACK TO NORMAL!
I HAD UNDONE THE BUTTERFLY THING!
SPROING
SPROING
AND NOW MY DAD IS GONNA RETURN TO A TOWN WHERE ALL THE CAFÉS HAVE BEEN BLOWN UP! AND HE IS DEFINITELY GONNA NOTICE THAT. AND THERE GO ALL MY PLANS TO WANDER THE WORLD!
BECAUSE THE ONLY THING I'LL EVER WANDER IS THE HALLWAY OF MY HOUSE!
BUT SQUIRRELY WASN'T LISTENING. HE JUST WANTED TO GET AS FAR AWAY AS HE COULD FROM WHO-EVER MIGHT BE CHASING THEM.

AND THAT WAS THE ENTIRE TOWN.

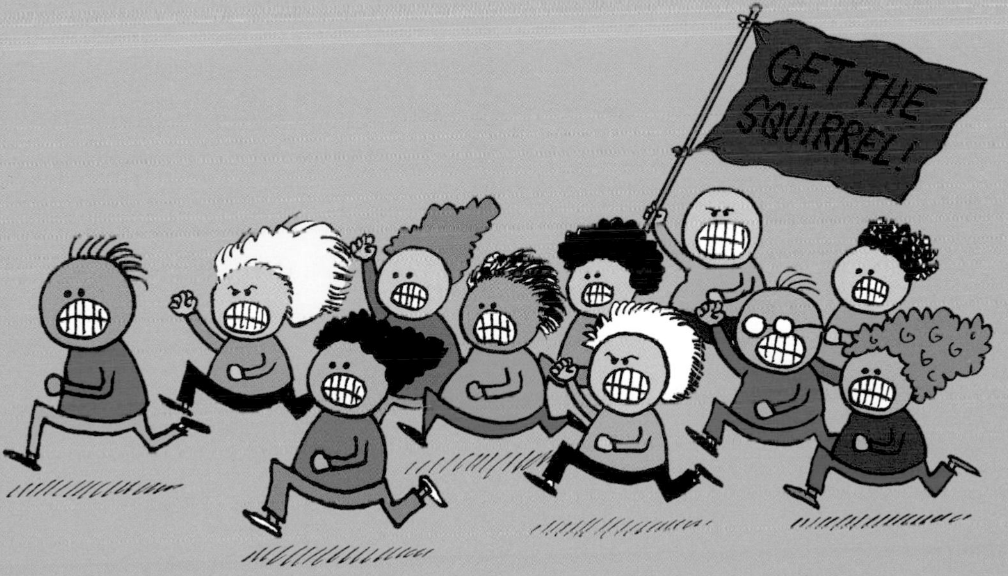
GET THE SQUIRREL!

CHAPTER NINE

WHICH IS...

ONE AFTER EIGHT

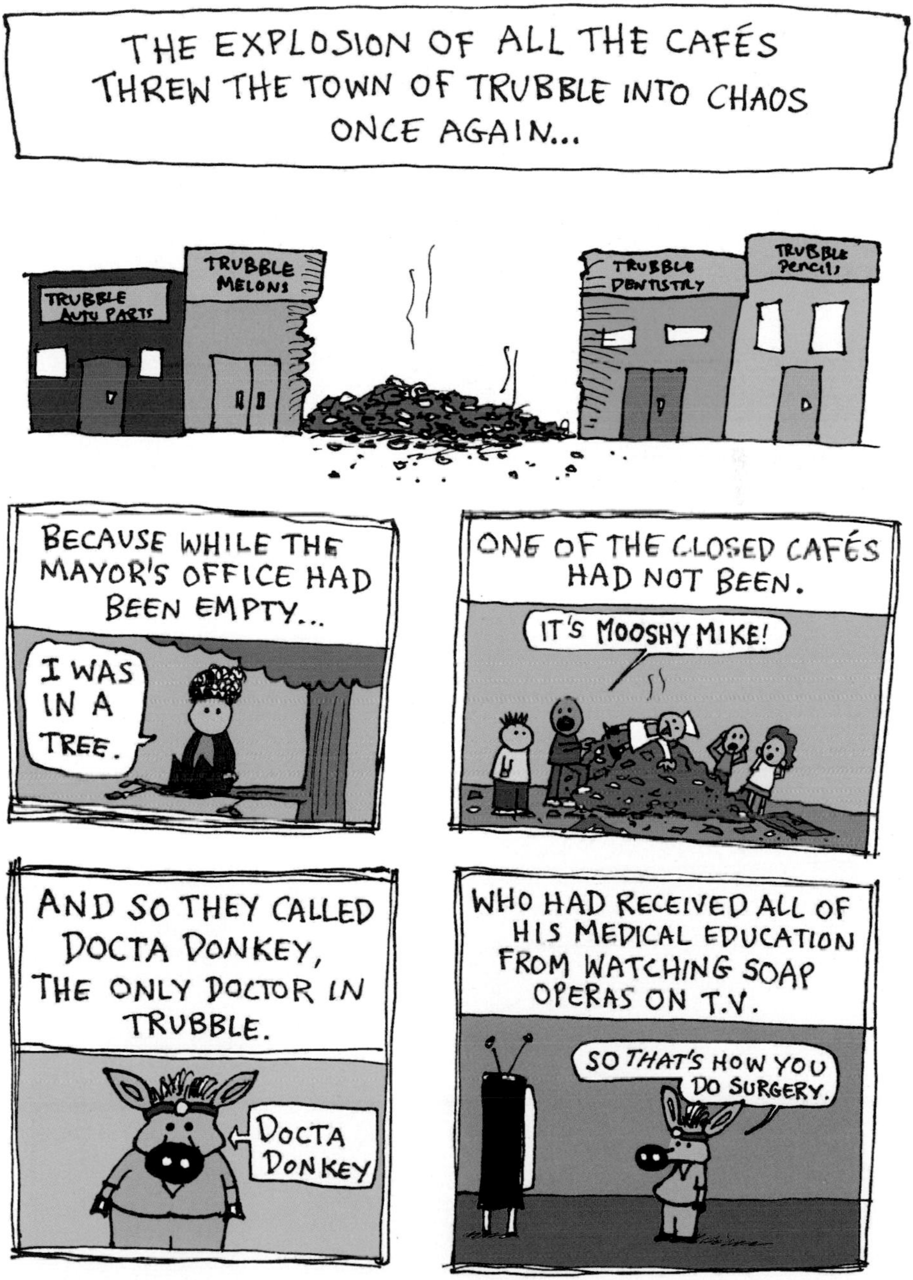
THE EXPLOSION OF ALL THE CAFÉS THREW THE TOWN OF TRUBBLE INTO CHAOS ONCE AGAIN...
TRUBBLE AUTO PARTS
TRUBBLE MELONS
TRUBBLE DENTISTRY
TRUBBLE PENCILS
BECAUSE WHILE THE MAYOR'S OFFICE HAD BEEN EMPTY...
I WAS IN A TREE.
ONE OF THE CLOSED CAFÉS HAD NOT BEEN.
IT'S MOOSHY MIKE!
AND SO THEY CALLED DOCTA DONKEY, THE ONLY DOCTOR IN TRUBBLE.
DOCTA DONKEY
WHO HAD RECEIVED ALL OF HIS MEDICAL EDUCATION FROM WATCHING SOAP OPERAS ON T.V.
SO *THAT'S* HOW YOU DO SURGERY.

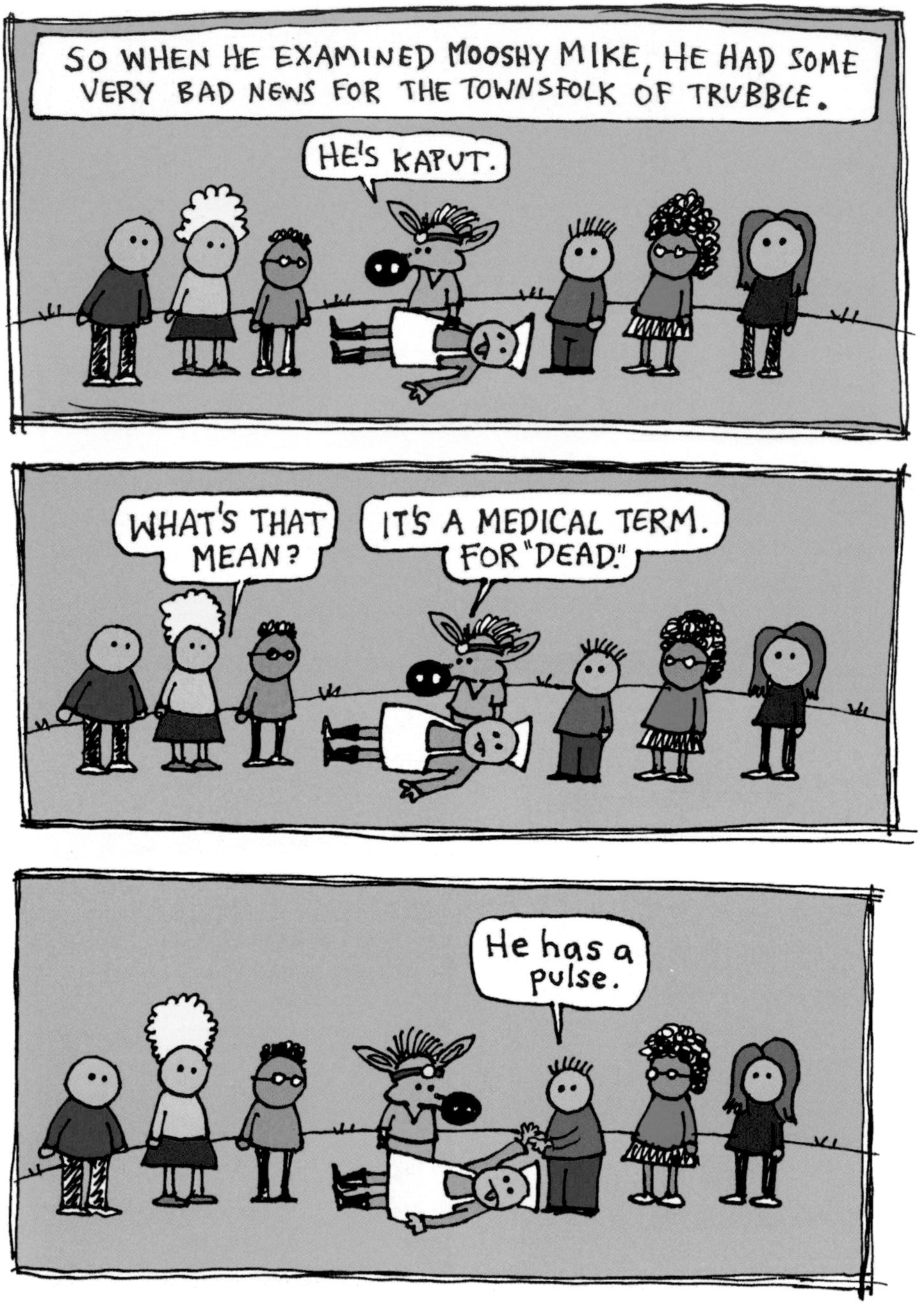
SO WHEN HE EXAMINED MOOSHY MIKE, HE HAD SOME VERY BAD NEWS FOR THE TOWNSFOLK OF TRUBBLE.
HE'S KAPUT.
WHAT'S THAT MEAN?
IT'S A MEDICAL TERM. FOR "DEAD."
He has a pulse.

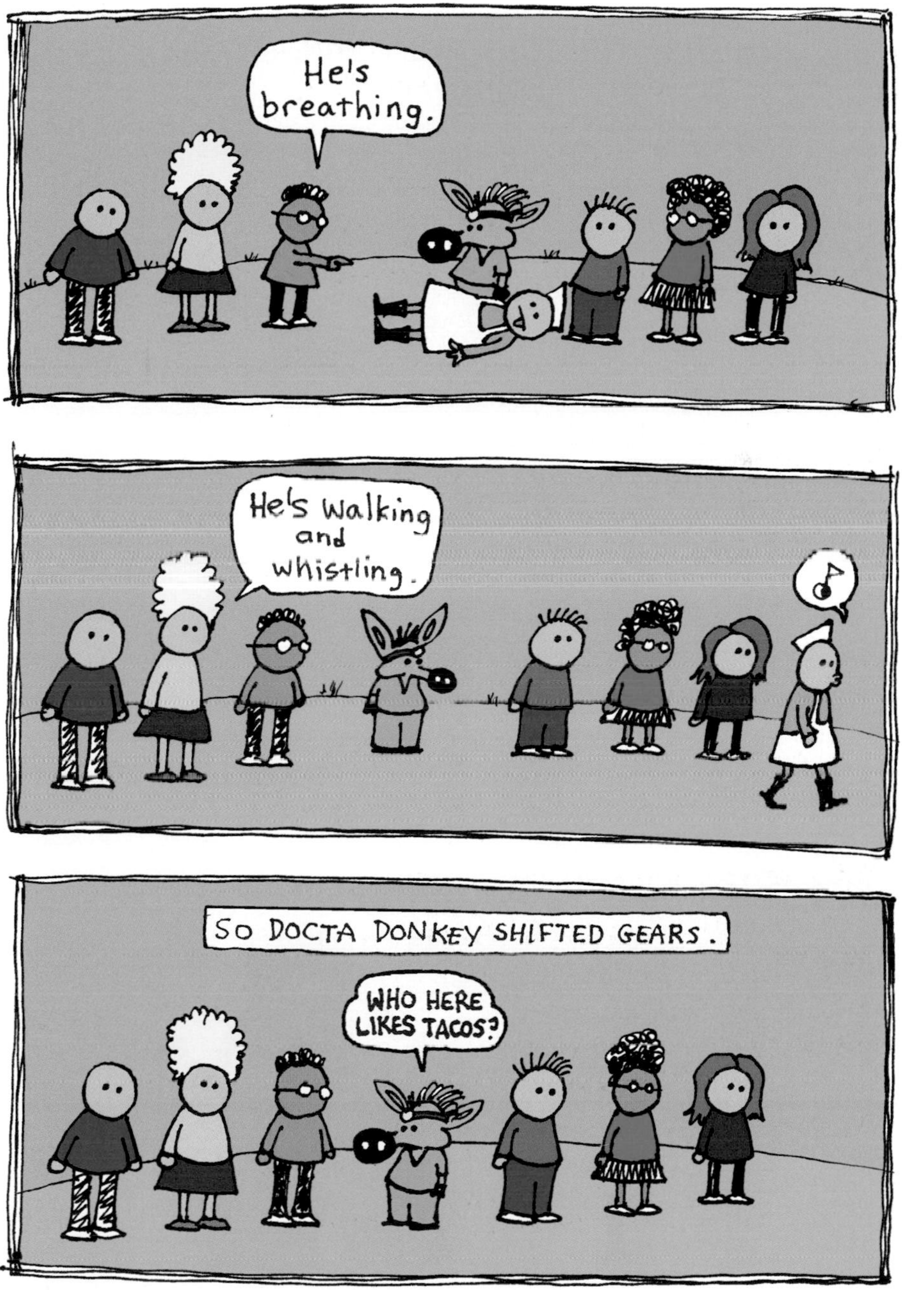
He's breathing.
He's walking and whistling.
SO DOCTA DONKEY SHIFTED GEARS.
WHO HERE LIKES TACOS?

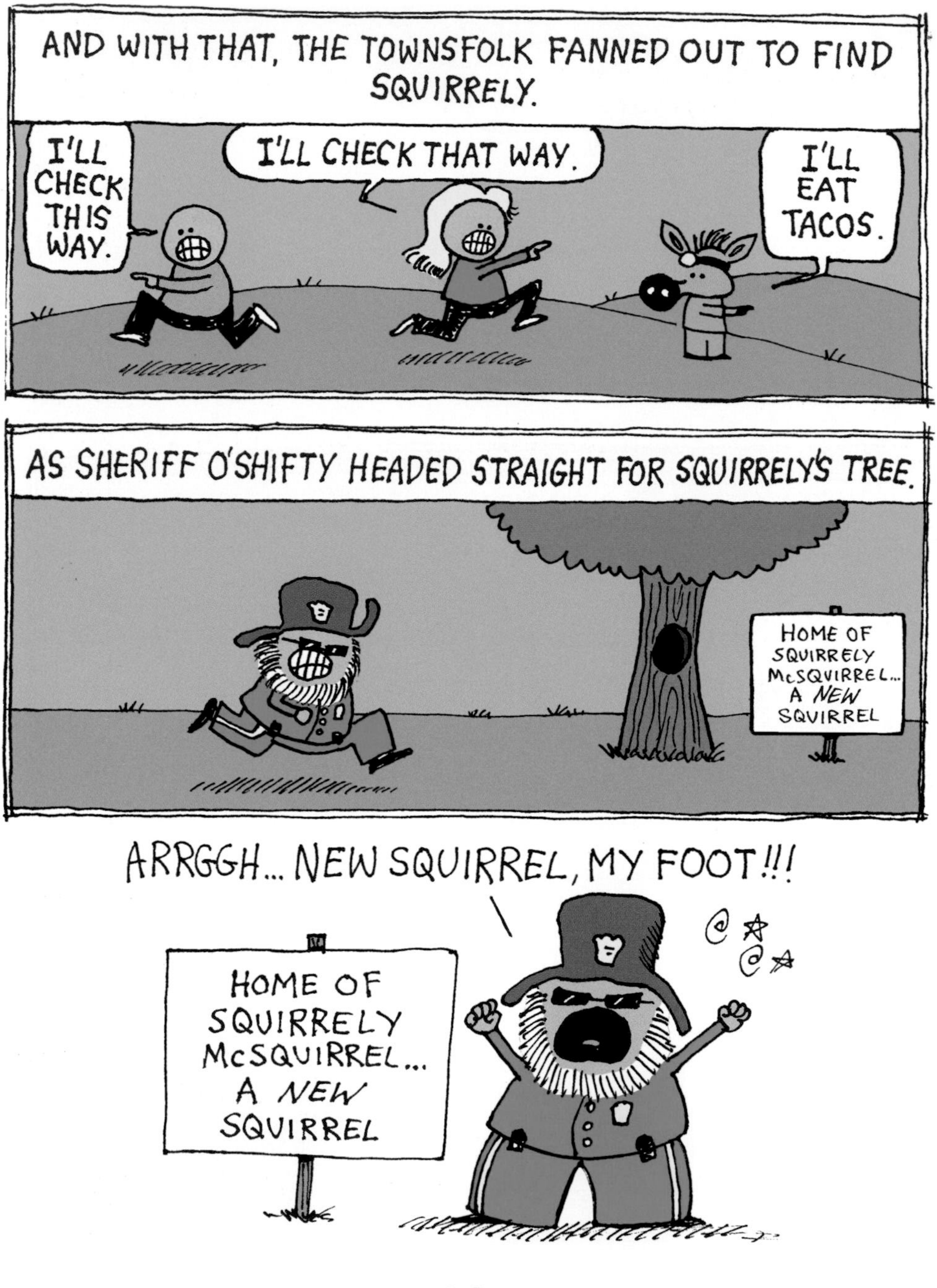
AND WITH THAT, THE TOWNSFOLK FANNED OUT TO FIND SQUIRRELY.
I'LL CHECK THIS WAY.
I'LL CHECK THAT WAY.
I'LL EAT TACOS.
AS SHERIFF O'SHIFTY HEADED STRAIGHT FOR SQUIRRELY'S TREE.
HOME OF SQUIRRELY McSQUIRREL... A *NEW* SQUIRREL
ARRGGH... NEW SQUIRREL, MY FOOT!!!
HOME OF SQUIRRELY McSQUIRREL... A *NEW* SQUIRREL

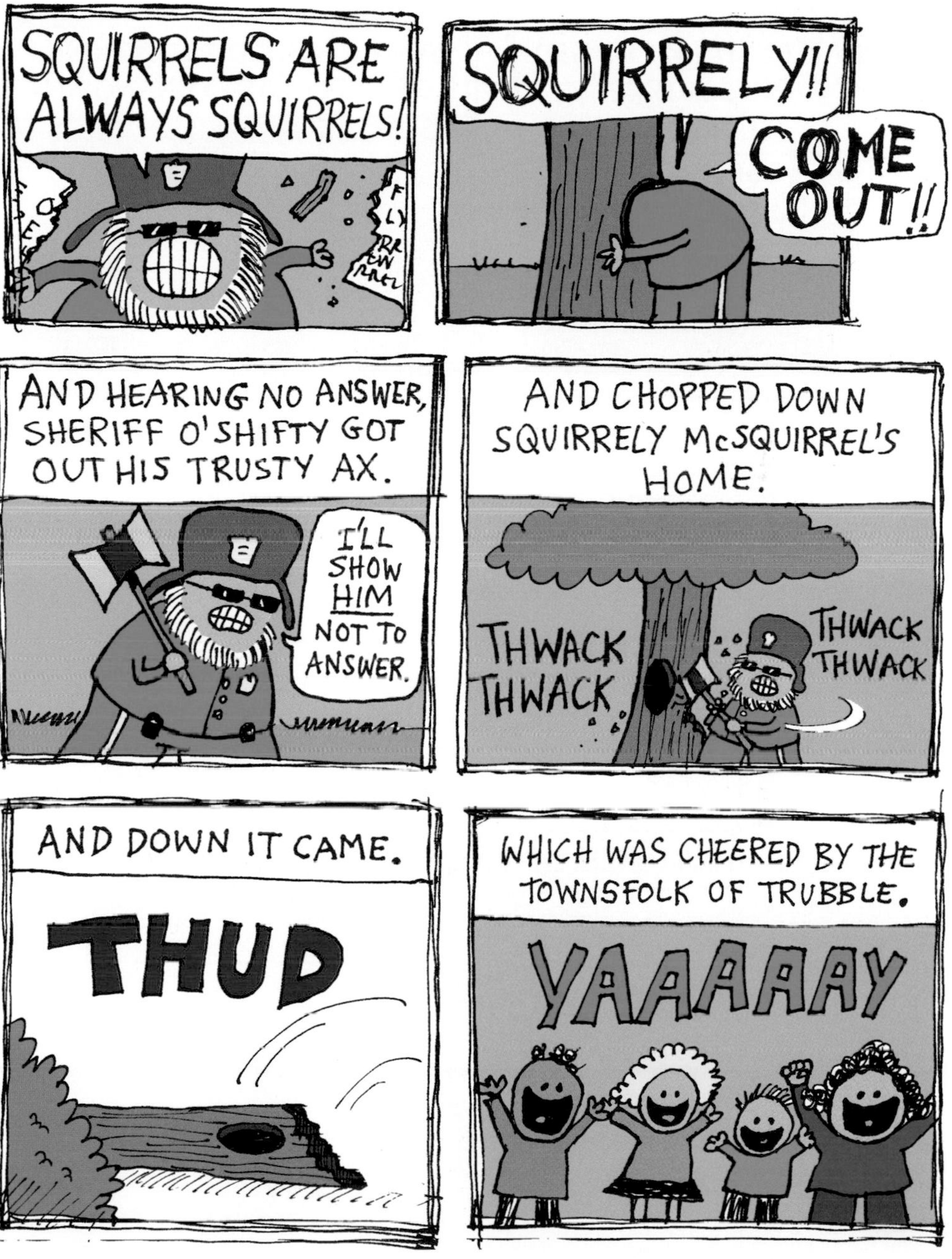
SQUIRRELS ARE ALWAYS SQUIRRELS!
SQUIRRELY!!
COME OUT!!
AND HEARING NO ANSWER, SHERIFF O'SHIFTY GOT OUT HIS TRUSTY AX.
I'LL SHOW HIM NOT TO ANSWER.
AND CHOPPED DOWN SQUIRRELY McSQUIRREL'S HOME.
THWACK THWACK
THWACK THWACK
AND DOWN IT CAME.
THUD
WHICH WAS CHEERED BY THE TOWNSFOLK OF TRUBBLE.
YAAAAAY

WHO PROMPTLY RUMMAGED THROUGH SQUIRRELY'S THINGS.

DIBS ON HIS TUBA!

I GET THE SOFA!

THE PIANO IS MINE!

AND CARRIED EVERYTHING OFF TO PARTS UNKNOWN.

EXCEPT FOR ONE SMALL THING.

SQUIRRELY'S PRIVATE DIARY.

SQUIRRELY'S MOST SECRET-EST SECRET SECRETS

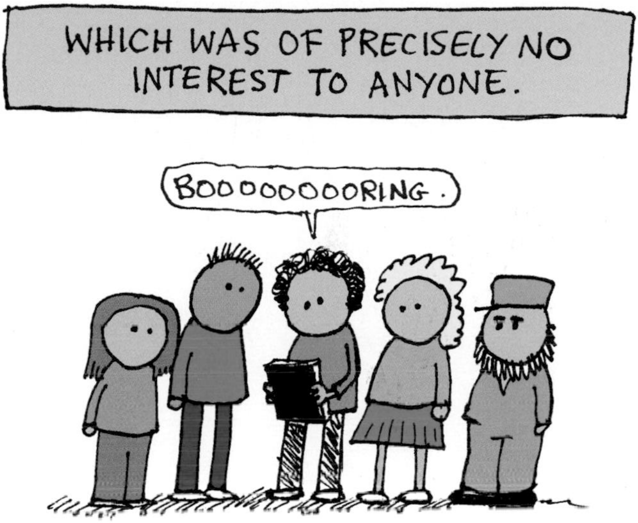
WHICH WAS OF PRECISELY NO INTEREST TO ANYONE.
BOOOOOOOOORING.

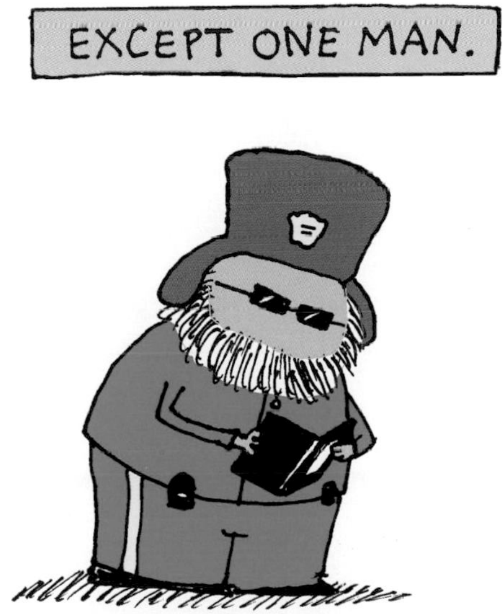
EXCEPT ONE MAN.

CHAPTER
TEN

IN WHICH...

YOU WILL LEARN THINGS YOU DIDN'T KNOW

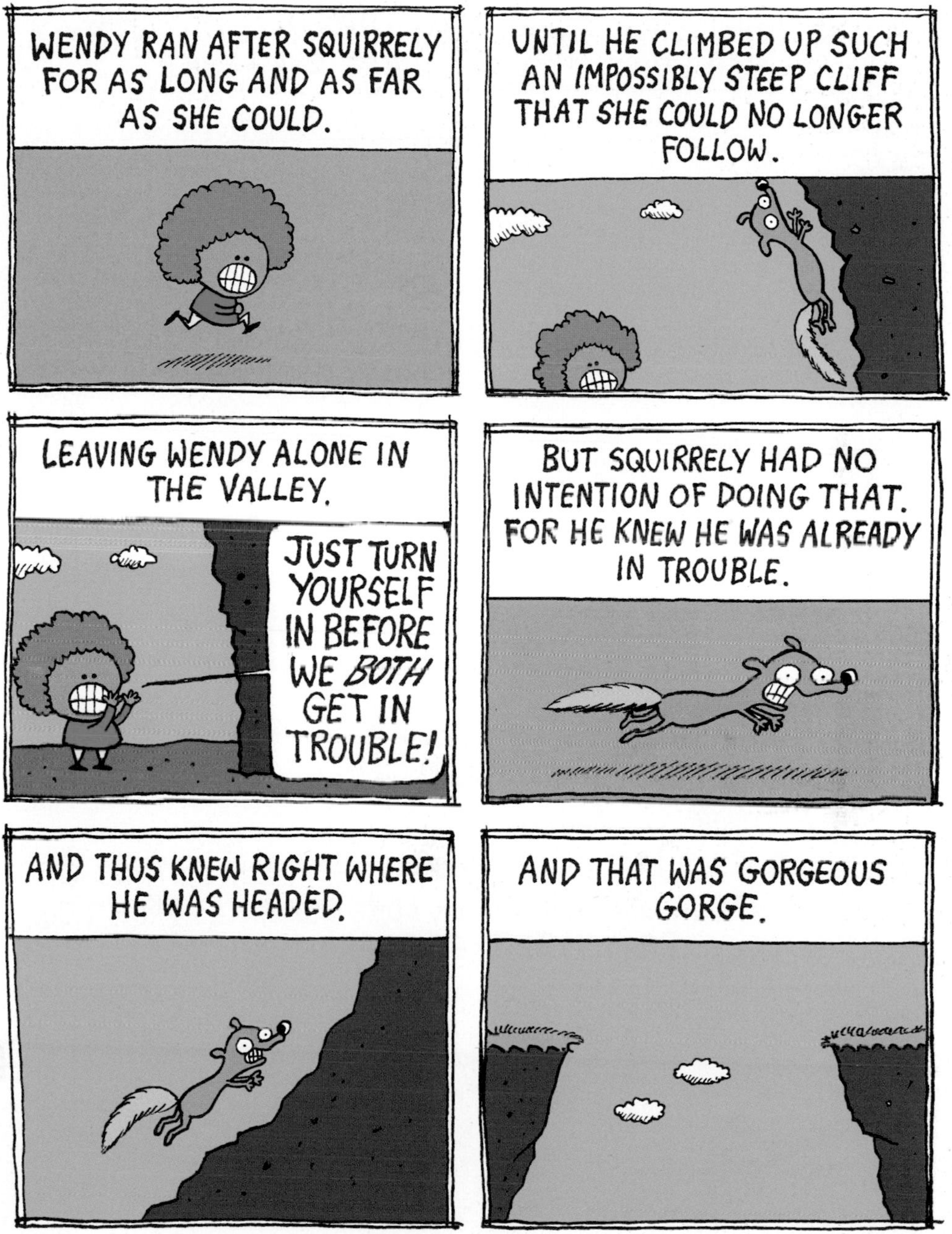
WENDY RAN AFTER SQUIRRELY FOR AS LONG AND AS FAR AS SHE COULD.
UNTIL HE CLIMBED UP SUCH AN IMPOSSIBLY STEEP CLIFF THAT SHE COULD NO LONGER FOLLOW.
LEAVING WENDY ALONE IN THE VALLEY.
JUST TURN YOURSELF IN BEFORE WE *BOTH* GET IN TROUBLE!
BUT SQUIRRELY HAD NO INTENTION OF DOING THAT. FOR HE KNEW HE WAS ALREADY IN TROUBLE.
AND THUS KNEW RIGHT WHERE HE WAS HEADED.
AND THAT WAS GORGEOUS GORGE.

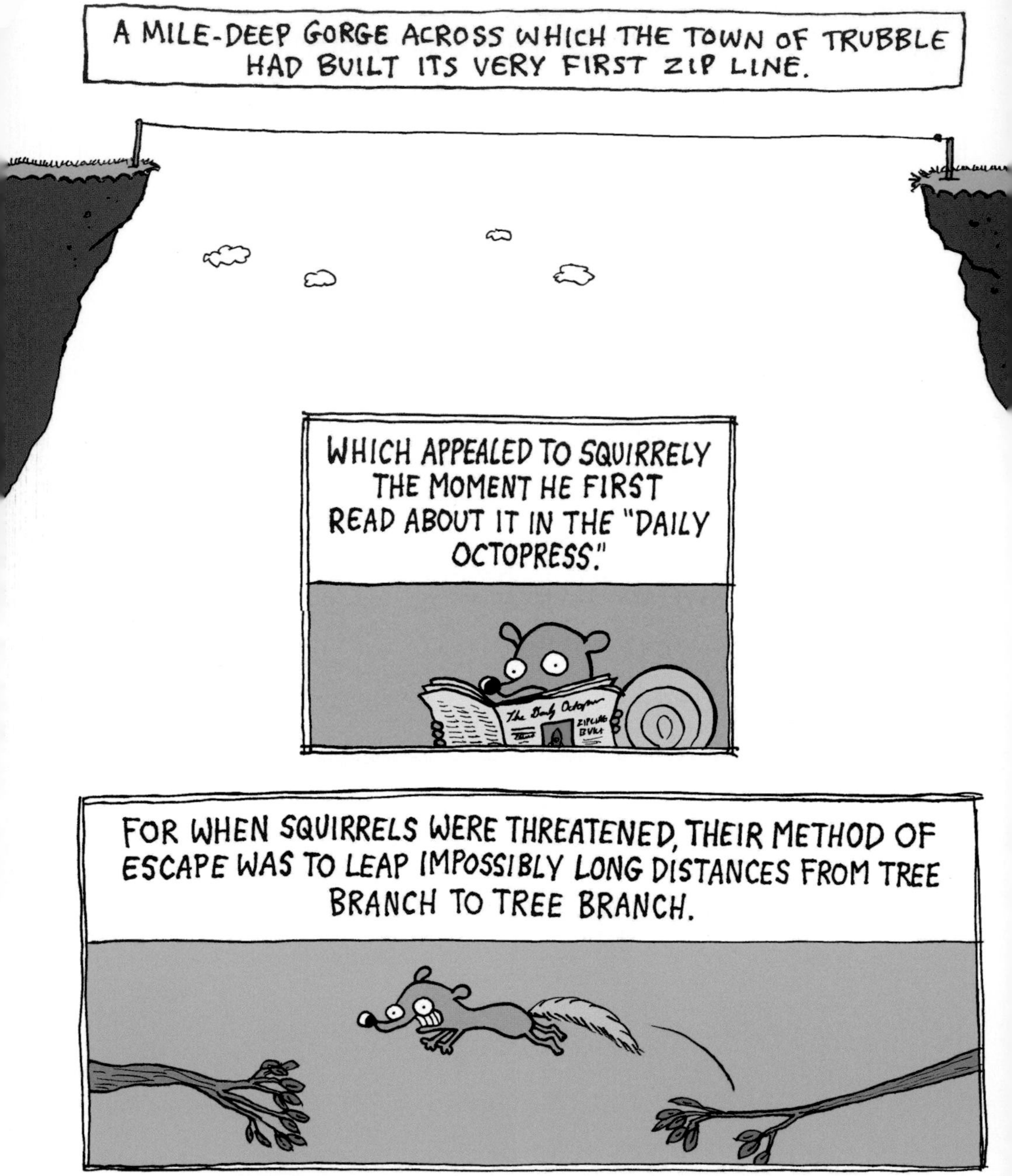
A MILE-DEEP GORGE ACROSS WHICH THE TOWN OF TRUBBLE HAD BUILT ITS VERY FIRST ZIP LINE.
WHICH APPEALED TO SQUIRRELY THE MOMENT HE FIRST READ ABOUT IT IN THE "DAILY OCTOPRESS."
FOR WHEN SQUIRRELS WERE THREATENED, THEIR METHOD OF ESCAPE WAS TO LEAP IMPOSSIBLY LONG DISTANCES FROM TREE BRANCH TO TREE BRANCH.

AND THIS WAS THE LONGEST DISTANCE OF ALL.
VERY LONG
A FACT SQUIRRELY ONCE DIAGRAMMED ON A PIECE OF NOTEBOOK PAPER.
ANALYSIS OF ZIP LINE (i.e., The Great Escape)
Typical branch leap: 2 to 10 yards
Zip line over Gorgeous Gorge: 1,430 yards
1,430 yds
Zip line > branch
AND SO WHEN THE FLEEING SQUIRRELY FINALLY SPOTTED THE ZIP LINE, HIS HEART WAS FILLED WITH JOY.
AND HE LEAPED FOR THE HANDLEBARS.

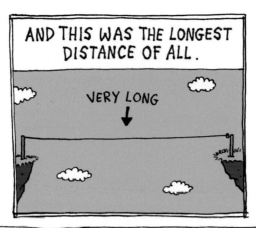

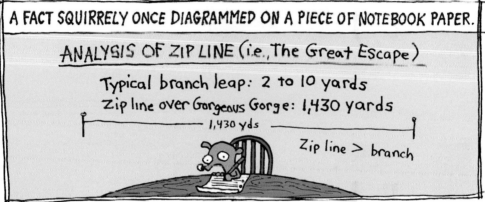

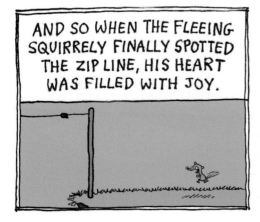

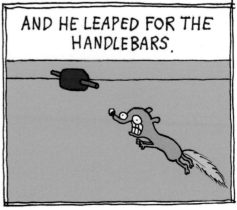

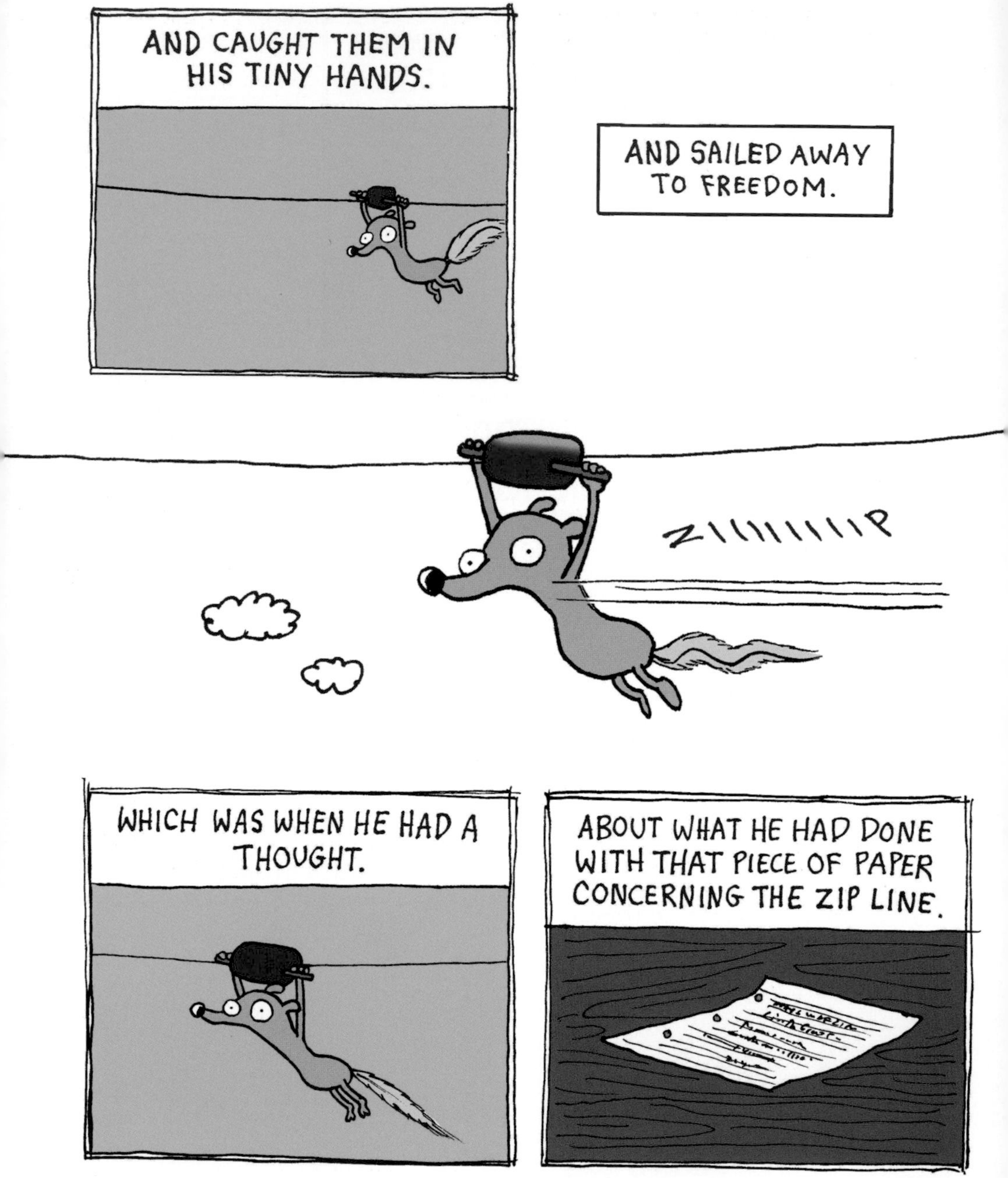
AND CAUGHT THEM IN HIS TINY HANDS.
AND SAILED AWAY TO FREEDOM.
ZIIIIIIIIP
WHICH WAS WHEN HE HAD A THOUGHT.
ABOUT WHAT HE HAD DONE WITH THAT PIECE OF PAPER CONCERNING THE ZIP LINE.

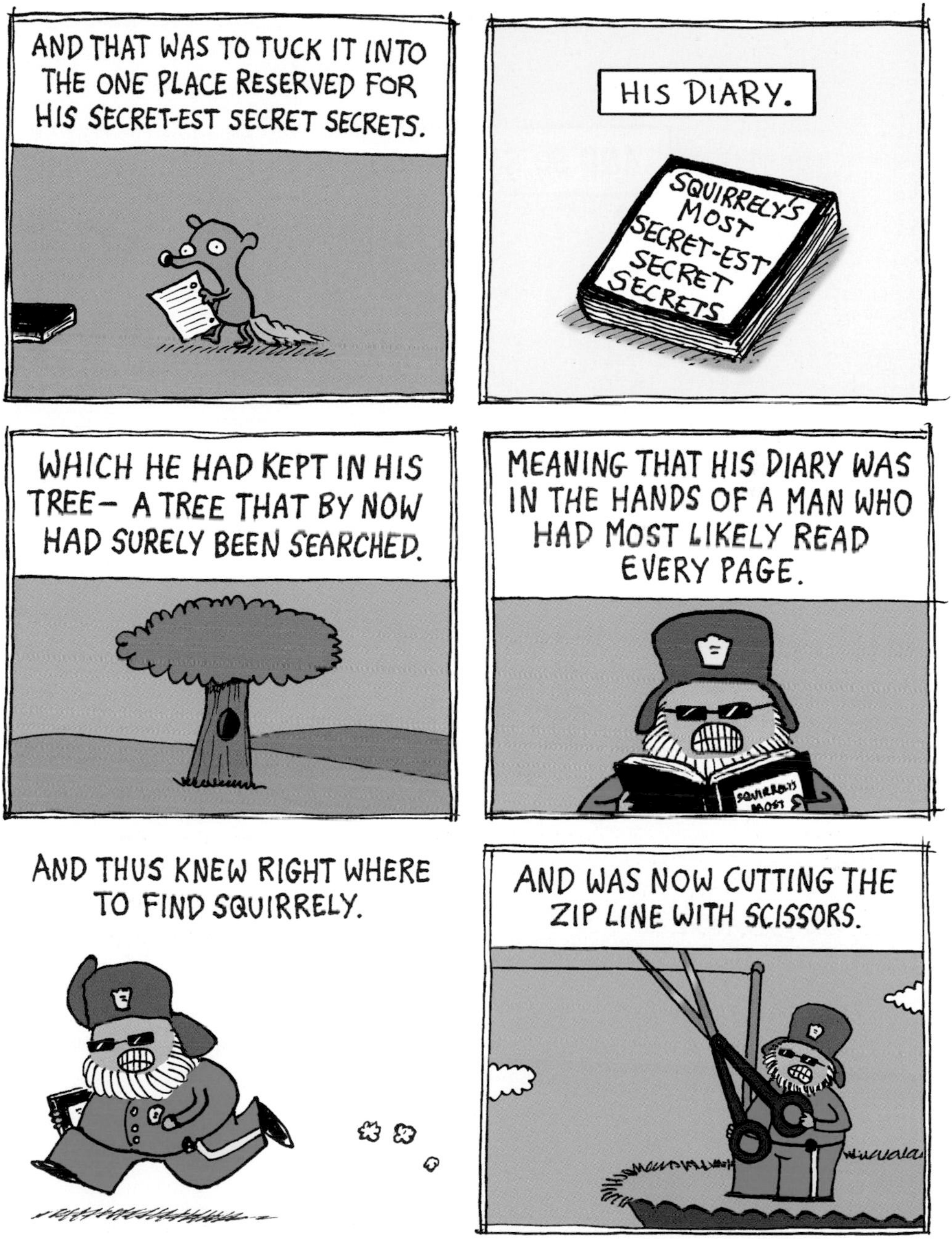
AND THAT WAS TO TUCK IT INTO THE ONE PLACE RESERVED FOR HIS SECRET-EST SECRET SECRETS.
HIS DIARY.
SQUIRRELY'S MOST SECRET-EST SECRET SECRETS
WHICH HE HAD KEPT IN HIS TREE— A TREE THAT BY NOW HAD SURELY BEEN SEARCHED.
MEANING THAT HIS DIARY WAS IN THE HANDS OF A MAN WHO HAD MOST LIKELY READ EVERY PAGE.
AND THUS KNEW RIGHT WHERE TO FIND SQUIRRELY.
AND WAS NOW CUTTING THE ZIP LINE WITH SCISSORS.

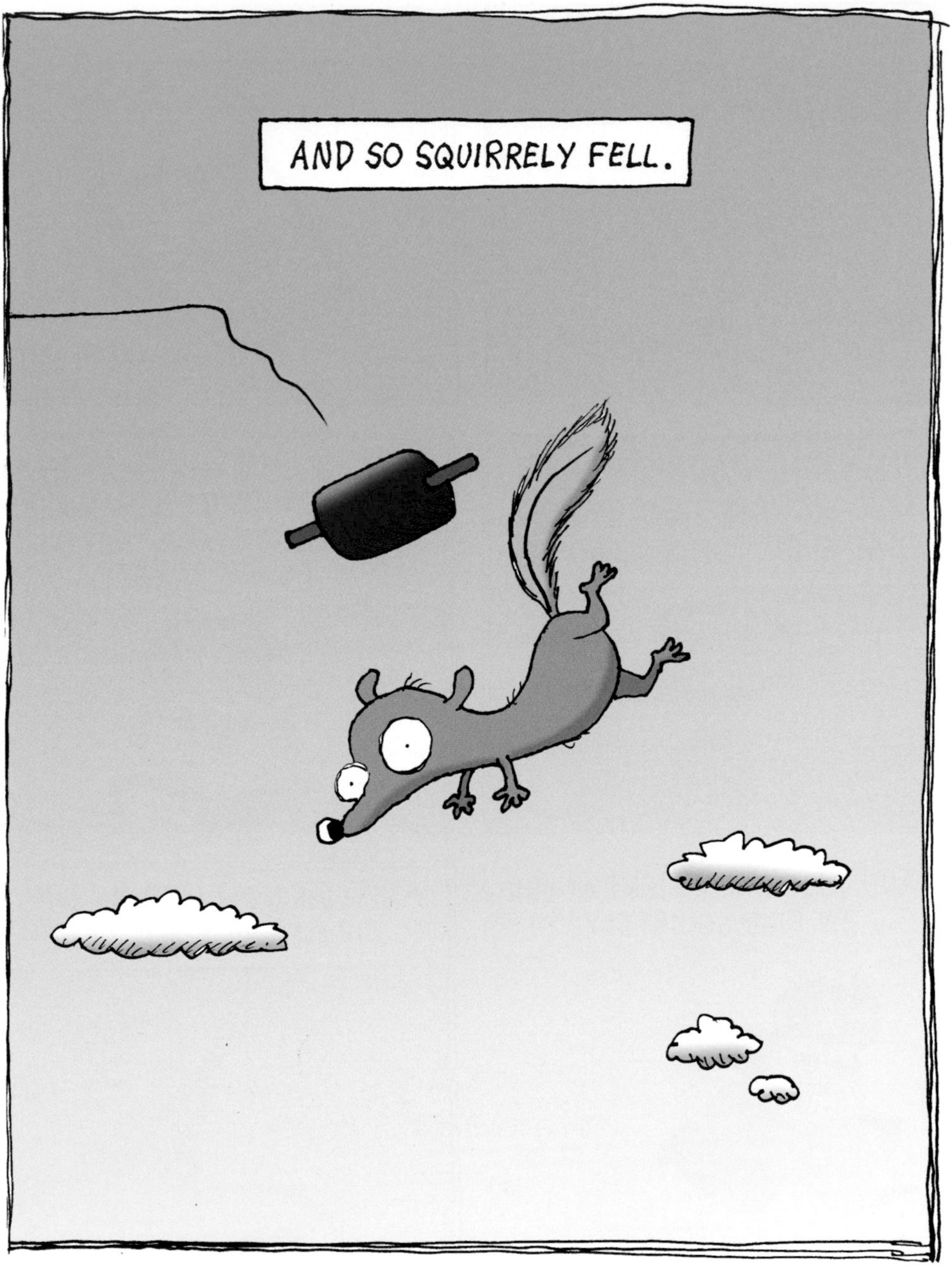
AND SO SQUIRRELY FELL.

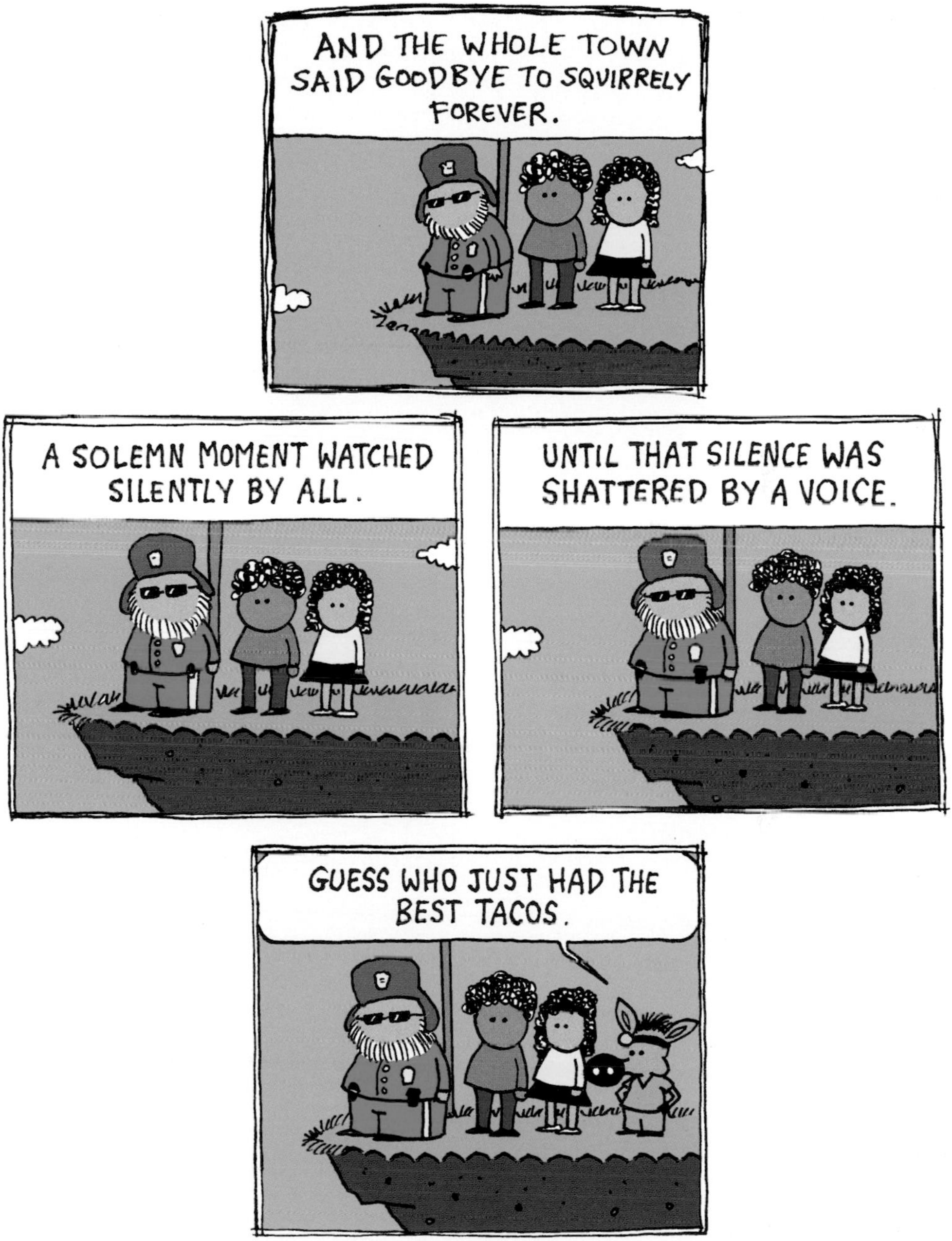
AND THE WHOLE TOWN SAID GOODBYE TO SQUIRRELY FOREVER.
A SOLEMN MOMENT WATCHED SILENTLY BY ALL.
UNTIL THAT SILENCE WAS SHATTERED BY A VOICE.
GUESS WHO JUST HAD THE BEST TACOS.

CHAPTER

ELEVEN

IN WHICH...

LETTERS FORM WORDS, WHICH YOU THEN READ

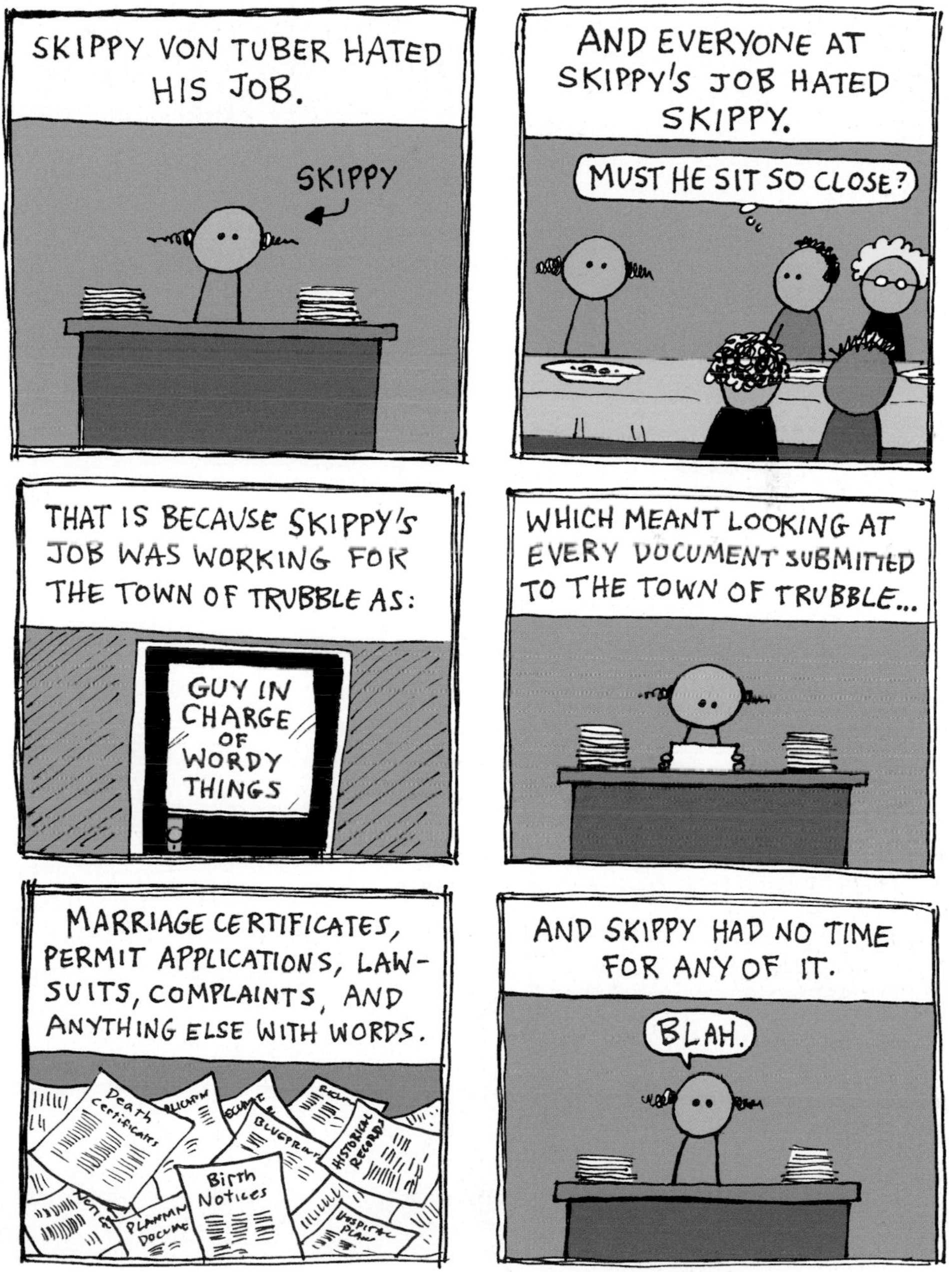
SKIPPY VON TUBER HATED HIS JOB.
SKIPPY
AND EVERYONE AT SKIPPY'S JOB HATED SKIPPY.
MUST HE SIT SO CLOSE?
THAT IS BECAUSE SKIPPY'S JOB WAS WORKING FOR THE TOWN OF TRUBBLE AS:
GUY IN CHARGE OF WORDY THINGS
WHICH MEANT LOOKING AT EVERY DOCUMENT SUBMITTED TO THE TOWN OF TRUBBLE...
MARRIAGE CERTIFICATES, PERMIT APPLICATIONS, LAW-SUITS, COMPLAINTS, AND ANYTHING ELSE WITH WORDS.
Death Certificates
HISTORICAL RECORDS
Birth Notices
AND SKIPPY HAD NO TIME FOR ANY OF IT.
BLAH.

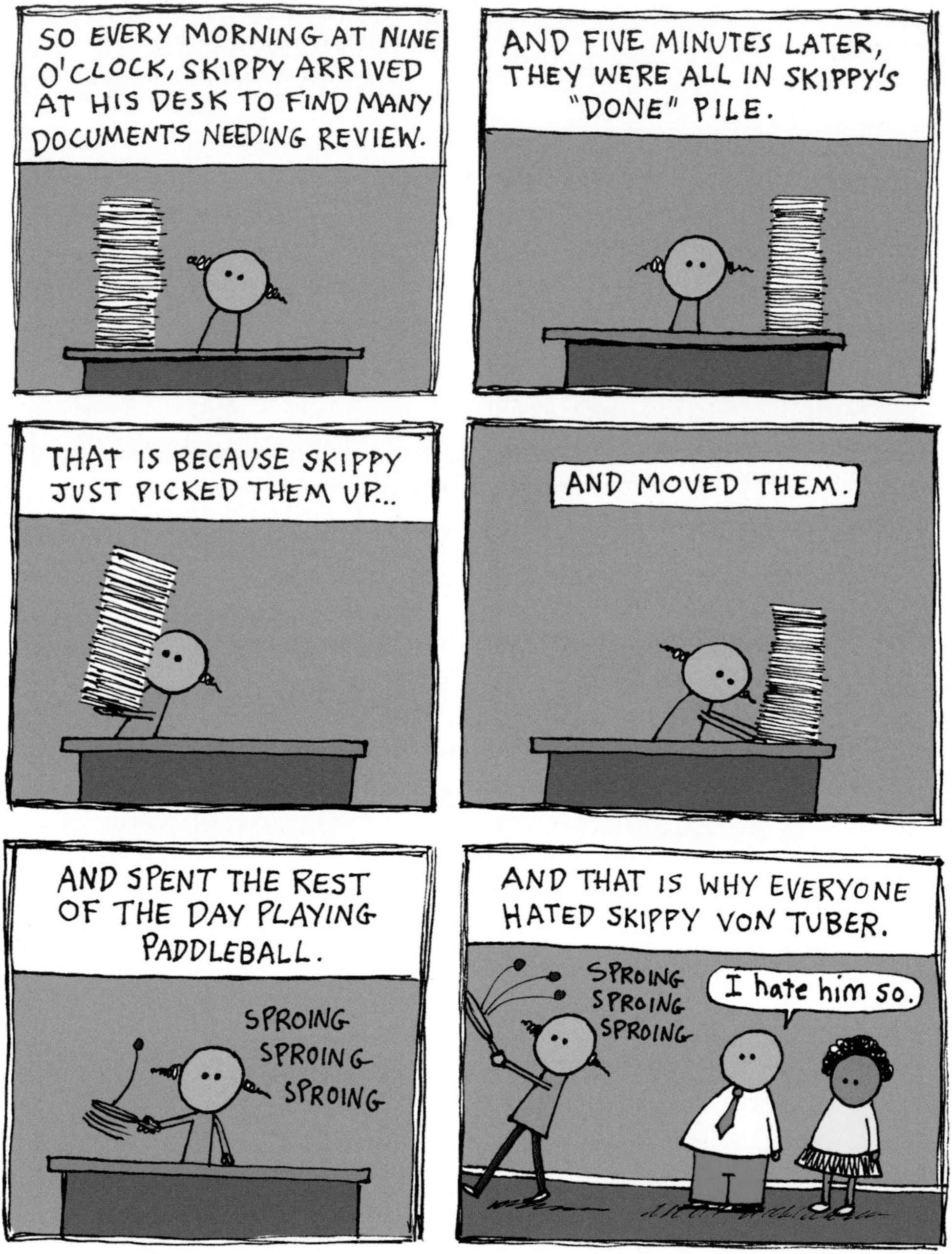
SO EVERY MORNING AT NINE O'CLOCK, SKIPPY ARRIVED AT HIS DESK TO FIND MANY DOCUMENTS NEEDING REVIEW.
AND FIVE MINUTES LATER, THEY WERE ALL IN SKIPPY'S "DONE" PILE.
THAT IS BECAUSE SKIPPY JUST PICKED THEM UP...
AND MOVED THEM.
AND SPENT THE REST OF THE DAY PLAYING PADDLEBALL.
SPROING
SPROING
SPROING
AND THAT IS WHY EVERYONE HATED SKIPPY VON TUBER.
SPROING
SPROING
SPROING
I hate him so.

AND THAT WAS NOT EVEN THE WORST THING ABOUT HIM. THE WORST THING WAS HIS PET PEEVE.
GRRRRR
AND THAT WAS THE WORD...
ANYWAYS.
BECAUSE ACCORDING TO SKIPPY, "ANYWAYS" IS NOT A PROPER WORD. THE PROPER WORD IS...
ANYWAY.
AND SO IF SKIPPY HAPPENED TO SEE "ANYWAYS" ON ANY DOCUMENT AS HE WAS LIFTING THE PILE FROM ONE SPOT TO THE OTHER...
OH NO.
HE TOOK NOTE OF THE WRITER'S NAME.
Melvin Slimski.
AND WALKED TO HIS HOUSE.

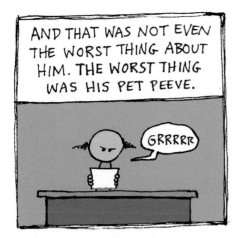

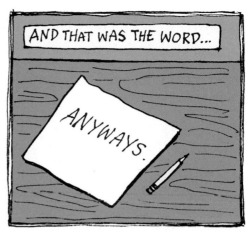

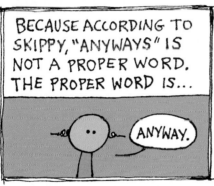

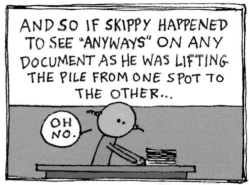

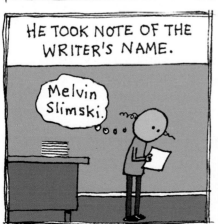

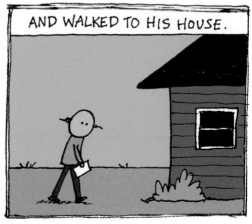

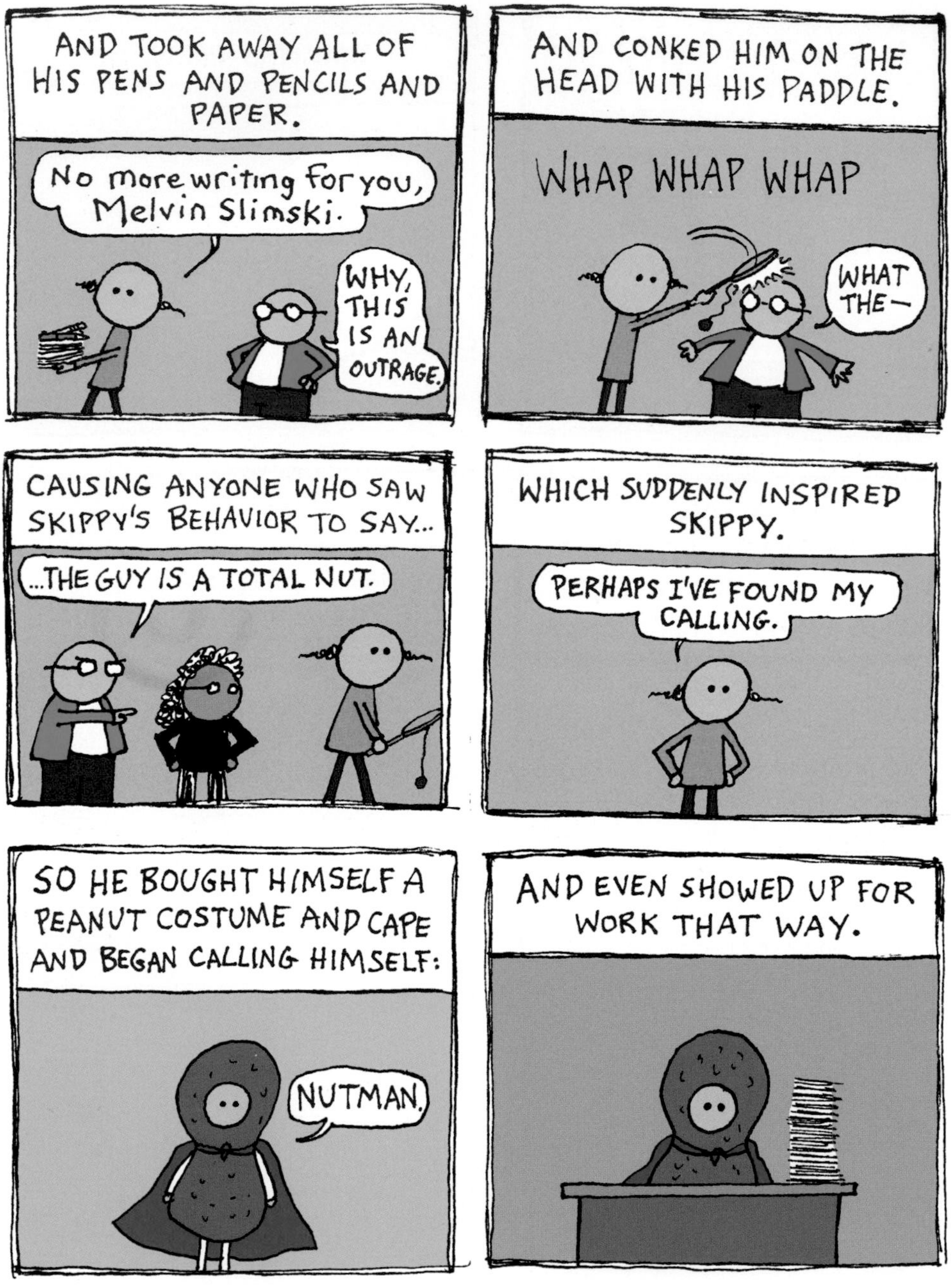
AND TOOK AWAY ALL OF HIS PENS AND PENCILS AND PAPER.
No more writing for you, Melvin Slimski.
WHY, THIS IS AN OUTRAGE.
AND CONKED HIM ON THE HEAD WITH HIS PADDLE.
WHAP WHAP WHAP
WHAT THE—
CAUSING ANYONE WHO SAW SKIPPY'S BEHAVIOR TO SAY...
...THE GUY IS A TOTAL NUT.
WHICH SUDDENLY INSPIRED SKIPPY.
PERHAPS I'VE FOUND MY CALLING.
SO HE BOUGHT HIMSELF A PEANUT COSTUME AND CAPE AND BEGAN CALLING HIMSELF:
NUTMAN.
AND EVEN SHOWED UP FOR WORK THAT WAY.

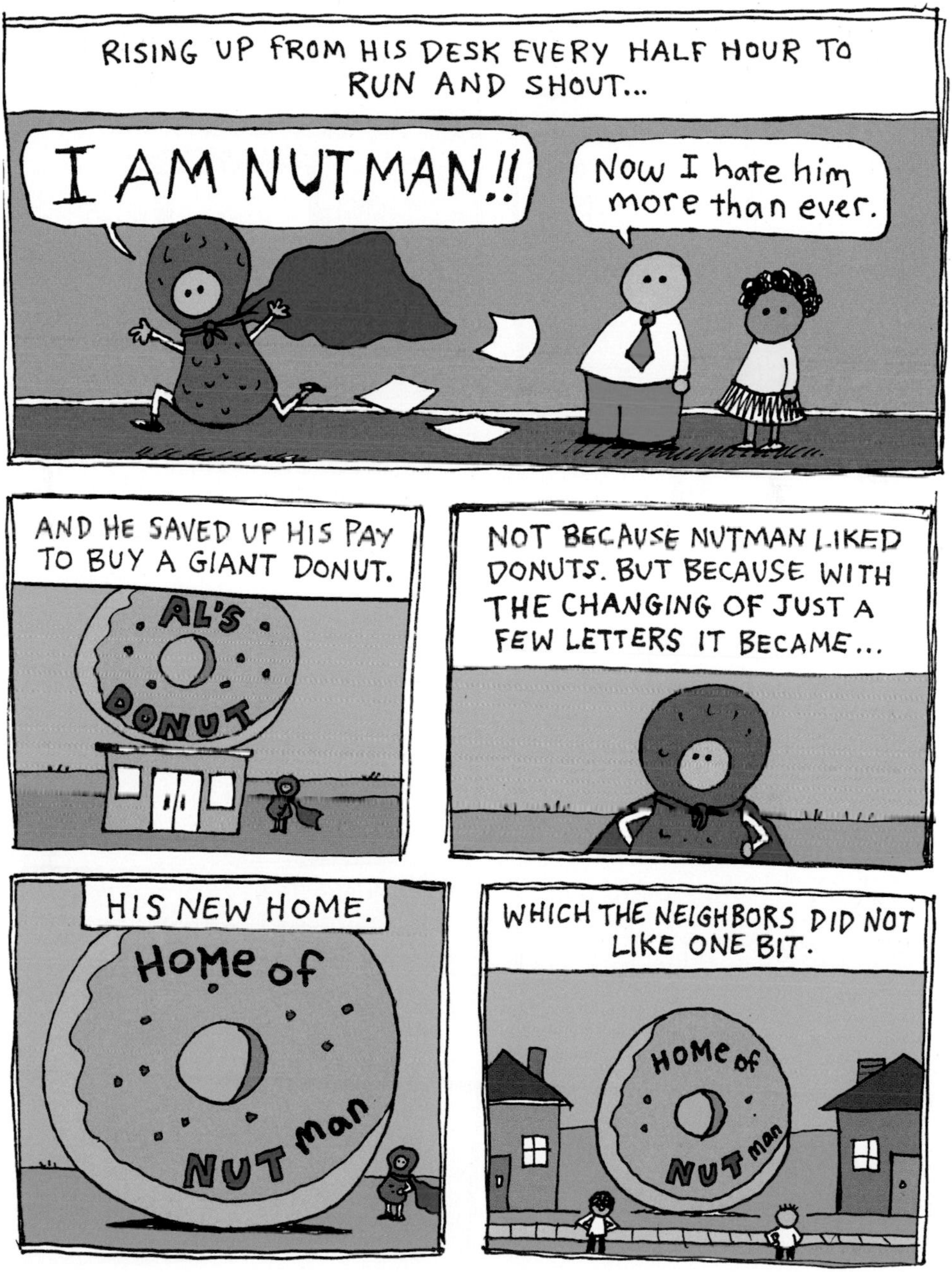
RISING UP FROM HIS DESK EVERY HALF HOUR TO RUN AND SHOUT...
I AM NUTMAN!!
Now I hate him more than ever.
AND HE SAVED UP HIS PAY TO BUY A GIANT DONUT.
AL'S DONUT
NOT BECAUSE NUTMAN LIKED DONUTS. BUT BECAUSE WITH THE CHANGING OF JUST A FEW LETTERS IT BECAME...
HIS NEW HOME.
HOME of NUT man
WHICH THE NEIGHBORS DID NOT LIKE ONE BIT.
HOME of NUT man

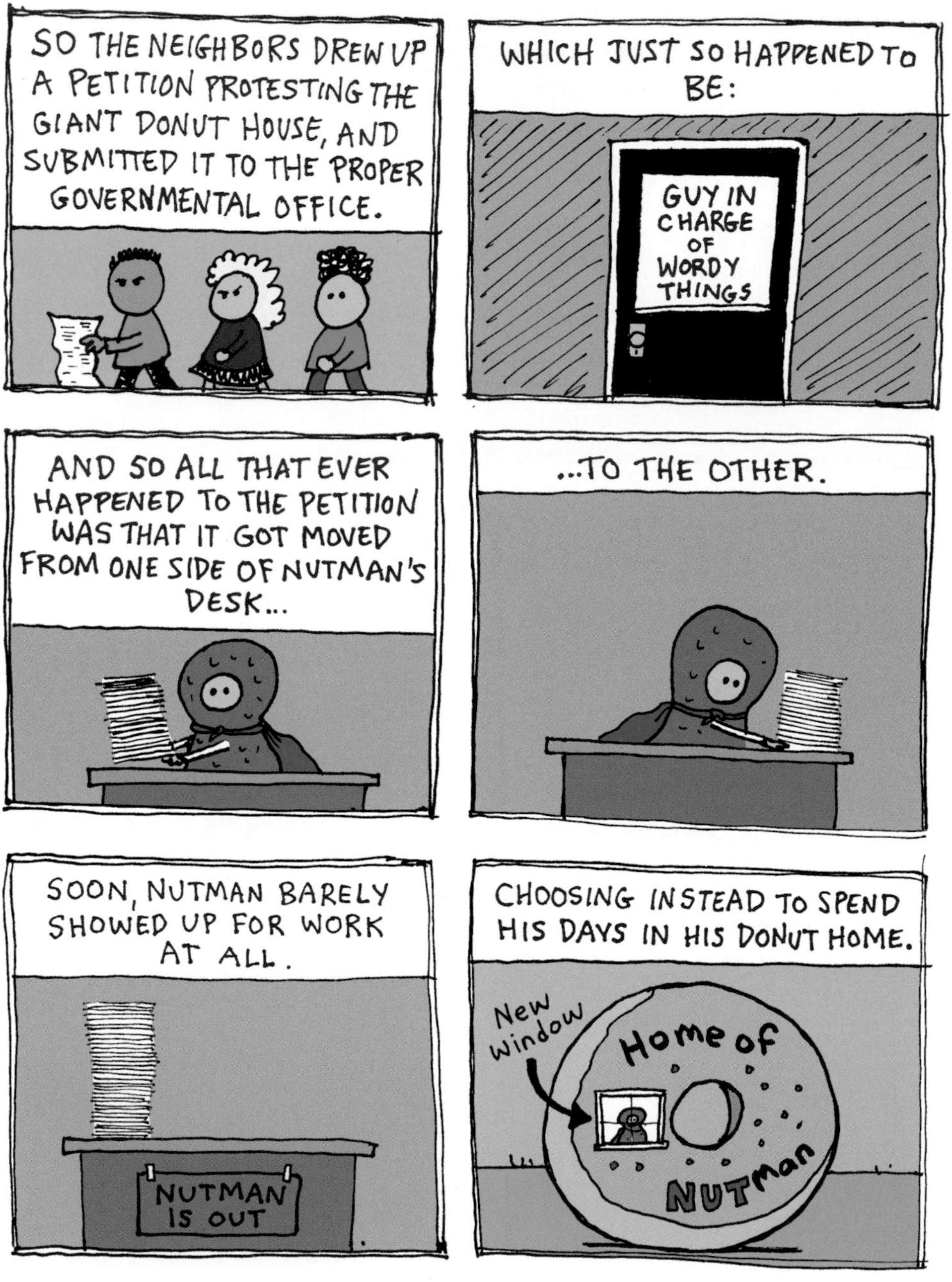
SO THE NEIGHBORS DREW UP A PETITION PROTESTING THE GIANT DONUT HOUSE, AND SUBMITTED IT TO THE PROPER GOVERNMENTAL OFFICE.
WHICH JUST SO HAPPENED TO BE:
GUY IN CHARGE OF WORDY THINGS
AND SO ALL THAT EVER HAPPENED TO THE PETITION WAS THAT IT GOT MOVED FROM ONE SIDE OF NUTMAN'S DESK...
...TO THE OTHER.
SOON, NUTMAN BARELY SHOWED UP FOR WORK AT ALL.
NUTMAN IS OUT
CHOOSING INSTEAD TO SPEND HIS DAYS IN HIS DONUT HOME.
New window
Home of NUTman

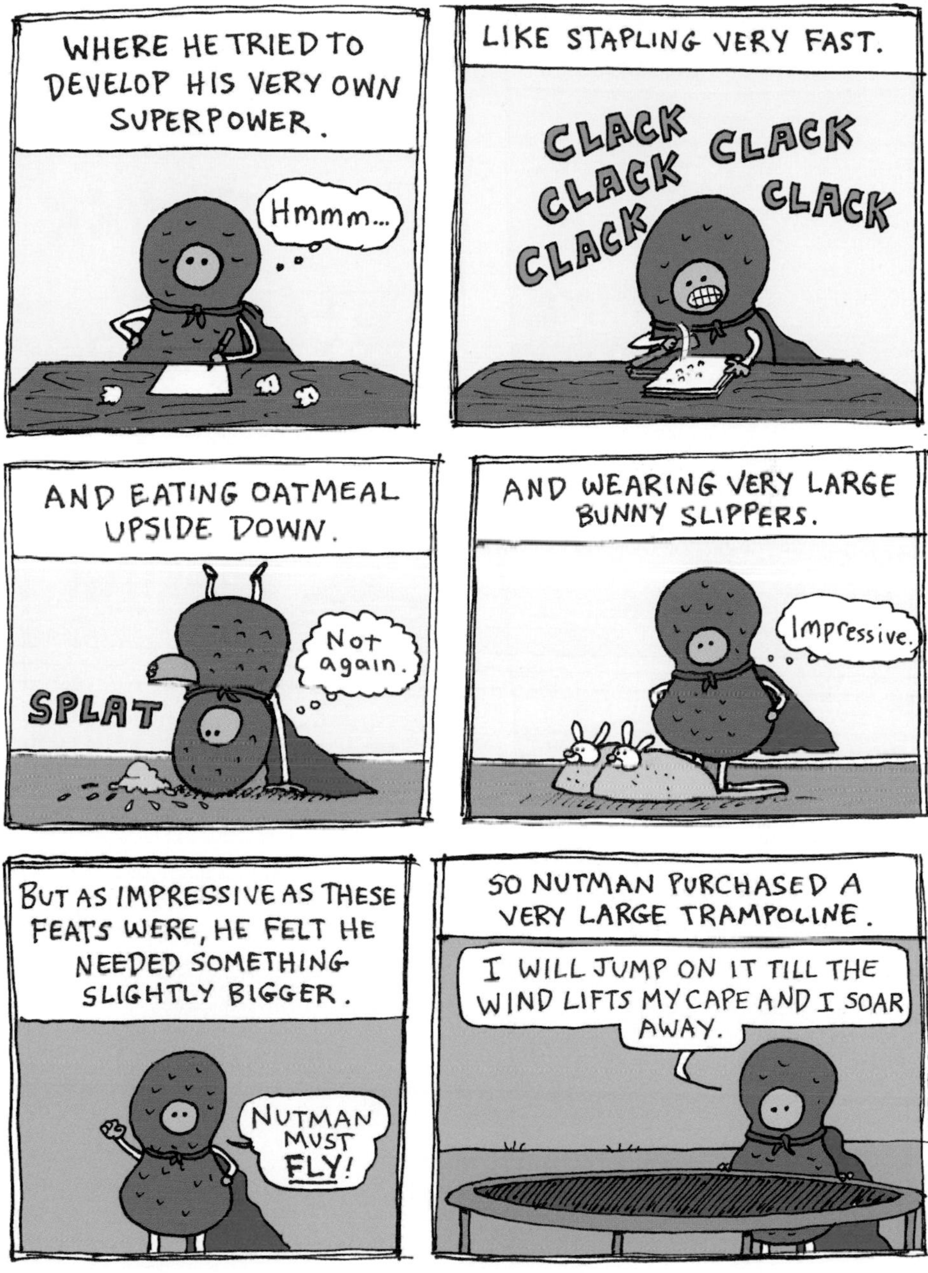
WHERE HE TRIED TO DEVELOP HIS VERY OWN SUPERPOWER.
Hmmm...
LIKE STAPLING VERY FAST.
CLACK CLACK CLACK CLACK CLACK
AND EATING OATMEAL UPSIDE DOWN.
SPLAT
Not again.
AND WEARING VERY LARGE BUNNY SLIPPERS.
Impressive.
BUT AS IMPRESSIVE AS THESE FEATS WERE, HE FELT HE NEEDED SOMETHING SLIGHTLY BIGGER.
NUTMAN MUST FLY!
SO NUTMAN PURCHASED A VERY LARGE TRAMPOLINE.
I WILL JUMP ON IT TILL THE WIND LIFTS MY CAPE AND I SOAR AWAY.

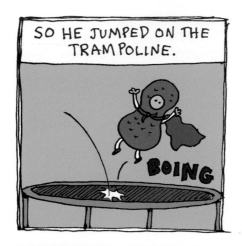

SO HE JUMPED ON THE TRAMPOLINE.

BOING

AND LANDED ON THE GROUND.

THWACK

AND HE JUMPED ON THE TRAMPOLINE.

BOING

AND HIT A GARAGE.

KADOINK

AND HE JUMPED ON THE TRAMPOLINE.

BOING

AND LANDED IN A TREE.

PLOOSH

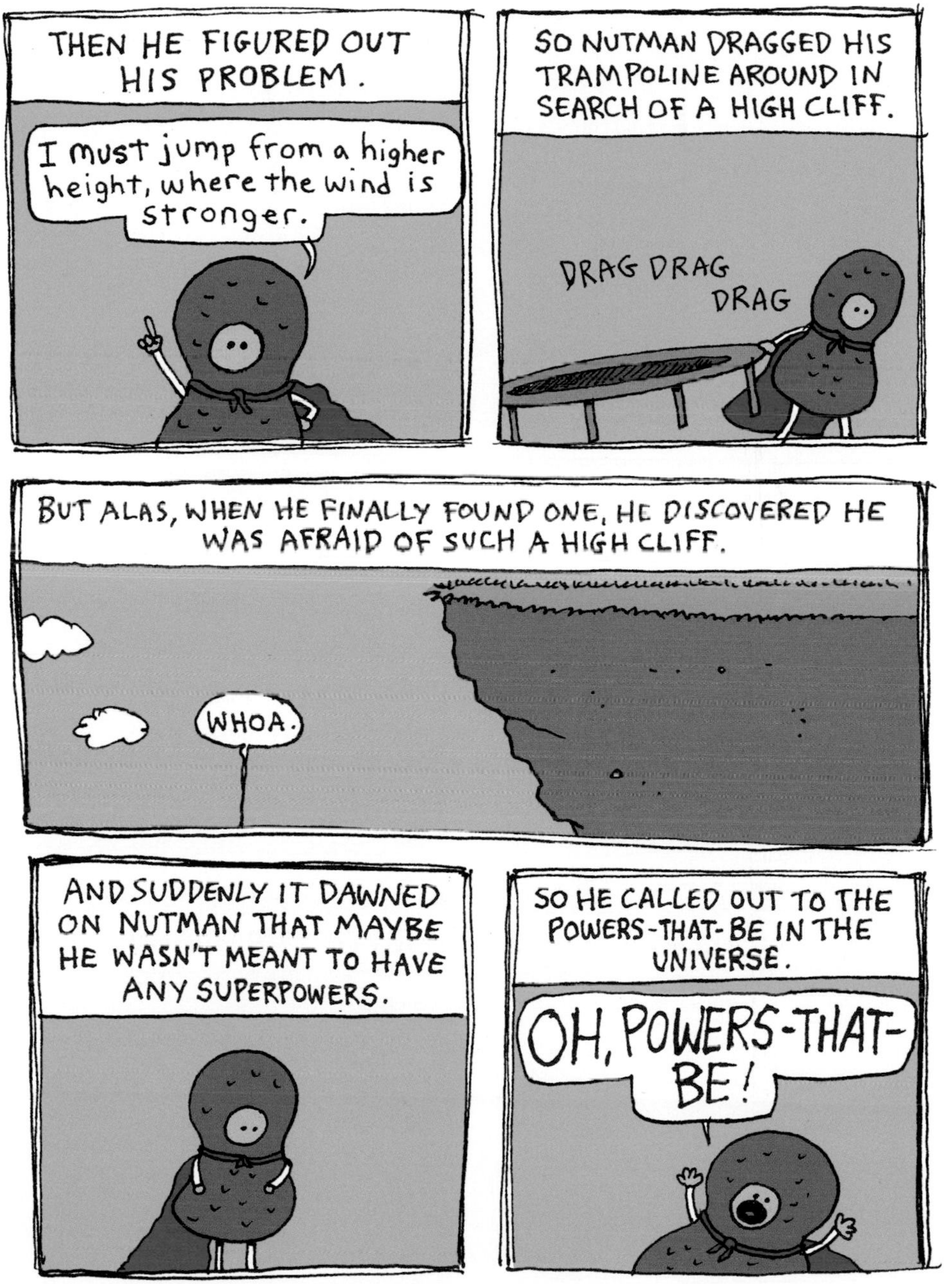
THEN HE FIGURED OUT HIS PROBLEM.
I must jump from a higher height, where the wind is stronger.
SO NUTMAN DRAGGED HIS TRAMPOLINE AROUND IN SEARCH OF A HIGH CLIFF.
DRAG DRAG DRAG
BUT ALAS, WHEN HE FINALLY FOUND ONE, HE DISCOVERED HE WAS AFRAID OF SUCH A HIGH CLIFF.
WHOA.
AND SUDDENLY IT DAWNED ON NUTMAN THAT MAYBE HE WASN'T MEANT TO HAVE ANY SUPERPOWERS.
SO HE CALLED OUT TO THE POWERS-THAT-BE IN THE UNIVERSE.
OH, POWERS-THAT-BE!

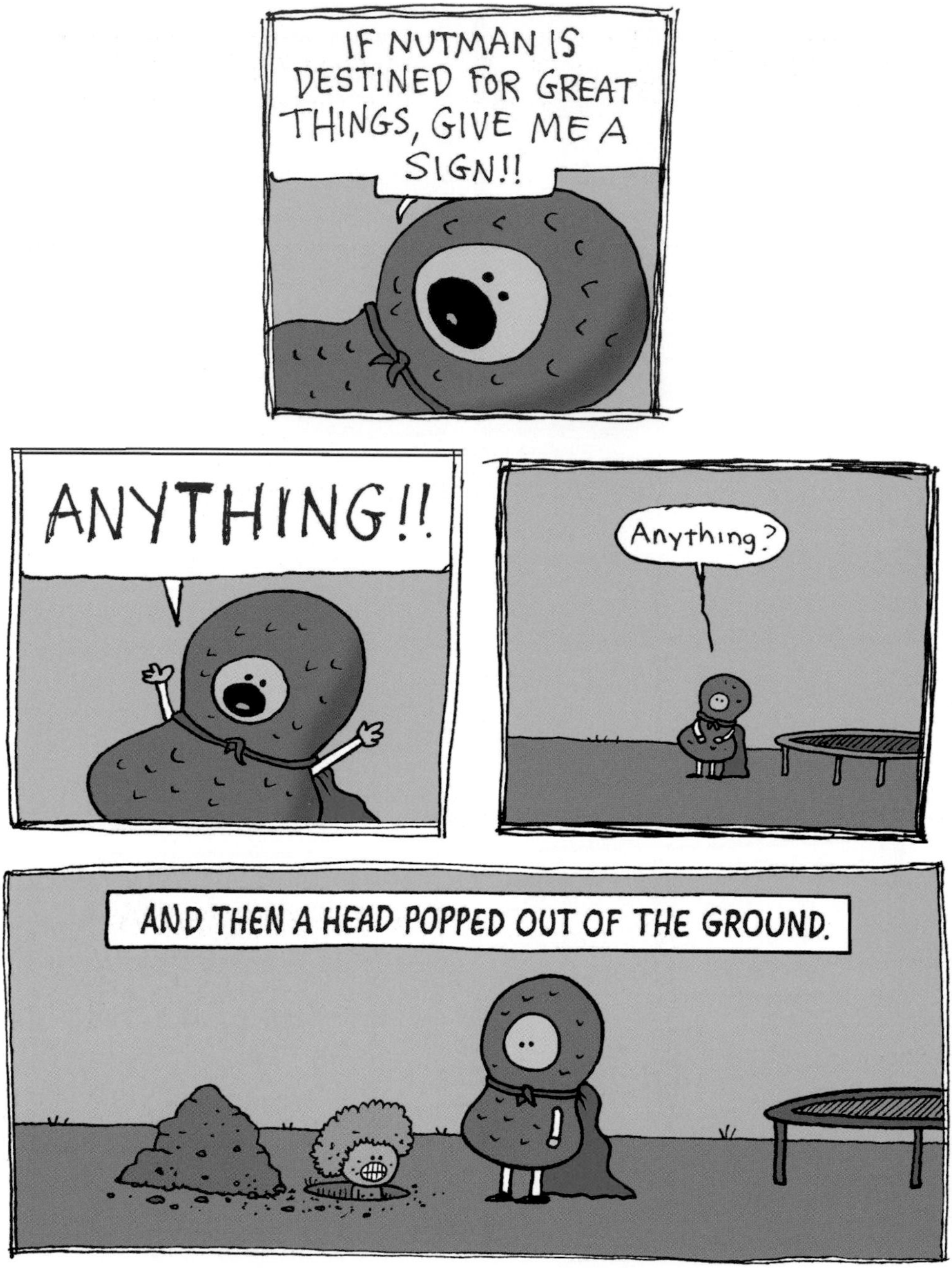
IF NUTMAN IS DESTINED FOR GREAT THINGS, GIVE ME A SIGN!!
ANYTHING!!
Anything?
AND THEN A HEAD POPPED OUT OF THE GROUND.

AND A SQUIRREL FELL FROM THE SKY.

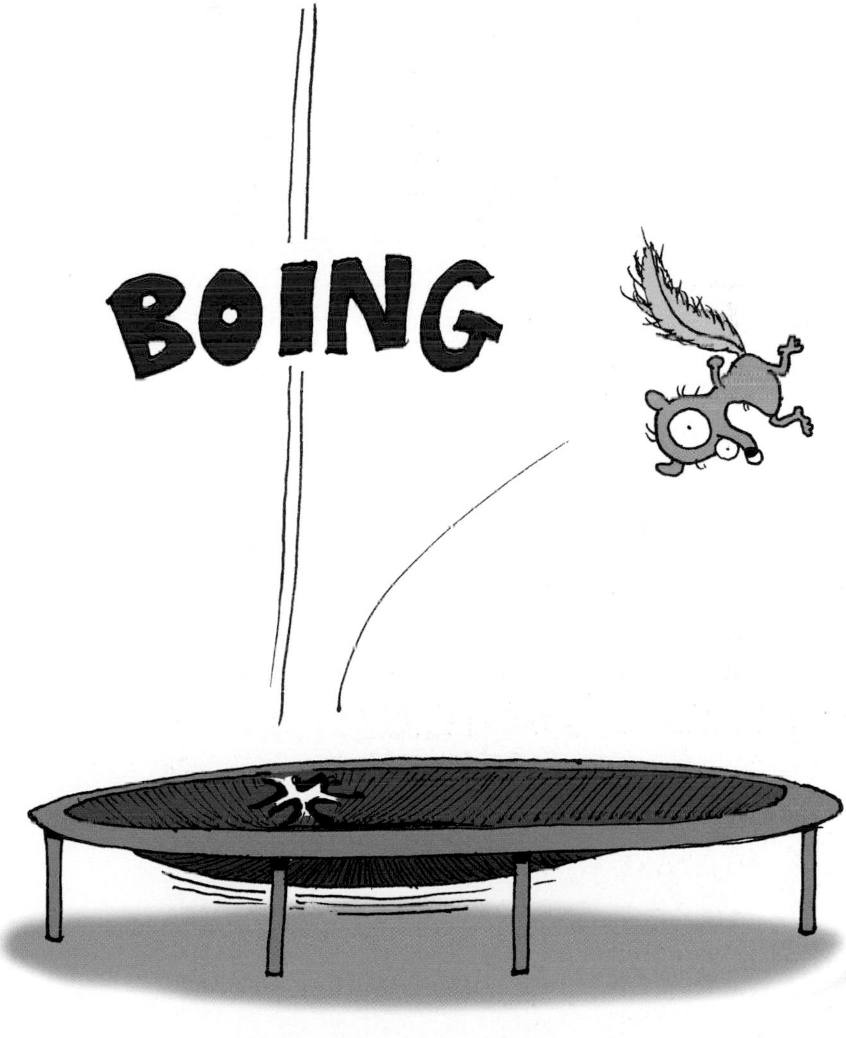
BOING

CHAPTER SOMEWHERE BETWEEN ELEVEN AND TWELVE

IN WHICH...

WE ARE SOMEWHAT INDECISIVE

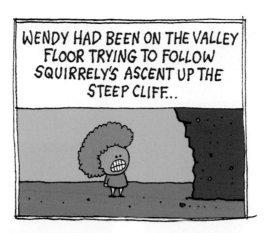

WENDY HAD BEEN ON THE VALLEY FLOOR TRYING TO FOLLOW SQUIRRELY'S ASCENT UP THE STEEP CLIFF...

WHEN SHE HEARD FOOTSTEPS APPROACHING.

SO WITH NOWHERE TO RUN, SHE DECIDED TO EMPLOY A SKILL SHE HAD LEARNED FROM WATCHING THE MOLES.

THE MOLES

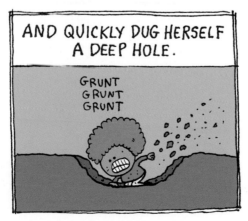

AND QUICKLY DUG HERSELF A DEEP HOLE.

GRUNT
GRUNT
GRUNT

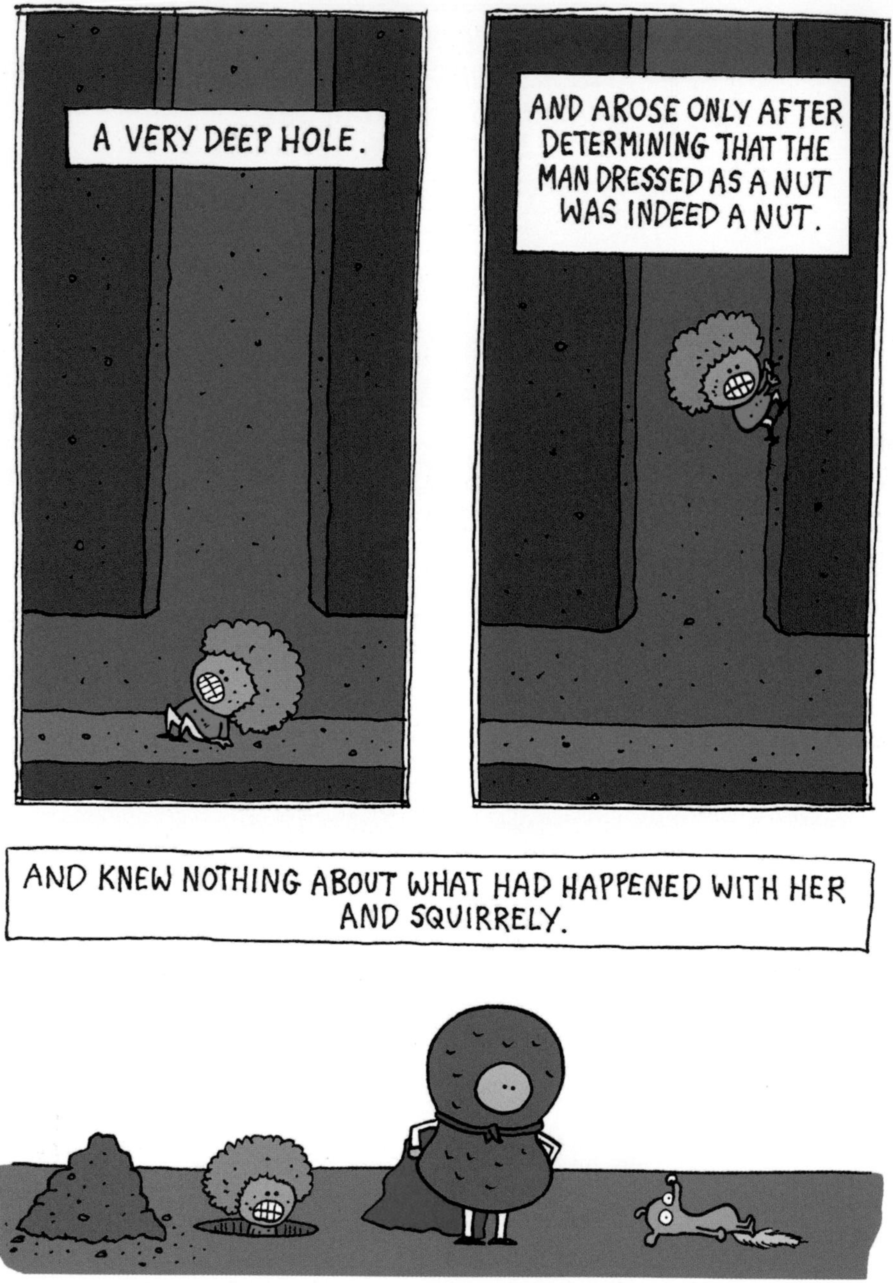
A VERY DEEP HOLE.
AND AROSE ONLY AFTER DETERMINING THAT THE MAN DRESSED AS A NUT WAS INDEED A NUT.
AND KNEW NOTHING ABOUT WHAT HAD HAPPENED WITH HER AND SQUIRRELY.

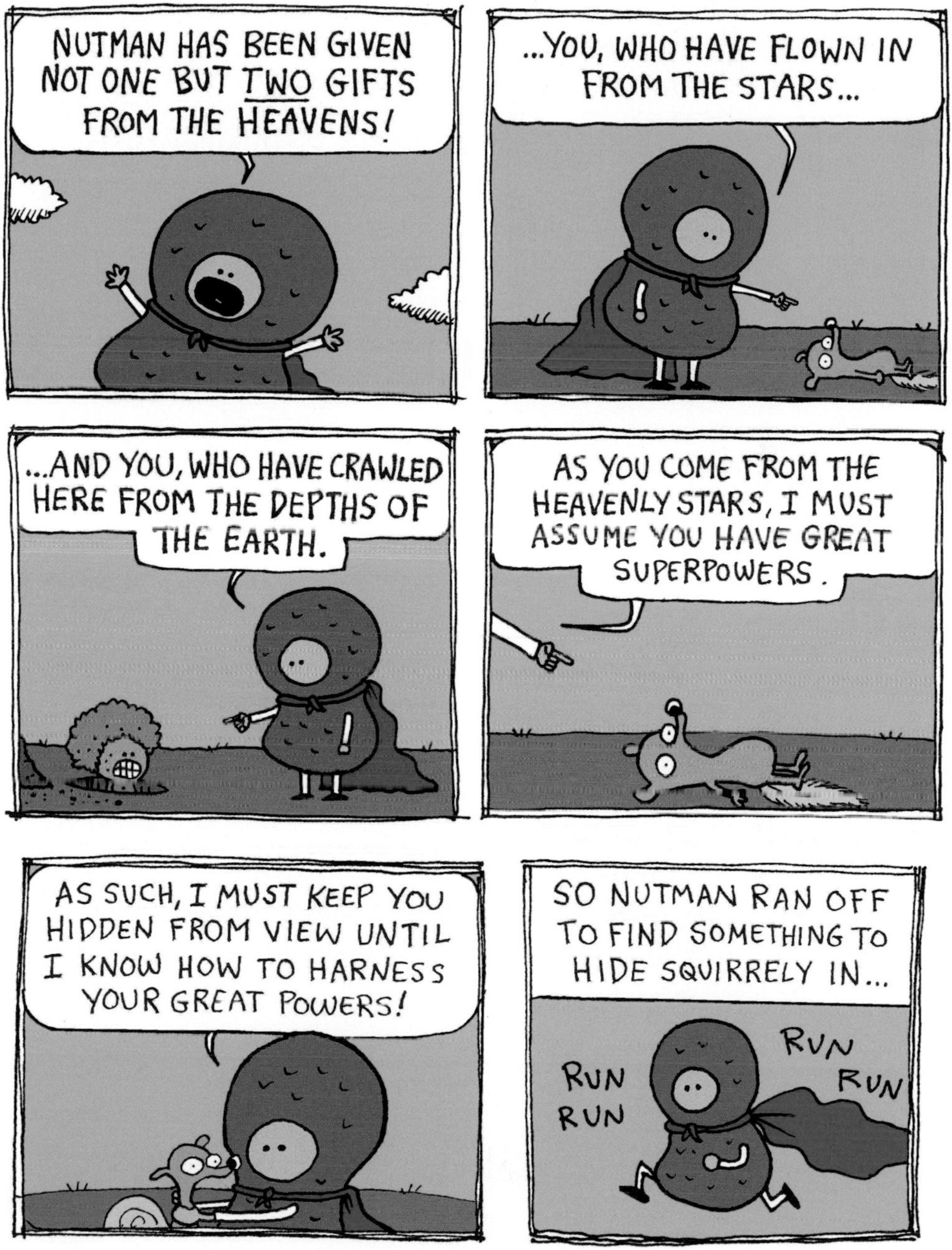
NUTMAN HAS BEEN GIVEN NOT ONE BUT TWO GIFTS FROM THE HEAVENS!
...YOU, WHO HAVE FLOWN IN FROM THE STARS...
...AND YOU, WHO HAVE CRAWLED HERE FROM THE DEPTHS OF THE EARTH.
AS YOU COME FROM THE HEAVENLY STARS, I MUST ASSUME YOU HAVE GREAT SUPERPOWERS.
AS SUCH, I MUST KEEP YOU HIDDEN FROM VIEW UNTIL I KNOW HOW TO HARNESS YOUR GREAT POWERS!
SO NUTMAN RAN OFF TO FIND SOMETHING TO HIDE SQUIRRELY IN...
RUN RUN
RUN
RUN

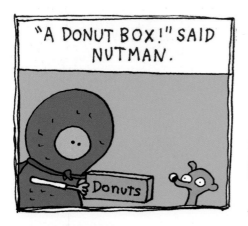

"A DONUT BOX!" SAID NUTMAN.

"I HAVE FOUND HUNDREDS SQUIRRELED AWAY IN MY NEW HOME," HE ADDED. "NO PUN INTENDED."

Home of
Nutman

SO NUTMAN SHOVED THE ALL-POWERFUL SQUIRREL INTO A DONUT BOX.

Shove Shove

Donuts

"As soon as I get you safely to my abode, we shall discuss our noble mission," he said to his donut box.

"Which I suspect involves something grand, like saving the world."

The world

THOUGH, SADLY, I HAVE RECONSIDERED YOU...

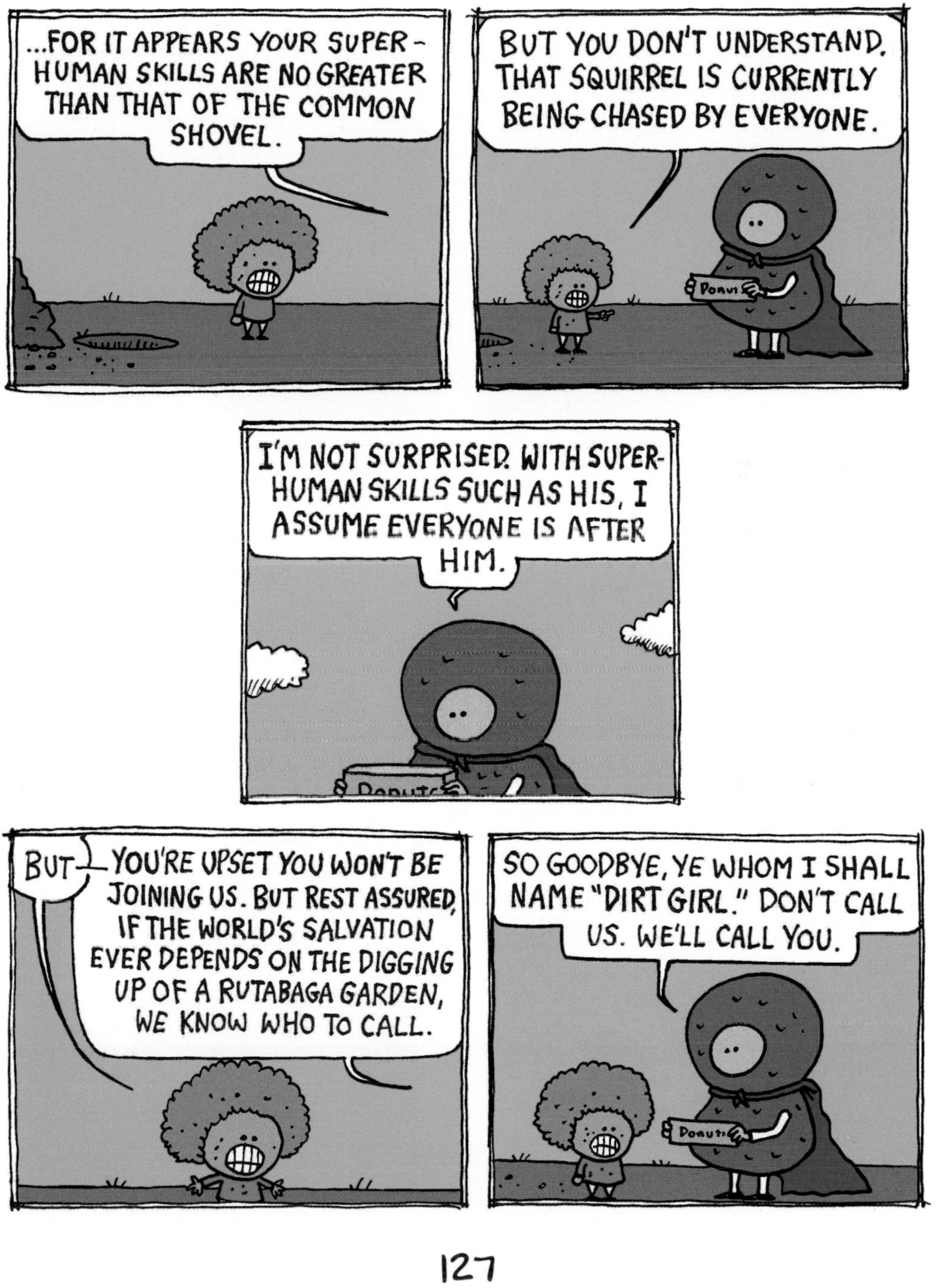
...FOR IT APPEARS YOUR SUPER-HUMAN SKILLS ARE NO GREATER THAN THAT OF THE COMMON SHOVEL.
BUT YOU DON'T UNDERSTAND. THAT SQUIRREL IS CURRENTLY BEING CHASED BY EVERYONE.
DONUTS
I'M NOT SURPRISED. WITH SUPER-HUMAN SKILLS SUCH AS HIS, I ASSUME EVERYONE IS AFTER HIM.
BUT-
YOU'RE UPSET YOU WON'T BE JOINING US. BUT REST ASSURED, IF THE WORLD'S SALVATION EVER DEPENDS ON THE DIGGING UP OF A RUTABAGA GARDEN, WE KNOW WHO TO CALL.
SO GOODBYE, YE WHOM I SHALL NAME "DIRT GIRL." DON'T CALL US. WE'LL CALL YOU.
DONUTS

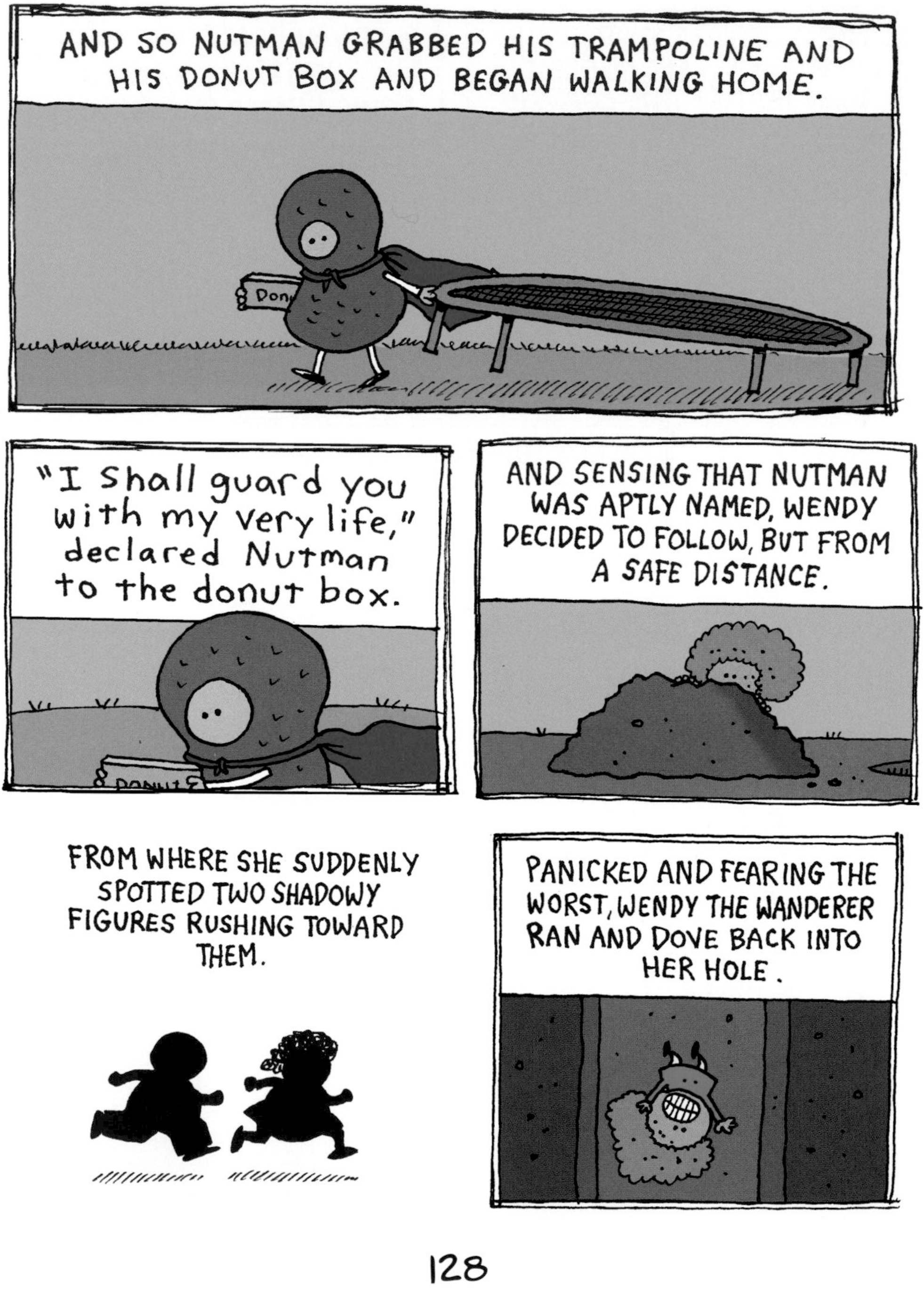
AND SO NUTMAN GRABBED HIS TRAMPOLINE AND HIS DONUT BOX AND BEGAN WALKING HOME.
"I shall guard you with my very life," declared Nutman to the donut box.
AND SENSING THAT NUTMAN WAS APTLY NAMED, WENDY DECIDED TO FOLLOW, BUT FROM A SAFE DISTANCE.
FROM WHERE SHE SUDDENLY SPOTTED TWO SHADOWY FIGURES RUSHING TOWARD THEM.
PANICKED AND FEARING THE WORST, WENDY THE WANDERER RAN AND DOVE BACK INTO HER HOLE.

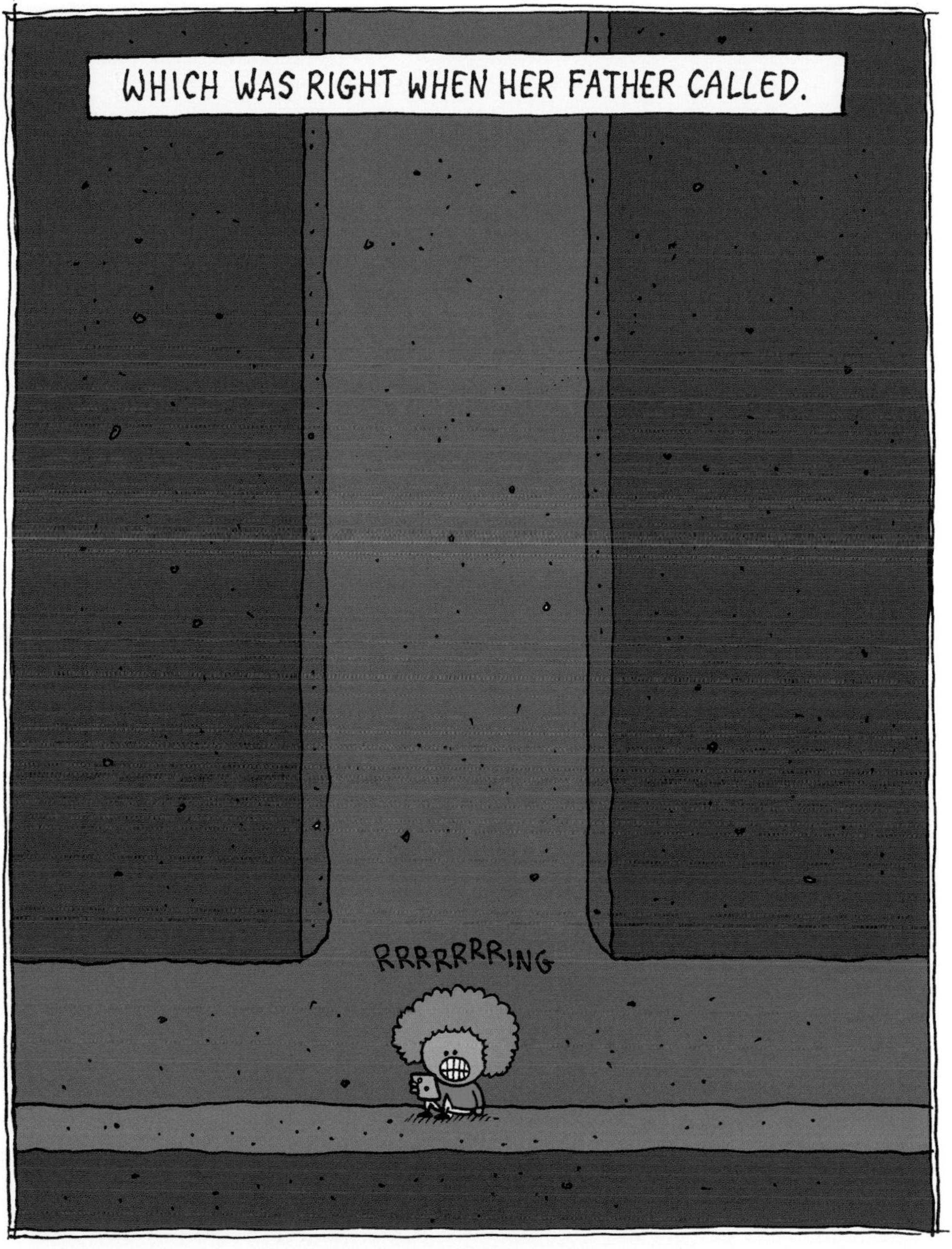
WHICH WAS RIGHT WHEN HER FATHER CALLED.
RRRRRRRING

CHAPTER TWELVE

IN WHICH...

YOU BEGIN TO REALIZE WHAT GREAT LITERATURE THIS REALLY IS

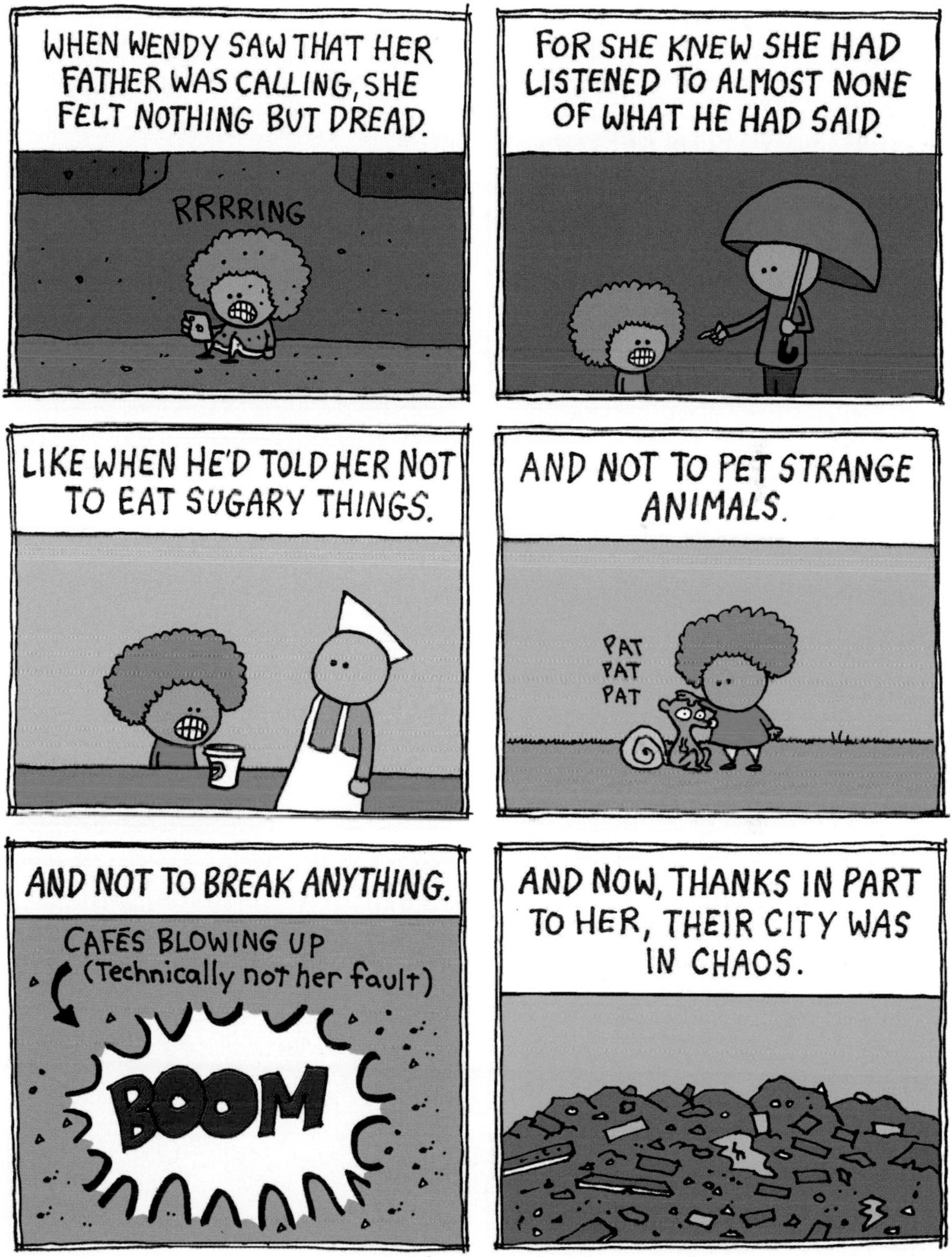
WHEN WENDY SAW THAT HER FATHER WAS CALLING, SHE FELT NOTHING BUT DREAD.
RRRRING
FOR SHE KNEW SHE HAD LISTENED TO ALMOST NONE OF WHAT HE HAD SAID.
LIKE WHEN HE'D TOLD HER NOT TO EAT SUGARY THINGS.
AND NOT TO PET STRANGE ANIMALS.
PAT
PAT
PAT
AND NOT TO BREAK ANYTHING.
CAFÉS BLOWING UP
(Technically not her fault)
BOOM
AND NOW, THANKS IN PART TO HER, THEIR CITY WAS IN CHAOS.

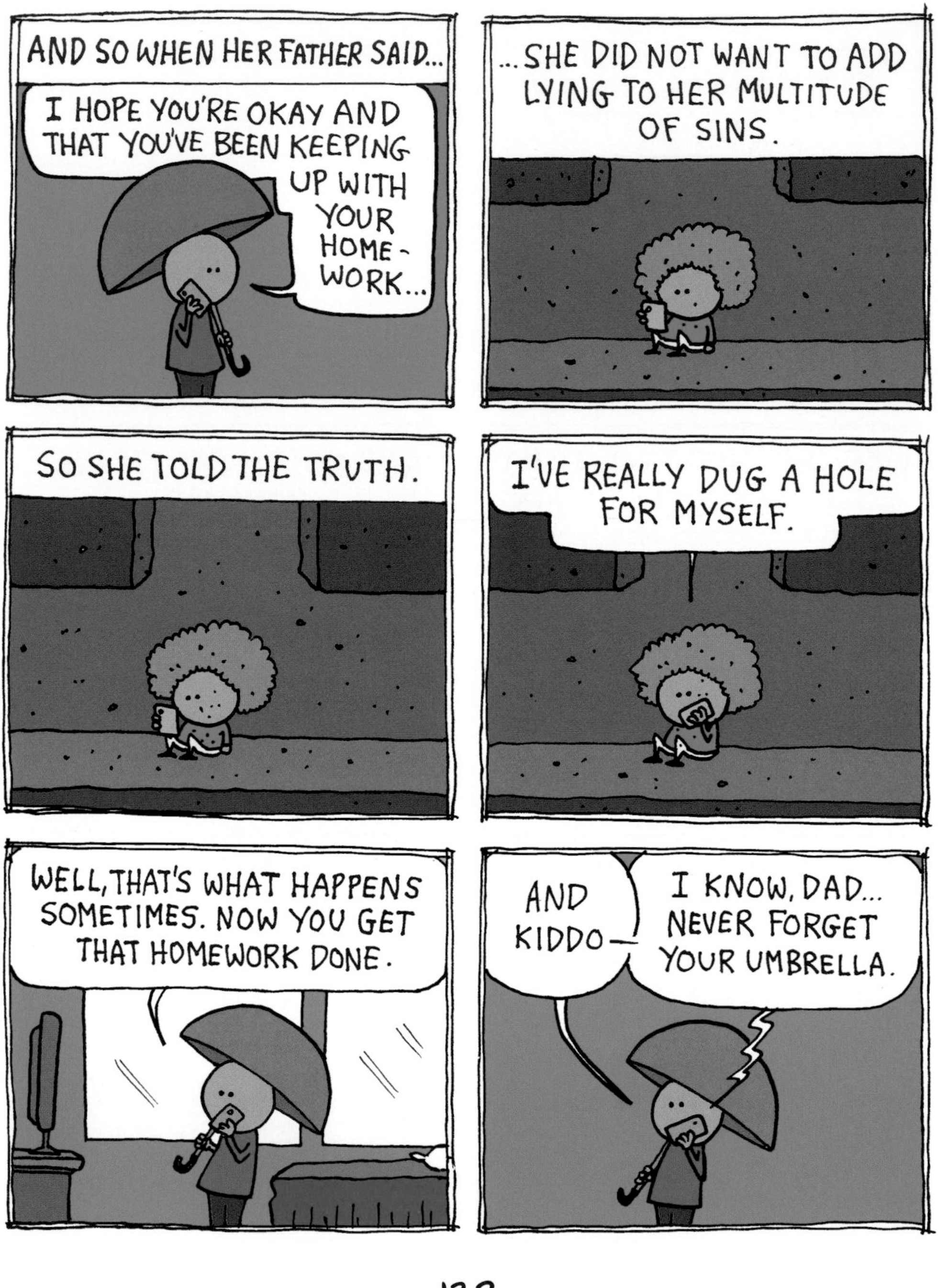
AND SO WHEN HER FATHER SAID...
I HOPE YOU'RE OKAY AND THAT YOU'VE BEEN KEEPING UP WITH YOUR HOME-WORK...
...SHE DID NOT WANT TO ADD LYING TO HER MULTITUDE OF SINS.
SO SHE TOLD THE TRUTH.
I'VE REALLY DUG A HOLE FOR MYSELF.
WELL, THAT'S WHAT HAPPENS SOMETIMES. NOW YOU GET THAT HOMEWORK DONE.
AND KIDDO—
I KNOW, DAD... NEVER FORGET YOUR UMBRELLA.

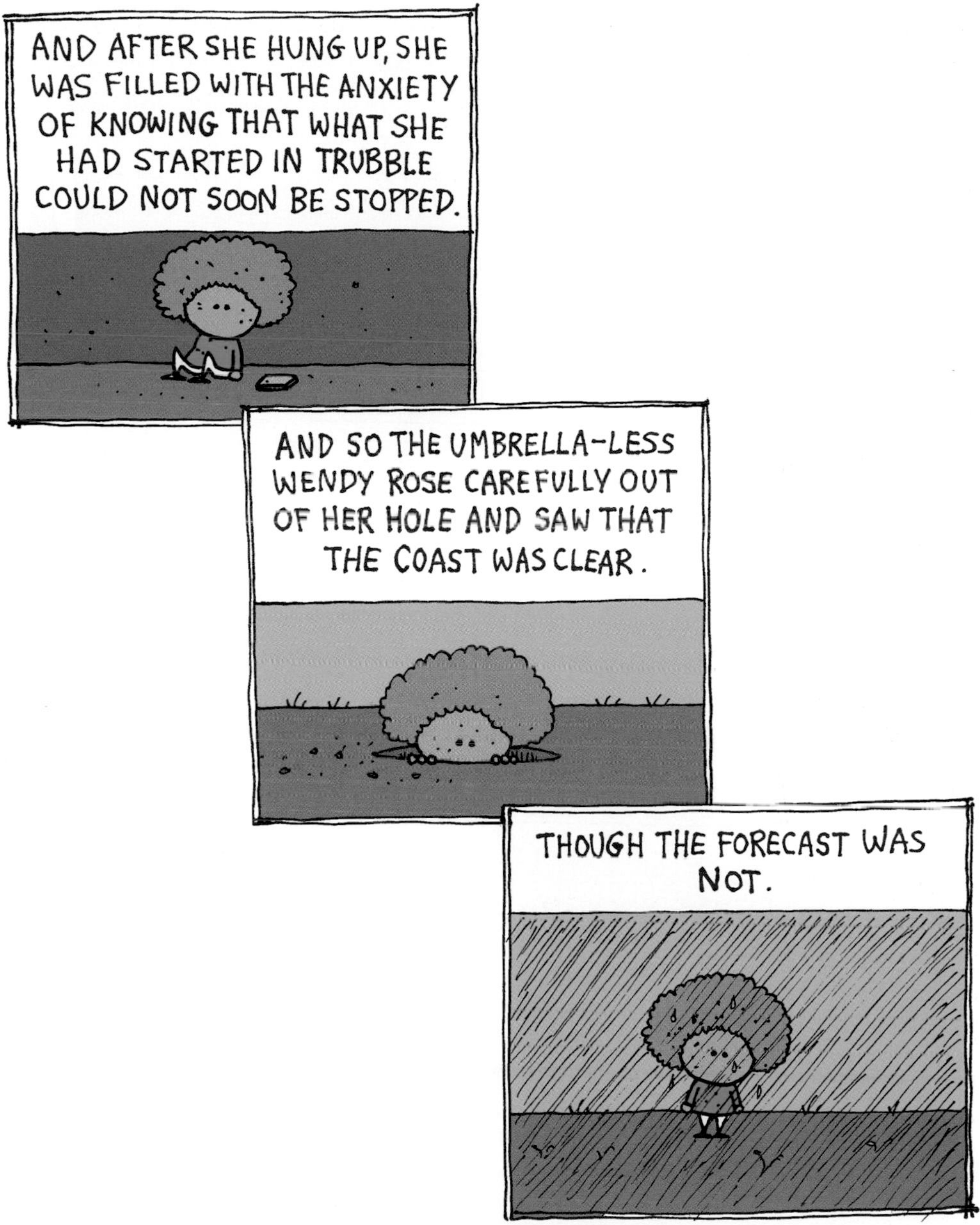
AND AFTER SHE HUNG UP, SHE WAS FILLED WITH THE ANXIETY OF KNOWING THAT WHAT SHE HAD STARTED IN TRUBBLE COULD NOT SOON BE STOPPED.
AND SO THE UMBRELLA-LESS WENDY ROSE CAREFULLY OUT OF HER HOLE AND SAW THAT THE COAST WAS CLEAR.
THOUGH THE FORECAST WAS NOT.

CHAPTER 13

IN WHICH...

YOU ARE MOVED TO WEEPY, WEEPY TEARS

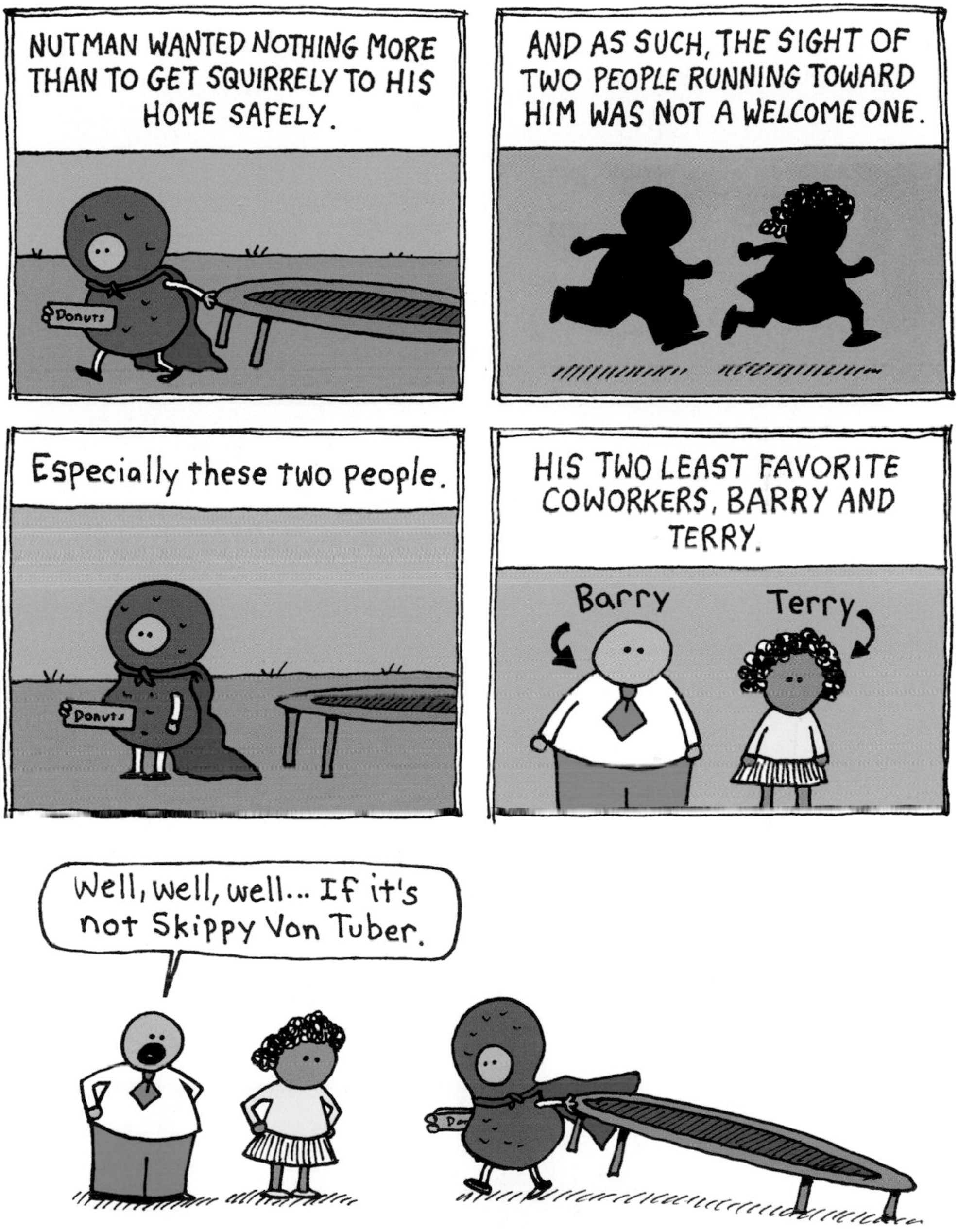

NUTMAN WANTED NOTHING MORE THAN TO GET SQUIRRELY TO HIS HOME SAFELY.
Donuts
AND AS SUCH, THE SIGHT OF TWO PEOPLE RUNNING TOWARD HIM WAS NOT A WELCOME ONE.
Especially these two people.
Donuts
HIS TWO LEAST FAVORITE COWORKERS, BARRY AND TERRY.
Barry
Terry
Well, well, well... If it's not Skippy Von Tuber.

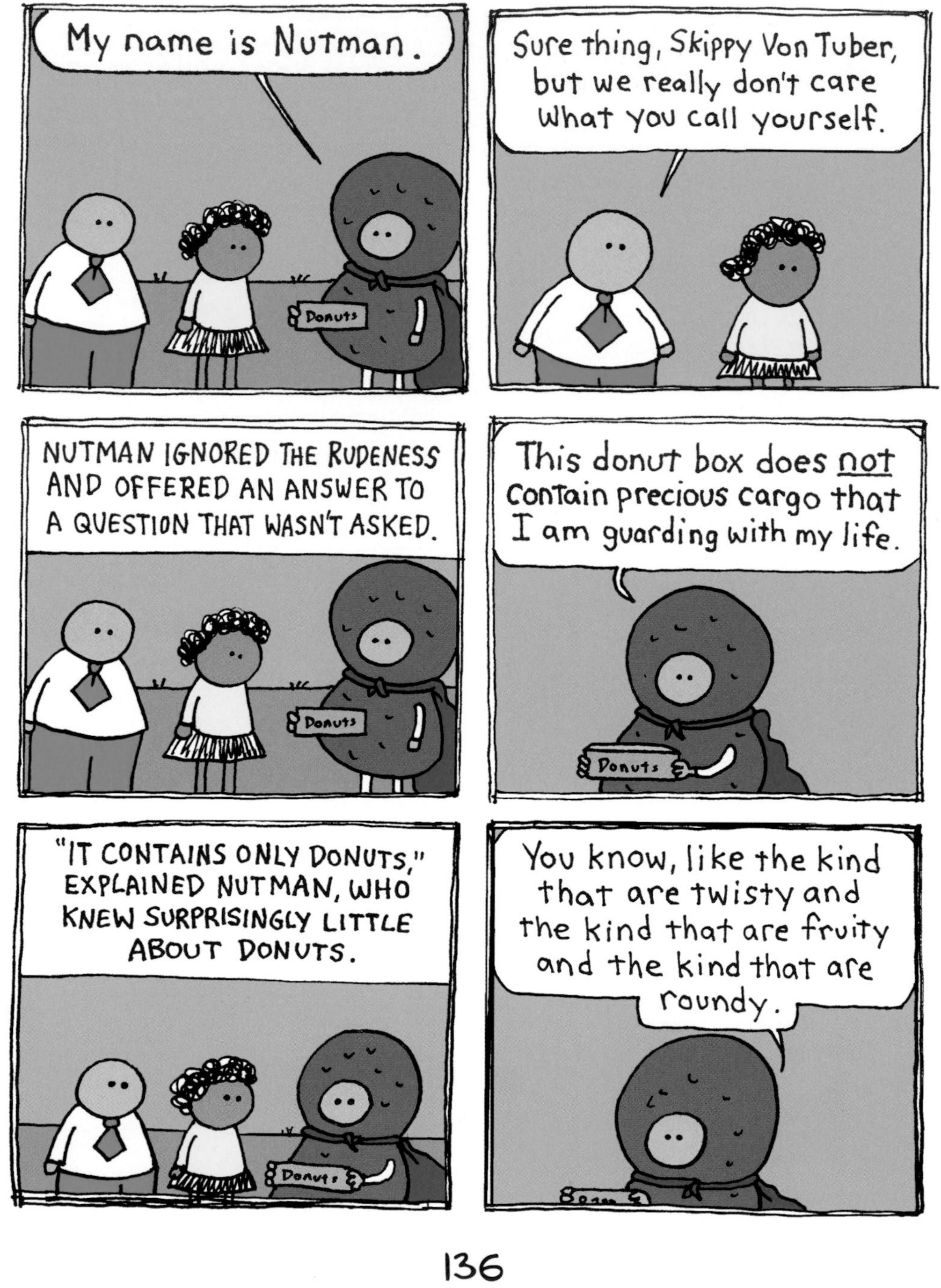

My name is Nutman.
DONUTS
Sure thing, Skippy Von Tuber, but we really don't care what you call yourself.
NUTMAN IGNORED THE RUDENESS AND OFFERED AN ANSWER TO A QUESTION THAT WASN'T ASKED.
DONUTS
This donut box does not contain precious cargo that I am guarding with my life.
Donuts
"IT CONTAINS ONLY DONUTS," EXPLAINED NUTMAN, WHO KNEW SURPRISINGLY LITTLE ABOUT DONUTS.
Donuts
You know, like the kind that are twisty and the kind that are fruity and the kind that are roundy.

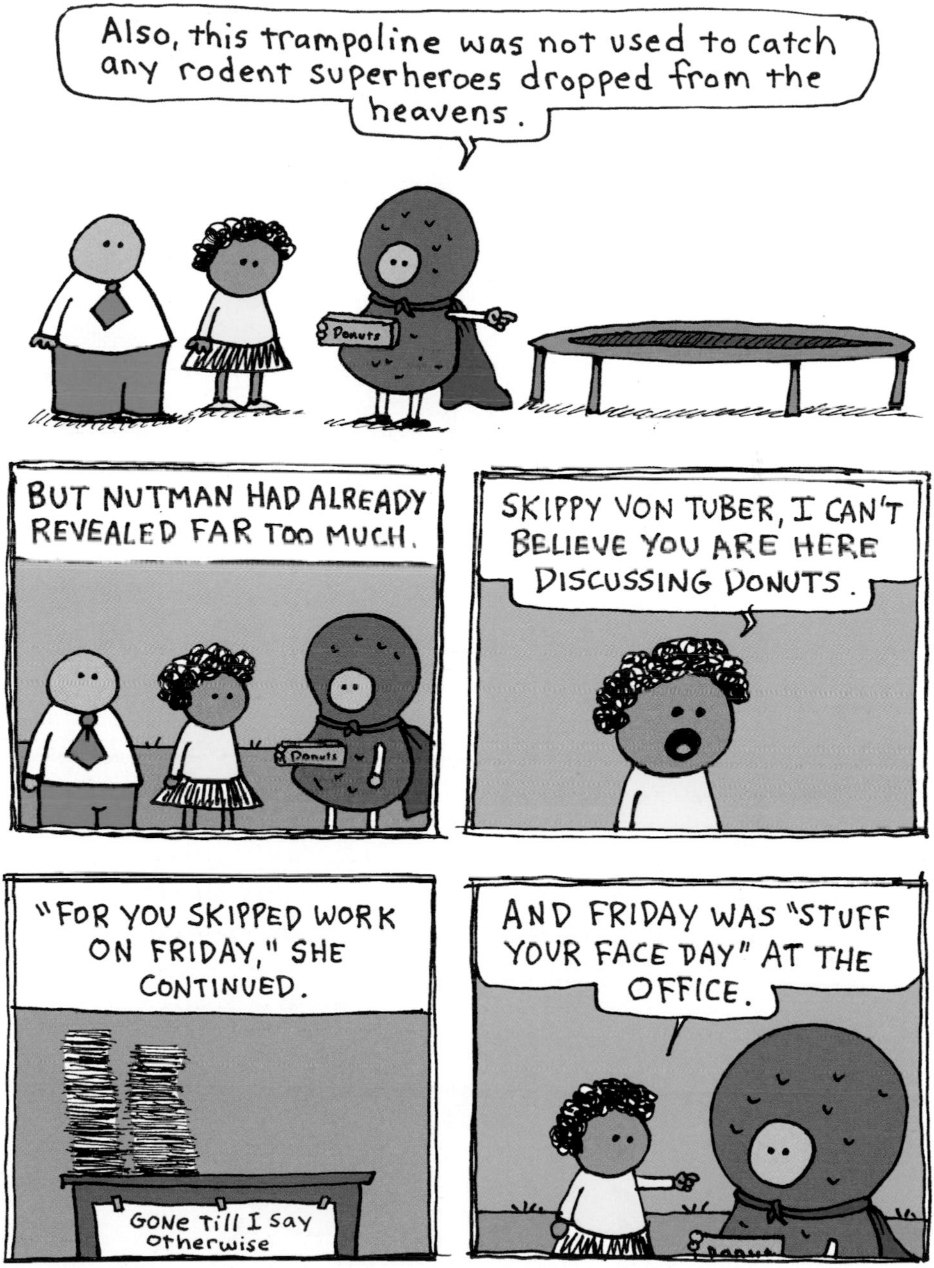
Also, this trampoline was not used to catch any rodent superheroes dropped from the heavens.
Donuts
BUT NUTMAN HAD ALREADY REVEALED FAR TOO MUCH.
Donuts
SKIPPY VON TUBER, I CAN'T BELIEVE YOU ARE HERE DISCUSSING DONUTS.
"FOR YOU SKIPPED WORK ON FRIDAY," SHE CONTINUED.
GONE Till I Say otherwise
AND FRIDAY WAS "STUFF YOUR FACE DAY" AT THE OFFICE.

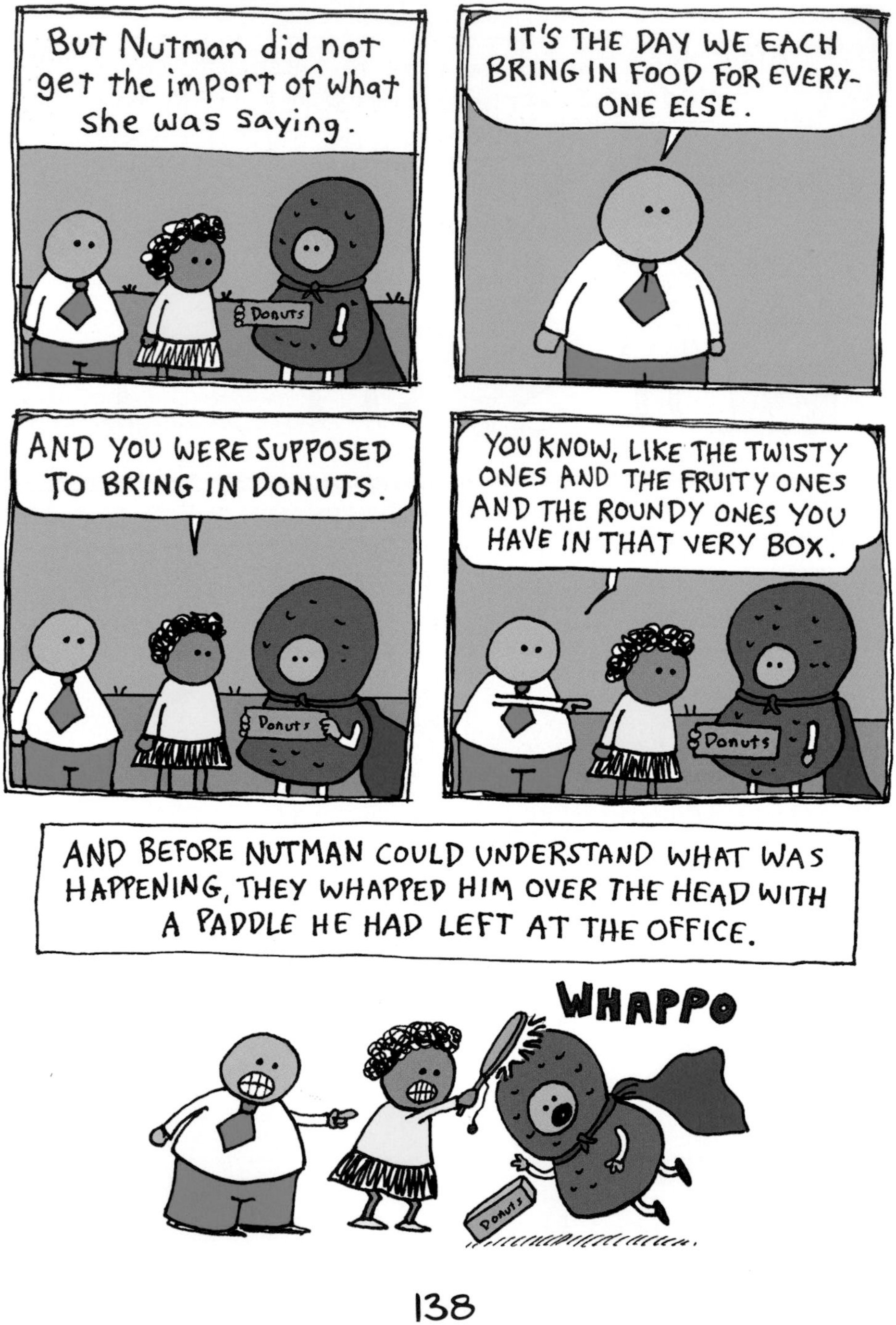

But Nutman did not get the import of what she was saying.
DONUTS
IT'S THE DAY WE EACH BRING IN FOOD FOR EVERY-ONE ELSE.
AND YOU WERE SUPPOSED TO BRING IN DONUTS.
Donuts
YOU KNOW, LIKE THE TWISTY ONES AND THE FRUITY ONES AND THE ROUNDY ONES YOU HAVE IN THAT VERY BOX.
Donuts
AND BEFORE NUTMAN COULD UNDERSTAND WHAT WAS HAPPENING, THEY WHAPPED HIM OVER THE HEAD WITH A PADDLE HE HAD LEFT AT THE OFFICE.
WHAPPO
DONUTS

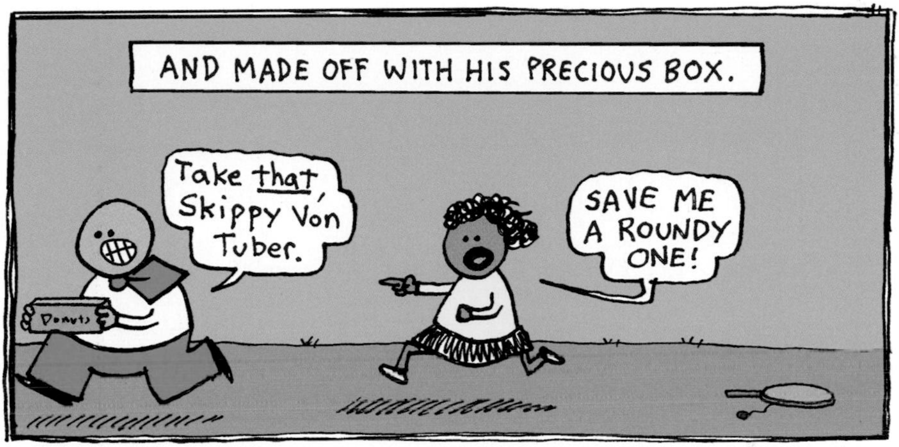
AND MADE OFF WITH HIS PRECIOUS BOX.
Take that, Skippy Von Tuber.
SAVE ME A ROUNDY ONE!

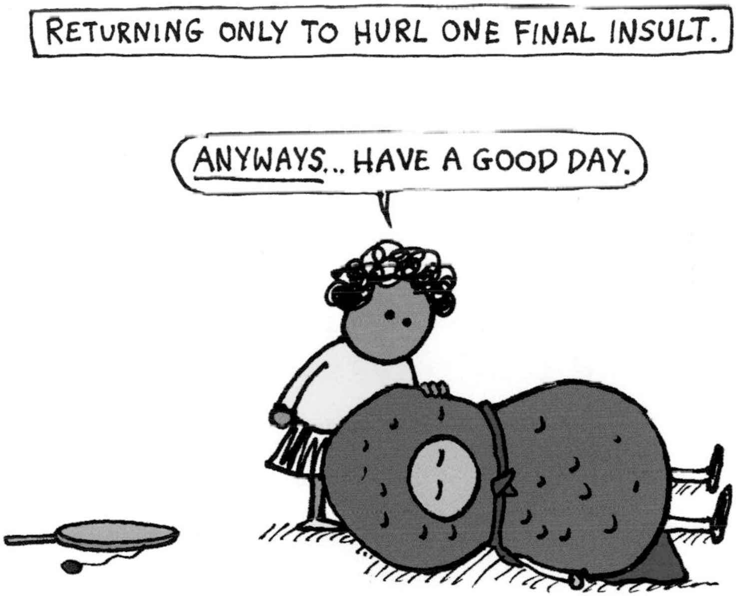
RETURNING ONLY TO HURL ONE FINAL INSULT.
ANYWAYS... HAVE A GOOD DAY.

CHAPTER FOURTEEN

IN WHICH...

THE ANSWERS TO ALL O' LIFE'S MYSTERIES ARE REVEALED

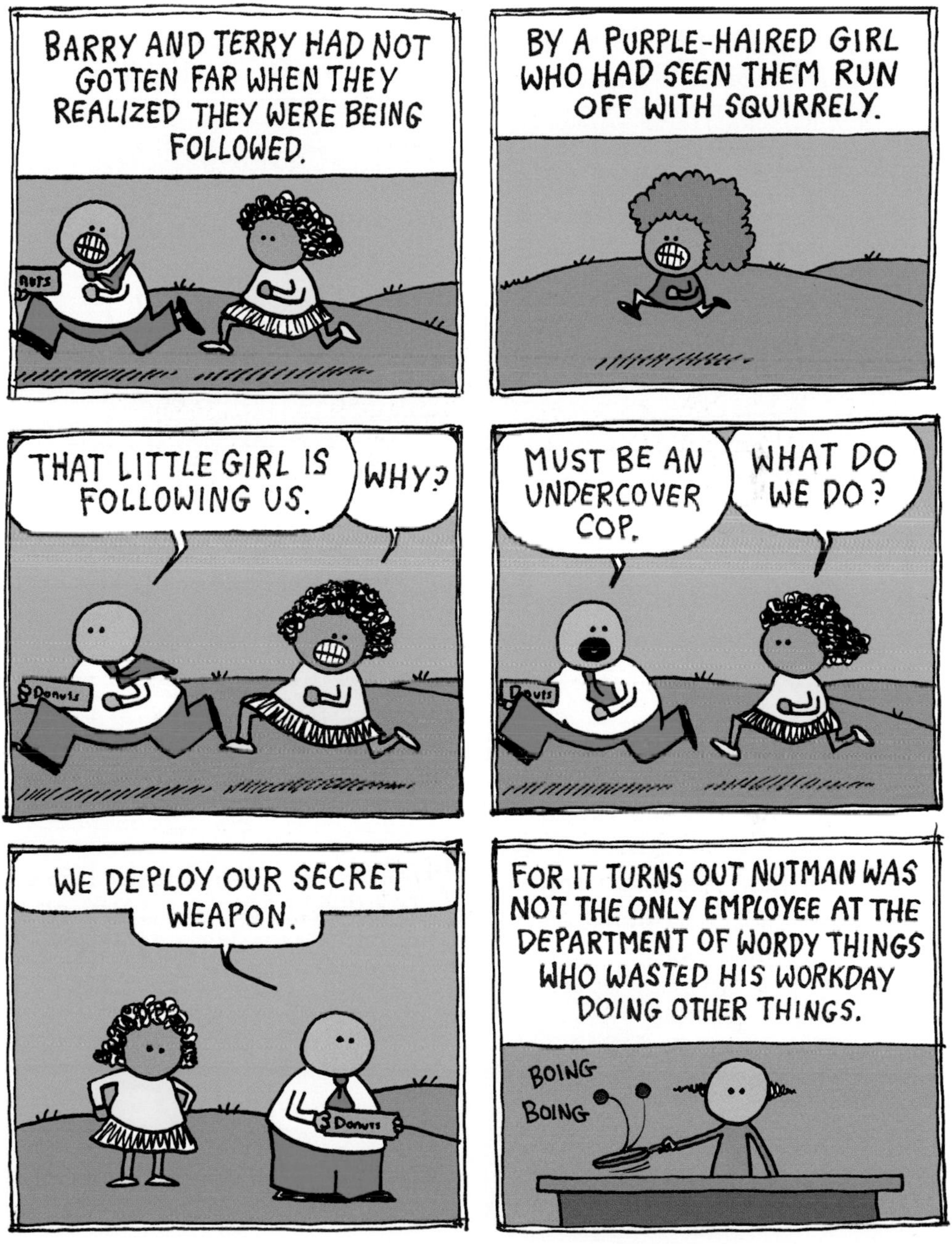
BARRY AND TERRY HAD NOT GOTTEN FAR WHEN THEY REALIZED THEY WERE BEING FOLLOWED.
BY A PURPLE-HAIRED GIRL WHO HAD SEEN THEM RUN OFF WITH SQUIRRELY.
THAT LITTLE GIRL IS FOLLOWING US.
WHY?
MUST BE AN UNDERCOVER COP.
WHAT DO WE DO?
WE DEPLOY OUR SECRET WEAPON.
Donuts
FOR IT TURNS OUT NUTMAN WAS NOT THE ONLY EMPLOYEE AT THE DEPARTMENT OF WORDY THINGS WHO WASTED HIS WORKDAY DOING OTHER THINGS.
BOING
BOING

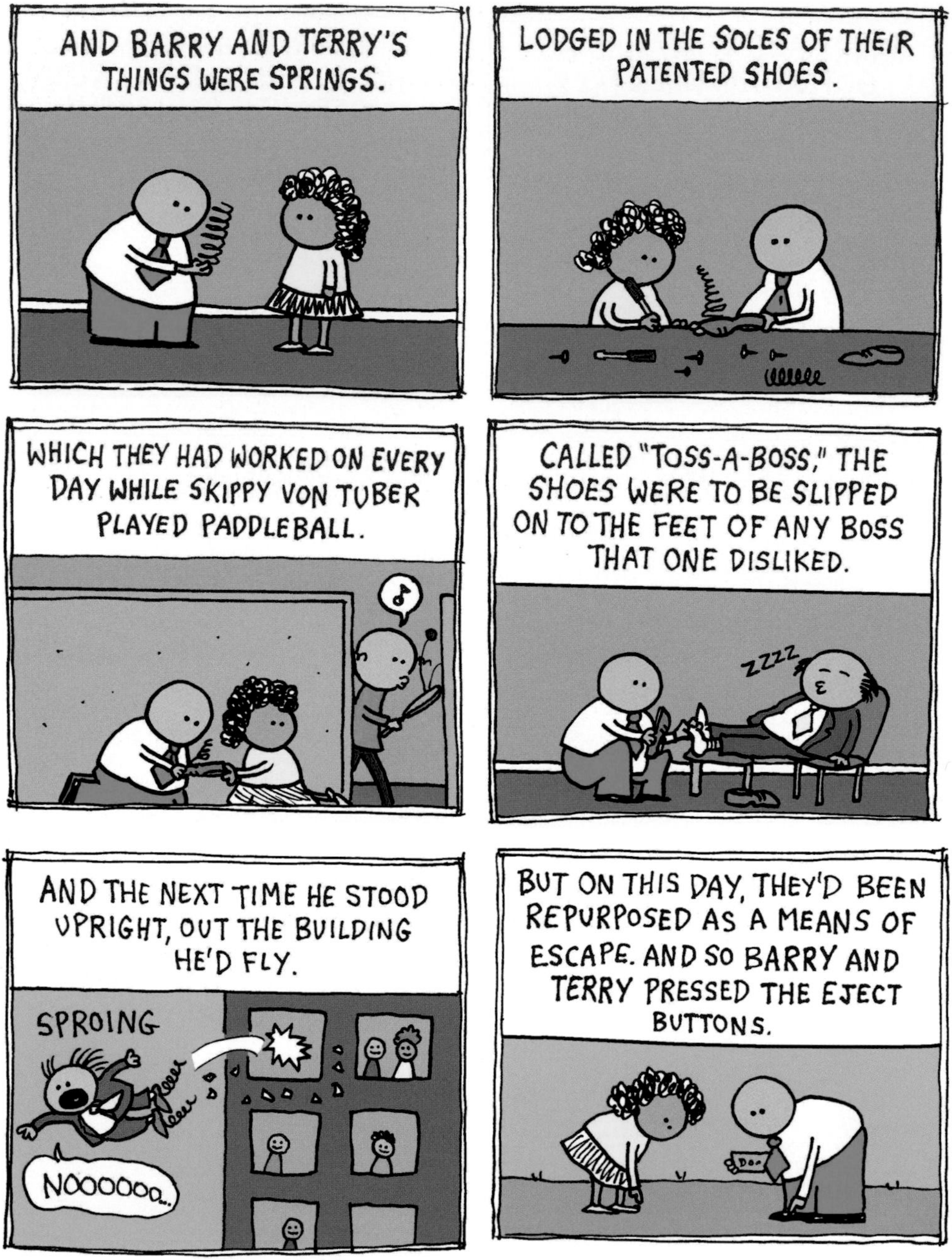
AND BARRY AND TERRY'S THINGS WERE SPRINGS.
LODGED IN THE SOLES OF THEIR PATENTED SHOES.
WHICH THEY HAD WORKED ON EVERY DAY WHILE SKIPPY VON TUBER PLAYED PADDLEBALL.
CALLED "TOSS-A-BOSS," THE SHOES WERE TO BE SLIPPED ON TO THE FEET OF ANY BOSS THAT ONE DISLIKED.
ZZZZ
AND THE NEXT TIME HE STOOD UPRIGHT, OUT THE BUILDING HE'D FLY.
SPROING
NOOOOOO...
BUT ON THIS DAY, THEY'D BEEN REPURPOSED AS A MEANS OF ESCAPE. AND SO BARRY AND TERRY PRESSED THE EJECT BUTTONS.

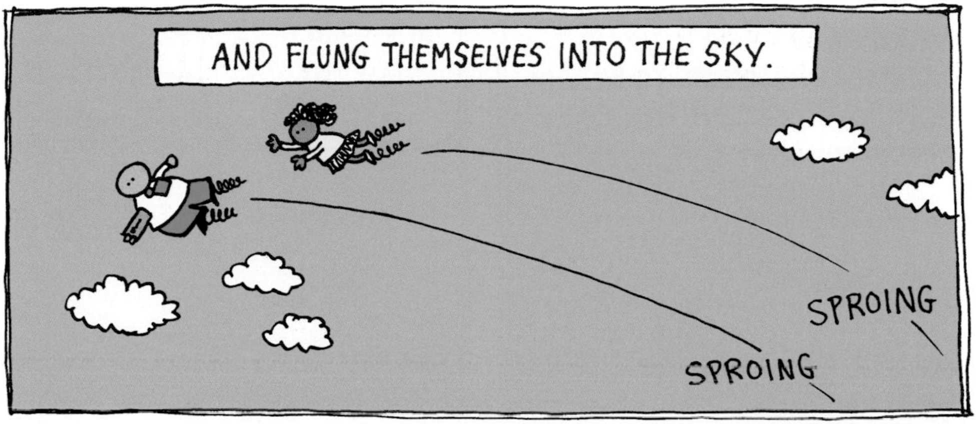
AND FLUNG THEMSELVES INTO THE SKY.
SPROING
SPROING

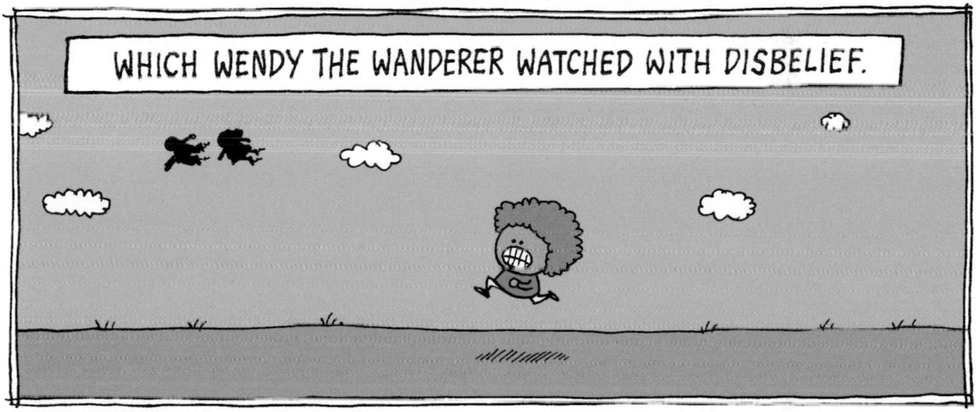
WHICH WENDY THE WANDERER WATCHED WITH DISBELIEF.

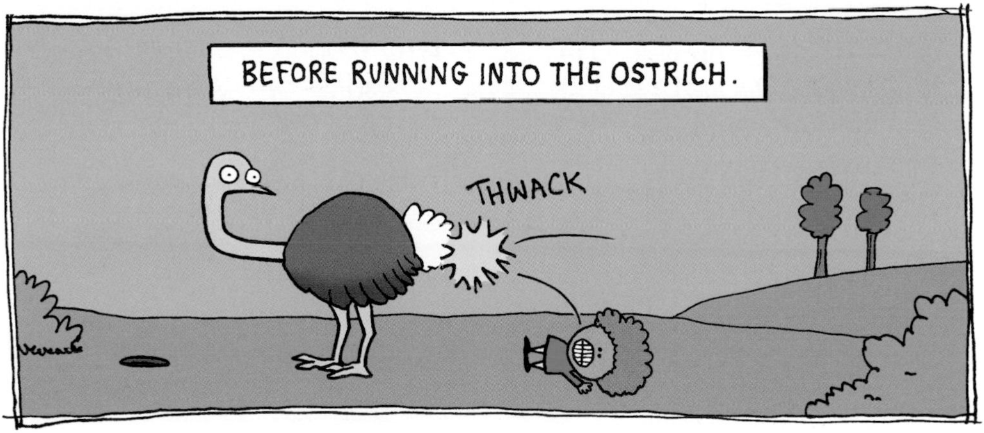
BEFORE RUNNING INTO THE OSTRICH.
THWACK

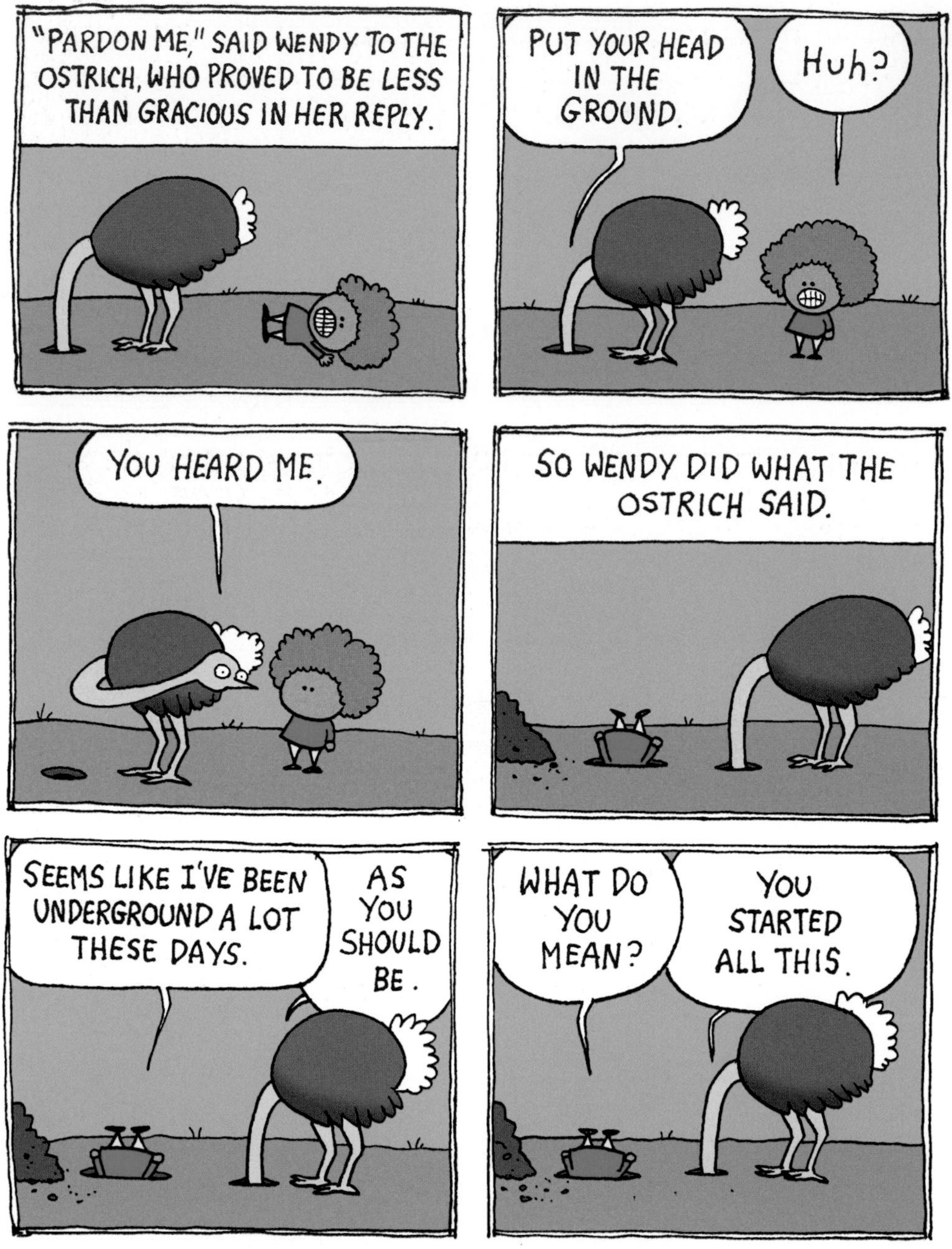
"PARDON ME," SAID WENDY TO THE OSTRICH, WHO PROVED TO BE LESS THAN GRACIOUS IN HER REPLY.
PUT YOUR HEAD IN THE GROUND.
Huh?
YOU HEARD ME.
SO WENDY DID WHAT THE OSTRICH SAID.
SEEMS LIKE I'VE BEEN UNDERGROUND A LOT THESE DAYS.
AS YOU SHOULD BE.
WHAT DO YOU MEAN?
YOU STARTED ALL THIS.

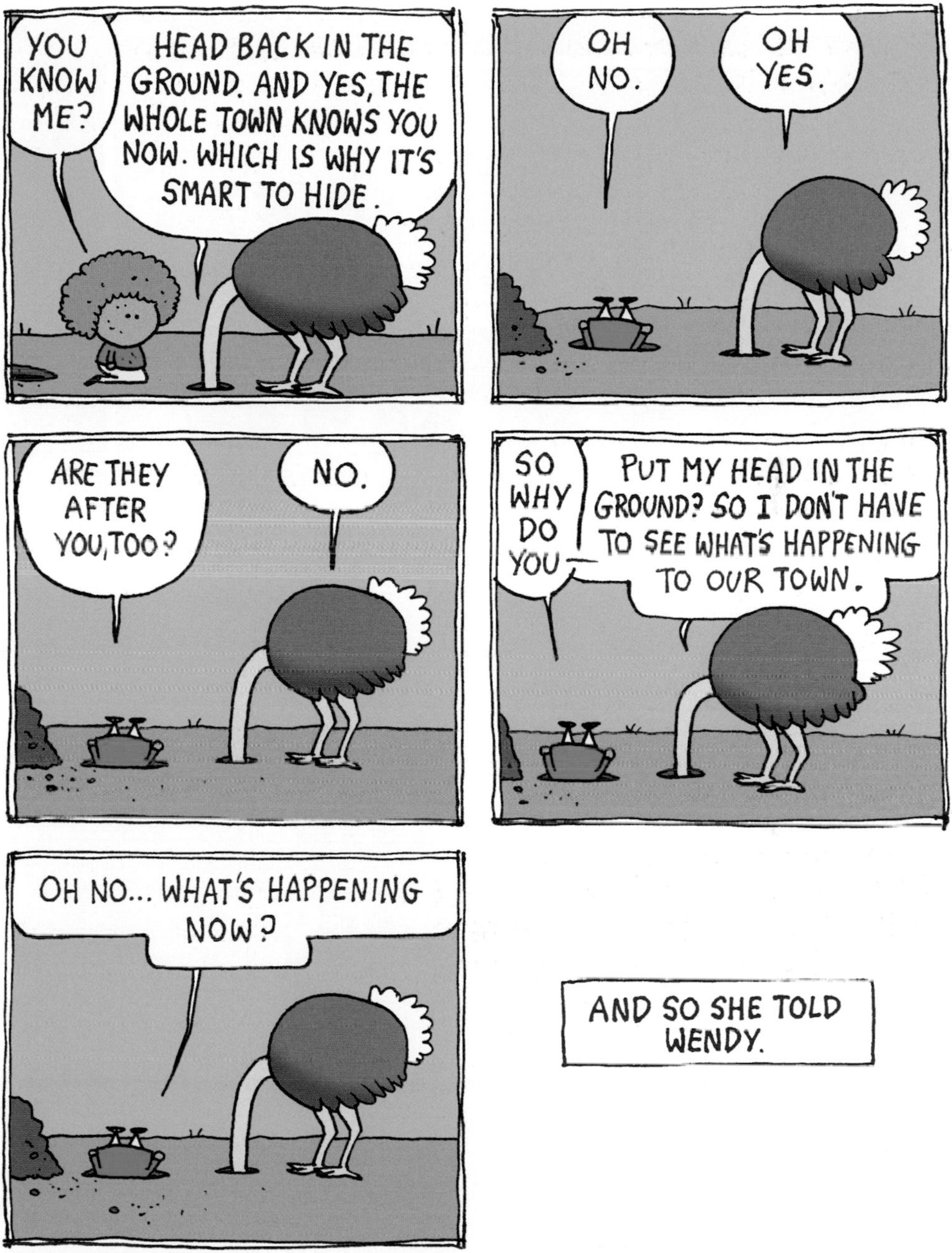
YOU KNOW ME?
HEAD BACK IN THE GROUND. AND YES, THE WHOLE TOWN KNOWS YOU NOW. WHICH IS WHY IT'S SMART TO HIDE.
OH NO.
OH YES.
ARE THEY AFTER YOU, TOO?
NO.
SO WHY DO YOU—
PUT MY HEAD IN THE GROUND? SO I DON'T HAVE TO SEE WHAT'S HAPPENING TO OUR TOWN.
OH NO... WHAT'S HAPPENING NOW?
AND SO SHE TOLD WENDY.

CHAPTER OSTRICH

IN WHICH...

THE BIRD DOES ALL THE YAPPING

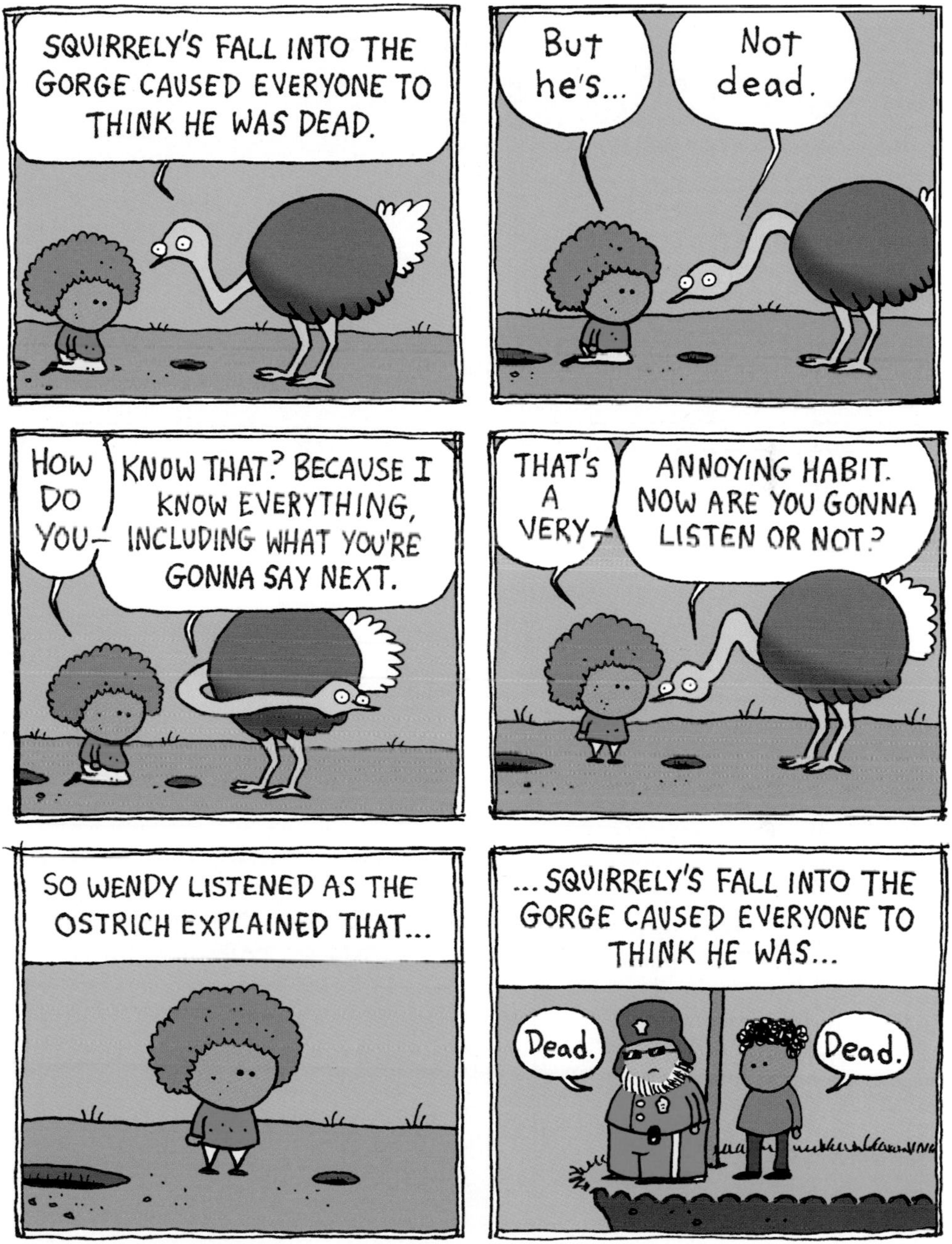
SQUIRRELY'S FALL INTO THE GORGE CAUSED EVERYONE TO THINK HE WAS DEAD.
But he's...
Not dead.
HOW DO YOU—
KNOW THAT? BECAUSE I KNOW EVERYTHING, INCLUDING WHAT YOU'RE GONNA SAY NEXT.
THAT'S A VERY—
ANNOYING HABIT. NOW ARE YOU GONNA LISTEN OR NOT?
SO WENDY LISTENED AS THE OSTRICH EXPLAINED THAT...
...SQUIRRELY'S FALL INTO THE GORGE CAUSED EVERYONE TO THINK HE WAS...
Dead.
Dead.

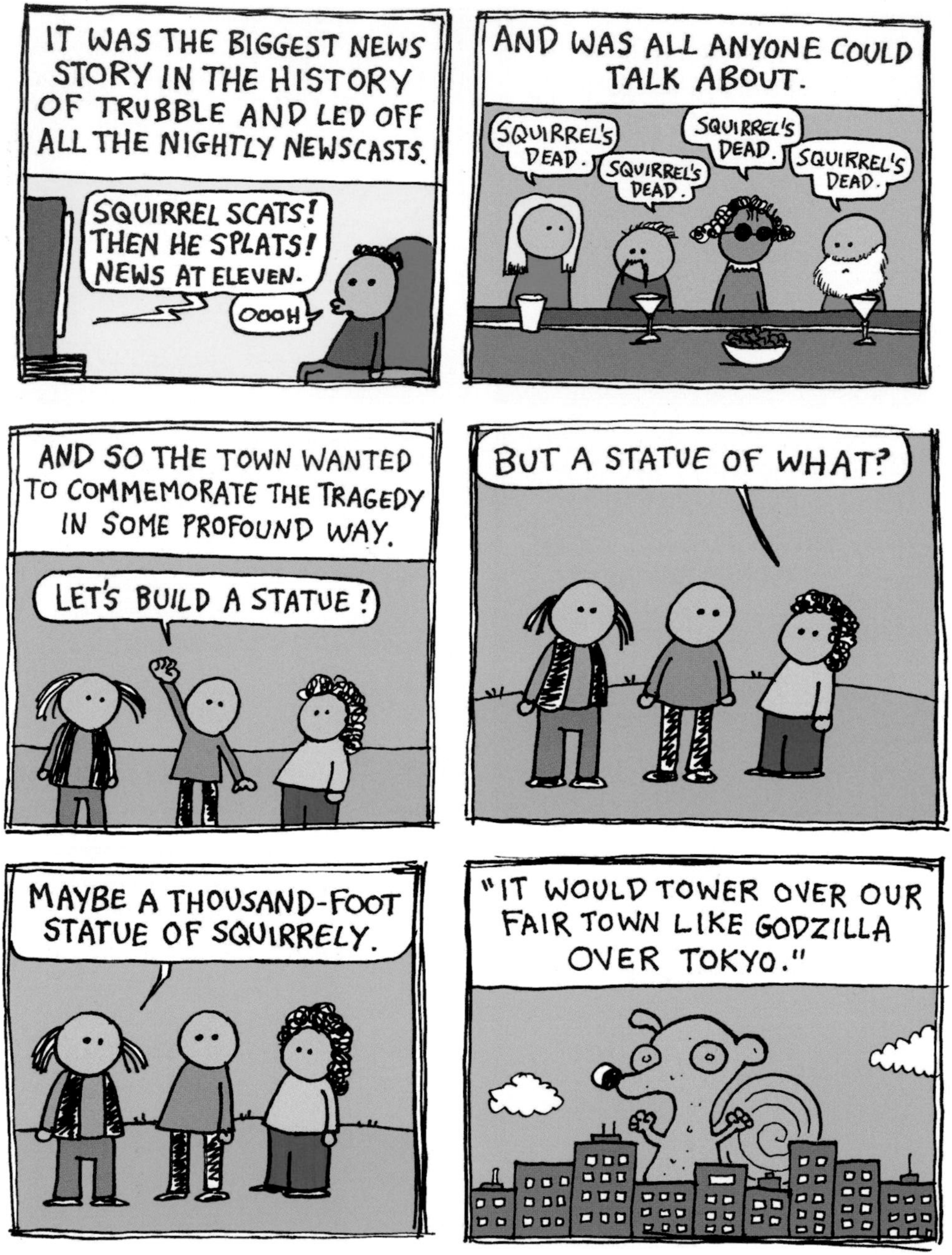
IT WAS THE BIGGEST NEWS STORY IN THE HISTORY OF TRUBBLE AND LED OFF ALL THE NIGHTLY NEWSCASTS.
SQUIRREL SCATS! THEN HE SPLATS! NEWS AT ELEVEN.
OOOH
AND WAS ALL ANYONE COULD TALK ABOUT.
SQUIRREL'S DEAD.
SQUIRREL'S DEAD.
SQUIRREL'S DEAD.
SQUIRREL'S DEAD.
AND SO THE TOWN WANTED TO COMMEMORATE THE TRAGEDY IN SOME PROFOUND WAY.
LET'S BUILD A STATUE!
BUT A STATUE OF WHAT?
MAYBE A THOUSAND-FOOT STATUE OF SQUIRRELY.
"IT WOULD TOWER OVER OUR FAIR TOWN LIKE GODZILLA OVER TOKYO."

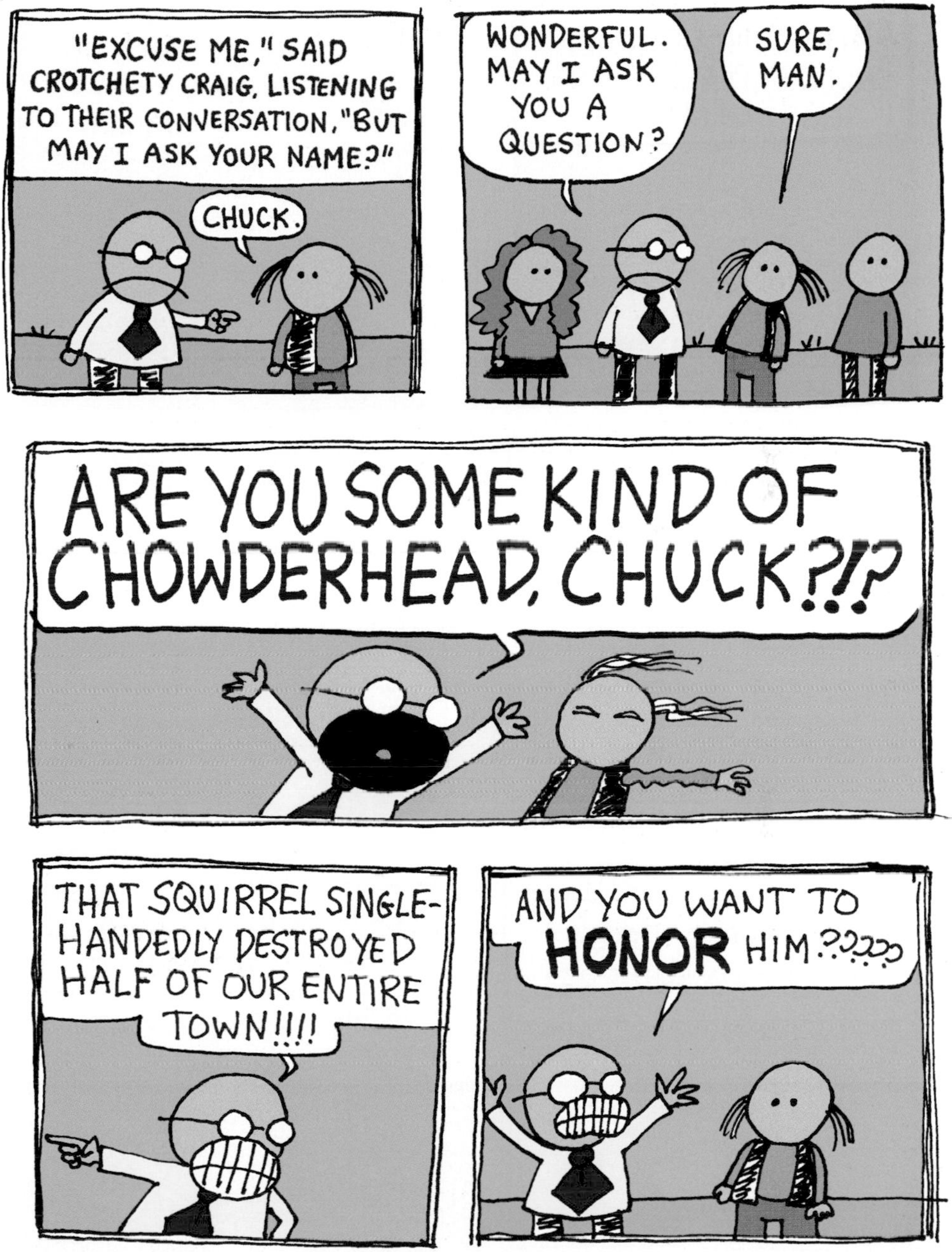
"EXCUSE ME," SAID CROTCHETY CRAIG, LISTENING TO THEIR CONVERSATION, "BUT MAY I ASK YOUR NAME?"
CHUCK.
WONDERFUL. MAY I ASK YOU A QUESTION?
SURE, MAN.
ARE YOU SOME KIND OF CHOWDERHEAD, CHUCK?!?
THAT SQUIRREL SINGLE-HANDEDLY DESTROYED HALF OF OUR ENTIRE TOWN!!!!
AND YOU WANT TO HONOR HIM?????

AND SO CHOWDERHEAD CHUCK EXPLAINED HIMSELF...

NO, I DO NOT WISH TO HONOR HIM.

FOR AT THE BOTTOM OF THE STATUE, WE SHALL PUT A SMALL PLAQUE.

SAYING WHAT??

IT SHALL SAY...

BAD SQUIRREL

SO YOU'RE GONNA HAVE A THOUSAND-FOOT STATUE OF A SQUIRREL...

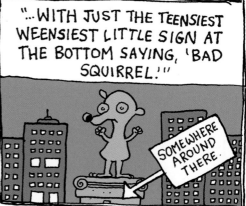

"...WITH JUST THE TEENSIEST WEENSIEST LITTLE SIGN AT THE BOTTOM SAYING, 'BAD SQUIRREL!'"

SOMEWHERE AROUND THERE.

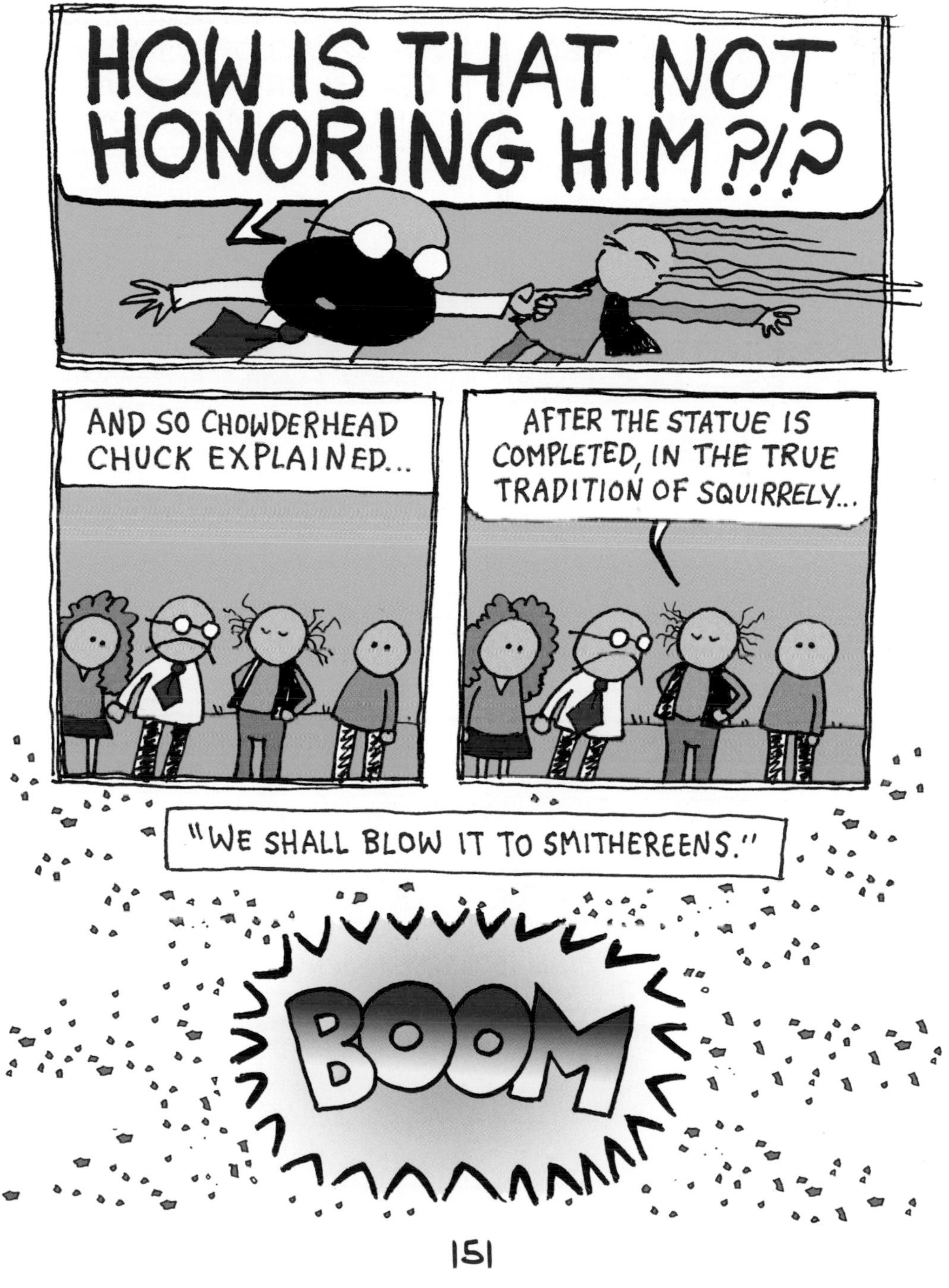
HOW IS THAT NOT HONORING HIM?!?
AND SO CHOWDERHEAD CHUCK EXPLAINED...
AFTER THE STATUE IS COMPLETED, IN THE TRUE TRADITION OF SQUIRRELY...
"WE SHALL BLOW IT TO SMITHEREENS."
BOOM

IT WAS AN IDEA SO SHOCKINGLY ABSURD THAT CROTCHETY CRAIG COULDN'T SPEAK.

AS NO PART OF HIS BRAIN COULD HANDLE THAT MUCH DUMBOSITY.

AND SO HE FELL TO THE GROUND.

Dead?

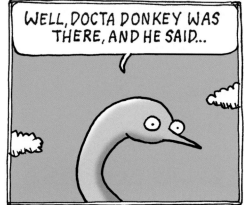

WELL, DOCTA DONKEY WAS THERE, AND HE SAID...

RELAX, FOR I AM A MEDICAL PROFESSIONAL, AND THIS MAN IS VERY MUCH ALIVE.

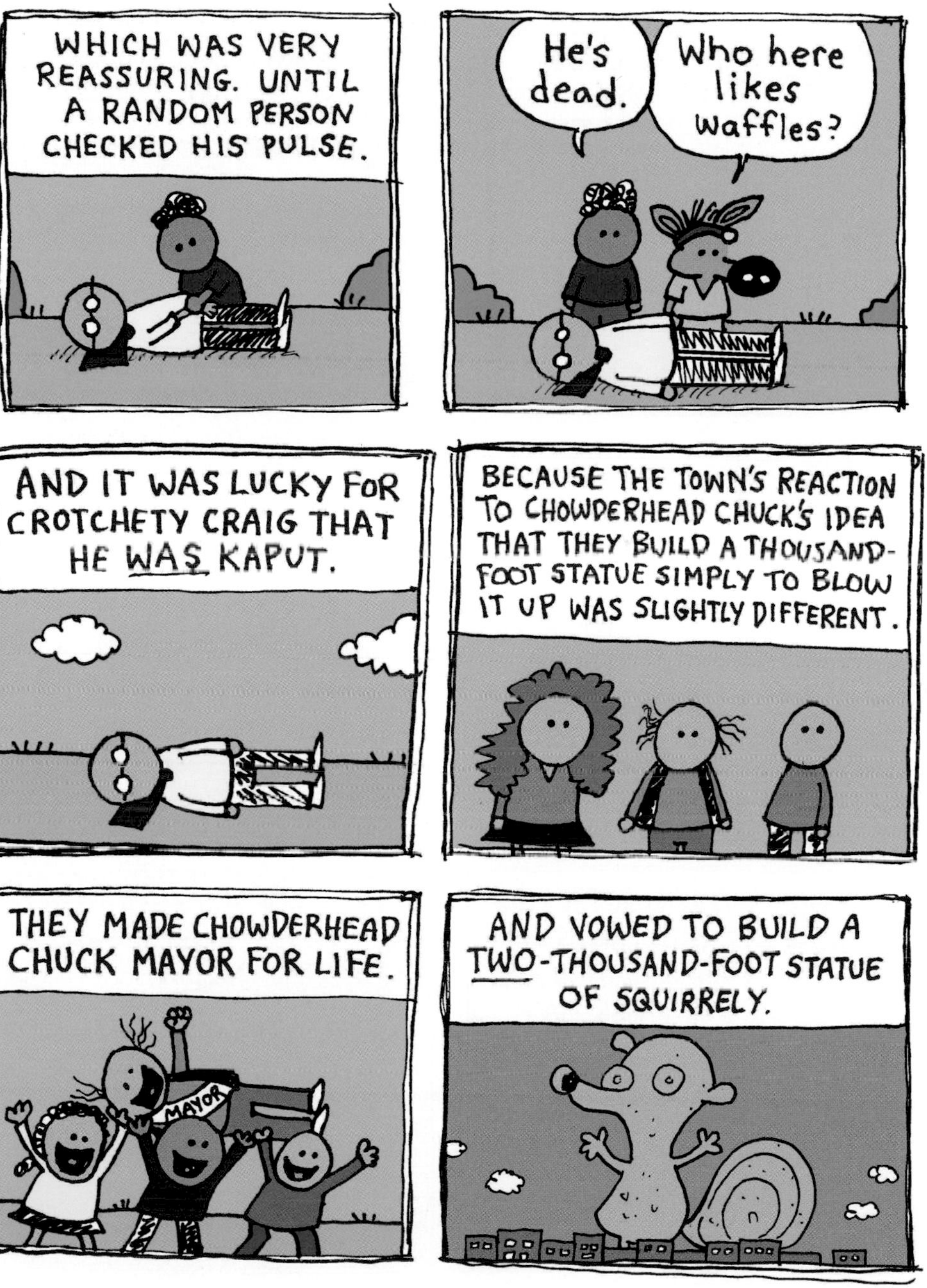
WHICH WAS VERY REASSURING. UNTIL A RANDOM PERSON CHECKED HIS PULSE.
He's dead.
Who here likes waffles?
AND IT WAS LUCKY FOR CROTCHETY CRAIG THAT HE WAS KAPUT.
BECAUSE THE TOWN'S REACTION TO CHOWDERHEAD CHUCK'S IDEA THAT THEY BUILD A THOUSAND-FOOT STATUE SIMPLY TO BLOW IT UP WAS SLIGHTLY DIFFERENT.
THEY MADE CHOWDERHEAD CHUCK MAYOR FOR LIFE.
MAYOR
AND VOWED TO BUILD A TWO-THOUSAND-FOOT STATUE OF SQUIRRELY.

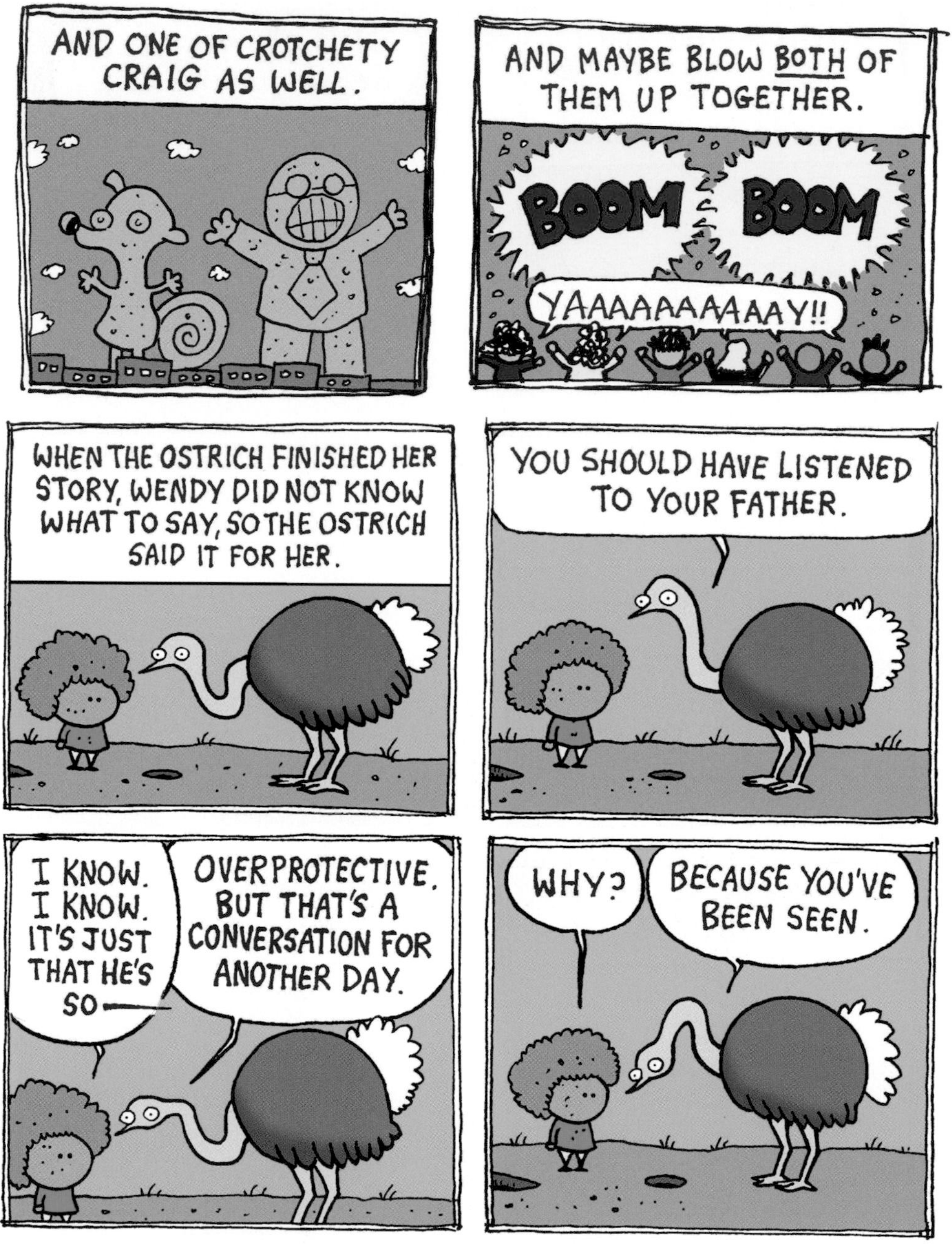
AND ONE OF CROTCHETY CRAIG AS WELL.
AND MAYBE BLOW BOTH OF THEM UP TOGETHER.
BOOM
BOOM
YAAAAAAAAAY!!
WHEN THE OSTRICH FINISHED HER STORY, WENDY DID NOT KNOW WHAT TO SAY, SO THE OSTRICH SAID IT FOR HER.
YOU SHOULD HAVE LISTENED TO YOUR FATHER.
I KNOW. I KNOW. IT'S JUST THAT HE'S SO—
OVERPROTECTIVE. BUT THAT'S A CONVERSATION FOR ANOTHER DAY.
WHY?
BECAUSE YOU'VE BEEN SEEN.

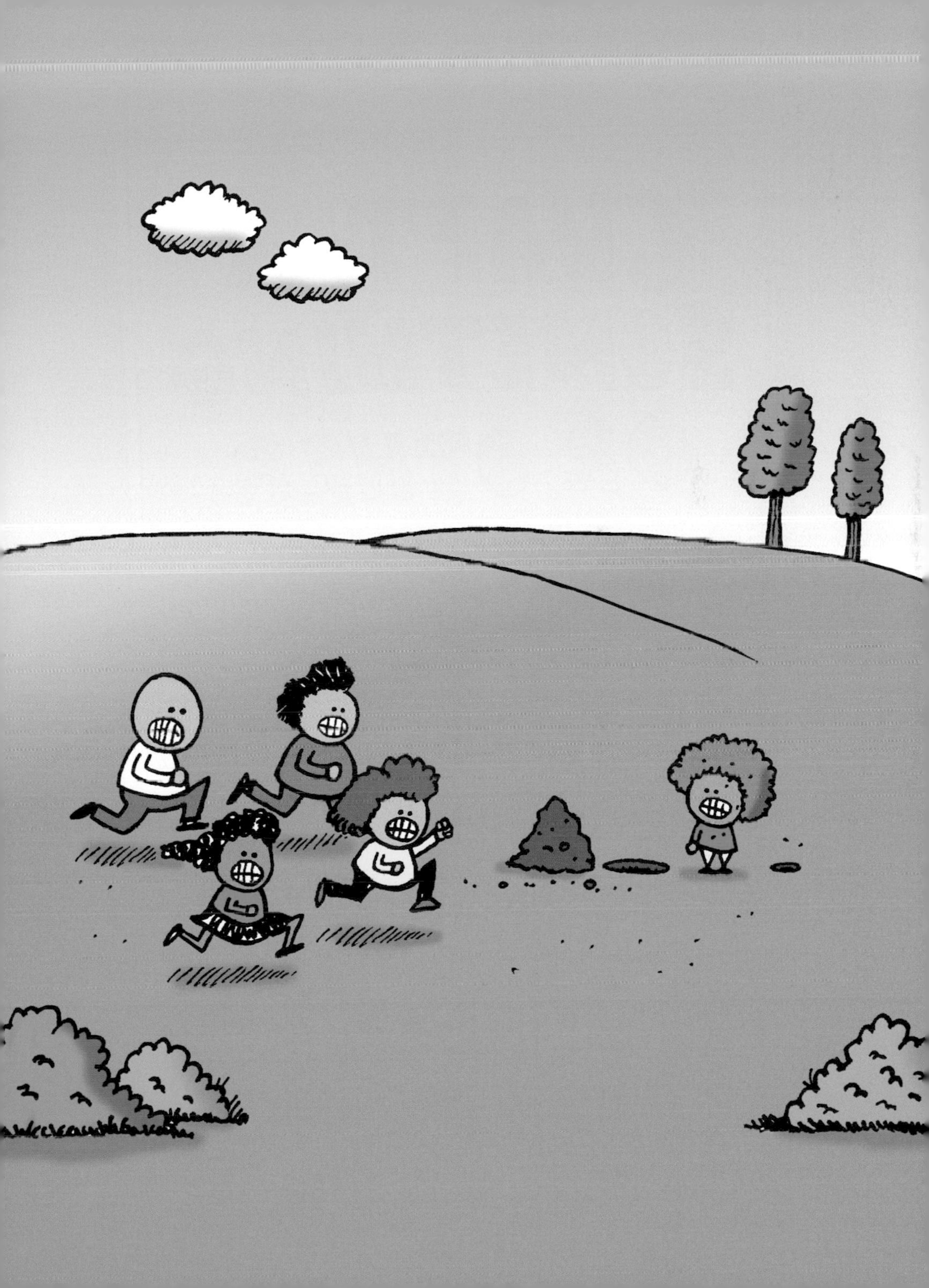

CHAPTER SOMETHING OR OTHER

IN WHICH...

WE LOSE TRACK OF THE CHAPTER NUMBERS

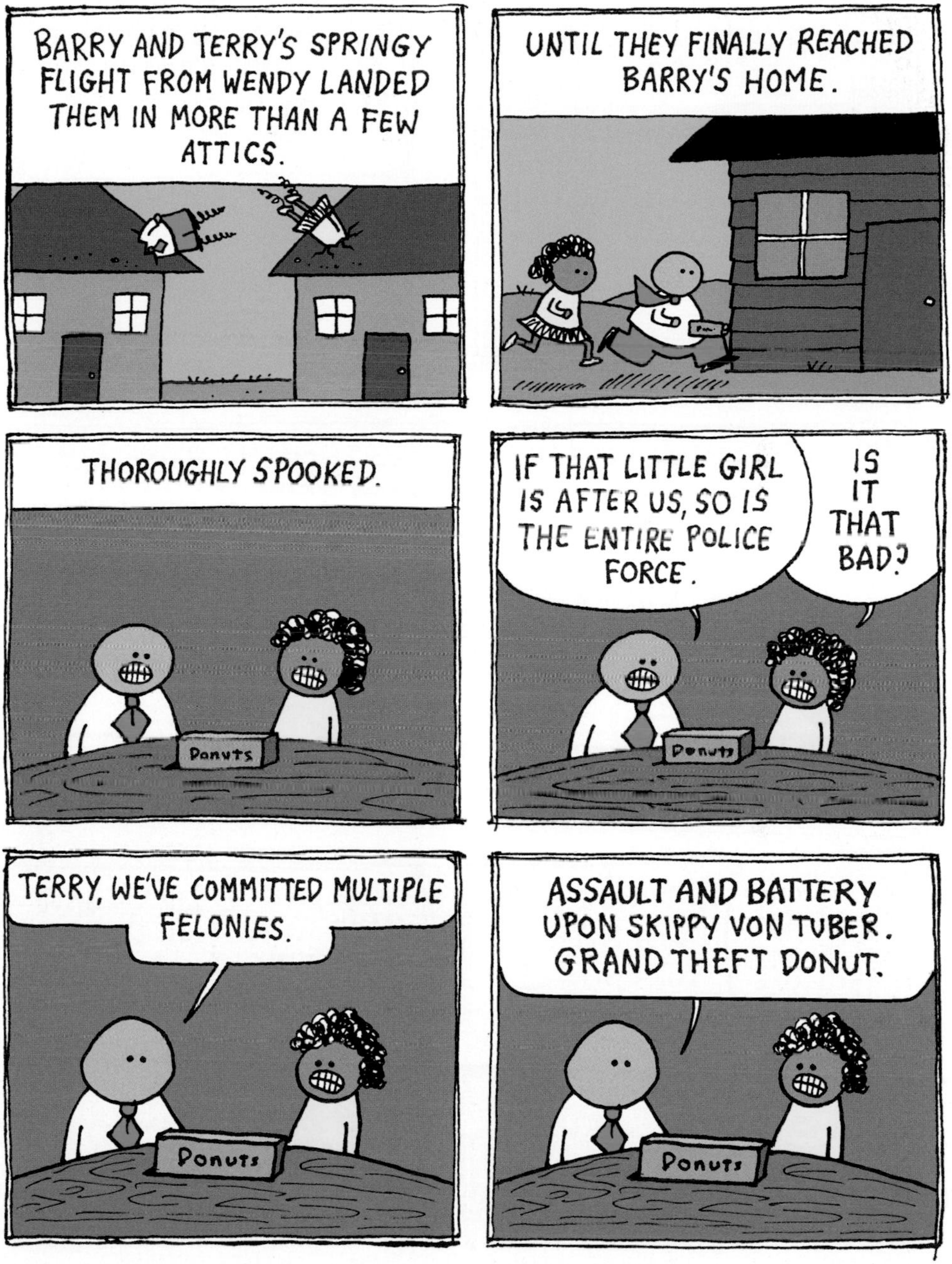
BARRY AND TERRY'S SPRINGY FLIGHT FROM WENDY LANDED THEM IN MORE THAN A FEW ATTICS.
UNTIL THEY FINALLY REACHED BARRY'S HOME.
THOROUGHLY SPOOKED.
Donuts
IF THAT LITTLE GIRL IS AFTER US, SO IS THE ENTIRE POLICE FORCE.
IS IT THAT BAD?
Donuts
TERRY, WE'VE COMMITTED MULTIPLE FELONIES.
Donuts
ASSAULT AND BATTERY UPON SKIPPY VON TUBER. GRAND THEFT DONUT.
Donuts

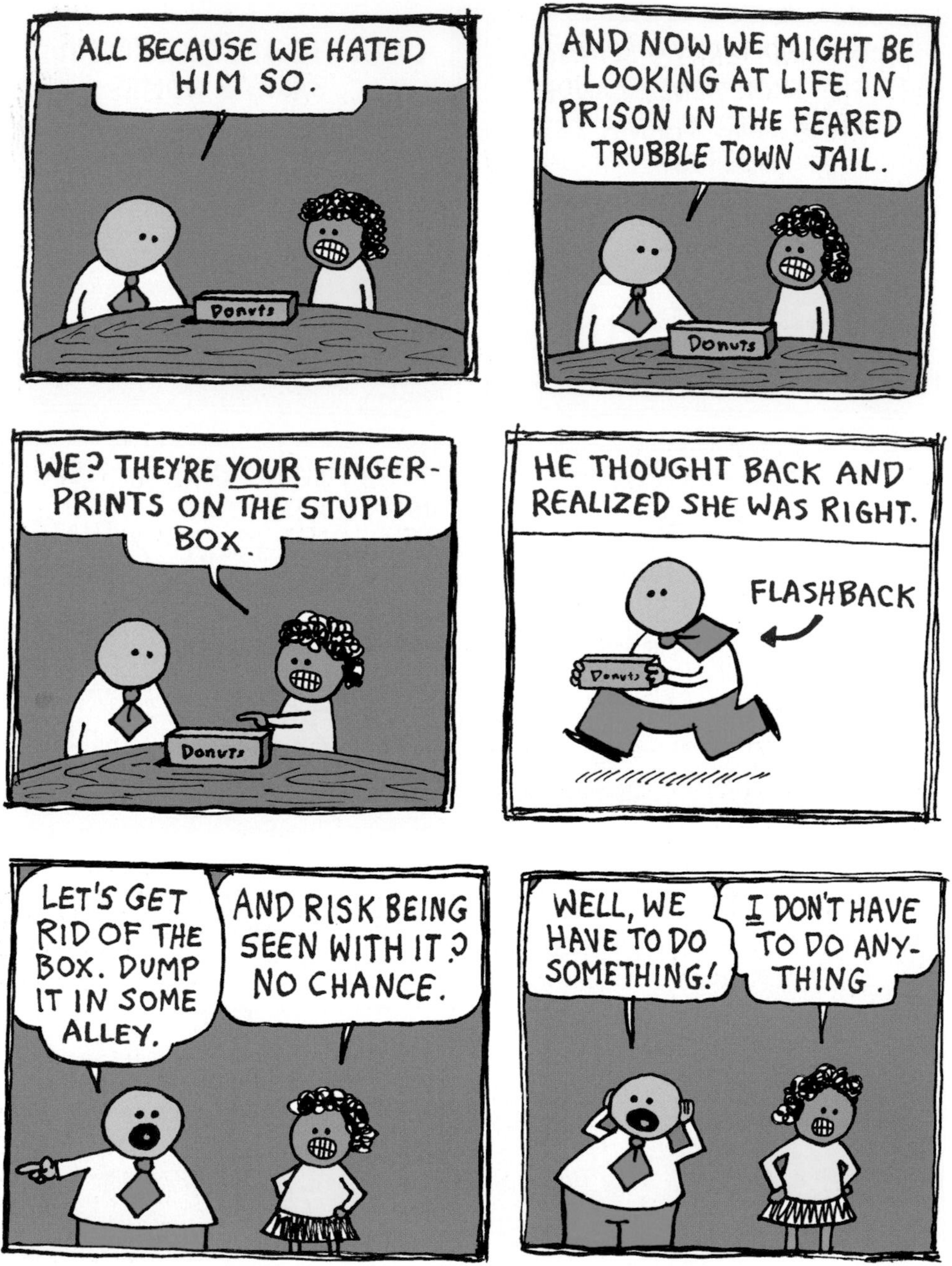

ALL BECAUSE WE HATED HIM SO.
AND NOW WE MIGHT BE LOOKING AT LIFE IN PRISON IN THE FEARED TRUBBLE TOWN JAIL.
Donuts
WE? THEY'RE YOUR FINGER-PRINTS ON THE STUPID BOX.
HE THOUGHT BACK AND REALIZED SHE WAS RIGHT.
FLASHBACK
LET'S GET RID OF THE BOX. DUMP IT IN SOME ALLEY.
AND RISK BEING SEEN WITH IT? NO CHANCE.
WELL, WE HAVE TO DO SOMETHING!
I DON'T HAVE TO DO ANY-THING.

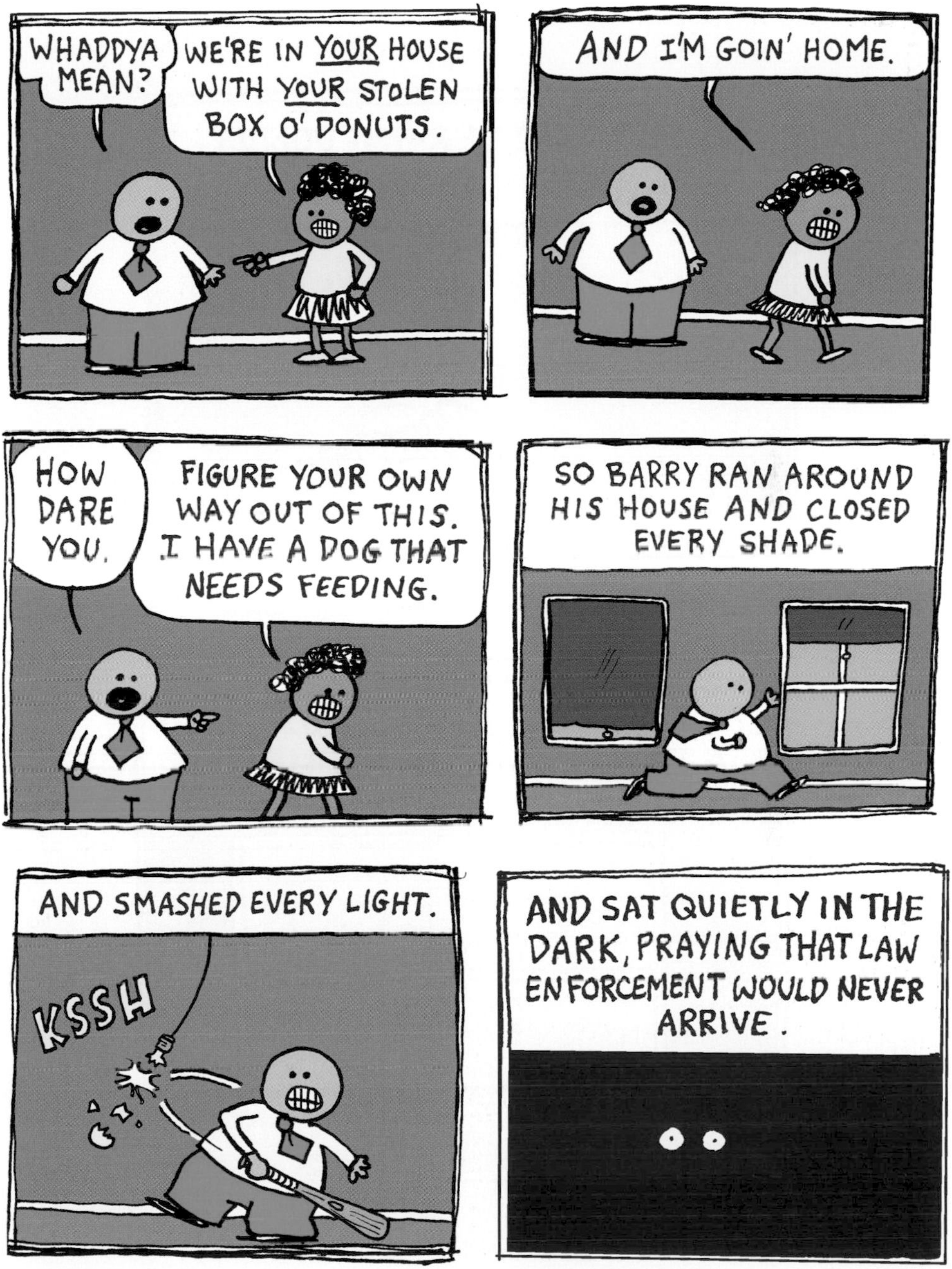
WHADDYA MEAN?
WE'RE IN YOUR HOUSE WITH YOUR STOLEN BOX O' DONUTS.
AND I'M GOIN' HOME.
HOW DARE YOU.
FIGURE YOUR OWN WAY OUT OF THIS. I HAVE A DOG THAT NEEDS FEEDING.
SO BARRY RAN AROUND HIS HOUSE AND CLOSED EVERY SHADE.
AND SMASHED EVERY LIGHT.
KSSH
AND SAT QUIETLY IN THE DARK, PRAYING THAT LAW ENFORCEMENT WOULD NEVER ARRIVE.

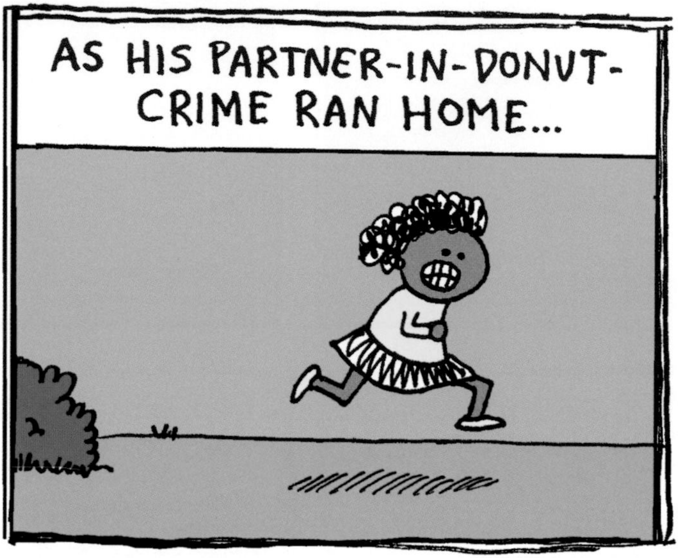
AS HIS PARTNER-IN-DONUT-CRIME RAN HOME...

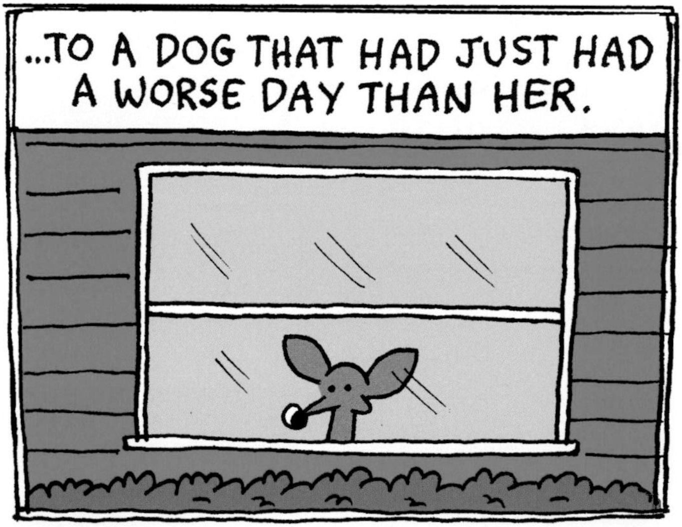
...TO A DOG THAT HAD JUST HAD A WORSE DAY THAN HER.

CHAPTER ONE-AFTER-THE-LAST-ONE

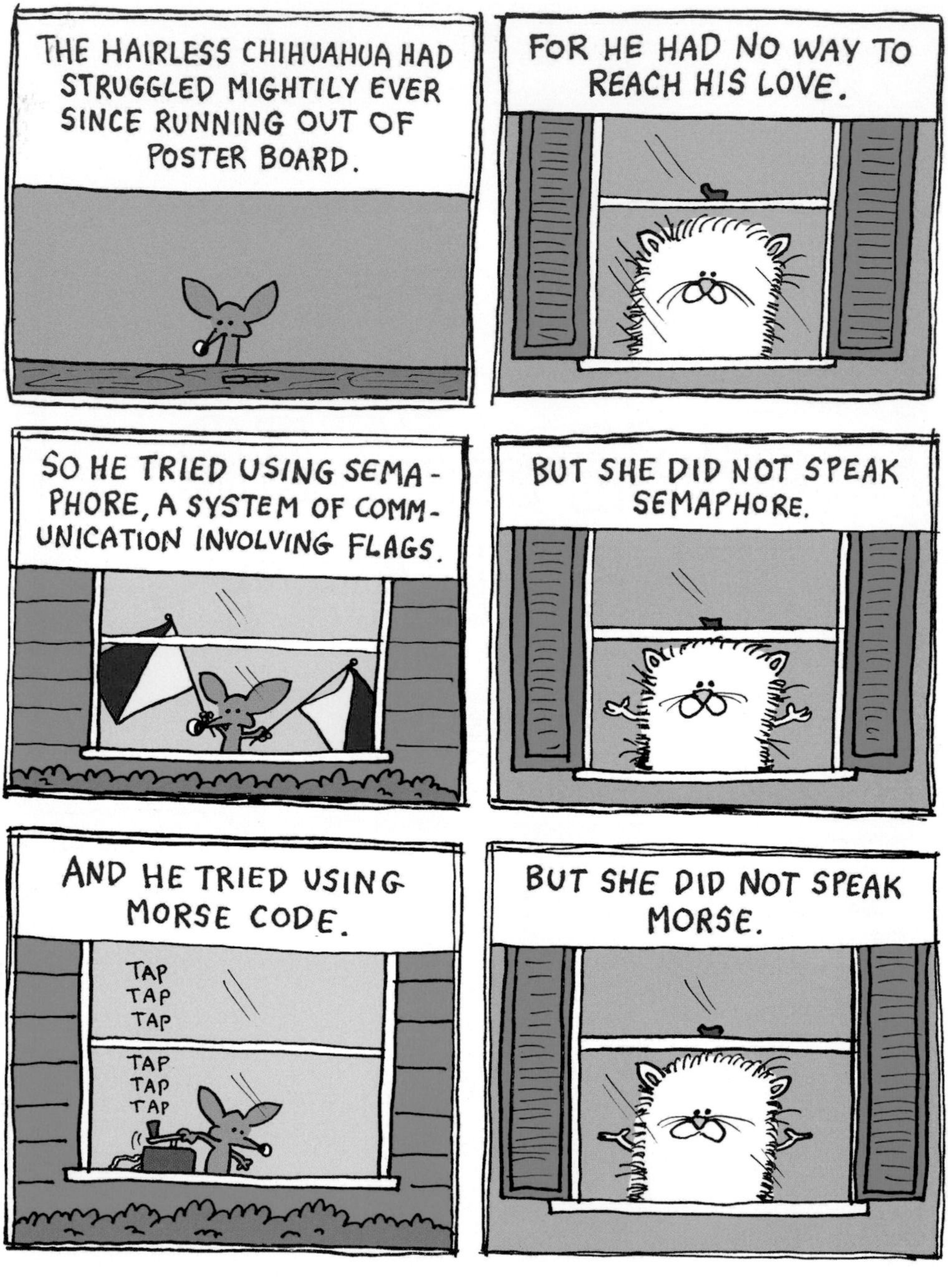
THE HAIRLESS CHIHUAHUA HAD STRUGGLED MIGHTILY EVER SINCE RUNNING OUT OF POSTER BOARD.
FOR HE HAD NO WAY TO REACH HIS LOVE.
SO HE TRIED USING SEMA-PHORE, A SYSTEM OF COMM-UNICATION INVOLVING FLAGS.
BUT SHE DID NOT SPEAK SEMAPHORE.
AND HE TRIED USING MORSE CODE.
TAP TAP TAP
TAP TAP TAP
BUT SHE DID NOT SPEAK MORSE.

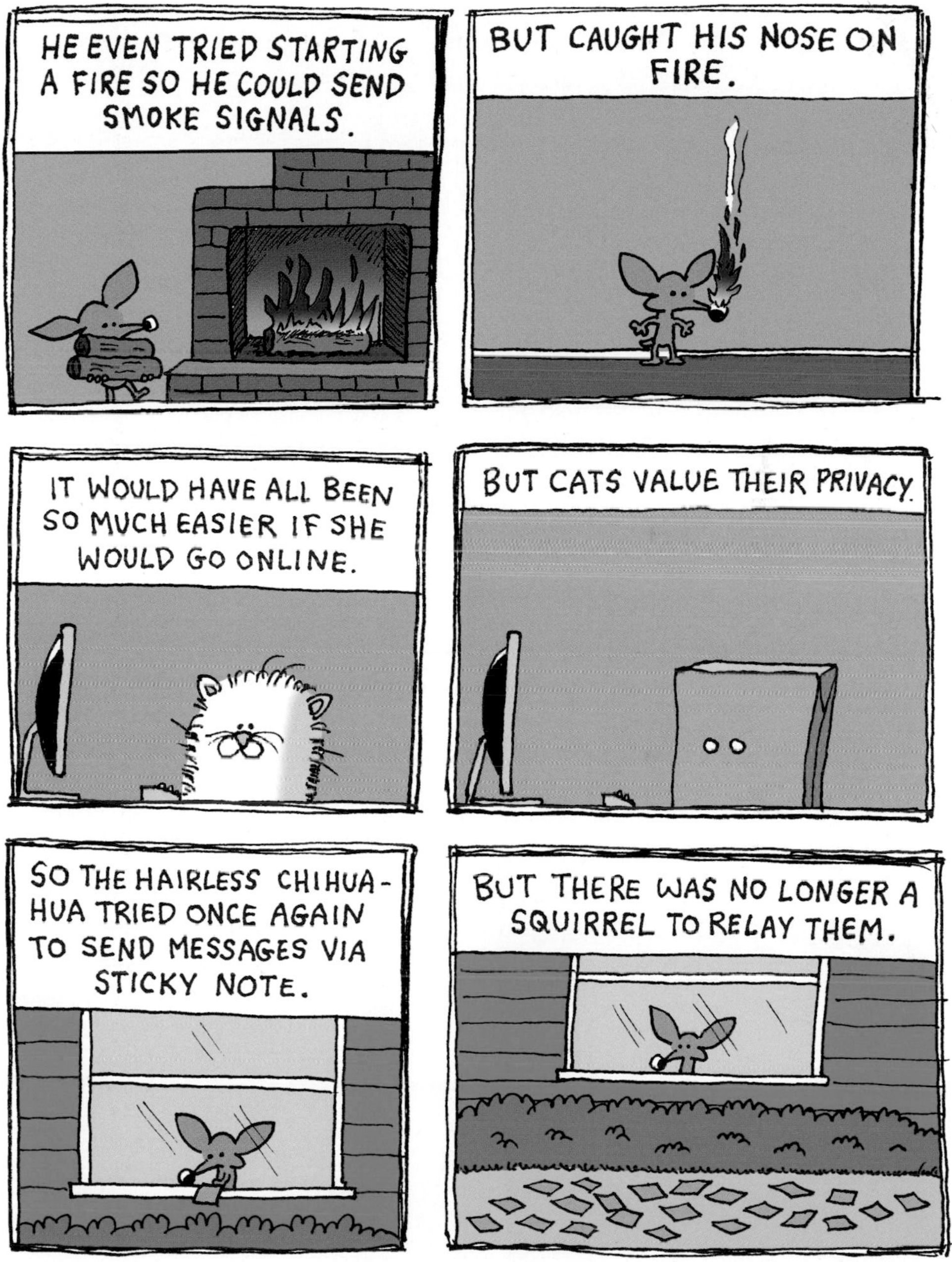
HE EVEN TRIED STARTING A FIRE SO HE COULD SEND SMOKE SIGNALS.
BUT CAUGHT HIS NOSE ON FIRE.
IT WOULD HAVE ALL BEEN SO MUCH EASIER IF SHE WOULD GO ONLINE.
BUT CATS VALUE THEIR PRIVACY.
SO THE HAIRLESS CHIHUA-HUA TRIED ONCE AGAIN TO SEND MESSAGES VIA STICKY NOTE.
BUT THERE WAS NO LONGER A SQUIRREL TO RELAY THEM.

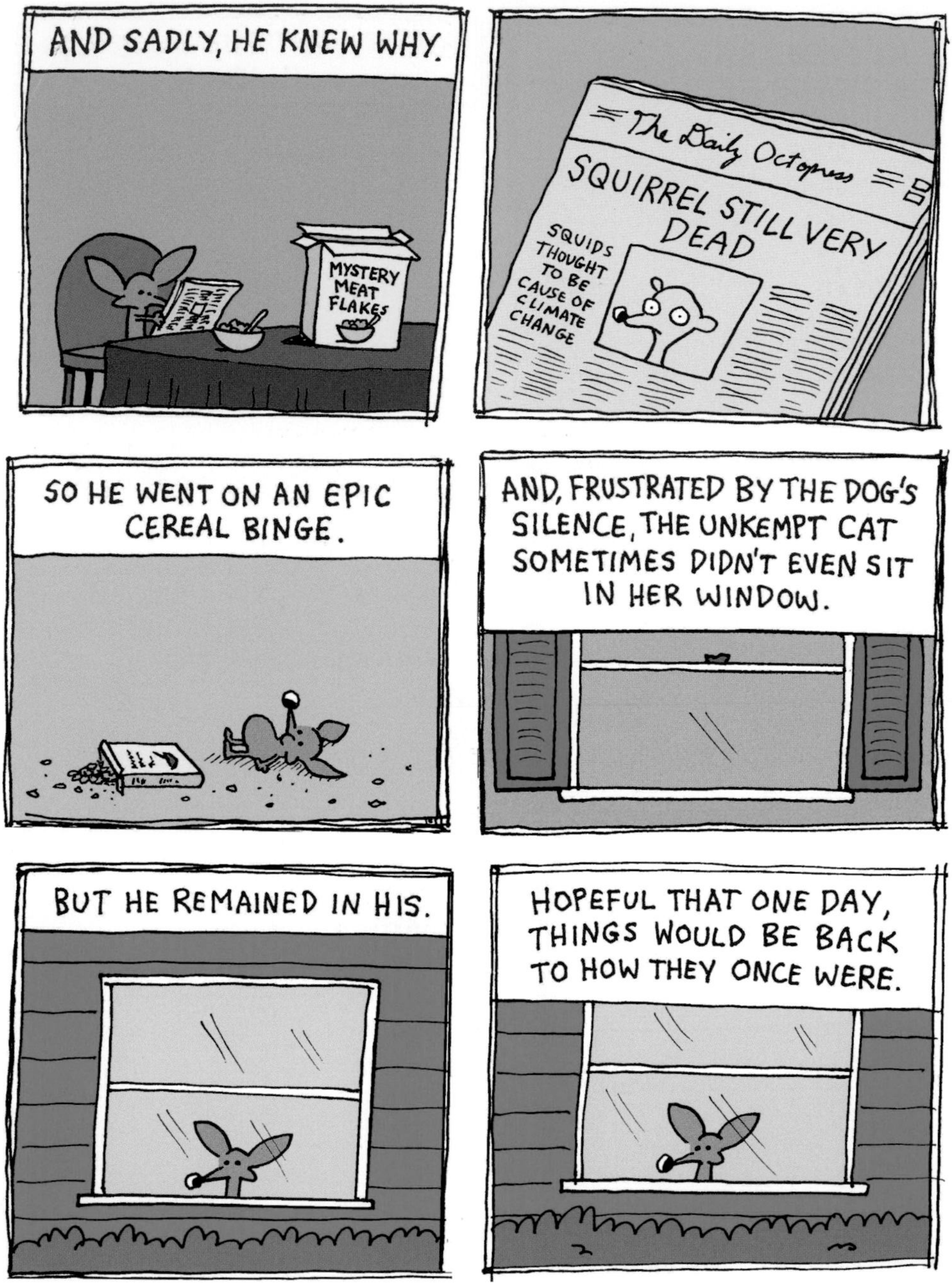
AND SADLY, HE KNEW WHY.
MYSTERY MEAT FLAKES
The Daily Octopus
SQUIRREL STILL VERY DEAD
SQUIDS THOUGHT TO BE CAUSE OF CLIMATE CHANGE
SO HE WENT ON AN EPIC CEREAL BINGE.
AND, FRUSTRATED BY THE DOG'S SILENCE, THE UNKEMPT CAT SOMETIMES DIDN'T EVEN SIT IN HER WINDOW.
BUT HE REMAINED IN HIS.
HOPEFUL THAT ONE DAY, THINGS WOULD BE BACK TO HOW THEY ONCE WERE.

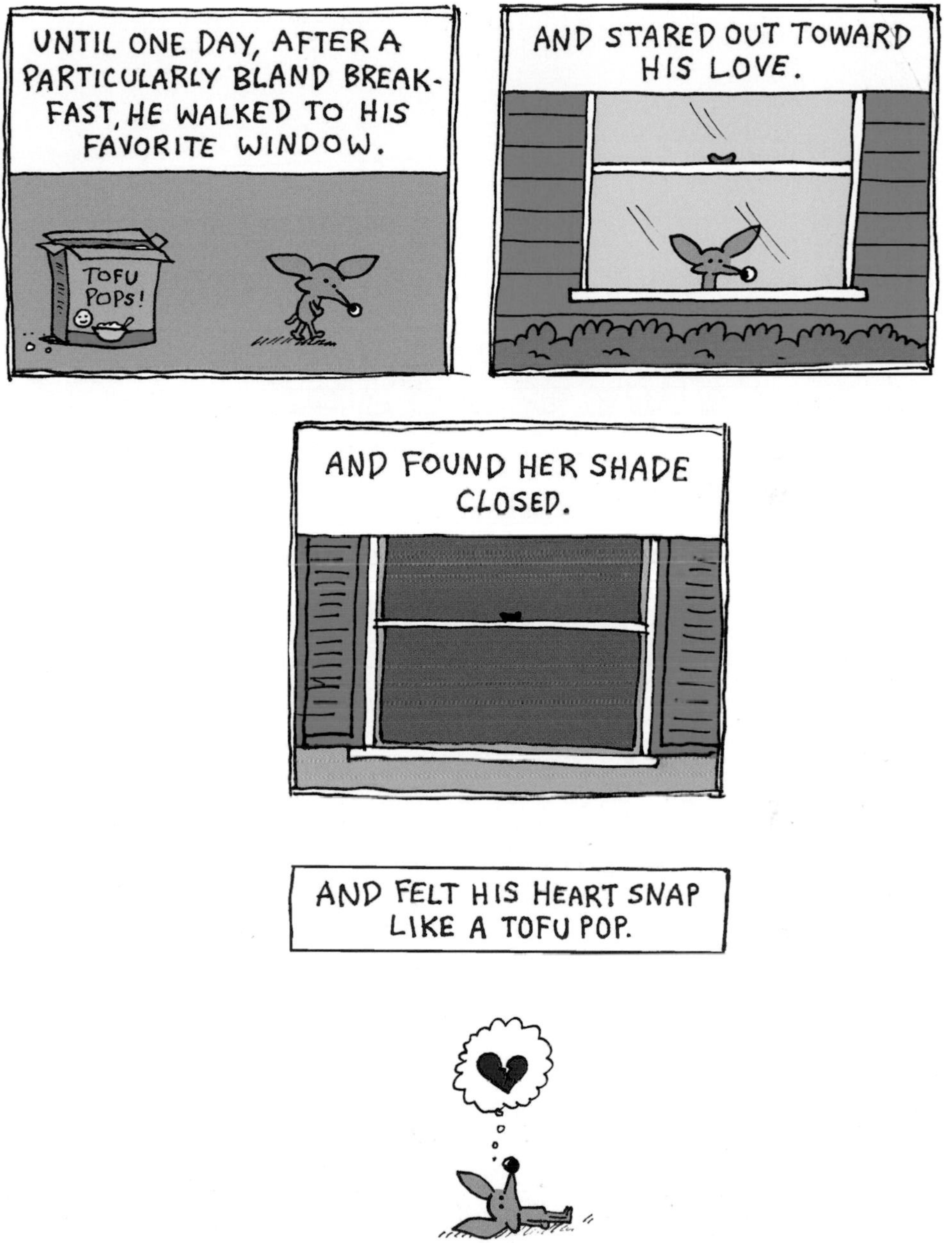
UNTIL ONE DAY, AFTER A PARTICULARLY BLAND BREAK-FAST, HE WALKED TO HIS FAVORITE WINDOW.
TOFU POPS!
AND STARED OUT TOWARD HIS LOVE.
AND FOUND HER SHADE CLOSED.
AND FELT HIS HEART SNAP LIKE A TOFU POP.

CHAPTER ANOTHER

IN WHICH...

THE PLOT,
TO THE DEGREE
IT EVEN EXISTS,
MOVETH
FORWARD

QUICKLY GROWING ACCUSTOMED TO LIVING HER LIFE UNDERGROUND, WENDY ELUDED THE MOB BY DUCKING INTO A MANHOLE.

RUNNING THROUGH THE TOWN'S UNDERGROUND PIPES.

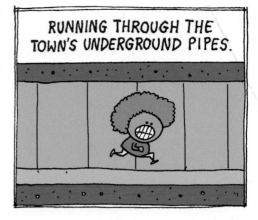

ARISING IN A NEIGHBORHOOD NEAR HER HOME.

AND THEN OBLIVIOUSLY PASSING THROUGH A SCATTERED ARRAY OF STICKY NOTES.

UNTIL SHE FINALLY ARRIVED HOME AND SAW NO ONE AROUND HER.

I WILL WALK CALMLY INSIDE AND ACT LIKE NOTHING HAS HAPPENED.

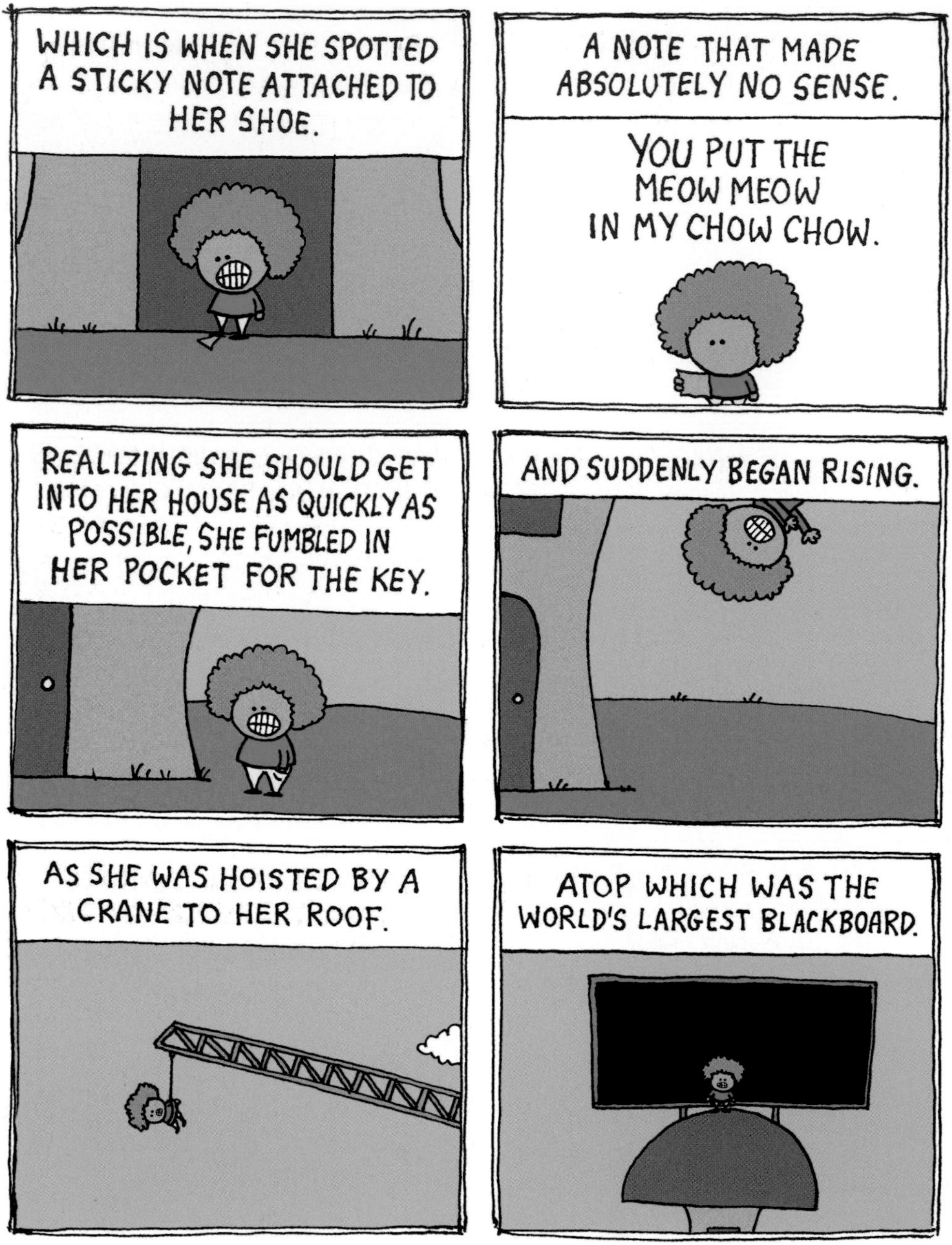
WHICH IS WHEN SHE SPOTTED A STICKY NOTE ATTACHED TO HER SHOE.
A NOTE THAT MADE ABSOLUTELY NO SENSE.
YOU PUT THE MEOW MEOW IN MY CHOW CHOW.
REALIZING SHE SHOULD GET INTO HER HOUSE AS QUICKLY AS POSSIBLE, SHE FUMBLED IN HER POCKET FOR THE KEY.
AND SUDDENLY BEGAN RISING.
AS SHE WAS HOISTED BY A CRANE TO HER ROOF.
ATOP WHICH WAS THE WORLD'S LARGEST BLACKBOARD.

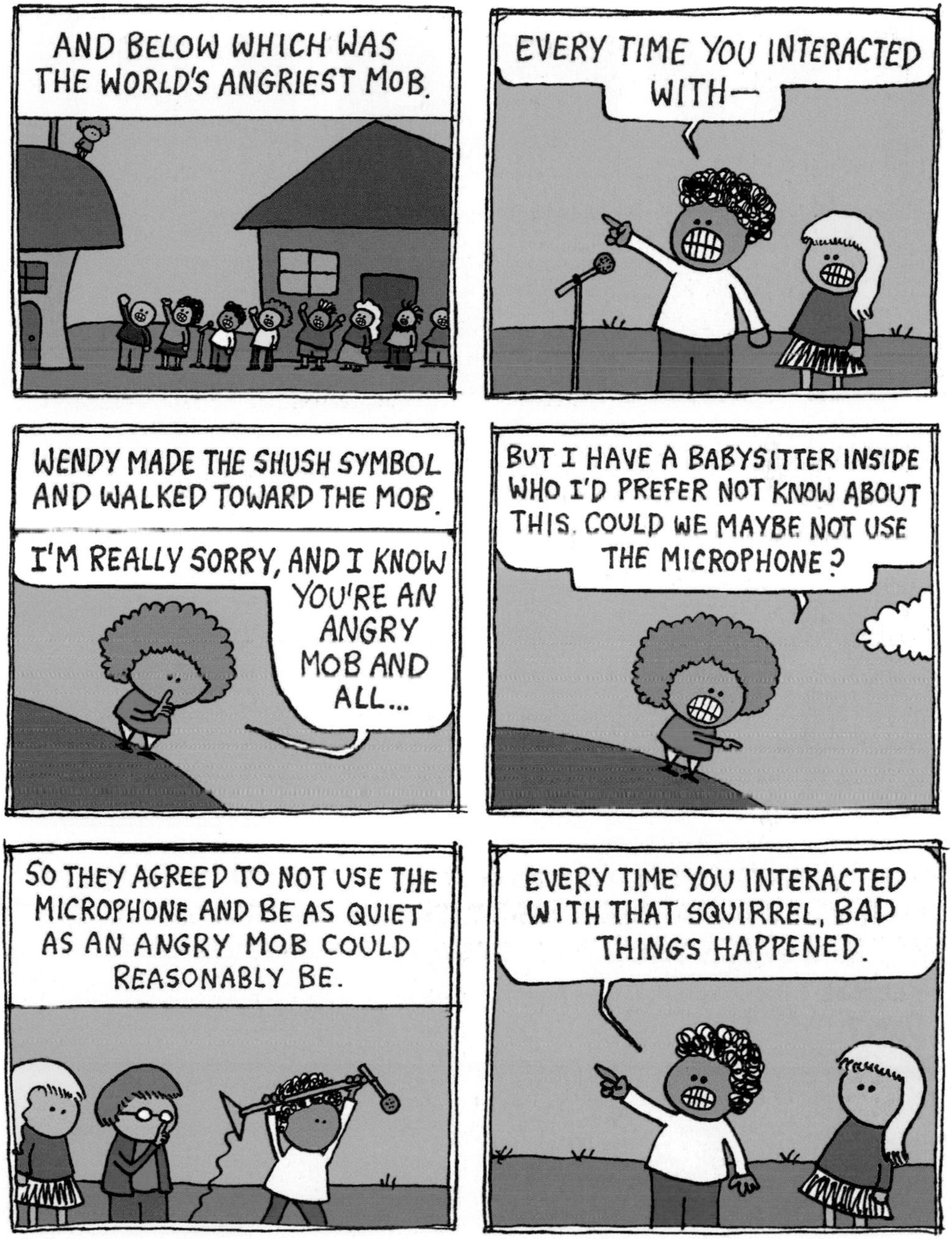
AND BELOW WHICH WAS THE WORLD'S ANGRIEST MOB.
EVERY TIME YOU INTERACTED WITH—
WENDY MADE THE SHUSH SYMBOL AND WALKED TOWARD THE MOB.
I'M REALLY SORRY, AND I KNOW YOU'RE AN ANGRY MOB AND ALL...
BUT I HAVE A BABYSITTER INSIDE WHO I'D PREFER NOT KNOW ABOUT THIS. COULD WE MAYBE NOT USE THE MICROPHONE?
SO THEY AGREED TO NOT USE THE MICROPHONE AND BE AS QUIET AS AN ANGRY MOB COULD REASONABLY BE.
EVERY TIME YOU INTERACTED WITH THAT SQUIRREL, BAD THINGS HAPPENED.

YEAH

AND YOU NEED TO PAY A PRICE!

AND SUDDENLY FEARFUL THAT THE PRICE WOULD BE THEM TELLING HER FATHER WHAT HAD HAPPENED, WENDY MADE A REASONED ARGUMENT.

PLEASE DON'T DO IT. PLEASE DON'T DO IT. PLEASE DON'T DO IT. PLEASE DON'T DO IT. PLEASE DON'T DO IT. PLEASE DON'T DO IT. PLEASE DON'T DO IT. PLEASE DON'T DO IT. PLEASE DON'T DO IT. PLEASE DON'T

UH... CAN WE SAY THE PUNISH-MENT FIRST?

SORRY.

YOU WILL WRITE "SQUIRRELS ARE NOT OUR FRIENDS" ON THE BLACKBOARD BEHIND YOU INFINITY TIMES.

AND HEARING THAT SPENDING INFINITY ON HER ROOF WAS HER ONLY PUNISHMENT, WENDY WAS RELIEVED.

BUT RAISED ONE POINT OF CLARIFICATION.

IF I MAY, I'M AFRAID I DON'T KNOW HOW TO SPELL "SQUIRREL."

WHAT IF YOU JUST WRITE "CHA-CHA"? IT'S MY FAVORITE DANCE.

AND SO, AS WENDY BEGAN HER PUNISHMENT, THE ANGRY MOB DISPERSED.

CHA-CHA CHA-CHA CHA-CH

AND OUT OF THEIR HOLES ROSE THE MOLES.

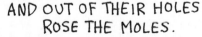

CHAPTER EIGHTEEN

IN WHICH...

WE GUESS THAT THAT'S THE CORRECT CHAPTER NUMBER

THE HAIRLESS CHIHUAHUA'S DESCENT INTO BAD MOODERY WAS SYMBOLIC OF WHAT WAS HAPPENING THROUGHOUT TRUBBLE.

FROM THE SCARED DONUT FELON...

...TO NUTMAN, STILL TOO WOOZY TO ARISE...

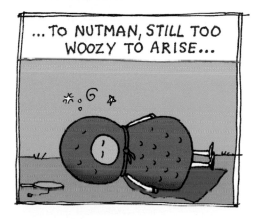

...TO THE SQUIRREL COWERING IN THE DONUT BOX...

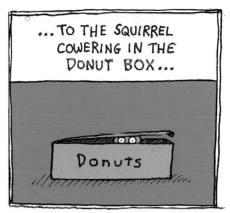

...TO THE STATUE OF THAT SQUIRREL THAT COULD BANKRUPT THE TOWN FOR THE NEXT TWO HUNDRED YEARS...

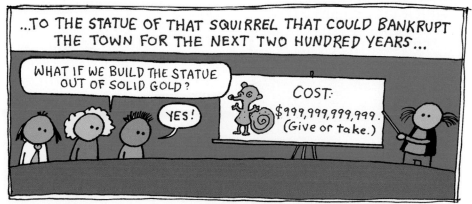

WHAT IF WE BUILD THE STATUE OUT OF SOLID GOLD?

YES!

COST:
$999,999,999,999.
(Give or take.)

... THINGS IN TRUBBLE WERE QUITE THE MESS.

WELCOME TO TRUBBLE. (Don't hope for much.)

AND THE MOLES OF M.O.T.H.E.R. COULD NO LONGER SIT SILENT.

MYRTLE! GIRDLE! LET'S SAVE OUR CITY!

AND SO THEY CAME UP WITH A BRAND NEW ORGANIZATION.

F.A.T.H.E.R.

FIX ANYTHING THAT HURTS EGG ROLLS

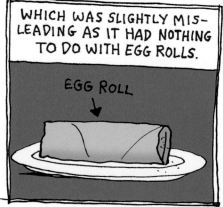

WHICH WAS SLIGHTLY MIS-LEADING AS IT HAD NOTHING TO DO WITH EGG ROLLS.

EGG ROLL

THEY JUST NEEDED WORDS THAT STARTED WITH AN "E" AND AN "R", BECAUSE THEY WERE TRYING VERY HARD TO SPELL "FATHER."

ENERGETIC RAISINS?

174

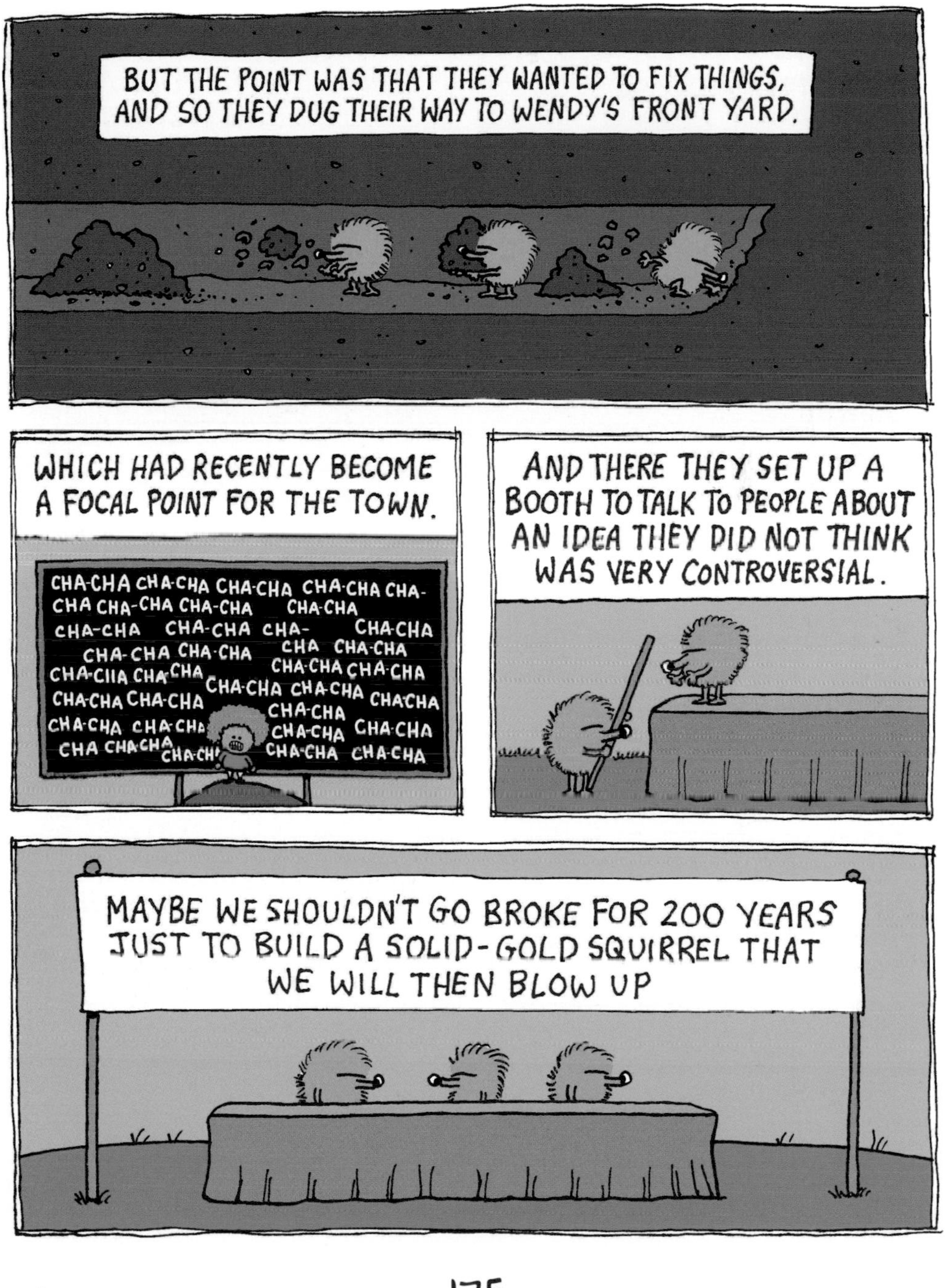
BUT THE POINT WAS THAT THEY WANTED TO FIX THINGS, AND SO THEY DUG THEIR WAY TO WENDY'S FRONT YARD.
WHICH HAD RECENTLY BECOME A FOCAL POINT FOR THE TOWN.
CHA-CHA CHA-CHA CHA-CHA CHA-CHA CHA-CHA CHA-CHA CHA-CHA CHA-CHA
CHA-CHA CHA-CHA CHA-CHA CHA-CHA
CHA-CHA CHA-CHA CHA-CHA CHA-CHA
CHA-CHA CHA-CHA CHA-CHA CHA-CHA CHA-CHA CHA-CHA CHA-CHA
CHA-CHA CHA-CHA CHA-CHA CHA-CHA CHA-CHA
CHA-CHA CHA-CHA CHA-CHA CHA-CHA CHA-CHA
CHA CHA-CHA CHA-CH CHA-CHA CHA-CHA
AND THERE THEY SET UP A BOOTH TO TALK TO PEOPLE ABOUT AN IDEA THEY DID NOT THINK WAS VERY CONTROVERSIAL.
MAYBE WE SHOULDN'T GO BROKE FOR 200 YEARS JUST TO BUILD A SOLID-GOLD SQUIRREL THAT WE WILL THEN BLOW UP

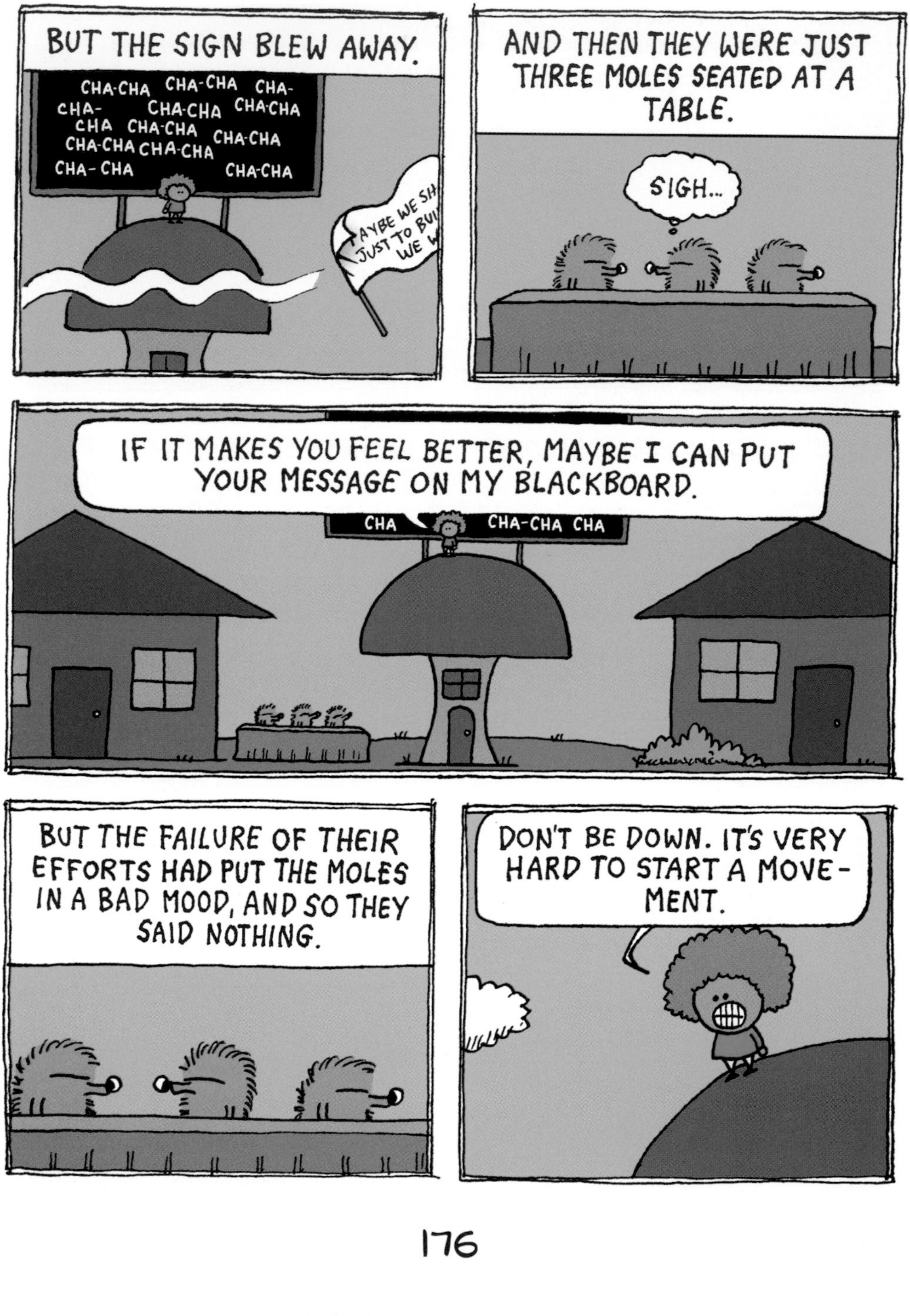
BUT THE SIGN BLEW AWAY.
CHA-CHA CHA-CHA CHA- CHA- CHA-CHA CHA-CHA CHA CHA-CHA CHA-CHA CHA-CHA CHA-CHA CHA-CHA CHA- CHA CHA-CHA
AYBE WE SH JUST TO BU WE W
AND THEN THEY WERE JUST THREE MOLES SEATED AT A TABLE.
SIGH...
IF IT MAKES YOU FEEL BETTER, MAYBE I CAN PUT YOUR MESSAGE ON MY BLACKBOARD.
CHA CHA-CHA CHA
BUT THE FAILURE OF THEIR EFFORTS HAD PUT THE MOLES IN A BAD MOOD, AND SO THEY SAID NOTHING.
DON'T BE DOWN. IT'S VERY HARD TO START A MOVE-MENT.

IF IT WASN'T FOR YOU, WE WOULDN'T <u>NEED</u> A MOVEMENT.

WHICH MADE WENDY FEEL BAD. AND SO SHE ERASED HER BLACKBOARD.

CHA-C' CHA

GIANT ERASER

AND WROTE AN INSPIRATIONAL MESSAGE.

HOP

HOP WHERE?

IT'S SUPPOSED TO SAY "HOPE." I JUST RAN OUT OF ROOM.

AND SUDDENLY FEELING HOP-LESS, THE MOLES BEGAN DIGGING A NEW HOLE.

WAIT. PLEASE. DON'T DISAPPEAR AGAIN.

GRUNT GRUNT

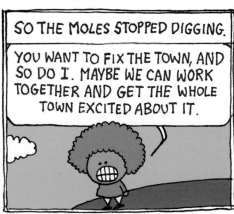

SO THE MOLES STOPPED DIGGING.

YOU WANT TO FIX THE TOWN, AND SO DO I. MAYBE WE CAN WORK TOGETHER AND GET THE WHOLE TOWN EXCITED ABOUT IT.

BUT THE TOWN WAS ALREADY EXCITED.

WOOOOOHOOOOOO

WHAT WAS THAT?

SOME RALLY. THEY WALKED BY EARLIER.

HOW MANY PEOPLE?

JUST A FEW.

AND SO THE MOLES WALKED TOWARD THOSE PEOPLE.

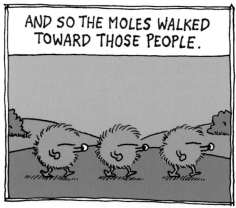

AND THERE WERE MORE THAN A FEW.

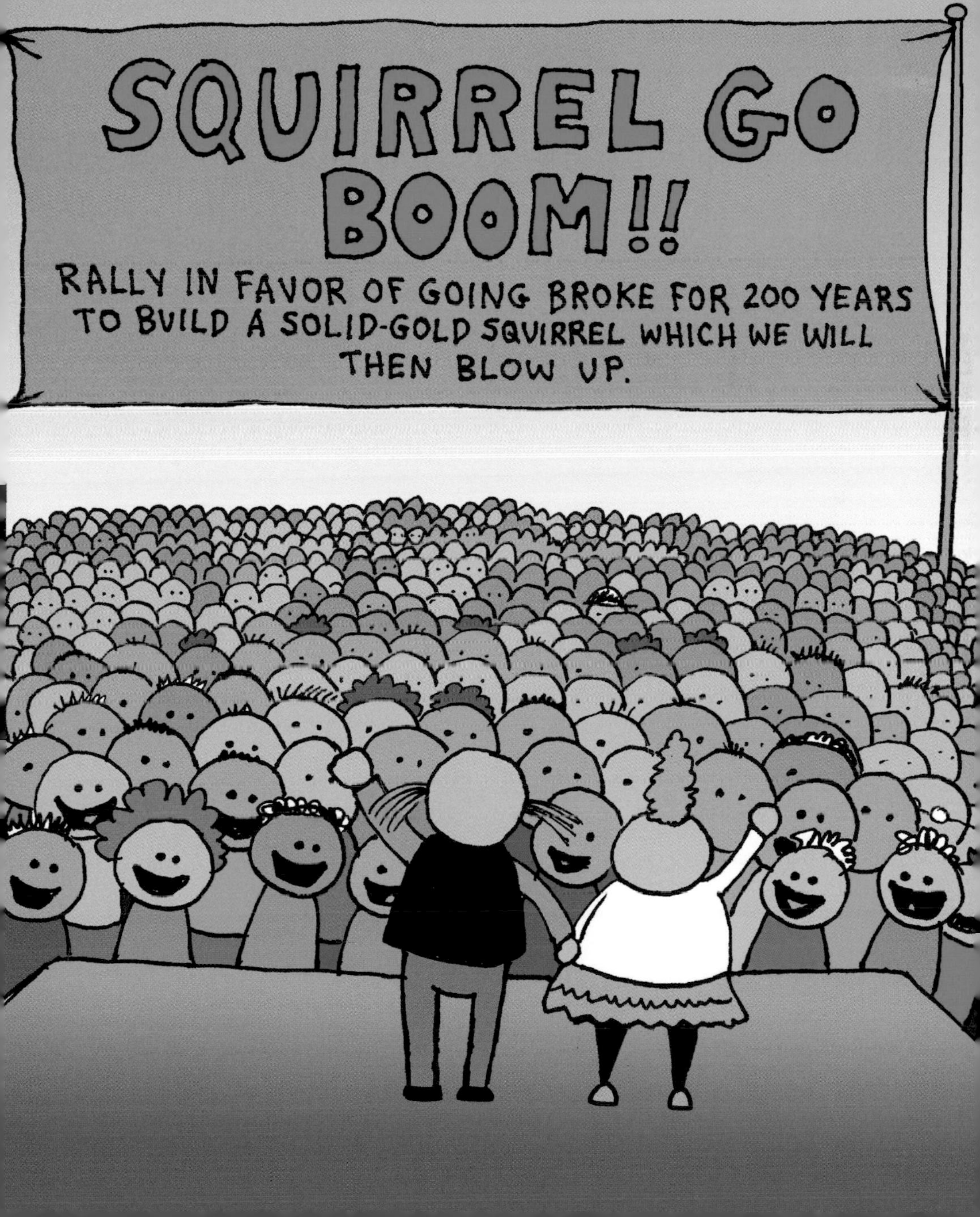
SQUIRREL GO BOOM!!
RALLY IN FAVOR OF GOING BROKE FOR 200 YEARS TO BUILD A SOLID-GOLD SQUIRREL WHICH WE WILL THEN BLOW UP.

CHAPTER CHAPTER

IN WHICH...

WE GET REPETITIVE

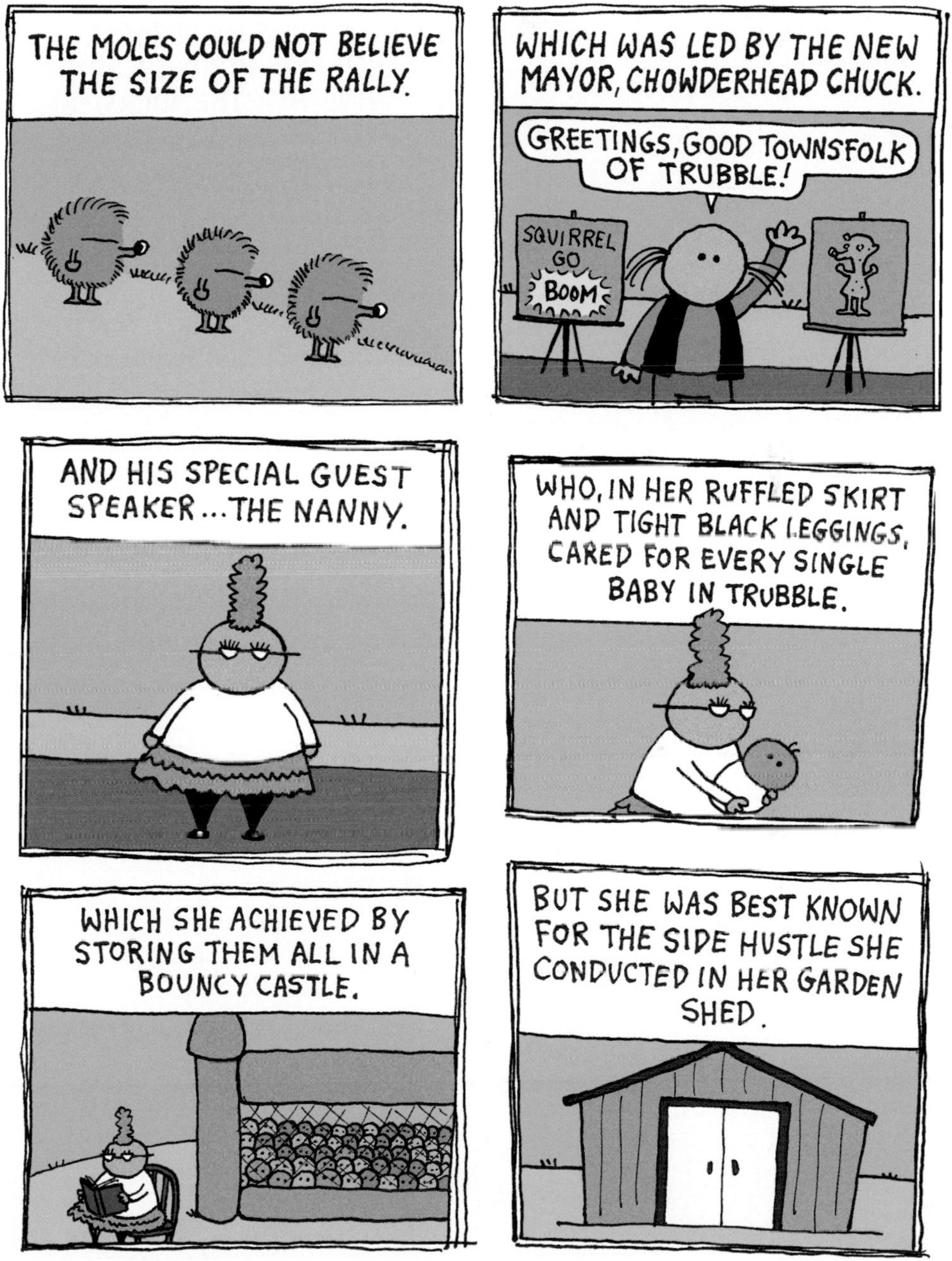
THE MOLES COULD NOT BELIEVE THE SIZE OF THE RALLY.
WHICH WAS LED BY THE NEW MAYOR, CHOWDERHEAD CHUCK.
GREETINGS, GOOD TOWNSFOLK OF TRUBBLE!
SQUIRREL GO BOOM
AND HIS SPECIAL GUEST SPEAKER ... THE NANNY.
WHO, IN HER RUFFLED SKIRT AND TIGHT BLACK LEGGINGS, CARED FOR EVERY SINGLE BABY IN TRUBBLE.
WHICH SHE ACHIEVED BY STORING THEM ALL IN A BOUNCY CASTLE.
BUT SHE WAS BEST KNOWN FOR THE SIDE HUSTLE SHE CONDUCTED IN HER GARDEN SHED.

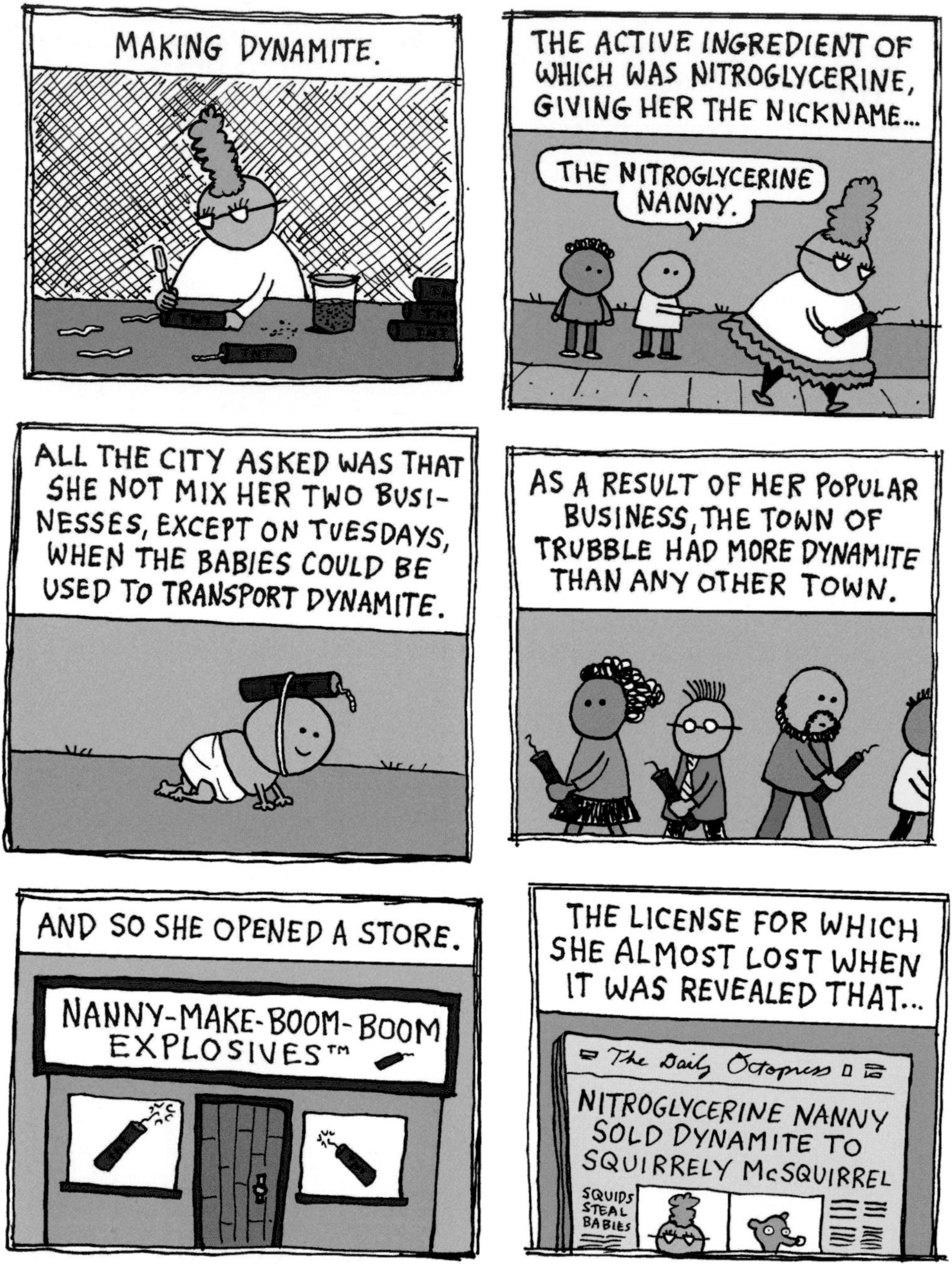
MAKING DYNAMITE.
THE ACTIVE INGREDIENT OF WHICH WAS NITROGLYCERINE, GIVING HER THE NICKNAME...
THE NITROGLYCERINE NANNY.
ALL THE CITY ASKED WAS THAT SHE NOT MIX HER TWO BUSI-NESSES, EXCEPT ON TUESDAYS, WHEN THE BABIES COULD BE USED TO TRANSPORT DYNAMITE.
AS A RESULT OF HER POPULAR BUSINESS, THE TOWN OF TRUBBLE HAD MORE DYNAMITE THAN ANY OTHER TOWN.
AND SO SHE OPENED A STORE.
NANNY-MAKE-BOOM-BOOM EXPLOSIVES™
THE LICENSE FOR WHICH SHE ALMOST LOST WHEN IT WAS REVEALED THAT...
The Daily Octopress
NITROGLYCERINE NANNY SOLD DYNAMITE TO SQUIRRELY McSQUIRREL
SQUIDS STEAL BABIES

BUT SHE GOT TO KEEP THE LICENSE BY ARGUING...

I'LL JUST STOP CARING FOR YOUR ANNOYING KIDS.

SO WHEN IT CAME TO DECIDING WHO WOULD BLOW UP THE GIANT SQUIRREL STATUE, THERE WAS REALLY NO DOUBT.

NITROGLYCERINE NANNY!

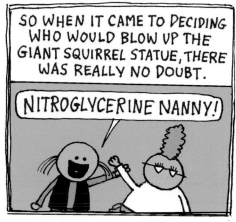

I WILL BLOW THAT SQUIRREL UP GOOD! REAL GOOD!!

WHICH MADE ZERO SENSE TO F.A.T.H.E.R., WHO THOUGHT IT KNEW BEST.

THEY'RE COMMEMORATING A SQUIRREL WHO THEY SAY BLEW UP THEIR TOWN.

WHO THEY THEN CHASED TO HIS UNTIMELY DEATH.

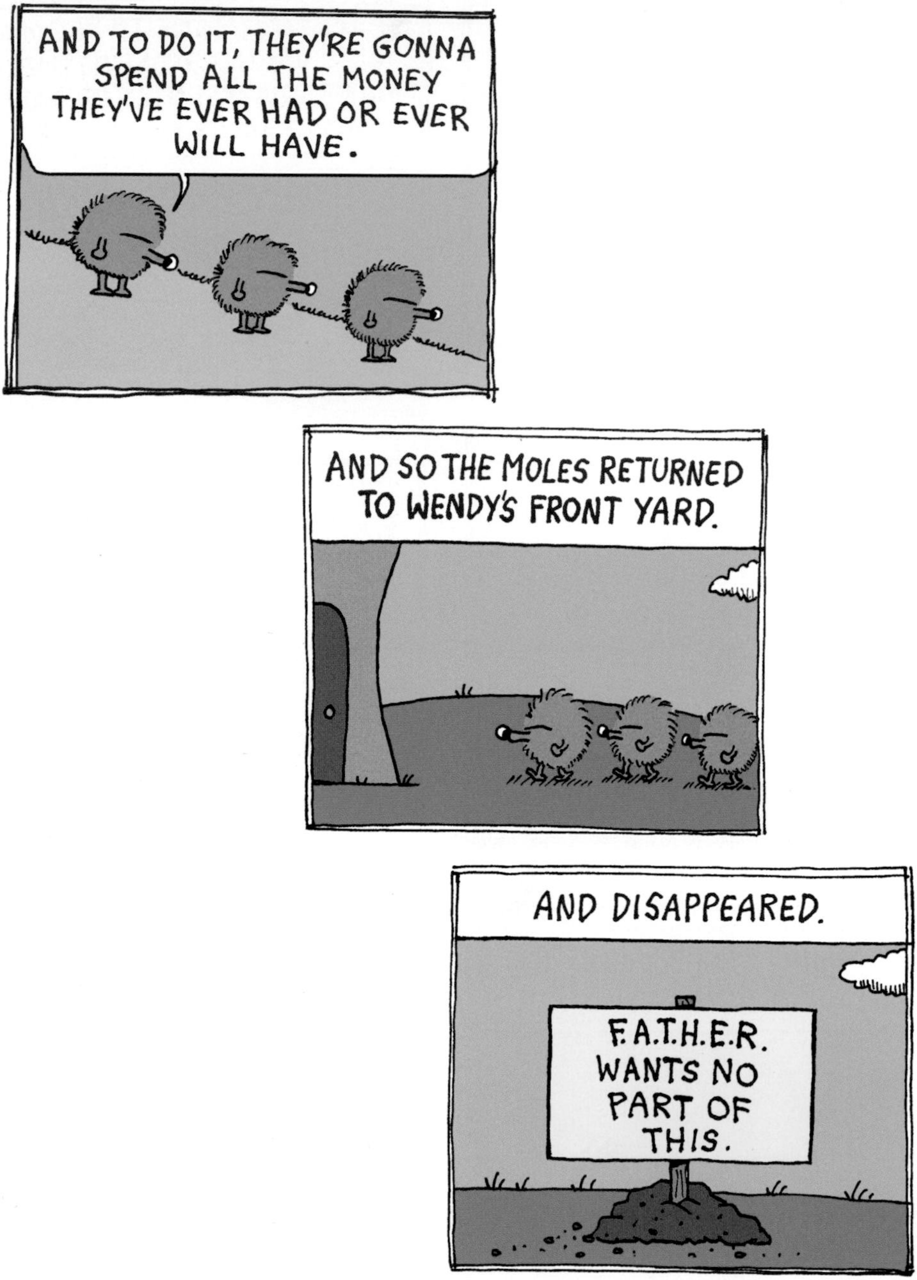
AND TO DO IT, THEY'RE GONNA SPEND ALL THE MONEY THEY'VE EVER HAD OR EVER WILL HAVE.
AND SO THE MOLES RETURNED TO WENDY'S FRONT YARD.
AND DISAPPEARED.
F.A.T.H.E.R. WANTS NO PART OF THIS.

CHAPTER EIGHTEEN

PLUS ONE EQUALS SOMETHING

IN WHICH...

WE SHOW WE CAN ALMOST COUNT

WENDY HAD NEVER FELT MORE ALONE.

FOR SHE WANTED DESPERATELY TO FIX HER TOWN BEFORE HER FATHER GOT HOME.

USED TO BE A CAFÉ

BUT WITH THE MOLES ONCE AGAIN UNDERGROUND, SHE WOULD HAVE TO DO IT ALONE.

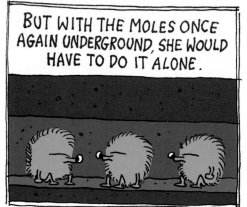

FROM A ROOF.

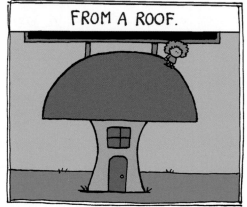

AND SO SHE DECIDED TO CREATE AN UPLIFTING TOWN SLOGAN, PROUDLY INCORPORATING HER MOTHER'S DESIGN OF THE HOUSE.

LET US BE LIKE A MUSHROOM RISING FROM THE ASHES.

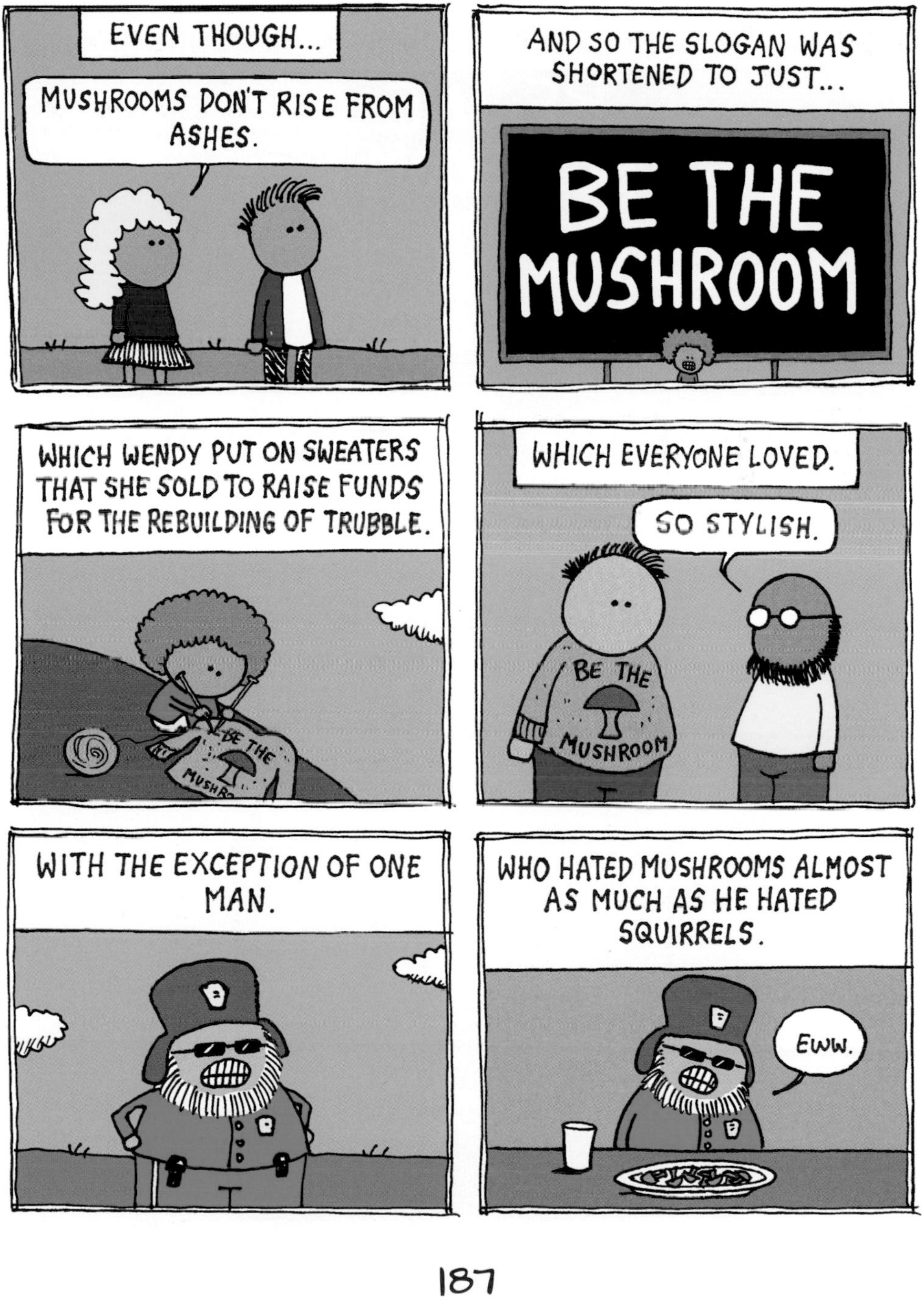
EVEN THOUGH...
MUSHROOMS DON'T RISE FROM ASHES.
AND SO THE SLOGAN WAS SHORTENED TO JUST...
BE THE MUSHROOM
WHICH WENDY PUT ON SWEATERS THAT SHE SOLD TO RAISE FUNDS FOR THE REBUILDING OF TRUBBLE.
BE THE
WHICH EVERYONE LOVED.
SO STYLISH.
BE THE MUSHROOM
WITH THE EXCEPTION OF ONE MAN.
WHO HATED MUSHROOMS ALMOST AS MUCH AS HE HATED SQUIRRELS.
EWW.

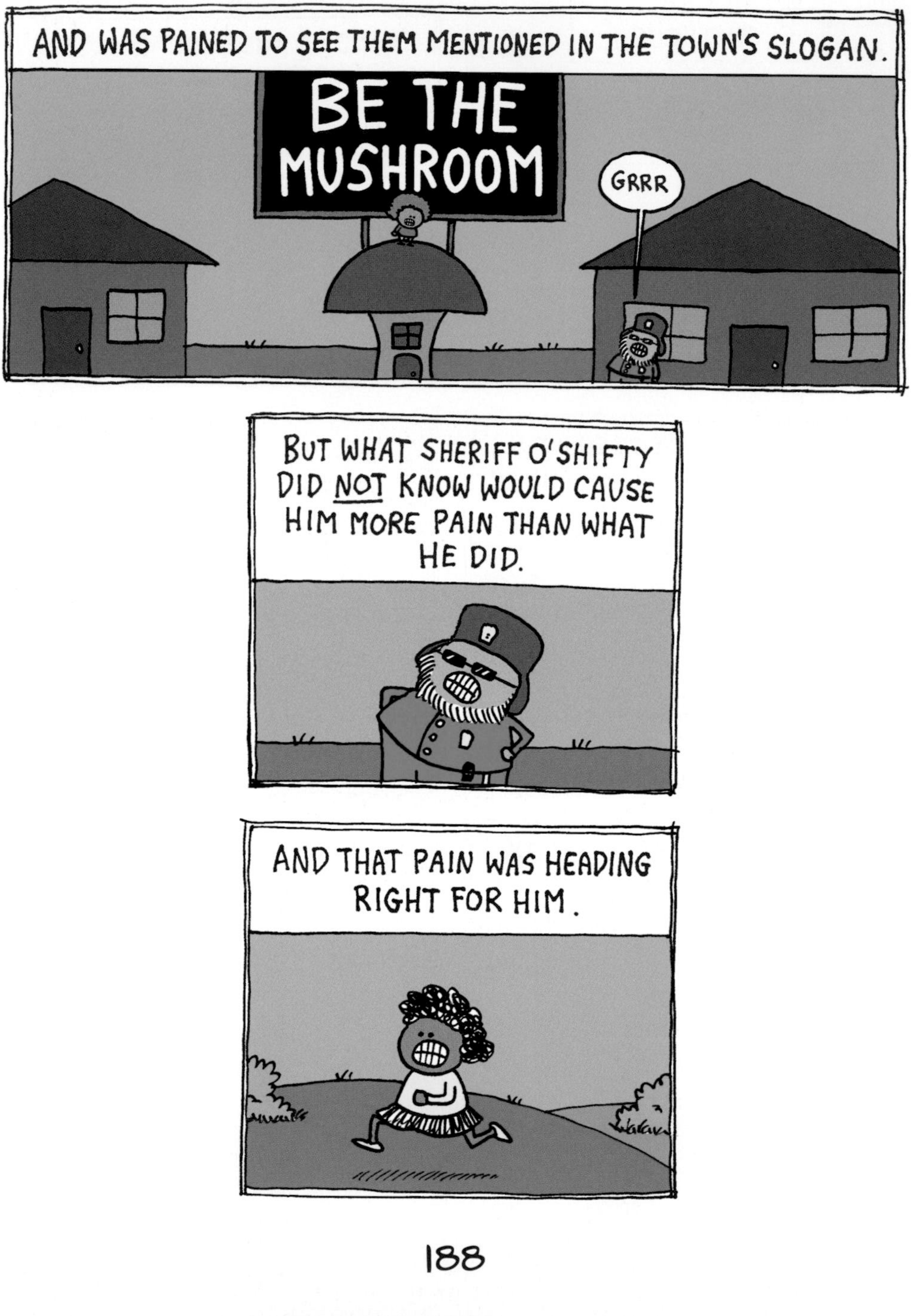
AND WAS PAINED TO SEE THEM MENTIONED IN THE TOWN'S SLOGAN.
BE THE MUSHROOM
GRRR
BUT WHAT SHERIFF O'SHIFTY DID NOT KNOW WOULD CAUSE HIM MORE PAIN THAN WHAT HE DID.
AND THAT PAIN WAS HEADING RIGHT FOR HIM.

CHAPTER SNAPPED HER

WHICH...

RHYMES NICELY AND TELLS YOU THAT A FEMALE CHARACTER IS ABOUT TO SNAP

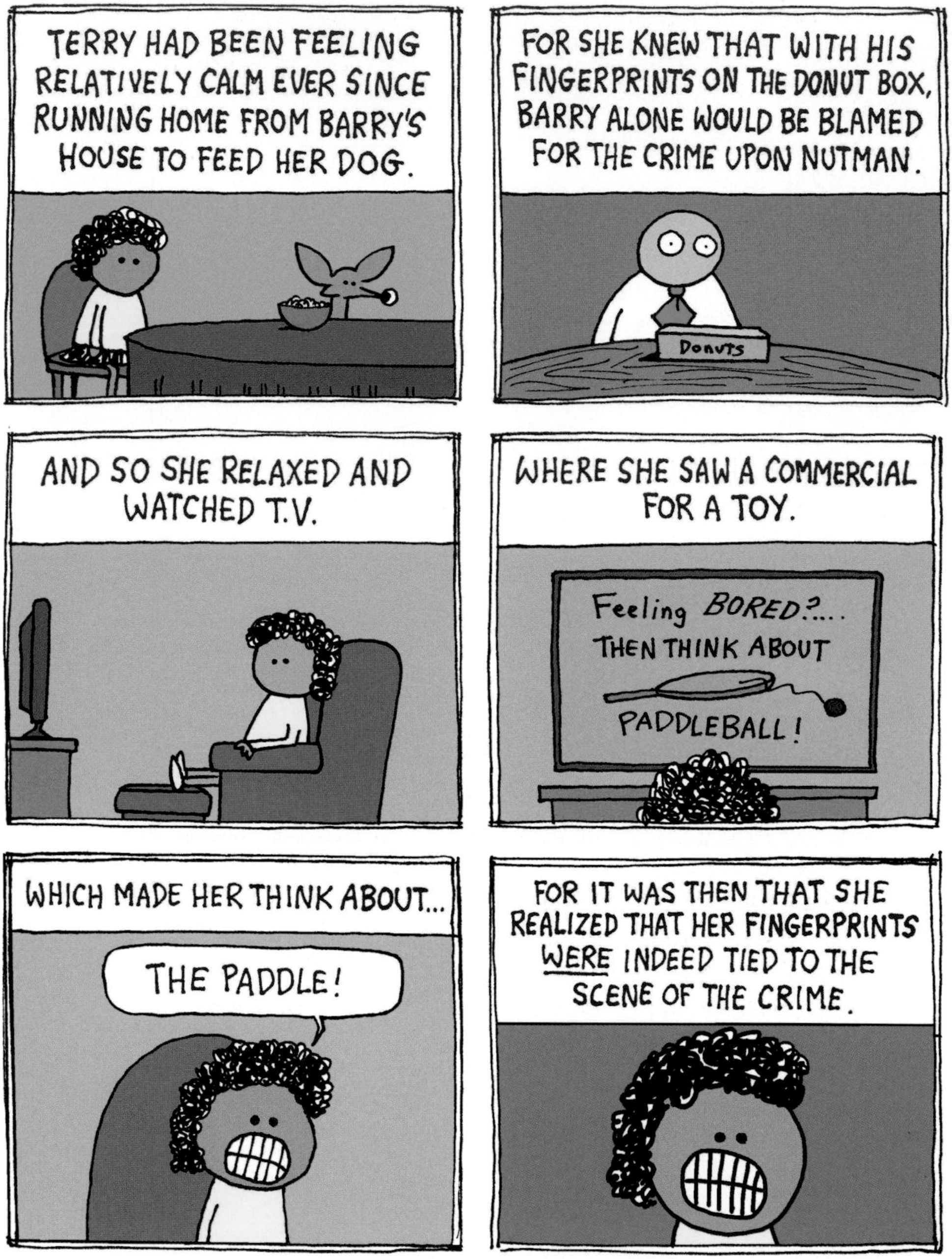
TERRY HAD BEEN FEELING RELATIVELY CALM EVER SINCE RUNNING HOME FROM BARRY'S HOUSE TO FEED HER DOG.
FOR SHE KNEW THAT WITH HIS FINGERPRINTS ON THE DONUT BOX, BARRY ALONE WOULD BE BLAMED FOR THE CRIME UPON NUTMAN.
DONUTS
AND SO SHE RELAXED AND WATCHED T.V.
WHERE SHE SAW A COMMERCIAL FOR A TOY.
Feeling BORED?....
THEN THINK ABOUT
PADDLEBALL!
WHICH MADE HER THINK ABOUT...
THE PADDLE!
FOR IT WAS THEN THAT SHE REALIZED THAT HER FINGERPRINTS WERE INDEED TIED TO THE SCENE OF THE CRIME.

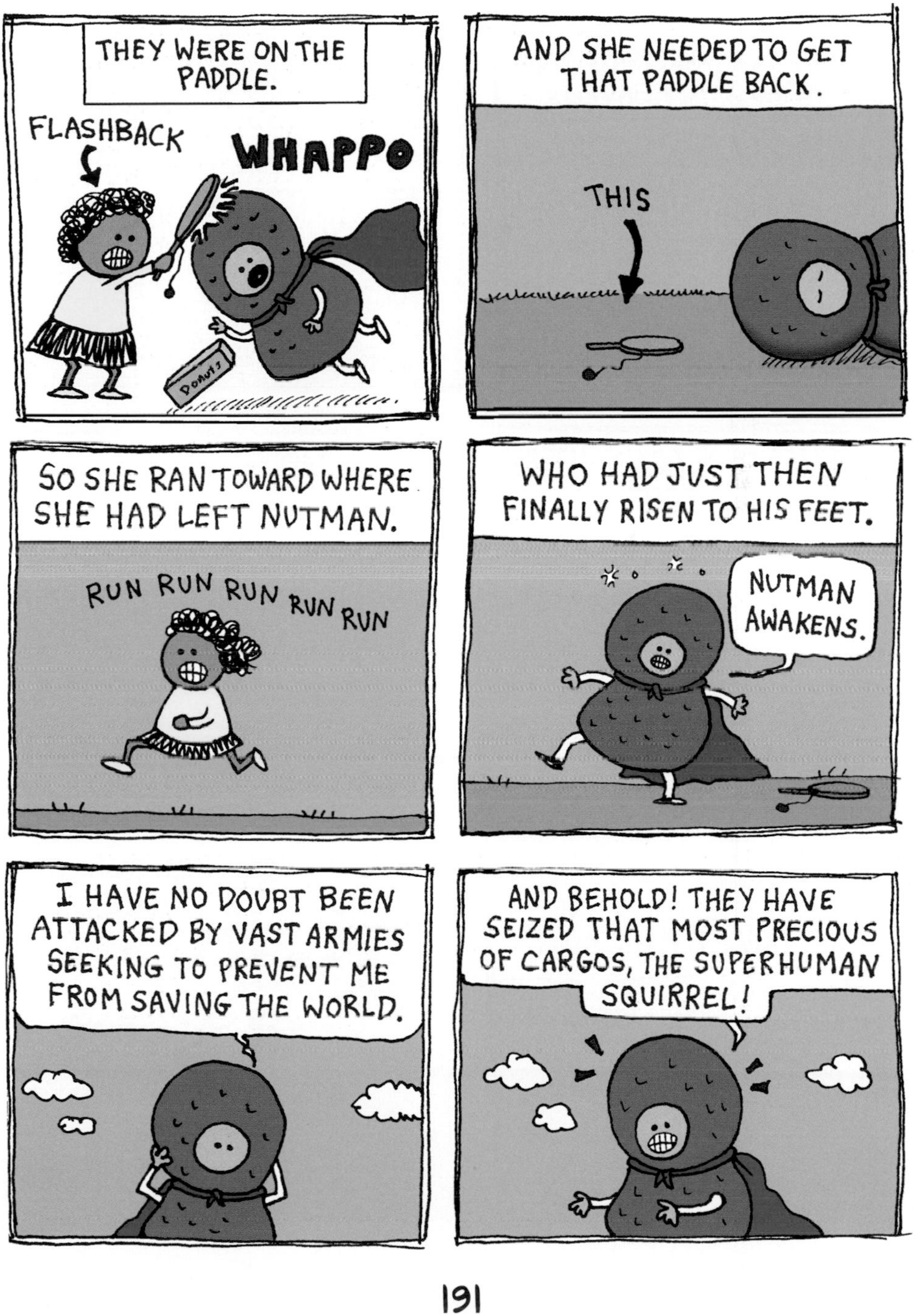
THEY WERE ON THE PADDLE.
FLASHBACK
WHAPPO
DONUTS
AND SHE NEEDED TO GET THAT PADDLE BACK.
THIS
SO SHE RAN TOWARD WHERE SHE HAD LEFT NUTMAN.
RUN RUN RUN RUN RUN
WHO HAD JUST THEN FINALLY RISEN TO HIS FEET.
NUTMAN AWAKENS.
I HAVE NO DOUBT BEEN ATTACKED BY VAST ARMIES SEEKING TO PREVENT ME FROM SAVING THE WORLD.
AND BEHOLD! THEY HAVE SEIZED THAT MOST PRECIOUS OF CARGOS, THE SUPERHUMAN SQUIRREL!

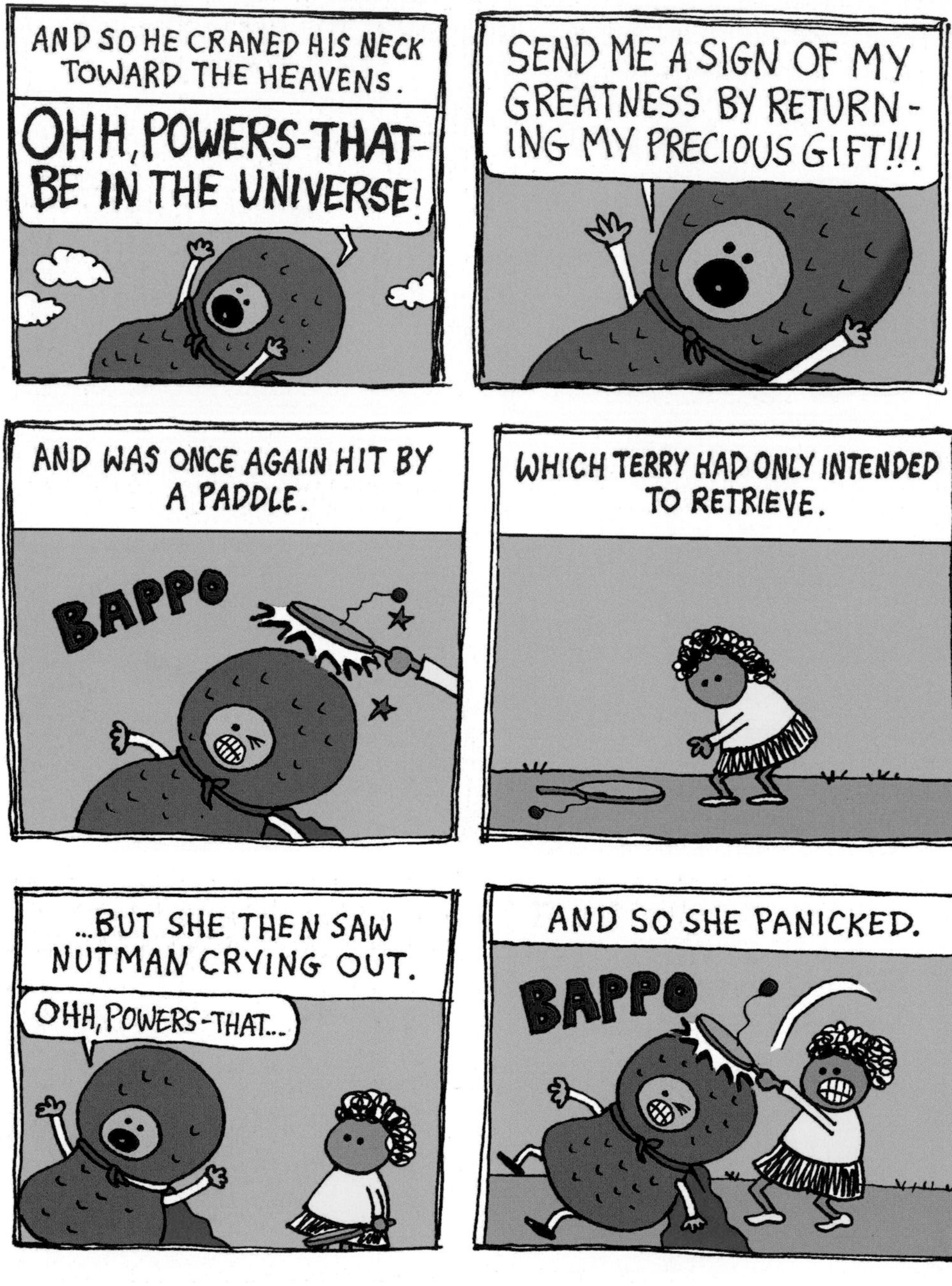
AND SO HE CRANED HIS NECK TOWARD THE HEAVENS.
OHH, POWERS-THAT-BE IN THE UNIVERSE!
SEND ME A SIGN OF MY GREATNESS BY RETURNING MY PRECIOUS GIFT!!!
AND WAS ONCE AGAIN HIT BY A PADDLE.
BAPPO
WHICH TERRY HAD ONLY INTENDED TO RETRIEVE.
...BUT SHE THEN SAW NUTMAN CRYING OUT.
OHH, POWERS-THAT...
AND SO SHE PANICKED.
BAPPO

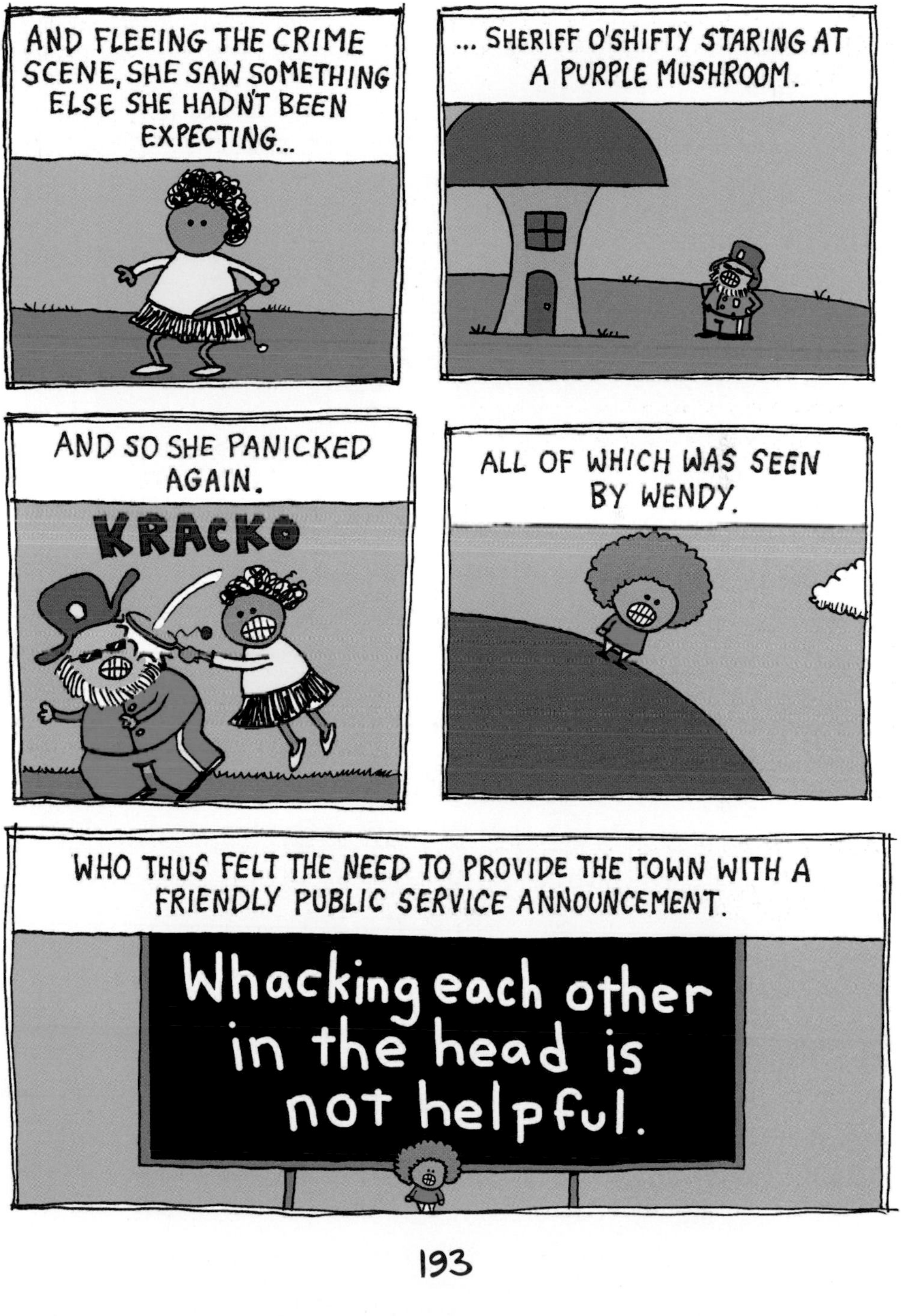
AND FLEEING THE CRIME SCENE, SHE SAW SOMETHING ELSE SHE HADN'T BEEN EXPECTING...
... SHERIFF O'SHIFTY STARING AT A PURPLE MUSHROOM.
AND SO SHE PANICKED AGAIN.
KRACKO
ALL OF WHICH WAS SEEN BY WENDY.
WHO THUS FELT THE NEED TO PROVIDE THE TOWN WITH A FRIENDLY PUBLIC SERVICE ANNOUNCEMENT.
Whacking each other in the head is not helpful.

CHAPTER SUPER BRIEF

IN WHICH...

WE ARE SUPER BRIEF

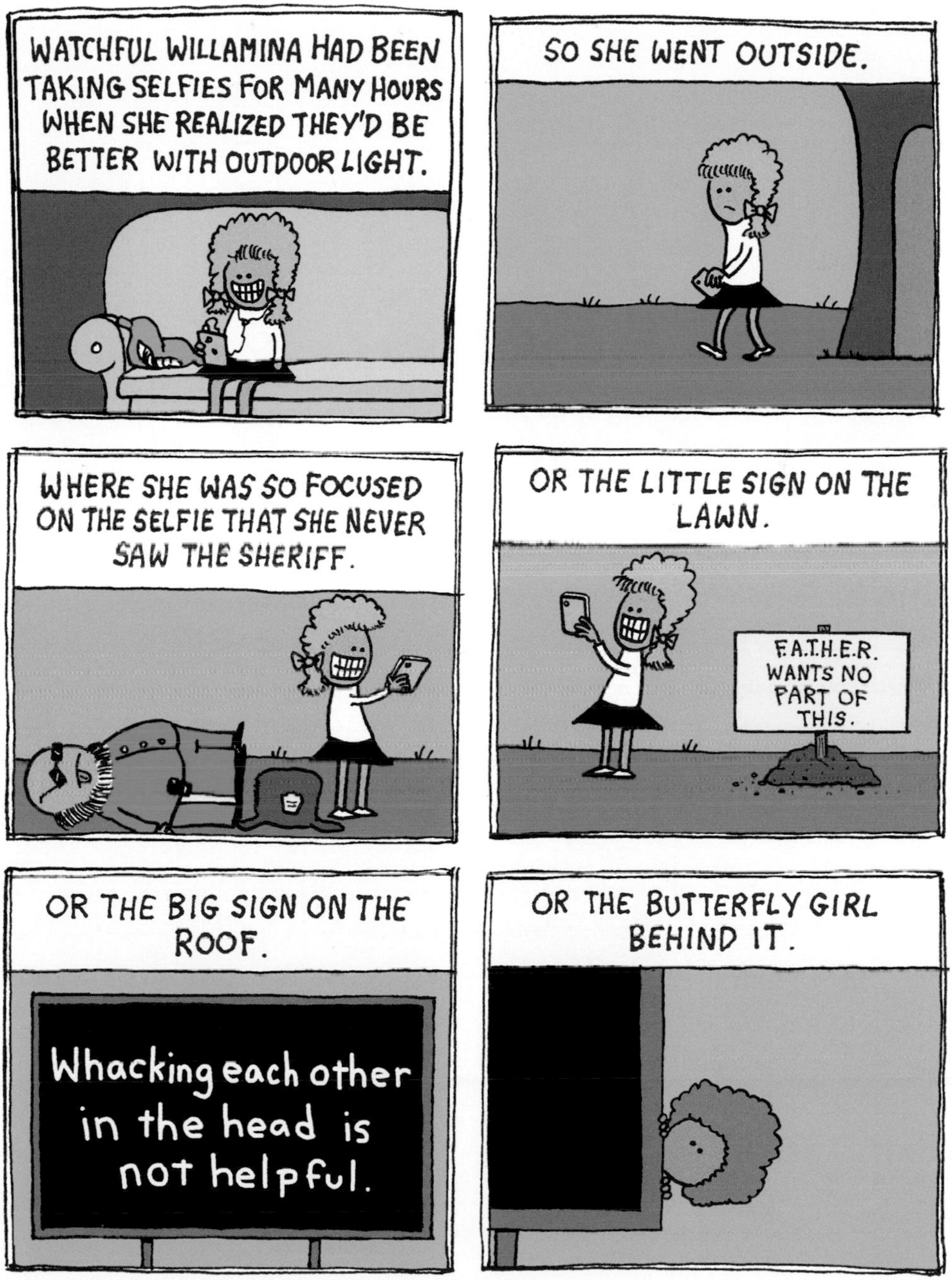
WATCHFUL WILLAMINA HAD BEEN TAKING SELFIES FOR MANY HOURS WHEN SHE REALIZED THEY'D BE BETTER WITH OUTDOOR LIGHT.
SO SHE WENT OUTSIDE.
WHERE SHE WAS SO FOCUSED ON THE SELFIE THAT SHE NEVER SAW THE SHERIFF.
OR THE LITTLE SIGN ON THE LAWN.
F.A.T.H.E.R. WANTS NO PART OF THIS.
OR THE BIG SIGN ON THE ROOF.
Whacking each other in the head is not helpful.
OR THE BUTTERFLY GIRL BEHIND IT.

CHAPTER PROBABLY TWENTY

IN WHICH...

YOU WILL BE GLUED
TO THE EDGE OF
YOUR SEAT, BUT
HOPEFULLY NOT
WITH ACTUAL
GLUE

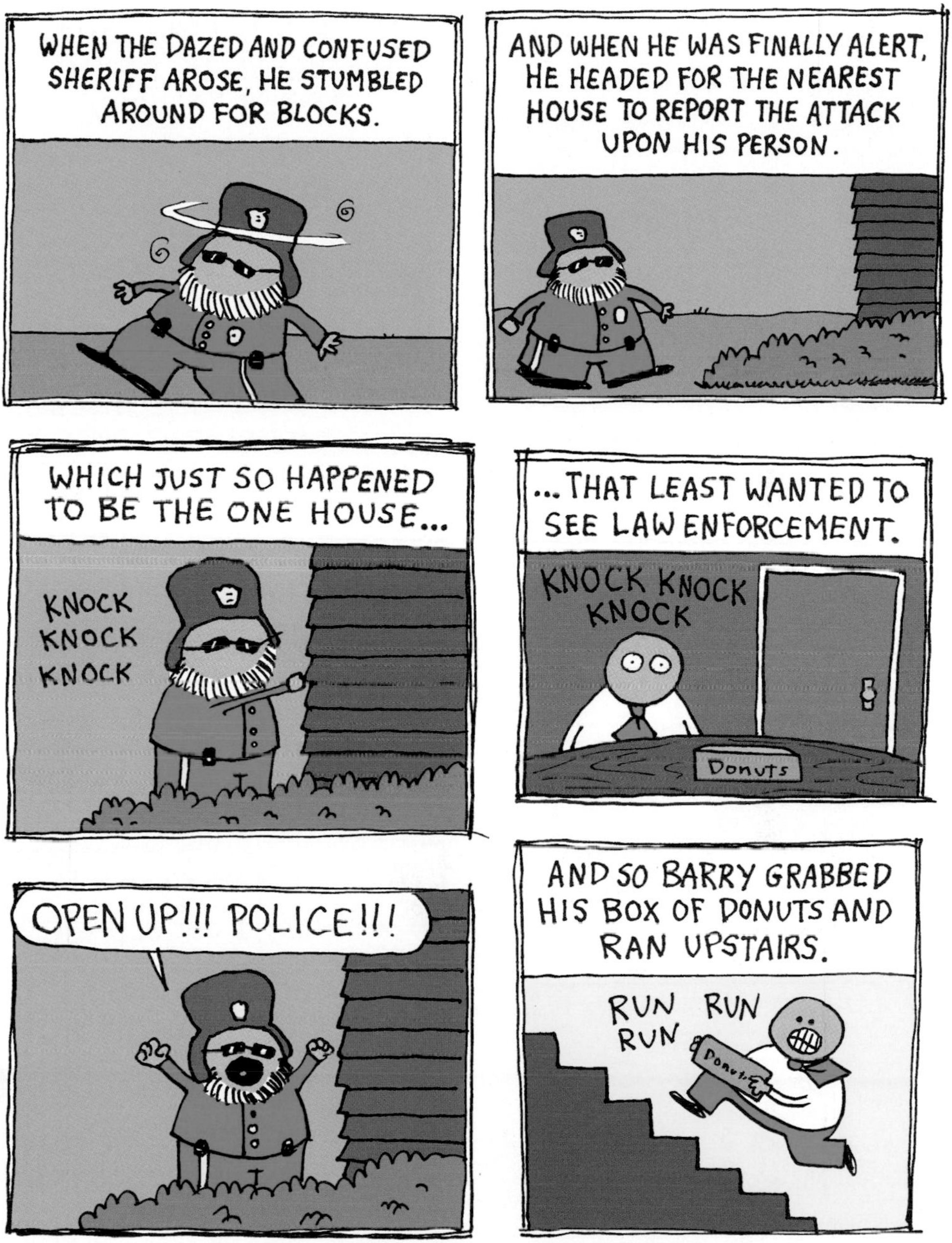
WHEN THE DAZED AND CONFUSED SHERIFF AROSE, HE STUMBLED AROUND FOR BLOCKS.
AND WHEN HE WAS FINALLY ALERT, HE HEADED FOR THE NEAREST HOUSE TO REPORT THE ATTACK UPON HIS PERSON.
WHICH JUST SO HAPPENED TO BE THE ONE HOUSE...
KNOCK KNOCK KNOCK
...THAT LEAST WANTED TO SEE LAW ENFORCEMENT.
KNOCK KNOCK KNOCK
DONUTS
OPEN UP!!! POLICE!!!
AND SO BARRY GRABBED HIS BOX OF DONUTS AND RAN UPSTAIRS.
RUN RUN RUN
DONUTS

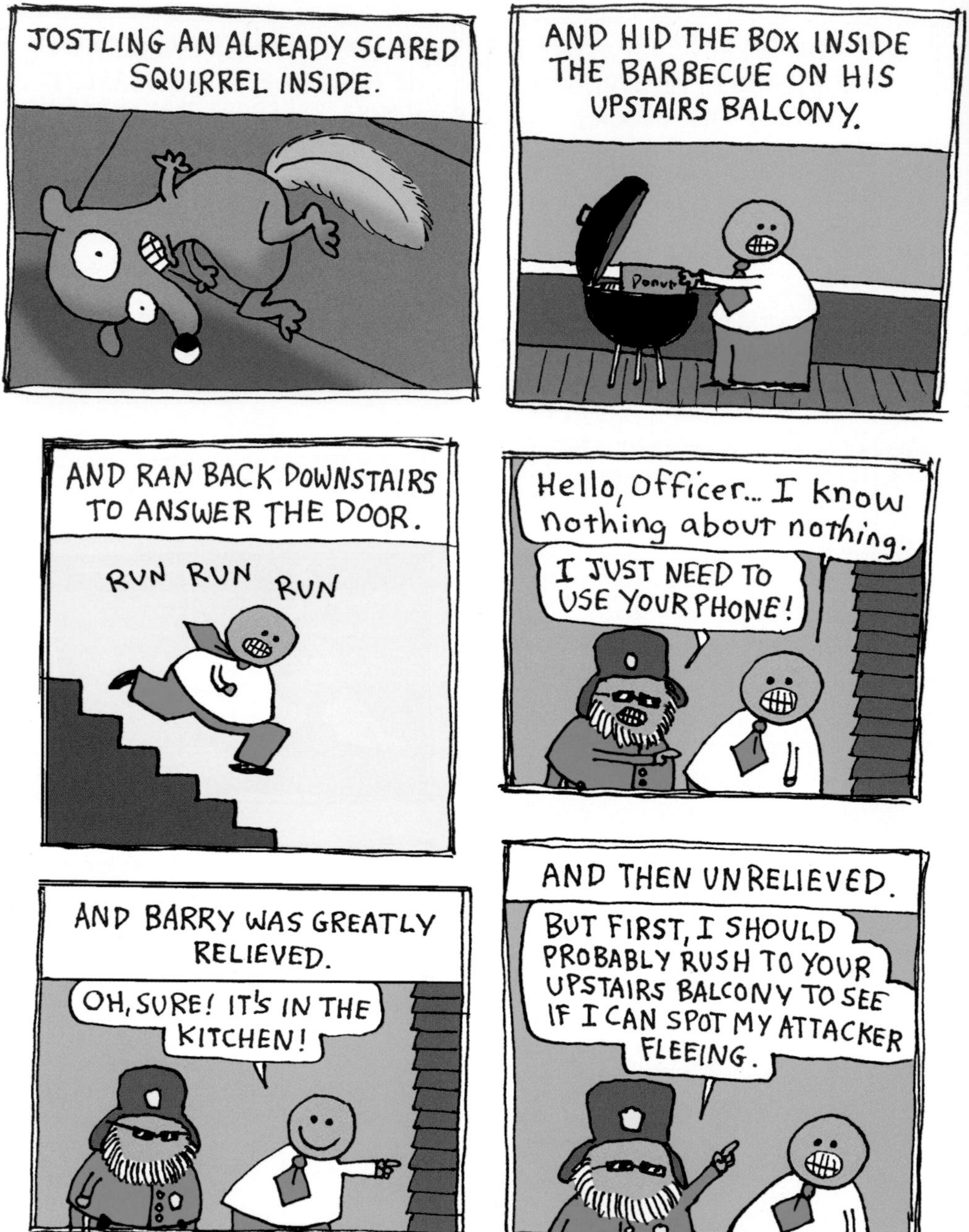
JOSTLING AN ALREADY SCARED SQUIRREL INSIDE.
AND HID THE BOX INSIDE THE BARBECUE ON HIS UPSTAIRS BALCONY.
DONUT
AND RAN BACK DOWNSTAIRS TO ANSWER THE DOOR.
RUN RUN RUN
Hello, Officer... I know nothing about nothing.
I JUST NEED TO USE YOUR PHONE!
AND BARRY WAS GREATLY RELIEVED.
OH, SURE! IT'S IN THE KITCHEN!
AND THEN UNRELIEVED.
BUT FIRST, I SHOULD PROBABLY RUSH TO YOUR UPSTAIRS BALCONY TO SEE IF I CAN SPOT MY ATTACKER FLEEING.

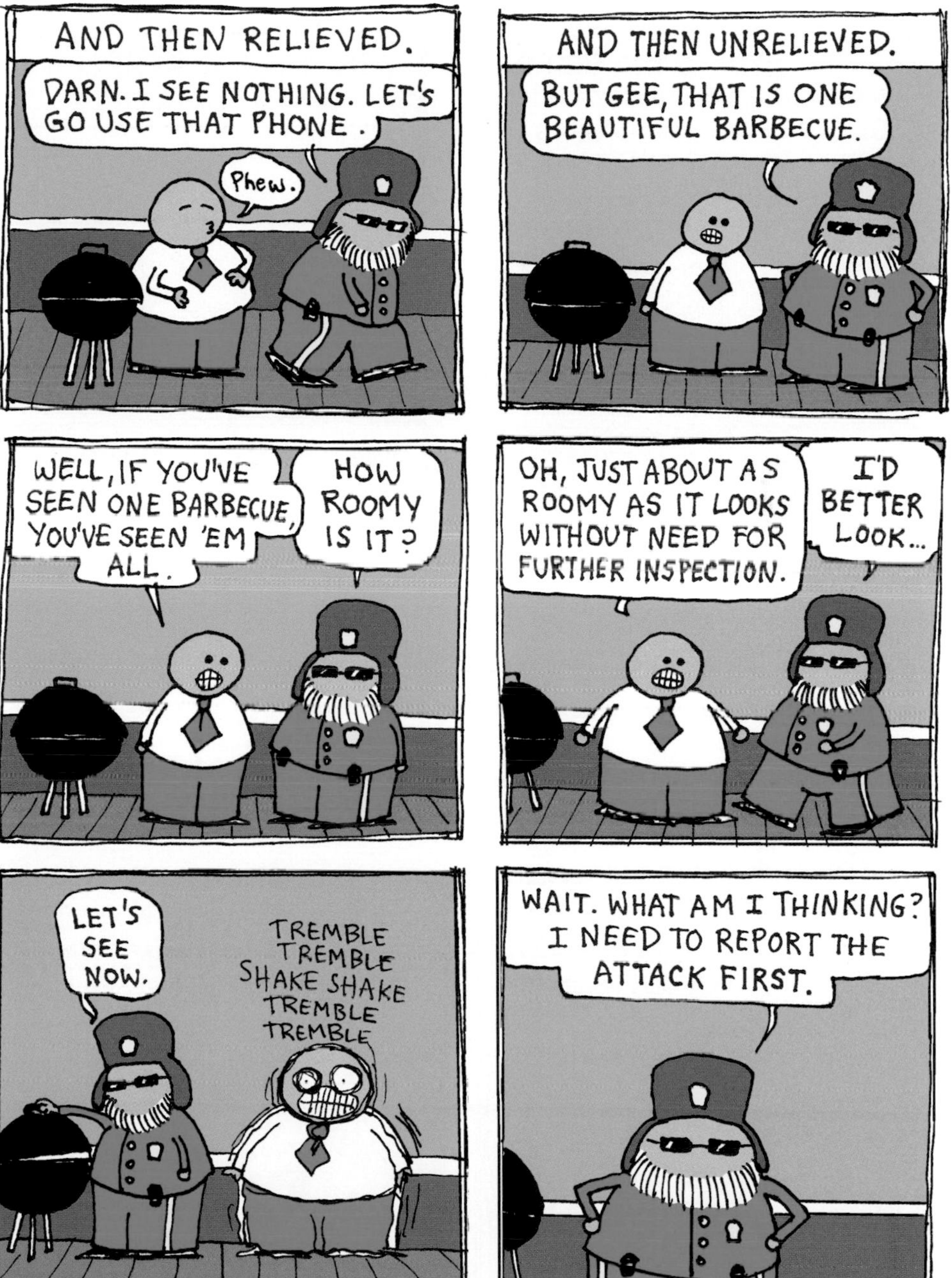
AND THEN RELIEVED.
DARN. I SEE NOTHING. LET'S GO USE THAT PHONE.
Phew.
AND THEN UNRELIEVED.
BUT GEE, THAT IS ONE BEAUTIFUL BARBECUE.
WELL, IF YOU'VE SEEN ONE BARBECUE, YOU'VE SEEN 'EM ALL.
HOW ROOMY IS IT?
OH, JUST ABOUT AS ROOMY AS IT LOOKS WITHOUT NEED FOR FURTHER INSPECTION.
I'D BETTER LOOK...
LET'S SEE NOW.
TREMBLE TREMBLE SHAKE SHAKE TREMBLE TREMBLE
WAIT. WHAT AM I THINKING? I NEED TO REPORT THE ATTACK FIRST.

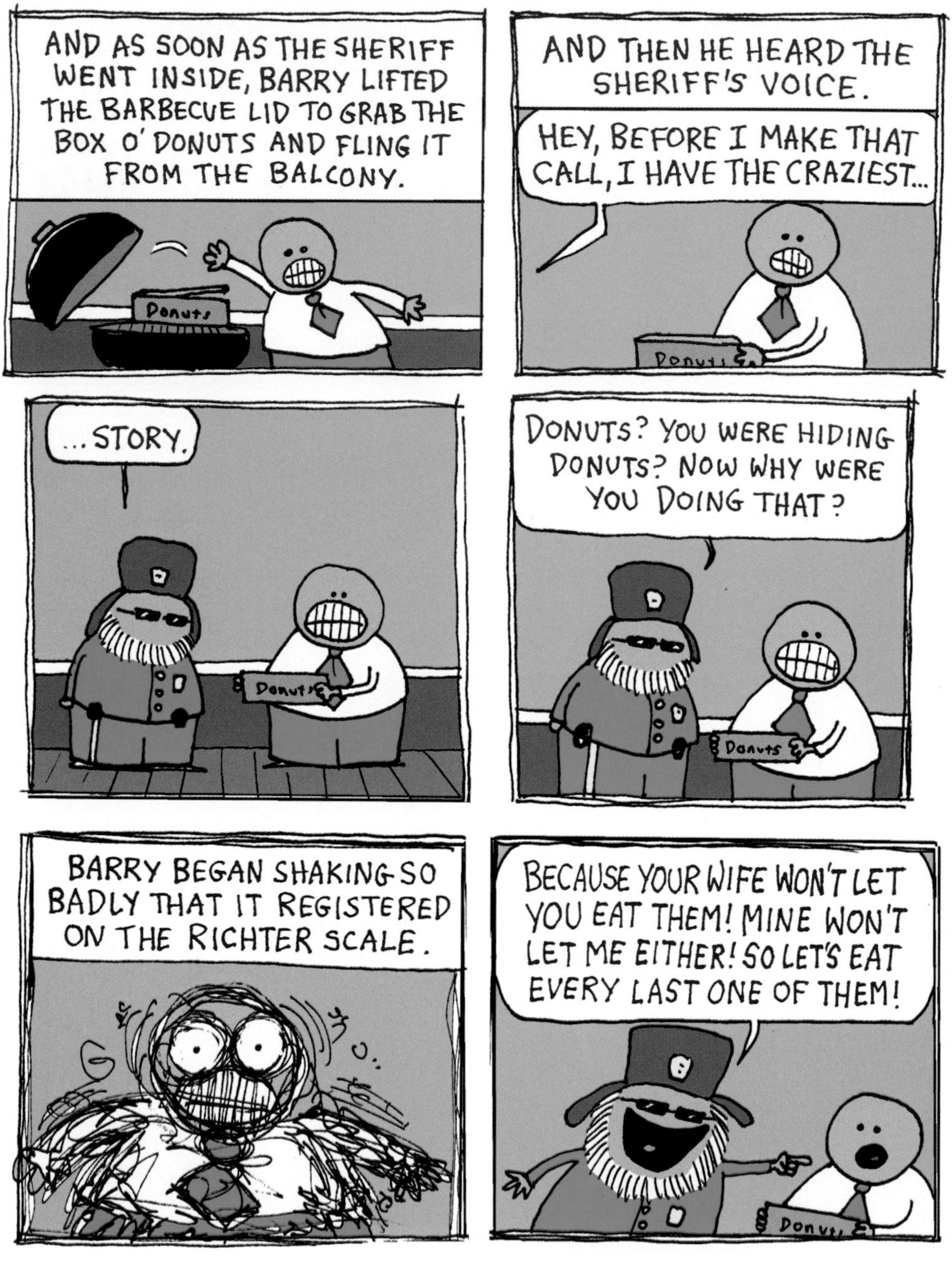
AND AS SOON AS THE SHERIFF WENT INSIDE, BARRY LIFTED THE BARBECUE LID TO GRAB THE BOX O' DONUTS AND FLING IT FROM THE BALCONY.
Donuts
AND THEN HE HEARD THE SHERIFF'S VOICE.
HEY, BEFORE I MAKE THAT CALL, I HAVE THE CRAZIEST...
...STORY.
Donuts
DONUTS? YOU WERE HIDING DONUTS? NOW WHY WERE YOU DOING THAT?
Donuts
BARRY BEGAN SHAKING SO BADLY THAT IT REGISTERED ON THE RICHTER SCALE.
BECAUSE YOUR WIFE WON'T LET YOU EAT THEM! MINE WON'T LET ME EITHER! SO LET'S EAT EVERY LAST ONE OF THEM!

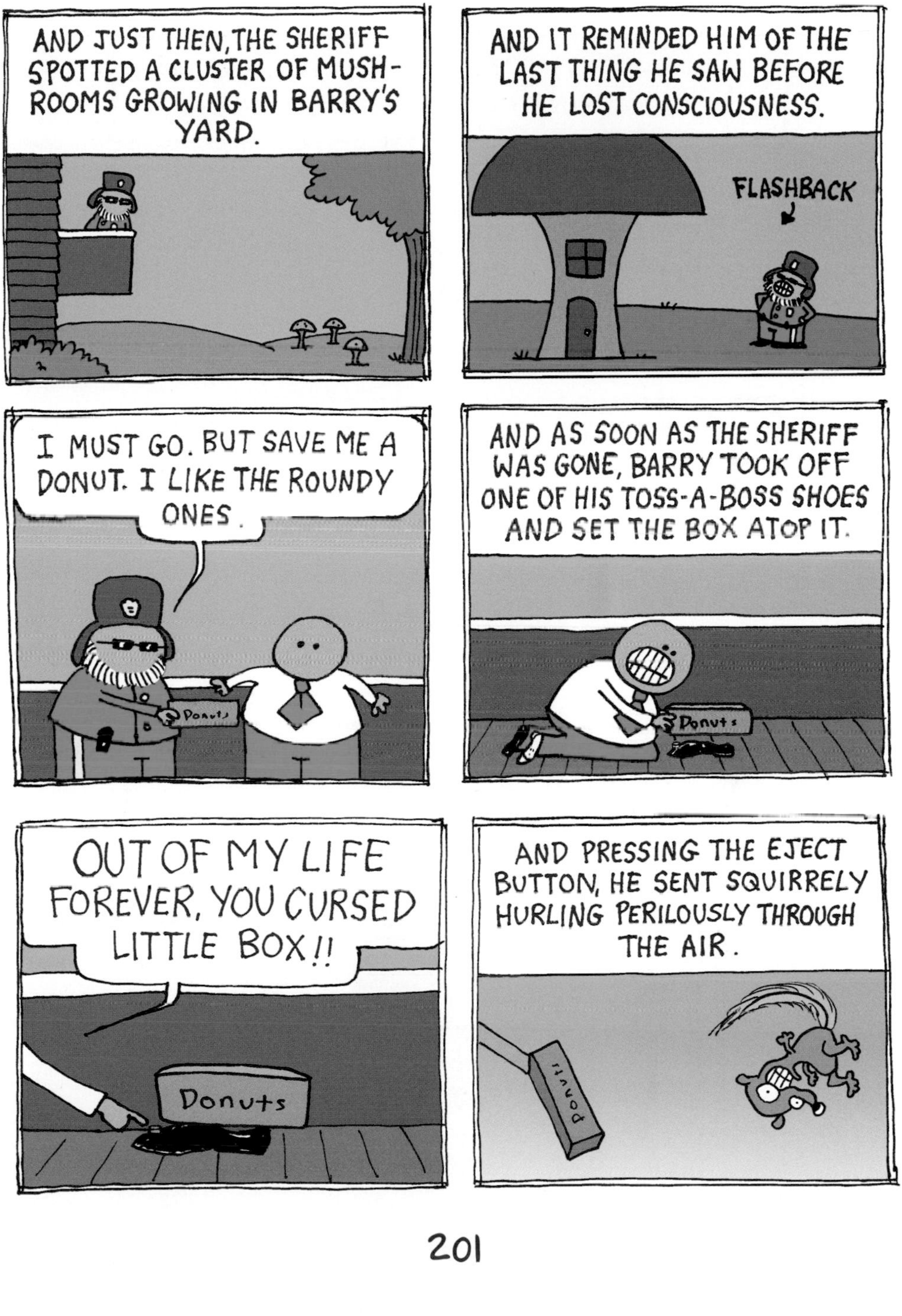
AND JUST THEN, THE SHERIFF SPOTTED A CLUSTER OF MUSH-ROOMS GROWING IN BARRY'S YARD.
AND IT REMINDED HIM OF THE LAST THING HE SAW BEFORE HE LOST CONSCIOUSNESS.
FLASHBACK
I MUST GO. BUT SAVE ME A DONUT. I LIKE THE ROUNDY ONES.
Donuts
AND AS SOON AS THE SHERIFF WAS GONE, BARRY TOOK OFF ONE OF HIS TOSS-A-BOSS SHOES AND SET THE BOX ATOP IT.
Donuts
OUT OF MY LIFE FOREVER, YOU CURSED LITTLE BOX!!
Donuts
AND PRESSING THE EJECT BUTTON, HE SENT SQUIRRELY HURLING PERILOUSLY THROUGH THE AIR.
Donuts

INADVERTENTLY TOWARD A MAN WHO WAS
NOW STANDING ON THE GROUND BELOW...

...TO WHOM SQUIRRELY MEANT MORE
THAN ANYONE ELSE IN THE WORLD.

AND WHO HAD JUST ASKED THE
HEAVENS FOR A SIGN.

PLOP

CHAPTER BLANK

IN WHICH...

WE RUN OUT OF CLEVER CHAPTER TITLES

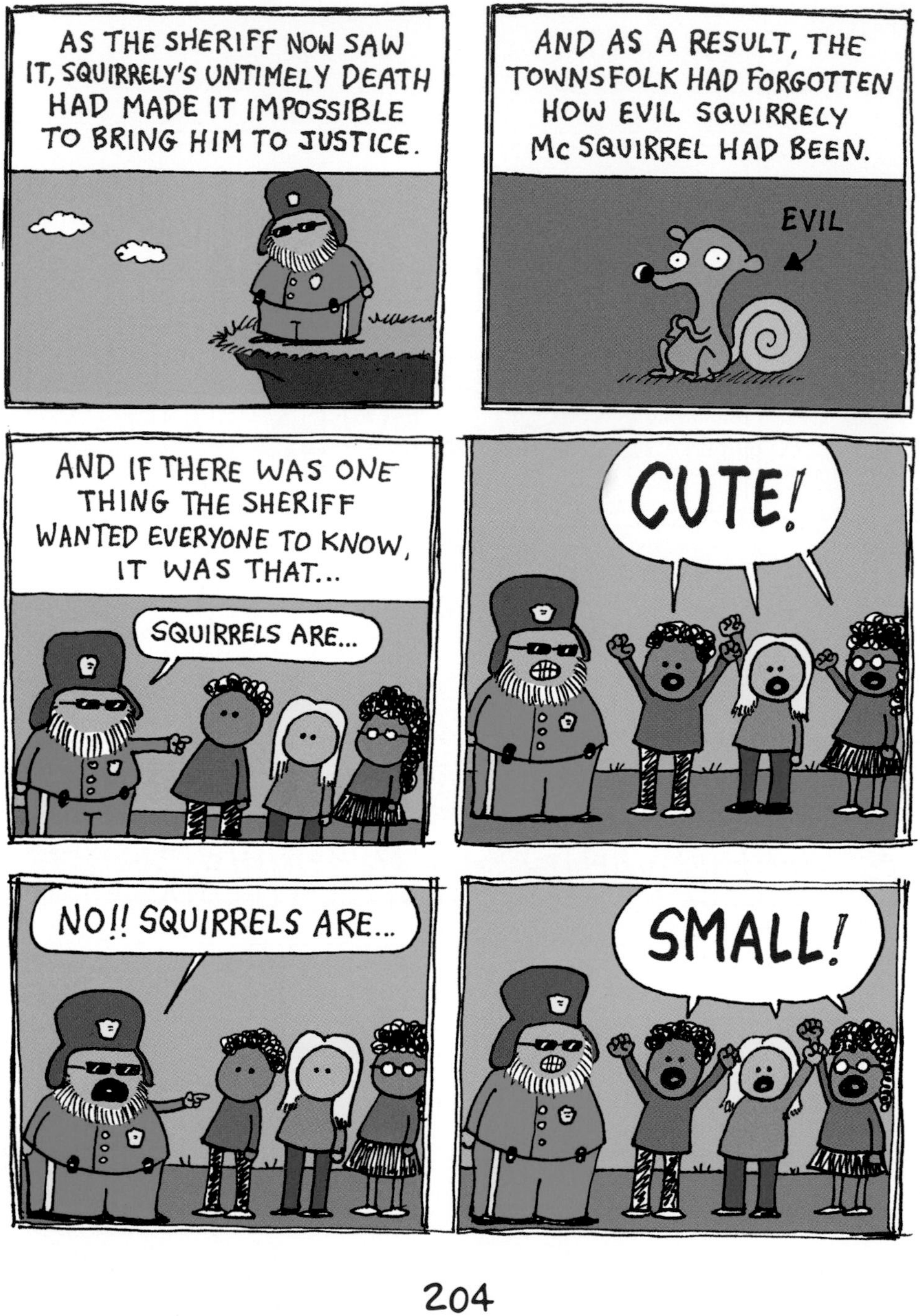
AS THE SHERIFF NOW SAW IT, SQUIRRELY'S UNTIMELY DEATH HAD MADE IT IMPOSSIBLE TO BRING HIM TO JUSTICE.
AND AS A RESULT, THE TOWNSFOLK HAD FORGOTTEN HOW EVIL SQUIRRELY McSQUIRREL HAD BEEN.
EVIL
AND IF THERE WAS ONE THING THE SHERIFF WANTED EVERYONE TO KNOW, IT WAS THAT...
SQUIRRELS ARE...
CUTE!
NO!! SQUIRRELS ARE...
SMALL!

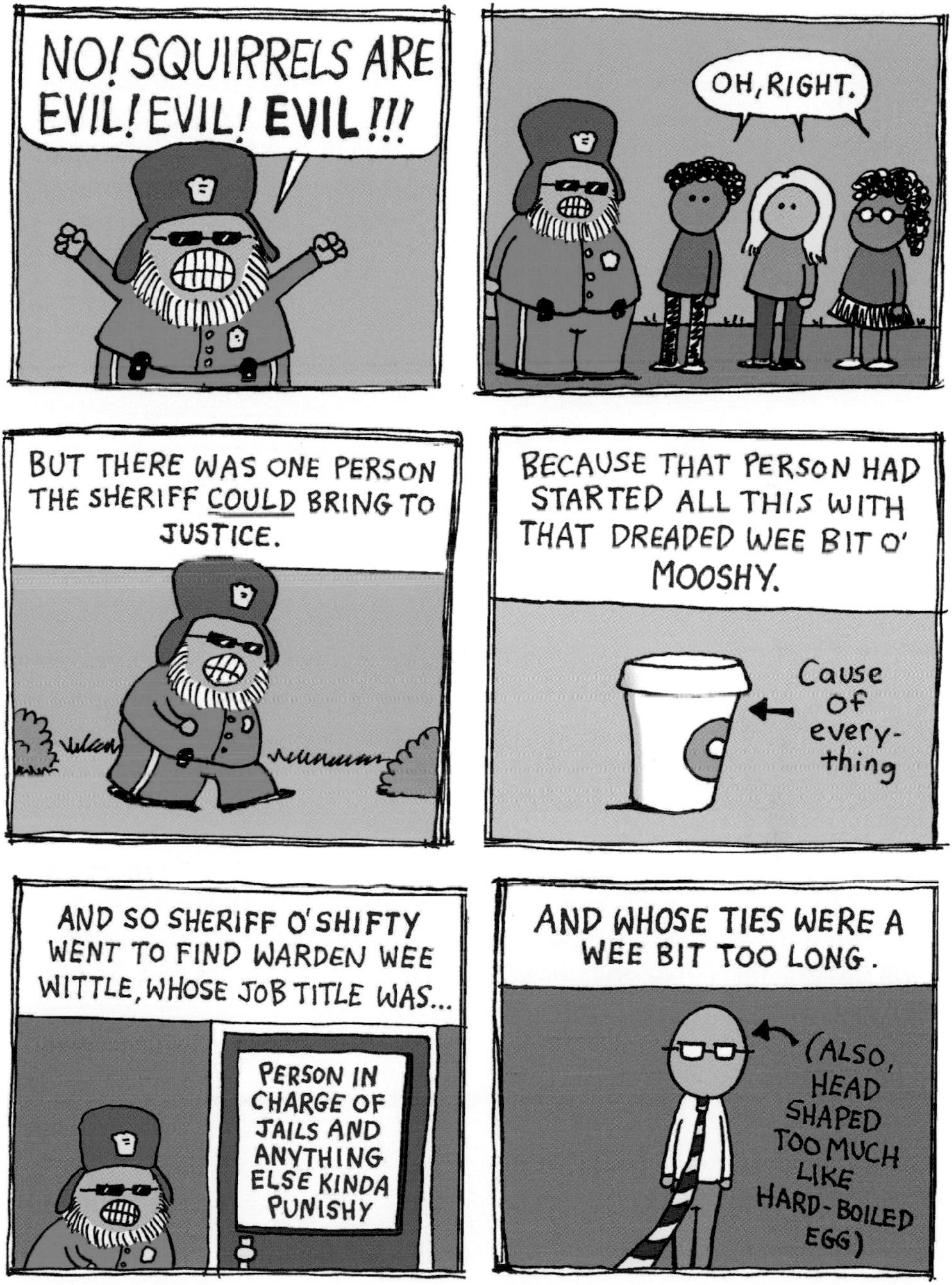
NO! SQUIRRELS ARE EVIL! EVIL! EVIL!!!
OH, RIGHT.
BUT THERE WAS ONE PERSON THE SHERIFF COULD BRING TO JUSTICE.
BECAUSE THAT PERSON HAD STARTED ALL THIS WITH THAT DREADED WEE BIT O' MOOSHY.
Cause of every-thing
AND SO SHERIFF O'SHIFTY WENT TO FIND WARDEN WEE WITTLE, WHOSE JOB TITLE WAS...
PERSON IN CHARGE OF JAILS AND ANYTHING ELSE KINDA PUNISHY
AND WHOSE TIES WERE A WEE BIT TOO LONG.
(ALSO, HEAD SHAPED TOO MUCH LIKE HARD-BOILED EGG)

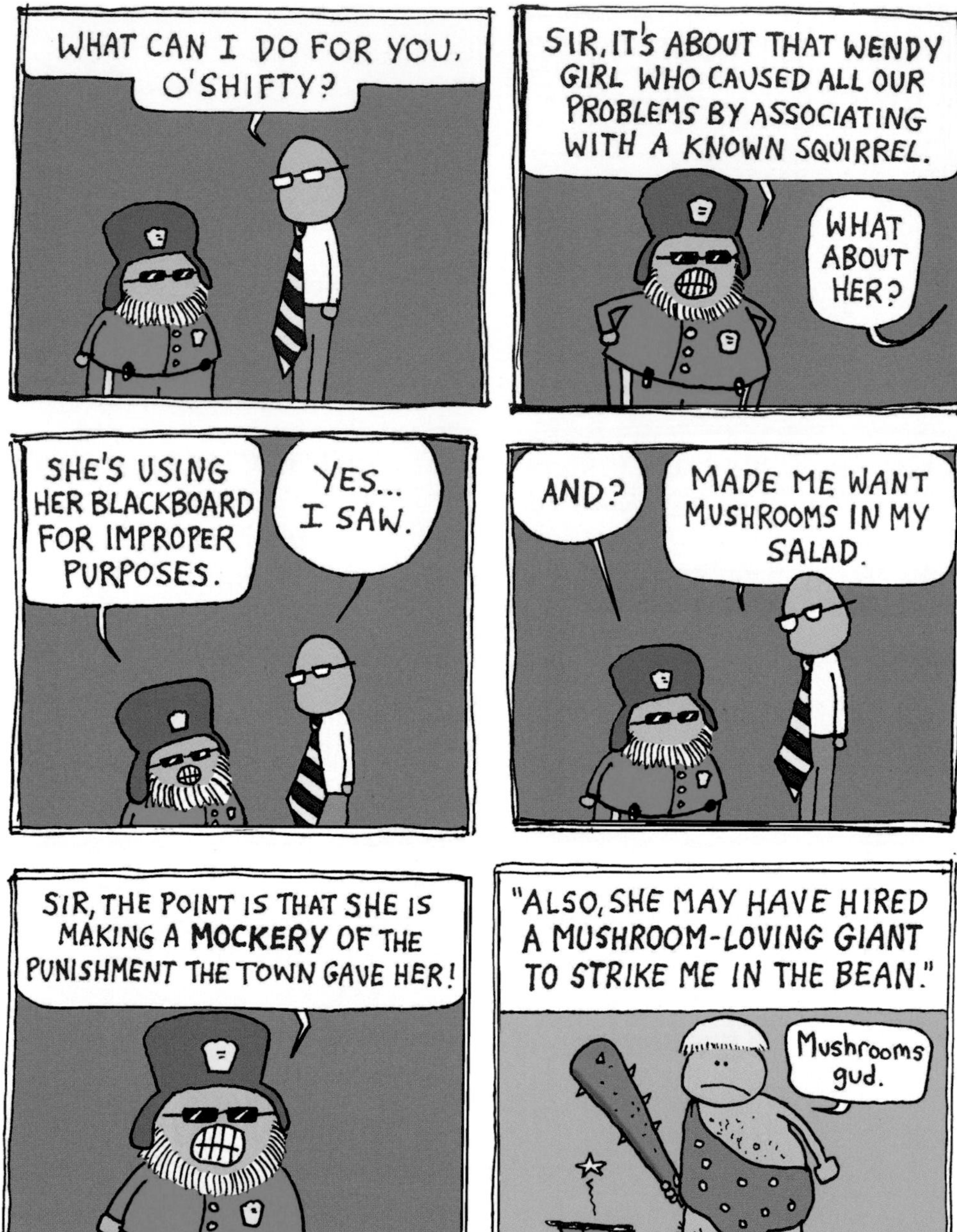
WHAT CAN I DO FOR YOU, O'SHIFTY?
SIR, IT'S ABOUT THAT WENDY GIRL WHO CAUSED ALL OUR PROBLEMS BY ASSOCIATING WITH A KNOWN SQUIRREL.
WHAT ABOUT HER?
SHE'S USING HER BLACKBOARD FOR IMPROPER PURPOSES.
YES... I SAW.
AND?
MADE ME WANT MUSHROOMS IN MY SALAD.
SIR, THE POINT IS THAT SHE IS MAKING A **MOCKERY** OF THE PUNISHMENT THE TOWN GAVE HER!
"ALSO, SHE MAY HAVE HIRED A MUSHROOM-LOVING GIANT TO STRIKE ME IN THE BEAN."
Mushrooms gud.

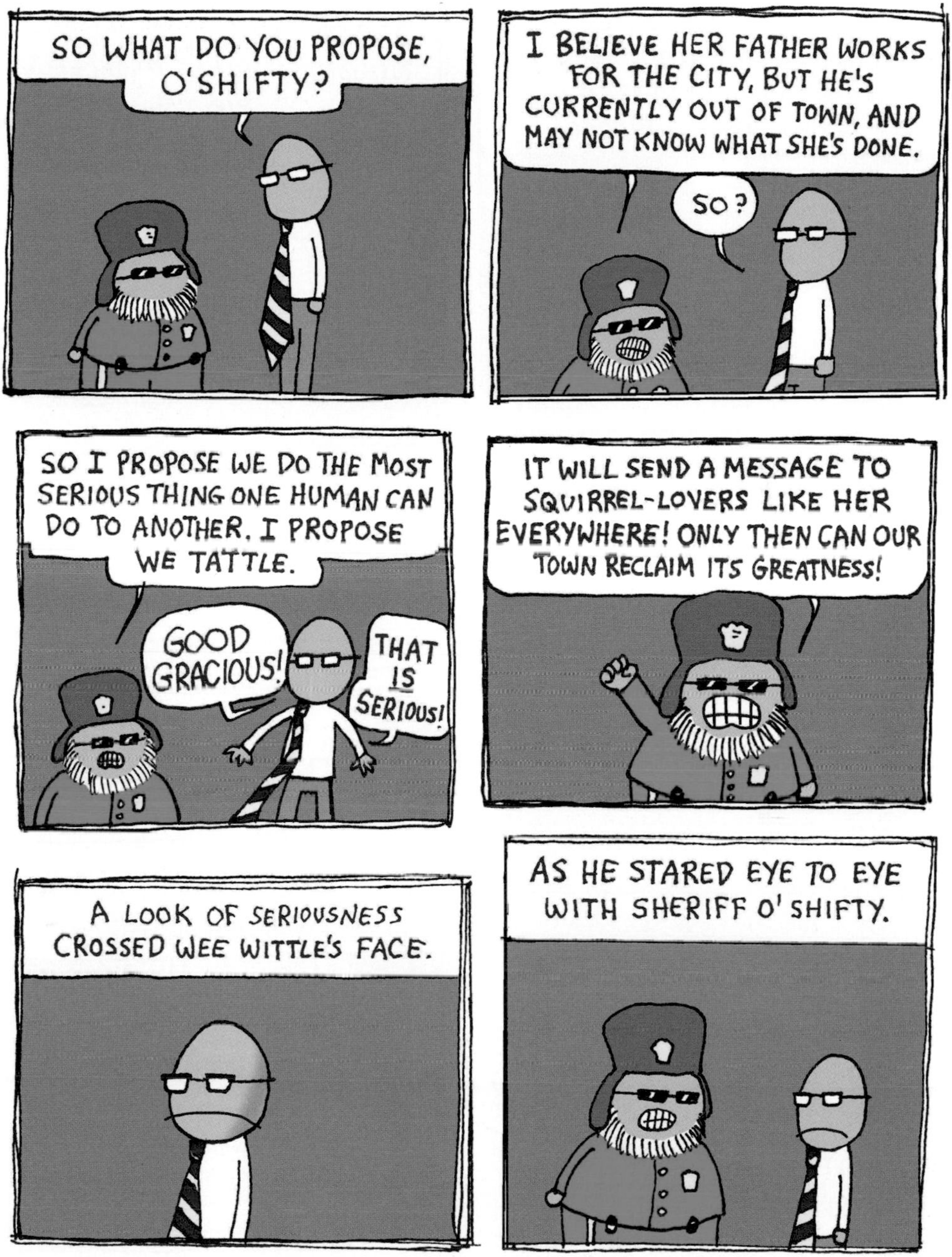
SO WHAT DO YOU PROPOSE, O'SHIFTY?
I BELIEVE HER FATHER WORKS FOR THE CITY, BUT HE'S CURRENTLY OUT OF TOWN, AND MAY NOT KNOW WHAT SHE'S DONE.
SO?
SO I PROPOSE WE DO THE MOST SERIOUS THING ONE HUMAN CAN DO TO ANOTHER. I PROPOSE WE TATTLE.
GOOD GRACIOUS!
THAT IS SERIOUS!
IT WILL SEND A MESSAGE TO SQUIRREL-LOVERS LIKE HER EVERYWHERE! ONLY THEN CAN OUR TOWN RECLAIM ITS GREATNESS!
A LOOK OF SERIOUSNESS CROSSED WEE WITTLE'S FACE.
AS HE STARED EYE TO EYE WITH SHERIFF O'SHIFTY.

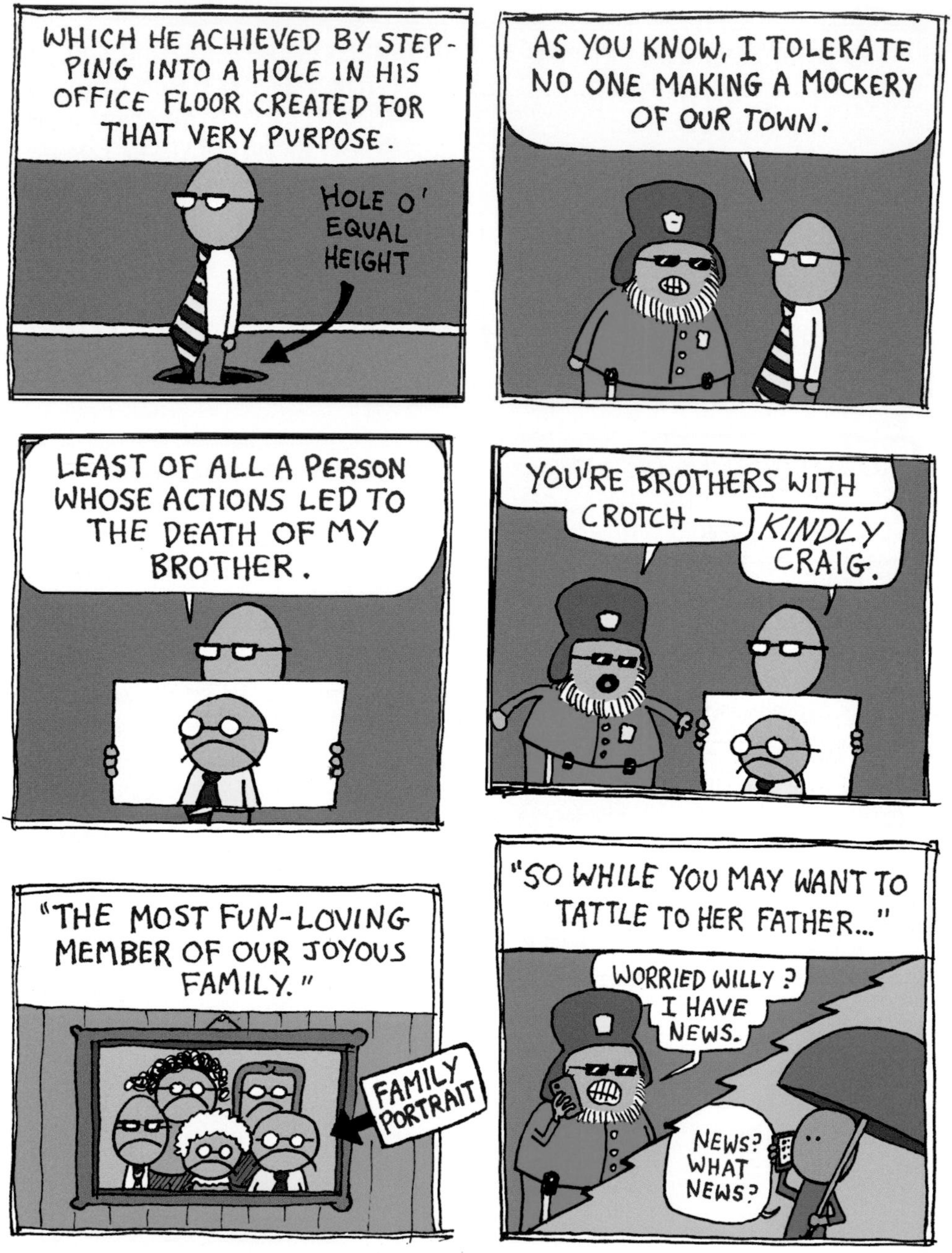
WHICH HE ACHIEVED BY STEPPING INTO A HOLE IN HIS OFFICE FLOOR CREATED FOR THAT VERY PURPOSE.
HOLE O' EQUAL HEIGHT
AS YOU KNOW, I TOLERATE NO ONE MAKING A MOCKERY OF OUR TOWN.
LEAST OF ALL A PERSON WHOSE ACTIONS LED TO THE DEATH OF MY BROTHER.
YOU'RE BROTHERS WITH CROTCH —
KINDLY CRAIG.
"THE MOST FUN-LOVING MEMBER OF OUR JOYOUS FAMILY."
FAMILY PORTRAIT
"SO WHILE YOU MAY WANT TO TATTLE TO HER FATHER..."
WORRIED WILLY? I HAVE NEWS.
NEWS? WHAT NEWS?

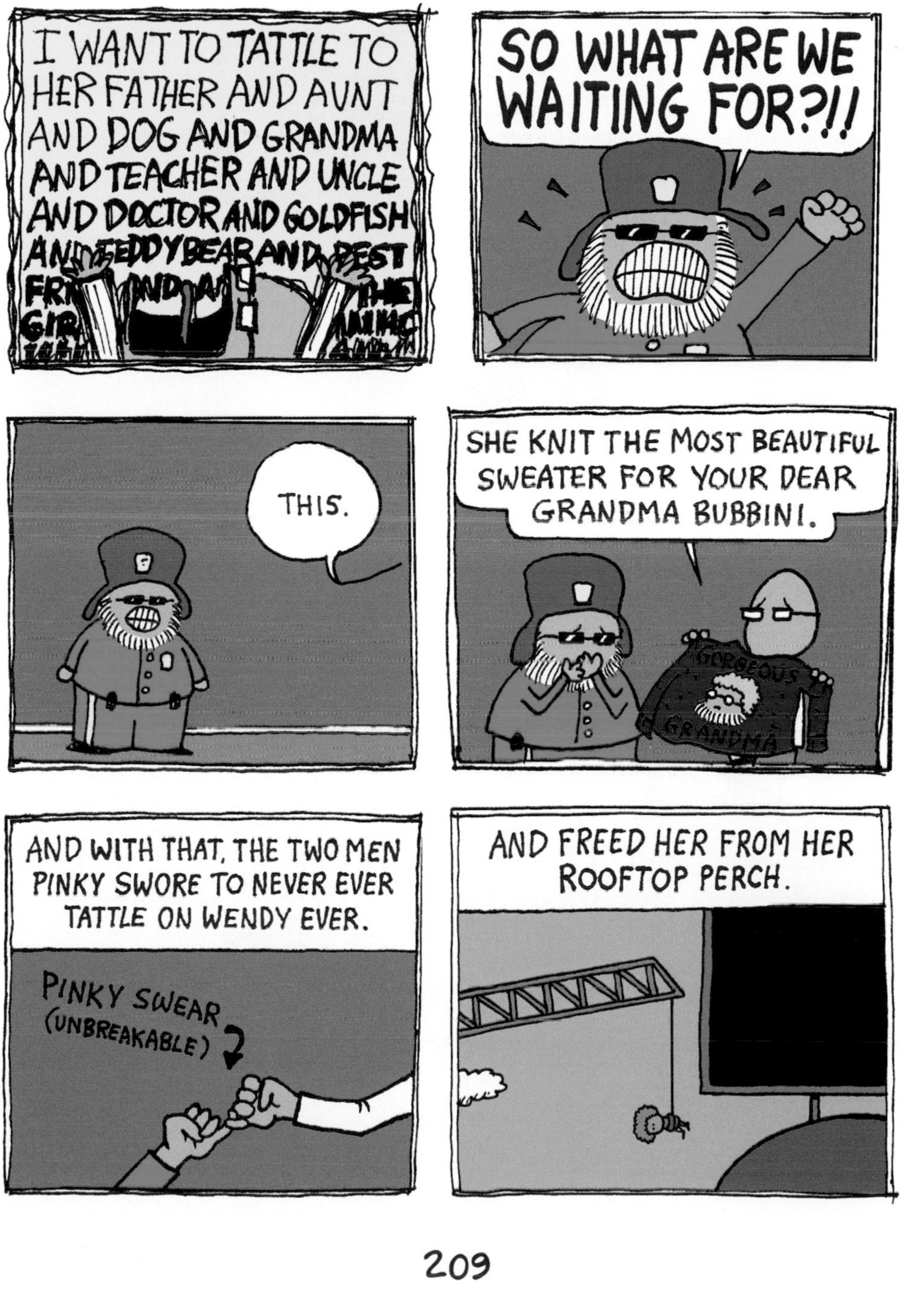
I WANT TO TATTLE TO HER FATHER AND AUNT AND DOG AND GRANDMA AND TEACHER AND UNCLE AND DOCTOR AND GOLDFISH
SO WHAT ARE WE WAITING FOR?!!
THIS.
SHE KNIT THE MOST BEAUTIFUL SWEATER FOR YOUR DEAR GRANDMA BUBBINI.
GORGEOUS GRANDMA
AND WITH THAT, THE TWO MEN PINKY SWORE TO NEVER EVER TATTLE ON WENDY EVER.
PINKY SWEAR (UNBREAKABLE)
AND FREED HER FROM HER ROOFTOP PERCH.

AND IN A BURST OF JOYOUS MERCY, THE TWO MEN THEN FREED EVERYONE FROM THE TRUBBLE TOWN JAIL AS WELL.

LET'S GO STEAL CARS!

ROB BANKS!

AND WHILE EVERYONE IN THE TOWN OF TRUBBLE HAD THEIR HOMES BURGLARIZED OVER THE NEXT TWENTY-FOUR HOURS, THAT WAS OF NO CONCERN TO SHERIFF O'SHIFTY AND WARDEN WEE WITTLE.

AWWW... THERE GOES MY DRYER.

YES. AREN'T PEOPLE WONDERFUL?

CHAPTER WHO-THE-HECK KNOWS

IN WHICH...

WE ARE CONFUSED

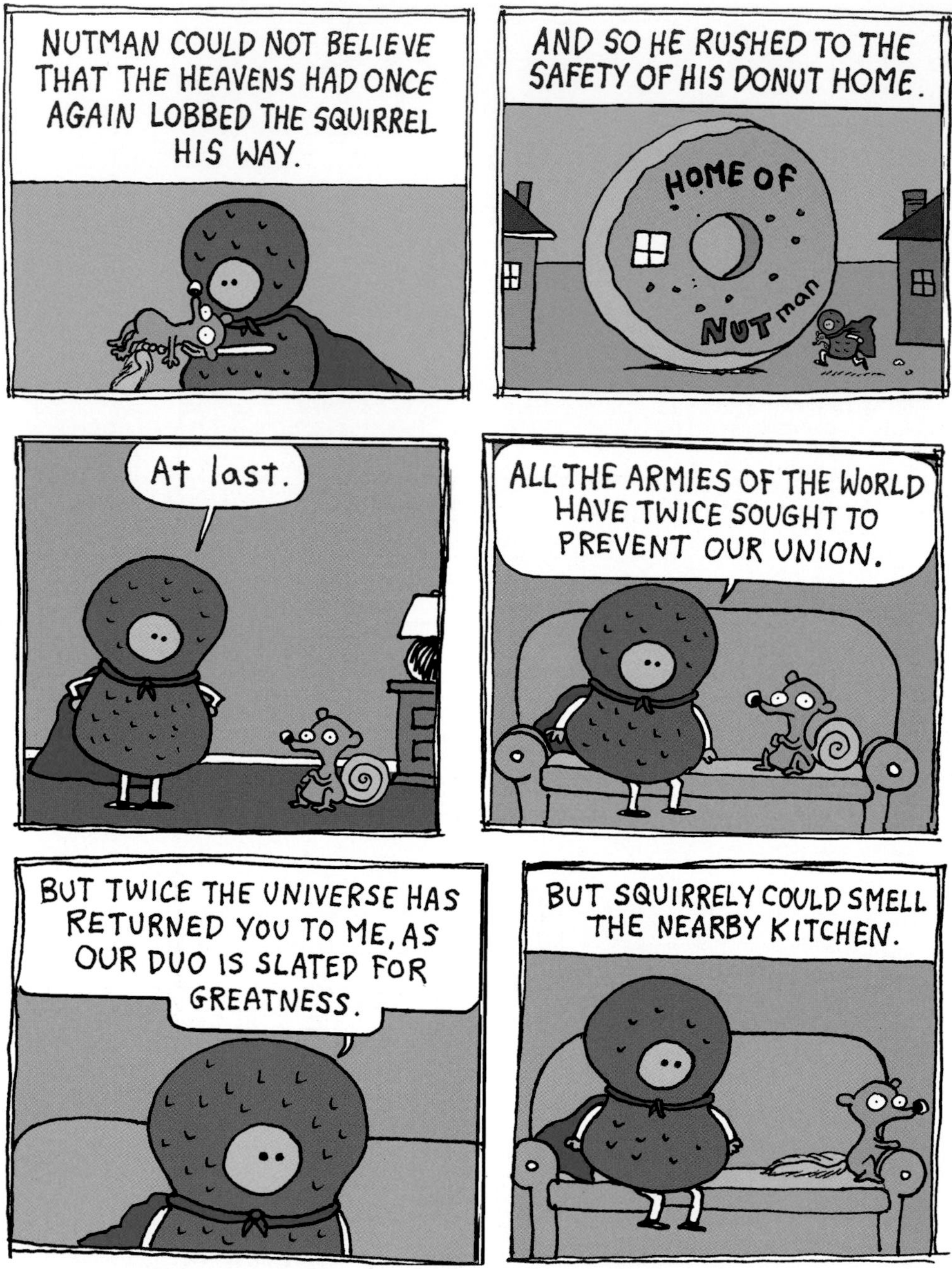
NUTMAN COULD NOT BELIEVE THAT THE HEAVENS HAD ONCE AGAIN LOBBED THE SQUIRREL HIS WAY.
AND SO HE RUSHED TO THE SAFETY OF HIS DONUT HOME.
HOME OF NUTman
At last.
ALL THE ARMIES OF THE WORLD HAVE TWICE SOUGHT TO PREVENT OUR UNION.
BUT TWICE THE UNIVERSE HAS RETURNED YOU TO ME, AS OUR DUO IS SLATED FOR GREATNESS.
BUT SQUIRRELY COULD SMELL THE NEARBY KITCHEN.

TELL ME, YE GIFT O' THE HEAVENS... WHAT IS OUR NOBLE MISSION?

SQUIRRELY POINTED AT THE KITCHEN.

IF I MAY BE SO BOLD, MAY I SUGGEST IT MIGHT HAVE SOMETHING TO DO WITH THE WORD "ANYWAYS"? AS YOU KNOW, IT'S NOT A REAL WORD.

BUT SQUIRRELY HAD LEFT FOR THE KITCHEN.

SO NUTMAN FOLLOWED.

PERHAPS THE UNIVERSE WANTS US TO BASH DOWN THE FRONT DOORS OF THOSE WHO USE THE WORD, IN ORDER THAT WE MAY SET THEM STRAIGHT.

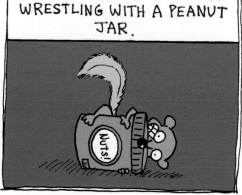

BUT SQUIRRELY WAS NOW WRESTLING WITH A PEANUT JAR.

NUTS!

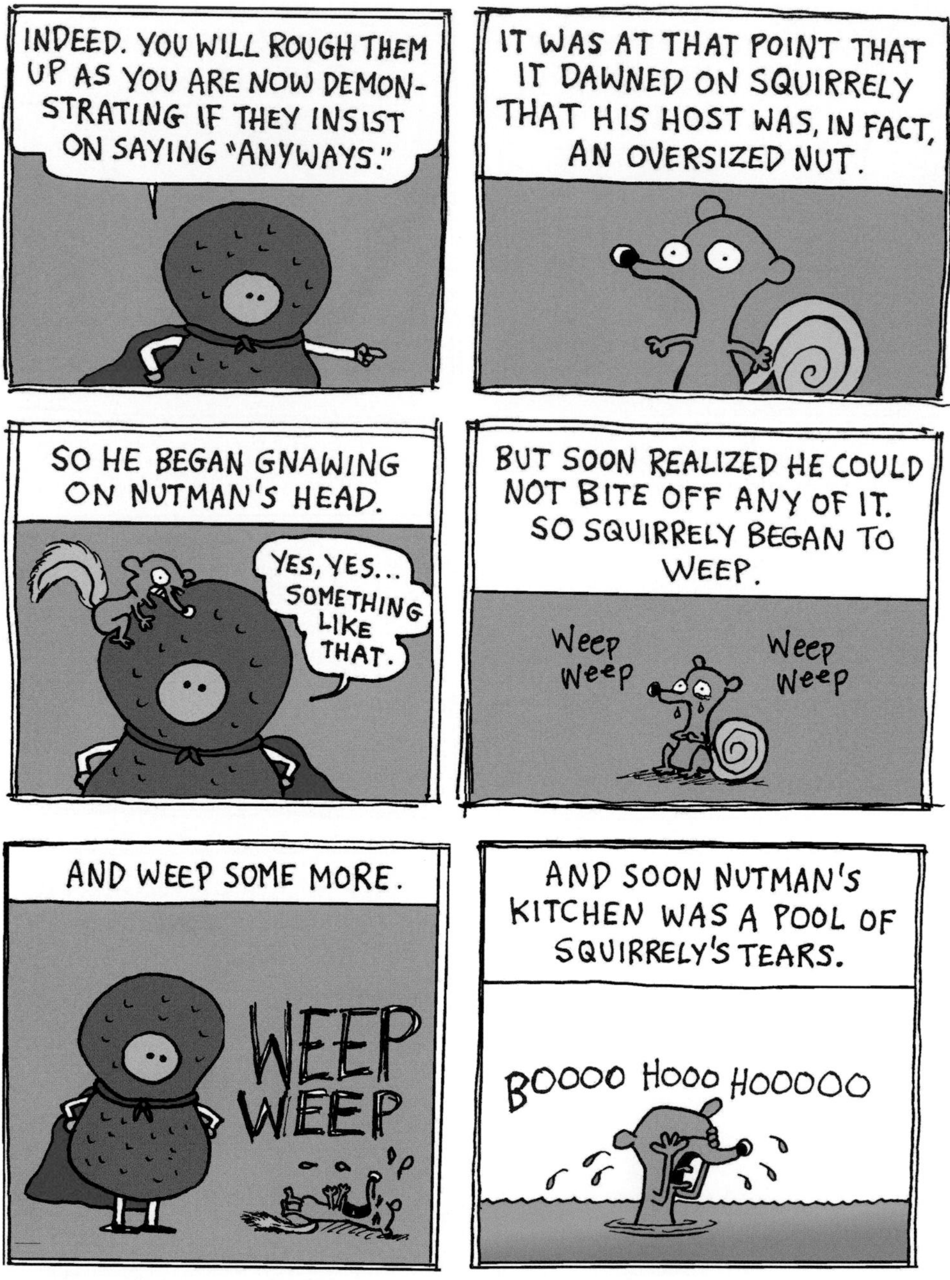
INDEED. YOU WILL ROUGH THEM UP AS YOU ARE NOW DEMON-STRATING IF THEY INSIST ON SAYING "ANYWAYS."
IT WAS AT THAT POINT THAT IT DAWNED ON SQUIRRELY THAT HIS HOST WAS, IN FACT, AN OVERSIZED NUT.
SO HE BEGAN GNAWING ON NUTMAN'S HEAD.
YES, YES... SOMETHING LIKE THAT.
BUT SOON REALIZED HE COULD NOT BITE OFF ANY OF IT. SO SQUIRRELY BEGAN TO WEEP.
Weep weep
Weep weep
AND WEEP SOME MORE.
WEEP WEEP
AND SOON NUTMAN'S KITCHEN WAS A POOL OF SQUIRRELY'S TEARS.
BOOOO HOOO HOOOOO

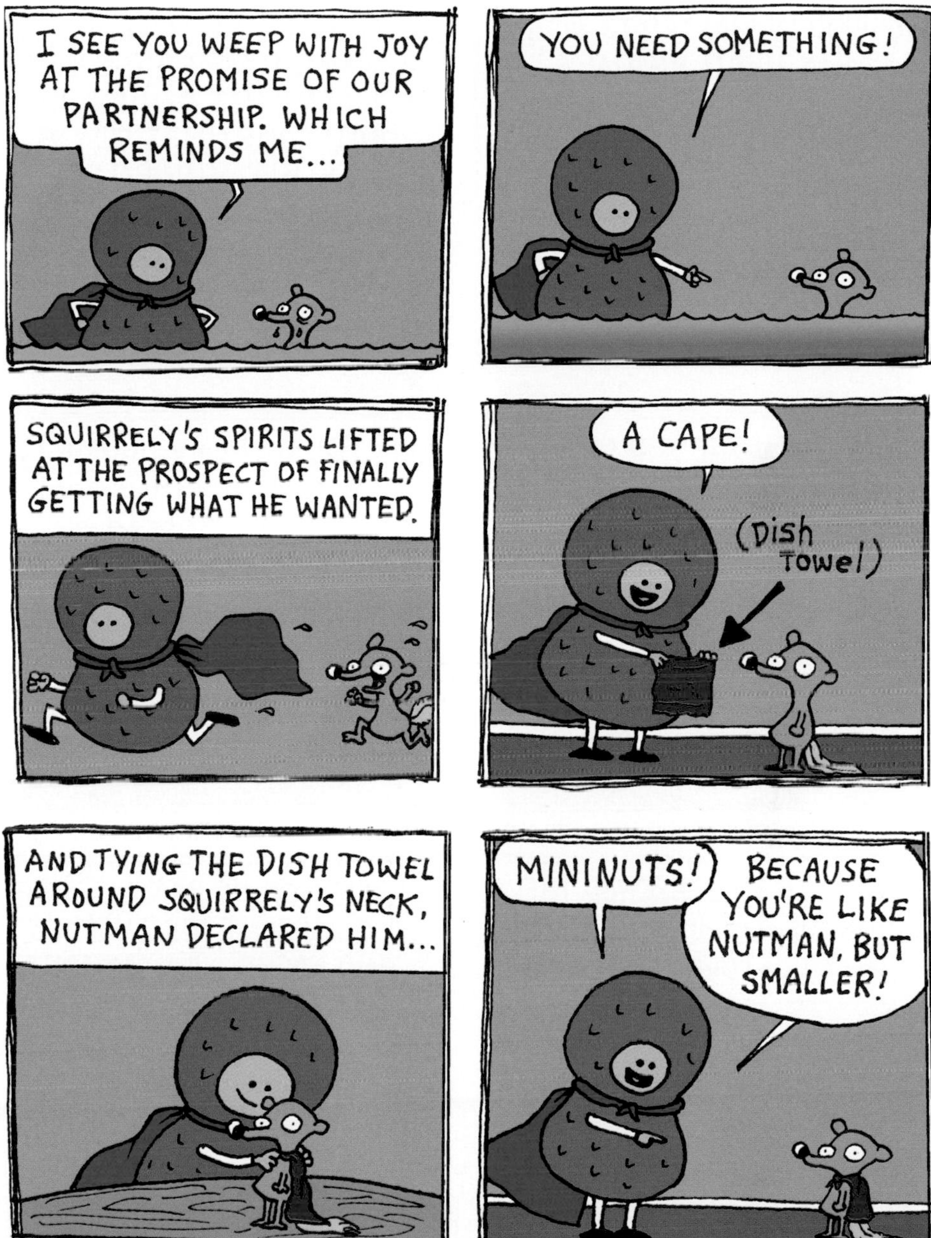
I SEE YOU WEEP WITH JOY AT THE PROMISE OF OUR PARTNERSHIP. WHICH REMINDS ME...
YOU NEED SOMETHING!
SQUIRRELY'S SPIRITS LIFTED AT THE PROSPECT OF FINALLY GETTING WHAT HE WANTED.
A CAPE!
(DISH TOWEL)
AND TYING THE DISH TOWEL AROUND SQUIRRELY'S NECK, NUTMAN DECLARED HIM...
MININUTS!
BECAUSE YOU'RE LIKE NUTMAN, BUT SMALLER!

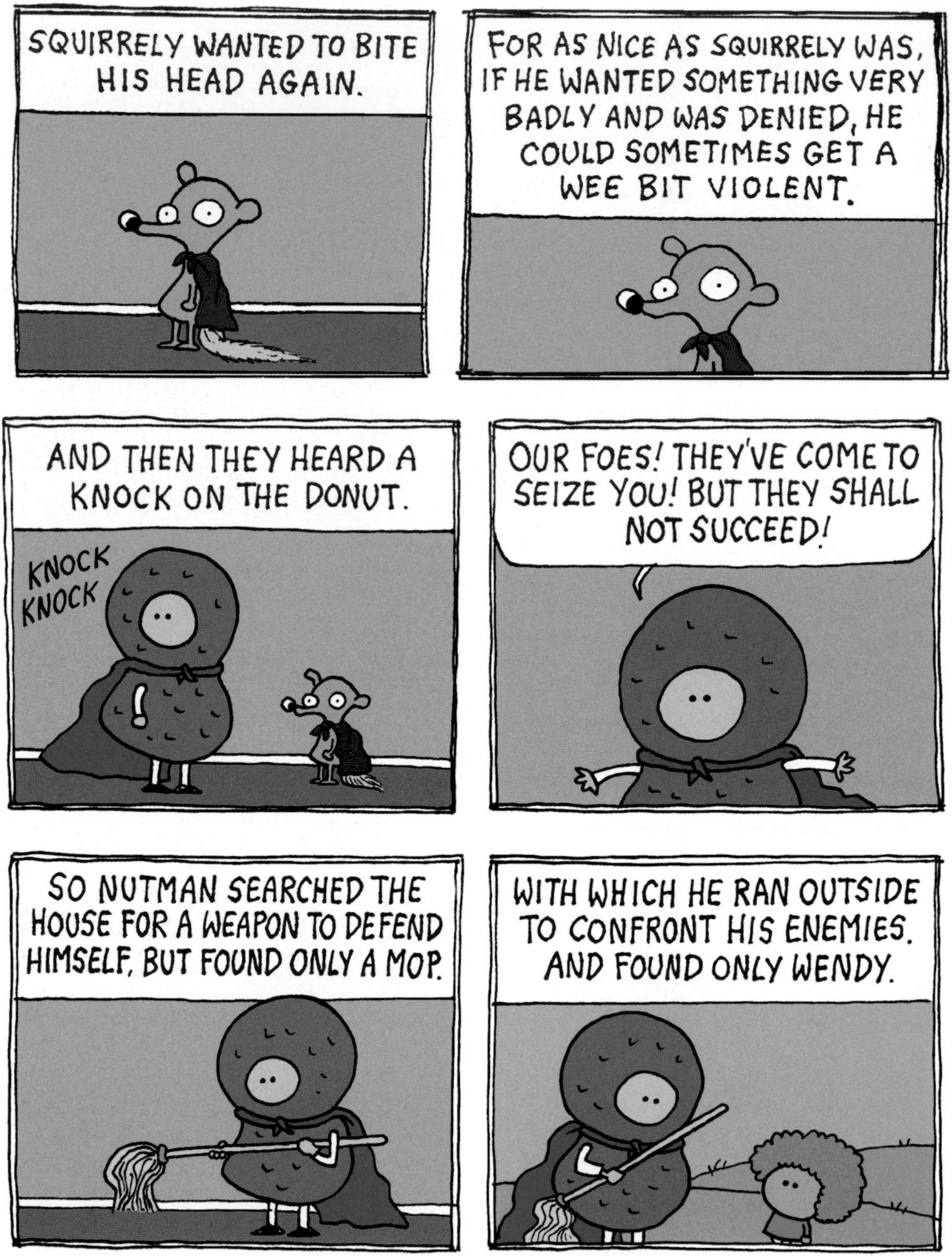
SQUIRRELY WANTED TO BITE HIS HEAD AGAIN.
FOR AS NICE AS SQUIRRELY WAS, IF HE WANTED SOMETHING VERY BADLY AND WAS DENIED, HE COULD SOMETIMES GET A WEE BIT VIOLENT.
AND THEN THEY HEARD A KNOCK ON THE DONUT.
KNOCK KNOCK
OUR FOES! THEY'VE COME TO SEIZE YOU! BUT THEY SHALL NOT SUCCEED!
SO NUTMAN SEARCHED THE HOUSE FOR A WEAPON TO DEFEND HIMSELF, BUT FOUND ONLY A MOP.
WITH WHICH HE RAN OUTSIDE TO CONFRONT HIS ENEMIES. AND FOUND ONLY WENDY.

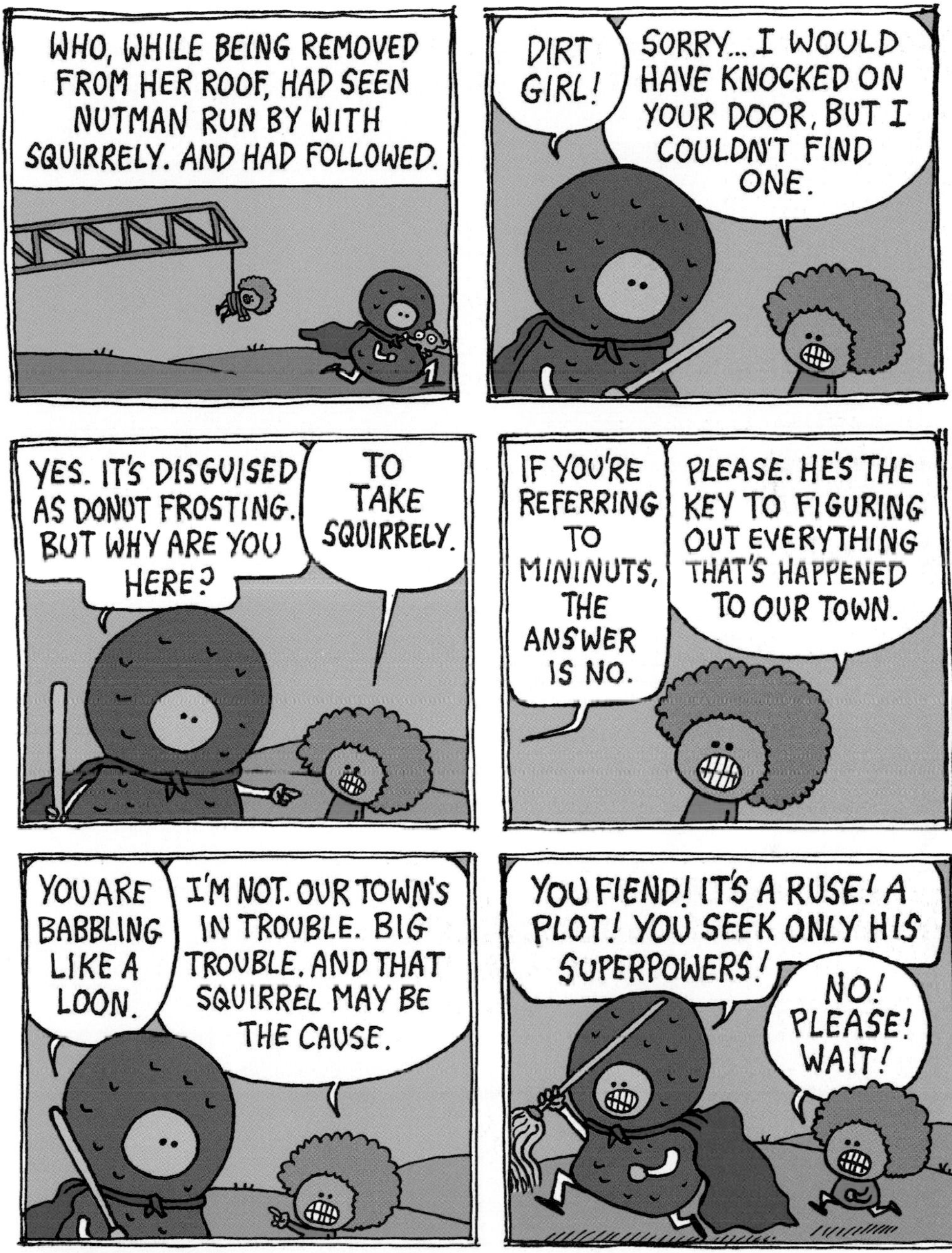
WHO, WHILE BEING REMOVED FROM HER ROOF, HAD SEEN NUTMAN RUN BY WITH SQUIRRELY. AND HAD FOLLOWED.
DIRT GIRL!
SORRY... I WOULD HAVE KNOCKED ON YOUR DOOR, BUT I COULDN'T FIND ONE.
YES. IT'S DISGUISED AS DONUT FROSTING. BUT WHY ARE YOU HERE?
TO TAKE SQUIRRELY.
IF YOU'RE REFERRING TO MININUTS, THE ANSWER IS NO.
PLEASE. HE'S THE KEY TO FIGURING OUT EVERYTHING THAT'S HAPPENED TO OUR TOWN.
YOU ARE BABBLING LIKE A LOON.
I'M NOT. OUR TOWN'S IN TROUBLE. BIG TROUBLE. AND THAT SQUIRREL MAY BE THE CAUSE.
YOU FIEND! IT'S A RUSE! A PLOT! YOU SEEK ONLY HIS SUPERPOWERS!
NO! PLEASE! WAIT!

BUT NUTMAN WOULD NOT LISTEN. INSTEAD, HE FLED BACK INTO HIS DONUT.

WHERE HE COMFORTED SQUIRRELY.

FEAR NOT. FOR I HAVE THWARTED DIRT GIRL.

LEAVING A DESPERATE DIRT GIRL TO SEARCH FOR THE DONUT DOOR.

ALAS. ALL OF THIS CRIME-FIGHTING HAS FATIGUED ME. LET US GET OUR REST AND BEGIN OUR NOBLE MISSION TOMORROW.

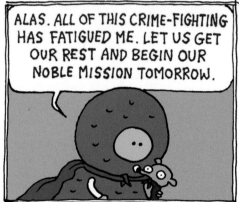

AND SO HE PLACED SQUIRRELY IN A BOWLING BAG.

IT IS SAFE, SECURE, AND FOR SOMEONE OF YOUR SIZE, THE EQUIVALENT OF A NICE STUDIO APARTMENT.

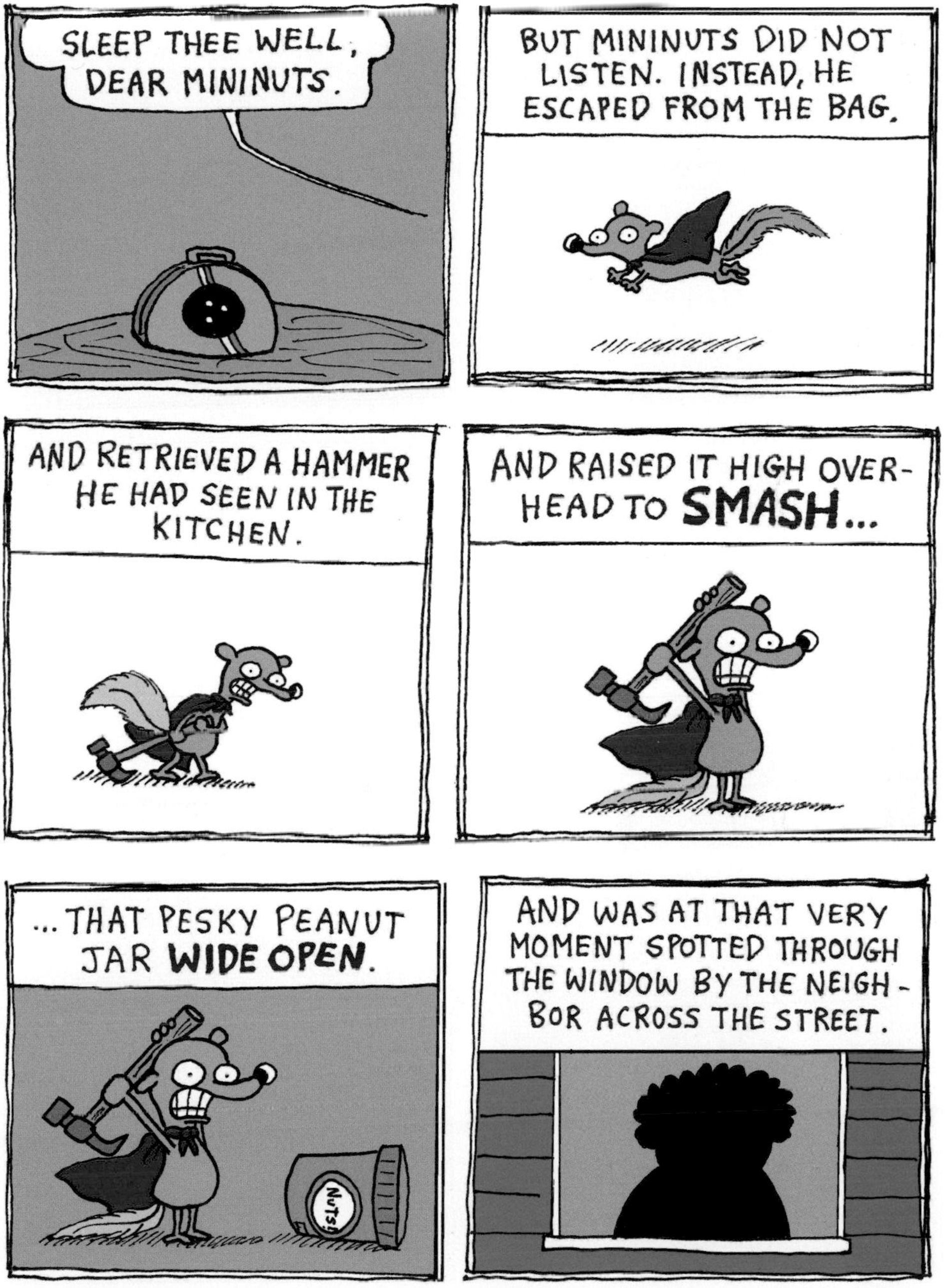
SLEEP THEE WELL, DEAR MININUTS.
BUT MININUTS DID NOT LISTEN. INSTEAD, HE ESCAPED FROM THE BAG.
AND RETRIEVED A HAMMER HE HAD SEEN IN THE KITCHEN.
AND RAISED IT HIGH OVERHEAD TO SMASH...
...THAT PESKY PEANUT JAR WIDE OPEN.
NUTS!
AND WAS AT THAT VERY MOMENT SPOTTED THROUGH THE WINDOW BY THE NEIGHBOR ACROSS THE STREET.

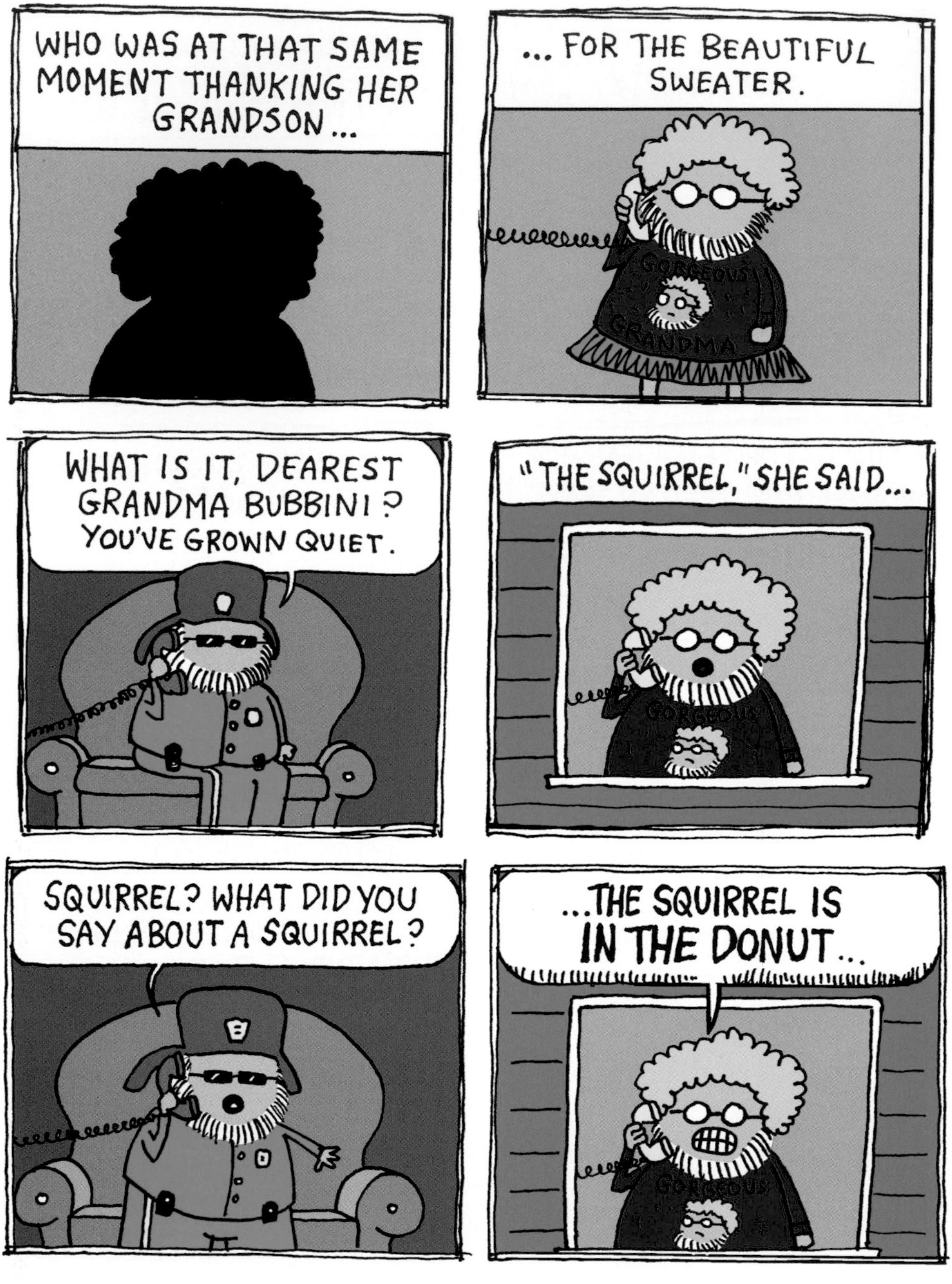

WHO WAS AT THAT SAME MOMENT THANKING HER GRANDSON...
... FOR THE BEAUTIFUL SWEATER.
GORGEOUS GRANDMA
WHAT IS IT, DEAREST GRANDMA BUBBINI? YOU'VE GROWN QUIET.
"THE SQUIRREL," SHE SAID...
GORGEOUS
SQUIRREL? WHAT DID YOU SAY ABOUT A SQUIRREL?
...THE SQUIRREL IS IN THE DONUT...
GORGEOUS

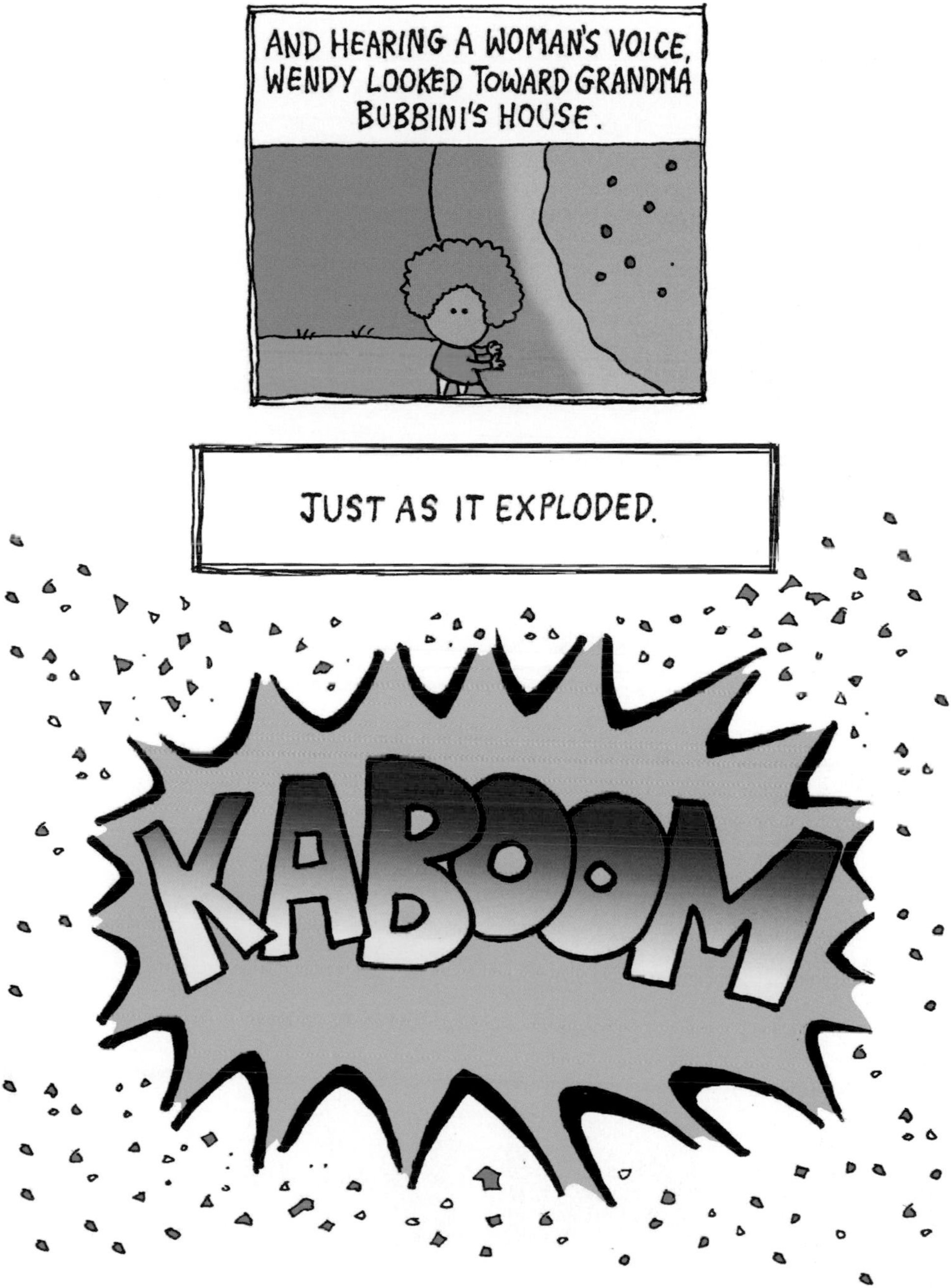
AND HEARING A WOMAN'S VOICE, WENDY LOOKED TOWARD GRANDMA BUBBINI'S HOUSE.
JUST AS IT EXPLODED.
KABOOM

CHAPTER PICK A NUMBER, ANY NUMBER

IN WHICH...

YOU'RE MORE KNOWLEDGEABLE THAN THE AUTHOR

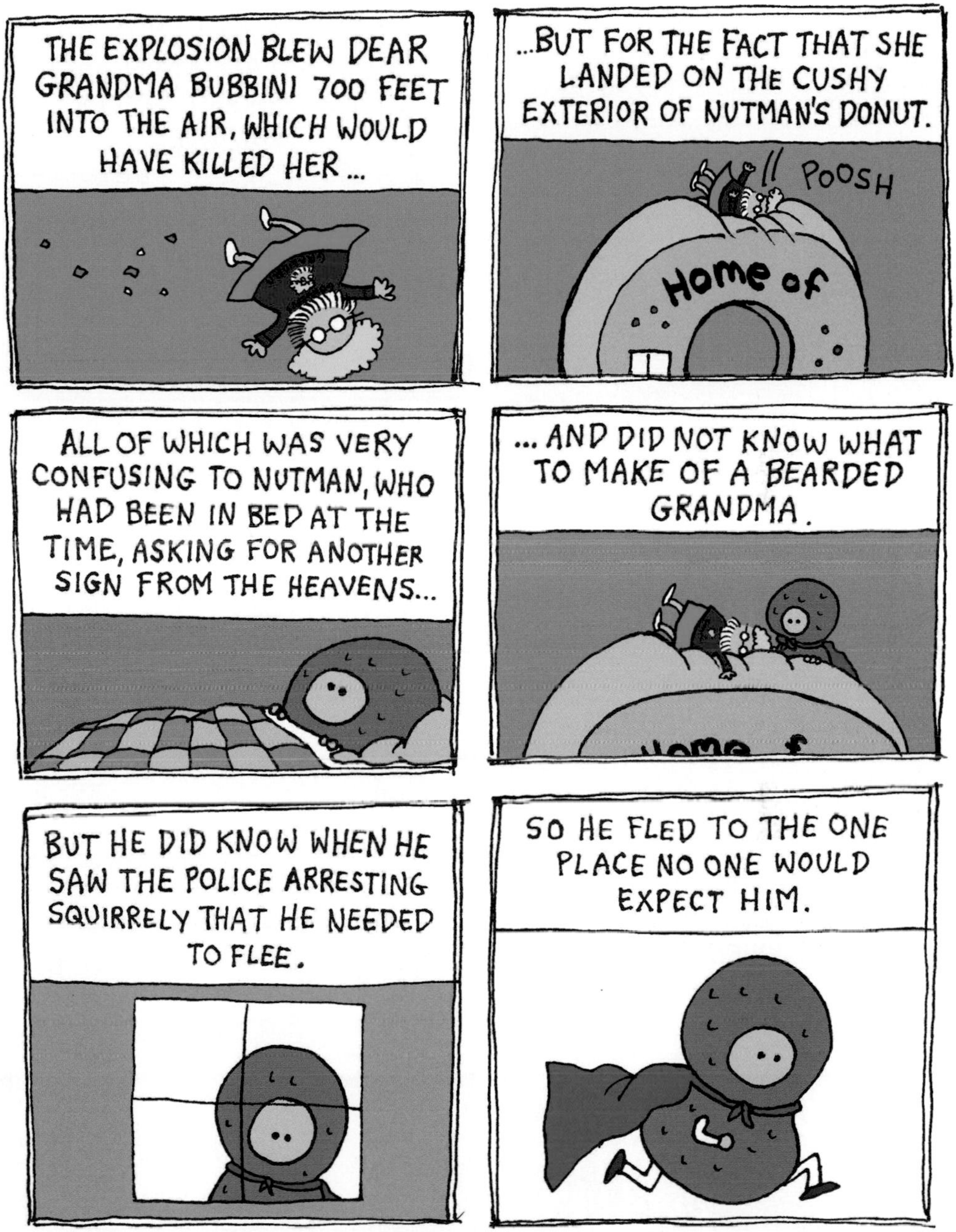
THE EXPLOSION BLEW DEAR GRANDMA BUBBINI 700 FEET INTO THE AIR, WHICH WOULD HAVE KILLED HER ...
...BUT FOR THE FACT THAT SHE LANDED ON THE CUSHY EXTERIOR OF NUTMAN'S DONUT.
POOSH
Home of
ALL OF WHICH WAS VERY CONFUSING TO NUTMAN, WHO HAD BEEN IN BED AT THE TIME, ASKING FOR ANOTHER SIGN FROM THE HEAVENS...
... AND DID NOT KNOW WHAT TO MAKE OF A BEARDED GRANDMA.
BUT HE DID KNOW WHEN HE SAW THE POLICE ARRESTING SQUIRRELY THAT HE NEEDED TO FLEE.
SO HE FLED TO THE ONE PLACE NO ONE WOULD EXPECT HIM.

WORK.

GUY IN CHARGE OF WORDY THINGS

WHERE, AS SKIPPY VON TUBER, HE DENIED ALL KNOWLEDGE OF THE VIOLENT LITTLE SQUIRREL.

WHAT? HE WAS IN MY HOUSE?

BUT TO THE REST OF TRUBBLE, IT WAS THE MERE FACT THAT SQUIRRELY WAS ALIVE THAT SENT SHOCK WAVES THROUGH THE TOWN.

LEADING TO THE QUESTION OF WHAT TO DO WITH THE ALREADY HALF-COMPLETED GOLD STATUE.

A PROBLEM ACCIDENTALLY SOLVED BY THE NITROGLYCERINE NANNY WHEN SHE WAS WORKING.

AND SAW ONE OF THE BABIES SHE WAS SUPPOSED TO BE WATCHING ESCAPE FROM THE BOUNCY CASTLE.

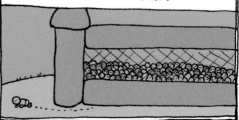

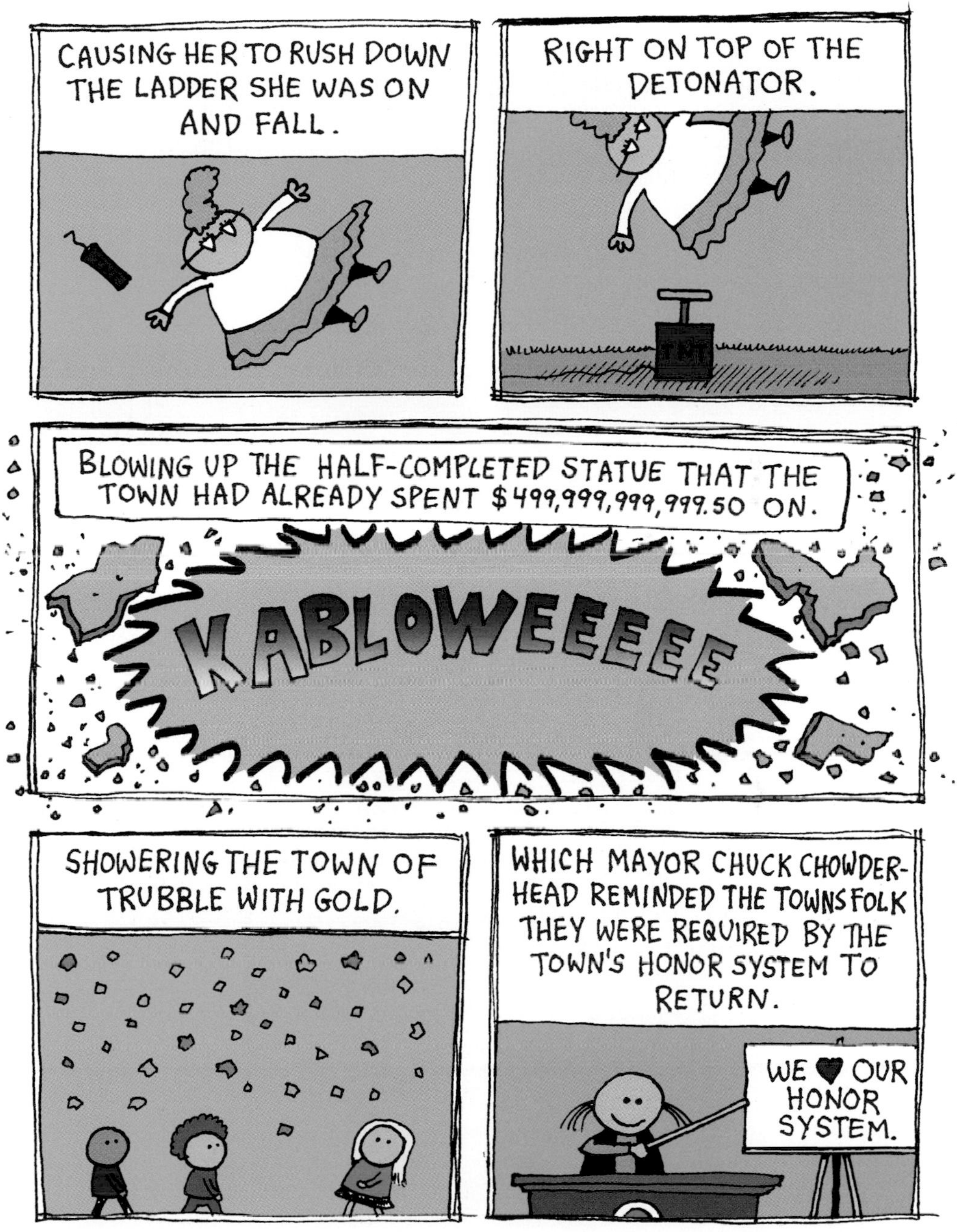
CAUSING HER TO RUSH DOWN THE LADDER SHE WAS ON AND FALL.
RIGHT ON TOP OF THE DETONATOR.
TNT
BLOWING UP THE HALF-COMPLETED STATUE THAT THE TOWN HAD ALREADY SPENT $499,999,999,999.50 ON.
KABLOWEEEEE
SHOWERING THE TOWN OF TRUBBLE WITH GOLD.
WHICH MAYOR CHUCK CHOWDERHEAD REMINDED THE TOWNSFOLK THEY WERE REQUIRED BY THE TOWN'S HONOR SYSTEM TO RETURN.
WE ♥ OUR HONOR SYSTEM.

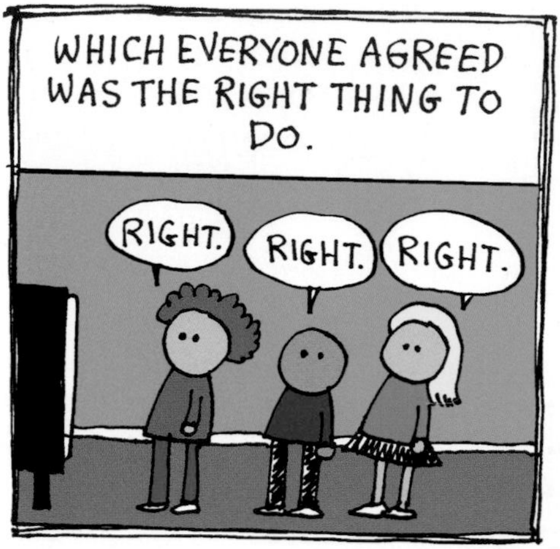
WHICH EVERYONE AGREED WAS THE RIGHT THING TO DO.
RIGHT.
RIGHT.
RIGHT.

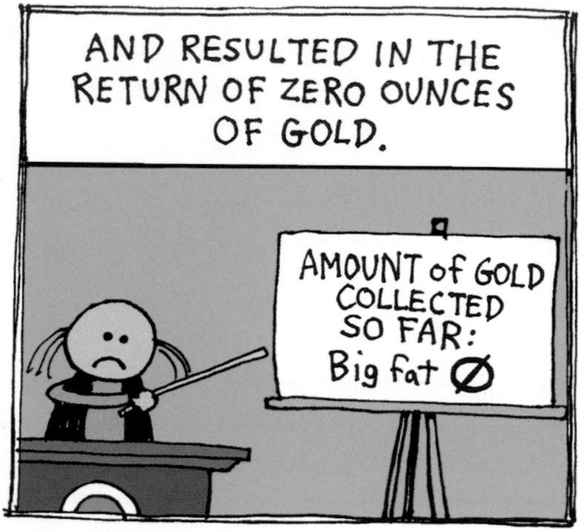
AND RESULTED IN THE RETURN OF ZERO OUNCES OF GOLD.
AMOUNT of GOLD COLLECTED SO FAR: Big fat Ø

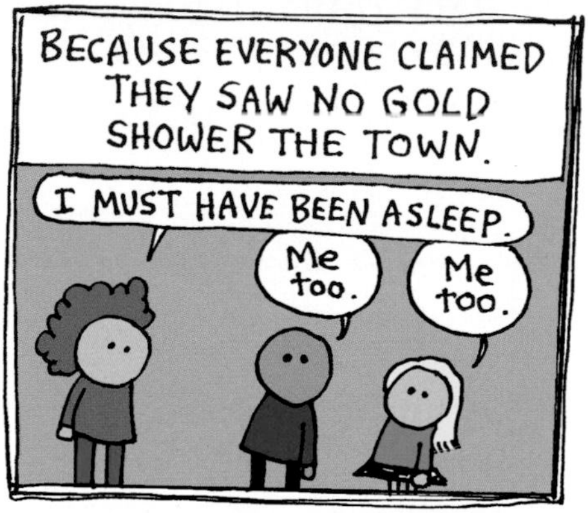
BECAUSE EVERYONE CLAIMED THEY SAW NO GOLD SHOWER THE TOWN.
I MUST HAVE BEEN ASLEEP.
Me too.
Me too.

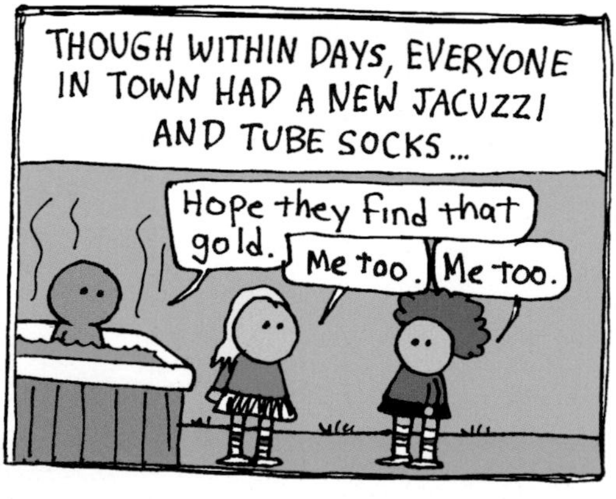
THOUGH WITHIN DAYS, EVERYONE IN TOWN HAD A NEW JACUZZI AND TUBE SOCKS...
Hope they find that gold.
Me too.
Me too.

... WITH THE EXCEPTION OF A SQUIRREL...

... WHO WAS AWAITING TRIAL IN A STEEL CAGE OVERHANGING AN ELECTRIFIED SHARK TANK.

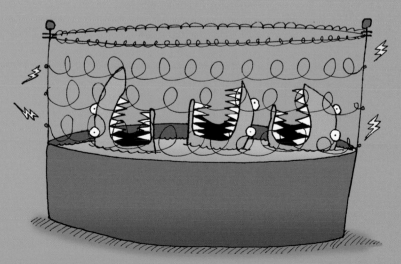

... AND A PURPLE-HAIRED GIRL...

... ABOUT TO TELL HER DAD EVERYTHING.

CHAPTER DOOM AND GLOOM

WHICH...

PRETTY MUCH TELLS YOU ALL YOU NEED TO KNOW

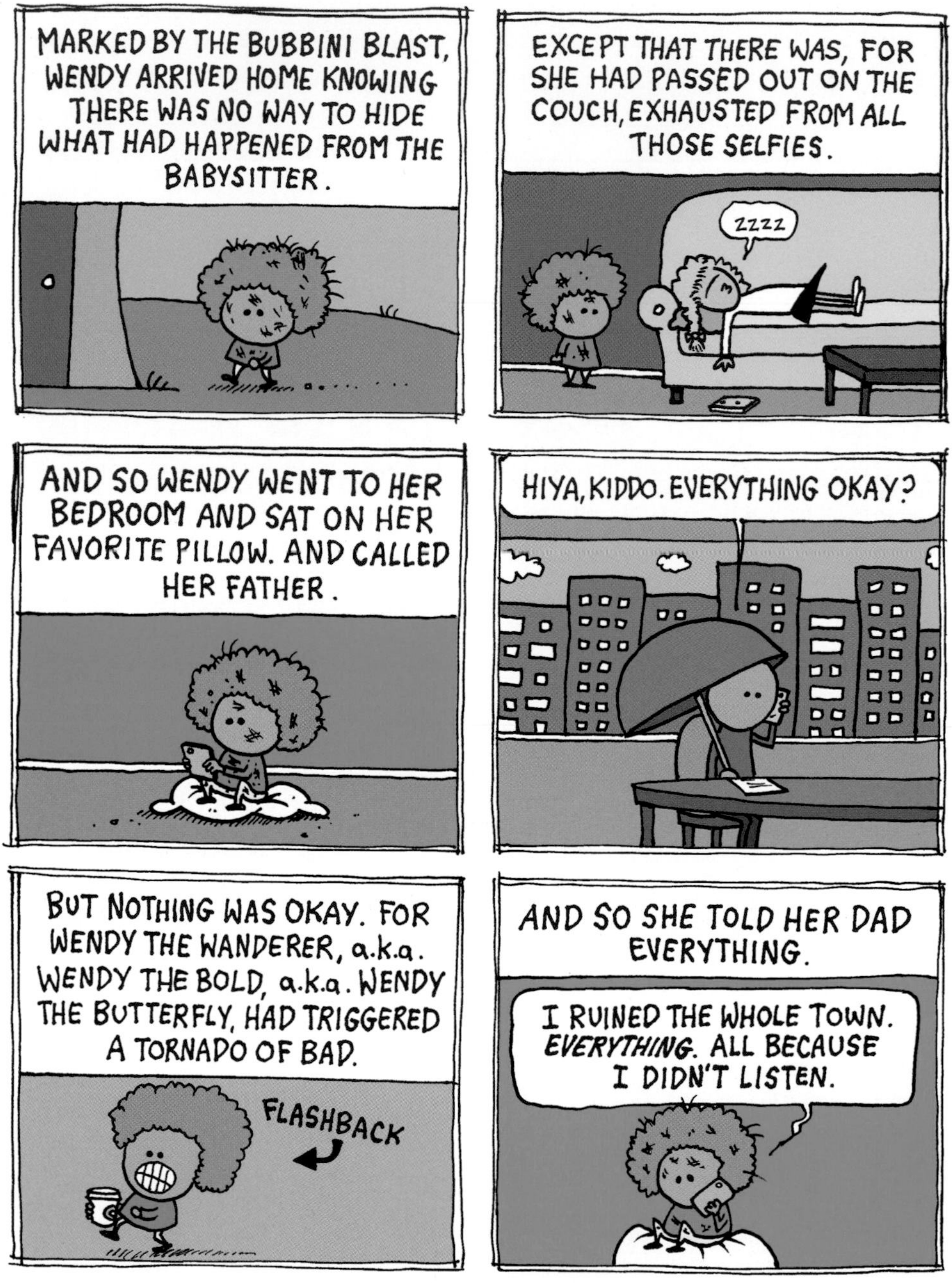

MARKED BY THE BUBBINI BLAST, WENDY ARRIVED HOME KNOWING THERE WAS NO WAY TO HIDE WHAT HAD HAPPENED FROM THE BABYSITTER.
EXCEPT THAT THERE WAS, FOR SHE HAD PASSED OUT ON THE COUCH, EXHAUSTED FROM ALL THOSE SELFIES.
ZZZZ
AND SO WENDY WENT TO HER BEDROOM AND SAT ON HER FAVORITE PILLOW. AND CALLED HER FATHER.
HIYA, KIDDO. EVERYTHING OKAY?
BUT NOTHING WAS OKAY. FOR WENDY THE WANDERER, a.k.a. WENDY THE BOLD, a.k.a. WENDY THE BUTTERFLY, HAD TRIGGERED A TORNADO OF BAD.
FLASHBACK
AND SO SHE TOLD HER DAD EVERYTHING.
I RUINED THE WHOLE TOWN. *EVERYTHING*. ALL BECAUSE I DIDN'T LISTEN.

AND NOW THE MAYOR'S OFFICE IS GONE. AND THE CAFÉS. AND GRANDMA BUBBINI'S HOUSE.

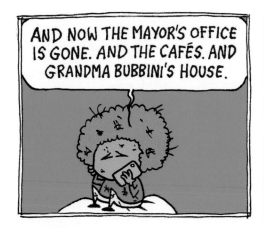

AND ON THE OTHER END OF THE LINE, THERE WAS SILENCE, WHICH ANYONE WITH A PARENT KNOWS SPELLS THE DOOMIEST KIND OF DOOM.

SILENCE = BAD

(Really, really bad)

EXCEPT THIS TIME. THIS TIME IT MEANT THAT TRUBBLE'S ONLY CELL PHONE TOWER (DAMAGED IN THE BUBBINI BLAST) HAD FALLEN.

KSSH

AND WAS NOW KAPUT.

Hello?
Kiddo?
Hello?

A FACT NOT KNOWN BY WENDY.

WHO, UPON HEARING THE DOOMIEST DAD SILENCE SHE HAD EVER HEARD, JUST PUT DOWN THE CELL PHONE AND CRIED.

CHAPTER 25
THE TRIAL
OF
SQUIRRELY

IN WHICH...

WE PROVE WE CAN NUMBER A CHAPTER LIKE A NORMAL PERSON

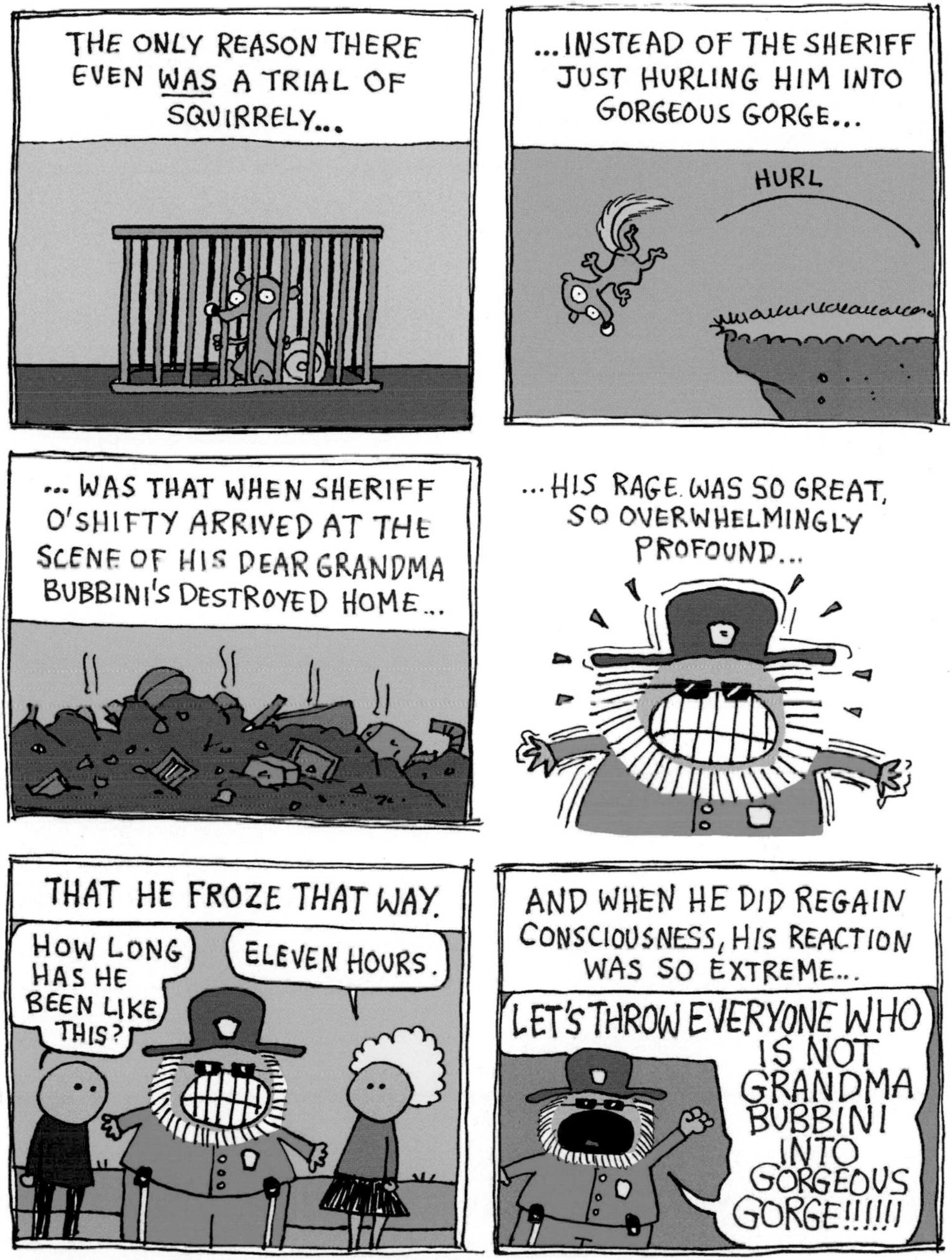

THE ONLY REASON THERE EVEN WAS A TRIAL OF SQUIRRELY...
...INSTEAD OF THE SHERIFF JUST HURLING HIM INTO GORGEOUS GORGE...
HURL
... WAS THAT WHEN SHERIFF O'SHIFTY ARRIVED AT THE SCENE OF HIS DEAR GRANDMA BUBBINI'S DESTROYED HOME...
...HIS RAGE WAS SO GREAT, SO OVERWHELMINGLY PROFOUND...
THAT HE FROZE THAT WAY.
HOW LONG HAS HE BEEN LIKE THIS?
ELEVEN HOURS.
AND WHEN HE DID REGAIN CONSCIOUSNESS, HIS REACTION WAS SO EXTREME...
LET'S THROW EVERYONE WHO IS NOT GRANDMA BUBBINI INTO GORGEOUS GORGE!!!!!!

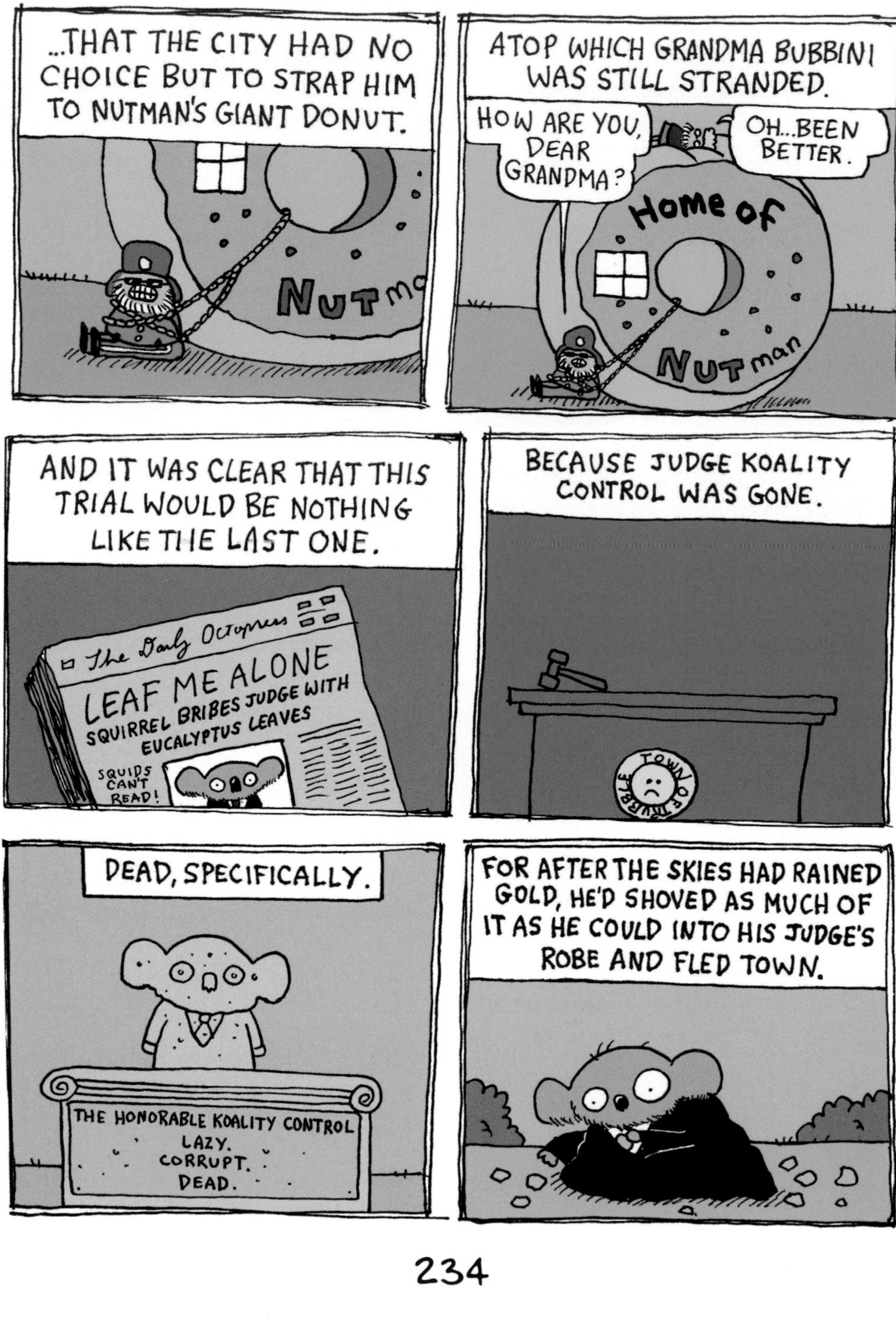
...THAT THE CITY HAD NO CHOICE BUT TO STRAP HIM TO NUTMAN'S GIANT DONUT.
NUTma
ATOP WHICH GRANDMA BUBBINI WAS STILL STRANDED.
HOW ARE YOU, DEAR GRANDMA?
OH...BEEN BETTER.
Home of
NUTman
AND IT WAS CLEAR THAT THIS TRIAL WOULD BE NOTHING LIKE THE LAST ONE.
The Daily Octopress
LEAF ME ALONE
SQUIRREL BRIBES JUDGE WITH EUCALYPTUS LEAVES
SQUIDS CAN'T READ!
BECAUSE JUDGE KOALITY CONTROL WAS GONE.
TOWN OF TRUBBLE
DEAD, SPECIFICALLY.
THE HONORABLE KOALITY CONTROL
LAZY.
CORRUPT.
DEAD.
FOR AFTER THE SKIES HAD RAINED GOLD, HE'D SHOVED AS MUCH OF IT AS HE COULD INTO HIS JUDGE'S ROBE AND FLED TOWN.

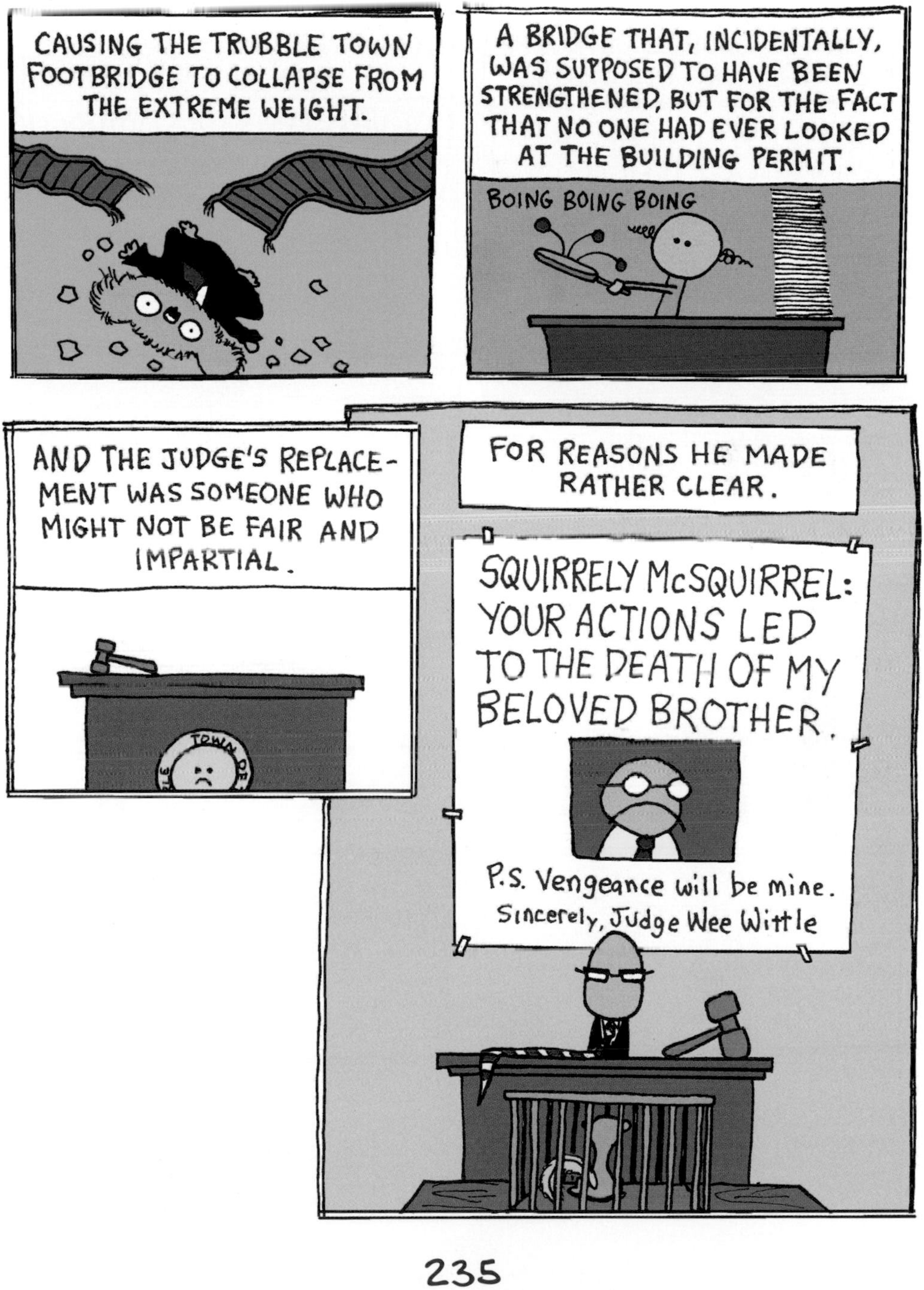
CAUSING THE TRUBBLE TOWN FOOTBRIDGE TO COLLAPSE FROM THE EXTREME WEIGHT.
A BRIDGE THAT, INCIDENTALLY, WAS SUPPOSED TO HAVE BEEN STRENGTHENED, BUT FOR THE FACT THAT NO ONE HAD EVER LOOKED AT THE BUILDING PERMIT.
BOING BOING BOING
AND THE JUDGE'S REPLACEMENT WAS SOMEONE WHO MIGHT NOT BE FAIR AND IMPARTIAL.
FOR REASONS HE MADE RATHER CLEAR.
SQUIRRELY McSQUIRREL: YOUR ACTIONS LED TO THE DEATH OF MY BELOVED BROTHER.
P.S. Vengeance will be mine.
Sincerely, Judge Wee Wittle

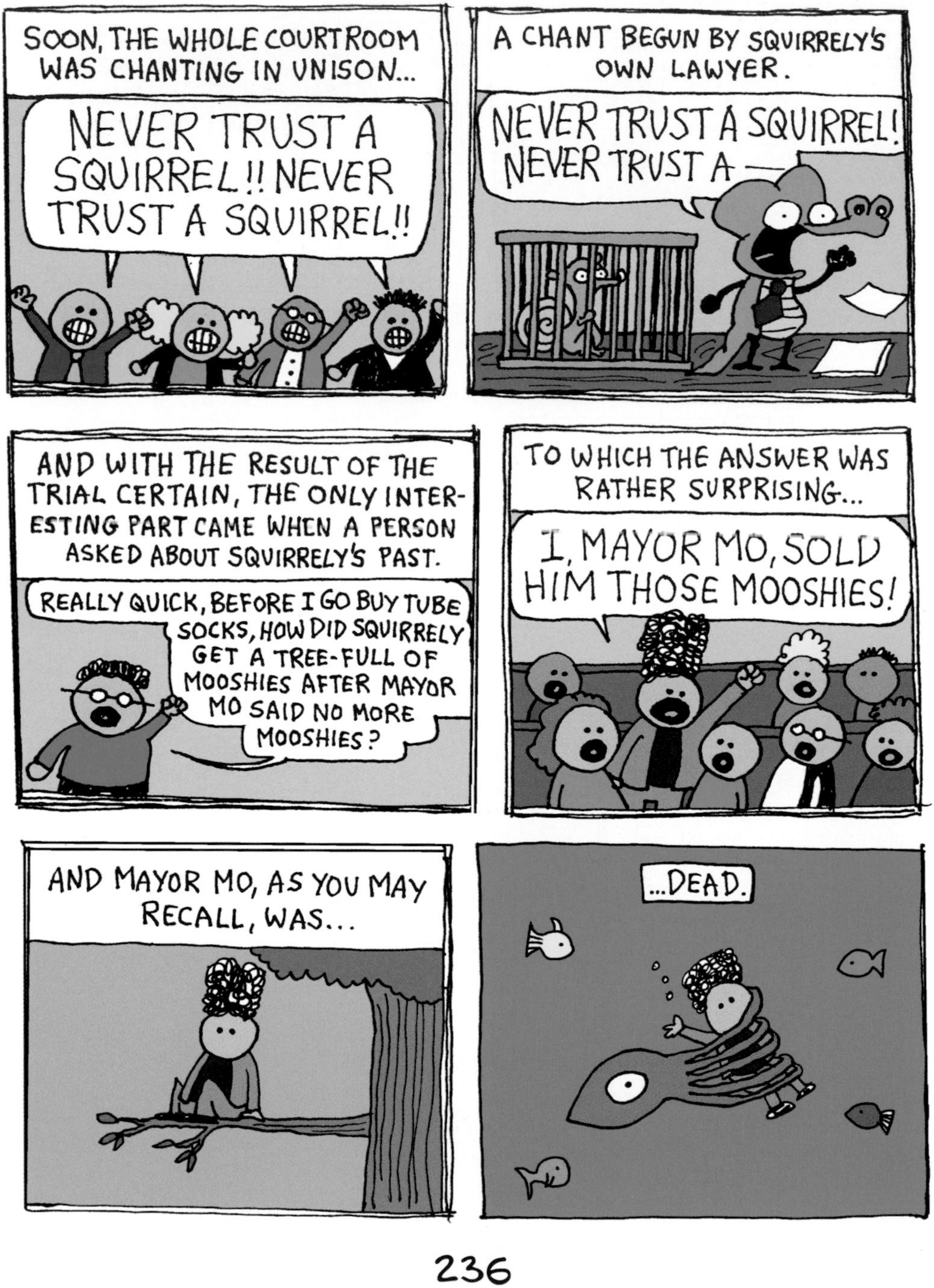
SOON, THE WHOLE COURTROOM WAS CHANTING IN UNISON...
NEVER TRUST A SQUIRREL!! NEVER TRUST A SQUIRREL!!
A CHANT BEGUN BY SQUIRRELY'S OWN LAWYER.
NEVER TRUST A SQUIRREL! NEVER TRUST A —
AND WITH THE RESULT OF THE TRIAL CERTAIN, THE ONLY INTERESTING PART CAME WHEN A PERSON ASKED ABOUT SQUIRRELY'S PAST.
REALLY QUICK, BEFORE I GO BUY TUBE SOCKS, HOW DID SQUIRRELY GET A TREE-FULL OF MOOSHIES AFTER MAYOR MO SAID NO MORE MOOSHIES?
TO WHICH THE ANSWER WAS RATHER SURPRISING...
I, MAYOR MO, SOLD HIM THOSE MOOSHIES!
AND MAYOR MO, AS YOU MAY RECALL, WAS...
...DEAD.

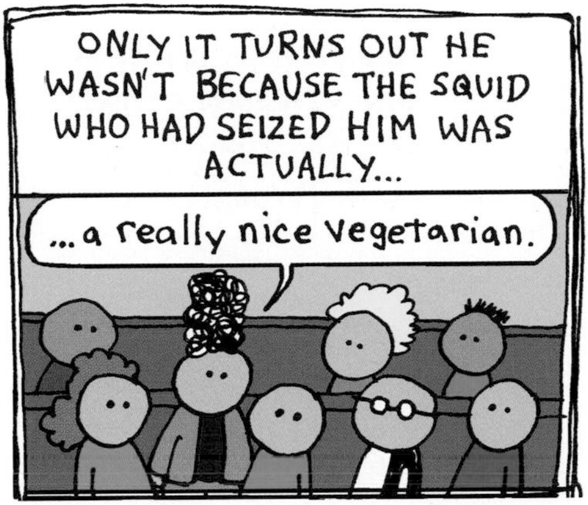
ONLY IT TURNS OUT HE WASN'T BECAUSE THE SQUID WHO HAD SEIZED HIM WAS ACTUALLY...
...a really nice vegetarian.

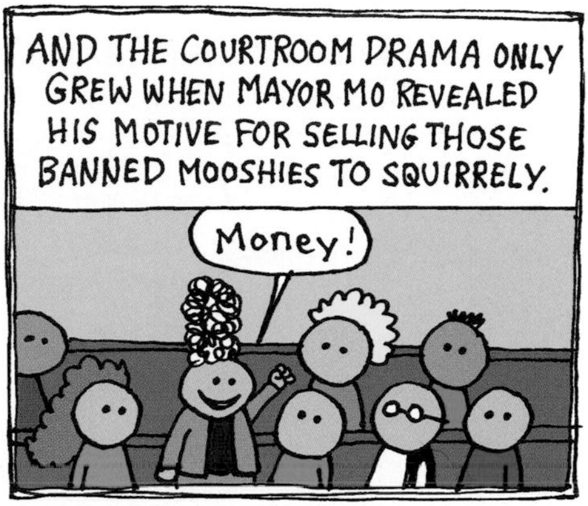
AND THE COURTROOM DRAMA ONLY GREW WHEN MAYOR MO REVEALED HIS MOTIVE FOR SELLING THOSE BANNED MOOSHIES TO SQUIRRELY.
Money!

BUT BY FAR THE BIGGEST SURPRISE IN COURT WAS THE APPEARANCE OF THE GIRL WITH HOMEMADE BUTTERFLY WINGS.

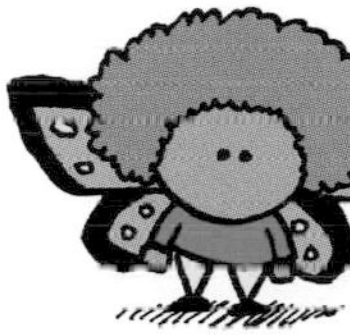

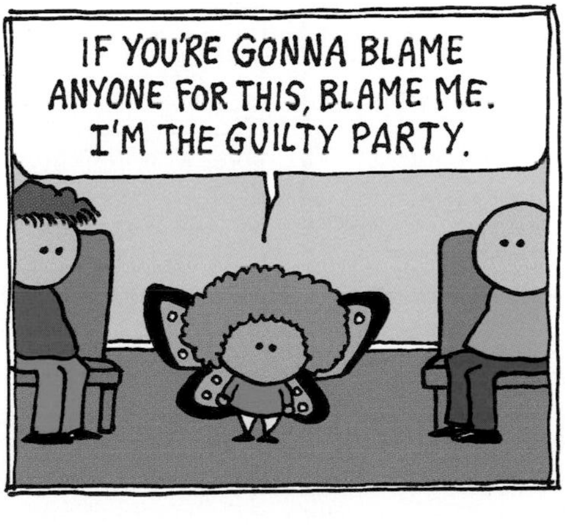
IF YOU'RE GONNA BLAME ANYONE FOR THIS, BLAME ME. I'M THE GUILTY PARTY.

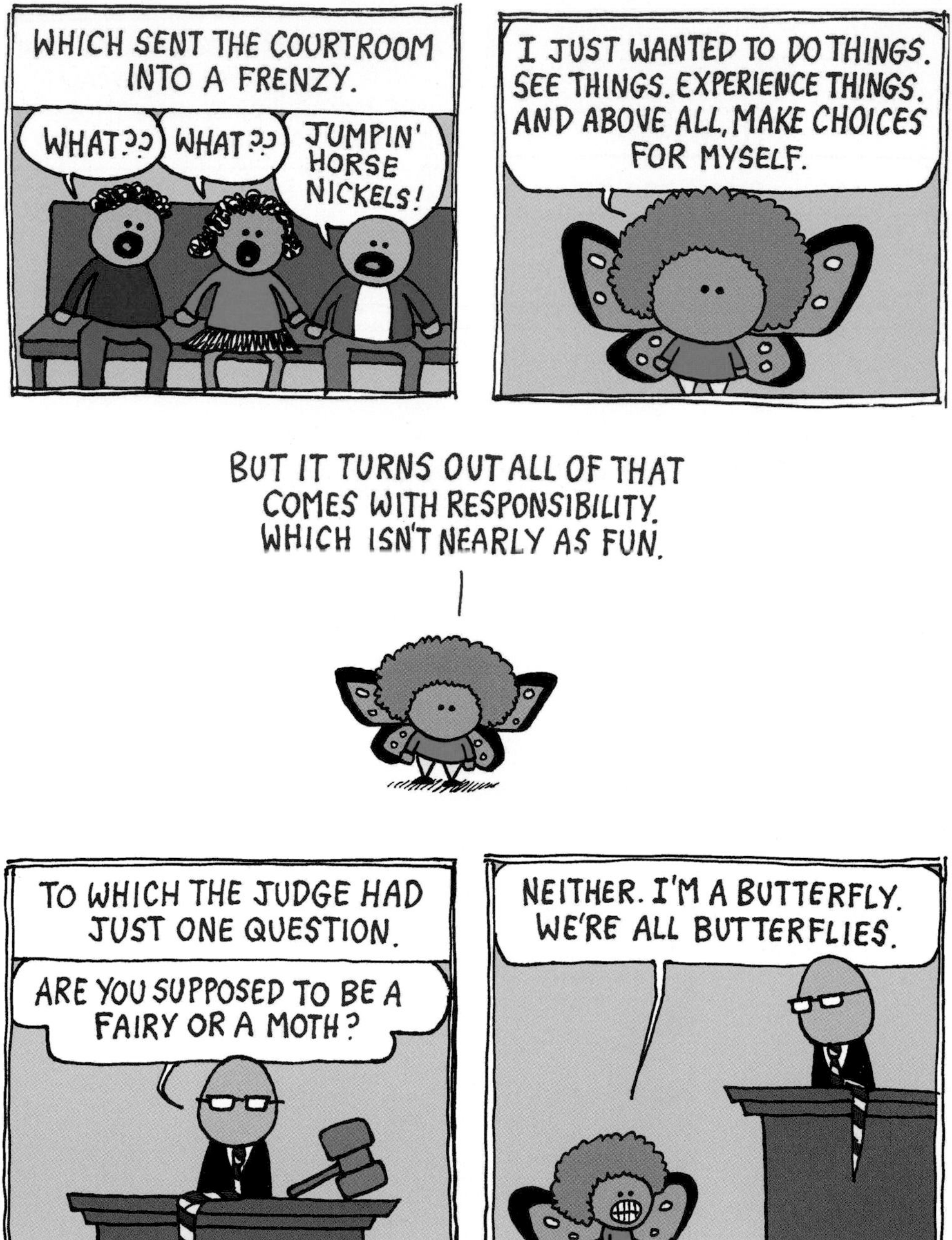
WHICH SENT THE COURTROOM INTO A FRENZY.
WHAT??
WHAT??
JUMPIN' HORSE NICKELS!
I JUST WANTED TO DO THINGS. SEE THINGS. EXPERIENCE THINGS. AND ABOVE ALL, MAKE CHOICES FOR MYSELF.
BUT IT TURNS OUT ALL OF THAT COMES WITH RESPONSIBILITY. WHICH ISN'T NEARLY AS FUN.
TO WHICH THE JUDGE HAD JUST ONE QUESTION.
ARE YOU SUPPOSED TO BE A FAIRY OR A MOTH?
NEITHER. I'M A BUTTERFLY. WE'RE ALL BUTTERFLIES.

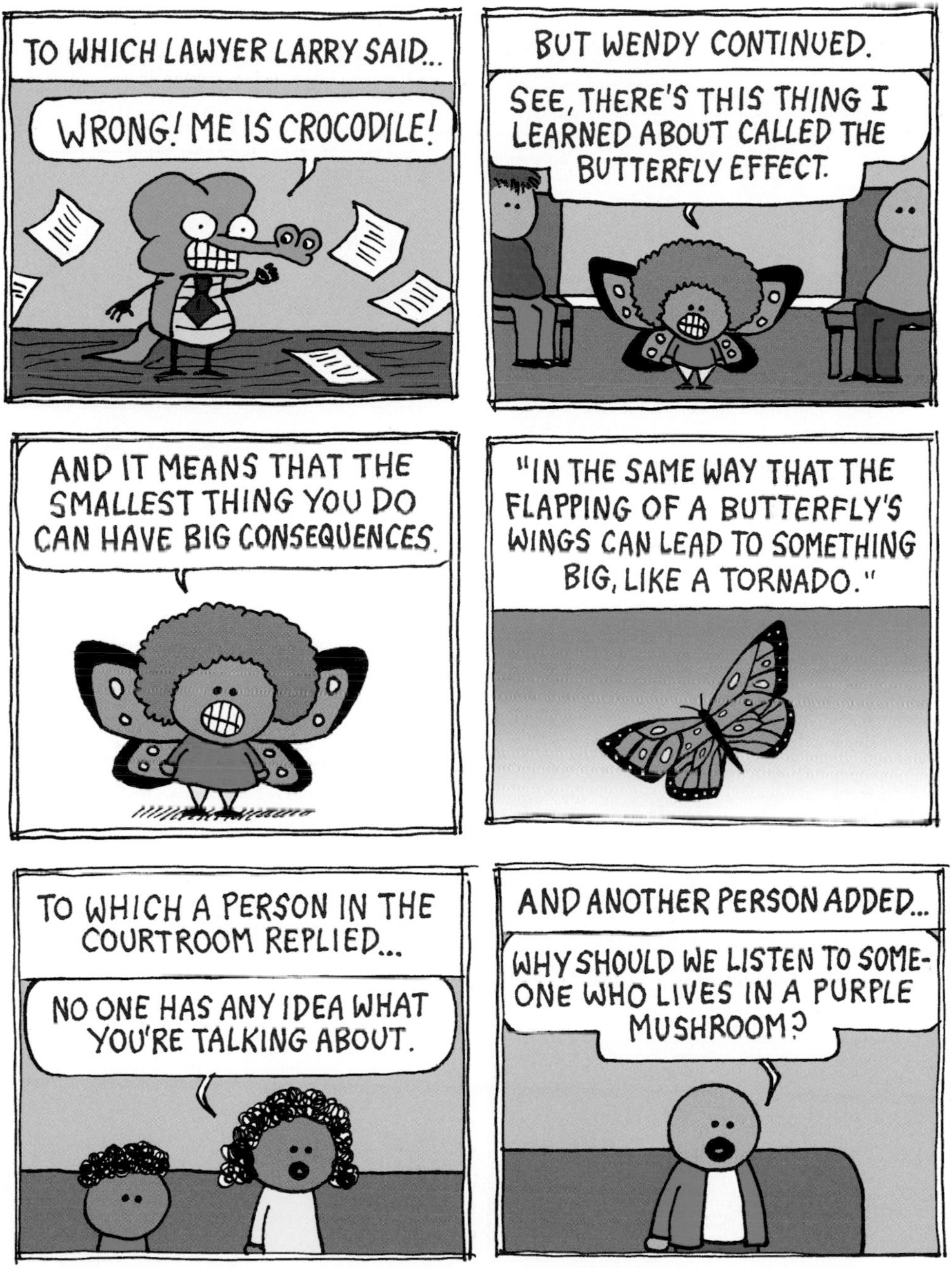
TO WHICH LAWYER LARRY SAID...
WRONG! ME IS CROCODILE!
BUT WENDY CONTINUED.
SEE, THERE'S THIS THING I LEARNED ABOUT CALLED THE BUTTERFLY EFFECT.
AND IT MEANS THAT THE SMALLEST THING YOU DO CAN HAVE BIG CONSEQUENCES.
"IN THE SAME WAY THAT THE FLAPPING OF A BUTTERFLY'S WINGS CAN LEAD TO SOMETHING BIG, LIKE A TORNADO."
TO WHICH A PERSON IN THE COURTROOM REPLIED...
NO ONE HAS ANY IDEA WHAT YOU'RE TALKING ABOUT.
AND ANOTHER PERSON ADDED...
WHY SHOULD WE LISTEN TO SOME-ONE WHO LIVES IN A PURPLE MUSHROOM?

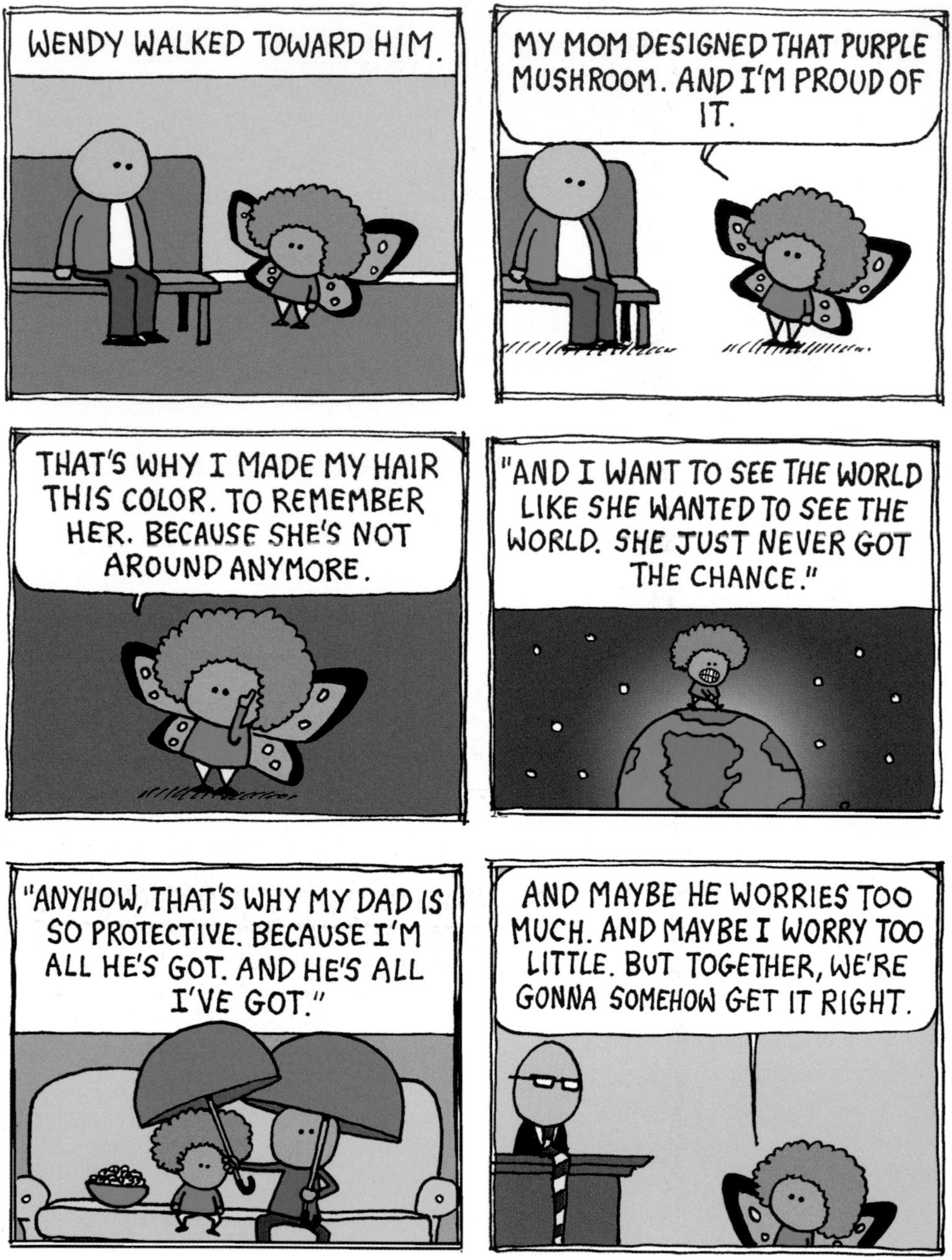
WENDY WALKED TOWARD HIM.
MY MOM DESIGNED THAT PURPLE MUSHROOM. AND I'M PROUD OF IT.
THAT'S WHY I MADE MY HAIR THIS COLOR. TO REMEMBER HER. BECAUSE SHE'S NOT AROUND ANYMORE.
"AND I WANT TO SEE THE WORLD LIKE SHE WANTED TO SEE THE WORLD. SHE JUST NEVER GOT THE CHANCE."
"ANYHOW, THAT'S WHY MY DAD IS SO PROTECTIVE. BECAUSE I'M ALL HE'S GOT. AND HE'S ALL I'VE GOT."
AND MAYBE HE WORRIES TOO MUCH. AND MAYBE I WORRY TOO LITTLE. BUT TOGETHER, WE'RE GONNA SOMEHOW GET IT RIGHT.

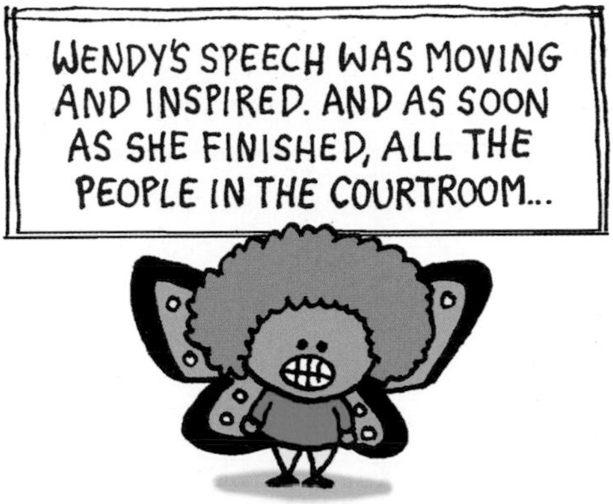
WENDY'S SPEECH WAS MOVING AND INSPIRED. AND AS SOON AS SHE FINISHED, ALL THE PEOPLE IN THE COURTROOM...

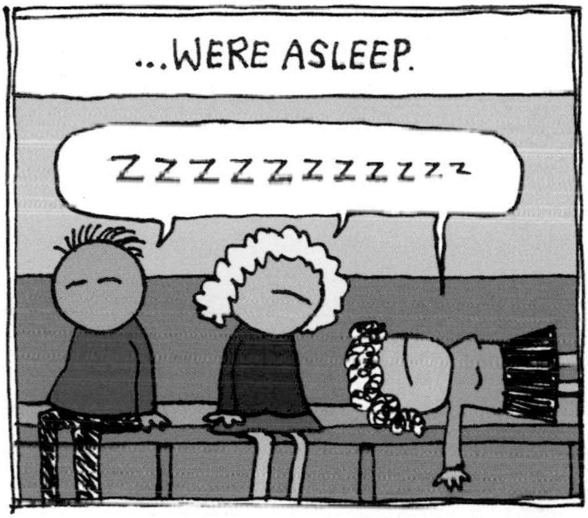
...WERE ASLEEP.
ZZZZZZZZZZZZ

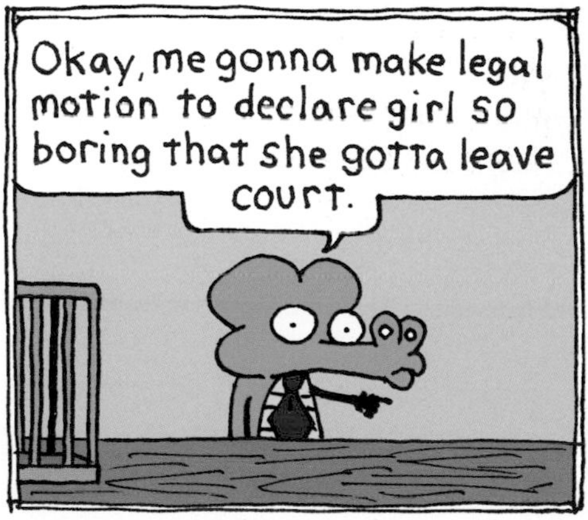
Okay, me gonna make legal motion to declare girl so boring that she gotta leave court.

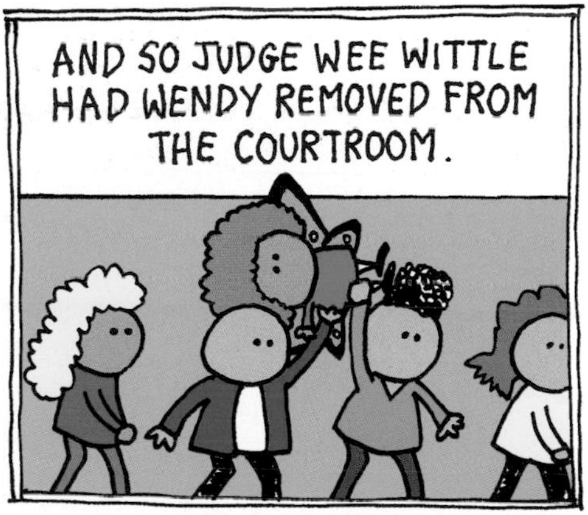
AND SO JUDGE WEE WITTLE HAD WENDY REMOVED FROM THE COURTROOM.

AND DECLARED THE LITTLE SQUIRREL...

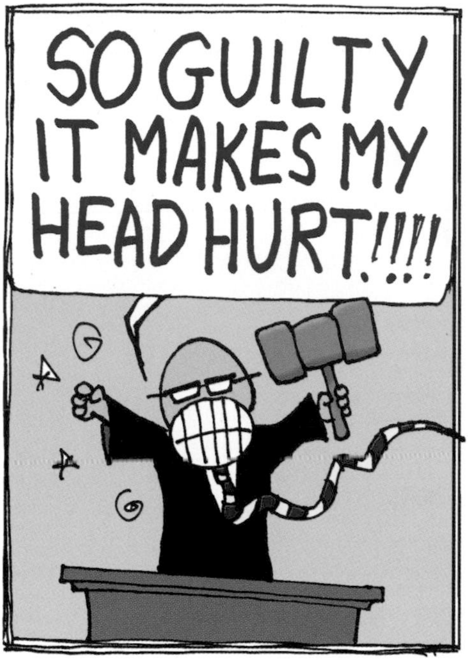
SO GUILTY IT MAKES MY HEAD HURT!!!!!

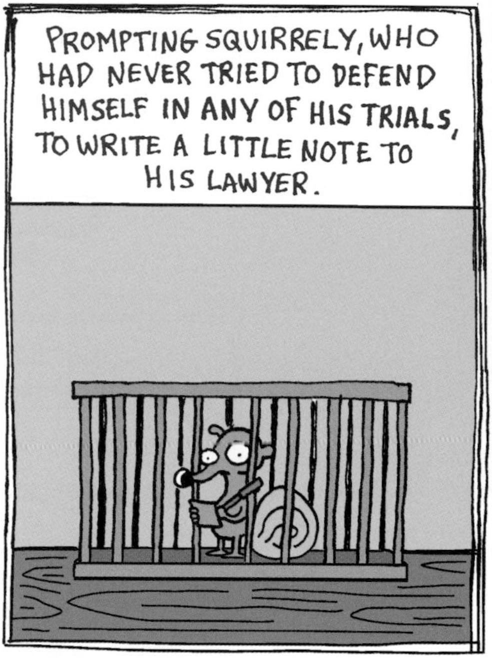
PROMPTING SQUIRRELY, WHO HAD NEVER TRIED TO DEFEND HIMSELF IN ANY OF HIS TRIALS, TO WRITE A LITTLE NOTE TO HIS LAWYER.

SAYING ONLY...

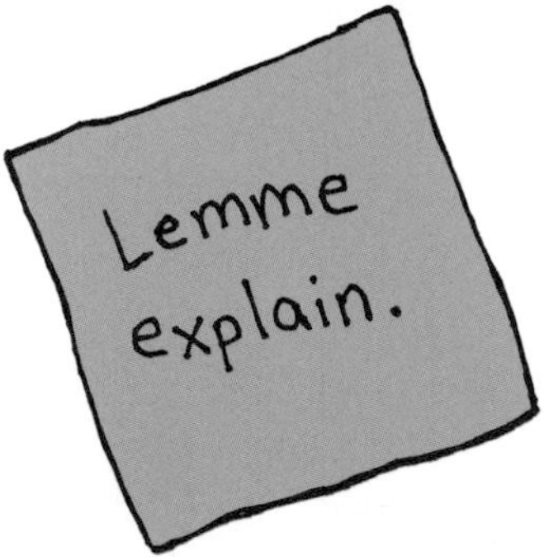
Lemme explain.

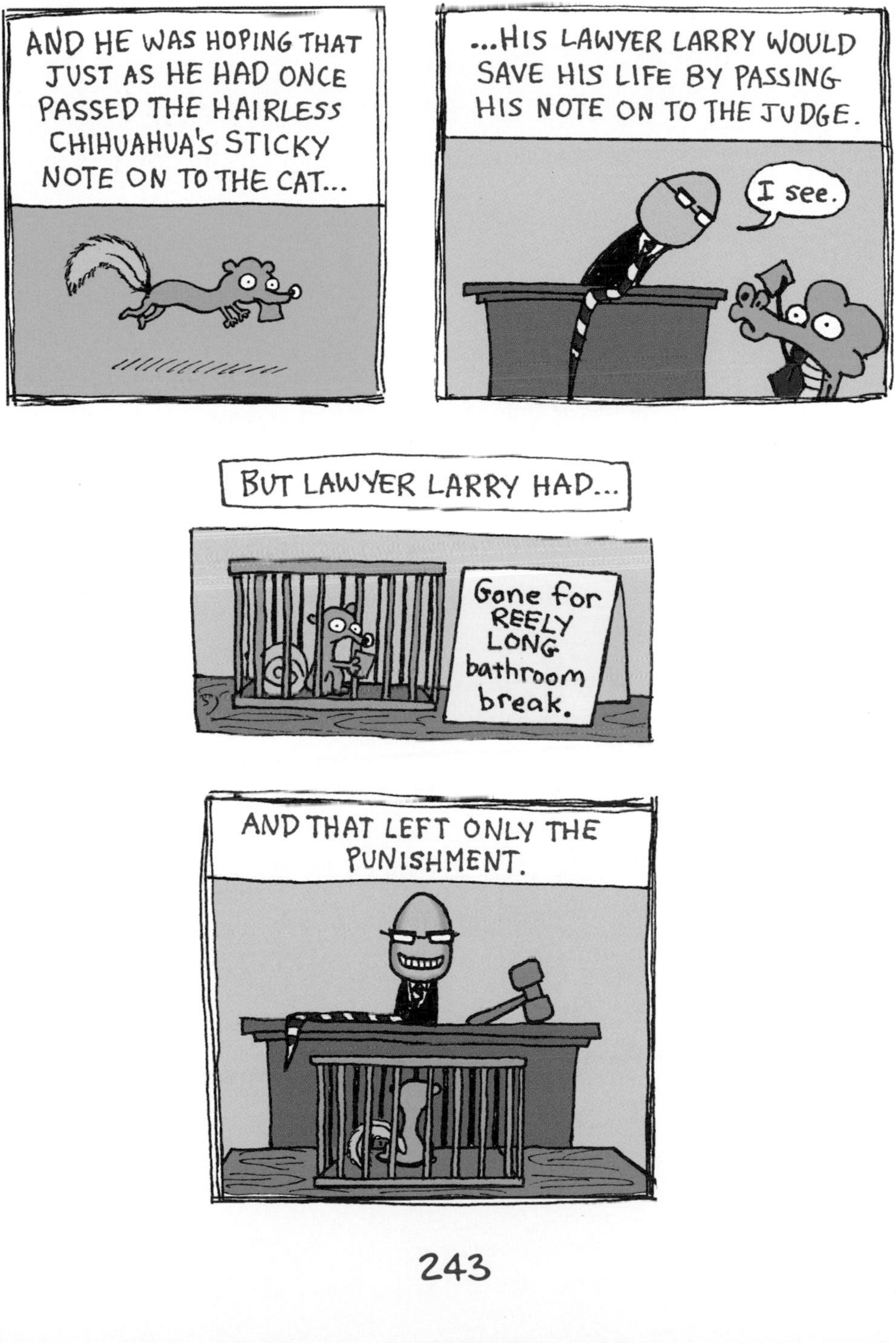
AND HE WAS HOPING THAT JUST AS HE HAD ONCE PASSED THE HAIRLESS CHIHUAHUA'S STICKY NOTE ON TO THE CAT...
...HIS LAWYER LARRY WOULD SAVE HIS LIFE BY PASSING HIS NOTE ON TO THE JUDGE.
I see.
BUT LAWYER LARRY HAD...
Gone for REELY LONG bathroom break.
AND THAT LEFT ONLY THE PUNISHMENT.

IN WHICH...

OUR DEAR
LITTLE
FRIEND
GOES
BYE-BYE

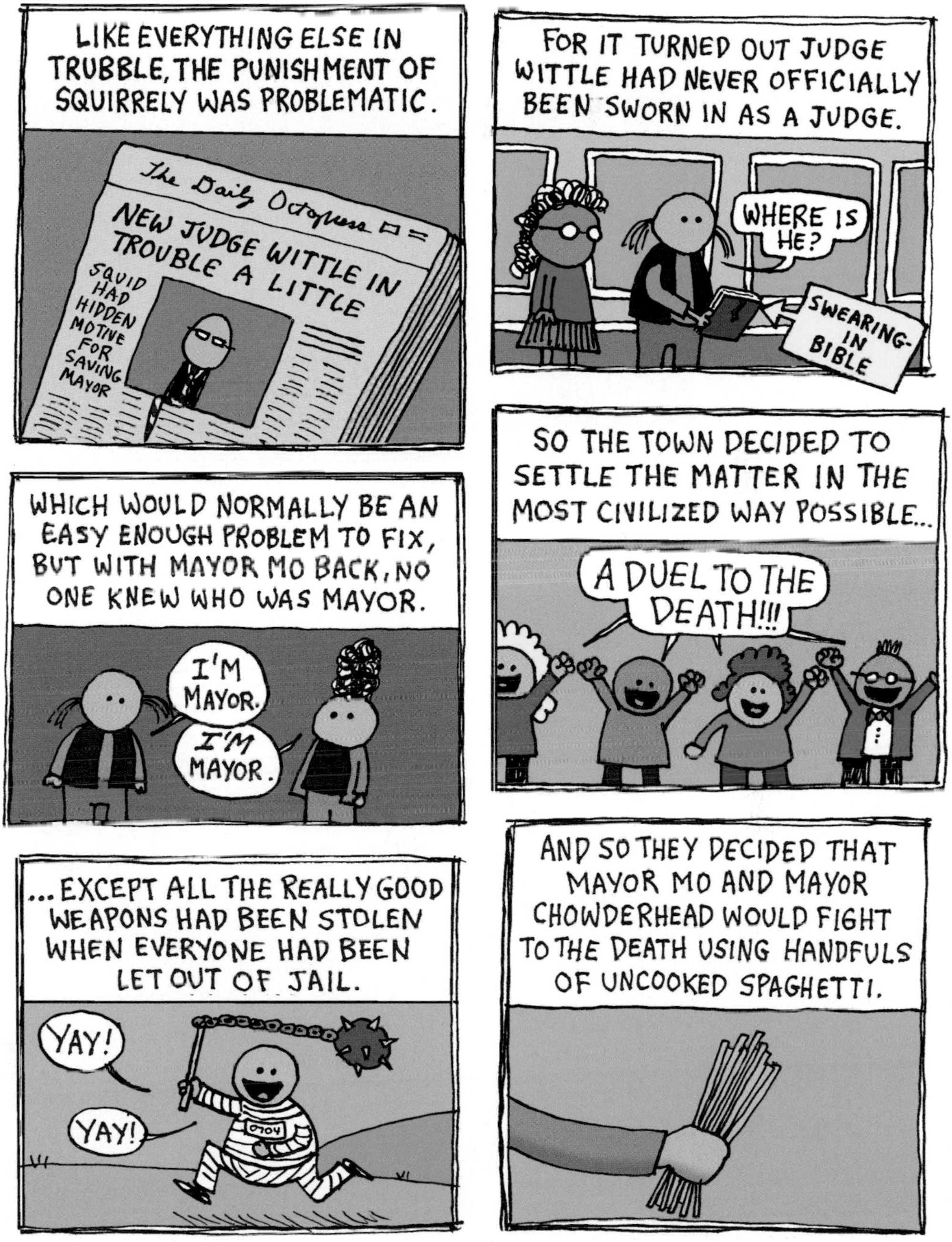
LIKE EVERYTHING ELSE IN TRUBBLE, THE PUNISHMENT OF SQUIRRELY WAS PROBLEMATIC.
The Daily Octopress
NEW JUDGE WITTLE IN TROUBLE A LITTLE
SQUID HAD HIDDEN MOTIVE FOR SAVING MAYOR
FOR IT TURNED OUT JUDGE WITTLE HAD NEVER OFFICIALLY BEEN SWORN IN AS A JUDGE.
WHERE IS HE?
SWEARING-IN BIBLE
WHICH WOULD NORMALLY BE AN EASY ENOUGH PROBLEM TO FIX, BUT WITH MAYOR MO BACK, NO ONE KNEW WHO WAS MAYOR.
I'M MAYOR.
I'M MAYOR.
SO THE TOWN DECIDED TO SETTLE THE MATTER IN THE MOST CIVILIZED WAY POSSIBLE...
A DUEL TO THE DEATH!!!
...EXCEPT ALL THE REALLY GOOD WEAPONS HAD BEEN STOLEN WHEN EVERYONE HAD BEEN LET OUT OF JAIL.
YAY!
YAY!
0704
AND SO THEY DECIDED THAT MAYOR MO AND MAYOR CHOWDERHEAD WOULD FIGHT TO THE DEATH USING HANDFULS OF UNCOOKED SPAGHETTI.

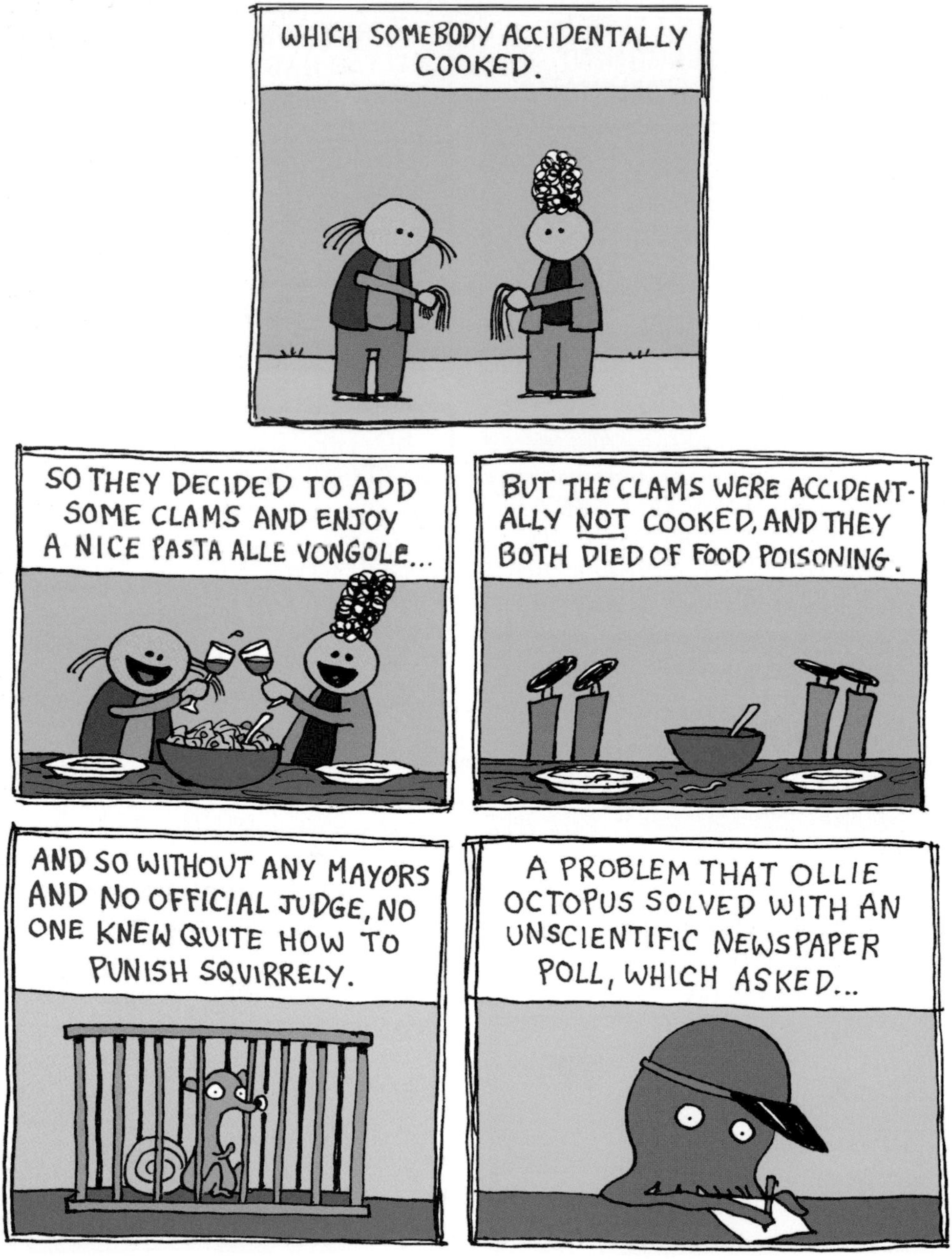
WHICH SOMEBODY ACCIDENTALLY COOKED.
SO THEY DECIDED TO ADD SOME CLAMS AND ENJOY A NICE PASTA ALLE VONGOLE...
BUT THE CLAMS WERE ACCIDENTALLY NOT COOKED, AND THEY BOTH DIED OF FOOD POISONING.
AND SO WITHOUT ANY MAYORS AND NO OFFICIAL JUDGE, NO ONE KNEW QUITE HOW TO PUNISH SQUIRRELY.
A PROBLEM THAT OLLIE OCTOPUS SOLVED WITH AN UNSCIENTIFIC NEWSPAPER POLL, WHICH ASKED...

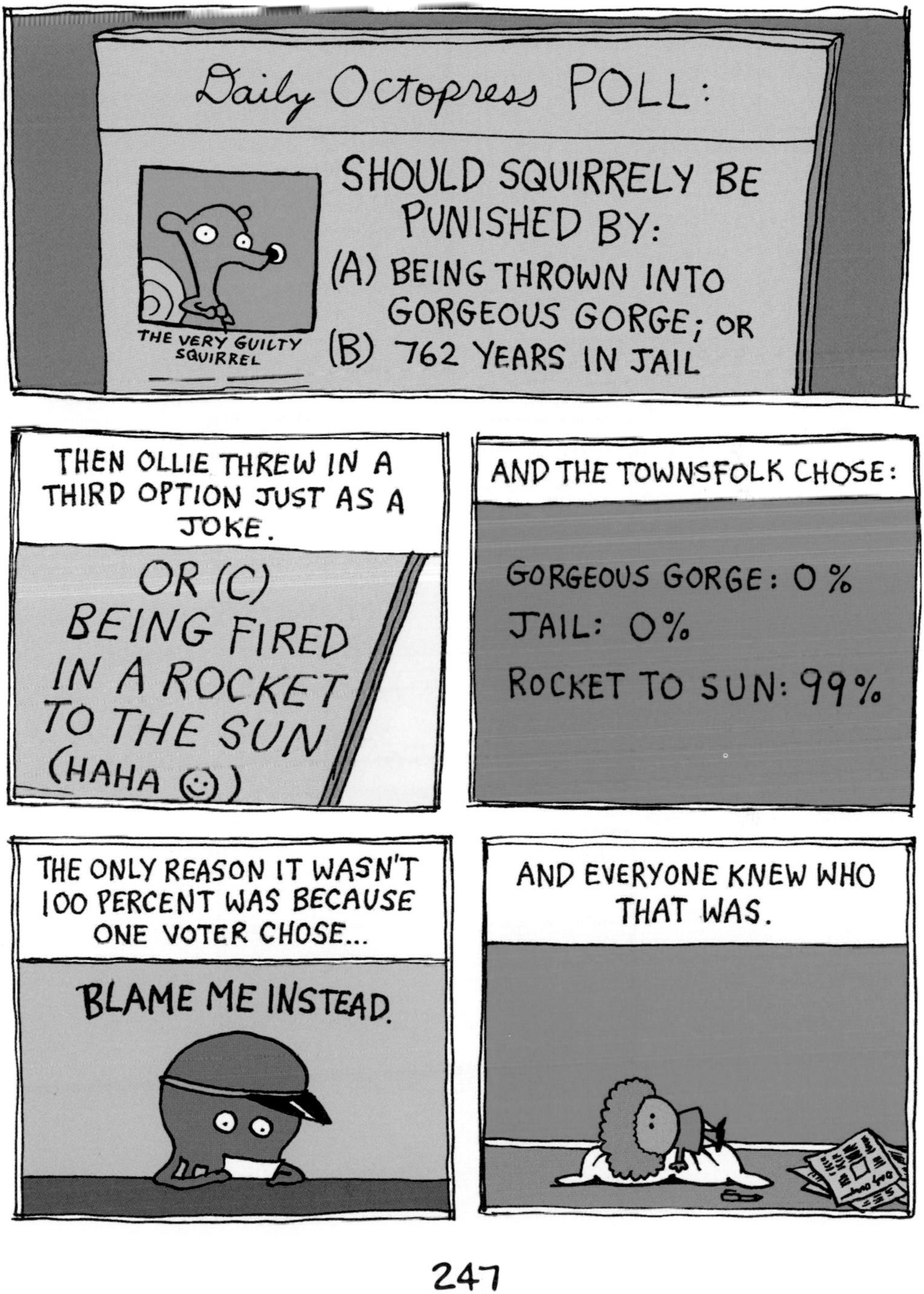
Daily Octopress POLL:
SHOULD SQUIRRELY BE PUNISHED BY:
(A) BEING THROWN INTO GORGEOUS GORGE; OR
(B) 762 YEARS IN JAIL
THE VERY GUILTY SQUIRREL
THEN OLLIE THREW IN A THIRD OPTION JUST AS A JOKE.
OR (C) BEING FIRED IN A ROCKET TO THE SUN (HAHA ☺)
AND THE TOWNSFOLK CHOSE:
GORGEOUS GORGE: 0%
JAIL: 0%
ROCKET TO SUN: 99%
THE ONLY REASON IT WASN'T 100 PERCENT WAS BECAUSE ONE VOTER CHOSE...
BLAME ME INSTEAD.
AND EVERYONE KNEW WHO THAT WAS.

BUT AFTER THE VOTING, THERE WAS ONE OBVIOUS QUESTION.

WHO HERE CAN BUILD A ROCKET TO THE SUN?

AND ONE NOT-SO-OBVIOUS ANSWER.

I CAN! I CAN!

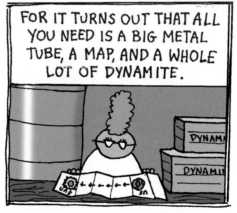

FOR IT TURNS OUT THAT ALL YOU NEED IS A BIG METAL TUBE, A MAP, AND A WHOLE LOT OF DYNAMITE.

AND SOON SHE WAS READY TO SHOW EVERYONE.

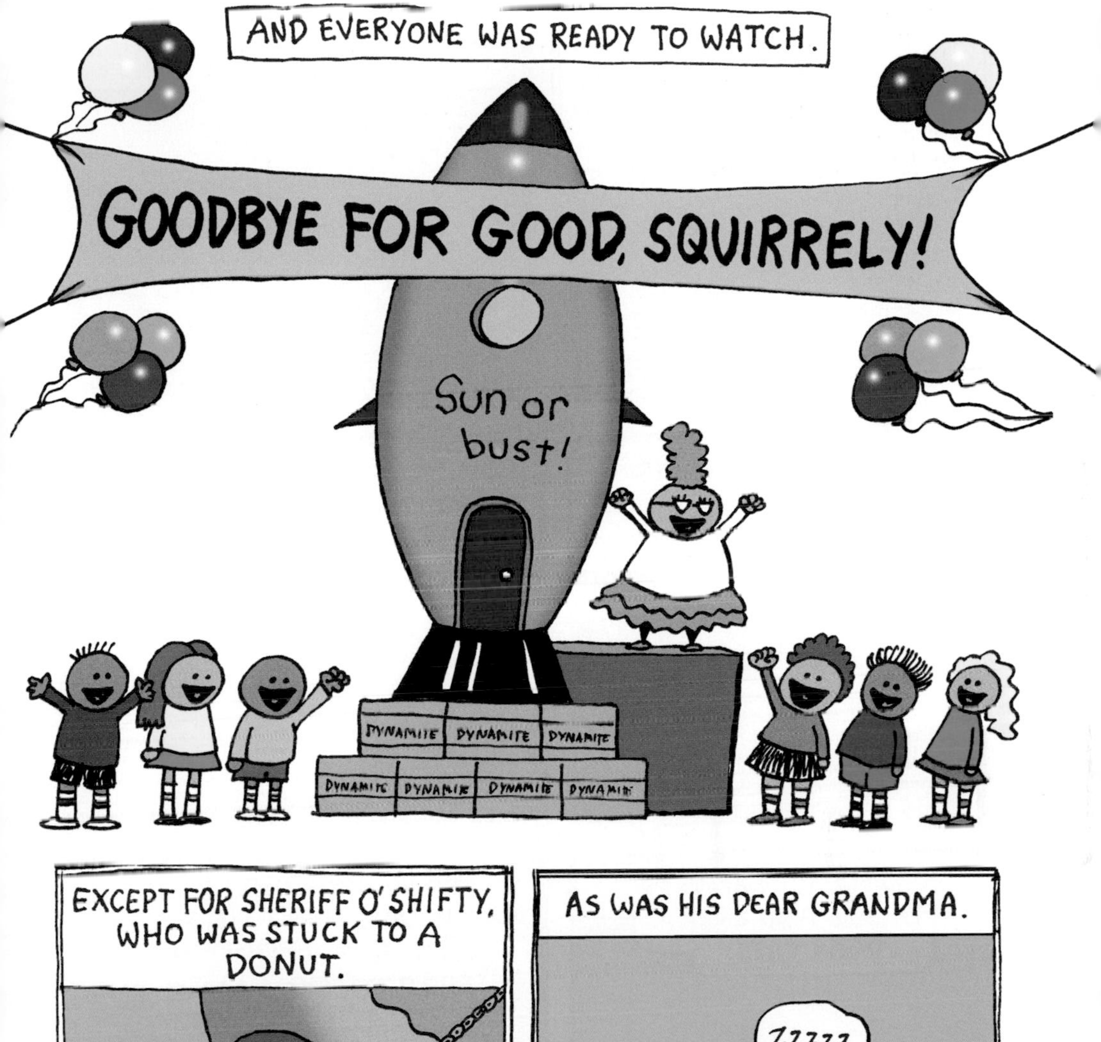
AND EVERYONE WAS READY TO WATCH.
GOODBYE FOR GOOD, SQUIRRELY!
Sun or bust!
DYNAMITE DYNAMITE DYNAMITE
DYNAMITE DYNAMITE DYNAMITE DYNAMITE

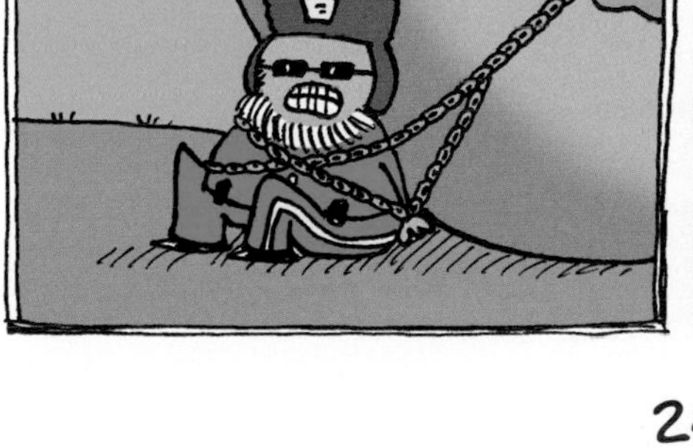
EXCEPT FOR SHERIFF O'SHIFTY, WHO WAS STUCK TO A DONUT.

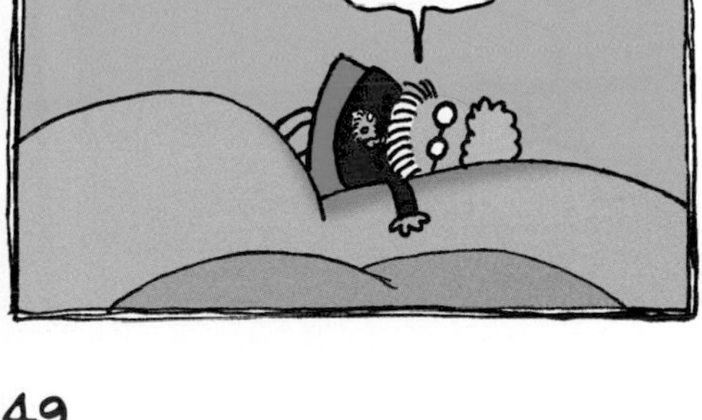
AS WAS HIS DEAR GRANDMA.
Zzzzz

THE SPECTACLE ITSELF WAS HELD IN A FORMER MELON PATCH LONG SINCE RAVAGED BY RODENTS AND OTHER SMALL ANIMALS.

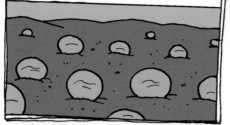

BUT NOW FILLED WITH EXCITED PEOPLE.

AND ONE SCARED SQUIRREL.

AND BECAUSE HE WAS STILL QUITE ANGRY OVER HIS EXPLODED CAFÉ, MOOSHY MIKE WAS THE PERSON CHOSEN TO ADDRESS SQUIRRELY.

SQUIRRELY, YOU EXPLODED MY CAFÉ AND EVERY OTHER CAFÉ.

AND YOU TRIED TO KILL THE MAYOR, WHO DIDN'T DIE, BUT THEN DID DIE, BUT SOMEHOW UNDIED, AND THEN DIED AGAIN.

250

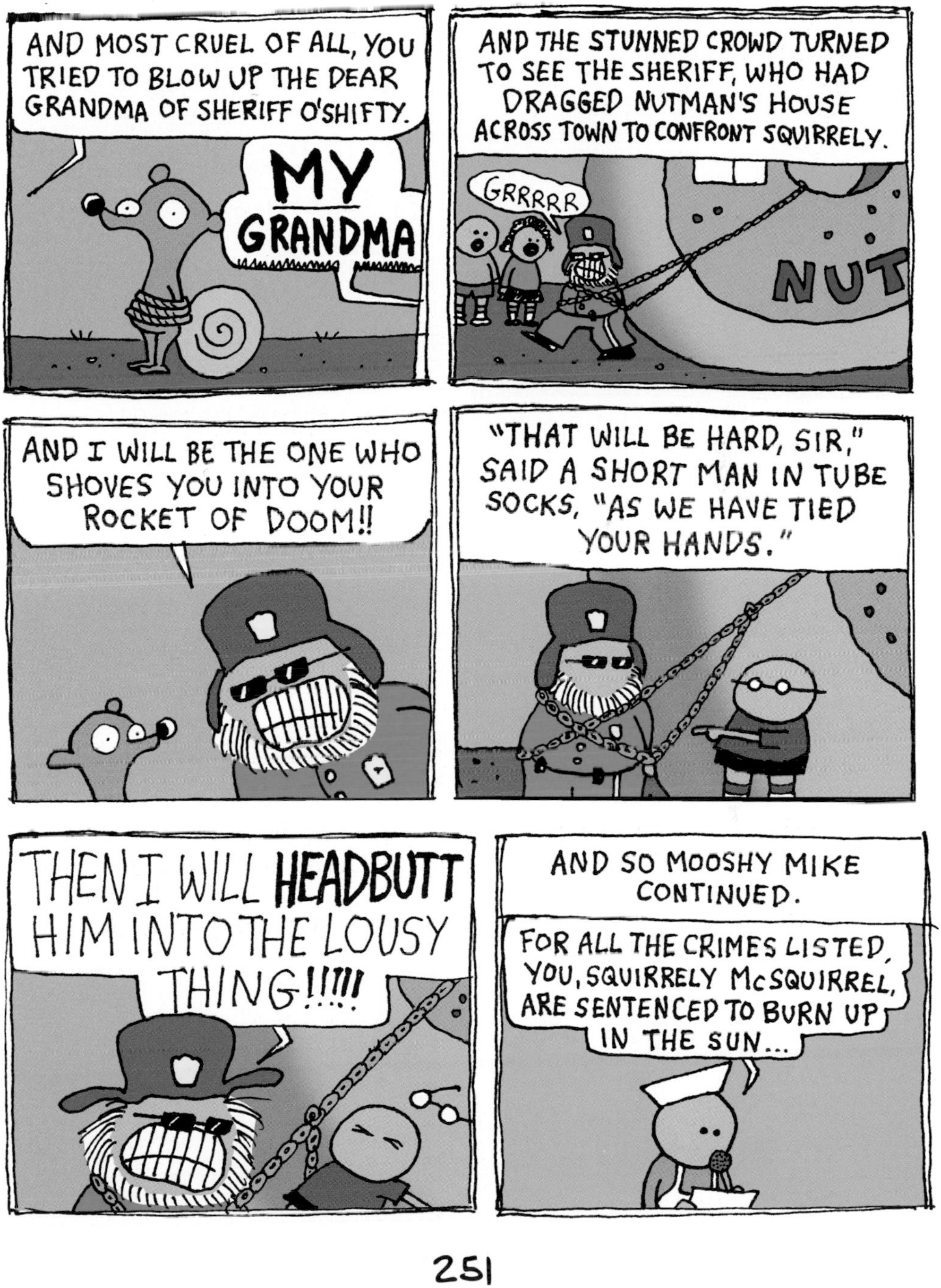
AND MOST CRUEL OF ALL, YOU TRIED TO BLOW UP THE DEAR GRANDMA OF SHERIFF O'SHIFTY.
MY GRANDMA
AND THE STUNNED CROWD TURNED TO SEE THE SHERIFF, WHO HAD DRAGGED NUTMAN'S HOUSE ACROSS TOWN TO CONFRONT SQUIRRELY.
GRRRRR
NUT
AND I WILL BE THE ONE WHO SHOVES YOU INTO YOUR ROCKET OF DOOM!!
"THAT WILL BE HARD, SIR," SAID A SHORT MAN IN TUBE SOCKS, "AS WE HAVE TIED YOUR HANDS."
THEN I WILL HEADBUTT HIM INTO THE LOUSY THING!!!!!
AND SO MOOSHY MIKE CONTINUED.
FOR ALL THE CRIMES LISTED, YOU, SQUIRRELY McSQUIRREL, ARE SENTENCED TO BURN UP IN THE SUN...

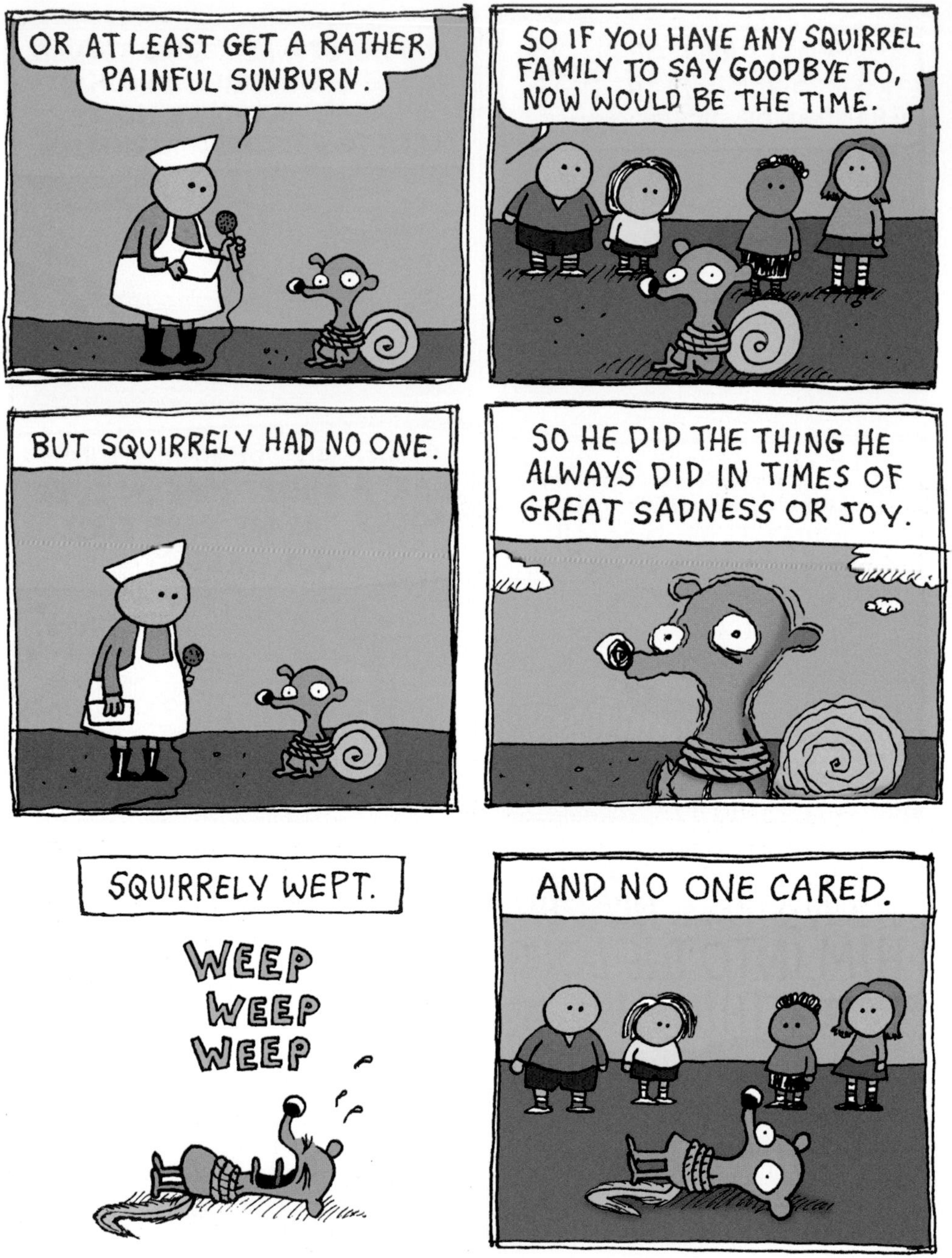
OR AT LEAST GET A RATHER PAINFUL SUNBURN.
SO IF YOU HAVE ANY SQUIRREL FAMILY TO SAY GOODBYE TO, NOW WOULD BE THE TIME.
BUT SQUIRRELY HAD NO ONE.
SO HE DID THE THING HE ALWAYS DID IN TIMES OF GREAT SADNESS OR JOY.
SQUIRRELY WEPT.
WEEP
WEEP
WEEP
AND NO ONE CARED.

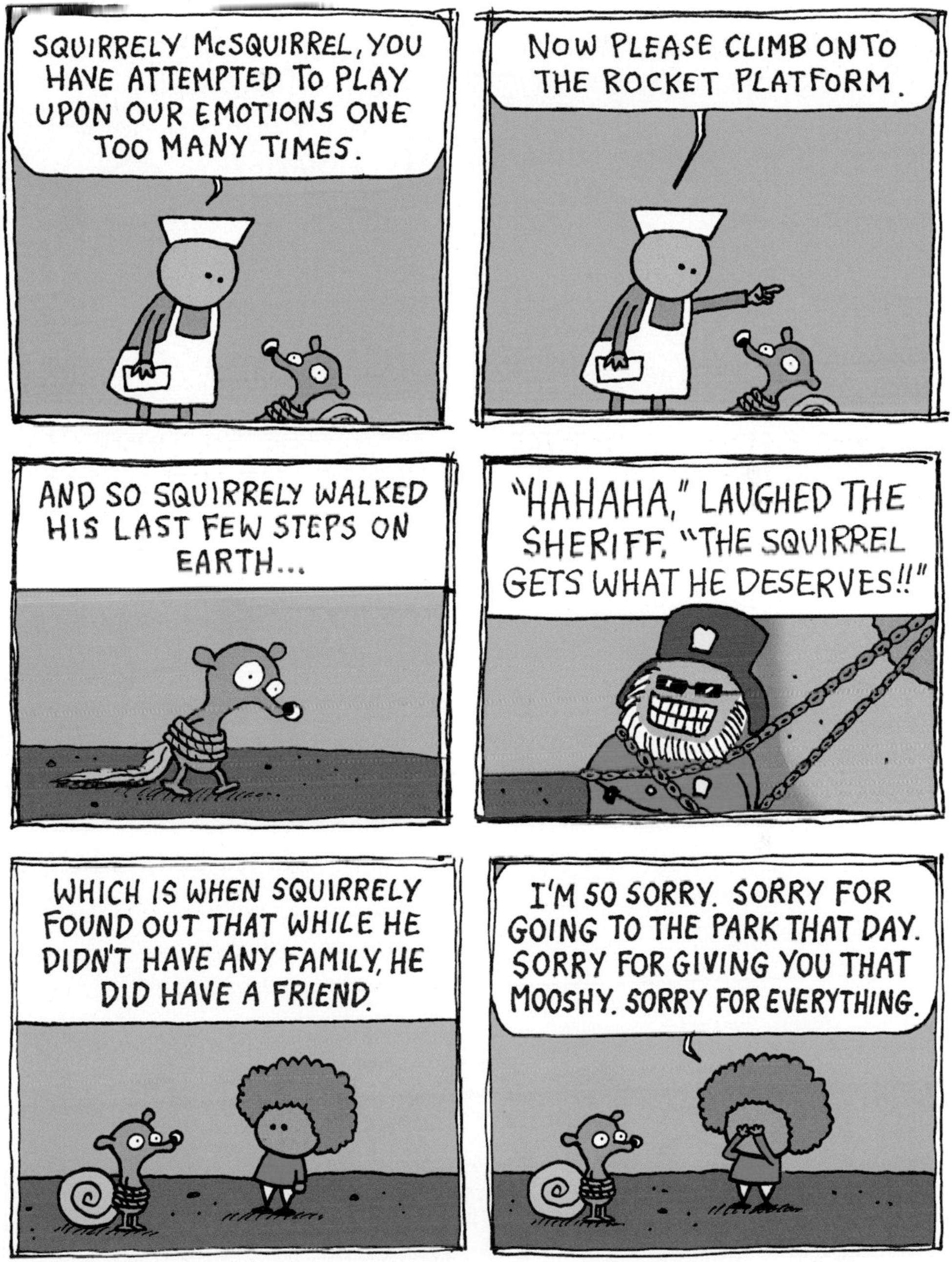
SQUIRRELY McSQUIRREL, YOU HAVE ATTEMPTED TO PLAY UPON OUR EMOTIONS ONE TOO MANY TIMES.
NOW PLEASE CLIMB ONTO THE ROCKET PLATFORM.
AND SO SQUIRRELY WALKED HIS LAST FEW STEPS ON EARTH...
"HAHAHA," LAUGHED THE SHERIFF. "THE SQUIRREL GETS WHAT HE DESERVES!!"
WHICH IS WHEN SQUIRRELY FOUND OUT THAT WHILE HE DIDN'T HAVE ANY FAMILY, HE DID HAVE A FRIEND.
I'M SO SORRY. SORRY FOR GOING TO THE PARK THAT DAY. SORRY FOR GIVING YOU THAT MOOSHY. SORRY FOR EVERYTHING.

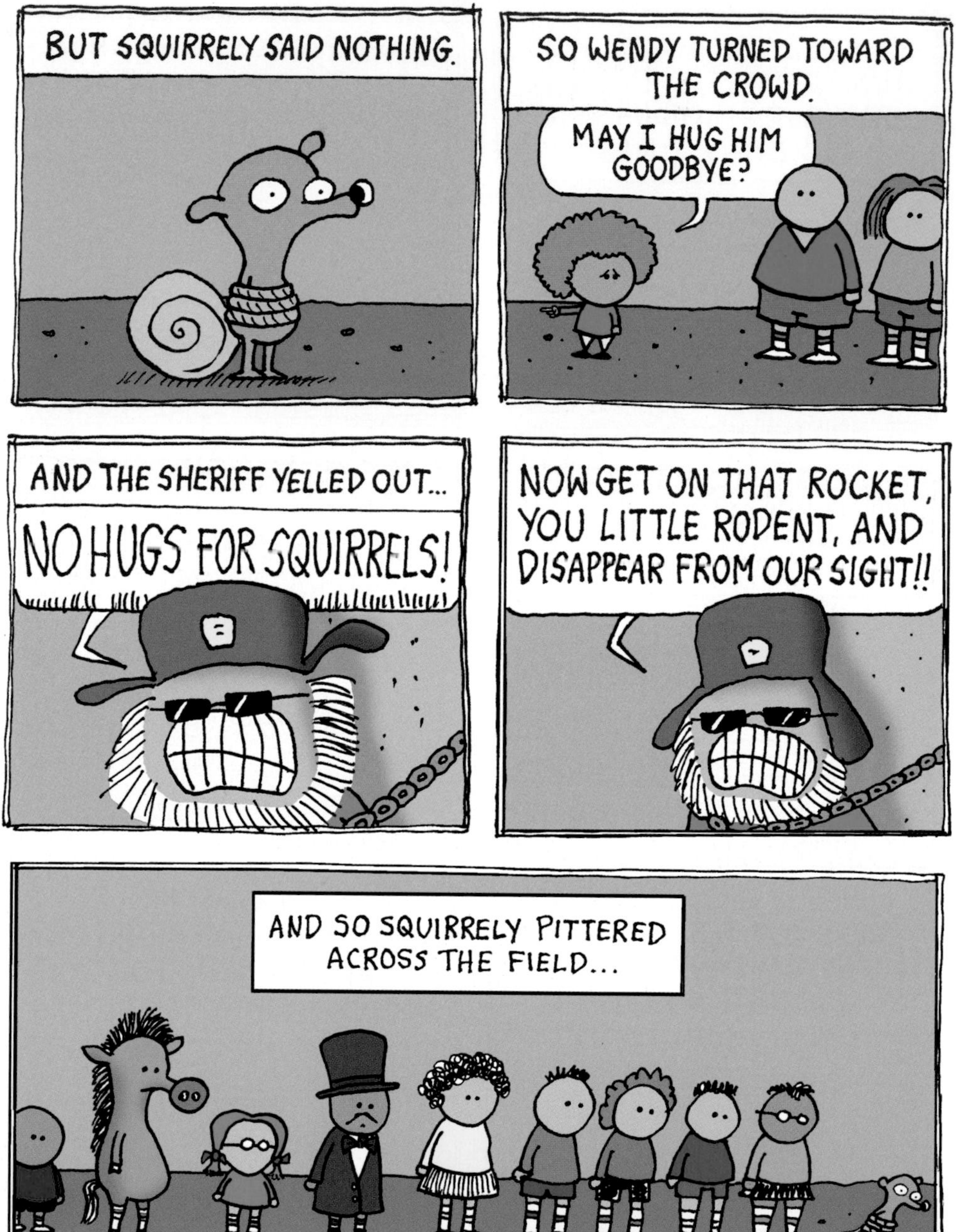
BUT SQUIRRELY SAID NOTHING.
SO WENDY TURNED TOWARD THE CROWD.
MAY I HUG HIM GOODBYE?
AND THE SHERIFF YELLED OUT...
NO HUGS FOR SQUIRRELS!
NOW GET ON THAT ROCKET, YOU LITTLE RODENT, AND DISAPPEAR FROM OUR SIGHT!!
AND SO SQUIRRELY PITTERED ACROSS THE FIELD...

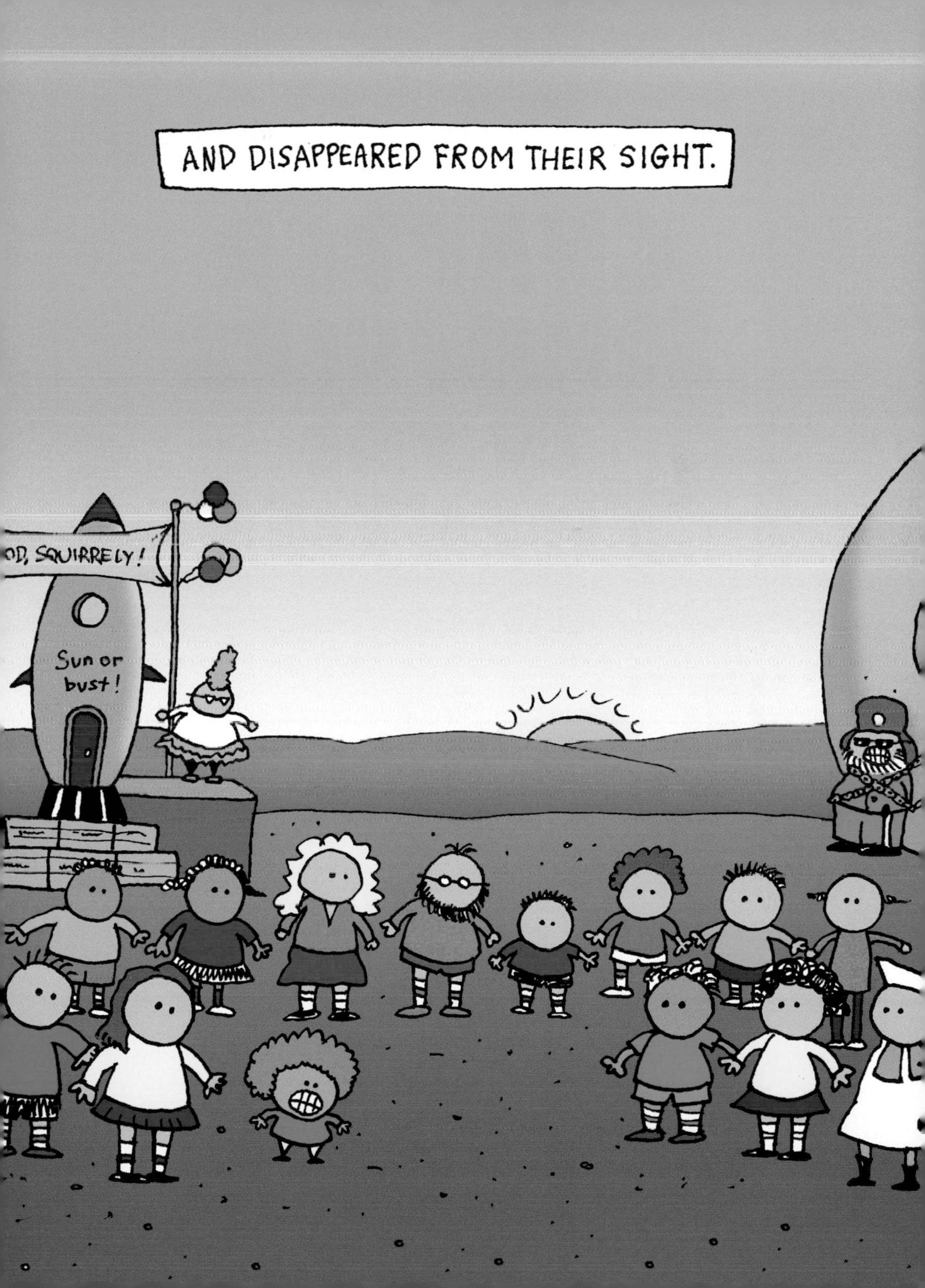
AND DISAPPEARED FROM THEIR SIGHT.
OD, SQUIRRELY!
Sun or bust!

CHAPTER SOMEWHERE IN THE TWENTIES

IN WHICH...

THINGS GET SUPER DEEP

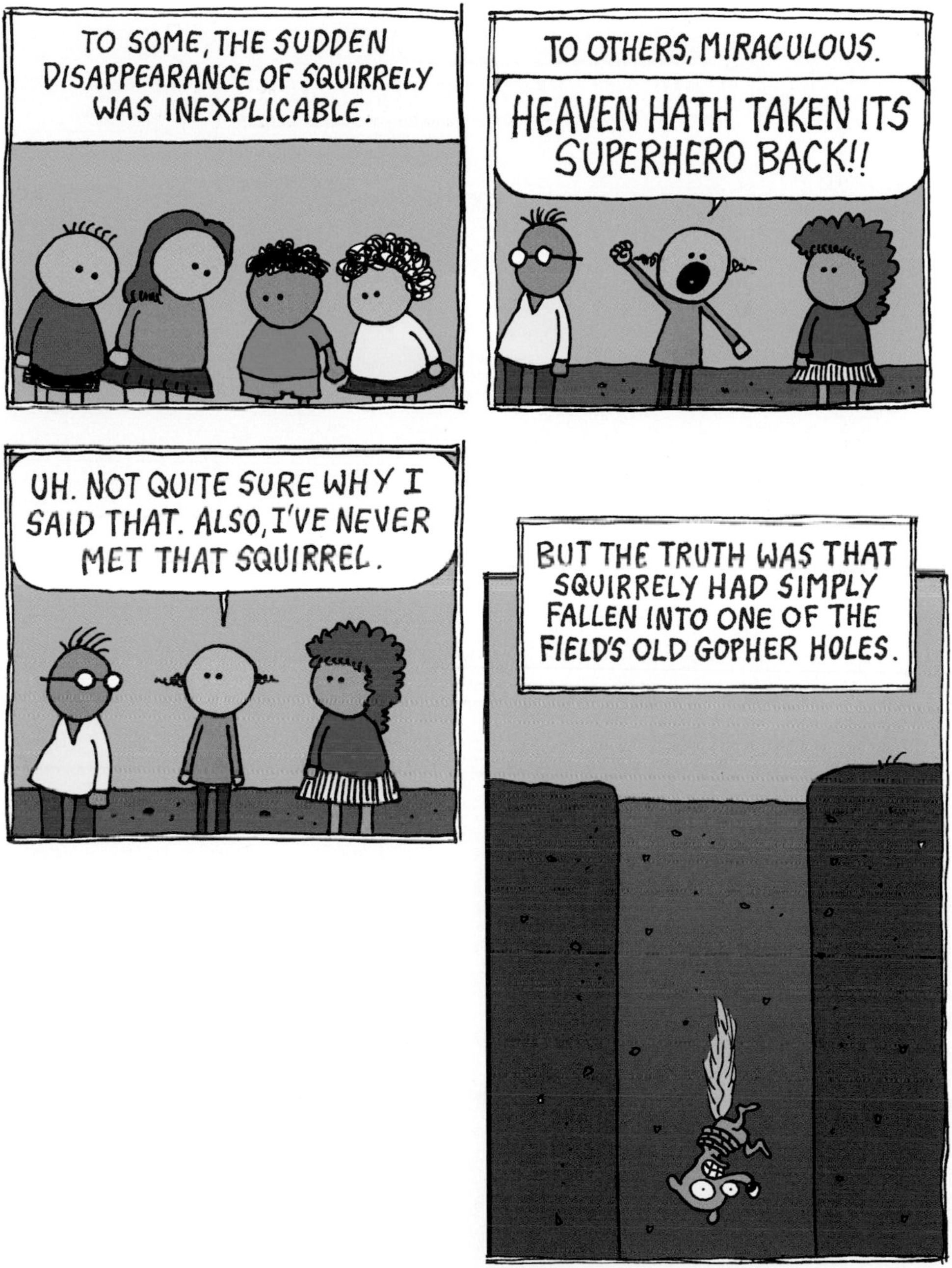
TO SOME, THE SUDDEN DISAPPEARANCE OF SQUIRRELY WAS INEXPLICABLE.
TO OTHERS, MIRACULOUS.
HEAVEN HATH TAKEN ITS SUPERHERO BACK!!
UH. NOT QUITE SURE WHY I SAID THAT. ALSO, I'VE NEVER MET THAT SQUIRREL.
BUT THE TRUTH WAS THAT SQUIRRELY HAD SIMPLY FALLEN INTO ONE OF THE FIELD'S OLD GOPHER HOLES.

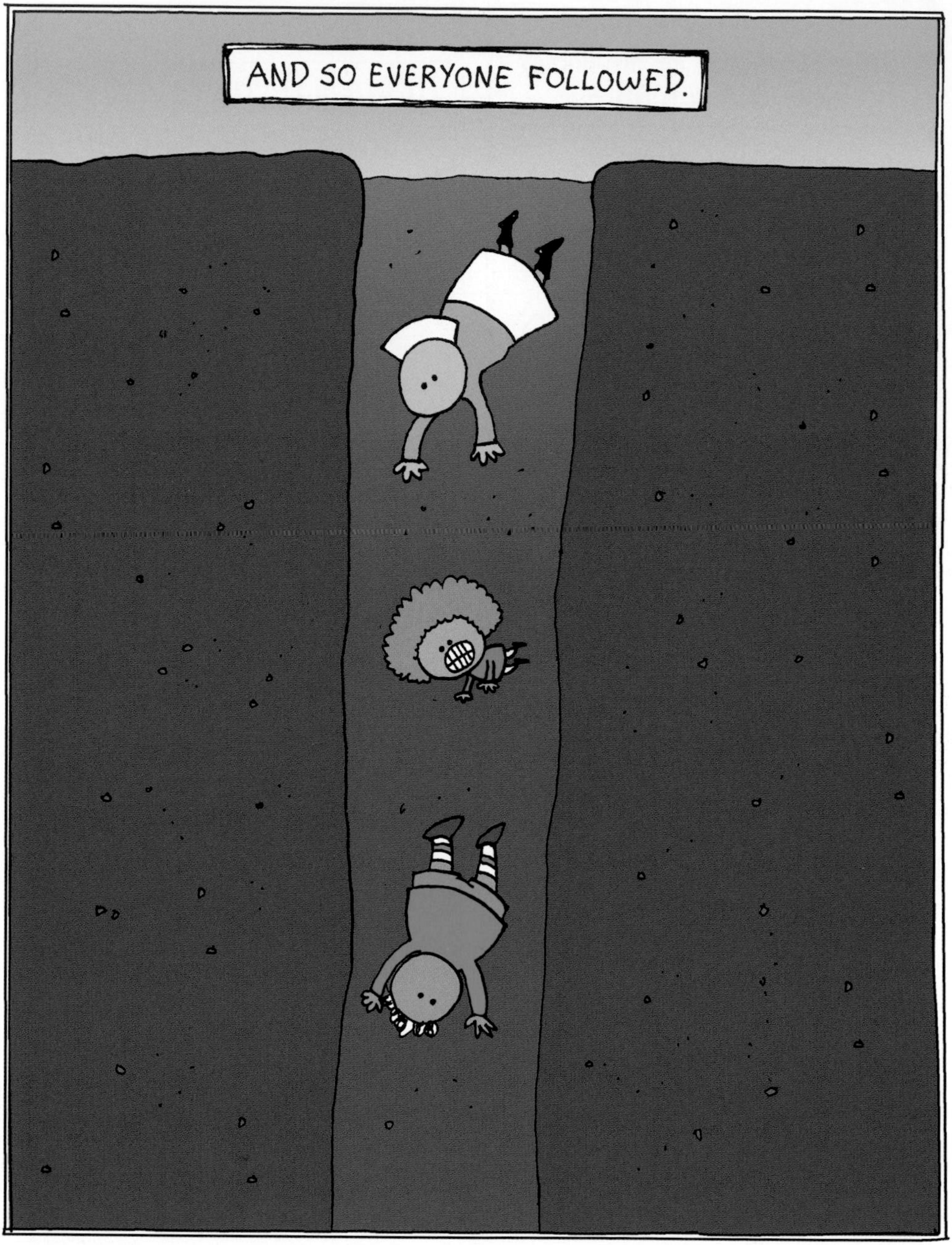
AND SO EVERYONE FOLLOWED.

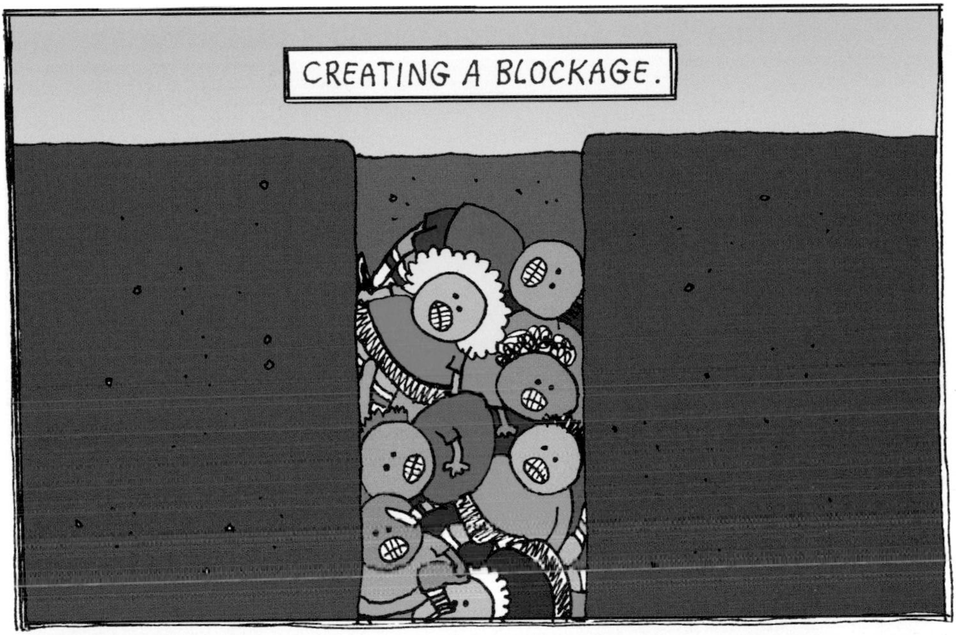
CREATING A BLOCKAGE.

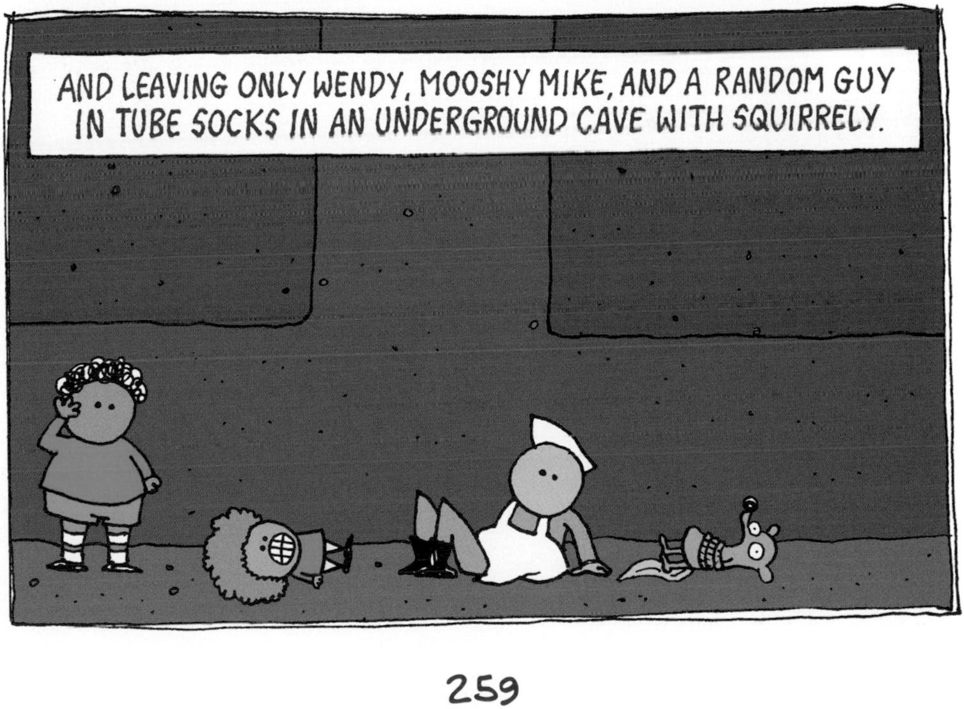
AND LEAVING ONLY WENDY, MOOSHY MIKE, AND A RANDOM GUY IN TUBE SOCKS IN AN UNDERGROUND CAVE WITH SQUIRRELY.

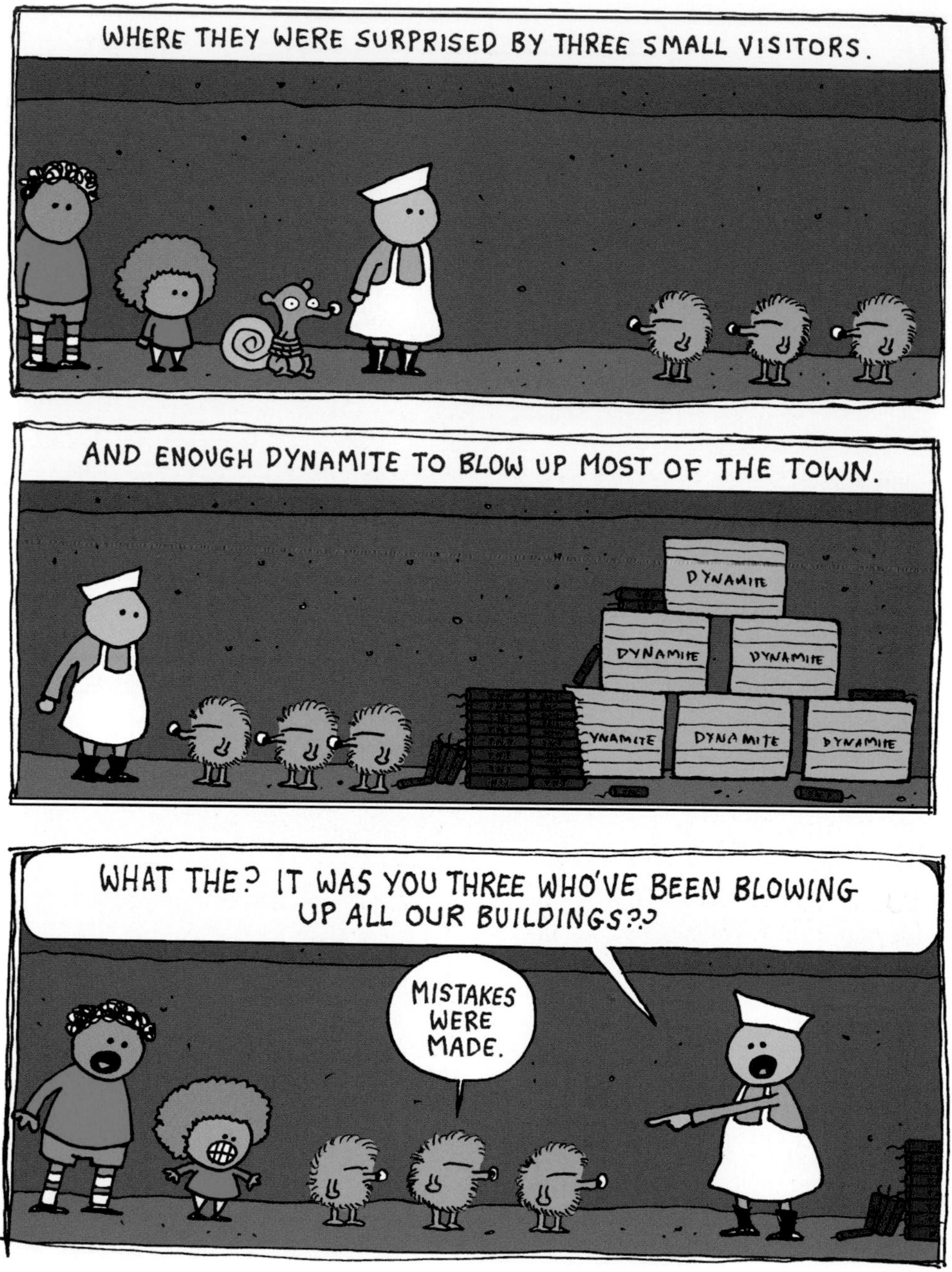
WHERE THEY WERE SURPRISED BY THREE SMALL VISITORS.
AND ENOUGH DYNAMITE TO BLOW UP MOST OF THE TOWN.
DYNAMITE
DYNAMITE
DYNAMITE
YNAMITE
DYNAMITE
DYNAMITE
WHAT THE? IT WAS YOU THREE WHO'VE BEEN BLOWING UP ALL OUR BUILDINGS??
MISTAKES WERE MADE.

AND THAT WAS MORE THAN MOOSHY MIKE COULD TAKE.

WHY, YOU LITTLE...

WAIT. PLEASE. WE CAN EXPLAIN.

EXPLAIN IT HOW?

WE'VE BEEN TRYING TO FIX THIS TOWN FOREVER... SIGN-UP BOOTHS, PETITIONS. BUT YOU ALL IGNORED US.

SO YOU GOT UPSET AND BLEW UP THE TOWN?

NO, BUT ALL THOSE EFFORTS REQUIRE MONEY. SO WE HAD TO GET JOBS.

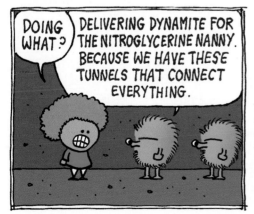

DOING WHAT?

DELIVERING DYNAMITE FOR THE NITROGLYCERINE NANNY. BECAUSE WE HAVE THESE TUNNELS THAT CONNECT EVERYTHING.

AND IT'S SAFER TO DELIVER IT THAT WAY?

YES. WELL, IT'S SUPPOSED TO BE.

261

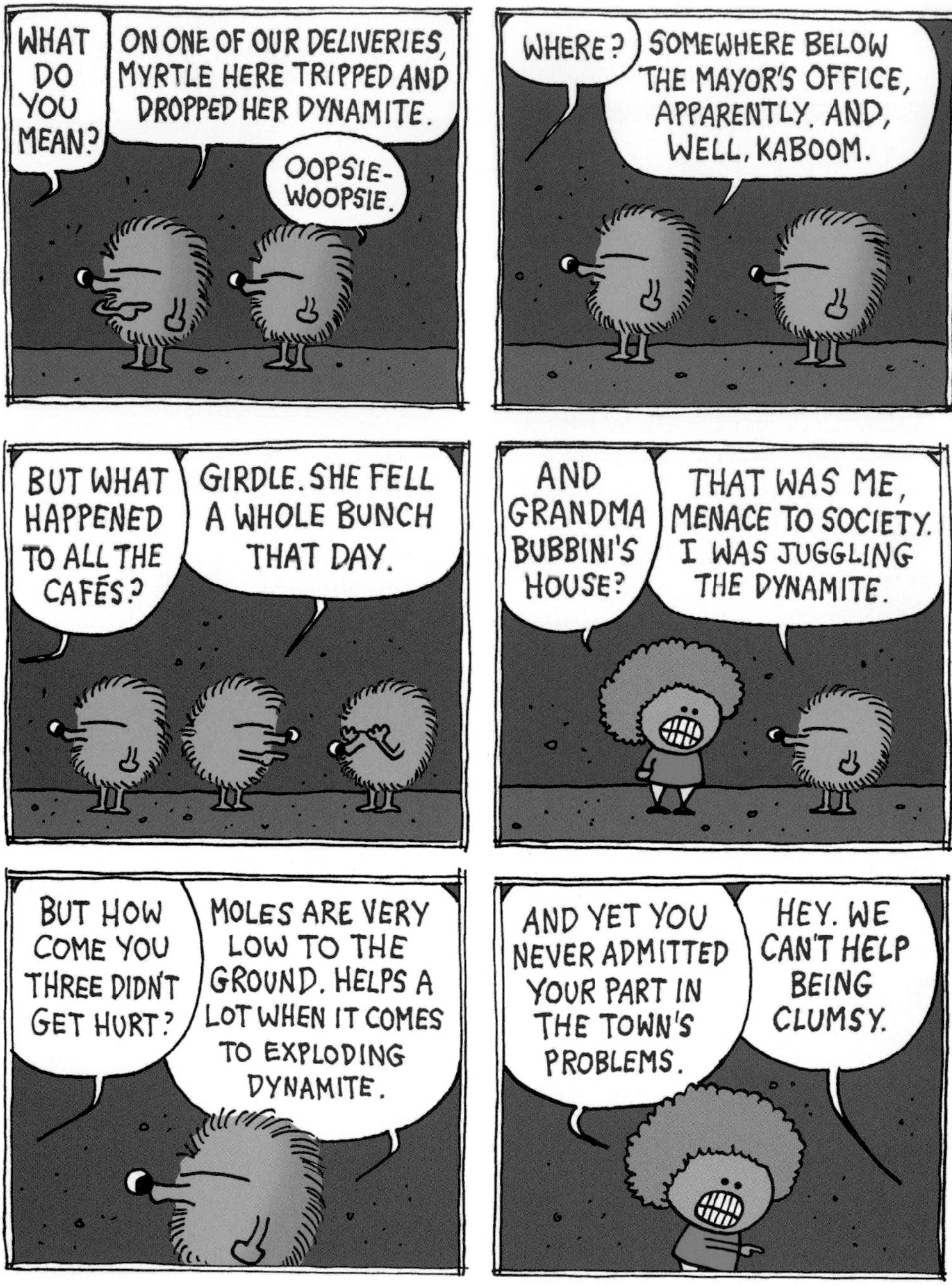
WHAT DO YOU MEAN?
ON ONE OF OUR DELIVERIES, MYRTLE HERE TRIPPED AND DROPPED HER DYNAMITE.
OOPSIE-WOOPSIE.
WHERE?
SOMEWHERE BELOW THE MAYOR'S OFFICE, APPARENTLY. AND, WELL, KABOOM.
BUT WHAT HAPPENED TO ALL THE CAFÉS?
GIRDLE. SHE FELL A WHOLE BUNCH THAT DAY.
AND GRANDMA BUBBINI'S HOUSE?
THAT WAS ME, MENACE TO SOCIETY. I WAS JUGGLING THE DYNAMITE.
BUT HOW COME YOU THREE DIDN'T GET HURT?
MOLES ARE VERY LOW TO THE GROUND. HELPS A LOT WHEN IT COMES TO EXPLODING DYNAMITE.
AND YET YOU NEVER ADMITTED YOUR PART IN THE TOWN'S PROBLEMS.
HEY. WE CAN'T HELP BEING CLUMSY.

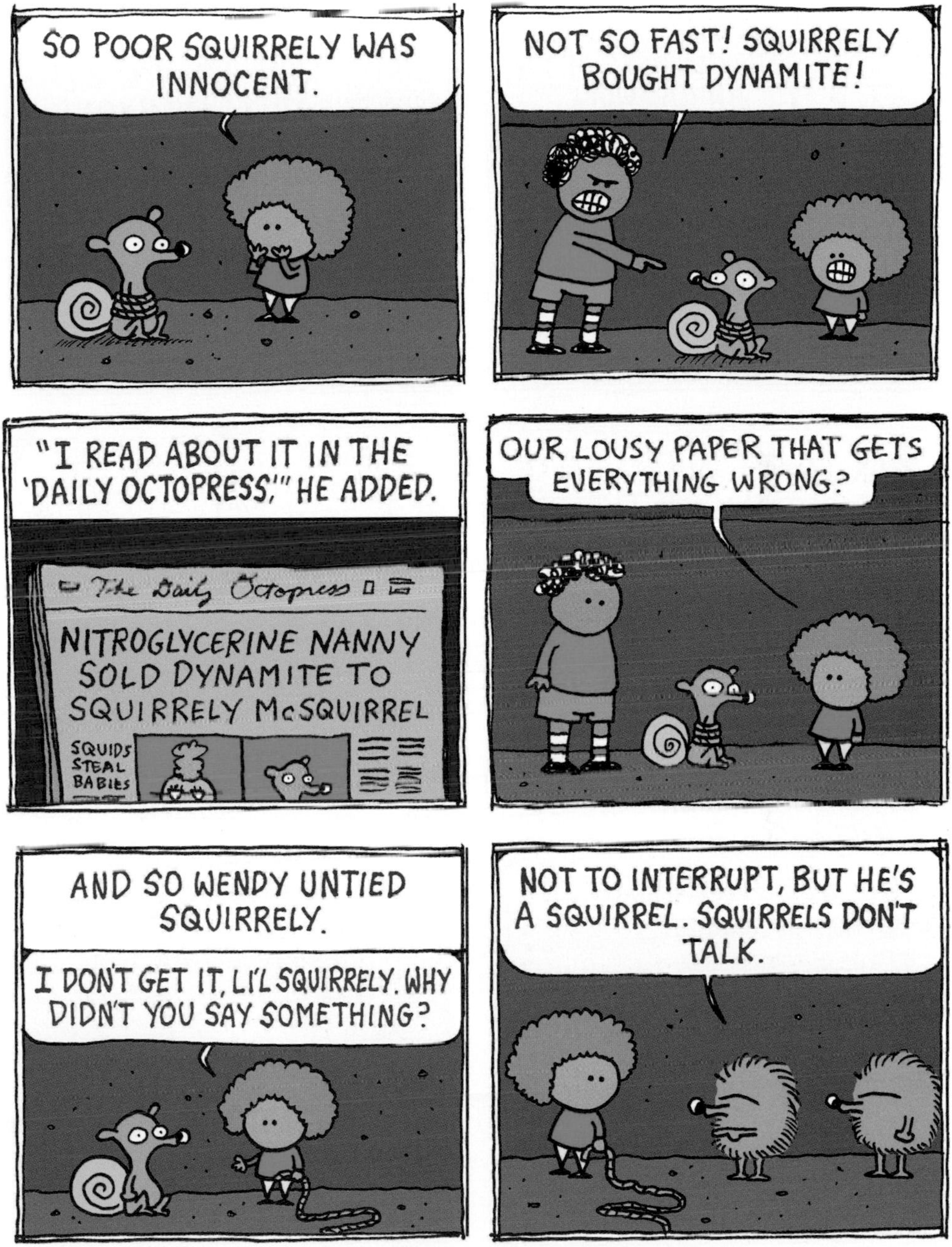
SO POOR SQUIRRELY WAS INNOCENT.
NOT SO FAST! SQUIRRELY BOUGHT DYNAMITE!
"I READ ABOUT IT IN THE 'DAILY OCTOPRESS,'" HE ADDED.
The Daily Octopress
NITROGLYCERINE NANNY SOLD DYNAMITE TO SQUIRRELY McSQUIRREL
SQUIDS STEAL BABIES
OUR LOUSY PAPER THAT GETS EVERYTHING WRONG?
AND SO WENDY UNTIED SQUIRRELY.
I DON'T GET IT, LI'L SQUIRRELY. WHY DIDN'T YOU SAY SOMETHING?
NOT TO INTERRUPT, BUT HE'S A SQUIRREL. SQUIRRELS DON'T TALK.

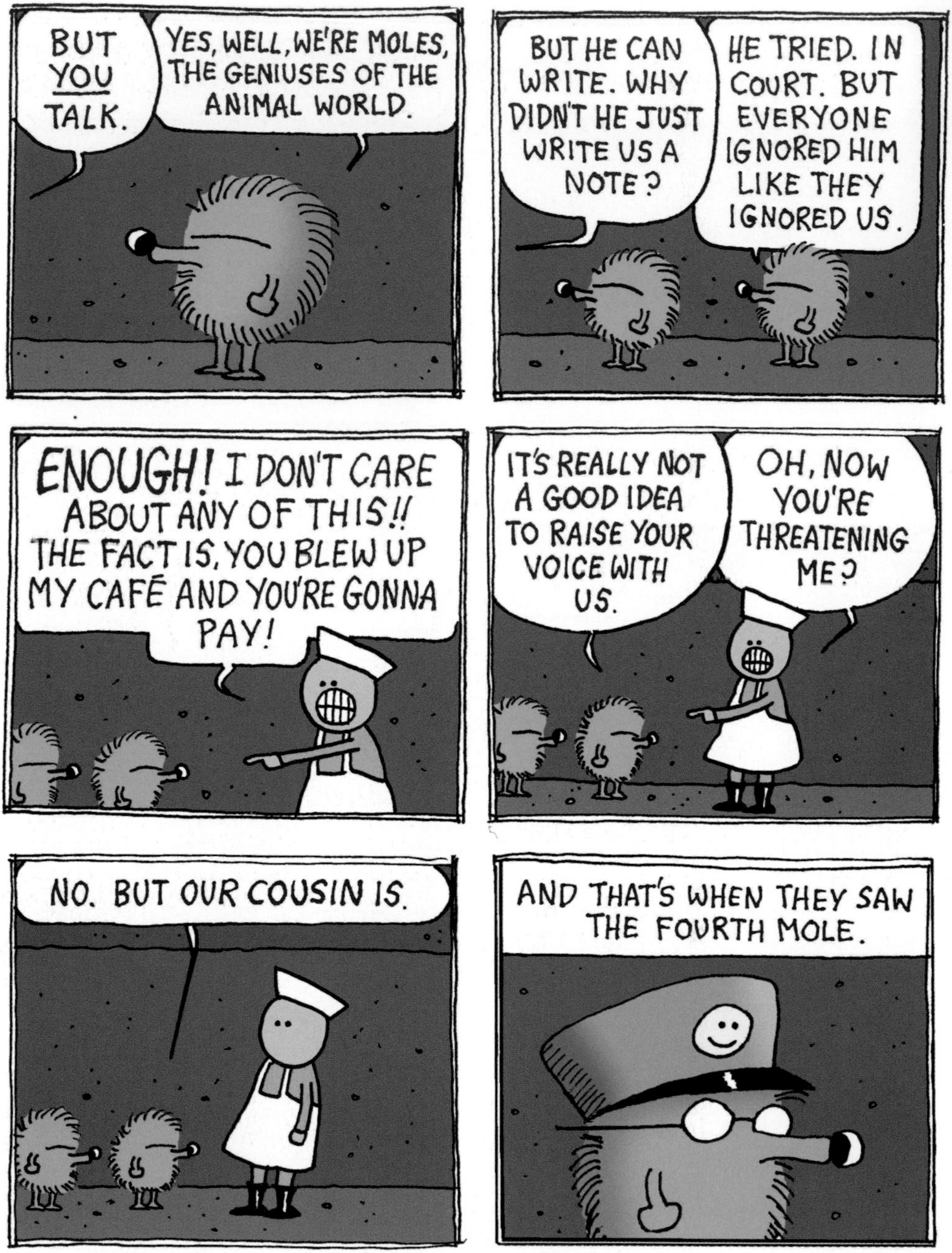
BUT YOU TALK.
YES, WELL, WE'RE MOLES, THE GENIUSES OF THE ANIMAL WORLD.
BUT HE CAN WRITE. WHY DIDN'T HE JUST WRITE US A NOTE?
HE TRIED. IN COURT. BUT EVERYONE IGNORED HIM LIKE THEY IGNORED US.
ENOUGH! I DON'T CARE ABOUT ANY OF THIS!! THE FACT IS, YOU BLEW UP MY CAFÉ AND YOU'RE GONNA PAY!
IT'S REALLY NOT A GOOD IDEA TO RAISE YOUR VOICE WITH US.
OH, NOW YOU'RE THREATENING ME?
NO. BUT OUR COUSIN IS.
AND THAT'S WHEN THEY SAW THE FOURTH MOLE.

WITH ONE ARM ON THE DETONATOR TO EVERYTHING.

THAT'S OUR COUSIN, "THE OPTIMIST." POORLY NAMED, THOUGH, AS HE'S OUR VERSION OF CROTCHETY CRAIG.

AND SO MOOSHY MIKE FOLLOWED THE FUSES AND SAW THAT THE OPTIMIST WAS ABOUT TO BLOW UP BUILDINGS ALL OVER TOWN.

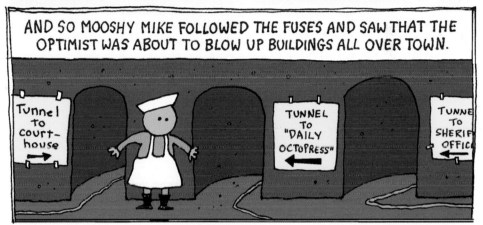

Tunnel to court-house

TUNNEL TO "DAILY OCTOPRESS"

TUNNE TO SHERIF OFFIC

HE'S GONNA BLOW UP EVERYTHING!

YES, WELL, UNLIKE US, HE REALLY *IS* UPSET OVER HOW THE MOLES IN THIS TOWN HAVE BEEN TREATED.

AND HE LIKES TO EXPRESS HIS FEELINGS IN A LESS-THAN-PEACEFUL WAY.

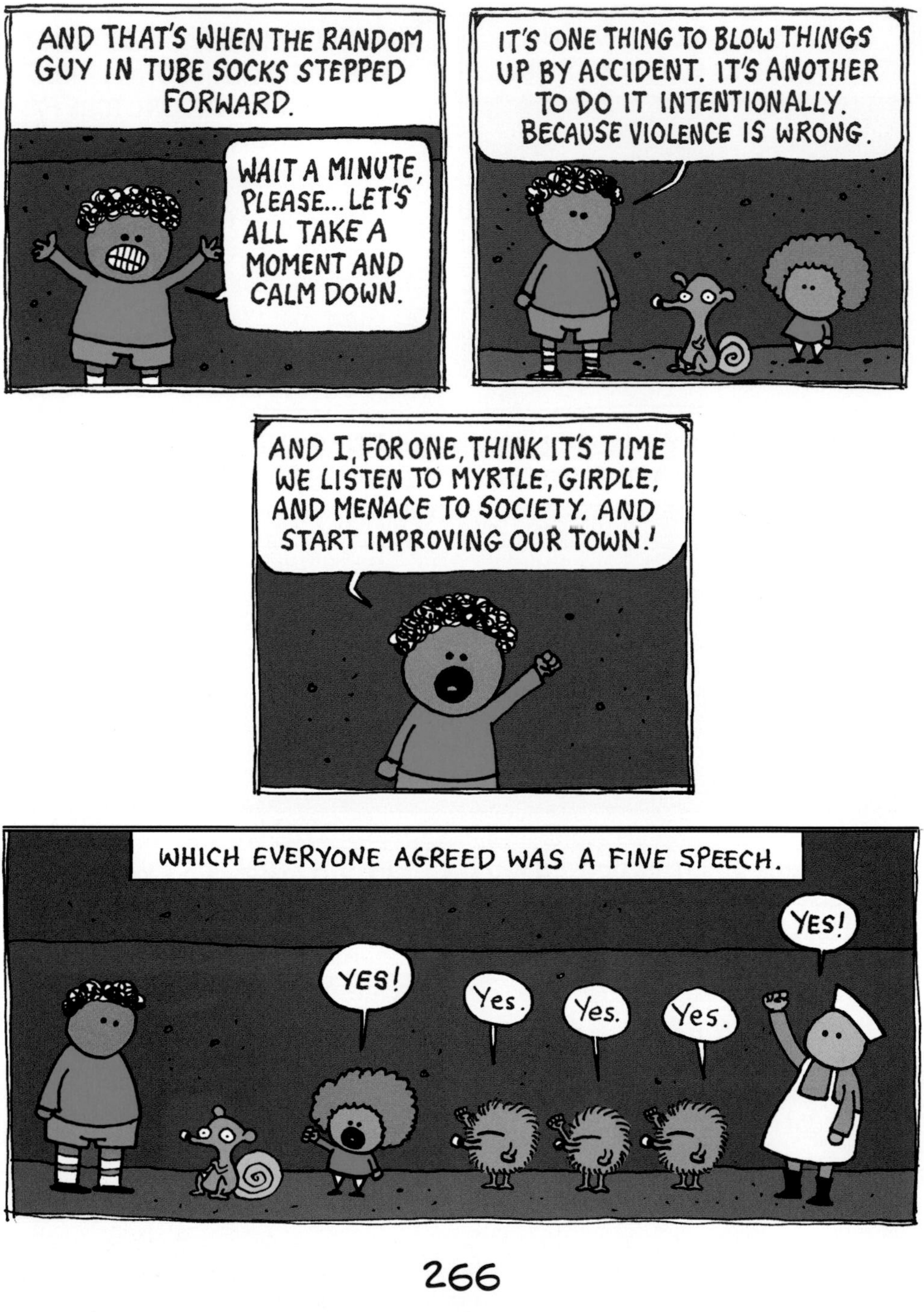
AND THAT'S WHEN THE RANDOM GUY IN TUBE SOCKS STEPPED FORWARD.
WAIT A MINUTE, PLEASE... LET'S ALL TAKE A MOMENT AND CALM DOWN.
IT'S ONE THING TO BLOW THINGS UP BY ACCIDENT. IT'S ANOTHER TO DO IT INTENTIONALLY. BECAUSE VIOLENCE IS WRONG.
AND I, FOR ONE, THINK IT'S TIME WE LISTEN TO MYRTLE, GIRDLE, AND MENACE TO SOCIETY, AND START IMPROVING OUR TOWN!
WHICH EVERYONE AGREED WAS A FINE SPEECH.
YES!
Yes.
Yes.
Yes.
YES!

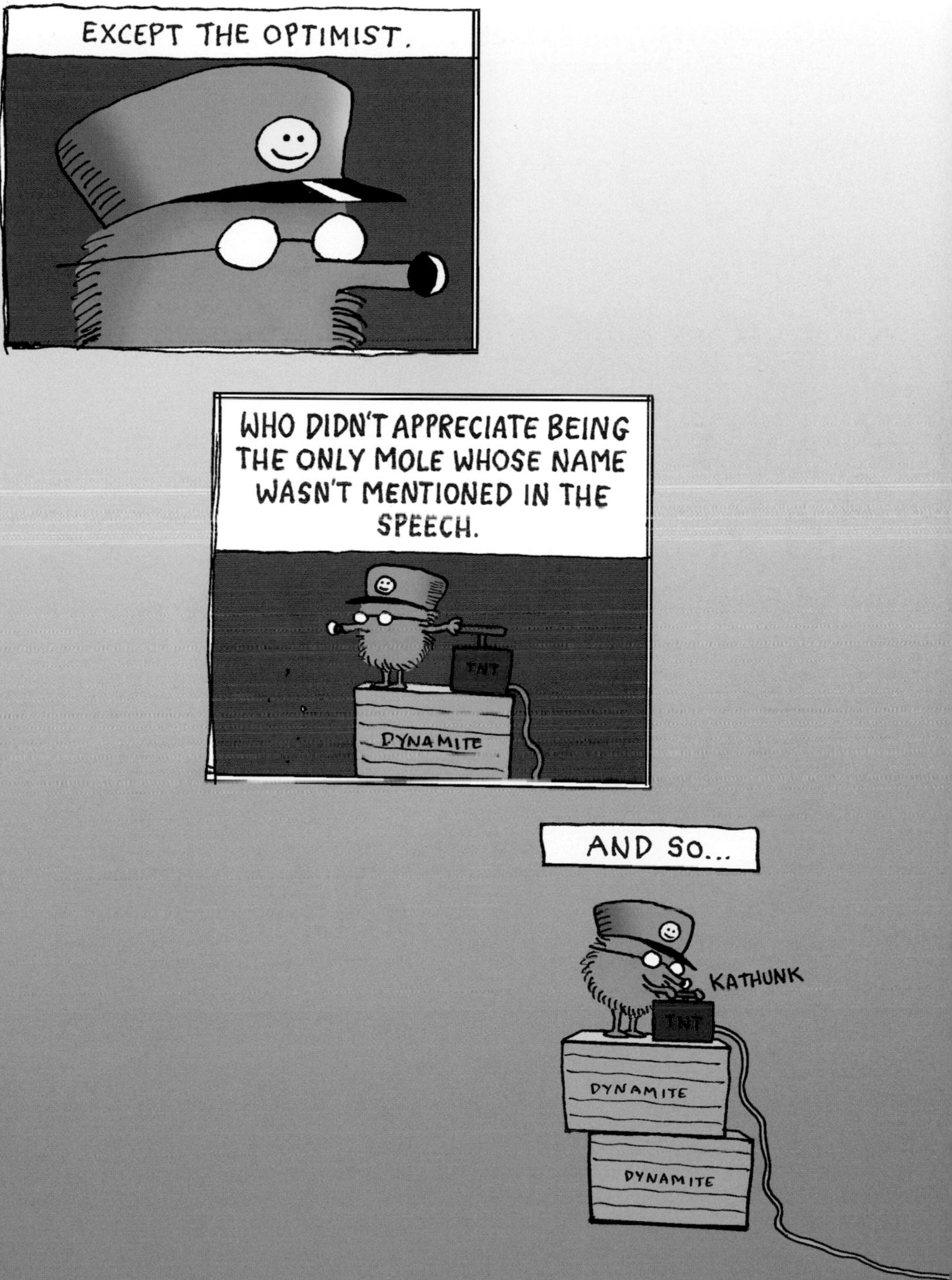
EXCEPT THE OPTIMIST.
WHO DIDN'T APPRECIATE BEING THE ONLY MOLE WHOSE NAME WASN'T MENTIONED IN THE SPEECH.
TNT
DYNAMITE
AND SO...
KATHUNK
TNT
DYNAMITE
DYNAMITE

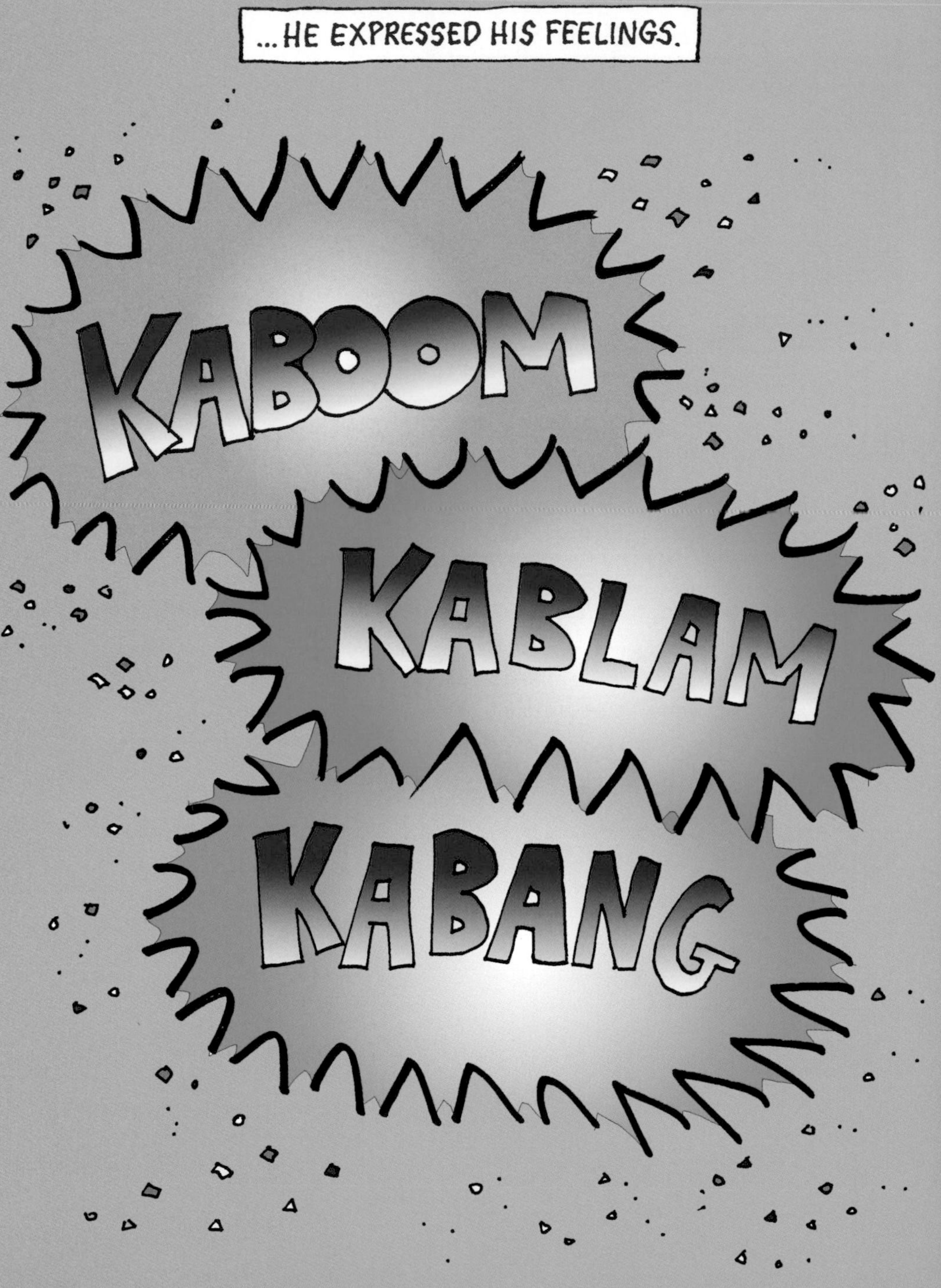
...HE EXPRESSED HIS FEELINGS.
KABOOM
KABLAM
KABANG

CHAPTER LAST

IN WHICH...

WE SAY, "IT'S ABOUT STINKING TIME."

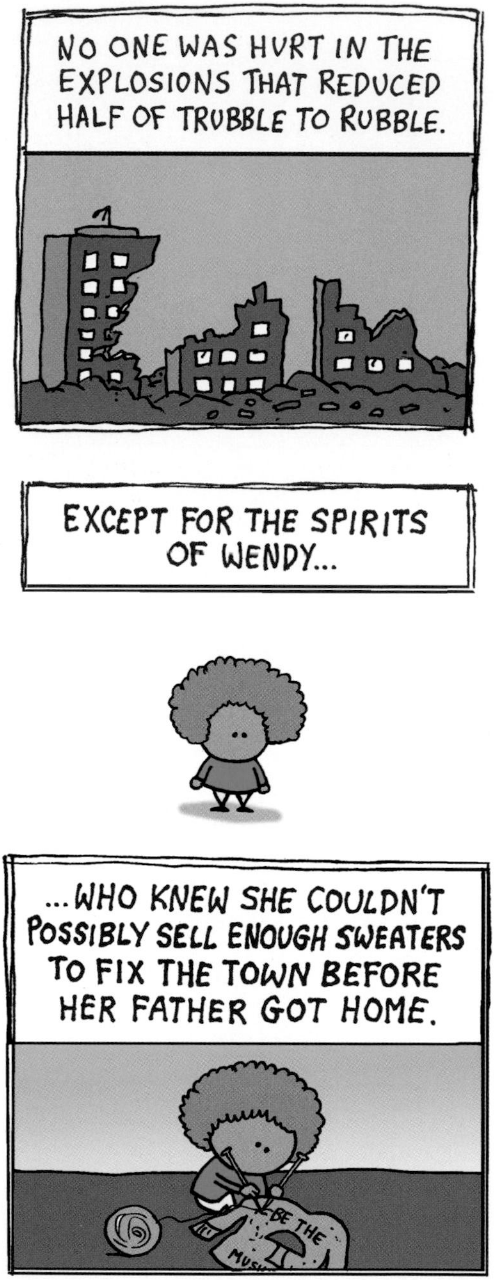
NO ONE WAS HURT IN THE EXPLOSIONS THAT REDUCED HALF OF TRUBBLE TO RUBBLE.
EXCEPT FOR THE SPIRITS OF WENDY...
...WHO KNEW SHE COULDN'T POSSIBLY SELL ENOUGH SWEATERS TO FIX THE TOWN BEFORE HER FATHER GOT HOME.
BE THE

THOUGH WENDY'S SPIRITS WEREN'T THE ONLY THING THE EXPLOSIONS SHOOK.

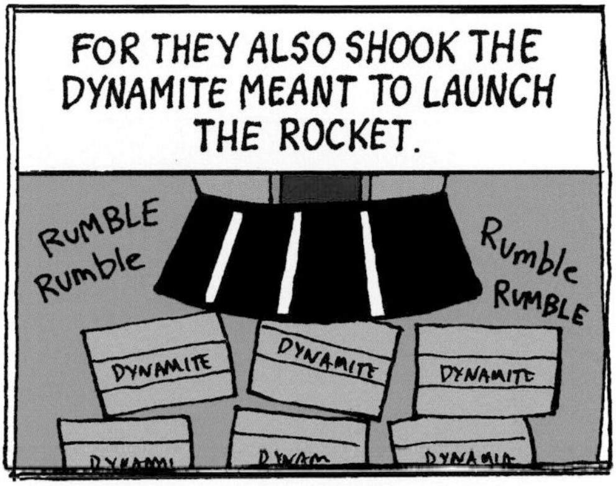
FOR THEY ALSO SHOOK THE DYNAMITE MEANT TO LAUNCH THE ROCKET.
RUMBLE Rumble
Rumble RUMBLE
DYNAMITE
DYNAMITE
DYNAMITE

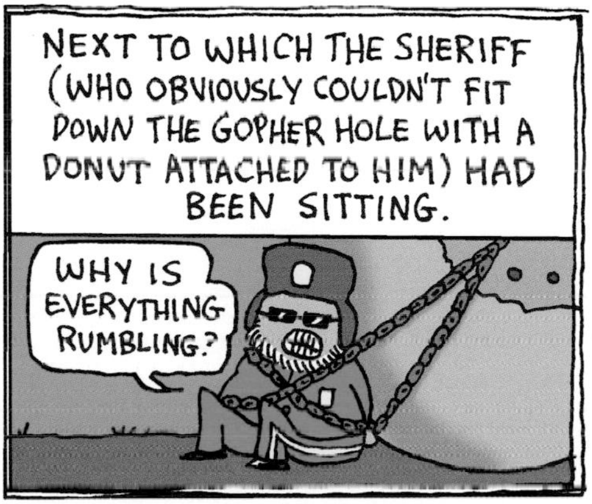
NEXT TO WHICH THE SHERIFF (WHO OBVIOUSLY COULDN'T FIT DOWN THE GOPHER HOLE WITH A DONUT ATTACHED TO HIM) HAD BEEN SITTING.
WHY IS EVERYTHING RUMBLING?

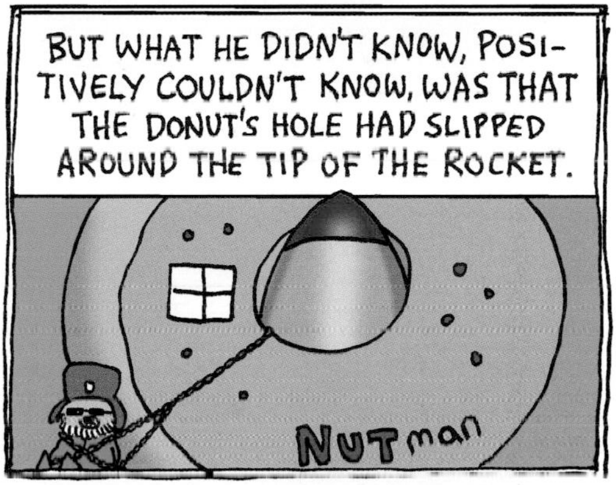
BUT WHAT HE DIDN'T KNOW, POSITIVELY COULDN'T KNOW, WAS THAT THE DONUT'S HOLE HAD SLIPPED AROUND THE TIP OF THE ROCKET.
NUTman

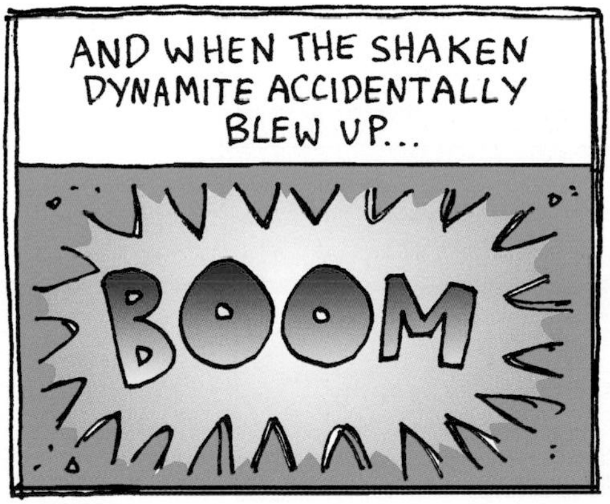
AND WHEN THE SHAKEN DYNAMITE ACCIDENTALLY BLEW UP...
BOOM

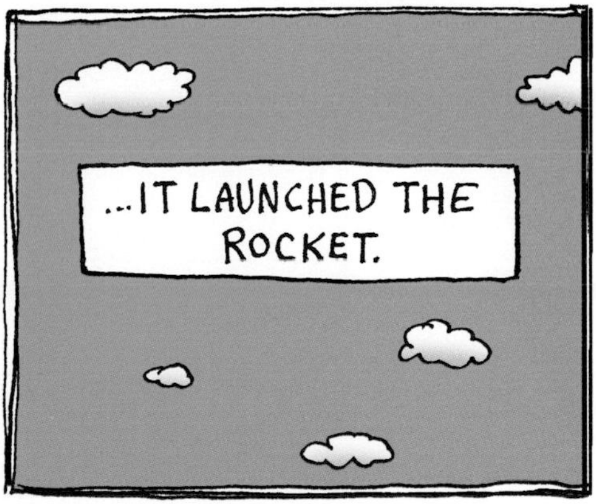
...IT LAUNCHED THE ROCKET.

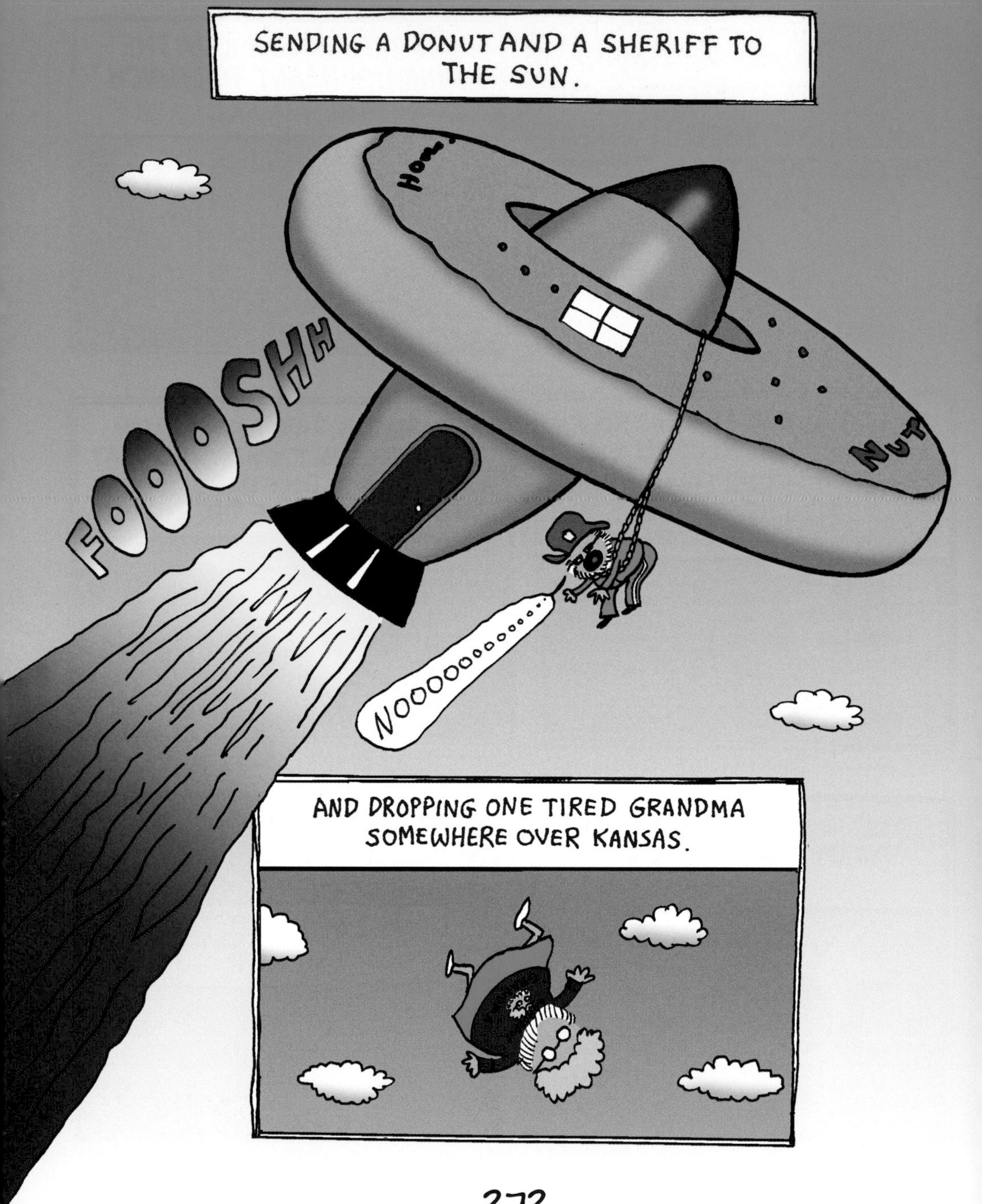
SENDING A DONUT AND A SHERIFF TO THE SUN.
FOOOSHH
NOOOOOOOOOOOOO
AND DROPPING ONE TIRED GRANDMA SOMEWHERE OVER KANSAS.

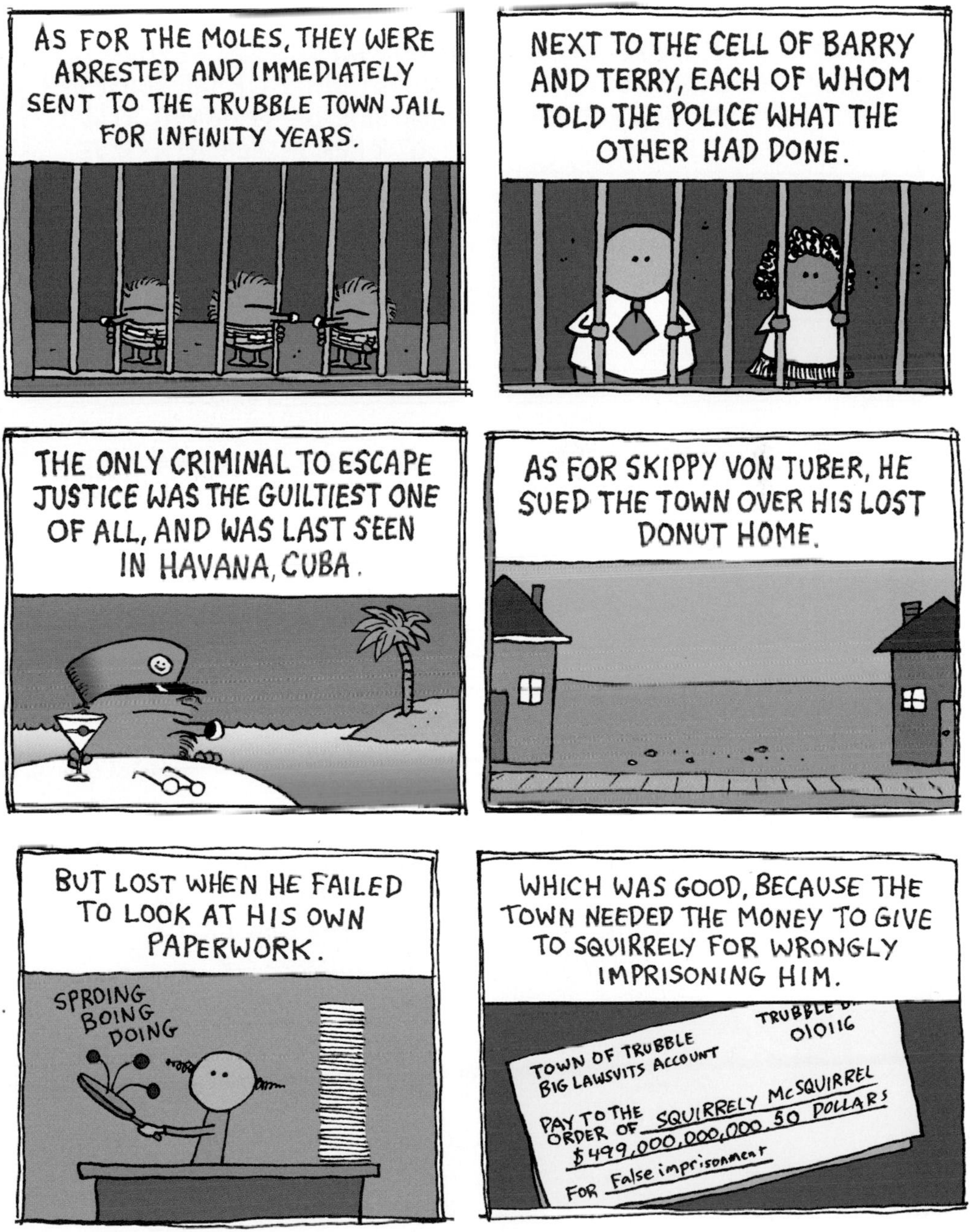
AS FOR THE MOLES, THEY WERE ARRESTED AND IMMEDIATELY SENT TO THE TRUBBLE TOWN JAIL FOR INFINITY YEARS.
NEXT TO THE CELL OF BARRY AND TERRY, EACH OF WHOM TOLD THE POLICE WHAT THE OTHER HAD DONE.
THE ONLY CRIMINAL TO ESCAPE JUSTICE WAS THE GUILTIEST ONE OF ALL, AND WAS LAST SEEN IN HAVANA, CUBA.
AS FOR SKIPPY VON TUBER, HE SUED THE TOWN OVER HIS LOST DONUT HOME.
BUT LOST WHEN HE FAILED TO LOOK AT HIS OWN PAPERWORK.
SPROING
BOING
DOING
WHICH WAS GOOD, BECAUSE THE TOWN NEEDED THE MONEY TO GIVE TO SQUIRRELY FOR WRONGLY IMPRISONING HIM.
010116
TOWN OF TRUBBLE
BIG LAWSUITS ACCOUNT
PAY TO THE ORDER OF SQUIRRELY McSQUIRREL
$499,000,000,000.50 DOLLARS
FOR False imprisonment

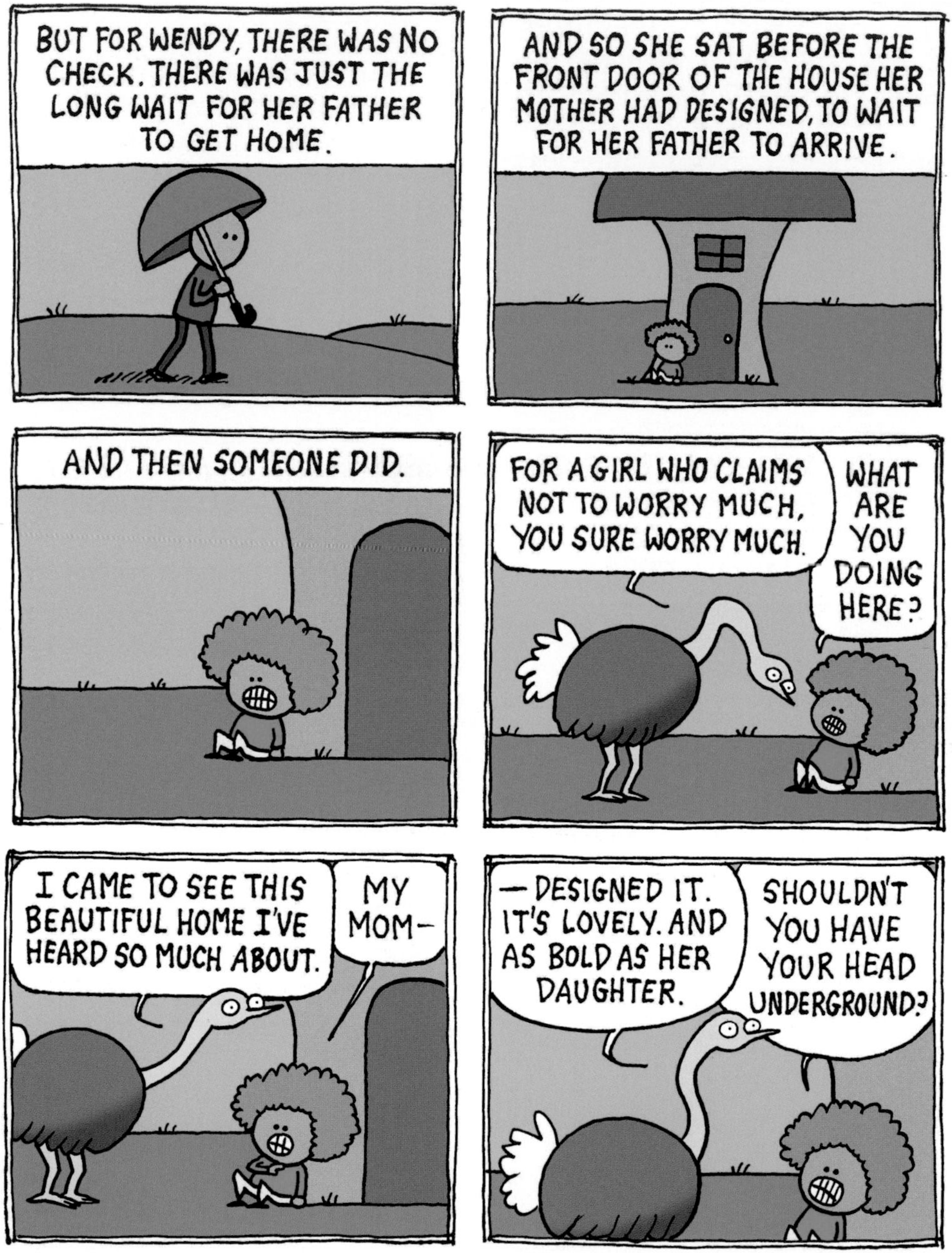

BUT FOR WENDY, THERE WAS NO CHECK. THERE WAS JUST THE LONG WAIT FOR HER FATHER TO GET HOME.
AND SO SHE SAT BEFORE THE FRONT DOOR OF THE HOUSE HER MOTHER HAD DESIGNED, TO WAIT FOR HER FATHER TO ARRIVE.
AND THEN SOMEONE DID.
FOR A GIRL WHO CLAIMS NOT TO WORRY MUCH, YOU SURE WORRY MUCH.
WHAT ARE YOU DOING HERE?
I CAME TO SEE THIS BEAUTIFUL HOME I'VE HEARD SO MUCH ABOUT.
MY MOM-
—DESIGNED IT. IT'S LOVELY. AND AS BOLD AS HER DAUGHTER.
SHOULDN'T YOU HAVE YOUR HEAD UNDERGROUND?

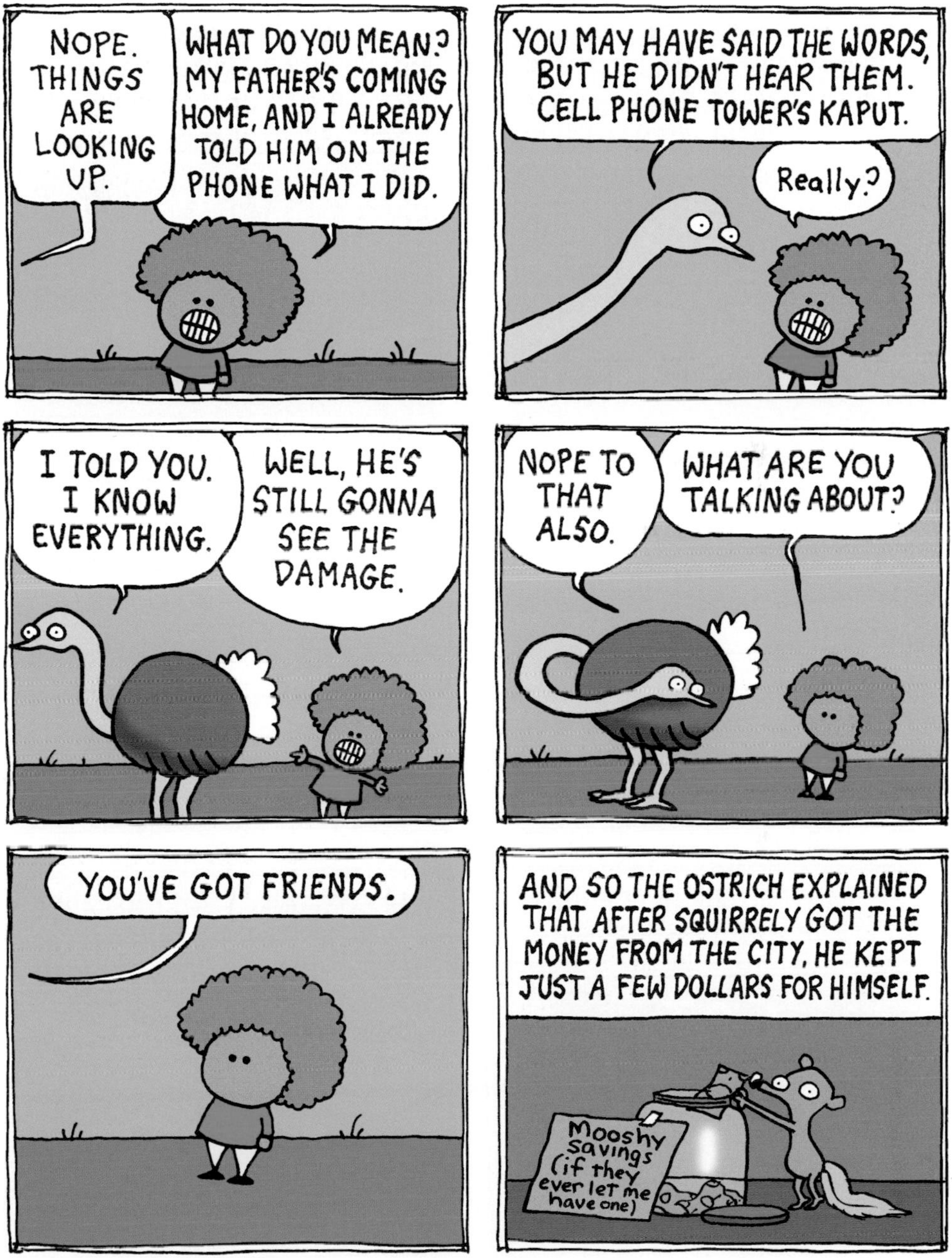
NOPE. THINGS ARE LOOKING UP.
WHAT DO YOU MEAN? MY FATHER'S COMING HOME, AND I ALREADY TOLD HIM ON THE PHONE WHAT I DID.
YOU MAY HAVE SAID THE WORDS, BUT HE DIDN'T HEAR THEM. CELL PHONE TOWER'S KAPUT.
Really?
I TOLD YOU. I KNOW EVERYTHING.
WELL, HE'S STILL GONNA SEE THE DAMAGE.
NOPE TO THAT ALSO.
WHAT ARE YOU TALKING ABOUT?
YOU'VE GOT FRIENDS.
AND SO THE OSTRICH EXPLAINED THAT AFTER SQUIRRELY GOT THE MONEY FROM THE CITY, HE KEPT JUST A FEW DOLLARS FOR HIMSELF.
Mooshy savings (if they ever let me have one)

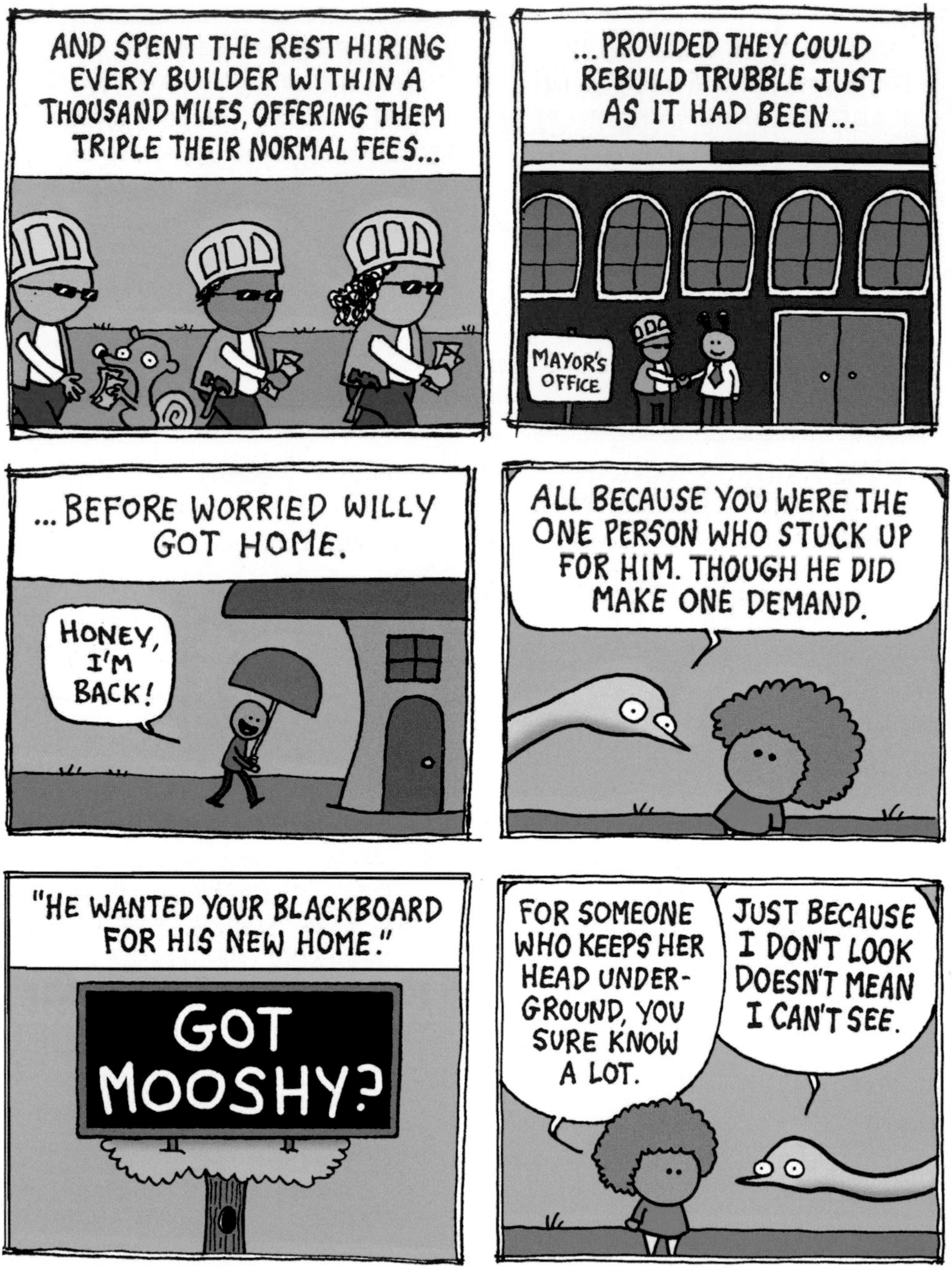
AND SPENT THE REST HIRING EVERY BUILDER WITHIN A THOUSAND MILES, OFFERING THEM TRIPLE THEIR NORMAL FEES...
...PROVIDED THEY COULD REBUILD TRUBBLE JUST AS IT HAD BEEN...
MAYOR'S OFFICE
...BEFORE WORRIED WILLY GOT HOME.
HONEY, I'M BACK!
ALL BECAUSE YOU WERE THE ONE PERSON WHO STUCK UP FOR HIM. THOUGH HE DID MAKE ONE DEMAND.
"HE WANTED YOUR BLACKBOARD FOR HIS NEW HOME."
GOT MOOSHY?
FOR SOMEONE WHO KEEPS HER HEAD UNDER-GROUND, YOU SURE KNOW A LOT.
JUST BECAUSE I DON'T LOOK DOESN'T MEAN I CAN'T SEE.

AND SO WHEN WORRIED WILLY RETURNED HOME, ALL WAS FINE.

EXCEPT FOR THE BABYSITTER.

WATCHFUL WILLAMINA

WHOSE MANY SELFIES POSTED ONLINE PROVED SHE HAD BEEN USELESS AND UNPROFESSIONAL, AND WHO WAS FIRED WITHOUT PAY.

AND PROMPTLY ELECTED MAYOR OF TRUBBLE.

YAAY   YAAY

MAYOR WILLAMINA

ALL OF WHICH LEFT ONLY ONE NAGGING QUESTION...

HAD SQUIRRELY REALLY BOUGHT DYNAMITE FROM THE NITRO-GLYCERINE NANNY?

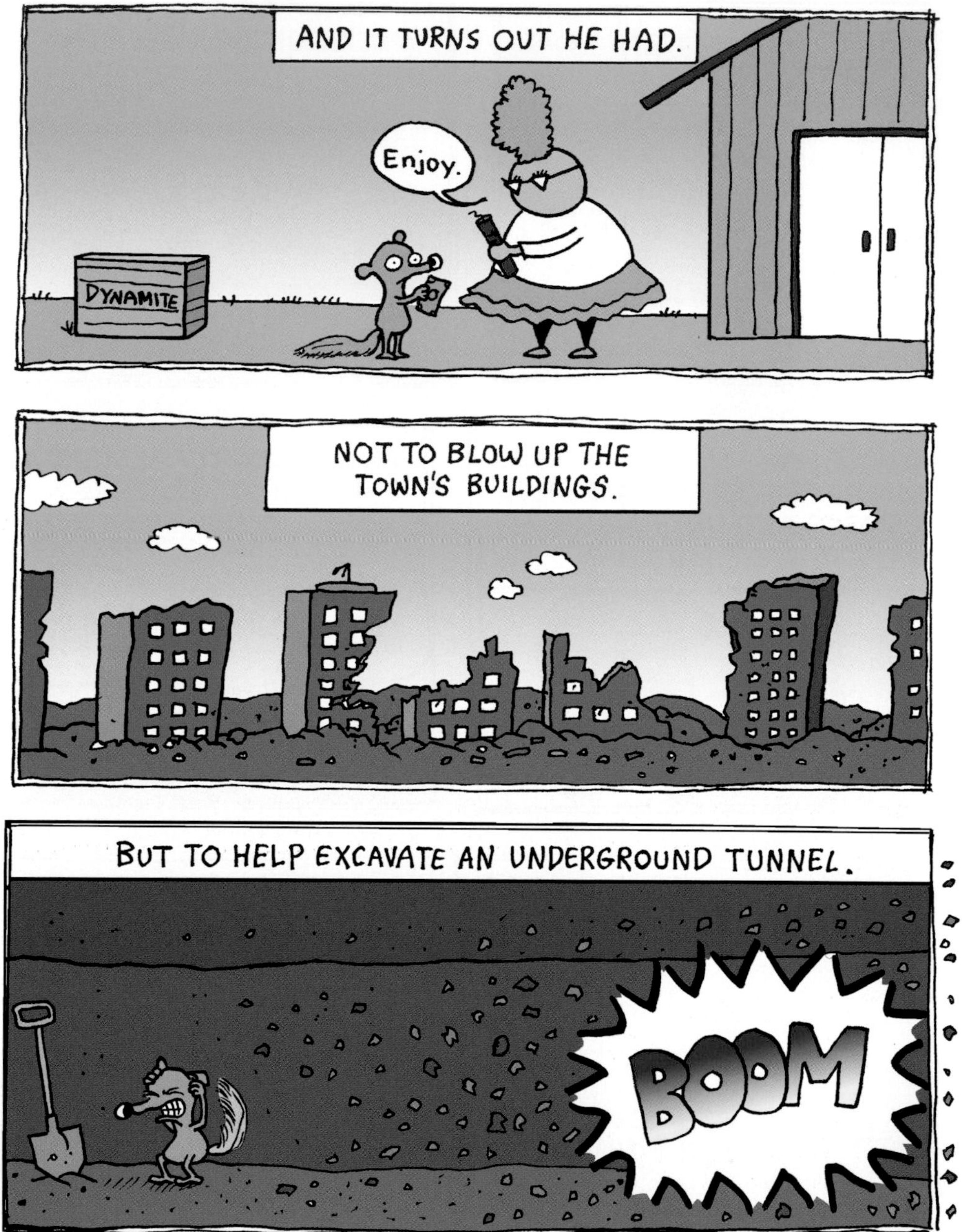
AND IT TURNS OUT HE HAD.
Enjoy.
DYNAMITE
NOT TO BLOW UP THE TOWN'S BUILDINGS.
BUT TO HELP EXCAVATE AN UNDERGROUND TUNNEL.
BOOM

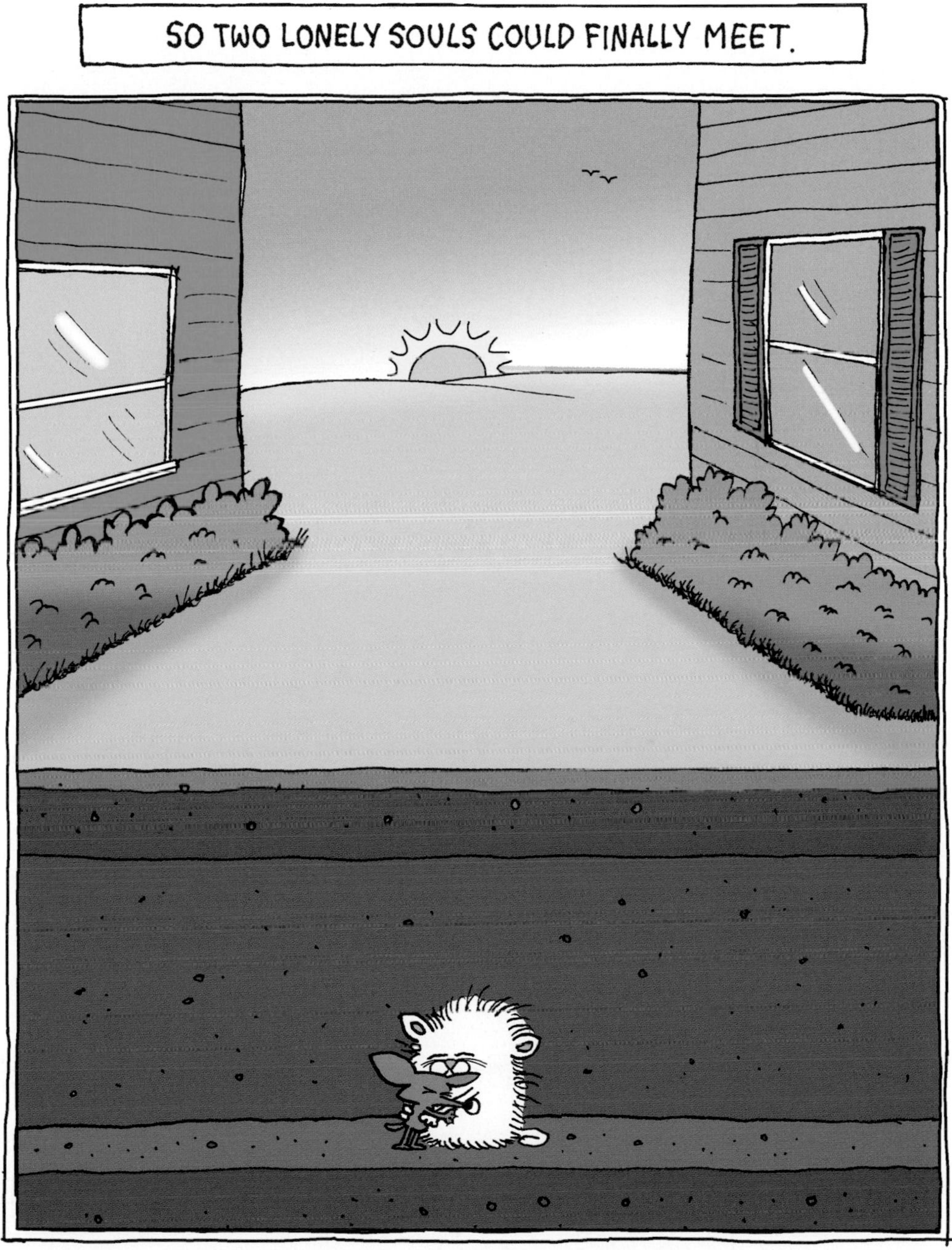
SO TWO LONELY SOULS COULD FINALLY MEET.

AFTERWORD

IN WHICH...

WE ADMIT WE DON'T REALLY KNOW WHAT AN AFTERWORD IS

EVERYTHING YOU JUST READ IN THIS BOOK IS TRUE, EXCEPT FOR THE PARTS THAT WERE MADE UP.

TRUBBLE TOWN

AND ONE OF THE PARTS THAT WAS MADE UP WAS THE NAME OF THE AUTHOR...

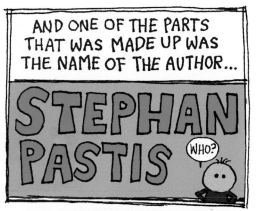

STEPHAN PASTIS

WHO?

"STEPHAN PASTIS" IS JUST A RANDOM NAME THAT THE PUBLISHERS OF THIS BOOK CHOSE FROM A PHONE BOOK.

THAT GUY.

SO IF YOU EVER SEE A PERSON NAMED "STEPHAN PASTIS" CLAIMING TO HAVE WRITTEN THIS BOOK, PLEASE KNOW HE IS LYING.

NO, REALLY... I WROTE IT.

FOR THE REAL AUTHOR...

IS...

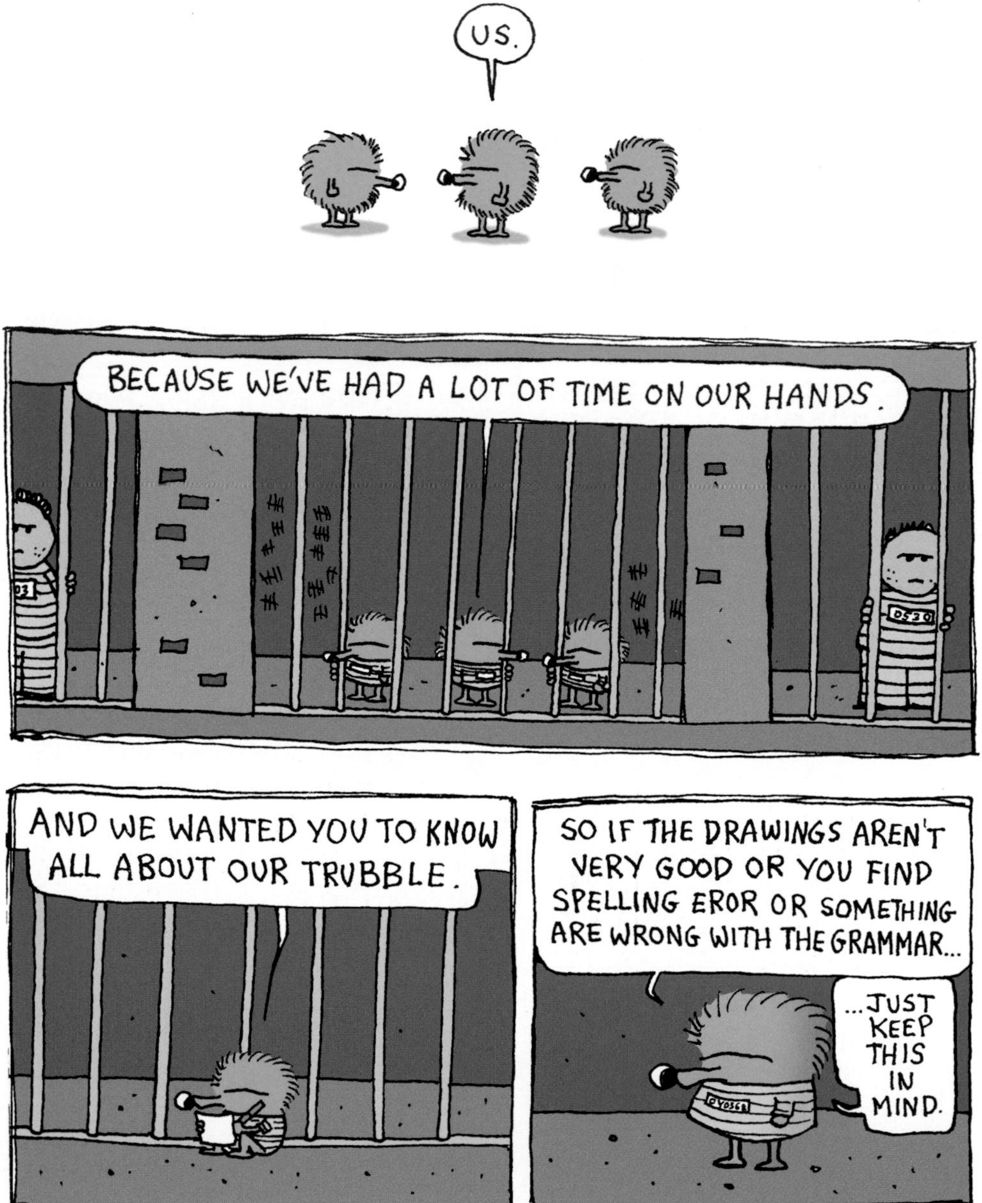
US.
BECAUSE WE'VE HAD A LOT OF TIME ON OUR HANDS.
AND WE WANTED YOU TO KNOW ALL ABOUT OUR TRUBBLE.
SO IF THE DRAWINGS AREN'T VERY GOOD OR YOU FIND SPELLING EROR OR SOMETHING ARE WRONG WITH THE GRAMMAR...
...JUST KEEP THIS IN MIND.

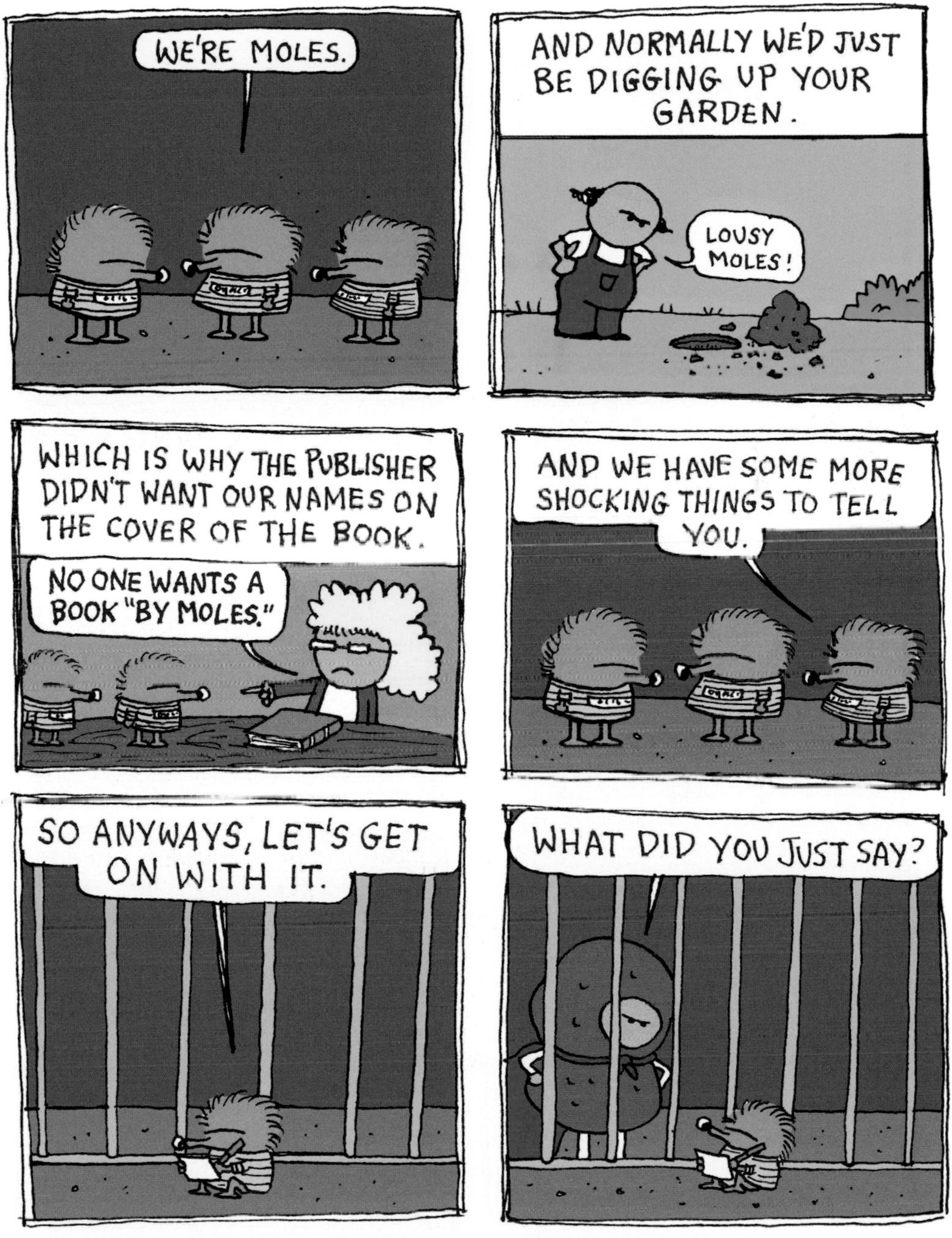
WE'RE MOLES.
AND NORMALLY WE'D JUST BE DIGGING UP YOUR GARDEN.
LOUSY MOLES!
WHICH IS WHY THE PUBLISHER DIDN'T WANT OUR NAMES ON THE COVER OF THE BOOK.
NO ONE WANTS A BOOK "BY MOLES."
AND WE HAVE SOME MORE SHOCKING THINGS TO TELL YOU.
SO ANYWAYS, LET'S GET ON WITH IT.
WHAT DID YOU JUST SAY?

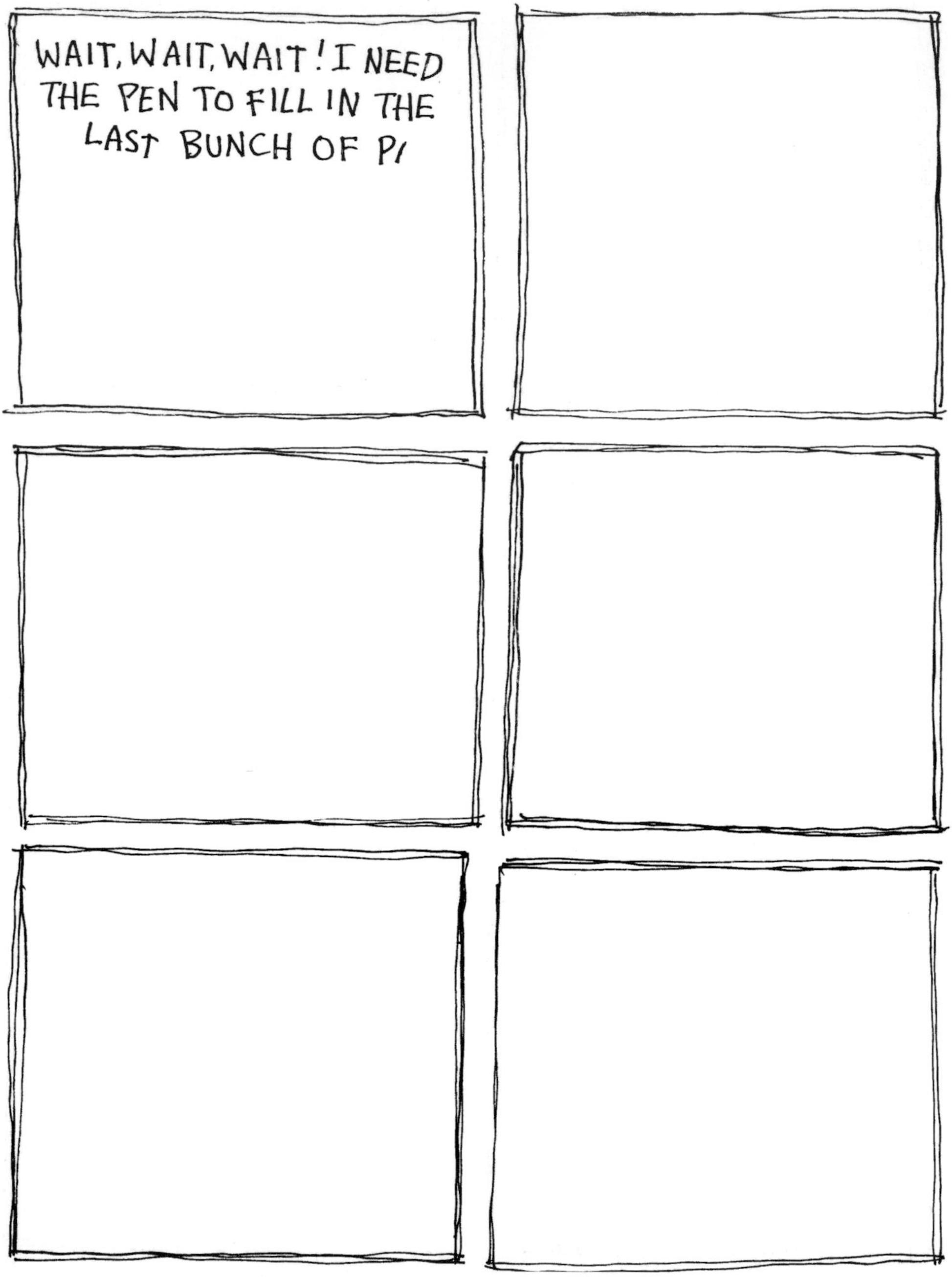
WAIT, WAIT, WAIT! I NEED THE PEN TO FILL IN THE LAST BUNCH OF PI

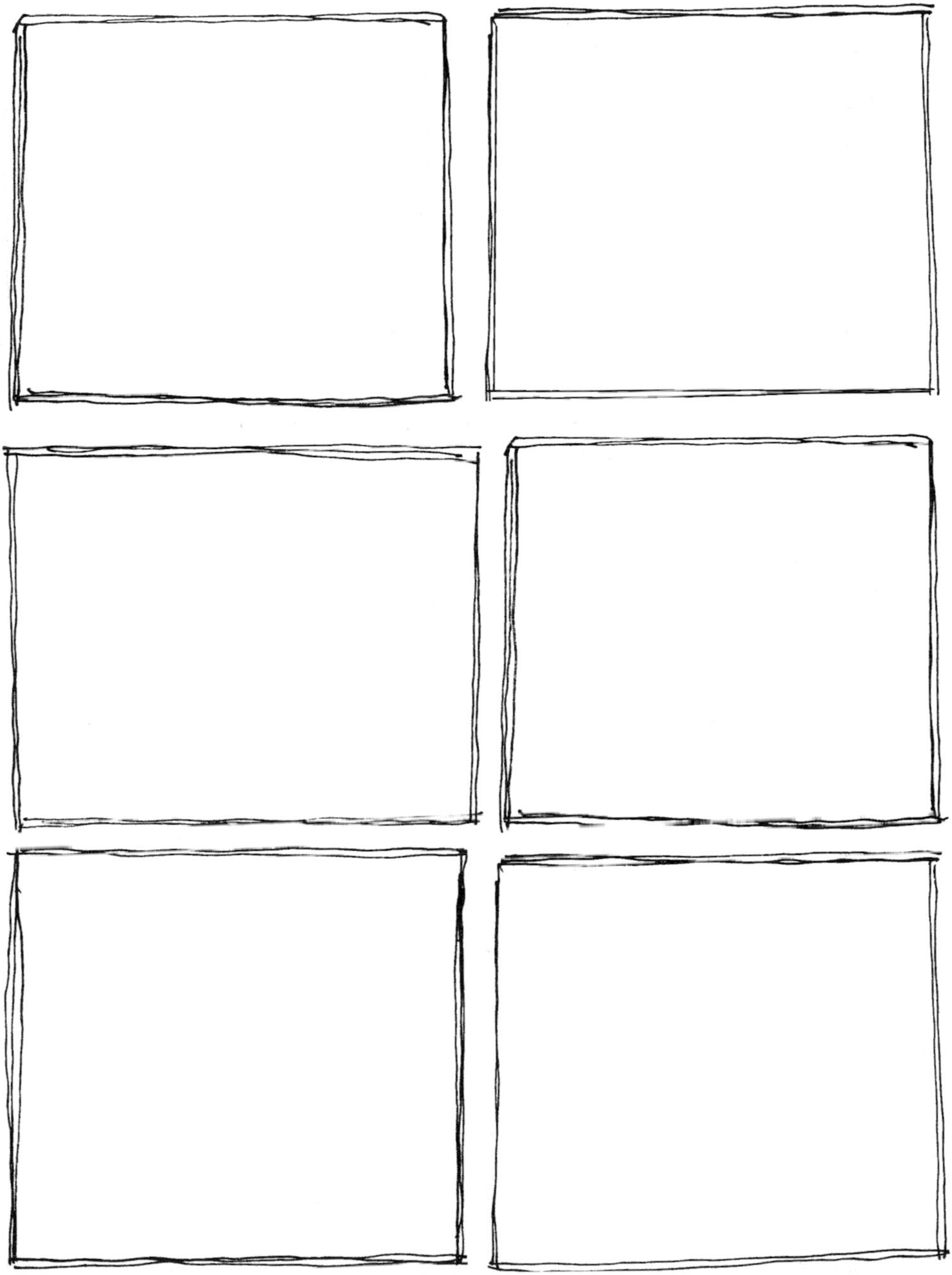

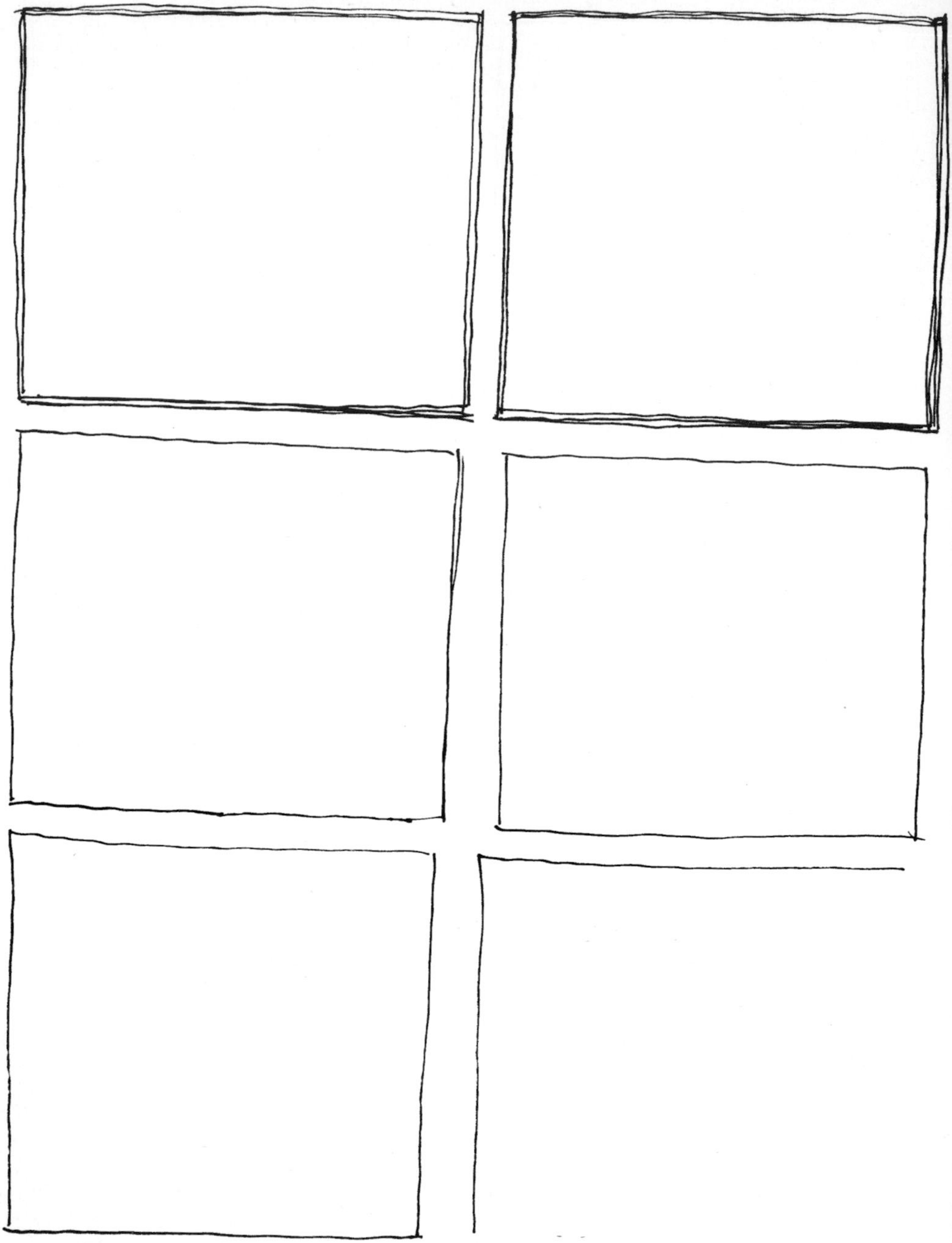

THE END
(Finally)

ABOUT
THE
AUTHORS

The moles are currently serving a prison sentence of infinity years in the Trubble town jail. This is their first published work.

If you would like them to speak at your school, they cannot.

They can be reached at: **trubbletownjail@gmail.com**

Please be aware that your message will be screened by jail personnel.